This book is dedicated to my children, Rachel, David, Jackie, and Jason – I love you and am so proud of each of you; always follow your dreams, and my parents, Myrna and Max, who have always supported me through all the paths I have taken and whose friendship I know I can always count on.

I would like to thank the following people who I am lucky to have as part of my life:

Martha and Steve

Mary Jo and Roy

Hesham

Charles

Maria and Jeff

Laura and Jay

Marcy and Alan

Elaine

Rabbi Susan

The community at CKS

Julie

Terry

TABLE OF CONTENTS

Chapter 1	The need for Change	Page 4
Chapter 2	Self Serving Reactions	Page 20
Chapter 3	The Art of Creating Scandal	Page 60
Chapter 4	Geo Politics at Home	Page 112
Chapter 5	The Pope's Slippery Slope	Page 160
Chapter 6	Redefining Political Demographics	Page 212
Chapter 7	Executive Hustle and Muscle	Page 239
Chapter 8	Tradition and Sexual Jealousy	Page 278
Chapter 9	Connecting the Dots	Page 299
Chapter 10	A Personal Touch	Page 325
Chapter 11	Don't Drink with Conservatives	Page 329
Chapter 12	Inside the Stinger	Page 358
Chapter 13	Machinations in the Orient	Page 418
Chapter 14	The Integrity of our Legal System	Page 452
Chapter 15	Globe-trotting Campaigning	Page 468
Chapter 16	A Parade of Witnesses	Page 502
Chapter 17	No Throne with the Drone	Page 533
Chapter 18	Candidates find their Niche	Page 560
Chapter 19	A Nation holds its Breath	Page 580
Epilogue	The Tip of the Iceberg	Page 587

CHAPTER 1

Cecily Bernard was on the phone with her daughter, Sondra, and they were discussing Sondra's upcoming wedding. It was Friday afternoon at 5pm on June 17, 2039.

"Oh mom, I can't wait for you to see the floral arrangement I picked out for the altar," Sondra said. "You'll love it."

"I am sure I will honey," Cecily replied. "Has Blake gotten his results from the Bar Association yet?"

"No, not yet."

"Well I am sure they will come any day."

"You know mom, if he passed, we are planning on starting a family right away."

"Are you sure about that? Why don't the two of you enjoy being married for a few years first?"

"We will not allow a baby to change our lives, mother. There is much we are planning to accomplish and we will not slow down."

"Of course not dear," Cecily answered, smiling to herself. "See you Sunday for dinner. Goodbye."

"Goodbye mom."

Just as Cecily hung up the phone, the doorbell rang.

"Mr. Braxton, are you quite finished?"

"There's that impudent Justice Manucci again," Chief Justice Braxton thought.

"Excuse me, Patrick, but I believe as Chief Justice, I am entitled to the right to speak."

"All right, let's try to remember that we are not adversaries," Judith Lackey said. "Back on point, when our founding fathers drafted the Constitution, they would never have been able to foresee the path our country has taken. Our opinions are supposed to change with the times."

"The real issue, as I see it, is whether someone not born in this country could effectively represent our society; all things considered, the answer is yes," said Samuel Kleinman, one of the more progressive Justices of the United States Supreme Court.

"That is all fine and well Sam, but how far do we really want to push the envelope?" replied Chief Justice James Braxton.

"If you are referring to me, Jim, I am certain I am a credit to this country," retorted Alex (Sasha) Levitsky. Braxton had to agree. Alex Levitsky, born of Slavic descent, was the first U.S. Supreme Court Justice to originate from outside of the United States. President Manny Sharpe had appointed him twelve years ago. Prior to that, he held the position of Croatian Ambassador to the United States. During his tenure as Ambassador, he and President Sharpe had developed a strong bond during the civil war going on in Croatia at the time, and the United States tried to offer as much diplomatic support as possible. When an opening on the Supreme Court presented itself, President Sharpe succeeded in pushing Levitsky's confirmation through Congress.

There had been questionable circumstances surrounding Sharpe's election win, to put it mildly. The Presidential election that year, 2024, marked the first one since the creation of the United States where the candidates represented only one political party. The previous two elections, in 2016 and 2020, had turned out to be disasters when the outcome of the popular vote differed from that of the Electoral College. Congress, under great pressure, petitioned the Supreme Court to amend the U.S. Constitution to eliminate the Electoral College and made the popular vote the sole factor in electing the President. The Supreme Court saw the necessity in this and ruled to do just that.

The political landscape had changed. Politics was not a prestigious career anymore; our new open door immigration policy which had come into effect during Sharpe's administration made being in office more demanding and next to impossible to get anything done because of the increased number of distinct immigrant groups each with their own unique needs as well as underscoring the need for someone more representative of those not born in the U.S. These trends, combined with the new popular vote process, were keeping more and more people from entering politics.

"One day you will realize not everything is about you, Sasha," said Andrew Turnbull, with more than a little disdain. Everyone on the Supreme Court knew the two did not get along, probably because Levitsky has taken away much of the attention from Turnbull, who had been the third African American appointed to the Court. Justice Turnbull could be intimidating; standing about 6'4'', he combined his large stature with an attitude of superiority to use to his advantage; Levitsky, however, refused to be bullied.

"Getting back to what James was saying, there is a big difference between a Supreme Court Justice and the leader of this country being born elsewhere," said Patrick Manucci, who hailed from Connecticut. "I mean, how could someone not born here really be able to relate to what it means to be American in their blood?"

Justice Patrick Manucci fancied himself a real legal scholar. Others, however, Braxton included, viewed him as somewhat of a joke, although they kept that opinion to themselves. His family possessed much power; based in New York, with questionable connections. Many people say he obtained his Supreme Court appointment through intimidation.

"Oh please Pat," replied Irene Salkin. "Just about everyone active in politics has ancestors that came from somewhere else. How many Native Americans can you name that held office in the last one hundred years? Besides, to me, the American work ethic is the most important value in a candidate, and there are people that possess that same work ethic all over the world. It's very likely that the masses will identify more easily with an outsider, and an outsider will likely be more able to meet their needs."

"That's true," added Samuel Kleinman, "and while it is our job to interpret the law, we can also include explanations of what would be deemed constitutional in our opinions. We are simply running out of qualified candidates who were born here."

"If I could put my two cents in," spoke Danielle Sorensen, who tended to be the most reticent of all the nine judges. "Does anyone really believe that a foreigner will be able to get anything done, that Congress will not fight him or her every step of the way?"

"Perhaps when we still had two major political parties," said Alex Levitsky. "But the trend since then has been toward unity in Washington. Winston, what do you think?"

Winston Bernard, the senior Justice on the court and a conservative, thought for a moment. "I can see both sides of the issue. Times change, and the law must change with the times; however, there is a certain pride and sense of nationalism that comes with being born in the United States, and no amount of time spent living here, no matter how much one loves this country or considers oneself a patriot, is a valid substitute."

"I wasn't lucky enough to be a member of this Court when the Electoral College was abolished, but I remember the outcry and all the rebellion back then when this Court upheld Congress's petition," Judith Lackey said. "The Supreme Court proved how progressive they were back then when this country needed it most. Why is this issue any different? We are in just as much of a political crisis now as we were back then."

"This is not an extension of that issue, Judith," Justice Bernard replied. "Many people believed that tampering had taken place involving the voting process at best and blackmail and bribery at worst. The public had abandoned all their faith in our election process, not to mention the eight most uneventful years politically. This issue provides us with other options."

The matter of a foreign born President had been working its way up the judicial system for a few years now and the case was President Harrington vs. the United States. It had been filed by the Executive Branch of the Federal Government in 2036, shortly after President Harrington's reelection. The President knew that this could not wait any longer; he made it his mission to push it through the Federal court system in Washington, where it met with rejection on its face and lost again in the Court of Appeals. Tenacious as always, the President petitioned the Supreme Court to hear his argument. The Court unanimously ruled to grant the case the writ of certiorari, and the President began to prepare.

The first thing Harrington had to do was to prepare a legal brief to submit to the Court. Knowing everything at stake, he employed all the people with legal backgrounds at his disposal to collaborate. Of course, once the word got out about what the process involved, public interest piqued. Many organizations wanted to weigh in and two came to the forefront. Worldwide Coalition Inc. (WCI), which was formed to foster diplomacy among nations, had its American chapter contribute written briefs in support of the new legislation. American Pride, a thinly disguised white supremacist fringe group, was up in arms, and came out vehemently against the measure, submitting briefs in opposition.

The Supreme Court had been deliberating for a week already and had made very little progress. There was great pressure for them to come to a decision quickly. They were getting ready to break for the summer in two weeks with the next election only a year and a half away. Campaigns take time to get organized; those who wanted this issue passed were very anxious. Braxton had been doing everything he could to see to it that this issue would be resolved before the summer break. Although it had only been done once before, the President had the authority to convene an emergency session of the Supreme Court if he or she believed it to be warranted. President Harrington indicated that he would consider this an emergency. The policy simply required a written decision to take effect; the Justices' individual opinions need not be written until the fall.

"Let's take another look at the three briefs we received," said Chief Justice Braxton.

Justice Sorensen went to retrieve the three briefs. Justice Braxton picked up the brief prepared by the President's staff.

He read, "Issue: Whether a person born in a foreign country is eligible to run for the office of President of the United States." Skipping down, he continued, "This clause in the Constitution was written 250 years ago; at that time a law like this would have been an absolute necessity. In today's world, this stipulation has grown into a hindrance to our ability to govern ourselves; our field of candidates is becoming more and more limited." Putting the brief down, Justice Braxton continued, "That is a valid point; a perfect example is the President himself."

The rest of the judges chuckled.

"Yes, but don't you think by allowing this, we are heading down a slippery slope?" Justice Turnbull said. "What's next, changing the required age of Presidential candidates from 35 to 20?"

"Where are we supposed to find good people anymore Andrew?" Justice Salkin retorted. "Look at Vice President White. The man barely made it through college. James, can we see the next brief – the one from the WCI?"

Irene Salkin had been a prosecutor in Boston before being nominated by President Harrington four years ago. Sometimes she still acted like she was in a courtroom trying cases.

Justice Braxton took that brief off the table. "The framers of the Constitution, if they were alive today, would be shocked at what dire straits we are in today politically. We have managed to modify our standards in other areas of public life; now is the right time for this antiquated law to be changed."

"There are other parts of Article 2 Section 1 Clause 5 of the Constitution," Justice Salkin said. "If the phrase about any candidate being a resident for fourteen years remains, the requirement will not be diluted so terribly. It is also possible to make the residency requirement greater than the current 14 years. Perhaps we should consider increasing it to 20 or 25 years."

"The fact is, we are a completely different country than we were in colonial times," Danielle Sorensen said.

"Yes, I am aware that women now enjoy the right to vote," spoke Judith Lackey, making a snide comment at Danielle Sorensen, who happened to be a descendant of Betty Friedan, the famous feminist. Being eternally proud of being related to Friedan, Justice Sorensen's comments and opinions often had undertones of the downtrodden female; she wore it like a badge of honor. "Why don't we take a look at the third brief."

Justice Braxton selected the third brief, written by American Pride. "We need to protect our interests from foreign influence, no matter how benign that influence may seem. A foreign born President would allow his or her biases to creep into the office no matter how much he or she tried to be impartial."

"What a load of crap." exclaimed Judge Levitsky. "Haven't the people at American Pride ever heard of checks and balances?"

"Another option available to us, as Judith mentioned, is to modify the amount of time that candidates have had to live here," said Justice Kleinman. "We could stipulate that only those who gained citizenship before turning 18 could emerge as candidates. If a person came here as a child, their perspective of this country would be completely different than if they had come in as an adult."

"We need more diplomacy among nations," pointed out Justice Braxton. "This may be a step in that direction."

"Aren't we just supposed to be interpreting the Constitution?" said Justice Manucci. "Diplomacy is for the people in office."

"Well that's one of our duties Pat," replied Justice Bernard in a condescending tone. Being the oldest Supreme Court Justice, Winston saw himself as something of a father figure; although not always the most patient one. "However, our duties have evolved and are not black and white. We must be ready to change with the transforming landscape which is turning more and more global. It would be negligent of us to ignore that fact."

"We already have more interaction with other nations than we did 20 years ago. How would having a foreign born President accelerate that process?" said Justice Turnbull.

"Someone born elsewhere would embody some of the values of the country in which they were born", said Justice Sorensen. "Maybe we could specify certain countries to exclude." Laughter emanated from around the room. She continued, "James, can we replay some of the oral arguments?"

The latest technology allowed the Court to use voice commands to access the audio files they needed; each Justice had access to the shared computer in their chamber; each file was designated with the date and subject and that was how they were identified.

Justice Braxton called up the oral argument from Louis Hirsch, head of Hirsch Studios. "The United States has always been a leader. We also have a history of tolerance and acceptance of those less fortunate. This change that is being proposed is a natural extension of that ideology. Would George Washington and our founding fathers have wanted us to have substandard leadership? Of course not. This is no different that running a business; you want the best and the brightest."

"Here's one from someone named Al Coogan, a construction worker from Louisville, Kentucky, who spoke at a town hall meeting there," said Justice Braxton.

"If it pleases the Court, I am dead set against this. If we believe in the system, there are plenty of worthy candidates that were born here. The answer is not to open up the office of the President to foreigners; the answer is to have government work together."

It was two minutes to eight, and the contact wasn't here yet. "I hope I haven't made a mistake in who I chose", Viper thought. This meeting place would not excite anyone: there were derelicts everywhere. Suddenly, a shadow appeared around the building in the Foggy Bottom section of Washington D.C.

"Right on time I see," said Viper.
"Just like you, Viper," said Wolf.
"Is everything in place?" asked Viper.
"Yes," said Wolf. "You will have the information you need tomorrow."
"OK, great. Just don't screw this up, or we will both be going up the river," said Viper.
"You got my money?" asked Wolf, ignoring Viper's comment; Wolf never could handle criticism.
"Half now, the other half when it is over. Good luck," said Viper.
Wolf picked up the briefcase and walked away, $50,000 richer.

The Justices had been deliberating all day, making it a week already. It was nine o'clock at night; exhausted, they decided to stop for the night. Chief Justice Braxton excused all the Justices. "Being it's Friday night, let's adjourn until Monday morning. Have a good weekend everyone."

The Justices all began to collect their notes and started to leave the room. On the way back to their private offices, Justice Braxton stopped to wait for Justice Kleinman. "Hello Sam. I know it's late, but how about a quick game of chess?"

"Ahh, sure James. It will help me unwind. Let me just stop by my office and then I will come in."

Ten minutes later, the two Justices were in Chief Justice Braxton's inner office.

"What is your impression of how things are going so far, Sam?" asked Justice Braxton.

"Well, our colleagues are reacting the way I expected. It seems like you are undecided so far. The only other person I am really unsure of is Judith."

Judith Lackey; now there was interesting story. Her ancestry dated all the way back to the American Indians. One of her distant cousins was Jim Thorpe, the decathlon winner who was stripped of his Olympic medals. Her grandfather was of Mexican heritage who made his bones in Miami and used his wealth to buy his family respectability. Judith had used all of her connections to help land her nomination as Supreme Court Justice.

"Well of course, she is a walking oxymoron," said Justice Braxton. "She comes from a family of foreigners; on the other hand, her son married into one of the oldest political families in Texas. As for myself, this has been one of the hardest cases for me to wrap my head around since I joined the Supreme Court 17 years ago. I am hardly getting any sleep at night. I realize that we are at a crossroads in our political system; at the same time, I do not want to be disloyal to the men and women who founded this country. Your move Sam."

"Oh, I don't think you have to worry about that. In the late 18th century, crossing the Atlantic was like going to the moon today. George Washington preached a policy of isolationism; we both understand how hard that would be to adhere to today. The Constitution was meant to be a living, breathing document," replied Sam. He continued, "It certainly seems like this case is going to be voted down. If either you or Judith vote against it, the consensus will be 5 to 4. To me, that would be a real disservice to our country. Our court is lopsided James; not at all representative of the citizens of the United States."

"The pendulum swings back and forth Sam," Braxton answered. "It is just your misfortune that the majority of the Justices on the Court now were appointed by conservatives. By the way, you forgot about Justice Sorensen. She has made a few contradictory comments, such as the one today about us being a different country than we were 250 years ago. I definitely had her pegged as being against the measure, but remarks like that make me unsure."

"Oh, she was probably just showing female solidarity for Irene." Justice Kleinman said. They both laughed. He continued, "I hope I preside long enough to see some forward thinkers on the Court."
 "Sam, Sam, always the liberal." Justice Braxton chuckled. "You would have been able to convince Attila the Hun to become a Democrat."
 "Well, I certainly would have tried, James. Checkmate!"

At the United States headquarters of Moritu Corporation in Dearborn, Michigan, there was a meeting going on in the executive boardroom. Hayao Yamamoto, the number one man at Moritu in the U.S. was in the middle of a video chat with his superiors back home in Tokyo.
"Have you heard anything about the Supreme Court deliberations yet Hayao?" asked Natsu Hakituri.
 "Not yet sir." replied Hayao.
 "You know what it would mean if the Court rules in favor of it, don't you Hayao?"
 "Yes, such a ruling would put me in an excellent position to obtain a nomination," Hayao answered distractedly.
 "Hayao, change your tone! If you become the next U.S. President the possibilities are endless."
 "Yes, sir."
 "You will keep us informed of any progress, won't you?"
 "Yes, sir. Goodbye."
 Hayao Yamamoto was the most senior Japanese executive currently working for any corporation in the United States, and certainly the most visible. He was 45 years old, came to this country when he was 19 where he was employed by the Moritu Corporation. Starting out in New York City, he quickly rose through the ranks with his superior intelligence. He had the foresight to engineer the relocation of his company's U.S. headquarters from New York to Dearborn, where overhead was a fraction of the cost, and had the good sense to funnel money back into the city of Detroit to help bring about its revitalization. For that, he was a local hero and a player on the national scale. He had no background in politics; however, having a proven track record

of achieving results and being immensely popular were a great one-two punch.

Due to Hayao's success in the Detroit area, Japanese people, both ones that had lived in the U.S. already and immigrants as well, began to migrate to that part of the country. They made their presence felt all over Wayne County and soon had taken over many positions of leadership; in their children's schools, in local government, and in opening up many new small businesses they wielded much power. If he got the chance to run for President, that would be a strong spring board for Hayao to start his campaign.

In Mexico, about 15 miles outside of Mexico City, Juan Pillar was visiting his cousin Vicente. They hadn't seen each other in two years.

"Juan do you think you have a chance of getting a nomination if the Supreme Court votes yes?" Vicente asked.

"Yes I do. I have served the U.S. Senate well for 10 years as a Senator from Georgia, and I am the highest ranking Mexican in federal government," replied Juan. "The Mexicans are one of the bigger ethnic groups demographically, and I am closely linked to President Harrington, who is very well liked."

Todd Russell was meeting with his advisers in the Governor's mansion in Springfield, Illinois.

"Governor, your latest numbers just came in. Your approval rating is down to 36%", said one of his advisers.

"What the hell is going on," the Governor fumed. "I was just re-elected a year ago on a wave of popularity."

"The people of Illinois have the misconception that you have just been going through the motions since the election."

"That's not true. I accomplished so much in my first term and now that I just have to maintain things, the people see me as a lame duck. The other problem is the changing sentiment in this country. The damn case that President Harrington put before the Supreme Court is hurting me as well. People, for the most part, are behind the measure. I, however, am an old time politician and people view me as ineffective. If I am going to have any chance at being

President I need to change my image and fast. Harold, set up a meeting with Chris Manning; she is the best public relations agent in the city."

"Might I also suggest Governor, that you get involved in some projects that will show you are taking an interest in the minority communities of our state," replied Harold, the Governor's top adviser. "For example, the Ukrainian community center in Evanston has been in the news lately because it is in disrepair due to lack of support. Getting behind causes like that is what I recommend to put you back on track."

"Good idea, Harold. Set it up. Ok, everyone, time to go to work."

U.S. representative Eric Layton from Colorado was having dinner with his wife at a posh restaurant in Washington D.C.

"Cindy, let's hope that this measure before the Supreme Court gets passed," he said.

"How would that work to your advantage Eric?" she asked.

"We both know that it would lead to several foreign candidates entering the race. The way I see it, they would split the votes of the people that would like to see a foreigner in the White House. The other front runner right now, besides me, is Todd Russell. I could beat him with my hands tied behind my back. He's older, part of the old political machine, and doesn't stand a chance with the new trend toward youth and vitality in politics. That leaves me, who will garner all the votes of traditionalists who still want a natural born citizen as their leader. I have a good record in the House, and I could then ride on President Harrington's coattails, pointing to the similarities in our political views."

"Not to mention the fact that you are devastatingly handsome, and have the female vote all locked up," Cindy Layton said, smiling enigmatically.

"Oh, Cindy, sounds like you are feeling frisky."

"I am."

"Check please!"

Down the hall and around the corner, Justice Winston Bernard looked around to make sure no one was watching. He opened the door to the stairs and descended four flights to the basement. When he got down there, he knocked on the door to the janitor's office.

"Who's there?",called out Lorraine Corvino, one of the custodians.

"It's me, let me in."

Stepping inside, Justice Bernard grabbed her and kissed her hard. "I thought that moron Braxton would never let us go. God, what a windbag."

"Oh Winston, don't let him get to you; we both know you are smarter than him. The only reason he is Chief Justice is because of who he knows."

"I know. You're right Lorraine. He just rubs me the wrong way. Ah, let's forget about him." He started to unbutton her shirt. This place always excited him. Maybe it was the dinginess of the space, or the smell of cleaning supplies mingled with the stench of day old garbage from the dumpster right outside, but he always felt trashy and wicked having sex down here. Lorraine was always after him to take her to a hotel, and once in a while he had to just to appease her, but even then he would always pick a dive; the cheapest, most tawdry ones he could find, which always seemed to reinforce the thrill of having an extramarital fling.

"By the way Winston, have you told your wife yet that you want a divorce?"

"No, it's not the right time. She is way too stressed right now planning my daughter's wedding." Wow, Lorraine sure does have a great body, Winston thought. I have certainly gone to pot, he thought unhappily. When I was an All American tennis player at Yale, I could stay on the courts all day. Now I am happy to do the elliptical for 30 minutes. That was one of the reasons he was carrying on with Lorraine; she made him remember what it was like to be youthful again.

"Well, you have been promising me you would tell her for some time now. Aren't you anxious to start our life together?"

"Of course I am. Once the wedding is behind us, I will be able to make a clean break. Let's try to enjoy ourselves now."

Chief Justice Braxton couldn't sleep and was enjoying a glass of brandy hoping it would help him relax. No issue had polarized the nation like this one since the Vietnam War and its aftermath, the counter culture movement. People felt very strongly about this; there was very little middle ground. Not surprisingly, the places where the people were the most at odds were the states that bordered either Canada or Mexico. Because of the proximity of these states to the other countries, differences of opinion were most common and there were the highest incidents of arguments and violence. In Maine, a tourist from Canada was killed in a bar when a disagreement took place over foreigner's rights. In Arizona, the mayor of a sleepy desert town was severely beaten by three men who had recently moved there from Mexico when the mayor was discussing his opinions in a restaurant. Indeed, people and governments were interested in the Supreme Court's deliberations every step of the way. The whole world was watching.

The people who were in favor of the change to the Constitution claimed that the logic coincided with the founding principles of this country, the fundamentals of capitalism, which were that the most enterprising will get ahead. They argued that this was a natural progression from that; there was no reason to exclude anyone from any political process. Furthermore, in keeping with our current open door immigration policy, we should allow all citizens to represent their country; this is even written on the Statue of Liberty.

Those against the measure use the historical argument that no one born elsewhere can have our best interests at heart; instead they will look for ways to be partial to their country of birth. They also point to the fact that this step is the first one down a slippery slope. If our President were to be from Canada, for example, he or she would likely fill government positions with U.S. citizens of Canadian origin, and the government would become more and more biased. This would create animosity in other governments everywhere, and a conflict would become more and more likely.

When Winston woke up, it was around 11 pm and Lorraine was still sound asleep. Getting dressed quietly, he slipped out of the office and made his way back upstairs. Entering the men's room for a minute to check his appearance, he hoped that his wife Cecily would be asleep when he got home. After 30 years of marriage, familiarity breeds contempt, and contempt was all she seemed to have for him these days. Yes, he would like to leave her, but despite what he told Lorraine, he had no intention of doing that. He much preferred to have his action on the side and keep up appearances. Besides, he had seen too many divorced men end up in the poor house. He knew Cecily was aware of what was going on. He had been having affairs for years; lately he only made the tiniest of efforts to conceal it. He also knew she would never leave him; he was her meal ticket and at this stage in her life she wasn't about to change. They had an unspoken agreement that as long as he kept it under the surface, she would turn a blind eye.

Their daughter, on the other hand, had no idea. No, Sondra was daddy's little girl, and always would be, even after she got married in six weeks. He would have to find a way to distance himself from his daughter without her realizing what he was doing. This was necessary; it was for her (and her fiancé's) own good. Newlyweds cannot grow together as a couple with extended family always around.

Winston exited the building and crossed the street to the parking garage. His colleagues had drivers, but he liked the control of driving himself, plus he did not want too many people knowing where he lived. Wow, there was a terrible odor in the stairwell. A homeless person had defecated there. He would have to call the Supreme Court police on Monday and chew them out for not being more vigilant.

Just as he was about to unlock his car, something pressed into his back, and then heard a voice in his ear. "If you know what's good for you, you won't resist. I have your wife, she is in the trunk of the car next to us, and if you fight or yell, she will suffer."

Justice Winston tried to look at the person behind him, but all he saw was a mask. Winston was guided into the backseat of the car, which was a Honda Civic - gray, nondescript. The kidnapper closed the door and started to walk around to the driver's side, then paused and whispered, "Oh I almost forgot." The judge winced when the dart was jabbed into his neck then felt nothing.

CHAPTER 2

When the Justice awoke to a fit of coughing, he realized the kidnapper had used smelling salts. It took a minute to clear his mind. He was blindfolded and bound to a chair. Listening for any sound at all, he heard breathing. "Who's there?" he called, panicking.

"Winston?"

"Cecily? Oh god, what have I done? What happened? Someone forced me into a car last night and told me you had also been abducted."

"I ended my phone call with Sondra when the doorbell rang. When I opened the door, someone was standing there with their back to me. The person turned around, and I saw a mask. They grabbed me before I could scream and plunged a syringe into my neck. When I woke up I had been blindfolded and tied up! Is this about one of your petty extramarital affairs? I've known about them for years. They finally caught up with you, you stupid idiot."

"Typical, jumping to the conclusion that we are here because of me. Did it ever occur to you that you might also have enemies?"

"From where? I am a housewife who volunteers at the hospital twice a week."

"I know. Don't worry Cecily. I will talk us out of this."

"Don't be so sure," a strange voice said.

"Who are you? I demand that you let us go immediately," said Winston.

Laughter came from across the room.

"Let's get started. Now, I am involved with some people who need information."

"What kind of information?"

"It involves the case before the Supreme Court, 'President Harrington vs. The United States Constitution'."

"You'll learn nothing from me," cried Winston.

Without warning, the kidnapper slapped the judge across the face, who cried out.

"Want to rethink your answer?"

"Go screw yourself."

The kidnapper walked over to Cecily Bernard. "Things are going to get a lot worse real quick, your honor, if you don't cooperate. I want to know which justices are voting which ways."

"Winston, don't say anything. He's bluffing." Cecily said.

Wolf took out a knife and cut the left side of Cecily's face – she screamed. "Does that sound like a bluff to you judge?", Wolf yelled.

"All right, all right, I will tell you what you want! Just don't hurt her."

"What a pussy," thought Wolf. "I'll be done in no time."

"OK, I want to find out which judges will vote to pass the law and which ones will reject it."

"Cecily, are you ok?"

"I'm ok Winston, just shaken up."

Winston addressed the kidnapper. "Please remove our blindfolds?"

"I can't do that. You'd be able to recognize me, and I would be forced to kill you. Simply give me the information and this will all be over soon and I will set you both free."

"Well, I will tell you what I can, but you realize that we are still in the middle of our deliberations and no one has made a definite ruling yet."

"I want you to predict how you expect each judge to rule, and you better be right or I will be back. I got to you very easily, and I can get to you again," Wolf replied impatiently.

"Chief Justice Braxton will vote against the measure; he is old fashioned about politics. He opposed the one party political system and spoke against the open door immigration policy."

"Justice Patrick Manucci will likely vote against the measure as well. Although it has never been proven, it has been rumored that his family has ties to organized crime, and the last thing that gangsters want is a foreigner in charge; one of the first things they would do would be to crack down on criminal enterprises."

"Justice Sam Kleinman will vote for the measure. He is a bleeding heart liberal and utopian; his view is that everyone should be equal under the law and fully supports immigrants' rights and privileges; his relatives came here and escaped the Holocaust."

"Justice Danielle Sorensen - I can't say for certain. If you looked at her track record, she typically rules conservatively. However, she is a feminist, and might surprise everyone and rule on the side of foreigner's rights, seeing that as a natural progression from women's rights. I would say she would rule against the measure."

"Justice Andrew Turnbull will vote against the measure. Surprising, I know. One would assume that as an African American he would want the political arena to be opened wider, but he is a firm believer in the fact that only an American born here would possess the level of patriotism required to lead our country."

"Justice Judith Lackey – she is the hardest colleague of mine to read. Her rulings are wildly inconsistent; she often argues both sides of the issue effectively in deliberations. I would say she will vote to pass the issue; her family tree has Mexican ancestors on it and she will want to honor their memories."

"Justice Irene Salkin will rule in favor of the measure. She considers herself to be a 'forward thinker'."

"Justice Alex Levitsky will vote in favor of the issue. Number one, he is a foreigner himself, and number two, he has a fondness for President Harrington, and tries to support him when possible."

"So, I gave you my opinion of how each justice will vote. Why don't you let us go now, and we will forget this all happened," Justice Bernard continued.

"Not just yet judge. It seems like the count is four to four. The people I am with are conducting important business. You left one judge out; yourself. Now, why don't you tell me how you plan to rule?" Wolf answered.

Winston, sweating profusely until now, began to shake. "I haven't been able to think it through yet. Now that you are an expert on me, why don't you tell me your name?"

"Just call me Wolf. Take your best guess."

Feeling sick now, Bernard's mind started to race. He searched for the answer that would keep him and Cecily alive. "I believe I am going to rule against it", replied the judge in a weak voice.

"I see. Well, you provided me much insight," Wolf responded and remained quiet for a moment. "Just one thing judge. You gave the wrong answer!"

The first shot knocked the judge backwards in his chair, just as his wife screamed. As blood started to gush out of Winston's head, Wolf finished her off too.

Officer Barnes walked along on his beat in Washington D.C. He covered the government buildings downtown which took him past the U.S. Supreme Court. It was 7 a.m. on Sunday morning and the streets were deserted. In the distance, right in front of the Supreme Court, he made out two large bundles in what appeared to be black garbage bags. When he got closer, he noticed they looked like two bodies. "Oh, no", he thought, "I will be filling out paperwork for a month." He took out his pocket knife and cut the first bag open. Inside he found a woman about sixty. Her skin still felt warm and elastic, which meant she had been dead less than three days. He sliced the second bag open and recognized the man immediately. Justice Bernard! Officer Barnes watched him often on television. "That must be his wife. I must call my lieutenant and the hospital; we should get the bodies out of here right away before the press gets wind of this before their family does." He took out his department issue phone which allowed him to get in touch with the precinct using voice commands and view the person on the other end automatically; Sergeant Galligan. He said, "Jim, I just came across Justice Winston Bernard's body and a woman I assume is his wife outside the Supreme Court. What should we do?"

"Well Tom, we need to call the Supreme Court police force – they maintain jurisdiction here. Let's do it right away so the family can retain some privacy. Luckily it's early in the morning. I will call them right now."

Half an hour later, a squad car with two officers and two forensic specialists from the Supreme Court police force arrived. The forensic experts got ready to take videos of the scene and study the area around the bodies. "The bodies were obviously dumped here. There is no blood or signs of a struggle. I want to get out of here right away, so give me the Moleculator", said the first man, officer Selridge. He appreciated the fact that they owned such a machine. The Moleculator is a new tool used in crime scene investigations that allowed samples to be taken from different surfaces such as tar and concrete to be analyzed later; it worked in two ways. First, it used vacuum technology to pull in any molecules, cells, and fibers that are loose on the ground. Second, it performed an analysis of the surrounding area to determine where there is a break in the composition of whatever surface is being checked. Twenty minutes later they had loaded the bodies into the trunk of their car, along with the samples taken from the Moleculator.

Once they got back on the road, the officers each breathed a sigh of relief. "Thank god we finished before the media arrived. That would have been a disaster. Twenty years ago, the technology didn't exist to finish a crime scene so quickly without leaving it cordoned off to return to it later."

Selridge and his partner arrived at the offices about fifteen minutes later. He wanted to get started right away, so he directed their actions by first carrying in the Moleculator and the two bodies. They brought all the items into their small forensics lab staffed with two part time forensics specialists which had always served their needs; this time however, the officers that arrived at the scene of the crime possessed their doubts.

After they cataloged the evidence, they sat down to collect their thoughts. Selridge and his partner, Officer Bill Carlstadt, tried to decide what to do. "The first thing we need to do is contact Chief Footerman; he'll want to contact the family before the story gets out and then make a statement to the media before tomorrow, because once Justice Bernard does not show up for deliberations tomorrow, word will get out real quick. Dick Maxwell and Whitney Danvers will want to take a crack at the forensics, but I am sure we will both agree that this will probably be a matter for the FBI. Now let's call the Chief," said Officer Selridge, the senior of the two officers.

Chief Footerman, captain of the Supreme Court Police force, was reading the news on his computer when his cell phone rang. He answered the phone on the second ring. "This better be important," he growled into the phone.

Officer Carlstadt apologized. "I am sorry, Chief, but Supreme Court Justice Bernard and his wife were found dead this morning on the street outside the Supreme Court building."

"Oh my god," remarked Chief Footerman, "this is going to be a disaster. Who found them and when?"

Officer Carlstadt answered, "D.C. police at 7am this morning. They called us right away, we went over the crime scene with the Moleculator and found no signs of a struggle. The bodies had been wrapped in black garbage bags, so it's clear they had been placed there after being killed, so we transported the bodies back to our offices."

Chief Footerman replied, "Good work. I will be there in twenty minutes."

It was about eight thirty am on Sunday and Wolf had almost finished. He packed the bodies last night, placed them in the trunk, drove into D.C. late last night and dumped them onto the street outside the Supreme Court. By then all the blood and signs of what took place were gone; having watched enough crime shows, he knew it wouldn't be difficult to destroy evidence and make the crime scene useless for the police. That included steam cleaning the carpet, changing clothes immediately after killing them and taking a shower. On Saturday afternoon around dinnertime, Wolf burned the clothes in the backyard, confident that people would assume that someone was barbecuing. He left fifteen minutes later, right on schedule.

Officers Carlstadt and Selridge were moving the bodies to the forensics area when Chief Footerman arrived. He was a small man physically but carried a big stick. "Hello men. Why don't you two get me up to speed?"

"It's like Bill told you on the phone, Chief. D.C police called us at just after 7, we went there, retrieved the bodies, collected the evidence, and brought it all here. We recorded everything, then called you," said Officer Selridge.

"How were they killed?"

"They were both shot, each of them one time in the head."

"Did you find anything unusual at the crime scene?"

"No. Whoever did this clearly knows something about forensics."

Chief Footerman rubbed his eyes wearily. "Ok, you two call Maxwell and Danvers while I figure out what I will tell the family."

At ten o'clock on Sunday morning. Wolf stopped at a diner just on the outskirts of Washington, looked inside and found Viper. They nodded hello to each other and Wolf ordered coffee. Viper had eggs, pancakes and sausage. "It's done, and now the fallout will start", said Wolf.

"Let me worry about that," replied Viper.

Without saying another word, Wolf took the briefcase and left, sticking Viper to pay for the coffee that had not come yet.

Chief Footerman took out his combination cell phone, computer, and television which could be folded into the size of a tissue box and said the words, "Winston Bernard, personal life." Instantaneously, a whole bio appeared on the screen. Skipping the part about his background, Footerman zoomed in on the part about Bernard's family. He saw that his parents and one brother died years ago, and that he and his wife had one daughter, Sondra, who would get married soon to a man named Blake Tristan. She lived in an apartment in Arlington, Virginia and worked for the American Civil Liberties Union. "Boy, I am sure her father loved that, being so conservative in his rulings", Footerman mused. He retrieved her phone number and wanted to get this over with as quickly as possible.

As Chief Footerman approached Sondra Bernard's apartment, he called her. A man answered, whom the Chief assumed to be her fiance. He asked to speak to Sondra, and a minute later she picked up. He introduced himself and said he would like to come over to speak with her. She asked if everything was all right, and the Chief replied that he would explain when he arrived in about five minutes.

The Chief took the elevator to the fourth floor. Stepping out, he saw that the door to Sondra's apartment had been opened with her standing outside waiting, a concerned look on her face. She ushered him inside and they sat down at the kitchen table where Blake Tristan soon joined them.

"Miss Bernard, I am truly sorry to tell you that your parents were found dead early this morning," Chief Footerman began.

Sondra Bernard turned white and started to shake. Blake reached over and took her hand to steady her.

"Oh my god," she said. "What happened?"

"An officer on the Washington D.C. police force found their bodies outside the U.S. Supreme Court building this morning at 7am. He called us immediately, and we went to gather the bodies and bring them to our offices", answered the Chief.

"Who would do this to them?", asked Sondra. "They were both good people."

"I can assure you ma'am, we will use all of our resources to get to the bottom of this."

"What was the cause of death?", asked Blake.

"Gunshot wounds in their heads," replied Chief Footerman.

"Oh my god. Does that mean we won't be able to have an open casket?"

"Well, we want our forensics experts to go over the body to gain insight about what happened. Once that is done, I can recommend an excellent mortician."

Still ashen, Sondra thanked him.

"Unfortunately, it's necessary that you come with me and officially identify the bodies, Miss Bernard. Mr. Tristan, of course you are welcome to accompany her," said the Chief.

"Please just give me a few minutes to compose myself," answered Sondra.

"Of course."

The ride for Sondra seemed intolerable. They arrived at the Supreme Court's police offices where officers Carlstadt and Selridge covered the bodies but left them the way they were. Chief Footerman warned her that the sight would be grotesque, but she told him to go ahead. When they pulled back the sheet on her father's body she sobbed once and said, "Yes, that is my father."

Next, she turned her attention to her mother's body. When they pulled back the sheet, and she saw her mother's mutilated face, she lost her composure. She started to cry uncontrollably. She nodded yes and Blake helped her leave.

Sondra went into the washroom and when she came out ten minutes later, she had calmed down.

"This is so unfair. Who is going to walk me down the aisle now? Our wedding is in six weeks," she said to Blake.

Blake pondered this for a moment. "What about your grandfather?" he finally said.

"Yes, he will be there for me." She turned to look at Blake, and her expression held a glint of something he never saw before; hatred. "Blake, I am going to make sure whoever did this gets brought to justice if it the last thing I do."

Chief Footerman drove them back to Sondra's apartment and turned to face them when he stopped. "You realize that come tomorrow, when your father does not show up at the Court, people are going to wonder. We need to decide how we want to report this to the media. Sondra, it is up to you. I would recommend that the notice come from me. However, reporters will be camped out at your door as soon as the word gets out. If you want, I'll wait until tonight if you want some time to find somewhere else to be for a few days."

"No, Chief. One thing I learned from my parents is to face things head on. Go ahead and contact the tv stations," Sondra replied after a pause.

When Chief Footerman got back to the police station, he sat down at his desk and wrote out a press release on his computer.
Washington D.C.
Sunday June 19th, 2039
12:00 pm

Two bodies were discovered early this morning by a Washington D.C. police officer around 7am while he conducted his routine duties. The bodies have been identified as Supreme Court Justice Winston Bernard and his wife, Cecily Bernard. The Supreme Court Police Department has taken possession of the bodies. More information will be provided as it becomes available.

He looked up the web page addresses for the national news networks as well as those of the local television stations. When he had them all, he sent out the notice. He leaned back for a moment, savoring the calm before the storm.

Chip Nesbit took a sip of his coffee as he researched a story about the latest robotic space launch which would be going further into space than any previous one when he saw a news item come through on the internet portal. Scanning it quickly, he did a double take. Justice Bernard's body found in D.C! His mind started spinning; this held the potential to tip the balance on the most visible case on the Supreme Court's agenda; President Harrington vs. The United States, which would determine whether a foreigner could run for President. Wow, this deserved top billing! A story like this demanded his immediate attention! He closed out of the web page by saying "Close page!" and spoke the name "Winston Bernard" at the screen. A complete biography of Justice Bernard appeared. Looking back at the press release from the Supreme Court police, Nesbit saw that Bernard's wife Cecily had been killed too. The only family left alive consisted of their daughter Sondra and Cecily's father. Chip saw that Sondra lived in Arlington, VA; he got on the phone and called his news bureau in D.C. Tom Sirois answered. "Hey Tom, Justice Bernard and his wife were found dead this morning. They have one surviving daughter, Sondra, who lives in Arlington, VA. Here is her address and phone number. Get over there and get an exclusive before anyone else does! Oh and take Felix and leave him there!"

Felix was the robot at each news bureau that took pictures and beamed them back to the home location, so the journalists would be alerted if he encountered something of interest.

Tom Sirois arrived at Sondra's apartment complex at just after 1pm and he saw no sign of any other reporters. He tried the front door and found it locked. He returned to his car and waited. About ten minutes later, a young couple walked out and after they left, Tom rushed to the door just before it closed and entered the building. He walked over to the electronic apartment directory and saw that Sondra lived in apartment 4c. When he got up there, he knocked on the door and heard footsteps. A man answered the door. "May I help you?" he asked.

Tom Sirois introduced himself as a journalist from the local affiliate of WNTL, the national news network. Before he asked any questions, or inquired about Sondra Bernard's whereabouts, the man said, "Get the hell out of here! We are in the middle of a tragedy! Show some compassion!" and got right in his face.

Before he answered, Tom heard a woman's voice from inside the apartment say,"It's all right Blake. Let me handle this."

Sondra Bernard walked to the door. Her eyes appeared bloodshot, and she trembled a little. "So you want an exclusive, is that it?"

"In fact, yes. In my business, Miss Bernard, you must beat everyone to the punch."

"Well, Mr. ?"

"Mr. Tom Sirois."

"Here's a punch and a kick for you. You will get an interview along with everyone else, when I give my press conference later today", and with that she slammed the door in his face.

Natsu Hakituri almost had finished his evening routine when he glanced at his computer screen and saw a headline in English that said "U.S. Supreme Court justice killed". He walked over to his computer which used voice commands exclusively. Keyboards and mice were things of the past – voice activation software had grown infinitely more sophisticated than even ten years ago. Online dictionaries and thesauruses also became increasingly popular that would give the user many more options when they didn't remember the correct word as well as built in translation software that translated between all the major languages. Hakituri used this software extensively; as the head of Moritu Corporation, he did business with influential people all over the world. The feature that the majority of people appreciated most of all however, was the elimination of buffering when downloading from the internet or streaming video or other media like there used to be. The companies responsible for the infrastructure of the internet came up with ways to increase their bandwidth to the point where even huge files could be opened all at once. Hakituri spoke to the screen, "U.S. Supreme Court justice killed," and the story appeared. Skimming over the details, he gleaned Justice Winston Bernard had been found dead. With no regard for the time, he immediately called Hayao Yamamoto in Dearborn. Hakituri was well versed about each one of the Supreme Court justices including their backgrounds, their political leanings, how they voted in the past, and which ones were likely to vote against the case consuming him lately. He felt like celebrating; Winston Bernard would almost certainly come out against having foreigners run for President. Furthermore, President Harrington would take his time and find a replacement justice with a liberal record who would tip the balance in favor of the measure, because as Hakituri saw it, with Justice Bernard on the bench the balance came down as five against four with the majority opposing the change to the Constitution. When Hayao answered, Hakituri wasted no time with small talk, assuming correctly that he knew. "This is a good thing for us, Hayao. One less obstacle in our way to the Presidency."

Hayao, who had been having a quiet breakfast, watching the news, expected this call. "Yes sir," he replied, hoping to get off the phone quickly; Sunday was his day off.

"You understand what must be done," Hakituri continued, and hung up.

Juan Pillar was still visiting with his cousin when he heard the news. Just like Natsu Hakituri, he realized what this meant for him and his mind began to race with the possibilities. "This changes everything. I planned to stay until Friday, but I want to get back now and jumpstart my campaign. Now I have a real shot! The first thing I will do is pick my campaign staff," he said to his cousin Vicente.

"That's great Juan. If, no sorry, when, you win, I hope you will find a spot for your cousin Vicente!" his cousin said jokingly.

"Don't worry, Vicente. I will find a vital position for you." They hugged each other and Juan left right away.

Almost three hours later, Sondra and Blake left to meet with President Harrington. Neither of them said a word to each other in the half hour it took them to get there. The driver, a Secret Service agent, swiped his card at the gate, and then they headed up the long driveway to the White House. They were ushered in the back entrance into a corridor where they waited for about ten minutes. Another Secret Service agent appeared and expressed his condolences to Sondra, then apologetically explained that he needed to scan them. Once they received clearance, they went upstairs to the President's office suite where they waited in an outer office. After about fifteen minutes, the door to the Oval Office opened and President Harrington emerged, hugging Sondra and shaking Blake's hand vigorously. The President stood about five feet eleven inches with blond hair and chiseled features making him quite handsome. He said to both of them, "I am so very sorry for your loss. Sondra, your father was a wonderful, wise man, and a great American. He will be missed, most of all by you." The President paused and walked over to face the window. "I understand that you two are getting married soon. I am sure that Winston would have walked Sondra down the aisle." He then turned to face them. "It would be an honor for me to take his place."

Sondra and Blake were stunned. Blake spoke first. "Mr. President, we cannot ask that of you. You have a country to run."

"I also must make time for things that are important, Blake. Sondra, did you have someone else in mind to give you away?" President Harrington replied.

"Yes, my grandfather, sir."

"I see. Well, at the risk of intruding on a private moment, perhaps you would allow both of us to walk you down the aisle," President Harrington said.

She wanted it to be an intimate moment, but saying no to the President? "That would be an honor, sir."

"Great. Just give the details about the wedding to my secretary on your way out. Now, let's talk about the press conference that's coming up. Perhaps you would speak first, Sondra, and then I would speak."

"That sounds fine to me as well", Sondra said.

"Great. We should go if you are ready. The press is already set up outside on the South lawn," President Harrington answered.

Blake cleared his throat. "Mr. President, please provide us with a security detail for a few weeks, mainly to shield us from reporters that already are camping out at our apartment."

"Of course Blake. I will take care of that right away." The President led the way through the White House to the doors that opened up onto the patio where all the reporters were. "Here we go." He opened the door and Sondra instantly felt besieged by all the cameras flashing in her face. She steadied herself and walked up to the microphone. "Earlier today, my parents, Cecily and Winston Bernard were found dead outside the United States Supreme Court building where my father served as a justice. The cause of death has not yet been determined, but I am confident that the police will sort this out. Thank you." A thousand questions filled the air, but Sondra simply turned and walked back to stand next to Blake. The President then took his turn at the mike. "Two great people were brutally murdered today. Rest assured that if this turns out to be politically motivated, the U.S. Government will use all of its resources to find the person or persons behind this. I will answer a few questions."

"Mr. President, who found the bodies?"

"A patrolman with the D.C. police."

"Who is going to be running the investigation?"

"The Supreme Court police force, for right now."

"Does that mean that they have a time limit on determining what happened?"

"No, it means that I am going to be monitoring their progress."

"Do you have any idea about who you will nominate to replace Justice Bernard?"

"No. I will answer two more questions."

"Will you nominate a liberal?"

"I don't know."

"Will you be attending Sondra Bernard's wedding?"

"If I am invited." The reporters and everyone else present chuckled. "Thank you." The President walked back to Sondra and Blake and all three went back inside the White House. They exchanged goodbyes and just before they left, the President said to them, "I meant what I said outside. I will see this through to the end. I give you my word."

Chief Justice Braxton had sent an email to the seven other Supreme Court justices, "Let's all meet tonight at 7pm at my house to discuss what happened today."

After all the justices had arrived at 7:05, Patrick Manucci said, "Well, there's one thing I am sure we will all agree on. President Harrington will certainly appoint someone who will rule in favor of having a foreigner run for President, namely a liberal."

Irene Salkin nodded in agreement. "This will also end our session until the fall as well. Hopefully by then the President will have appointed a new justice."

Chief Justice Braxton said, "I know all our hearts go out to Sondra. I can remember when Winston would bring her around to our offices as a cute little child. What a tragedy, right before her wedding."

Andrew Turnbull chimed in, "I know. What do you all think about who is responsible? Even though they murdered Cecily too, I find it hard to believe that this was personal. The nature of our business means that whichever way we rule on a case, we make enemies. Winston had been a justice for thirty years with some very high profile cases. He is bound to have angered many people; someone probably snapped."

Samuel Kleinman said, "If that's the case none of us are safe. In my opinion, it's more likely that whoever did this is unhappy about a current case with which we are involved."

Judith Lackey answered, "I agree. Maybe we should talk to the President about getting more protection."

All the justices agreed. Chief Justice Braxton said he would contact the President in the morning.

Danielle Sorensen added, "It certainly seems coincidental that this happened during the most controversial case we have had in years. There are many people and groups that stand to gain based upon how we end up ruling, on both sides of the argument."

Justice Judith Lackey replied, "We don't need to play police officers here. Winston was a national figure; there will be lots of resources used to investigate."

Sasha Levitsky said, "I just hope President Harrington appoints someone quickly, and they get approved quickly too. We will be under great pressure to reach a decision soon, so those who end up running for President will be able to start their campaigns."

Chief Justice Braxton said, "Let's not forget about the other smaller cases in front of us. While we can't reach a majority until a ninth justice has been appointed again, we can continue deliberating on those cases for another week and the new justice can become familiar with those cases when the new term starts. We will convene tomorrow at 9am for our regular session."

That night, around 8pm in Dearborn, Hayao Yamamoto placed a call to Florida. When the woman answered, Hayao said, "Hello Alex. This is Hayao. How are you?"

Alex Ramirez answered, "I am great Hayao. How are you?"

"I'm fine. How is life in Florida these days? I understand you are doing a fine job as Governor. The state is in better fiscal shape than it's been in years, and Florida's image in great – tourism is at an all time high."

"Well, thank you Hayao. Rumor has it that Moritu Corporation is thriving too. What can I do for you?"

"Well, I have a business trip to Florida in a few days and there is something I would like to discuss with you. Would you be available later in the week?"

"Which day did you have in mind?"

"How about Wednesday?"

"Perfect. Can you make it to the Governor's mansion in Tallahassee? I could prepare lunch for us. Say around noon?"

"That sounds great. I will see you then. Goodbye."

As he hung up the phone, he felt optimistic that things would fall into place.

The next morning Todd Russell met with his advisers again. "This may change everything, people. With Winston Bernard gone, the Supreme Court may vote down the measure, keeping Hayao and Juan Pillar out of the race. With them gone, I may actually stand a chance. Harold, have you called Chris Manning?"

"I left her a message sir."

"Well, if you don't hear from her by this afternoon, call her again. The other thing I need to contemplate is selecting a running mate. We need someone to offset my views; people perceive me as conservative, a liberal or moderate would complement my political ideology well. Also, let's try to find a person from another part of the country to maximize our demographics. Harold, will you develop a list of viable candidates?"

Harold nodded.

Governor Russell continued, "Now, let's turn our attention to the problems facing us here in Illinois. I realize things have been pretty much status quo since my reelection, but someone tell me, what is the biggest problem facing our state right now?"

One of the junior staffers answered, "Mr. Governor, that would probably be the Department of Education. Our administration has cut the state income tax and as a result been funneling less money to the towns to supplement their school budgets. Property taxes have risen, and some districts have opted to cut services instead."

The Governor replied, "Well, we need to make it look like we working with the mayors to come up with a solution. Alan, you are the liaison to that Department. Please make an appointment with Ed Zaslaw. This meeting is over."

As everyone started to leave, Governor Russell called one of his staffers over, a woman named Rose. "Rose, do you have a minute?" She nodded yes. The Governor waited until everyone had left and then got up to close the door. "Rose, do you still keep in touch with Joe Berry? I remember you once mentioned that you went to college together and participated in some campus organizations with him."

"As a matter of fact, Governor, I do. We communicate occasionally on the networking site 'PastConnect'".

"Please get in touch with him privately and tell him I would like to meet with him. Please also make it clear that just the three of us will be aware of this."

"Of course Governor. I will get in touch with him today." With that, the Governor exited the room.

At ten am on Monday morning the two forensic experts on the Supreme Court police force, Dick Maxwell and Whitney Danvers had been up all night going over Justice's Bernard's body and the evidence collected at the crime scene using the Moleculator. Chief

Footerman had just arrived and, after making his coffee, barged into the morgue for an update. "Well, what have you two found?" Danvers answered, "The shots came at close range in the head with a handgun, and we removed both bullets from their brains. We found no defensive wounds; both bodies had marks on their wrists from being bound. They must have been blindfolded too, and tightly; there were marks on their foreheads. We would place the time of death as sometime Saturday afternoon."

"What about the toxicology report?"

Maxwell said, "They had been given serum which would have affected them for about 16 hours."

The chief answered, "Let's check the garage where Justice Bernard parks and find out if his car is there. If it is, that means whoever abducted the judge and his wife likely picked up his wife first; in order to use that to threaten the judge and the judge would have gone more willingly; if he had no bargaining chip, I have a feeling that the judge might have resisted. So, working backwards, if the time of death had been, let's say 3pm, and whoever did this was after some information, they would have wanted the drugs to wear off around one or two pm. Which means that they were probably abducted around 11pm on Friday night. Let's talk to the other justices to see what time their session ended on Friday and find out if anyone saw Justice Bernard after that."

Officer Danvers thought for a moment about the best way to correct the Chief. "One thing Chief. It's possible that the kidnapper revived Justice Bernard and his wife rather than letting the serum wear off."

Chief Footerman said, "We will have a better idea of the timeline after we get some answers. Danvers, you canvass the parking garage. Maxwell, get over to the Supreme Court building and see what you can find. Let's meet back here after lunch."

Half an hour later Officer Maxwell arrived at the Supreme Court. He always felt overwhelmed when he went in – opinions were rendered here that affected the entire world!

Approaching the security desk, he showed his badge to the guard sitting there, took off his holster and gun, put it on the conveyor belt, and walked through the metal detector then went down to Chief Justice Braxton's office and knocked on the door.

Justice Braxton said, "Come in!"

Maxwell poked his head in the door and said hello. Chief Justice Braxton recognized him as part of the Supreme Court police but didn't remember his name. "Come on in officer. I assume you are here to discuss Justice Bernard's case."

"I am as a matter of fact. Did the court conduct a session on Friday?"

"Yes, we met in the afternoon and evening."

"What time did your deliberations end?"

"Around nine o'clock pm. We were all exhausted by then."

"Do you remember, did Justice Bernard leave the room right away?"

"As a matter of fact, I do. Yes, he walked out with Justice Salkin and they headed down the hallway together. I exited the room last that night and turned off the light. I saw the two of them as I exited the room; their offices are right next to each other."

"Thank you judge. Are all the other justices here?"

"Yes, they are. We have an afternoon session today which will be one of the last ones before our summer recess."

"Ok, good. I am going to have to speak with them all individually, starting with Justice Salkin."

"Of course, Officer. We will cooperate in any way we can."

"Thank you." Officer Maxwell turned to leave. As he got to the door to leave, he turned. "One last question judge. Besides the nine of you did you notice anyone in the building?"

"Not that I know of. Good day officer."

Officer Maxwell next went to Justice Salkin's office. She invited him in and asked him to sit. He told her the reason for his visit.

She said, "What a tragedy. I am just shaken to the core; Winston was a colleague and a friend." Wringing her hands, she continued, "My heart goes out to his daughter. Losing both parents just weeks before her wedding; I cannot even imagine the sorrow she is feeling."

Maxwell nodded in agreement. He waited a minute then said, "I am sorry to have to bring this up, but I am trying to recreate Judge

Bernard's schedule on Friday. I spoke to Justice Braxton, and he said that when you ended Friday's session, he saw yourself and Bernard walking down the hall together."

"That's right. Our offices were right next to each other."

"Had he been acting strangely or unusually in any way?"

"No, he seemed to be the same as always." She paused. "You know what, now that I think of it, I heard him on the phone when I left for the night. He typically left right away."

Maxwell considered this for a moment. "Do you have any idea if there was anyone else in the building that night?"

"Not to my knowledge."

"Thank you for your time."

Chief Footerman sat at his desk trying to wrap his head around this case and trying to make sure they would cover all the angles when the phone rang. The caller id showed a private number. He picked up the phone and for a minute, no one said anything. Just as he was about to hang up, a voice said, "Hello, hold for the Director of the FBI." A second later, Director James Grey came on the line. "Hello Mr. Footerman. Terrible thing about Winston Bernard."

Footerman agreed.

Director Grey continued, "Mr. Footerman, perhaps we could work together on this. I understand you have collected evidence from the crime scene. Was anything you found significant?"

"Unfortunately not. There were no fingerprints on the bags and no physical evidence found anywhere."

"I would like to ask for a favor. We would like to have the body in our possession, today, as soon as possible. There are some time sensitive tests we would like to run, and then we will return the body to you."

Chief Footerman's face turned red. Of all the nerve! However, he did not want to take on the FBI. "Of course; we are on the same team. When can you get here?"

The Director answered, "We will have someone there in fifteen minutes. Thank you for your cooperation." The line went dead.

Sure enough, fifteen minutes later he heard the FBI van arrive. Two men came in and with hardly a word took Bernard's body away.

Chief Footerman got back to his work; at one pm he noticed Danvers and Maxwell had returned.

"Well, you two, what have you found?"

Danvers went first. "I didn't find much at the parking garage. I saw Bernard's car and had it impounded and arranged for our forensics team to go over it. They didn't find any debris or signs of a struggle."

"Maxwell?"

"Well, I spoke to all the judges. Irene Salkin saw him last; after the session ended on Friday around nine pm, the two of them walked back to their offices together. She said there was something out of the ordinary however; she said that Bernard almost always left right away after the judges had finished deliberating for the day. Friday, however, he made a phone call and hadn't left when Salkin went home 15 minutes later."

"Was anyone else in the building besides the judges?" asked Footerman.

"Not to anyone's knowledge, but Justice Kleinman did say that there is a janitorial crew that works in the evenings; perhaps a custodian cleaning up."

"Or hanging around for another reason. All that thinking can sure make a man horny. What have we learned about Bernard?"

Danvers quickly looked him up online. "Athlete in college; I've seen him around, tall and slender. Married for 37 years. After that long, highly unlikely that he is staying in shape for his wife."

Looking at Maxwell, he said, "I would be willing to bet that if you check his phone records, he called his wife on Friday night to tell her that he had some things to finish up at work. Did you find out the name of the company that cleans the building?"

"Yes, Magnus Industries. They do buildings all around D.C."

Footerman said, "Ok let's get started. Maxwell, get the forensics team over to the Supreme Court building once they have finished with the judge's car. Maybe Bernard got sloppy and had a tryst in his office. Then, send them out to the judge's residence. Perhaps our kidnapper got sloppy also. Danvers, track down Bernard's phone log and see who he called. Then get the phone log from Bernard's house and their cell phones too. After that, get more information about the cases that the Supreme Court is working on. Clearly the obvious one to investigate is the case put forth by President Harrington, but we need to cover all our bases. I, in the meantime, will contact Magnus Industries and see if anyone worked at the court on Friday and speak to them. We will meet back here tomorrow morning at 10am."

   At the FBI headquarters in Quantico, Winston's body was ushered into the private section of the building that housed Director Grey's office and his private crime laboratory, which required special clearance to enter. In the law enforcement community, the facilities and equipment there are top secret and rumored to be unlike any others; so much so that the heads of other agencies around Washington, such as the CIA and NSA, didn't even have a clue about them. Director Grey walked in and addressed his top two scientists. "You know what to do. Winston had been a personal friend; he also possessed the foresight to submit to a full brain scan several years ago. I asked the Chief of the Supreme Court police about the time of death; they said around 4pm on Saturday. That gives us about 4 hours to run the comparative brain scan, so let's get started."

   Chief Footerman called Magnus Industries and spoke to the foreman on duty. "Can you tell me who cleans the Supreme Court building on Fridays?"
   The foreman answered, "It's usually Rick Heller and Brian Gorsky, but Gorsky called out sick, so Lorraine Corvino filled in for him."
   "Lorraine Corvino? Does she work in that building often?"
   "About once a week. Why?"
   "No reason. Just a lead I am following up on. What time do they usually finish?"
   "Around seven."

"I'd like to talk to both Heller and Corvino. Where are they now?"

"They are both on jobs. Heller finishes up in about an hour and Corvino has three hours to go."

"I will see Heller first. Where is he?"

"He is at a bar in downtown Washington and Corvino is at the Edgeview School."

"Thank you."

When the Chief arrived at the Smokehouse Bar, he saw a man with a ponytail and tattoos on his forearms sweeping the floor.

"Mr. Heller?"

"Who's asking?"

"I am Chief Footerman from the U.S. Supreme Court police."

"Oh, I guess you want to talk about that stiff judge who got waxed the other night."

"How eloquent," Footerman thought. "Yes, I understand that you were working Friday night when he was last seen. Did you notice anything unusual going on?"

"Nah, I worked with that wench Corvino. We had finished around nine pm. The only chamber we did not clean was the deliberation room. Me and Corvino went down to the janitors' room, and I got changed – behind the partition. When I finished I noticed that she didn't leave right away. She said she felt tired and wanted to just sit for a few minutes. So I left."

"Thank you. If I need anything I will be in touch."

Footerman arrived at the Edgeview School at about six pm. He walked in the front door and made a mental note to talk to the principal about security. He heard shouts coming from the gymnasium and wondered what about the noise since it was the end of the school year. There was a vacuum running from the other end of the school and walked off in that direction. When he turned the corner of the hallway, the woman vacuuming had her back to him. Rather than sneaking up on her, he found the light switch for the hallway and flicked it off and on twice. The woman noticed it and turned around. Footerman waved and held up his badge. She turned off the vacuum and took the earplugs out of her ears.

"Thank you for not startling me. People can be so inconsiderate."

Footerman asked, "Are you Lorraine Corvino?"

"Yes, what can I do for you, Mr.???"

"Chief Footerman from the U.S. Supreme Court police. I assume you know why I am here?"

"I would have to be living under a rock if I didn't. What a tragedy about Justice Bernard and his wife."

Footerman said, "I understand you worked at the Supreme Court building on Friday night. How often do you work there?"

"Usually once a week. My boss likes to move us around so we don't get too comfortable with the people working in the buildings we clean."

"How long have you worked for Magnus Industries?"

"Twenty one years."

"Really? You must have seen Justice Bernard quite a bit over the years."

"We saw each other in passing." Footerman noticed she looked down and wrung her hands when she said this.

"Did you notice anything out of the ordinary last Friday?"

"No. We finished work around nine o'clock and then we – my coworker Rick Heller and I – went down to our office in the basement. He left before I did and I left a few minutes later."

Footerman said, "Working in the same building for so many years a person must observe a lot. You mentioned that you saw Bernard in passing. What was he like?"

At this question Corvino blushed a little; she would not make a very good poker player. "He always acted cordially but aloof to me."

"Did you ever see him talking on his cell phone?"

"I am not an eavesdropper, sir."

Footerman sighed. "Thank you for your time Miss Corvino. Here is my card. If you remember anything that would be helpful to our investigation, please call me."

As he walked out of the school, Footerman looked at his watch. He decided to go straight home to be home in time to watch the news at seven pm.

Director Grey walked into the top secret crime lab at around nine pm. "Well, what have you found?" he asked his scientists.

They looked up, surprised. "Justice Bernard's baseline scan showed his blood distributed evenly throughout his brain, and a pooling of fluid on the right side of his brain." One of the scientists pointed to the pictures on the board to the left. "In comparison, when he was asked to show various emotions at his planned brain screening, the emotions that most closely resemble his brain activity at the time of death are bewilderment and fear. The electrical impulses demonstrate anger as well, but as a minor response overtaken by the other two."

"Did you perform the noetics test?"

"Yes we did. His brain has lost 4 ounces since his death. Considering the human brain weighs only about 24 ounces, that is an awful lot. That would seem to indicate that his mind took off in a million different directions right before his murder."

Director Grey asked, "How can you be sure? You don't know what his brain weighed right before he died."

"That's true, but when we performed the brain scan on him in our lab, we tried to simulate as many scenarios as possible. One of the scenarios we enacted involved fear and fright, in which Bernard's mind was racing. Taking into account that his emotions most closely resembled that, we can surmise that he lost about 4 ounces."

The director looked at them both for a minute. He then simply thanked them and walked out, excusing himself as he left.

Five minutes later, back in his interior office, Director Grey's head spun. He did not pretend to understand the work that went on in that lab. He scoured the country for the top young minds and then let them ply their trade. In recent years, they made the most strides in brain analysis. Of course, this was all top secret. Not even his deputy directors had access to the lab or what went on inside. Anyway, his scientists had come up with a way to take images of the brain to view the emotional activity for comparison purposes when collecting evidence in crimes like this one. Furthermore, they had also found a way to use noetics, the concept that thoughts have weight, in determining someone's neural activity at the time of death. In the case of Justice Bernard and those others that had submitted to healthy brain scans, the FBI Director had made sure that scans were taken with different emotions and their brains weighed with these different emotions. Now he had his work cut out for him with the results from Bernard's scan. The scientists had said that his brain had recorded fear and bewilderment, and that his brain had lost 4 ounces. This led Grey to believe that he had never met the person or persons who had kidnapped him and Cecily, and that he had desperately tried to think of a way out and for the right thing to say.

Winston had played around on Cecily; he just wasn't sure with whom. Maybe one of the other judges, or multiple women. It might also be related to one of the cases that the Supreme Court had dealt with. If he had to bet of course, he would say that it involved the case about a foreigner running for President. He had seen it all in his 30 years at the FBI, and he had never seen the country in such sorry shape. Politics had always been a dirty business and politicians could never be trusted, it was the nature of the beast. Now, however, it had turned into such an undesirable trade that they had to stoop so low to entice people from other countries to lead us. Oh well, none of this concerned him – yet. He predicted that this investigation would be too much for the Supreme Court police and the FBI would step in; then he could conduct the investigation the right way. For now, however, he would have to wait until it became apparent that the Supreme Court police were out of their league.

Eric Layton sat in his office at home thinking. The death of Justice Bernard was a tragedy, and one that could turn out to be a blessing or a curse for him. If President Harrington appointed a liberal, the measure would certainly pass. If it did, the new candidates would cut into his votes tremendously. The public saw him as a savior, a man who genuinely wanted to do some good, which seemed to be in short supply these days. They would feel the same way about the candidates from the other countries. On the other hand, there would be some people that would vote for him instead of the other candidates because they vehemently opposed an outsider being President. Conversely, if the new justice that gets appointed is a conservative that would definitely put him in the position of being the frontrunner. That was unlikely, however. President Harrington had brought the case to the Supreme Court in the first place. Layton had to figure out a way to turn this to his advantage. He appealed to people as an upstart, someone who brought a sense of youth and energy to politics that had been missing for years. Perhaps he could campaign with the message that only an American could truly be a leader. He looked at his watch; three o'clock. He had promised his son, Jack that he would take him to the park. Besides, it would make for a good photo op.

Governor Russell's phone buzzed. He picked up the phone on the second ring. "Hello?"
"Hello Governor, it's Rose. I have Joe Berry on the line." He heard her press the transfer button.
"Hello?" he said again.
"Governor Russell, this is Joe Berry. How are you today?"
"I am fine Joe. How are you?"
"Fine. I understand from Rose that you wanted to speak to me?"
"Yes I did. Are you on a secure line?"
Puzzled, Joe answered yes. The Governor got up to close the door. "Joe, I have a proposition for you. As you well know, I am planning to run for President. As of late, my approval ratings have gone down, and I can hardly use this as a springboard for my campaign. Now, with a new nomination coming for the Supreme Court, I am going to need all the help I can get. What I am proposing to you Joe, is that you work on my campaign, strictly from behind the scenes, as my lead public relations specialist. Your reputation in the industry precedes you, and Rose told me that the two of you still keep in touch, so we can communicate through the website. You would have to stay exclusively in the background, however, as I have my own staff who ostensibly handles all those aspects. Any suggestions that you have I could work back in to my people during our meetings. We could communicate in the evenings and on the weekends during non-business hours. Are you interested?"

Joe Berry didn't say anything for a minute. He worked for one of the biggest public relations agencies in Washington D.C. and came highly recommended. He had worked on accounts all over the country but had never been approached with an offer like this. Regarding Russell's reputation, since his first term ended, he has been viewed by the people in Illinois as completely apathetic and disinterested in their problems. He did need all the help he could get. Joe did not work behind the scenes though. He enjoyed the limelight and wanted people to understand how good he was at his job.

"If I take on this task, Governor, what type of compensation did you have in mind?"

"One million now, and one million if I get elected."

That's a lot of dough. Maybe I can make an exception. "All right, Governor. I'd like to help you out, and Rose is a good friend. The first thing we need to do is make you more visible. Why don't you start visiting some schools and make education reform a priority. I understand that the school budgets are suffering, why don't you look into shared services, it's worked in other states. Next, we have to get some commercials on tv. We have the summer to fix things. I am sure by the fall there will be a new justice and the Court will have made a decision, and once that happens the race will be on."

"You are absolutely right. Thank you, Joe. I am looking forward to working with you."

The next morning, Chief Footerman reconvened with his officers working on the case. He told them what he had learned and said that Lorraine Corvino had seemed nervous, blushing and wringing her hands. She had denied knowing Bernard but yet still showed much emotion when he questioned her. The chief asked Danvers to do a background check on her. He had another assignment for Dick Maxwell. He asked Maxwell to get in touch with Director Grey at the FBI and find out when they could get the body back. Once they had both left, he thought about what to do next. He decided to review the crime scene data and the forensics report. Touching the screen on his desk, he brought up the folder about the case and said "forensics report." Reading down, the report said that both Justice

Bernard and Cecily had been shot in the temple, with the bullet entering Justice Bernard's skull on the left and just the opposite for Cecily. Footerman stood up for a second. He pointed an imaginary gun. If an average person were about to kill two people, even premeditated, he would not have been so precise. This told him that whoever did this was not a stranger to handling firearms. He called two detectives into his office. Addressing both of them at the same time, he asked them to go out to the crime scene and canvass the neighborhood for any logical places where the killer may have disposed of the gun. With someone like this, he or she would have wanted to get rid of it as soon as possible. He suggested they look in any dumpsters in the area as well as the sewers and any other remote places. He wanted all the resources available to him working on this high profile case; the perception being that his police force shouldn't be taken seriously, and Footerman wanted to show everyone that he possessed the skills of a good cop and leader. He was no flunkie; he had solid training in law enforcement and had been a candidate for the FBI, the gold standard of law enforcement. If his force handled this right, it would bring much credibility to the Supreme Court police. Once again he went through the series of events. Bernard and Cecily were kidnapped Friday night, held hostage until Saturday, killed around 3pm on Saturday afternoon, and their bodies left in DC before 7am Sunday morning. That means that they must have been taken somewhere within an hour or two of the city to have time to elicit the information they needed and still have time to clean up the area and get back by 7am. The kidnapper or kidnappers likely went to a private residence with a garage or abandoned building with a secluded entrance; pulling up a map of the metro DC region, Footerman drew a circle around the area that could be reached within two hours. Trying to canvass every empty building or house would require way more manpower than he had however; he would reach out to the Washington DC police; maybe they could lend him some officers to investigate any people that have criminal records in the area. He would call Chief of Police Pruitt; they had always had a good working relationship. When he picked up the phone to call Pruitt, he heard Maxwell on the phone talking to

Director Grey. "We would like the body back, Director, as soon as possible." He listened for a minute, and then said, "Great. Thank you so much. Good bye." He hung up the phone and waited for Footerman to get off the phone too. When he did, he told Footerman that the FBI would return the body after lunch. Footerman was pleased; things seemed to be coming together. Pruitt had promised him five detectives starting tomorrow; now he wanted to review his theory with Danvers and Maxwell.

On Tuesday at 11am Hayao spent some time in Dearborn going over how he would present his proposal to Alex Ramirez. It was common knowledge that she held a thirst for power and wouldn't need much convincing. She would make the perfect running mate being very popular and had accomplished much as Florida's governor. It would be a balanced ticket; those that wanted to shake up the system would be in favor of a foreigner and a woman, and those that supported the status quo would approve of Ramirez; after all, there were really no other viable candidates on the horizon. Ramirez probably expected to be asked; he had once said in an interview that he would favor a female as his potential Vice President. His secretary buzzed him right then. "Mr. Yamamoto, it's President Harrington." He wants to talk about our exports for the last quarter. "Thanks, Lisa. Put him through. Oh, and Lisa, make sure the jet is fueled up, and please cancel all my appointments for tomorrow. Hello, Mr. President."

Sondra Bernard was home in her apartment by herself. Blake had gone out to do a few things. Her parents' funerals would be on Saturday; she had decided to have them both at the same time; she could not go through that agony twice. Phone calls have been nonstop, many from strangers. God, her head hurt. Blake has been wonderful, giving her just the right amount of space. He had encouraged her to go out with him today, but she didn't feel ready. She would be besieged by reporters and couldn't handle that yet. President Harrington had assured her that he would do what he could to keep them away from the funeral. The people at the ACLU where she worked had been wonderful also; her boss had given her three weeks off for bereavement time and said she would be paid during that time. Now that it had been a few days, she was certain the murders involved a case the Supreme Court had before them. The Supreme Court police had the case right now, but she hoped that the FBI would take over sometime soon which they had before in situations where there had been no progress. They had the authority to do that, and her father had been a personal friend of Director Grey. The FBI had resources that no other agency had, and Grey would give it all he had to get to the bottom of this. The phone rang. It was Meredith, one of her closest friends. "Hi Sondra. How are you holding up?"

"Oh, I am all right, Meredith. As best as can be expected, I suppose, under the circumstances. How are you?", she asked, trying to sound as upbeat as possible.

"I am fine, honey. I will be flying out on Friday, but if you need me I can come earlier."

No, Sondra thought. As much as she liked Meredith, she did not want to be entertaining right now. "No, Meredith, Friday is fine. I really appreciate you coming."

"You know that I wouldn't stay away. I will see you on Friday. Take care of yourself and say hello to Blake. Bye Sondra."

"Bye Meredith."

Viper had the news on, and the latest report on the Bernard murders revealed that the Supreme Court police were tracking down leads and enlisting the help of the Washington DC police force. "What boobs," Viper said to the television. For the time being there was nothing to worry about, no progress would be made until the FBI took over, which could happen at any time. With so many possible suspects, it would take them forever to make any headway. Besides, a contingency plan existed if the FBI got too close. Viper would worry about that if and when the time came. It remained critical that Wolf not get sloppy and that all tracks were covered and nothing could lead back to them. "Enough wasting time," Viper remarked silently. Many tasks still needed to be addressed.

President Harrington listened as Chief Justice James Braxton answered his question. The President had called him to see how things were going with their caseload in the wake of what happened as well as to make sure that each justice had received the security detail President Harrington had ordered. "Thank you Mr. President. The secret service agents are doing a terrific job; they are making us feel safe in the wake of all this anxiety. Obviously, none of us can keep our minds on our deliberations; fortunately we have our summer recess in a week." He paused. "Do you have any idea about who might replace Winston?"

President Harrington had expected this question. He didn't want to tip his hand but also wanted to make it clear to Braxton that he would pick someone that would support the President's agenda. "There are many qualified people out there Jim; the person I select will be fair and a forward thinker."

Braxton was disappointed. He hoped that President Harrington planned to try to keep the Court in balance. Braxton knew he wanted foreigners to be able to run for President, but many politicians kept the integrity of the Court intact, regardless of their political ideologies, replacing liberals with liberals, etc. The President had made it clear with his comment, however, that he would be appointing someone who would most likely support his agenda, a forward thinker! Oh, well, he couldn't do anything about it. Maybe the Supreme Court could find some common ground; it did not have to be all or nothing. Perhaps, like someone suggested, they could make it clear that the legislation include a residency requirement or something similar for the justices to view the measure as upholding the Constitution. Well, this would have to be put on the back burner now. There were other cases on their docket that they could devote some time to this week. They had already finished deliberating for the day; he would tell the other justices about the conversation with the President tomorrow.

When President Harrington hung up, he believed that he had conveyed his message that he intended to nominate a liberal to fill Bernard's seat. There would be opposition; moreover, he would be expected by some people to keep the mix the same on the Court. However, this should not come as a surprise. After all, he was the one who had filed the case in the first place! Did they think that he wouldn't seize this opportunity? Wait a minute, would anyone think...? No, impossible. His character has been unassailable. He had never had any shady dealings and all of his records were open for the public to see. He had to give some thought to whom he would nominate. Democrats and Republicans no longer existed as parties, but the conservatives in Congress would still automatically be opposed to whoever he nominated; that much hadn't changed since the U.S. had done away with political parties. He had a strategy. His first nominee would be a viable candidate, but would have something minor wrong with them, like perhaps that they had hired a domestic worker and paid them under the table for example. Congress would have someone to shoot down, and then he would be in the clear to nominate the person he really wanted; Isaac Adler, a brilliant man; more importantly, a forward thinker. He would tip the balance in favor of a foreigner running for President. This measure was for the good of the country; did the people really want someone like Todd Russell in charge? Our society has been going downhill for years. President Harrington also wanted to be remembered as the one who saved the country from further decline. Manny Sharpe had been a lame duck President. Oh, he had a nice smile, made people feel good, but his role amounted to that of an ambassador for the new political structure, the one party system. He and his administration knew that the most important thing for them to do had to be to make things work as smoothly as possible and generate the most good for the most people even if that meant it would be a problem in the future. He had inherited a lot of those issues. Foreign affairs were on an even keel right now; that fact allowed him to introduce the case before the Supreme Court. The domestic economy needed attention. Americans were not getting the jobs done at home anymore and the U.S. needed a global perspective to keep up with these other countries. As President, he maintained the unique position to see that and believed Isaac Adler would see it too. He did have someone in mind to be the justice that the Senate would reject as well; Darren Conklin. Darren was a good man with a good record. He did have a skeleton in his closet however. He had a child out of wedlock, which hardly anyone knew, having abandoned his daughter. When the time came, if it looked like Conklin would be approved, it could be arranged that an anonymous source could alert the media to this, and then a character debate would begin, which would surely result in his rejection as a Supreme Court justice. He liked Conklin, and he would make a fair justice, but Adler towered above Conklin, and would be an asset to the Supreme Court. Yes, Conklin would be the sacrificial lamb.

Wednesday June 22th 11am, EST
Hayao Yamamoto's plane touched down, and a few minutes later they had arrived at the gate. He closed his laptop and stood up and stretched. He had just spoken to Natsu again a few minutes ago, who had reiterated his message. Natsu deserved his respect, but Hayao had grown tired of his old fashioned ways. Ten minutes later, having been whisked through the airport by his handlers, one of the perks of being a top executive, he sat in his limousine. His phone rang. It was his secretary, telling him that the Governor of Michigan had called to ask him to hire one of his cronies. Morons, all of them. When he won the election he would make life as difficult as possible for the politicians in Michigan; all they cared about seemed to be getting jobs for their friends and getting laid. He returned to the moment; his meeting with Ramirez. Half an hour later, they arrived at the Governor's mansion in Tallahassee Florida. The house was stunning, like an old antebellum estate. When he rang the doorbell, a member from Governor Ramirez's security detail answered the door. A handsome man, Hayao couldn't help but notice; some urges never completely went away. The man showed him into the Governor's private sitting room. Two minutes later, Governor Ramirez entered the room. "Hayao, it is so nice to see you. It has been way too long!"

God, how he hated small talk, but he forced himself to engage. "I agree, Alex," he said as he hugged her. She gave him a tour of the mansion, during which he pretended to be interested. Fifteen minutes later they returned to the sitting room to indulge in the pastries and coffee on the table. Hayao decided to get right down to business. "You must have some idea of why I am here Alex." She nodded. "I don't mean to sound callous, but the death of Justice Bernard changed the whole political landscape. Regardless of how he would have ruled on the case introduced by the President, it is almost guaranteed that the President will appoint a liberal to replace him, and Congress will be under enormous pressure to approve. I predict by the time the Supreme Court reconvenes in the fall, we will have a new liberal as the ninth judge. That leads me to my next point. Once the measure passes, there would be a scramble to find some good candidates that were not born in this country." He paused. "Through no fault of my own, I have become probably the most prominent Asian person in the Unites States, and a logical choice for President. If I am nominated, I am definitely interested, and I would like you to be my Vice Presidential candidate." He looked at her to see her reaction; she did not seem particularly surprised, nor did she admit it.

"I would be lying if I said this came out of left field. You have been laying the groundwork for at least a year now. Having a woman on your ticket would lock up the liberal vote in this country. As far as the conservatives, you would have already lost them, as they would never vote for a foreigner in the first place. So, when you called me, I knew." Alex folded her arms.

Hayao said, "So, what is your answer?"

"Did you really think I would say no?" She smiled.

He replied, "Welcome aboard. It's too soon to make an official announcement, obviously, but you have my word that if the measure gets passed, and if I receive a nomination, that you will be my running mate. I believe we will have an excellent chance of winning."

The body had been returned to the Supreme Court police yesterday, and it looked intact. No one could tell what the FBI had done. As Pruitt had promised, more police took to the streets canvassing the neighborhoods. So far, no leads had been unturned. Footerman planned to reach out to other surrounding police departments this morning too. He still held suspicions about the janitor, Corvino, possessing the ability to sense when people were lying after so many years on the job. He definitely wanted to speak to her again. For now, however, he had phone calls to make. The kidnapper had taken the justice and his wife to a place within two hours of Washington DC, Footerman was positive. He brought up a map of the surrounding communities in metro DC and drew a circle with his finger of those within 90 miles. He would personally call each one and ask them to put the word out to their citizens to report anything unusual. The murder weapon also needed to be found. Ballistics had come back; it had been a handgun, but could not be narrowed down any further based on the bullets. That was the other reason why he wanted to zero in on where they had been taken to, it would be likely that the kidnapper had disposed of the murder weapon there as well.

   The justices had convened at the Supreme Court building again now that the police had finished. They only wanted to have a short meeting. Chief Justice Braxton said, "I think we should finalize our opinions and rulings now so that when we resume in the fall, we can hit the ground running." All the judges nodded in agreement. He continued, "Ok then. Since this is likely the last time we will meet for this term, I wish you all a peaceful summer. I know that some of us will be at the funeral on Saturday, but we won't get a chance to talk then. Let's hope President Harrington is prudent with his appointment." He then turned and left the room, and the justices all followed.

   All over the metro DC area and beyond, in Maryland and Virginia, the case of Winston Bernard and his wife had become a priority. Each police department had gotten a phone call from the Supreme Court police force asking for their help, to put the word out to the residents of their towns to report anything unusual. After 48 hours, crime investigations became more difficult, and a dragnet had been thrown down, but at this point it might have been too late; the person or persons responsible had probably already disappeared. Law enforcement officers were like animals; highly territorial, and each one wanting to take credit; cooperation between police forces and even precincts within the same police force was rare. For that reason, those on the inside believed that this really should be a case for the FBI, but for now the Supreme Court police had jurisdiction. That would change once the case came to a standstill. No leads had been turned up yet, and there were always those crazies who wanted to be a part of the media circus surrounding a big crime like this. Sergeant Fenwick was daydreaming about how he would spend his time when he retired in two years when the phone on his desk rang. His secretary said, "Another wacko on the phone who claims to have seen something the other night." "Put him through." When the call went through he said, "Laurel police department. Sergeant Fenwick speaking."

Friday June 24nd 2pm
Chief Footerman sat in his office thinking and brooding. They had not found the murder weapon yet, and this case seemed to be slipping away from him. They had checked every alleyway, dumpster, and other logical place all over the city. Furthermore, no word had come in from any of the other departments about a matching handgun either. He knew at some point the Potomac River would have to be searched; he did not have the manpower or the equipment for that. Just then the phone rang. It was Director Grey from the FBI. "Hello Chief, how are things going?"
"Just fine Director." Awkward silence for a few seconds.
"I guess you know why I am calling Chief. Have you made any progress on the case?"
"Smug fucking prick," thought Chief Footerman bitterly. "Yes we have. There was a janitor working at the courthouse the night of the kidnapping that seems suspicious to me. She became very fidgety during questioning. Her name is Lorraine Corvino. Also, we have constructed a timeline for when we believe that the Bernard's were abducted and killed, as well as getting back our ballistics report, which shows that the bullets came from a handgun."
Director Grey smiled and paused for a few seconds. "Do you believe that Lorraine Corvino is the shooter?"

"No. Her alibi checks out; furthermore, I believe that the murders had been committed by a person with much experience with firearms, and after investigating Corvino's background, she has no such experience. I am not discounting her as a suspect, however. Justice Bernard had a serious reputation as a philanderer, but he would never have left Cecily, certainly not for a custodian. If he has been stringing her along, she may have snapped."

"Good point Chief. One more question. Have you retrieved the murder weapon?"

His blood boiling, the Chief answered, "No not yet."

"All right Chief. I will touch base with you next week. Are you going to the funeral tomorrow?"

"Yes, I will see you there."

Saturday, June 25rd 11:30 am at Arlington National Cemetery

"I am roasting in this suit. What a rotten day for a funeral," Blake Tristan thought morbidly to himself. Then he looked over at Sondra, delirious with grief and reminded himself to be sympathetic. To take his mind off things, he looked around at all the attendants. President Harrington was here, all eight justices of the Supreme Court, and the Director of the FBI, who Blake knew had been a personal friend of Winston's. He had helped Sondra finalize her eulogy last night and had encouraged her to keep it on the short side; he thought the final draft to be very tasteful. Now the issue would be if she could deliver it. He had told her if she couldn't he would. She would speak first, then Sondra's grandfather, Hugh Urbanik, and finally President Harrington. After the funeral and the burial here at the cemetery the reception would follow at the National Press Club in downtown DC. On Monday, he made a mental note to get in touch with the Supreme Court police force and find out if the investigation had progressed. He was grateful that several of Sondra's friends had come to be with her today; that had helped take her mind off things a little bit. Just then, a man tapped Blake on the shoulder. "Mr. Tristan, I am so sorry for your loss. I am an old college friend of Winston's, Fred Lively. Winston couldn't have been more proud of Sondra, and so happy that her life seemed to be coming together so nicely; it is a real tragedy that he and Cecily won't be there for the wedding." They shook hands and Lively went off to offer his condolences to Sondra. The rest of the half hour went by in a blur, and the next thing Blake knew it was noon and time to take their seats under the tent. Sondra had insisted that the funeral be held outside. The priest walked up to the podium and introduced himself; he spoke for a minute and then beckoned Sondra up to the podium; she managed to get through her eulogy with a few pauses to compose herself. Hugh spoke next and then the President, and both of their speeches were short, thank God.

Monday morning, June 27th 9am
The phone rang at the Supreme Court police office. Chief Footerman answered; it was Blake Tristan. "Great! Another country heard from", Footerman grumbled.
"What can I do for you Mr. Tristan?"
"I hoped that you could give me an update on the case, Chief. Sondra and I could use some good news." Chief Footerman responded, "We have a few leads that we are following up on, and we have included all the surrounding police departments within 90 miles to assist in the investigation. How is Sondra doing? She handled herself beautifully on Saturday."
"She is fine, thanks for asking. Listen Chief, please try to keep us posted."
"I will. Goodbye Mr. Tristan."
President Harrington's private phone line rang; only a few people had this number. He answered the phone. Director Grey said, "Hello, it's me. Those bumbling idiots at the Supreme Court police force have gotten nowhere; they have not even recovered the murder weapon yet. Can you please step in and hand us the case?"
President Harrington had to calm down for a minute before he answered; Grey was a good director but an arrogant prick! "They are not idiots. They don't have two thousand people at their disposal like you do. I will call Footerman this morning and tell him." Without a goodbye, the President hung up.

Tuesday June 28th 11 am

Danvers walked into Chief Footerman's office to discuss any new developments in the case; the minute he saw the expression on the Chief's face, he knew something had gone wrong. "What is it Chief?"

"President Harrington called. The FBI is taking over the case." His eyes were dark; Danvers knew that he should stay away from him.

He said, "I am sorry; you do realize we did our best."

The Chief simply replied, "Anything else?" Danvers simply shook his head and walked out, closing the door behind him.

July 30th, one month later

Blake and Sondra finally had some privacy in their apartment, and they were both exhausted. Tomorrow was their wedding, and it had been beyond hectic for the last week. Between all the out of town guests arriving, and the media spotlights, they had not had a minute for themselves. Finally, now, just back from the rehearsal dinner, they could relax for a few minutes. Sitting next to each other on the couch, they just wanted to hold hands. Blake looked over at Sondra. "What are you thinking?" he asked.

"I'm thinking I can't wait to get the hell out of here for a week when we leave tomorrow night for Paris. I am so glad that you talked me out of cancelling out honeymoon. We both need a mental break from our lives."

"I know; and just wait and see what I planned for us; we are eating at the finest restaurants in the city, each one better than the one before!"

"Oh, Blake, you are the greatest!"

CHAPTER 3

Tuesday September 6th

President Harrington answered the phone. It was Abigail, one of his staffers, assigned to report back to him on the happenings at Congress, and right now priority number one at Congress involved appointing a new Supreme Court justice. The President asked, "How is it going with Conklin, Abby?" He liked Abby, she possessed a lot of potential. She replied, "It seems to be going pretty smoothly, sir. There does not seem to be any major issues as of yet, and I believe the hearings are coming to a close." President Harrington thought for a minute, and then simply said, "Thank you Abby. Keep up the good work." As soon as he hung up, he made a call from his private phone, checked daily for any listening devices or interference. When the person said hello, Harrington said, "Hello, Treetop. I have a job for you, one that must be handled swiftly and with the utmost discretion."

Todd Russell was in a good mood. Darren Conklin's confirmation hearings were moving right along and it looked as if he would be approved. Conklin was likely to rule against the case for a foreigner running for President, which would be good for him. Joe Berry seemed to be working his magic; Russell's numbers were improving each week, and he could feel himself peaking at just the right time. Screw Eric Layton, he thought. Russell would carry the Midwest! Maybe he would offer Layton a Cabinet post to be magnanimous. Let's not get ahead of things. He knew he must continue doing a good job in Illinois, otherwise he could hire all the public relations experts in the world and it wouldn't make a difference. With that thought, he got back to preparing his remarks for his visit to the group home today on the south side of Chicago.

Eric Layton started to pack, getting ready to return to Washington after two weeks at home with his wife Cindy in Colorado. They conducted a long distance relationship; it seemed to work for them. They saw each other every other weekend, and on and off during the summer. Jack had gotten used to it and having a senator for a father more than made up for Eric's absence. He too seemed pleased about the way that the Conklin hearings were going. Of course, being a senator, he had a spot on the inside and could help influence the proceedings. It called for discretion since it was common knowledge that he made it on the short list of candidates for the next election. He did not worry about Todd Russell. Sure Russell was doing well in the polls, but he didn't enjoy nearly the same national recognition that Layton did. He also gave no thought to Juan Pillar. First of all, it seemed unlikely that Conklin would rule in favor of the case, and even if it passed, when push came to shove Americans would not vote for a foreigner. He heard Cindy on the phone in the other room. She whispered; he knew that she planned his goodbye dinner for tonight. He would do his best to act surprised; he suspected they would go to Grimaldi's, one of the best seafood restaurants in Colorado, with several dishes that he craved while away. He needed to make sure that he continued his exemplary service record when he got back to Washington because when the Supreme Court finally reached their decision, he wanted to be able to start his campaign right away. After all, there would only be six months to position himself for the candidacy, as the election would be held in November 2040, and it was already September 2039. Americans possessed very short memories; all the good things he did would be forgotten if he screwed up now. Just then, Cindy walked in the room. "Hi honey," she said. "What do you say later this afternoon we go see a movie and then go for a drive and pick up something at Grimaldi's tonight for dinner?"

"That sounds great!"

Sondra Tristan looked out the back window of her apartment and sipped her coffee. She and Blake had been married now for six wonderful weeks. They would always cherish their heavenly honeymoon, and she temporarily forgot about her parents' murders and enjoyed herself. She and Blake would always remember their time in Paris. Since they got back, however, time has seemed as if it has been standing still. She knew that the investigation proceeded very slowly; the FBI took over the case right around the time of her wedding, and at first gotten no further than the

Supreme Court police. Then they caught a break. A gun washed up out of the Potomac River, and an innocent bystander turned it over to the police. Since the police were on high alert regarding the Bernard case, they passed the weapon over to the FBI, and their agents immediately determined that the gun matched the one used in the murders. Once they checked the bullets, they confirmed the match. The killer cleverly filed off the serial number on the gun. This represented a temporary setback, however. The FBI maintained the technology to outline the filed off serial number using reagents. They were able to match the serial number to a gun store in Georgia; the only problem turned out to be that the owner of the store failed to record the name of the customers for the past five years; he would likely be prosecuted for that and possessed no recollection of when the gun had been purchased or by whom. She felt beyond frustrated and didn't know where to turn. Blake has been wonderful, patient beyond belief. None of her father's contacts even tried to help. She wanted to meet again with Director Grey and ask him to change the team assigned to the case. She would call him in a little while. Right now, she had to finish getting ready for work.

FBI headquarters, Quantico, VA

Director Grey held a meeting with the men assigned to the Bernard case. He said, "Well, we have gotten nowhere gentlemen. Sondra Tristan wants to meet with me tomorrow. Let's review what we learned so far."

The lead agent spoke. "We determined that the gun was purchased from a gun store in Georgia, but not when or by whom. All the local police forces within the vicinity where the killer possibly took the judge and his wife turned up nothing."

"Are there any leads about the assailant?"

The agents looked at each other. One of them said nervously, "As a matter of fact we do. We identified Presidential hopeful Juan Pillar as a person of interest."

The Director was mildly surprised, but recovered right away. After so many years on the job, he understood that even the most innocuous people could always act in surprising ways. "What gives you the idea he might be involved?"

The agent continued, "Well, the gun comes from a store in Georgia where Pillar is from. Furthermore, he is planning on seeking the nomination for President if possible, and most likely anticipated that Justice Bernard would vote against it. With Bernard gone, Pillar would predict that President Harrington would appoint a liberal to vote in favor of the measure, allowing Pillar to enter the race."

Director Grey thought for a minute. "All circumstantial. We are the FBI gentlemen. We deal in hard evidence, not gossip. What else do you have to link Pillar to the gun?"

The agent looked down at the floor. "Nothing else right now, sir."

Director Grey clenched his teeth and said, "Good day gentlemen."

President Harrington insisted that only two secret service agents accompany him, the absolute minimum allowed by law. It was Tuesday night and he had arrived in New York this afternoon for a meeting with the Governor tomorrow. He told the agents he wanted to run down to the gift shop and buy himself a souvenir. They swept the store in the lobby and agreed to let him walk down the hall from the elevator to the shop by himself because they would be able to see him the whole way. He would then meet Treetop. He would only have about ten seconds, so everything needed to go smoothly. The explicit instructions were written on a pad. He needed Treetop to dig up dirt on Darren Conklin and told Treetop where to look. He mentioned that he would leave the instructions inside the top newspaper, and as soon as the President left the store, Treetop should come in and grab it. One of the agents knocked on his door. Here they go. He put his wig on and went to the elevator. This disguise seemed so convincing that he thought no one would ever recognize him. The agents were dressed casually so that once they entered the lobby, all three of them would not be conspicuous. President Harrington walked into the store and went straight for the miniature Statue of Liberty replicas. He saw the New York Times pile and went over to them. Picking one up, he deftly put the note inside the next copy from the top, went to the register and paid the bill. The cashier showed no hint of recognition. He then left the store and saw Treetop out of the corner of his eye, walking toward the shop. President Harrington knew he could count on Treetop to complete this assignment.

Hayao Yamamoto was on the phone with Alex Ramirez. They too were discussing Conklin's confirmation hearings. Hayao said, "How do you think things are going so far?"
She replied, "He seems to be sailing along. It's likely that he will vote down the measure. I am not sure why the President appointed him in the first place."
Hayao answered, "Yes that does seem strange. Maybe he knows something we don't. Perhaps Conklin has hinted that he has become more liberal as of late." He paused. "I'm not worried. The President wants this measure passed. I am confident that he thought this through."
Before she said goodbye and hung up, Ramirez thought, "I hope you are right. Otherwise, we need a contingency plan."

Wednesday, September 7th
Sondra Tristan arrived at the FBI Headquarters at 10 am; she had taken the morning off at the ACLU. The guard on duty obviously expected her and buzzed her right in through the gate. She drove up the winding road looking around at the surroundings. "Boy, the government spared no expense on this place!" she thought. She finally got to the building and parked her car. She entered the lobby and walked around in awe. The entire lobby was glass and the view knocked her socks off. The grounds were surrounded entirely by forest for miles; the location definitely would intimidate. Suddenly a man in a dark suit approached her.
"Mrs. Tristan, hello. Please follow me and I will escort you to Director Grey's office." Sondra and the agent walked to the elevators; once inside, the man announced, "Director Grey." The elevator started to move, as the agent explained that the elevator ran on voice recognition software, included as a security measure. The elevator rose to the top floor and the doors opened. They were

greeted by an armed guard who let them pass without a word. They entered an ante chamber which was staffed by three women who sat at three desks about five feet apart from each other. Continuing straight ahead, they passed another set of double doors which revealed the Director's expansive office. More like a suite of offices really. There were two conference rooms, a full service kitchen, bathroom complete with shower, and a smaller office for visitors. As soon as he saw her, Director Grey stood up from his desk and walked over to her.

"Sondra, how are you?" He kissed her hello. "Can I get you anything? Something to drink perhaps?"

She replied, "I would love a diet coke, thank you."

The Director buzzed one of the women sitting out front. "Diane, would you please bring Mrs. Tristan a diet coke? Thanks. Please sit down Sondra." She sat in a plush armchair in front of a coffee table as the Director sat across from her. "Let's get started. I know you want to discuss the case. Fire away."

Sondra said, "I understand that the investigation has stalled. Your agents have been working hard but come up with nothing so far. What you are planning to do?"

The Director replied, "Well Sondra, I am going to switch teams and bring in a very experienced field agent by the name of Ed Billet. He will lead the team, and if anyone can get results, he can. He happens to be here today. I thought you would like to meet him." She nodded. "Diane, would you ask Ed Billet to join us?" Turning back to Sondra, Director Grey said, "When he gets here, we can discuss his approach on how to proceed."

Ten minutes later, a lanky brown haired man walked into Director Grey's office. Sondra briefly thought, "Too bad I am married!" He nodded hello to Director Grey and walked straight over to Sondra, introduced himself, offered his condolences, and sat down next to her. She could tell right away that he was a no nonsense guy.

The Director spoke. "Let's get right to the point Ed. Sondra here is concerned that the investigation has hit a dead end. The team has found the gun but has not been able to produce any credible leads from the ballistics information. We need to step back and reevaluate. Ed, I would like you to take over this case."

Ed Billet looked at the Director. "With all due respect sir, it doesn't sound like you allowed the agents enough time. Did you suggest that they go back and retrace their steps?"

"No, I believe that we need a fresh perspective, and this is how I want to proceed. This is a very high profile case; you are a very seasoned detective, qualified to handle this. What do you say?"

Billet let this sink in for a minute. He had scaled back his workload in the last few years and liked it, having more time to pursue outside interests and wasn't sure he wanted to be thrown back into the soup. Still, it would be difficult to say no to the director. Although he would deny it, Director Grey was a vindictive man; he would find a way to get back at Billet if he refused. "Ok, sir, I will take over the case. I'd like to meet with the agents to see what they have found. Are they around today?"

"Yes", the director said. "I asked them to make themselves available today; I had a hunch that you would want to sit down together. Feel free to get going." That amounted to the director barking an order. He shook Sondra's hand on the way out. "I will keep you updated, Miss Tristan. Enjoy your day."

"This was good," Sondra thought. She got good vibes from Agent Ed Billet. He projected an air of confidence unlike the other agents working on the case. She felt reassured that he would be able to get to the bottom of this.

Treetop had his work cut out for him. He knew what he must look for; the illegitimate daughter of Darren Conklin. He didn't know her name or what she looked like; only that she had been born between 20 and 22 years ago, according to President Harrington. Fortunately, he had virtually unlimited resources. He started by contacting Allison Terrine, the head of the U.S. Department of Social Services. When she answered, he said, "Hi Allison, it's Treetop. How are you?" Knowing he was the President's hatchet man, she answered, "I'm fine, what can I do for you Treetop?"

"Well, I need some information. I am looking for a female baby born between 20 and 22 years ago, either adopted or turned over to an orphanage, and I need it yesterday."

Thinking for a minute, she said, "I can get it for you by tomorrow, but the list is going to be quite long. It will take you awhile to narrow it down."

"Could you also include the names and locations of the orphanages and adoption agencies?" "Sure shouldn't be a problem," and she hung up without saying goodbye.

President Harrington asked his secretary to get Director Grey on the phone. A few seconds later the Director came on the line.
"Yes Mr. President?"
"Hello James. What is the latest regarding the investigation into the Bernard case?"
"Well, we have not made too much progress yet, sir. As a matter of fact, today I turned the case over to agent Ed Billet."
President Harrington knew Billet. He had helped bring down some major cases over the years. "Good move James. Billet will put everything he has into solving this, and quickly. Please continue to keep me posted."
"Yes, sir. Goodbye."

Thursday Sept. 8
Ed Billet pulled into his driveway in suburban Virginia. He wasted no time on the Bernard case and started by re-interviewing all the justices and the custodians, either personally or through one of the members of his team. He thought about the people of interest. For starters, all the possible Presidential candidates were potential suspects; they all possessed motives for wanting to tip the balance of the Supreme Court. High ranking officials of the special interest groups needed to be looked at as well; no one could be sure how Justice Bernard would rule. He had not been consistently liberal or conservative over the years. He hated that this crossed his mind, but even President Harrington could be behind this. Ed Billet knew from experience that he contained a ruthless streak. He filed the lawsuit before the Supreme Court; his legacy was riding on the outcome. Getting out of his car, his looked at his dark house. Since his mom passed away last year, he had been living alone. He missed her, but caring for her consumed all his time. He began

playing golf and done some travelling also. Well, life goes on. He started walking to his front door when a car came careening around the corner. He saw the headlights and he took cover behind his bushes to avoid a hail of bullets. When he heard the car way down the street, he picked up his head. In the sky he saw a smoke bomb that spelled out a message: "BACK OFF OF THE BERNARD CASE." Boy, word sure got around fast! He shook himself off and looked up again. Anyone could produce those smoke bombs; moreover, they evaporated after a few minutes, so they could not be traced in any way. He was no stranger to either giving or getting intimidation.

When Billet arrived at FBI headquarters the next day, he went straight into Director Grey's office. His secretary motioned for him to enter. The Director was on the phone and waved Ed to sit. He said 'yes' and 'no' several times and Ed gleaned nothing from his end of the conversation. The Director said, "I will look into it, goodbye", and then turned to him. "Ah, Edward, how are you today?"

"Well, sir, I could be better. Someone shot at last night." Not appearing surprised, Director Grey nodded.

"Are you alright?"

"I am fine. I reacted just in the nick of time; besides, it seems like whoever orchestrated he attack tried to scare me; they also sent a message using an evaporating smoke bomb which said, 'back off of the Bernard case'."

"No surprise. On a case like this crazies will always come out of the woodwork."

"Yes, but so quickly? Only a handful of people are aware that I took over; it's only been two days."

"Come now, Edward, don't be naive. Even the FBI has leaks."

"Who knows about the change?"

"By now, I am sure everyone here at headquarters. Sondra Tristan, and President Harrington."

"How did the President find out?"

"He called me Tuesday afternoon to see how the investigation was going."

"Why did you tell him that I am involved now?"

"It's not a secret. I am sure all the news bureaus are aware of it by now with the loose lips around here. Besides, he is very interested in our progress." Billet thought for a minute. If anything, the fact that the President knew reinforced his notion from last night which the Director would understand.

Billet said, "How does one go about investigating the President of the United States?"

"With great aplomb, Edward."

Juan Pillar was on edge. The Conklin confirmation hearings seemed to be going well, and he knew Darren Conklin. A fair judge, but he could not sure which way he would rule on the case 'Michael Harrington vs. the United States'. Conklin appeared to be one of those people Pillar liked to refer to as a 'cookbook conservative', someone who took ingredients from different ideologies when it suited their interests. It was very difficult to predict how he would rule, and if you looked at his past decisions, they were not consistent and all over the place. He had been very surprised when the President appointed Conklin. Still, he had been getting his campaign in place. He assembled a good campaign staff and began making public appearances, trying to becoming more visible. He had much work to do since his primary adversary for the foreign vote would be Hayao Yamamoto. The Oriental community held much more influence in the U.S. than the Latino community; he made sure to include some Asian people on his teams. He really had to make his presence felt. In order for him to win, he must carry his share of the vote of people born here, as well as that of naturalized citizens. That is where he needs to beat Hayao. He would stress his background in government, in contrast to Hayao with no such background. He said out loud, "Tv, confirmation hearings!" The hearings came on a second later.

President Harrington picked up his cell phone, the one off the grid and dialed Treetop.
When Treetop answered, President Harrington said, "Hello Treetop. What progress have you made?"

"Well, sir, I obtained the list of adoptions and those kids taken in by orphanages during that time period. I narrowed the list to those girls that were surrendered to the two most reputable adoption agencies and orphanages in Houston, where Conklin is from. There are fifty four names on that short list."

"Well Treetop, you'd better get busy. I need this information as soon as possible." The line went dead.

Treetop realized he had to get started. He called the first adoption agency, using the call forwarding capability. When the operator at the agency answered, the number that appeared on her phone appeared as the Department of Justice. Once people saw that, it wasn't hard to get whatever information he needed. "Hello, ma'am. I am calling from the Department of Justice and I need some information. I am looking for some information about all of the adoptees from 20 years ago."

"20 years ago? Why would you possibly want that?"

"Ma'am, this is a government matter that does not concern you. What is your name by the way?"

"My name is Joan. I am sorry if I seemed nosy. Let me connect you to our Director." A minute later another woman answered the phone. "Hello, this is Margaret. My assistant explained what you are looking for, and I would be happy to oblige." Smiling, Treetop said, "I need the names of the babies that were adopted and the names and addresses of the people that adopted them."

"Of course. I will email it to you. What is your email address?"

"No ma'am. I need you to read me this information over the phone right now."

"Well, it will take me some time to compile this information."

"That's ok, I will hold on while you do."

Treetop repeated this process with the other agency and the two orphanages. When he had finished, there were twenty two names that matched the names on the list he got from the DOJ. Fortunately for him, there were only four female babies out of the twenty two. He called the first two numbers; both were apartments where the tenants had moved; he would need to talk to the superintendents to research the old records for forwarding addresses. The next name on the list, Donna Miller, was home.

Treetop asked her a few questions, but she denied ever having known Darren Conklin. She sounded convincing and he thought her to be telling the truth. The next and last contact on his list, Gerry Fiske, still lived in Houston. When Treetop asked her about Darren Conklin, he sensed right away he had found the mother of Conklin's child. He said, "Gerry we need to talk face to face. It's a matter of national security."

Viper placed a risky but necessary phone call; when Wolf answered, Viper asked, "Did you scare Billet?"
 "Yes, I made sure it could not be traced."
 "I hope so, and hope that he will back off; if not we will step it up and go to our next plan."
 "Viper, sometimes you scare even me."
 "Good."

Saturday, September 10th
 Treetop waited for Gerry Fiske to arrive at the location upon which he had decided. He stayed out of sight. Ten minutes later, he saw a redhead walk up and look around as if she was waiting for someone. Treetop quickly walked up to her and said, "Gerry? I'm the person you spoke with on the phone. Why don't we go sit in my car?" When he saw the look of distrust in her eyes, he added, "Don't worry, I will sit in the front and you can sit in the back with the door open, and you can hold my car keys."
 "Gerry, are you aware that Darren Conklin is about to be confirmed as a justice for the United States Supreme Court?"
 "Yes, I was aware of that. How does any of that relate to me?"
 "Well, let's just say that there are some people that possess doubts about him, and the fact that he has an incident in his past that sheds doubt on his moral character would most likely prevent him from being approved by Congress."
 Gerry looked at him incredulously. "You want me to go public with the fact that he has an illegitimate child? I will be ruining three lives; his, mine, and our daughter's! No way!"
 "We can protect her identity; the media will not be able to find her. As for Conklin, he is not what's best for our country. This is

your chance to do something patriotic. Besides, you will be able to do the talk show circuit after this, and maybe write a book. You will be set financially for the rest of your life!" He could see that he had pushed the right button.

"Do you promise that my daughter's identity will not be found out?"

"I will do everything in my power to prevent it."

"Ok, then I will go public. What is the next step?"

"You will hold a press conference. When you get in touch with the local media, they will want to know what it is about. You can leak the report that it has something to do with Conklin. That should stir up enough of an interest to attract the national networks. We will keep your statement simple. You had a brief affair with Darren Conklin 20 years ago, got pregnant, decided to keep the baby and put it up for adoption. Let it be known that it was a girl. Then be prepared for the questions. You will be asked if Conklin knew about the pregnancy. Answer honestly; yes, he did, and that you both agreed to put the baby up for adoption. His family's influence made it possible for you to use the services of one of the top adoption agencies in the city of Houston. It's up to you whether or not you give the agency's name; the reporters will be able to get that information on their own in a day or two. I will also make it my business to make sure that the records stay sealed. This controversy will only last for a while. After your book comes out and Conklin is no longer in the running for the Supreme Court, your daughter will not be in any danger of having her identity exposed. So you see, everybody wins. Your daughter's privacy is protected, you will become a rich woman, and the country will gain an appropriate Supreme Court justice."

"Ok, mister, you got a deal."

That night, Treetop called President Harrington. "It's all set sir. She agreed."

"Excellent work, Treetop. We will talk again when the next crisis arises."

Tuesday, September 13th

Treetop got in touch with Gerry Fiske. "Gerry, you know who this is. Everything is in place; go ahead and arrange for the press conference. It is guaranteed that the records will stay sealed."

The phone at WDXR Houston rang, and the secretary at the desk answered. "WDXR, we handle exclusives! How can I help you?"

"My name is Gerry Fiske, and I will be holding a press conference today at 3pm. You are not going to want to miss this one, trust me."

The secretary said, "Let me pass this call on to one of our reporters." She transferred the call to Ernie Webber because he secretly was her crush. He answered, "Ernie Webber." Gerry Fiske repeated, "I am Gerry Fiske, and I will be holding a press conference today at 3pm in front of town hall." Webber thought for a moment.

"Nothing personal lady, but I need a little more than that. What is this press conference about?" Gerry wisely did not give out too much information.

"Let's just say it involves Supreme Court nominee Darren Conklin." She then hung up, and proceeded to call all the other networks in Houston, the major newspapers, and internet news services.

Word of the press conference spread like wildfire. All four major candidates, Hayao, Pillar, Layton, and Russell, learned of it right away through their press people on staff. They were all speculating about what it could mean since it involved Darren Conklin. Russell was the only one that had legitimate concerns. He had been counting on the chance that Conklin would not vote the way everyone predicted; chances were, if he got voted down, President Harrington would appoint someone who would definitely support the measure to allow a foreigner to run for President. The whole thing smelled suspicious. Why would President Harrington appoint someone with a skeleton in his closet? The other three candidates were optimistic. None of them were crazy about Conklin for the same reason that Russell wanted him to be confirmed; they were unsure of his true stance on the issue. They recognized they were getting ahead of themselves, however. Better to wait and hear what this woman had to say first.

Ed Billet was at the crime scene in front of the Supreme Court building going over every inch of sidewalk and street with a fine tooth comb and watching the press conference on his phone. The woman, Gerry Fiske, was cute, but obviously struggled with life; she had a weathered look to her. She prepared to speak. "I called this press conference to bring something to light about Darren Conklin. I had an affair with him 22 years ago, which resulted in my getting pregnant, having a daughter, and placing her up for adoption. Justice Conklin was fully aware of this situation, and his family used their connections to work with the best adoption agency in Houston." After a long murmur from all the reporters, they started firing questions at her.

"Ms. Fiske, do you still have contact with that child?"
"No".
"Which adoption agency did you use?"
"The Sunshine Agency."
"Do you ever speak to Mr. Conklin?"
"Not since the adoption became final. One more question."
"Why are you coming forward with this information now?"
Treetop briefed her on how to answer this.
"It is not my intention to damage anyone's reputation. But the country needs to be familiar with the character of its appointed officials, and this event certainly says much about Mr. Conklin's character. Good day."

Hayao called Natsu immediately. He was expecting the call. "This will be positive for us, Natsu. There's no telling how Conklin would rule. I am certain that the President will now nominate someone who will definitely be in favor of a foreign born President."

"I agree. Did you hear anything further from Alex Ramirez?"
"No, not yet. There really isn't anything else for us to discuss. Switching gears, Moritu's earnings for this quarter are way up."
"Excellent, Hayao. Keep up the good work."

Todd Russell was beside himself. Gerry Fiske's announcement would almost certainly mean Conklin would not be confirmed. That stupid whore! Someone put her up to this. Knowing the President's stance, he would undoubtedly appoint someone who would be of the same mindset. This campaign was turning into one setback after another. When Justice Bernard had been killed, Russell wasn't certain how he would be affected. On the one hand, Bernard usually ruled conservatively. However, his daughter and future son-in-law at the time were bleeding heart liberals, and he knew they influenced him tremendously. Hiring Joe had been a great move based on his higher approval rating. They still had much work to do. He sent word that he wanted to speak to Rose, the staffer who went to college with Joe. About ten minutes later, Rose walked into his office. "You wanted to see me Governor?"

"Yes, Rose, please come in and sit down. Rose, I would like for you to send a message to Joe Berry on the website that you both use. Ask him what else he is planning for our campaign, and also ask him how this announcement about Conklin will change things. Let me know as soon as you hear from him. Thank you."

"Of course, sir."

Later that night, as Governor Russell sat in his study his phone rang.

"Yes, Rose, did you hear back from Joe?"

"Yes I did. He said that he is planning a lot more interaction with the public and more speaking engagements; you need to be as visible as possible. He also said that this may set us back a little, but we should be able to overcome it. He said that he will be in touch."

"Great. Thank you Rose."

Darren Conklin went crazy after he heard that Gerry Fiske planned to hold a press conference. His staff had never seen him get so excited. "Someone put her up to this! She never would have come forward on her own!" His hearings had been going so well! Well, now it became time for damage control. He would get his staff right on it. He would issue a statement through them, something to the effect that he was a young man when it happened, and he made sure that the child would end up in the best situation possible. Neither he nor Gerry were ready to raise a kid at that time in their lives. If he spun it right, perhaps his character wouldn't be called into question too much. After all, Clarence Thomas had been confirmed back in the 1990's, and what he had been accused of had been pretty dastardly. How could this happen? Why would someone try to sabotage his appointment? He possessed a fine record, and if this pertained to the case regarding the right of foreigners to run for President, he never disclosed how he would rule. Therefore, the situation with Gerry Fiske must have been orchestrated by someone who would rather see someone else fill the empty seat on the Supreme Court. This certainly had the feel of a conspiracy.

Wednesday, September 14th
Billet found nothing of significance at the crime scene. His next stop was the Supreme Court police to talk to the chief, a man named Footerman. Billet knew that they had turned over all the evidence to the FBI, but he wanted to see if they failed to tell the FBI anything. He anticipated encountering some bitterness; no one likes to lose a case, especially one as high profile as this one. Still, Footerman should be able to realize what was at stake here. When he arrived, Footerman's secretary buzzed the intercom to tell Footerman, he kept him waiting for fifteen minutes as a power play. When he finally entered Footerman's office, he didn't stand up to greet him. That's fine. Billet decided to get right to the point. "Hello, Chief. I am sure that you know why I am here. I would like to discuss the Bernard case. I have taken over the case for the FBI, and I am wondering if any information surfaced that you and your staff believes is pertinent to the investigation. Anything at all, even if you already shared it with the other agents from the FBI."

Footerman stared off into space for a few seconds, as if pondering whether to cooperate or not. Finally he spoke. "When we conducted our interviews with the people that were there that night at the courthouse, one of the janitors seemed suspicious to me. Lorraine Corvino acted nervous when I spoke to her, and if you ask me, some kind of hanky-panky went on between her and Justice Bernard. He was known to be a ladies' man; I am sure that if he even flirted with her once, she would pursue him with everything in her arsenal to carry on with a judge. Bernard never would have left his wife, however. Maybe Corvino felt jilted and decided to exact revenge."

"Did you look into her background? This was a very well thought out and executed plan. Does she have a criminal record? Does she even own a gun?"

"Yes, we looked into her background; shoplifting; that's it."

"She hardly sounds like a hardened criminal."

"Maybe she hired a professional." Billet thought for a minute. It was obvious that the Supreme Court police had not investigated much on this case. He decided that he would just start all over again. "Thanks for your time, Chief." They shook hands and he left.

The Senate held a meeting to discuss Darren Conklin. Up until now, it appeared that he would be a lock for the Supreme Court. The Senate Judiciary Committee passed a recommendation that Conklin be confirmed. That committee would not meet again regarding Conklin, and the vote now went to the Senate floor. This new information about Conklin would change the opinions of many of the senators. Although there were no more political parties, the Senate consisted of many conservatives, people who feared the country had gotten off track. They were probably the majority right now. The Senate floor was called to order. Cole Simmons, a Senator from down South, spoke first. "This is an outrage! I do not want someone sitting on the bench who has abandoned his responsibilities and hid his past! Those are two moral flaws!"

Mark Summers from Maine spoke next. "Hold on a minute. Darren Conklin has a stellar record as a judge. Isn't that what really counts? Besides, it's not like he committed a crime; he made a mistake and then took steps to find the best solution. I do not want to start a debate about adoption, abortion, etc., but is what he did so bad?"

The head of the Senate spoke next, and tried to quiet everyone down, who had all started to talk at the same time. "By a show of hands, who believes that this warrants a session on Conklin's moral character?" A clear majority raised their hands. He sighed. "Alright, let's get started."

Four hours later, the Senate session ended. The Senators emerged into the press room, which teemed with reporters, who had been waiting there since nine o'clock in the morning, believing that the deliberations would not take all day. The Senate designated Senator Simmons to speak, as he felt most strongly. As he approached the podium, he kept his expression somber. "Good afternoon everyone. After careful consideration, we decided to oppose Judge Darren Conklin's appointment to the United States Supreme Court. The decision passed by majority vote, and we entered our decision into record. I will now take questions."

"Senator, how many of you voted against Conklin?"

"71 opposed to 29 in favor of."

"Do you imagine someone has set Justice Conklin up?"

"I am not a conspiracy theorist, sir."

"Does the President have someone else in mind?"

"I don't know, please ask him yourself. Good day everyone." He walked away, and the reporters all started reading their stories into their voice activated computers.

President Harrington's press secretary had just left his private office. She made it clear that he needed to make a statement. He realized she was right, and he had one prepared, but he needed to make a phone call first. He took out his private cell phone and dialed the number he knew by heart. When the man said "Yeah?" President Harrington said, "Hello Treetop. My plan worked, thanks to you. Excellent work as always. I am sure I will be calling on you again in the future. Consider yourself a patriot, Treetop." He hung up; Treetop was a man of few words. He looked in the mirror, fixed his tie then felt ready. He walked down the hall and into the press briefing room; as soon as he walked in, everyone started firing questions at him. He ignored them and walked over to the podium where he raised both his hands to signal everyone to please be quiet. "Ladies and gentlemen, hello. As you all know, I am here to discuss Darren Conklin. My personal opinions aside, the Senate has made a decision to reject his appointment to the Supreme

Court despite the recommendation of the Senate Judiciary Committee, in light of the new information about Justice Conklin. Their decision is binding and I will make no attempt to appeal or reverse it." He paused to allow everyone to reflect briefly. "My responsibility now is to find another appointee, one who the Senate will hopefully find more suitable. I will now take questions." "Mr. President, have you spoken to Mr. Conklin?"

"Yes, and he will not be making a public statement or discussing this. He wishes to continue on in his duties and is confident that any actions he has taken were in the best interest of all concerned. He will abide by the Senate's decision and requests that everyone respect his and his family's privacy."

"Mr. President, do you have any idea who the next appointee will be?"

"No, not yet."

"Well, who else did you consider when you ended up nominating Justice Conklin?"

"I am not at liberty to say; I will be starting the process all over again."

"Mr. President, would you ever consider someone in your cabinet for the position?" They were referring to Jo Sylvester, President Harrington's ultra-liberal chief of staff, and former judge.

"I wouldn't rule it out. Good day everyone." He ended the press conference by walking out amidst a barrage of questions.

The eight Supreme Court justices were in session when they heard the Senate's decision. None of them were surprised. In addition to being mostly conservative, the majority of the senators did not like President Harrington and would take every opportunity to shoot down his measures. Judith Lackey spoke first. "We should be as close as possible to publishing our opinions about this case by the time the new justice is confirmed. We spent plenty of time deliberating, and we should have formed our answers by now. Our goal is to bring the new justice up to speed as quickly as possible. The election is only just over a year away; it takes time to build a campaign."

"Yes, I agree, it is time", said Chief Justice Braxton. "That is not to say we won't give the new justice time to catch up; we will. But if we try to explain what we covered so far, hopefully the process will go faster. Besides, whomever the President appoints should possess some idea of how our process works."

Justice Manucci chimed in, "You two figured it all out, right? What if some of us still haven't made up our minds? This kind of decision cannot be rushed! Furthermore, I am not sure we finished deliberating. The only absolute here is that the President is trying to rush us! I do not believe that we resolved anything; for example, do you all have opinions as to whether this violates the Constitution?"

Andrew Turnbull addressed his colleagues. "Technically, it does, but as we said before, look at how different our society is now from 260 years ago? Our job is to maintain our traditions but also change with the times."

Irene Salkin, the liberal from Boston added, "Yes, and I am convinced we are in a crisis here! Our leadership pool keeps dwindling!"

Samuel Kleinman stood up, as he sometimes did when he wanted to make an important point. "What we should remember, folks, is that we must rule based on what we think is best for the country at this particular time. The Constitution is a guide, one which can and should be modified. If we stick to that, we will make the right decision."

Chief Justice Braxton said, "Why don't we take the rest of the day to contemplate privately, and tomorrow maybe we can come up with some concrete proposals to discuss. Adjourned."

Ed Billet went back to FBI headquarters to look through the evidence again. He looked at the bullets, the gun recovered from the Potomac River, and the bodies. He would read the results from the brain scan tomorrow. Right now, the biggest lead came from the bodies. The trajectory of the bullets entering both the Bernards' brains indicated that the shooter fired the gun so that they would die quickly from all the blood loss caused by the size of the wound made by the bullets which lodged themselves in their heads. Also, they had both been tied and blindfolded, as evidenced from the marks on their hands and around their eyes. The killer had definitely been a pro. Billet's wanted to take a trip to Atlanta to get some information from the store that sold the gun to the murderer. Even though the gun had been purchased using cash, the store kept a record of when it was sold based on its serial number; it had been purchased two months before the murder. While the people in the store didn't remember the person who bought it, Billet would investigate the local businesses in the area, as well as the local residents hoping someone would remember something. He also wanted to review their brain scan on Winston Bernard since Director Grey already performed the state of the art scan on him. He would be able to surmise whether he knew the assailant or not, and get an idea for the emotions he had been experiencing when he was killed. Lastly, he and his team would personally canvass all the communities within two hours of the location where the bodies were left. This would be done to make sure that the police departments in turn had patrolled their neighborhoods to speak to their town's citizens, to see if anyone reported anything unusual. He had his work cut out for himself, but at least now he a plan existed. He pulled the contents of the bag from the Moleculator, the tool that the Supreme Court police used to sweep the sidewalk at the crime scene. There was some dirt, some candy wrappers, and a bee. Not much. Alright, time for the next step. He picked up the phone on the wall and dialed the neuro evidence lab. When the man picked up, Billet said, "Hello, this is Ed Billet. I would like to see the results from the Bernard's brain scans."

   President Harrington called together a meeting of the task force whose job it had been to present the President with a short list of potential people to fill the opening at the Supreme Court when Winston Bernard had been murdered. Getting right to the point, he said, "Okay everyone. I realize I just told the press that I would start at the beginning with regard to finding a new Supreme Court nominee. Time is of the essence here, the next Presidential election hangs in the balance; we need to fill the spot quickly. However, since the whole country is watching, we must also make sure that no one doubts that our process is thorough. Therefore, I would like the list of potential nominees on my desk one week from this Friday, on September 23rd. I will take the weekend to make a decision, and announce my choice on the following Monday, September 26th. That is all." While he walked out, the President pulled Matt Eldridge, the head of the committee, aside and said quietly, "Matt, there is no need to reinvent the wheel. Do you understand?"

"Yes, Mr. President."

Sondra Tristan was surprised about Darren Conklin. Her father always said that nobody was perfect, and those that wanted to enter public life should have the luxury of having certain things overlooked. I guess the Senate never got the memo. Ironic, isn't it? She hoped President Harrington selected a better candidate this time around; although her father never mentioned it, she suspected that he would have ruled in favor of allowing a foreign born person to run for President. Her mind started to wander, and she became sad for a moment, remembering her parents. Forcing herself to refocus on her work, she planned out the rest of her day. She would work until 5pm, exercise at the gym on her way home, and then go out with Blake tonight to dinner and a movie. God, Blake was wonderful! She felt better all of a sudden.

Juan Pillar was talking to his cousin Vicente about the news. Vicente said, "You are back in the game, cuz. This time I am sure that President Harrington will pick someone who will almost certainly be in favor of the measure. Don't worry."

"I hope you are right. Oh, let's be optimistic. I am going out to enjoy myself tonight Vicente, and you should do the same!"

Billet went into the private crime lab and the tech had the readout from the brain scan all ready. He took the readout over to the table and unfolded it completely. He looked at the key in the corner. After a few minutes, he had a feel for what justice Bernard experienced which included surprise, bewilderment, and fear. Billet now believed that he had not known the assailant. Great, he thought. My job just became all the more difficult. Scratching his head, he thought to himself that since he was here he should check the box of items the Supreme Court police found at the crime scene. As he looked through it, he saw a bee that apparently had been collected by the Moleculator. He went to the nearest office phone and dialed the forensic team. When one of them answered, Billet said, "Hi, this is Billet. Tell me, is it possible to extract human DNA from bees?" When the man answered yes, Billet said that he would be right there.

Five minutes later he walked into the forensic suite. The scientists there were busy, but this needed to become their top priority. Billet cleared his throat. Everyone looked at him. "I am afraid I am going to ask you to switch gears. Evidence related to the Bernard murders has been obtained, and Director Grey will want this handled immediately. I need to see any DNA available extracted from this bee preserved so that it can be compared to the national DNA database. Please contact me as soon as the results are available."

One of the men said, "Excuse me, but we must receive approval for this from the Director personally."

"Fine. Consider it done."

Friday, September 16th

Ed Billet approached the White House visitors' entrance. No matter how many times he came here on business, it always intimidated him. He had an appointment with the President this morning to officially discuss the case, but he really came to size Harrington up to see if he was somehow involved with the news about Darren Conklin coming out, which could mean that he might have had something to do with the murder of the Bernards. His name showed up on the list at the guardhouse. He drove up and parked in the visitor lot on the east side. He walked up to the main entrance and proceeded to the President's private office. Ten minutes later, President Harrington arrived. They shook hands; President Harrington remembered Billet from a visit to FBI headquarters last year. "I guess you know why I am here sir. Director Grey wanted me to update you on the case. We found a match on the gun, bought from a gun store in Atlanta, but no leads as it had been purchased for cash. A bee was found at the crime scene, and the techs at the FBI are testing it for any human DNA that could be extracted. I should get those results on Monday."

The President replied, "Well done Ed. Director Grey always speaks highly of you. By the way, he mentioned that someone took shots at you. Please be careful."

"Thank you sir. Isn't it crazy about the new information concerning Darren Conklin? Well, I am sure that his replacement will be just as competent. I wonder how Conklin would have ruled on the right of foreigners to run for President, and Justice Bernard for that matter. One can only speculate."

President Harrington was quiet for a minute. Then he said, "I suspect that Bernard would have ruled against it, and Conklin in favor, but he has a history of wavering, so one cannot be sure."

"Well sir, I don't want to waste more of your time. Good day."

"Good day Ed." Billet had all the information he needed.

The Supreme Court justices reconvened yesterday for their normal session. The minute they walked in, the feeling in the air persisted that things would be finalized today, at least among the eight of them. Chief Justice Braxton took over right away, in the hopes of steering the process toward a resolution. "Has everyone had a chance to review things?" Everyone nodded. "Can anyone offer any alternatives to a straight yes or no vote?" Samuel Kleinman spoke.

"I thought of an alternative. I suggest that in order to run for President, it's acceptable to be born elsewhere, that person must have lived in this country for at least five consecutive years." Justice Levitsky also had something to say.

"I would also like to include that the person running must take a government course, or will be required to during his or her campaign." All the justices were silent, but they all appeared to be in agreement. Justice Braxton spoke again.

"Does anyone else want to add anything?" Everyone kept silent. "In that case, we can consider this case to be unofficially decided; why don't we all retire to our chambers and write our opinions. Please remember that our written responses should reflect the legislation as it stands now. Any recommendations should be made to President Harrington when he inquires as to what clauses should be added to make it amenable to us."

Monday, September 19th
Ed Billet called the forensics lab at the FBI first thing Monday morning. "Have you got the results from the bee? Were you able to extract any human DNA? If so, were you able to identify it?"
The tech said, "Why don't you come in, Ed, so we can talk."
Forty minutes later, Billet walked into the lab. "Well, what else did you find?" The tech finished what he was doing and motioned Billet over to the table.
"Not only did I manage to extract the DNA, I hit the jackpot. There were two sets of human DNA available that I isolated, one female and one male. You take it from here." He handed Billet the packet.
DNA was used everywhere these days; it was encoded on cards that were used to compare it to DNA stored about every person in the United States. One's unique DNA code had become the new social security number; no two people had the exact same code. A national database contained everyone's DNA combination; a DNA sample when babies were born. For those that were born before this practice had been implemented, virtually every activity of day to day life required a DNA check. DNA was used for identification everywhere, from supermarkets to banks to liquor stores. People were basically forced to carry their DNA cards with them. Billet went downstairs to the FBI's computer center. He took the two DNA cards out of the folder and inserted the first one into the slot on the side. The DNA reader booted up immediately. Two minutes later Billet had his match. It was a woman named Kelly Visque. He printed the information sheet about her. He took out the next card and inserted it. The result this time returned a man named Peter Marvin. Now Billet switched computers to bring up the national people search database. He started with Peter Marvin and 2368 names were returned. Great, he thought. I sure have my work cut out for me. He then checked the name Kelly Visque; only 72 names came back. Billet decided to start with the bigger list. His

team of agents would be enlisted to get in touch with every person on the list and report back to him in one month with any leads they deemed worth investigating. He would tackle the list of people named Kelly Visque. He picked up the phone in the computer lab, called one of the agents and asked him to round the team up for a meeting in the conference room. One hour later Billet returned to his desk and started calling all the Kelly Visques across the country. The FBI was prohibited from including people's photographs in the DNA and name search databases; that made his job harder, as he couldn't identify people using a picture. He called the first name on the list, which was in alphabetical order by state. He sorted the data this way so that if anyone on his team needed to visit any of these people, they could be divided up geographically. This was a Kelly Visque that lived in Colorado. A childlike voice answered. "Hullo?" Billet asked, "Is your mom or dad home?"

"Just a minute. I will get my mom." A moment later a woman came on the phone.

"Hello?" She sounded pretty, Billet thought. Probably one of those outdoorsy types.

"Ms. Visque? This is Agent Ed Billet with the FBI. I'd like to ask you a few questions." There was a pause on the other end of the line.

"May I ask what this is about?"

"Where were you on June 17th through June 19th of this year?"

"I would like to understand why you are asking before I answer. In fact, how can I be sure that you are really an agent at all?" Billet got this response all the time.

"Look up the phone number for the FBI headquarters in Washington, and when you get through dial extension 41368. I will be waiting for your call."

Her call came through five minutes later. "Ok, so you are for real. What is going on and what happened in June?"

"I am working on the case involving the murder of Supreme Court Justice Bernard and his wife." Kelly Visque was stunned.

"What could that possibly have to do with me?"

"Please, if you could just tell me where you were that weekend we could clear this whole thing up."

"Fine. On June 17th I worked until 5pm, then I took my son to his Boy Scout meeting. On Saturday and Sunday, June 18th and 19th, I attended my daughter's soccer tournament. Her team came in second."

"Congratulations. I will need the names and phone numbers of people who can corroborate this." She gave him the information and hung up without saying goodbye. He spent the next hour going through the list and managed to confirm this woman's alibi. He looked at the other people named Kelly Visque and decided to skip to the ones that lived near DC. The next two on his list were children, one a boy who was seven from Virginia and one a fifteen year old girl from Delaware. He quickly ruled them out. He called the next name, who turned out to be a woman who lived in Bethesda Maryland. She too, reacted suspiciously when she found out he was calling from the FBI. He asked her the same question. When she answered that she had been in town that Saturday, his ears perked up. "What were you doing in DC?"

"Just visiting some of the museums. I went to the Spy museum that day. Would you mind telling me what the hell is going on?"

Billet replied, "It would be better if we spoke face to face. What is your address?"

Billet arrived at her townhouse an hour later. A blonde woman opened the door; she appeared to be just a little shorter than him, but he noticed right away how muscular she was. She could have easily maneuvered the bodies around. "Ms. Visque, I would like to ask you a few questions regarding the murders of Supreme Court justice Bernard and his wife. You see, there was DNA found at the crime scene and one of the matches was a woman named Kelly Visque. Is it possible that your DNA was at the crime scene?"

"If so, I have no idea how it got there."

"What do you do for a living, Ms. Visque?"

"Please, I insist anyone accusing me of murder call me Kelly. I am a personal trainer at Star Fitness." She looked Billet over.

"If you ever wanted a one on one session I would be happy to oblige." Ignoring her, Billet thought, going to bed with her would be dangerous.

"You see, Kelly, we were able to extract human DNA from a dead bumblebee found at the exact location where the Bernards' bodies were dumped. How would you explain that?"

"I do remember being stung that day. It happened in the afternoon, shortly after lunch. You know, bumblebees can sting more than once. What time were the bodies found?"

"Sunday morning, but we suspect they were placed their Saturday afternoon. What were you doing in town?"

"I met a friend for lunch and then went to the spy museum by myself."

"What is your friend's name?"

"Richard. Also known as married Richard. Please be discreet."

"Of course. What about the museum that you went to? Did you use a credit card?"

"No, I paid in cash. I am sure that being a spy museum, no one would remember me being there. Ha ha ha!"

"I assure you, Ms. Visque, this is not a laughing matter to me. What about Sunday June 19th?"

"I slept late, had an argument with my paperboy, and then worked at Star Fitness."

"I will be checking up on your alibis. Good day."

Thursday, September 22nd, 10 am

Billet reconvened with the other FBI agents on his team. He had given them the assignment of verifying Kelly Visque's story, as well as continuing to track down the correct Peter Marvin. They gathered in the Director's conference room, and Billet spent no time with pleasantries. "Ok, what have you all found?" They all started to speak at once, so Billet held up his hand to regain control. "One at a time. Let's start with the alibi for Kelly Visque." The team leader for the group stood up.

"Her alibi for lunch checks out. However, we spoke to the people she works with. Apparently, she is quite outspoken when it comes to politics. She is strongly against foreigners running for office, and has attended meetings of the American Pride. No one at the spy museum remembers her, and she has a criminal record, for grand theft auto."

"Did you show her mug shot and any other current pictures to the gun store in Atlanta?"

"Yes; they do not recognize her."

"I want her watched. Keep a car outside her townhouse and put a trace on her phone." Billet then turned to the other group, the one looking into the name Peter Marvin.

"Any luck?"

"Not yet. We eliminated all those under 12 and all those over 70." The spokesman paused for a second.

"One thing we did find, is that Juan Pillar has a friend named Peter Marvin who lives in the metro DC area. We are going to talk to him today, but we first want to give Mr. Pillar's people a heads up. We think that word should come from the Director himself, because Pillar will undoubtedly be outraged that we would even pursue this."

"Alright, I will speak to the director. Good work everyone. Keep tracking down those people named Peter Marvin and eliminate those that you can. We will meet back here in a week."

Friday, September 23rd

The President gathered his staff to discuss the new nominee for the Supreme Court. "Well, who did you come up with?" One of the men cleared his throat.

"We have given it much thought sir. We believe the best person for the job is Isaac Adler. He has the experience and the intelligence to be a valuable asset to the court." The President smiled inside. He thought they would come up with Adler.

"I will ask my press secretary to put out a press release and then I will hold a press conference later today. I want to push this through as quickly as possible. Thank you all. Dismissed." President Harrington buzzed his press secretary. "Could you please write a press release explaining that Isaac Adler is the new nominee for the Supreme Court, and get the word out that I will give a press conference today at 1pm. Thank you." Next, he called his personal assistant. "Please get me the number where Isaac Adler can be reached right away." He wanted to make this phone call himself. Ten minutes later he was talking to Adler, a superior court judge and an old friend of the President. "Isaac, it has been way too long. How are you old friend?"

"I am well sir, how are you?"

"Fine thanks. Isaac, I am calling to ask you something. My administration is looking to fill the empty Supreme Court seat and would like to nominate you. We can't imagine anyone who is more qualified than you are. Are you interested?" Isaac Adler was ecstatic, but he did not want to seem too desperate.

"I am honored sir. Taking this position would mean uprooting myself and my wife; I would like to spend the weekend thinking about it. Can we talk on Monday?"

"Of course Isaac. Your name has already been released to the press, and I am going to be holding a press conference today, so just be prepared for the onslaught. I will call you Monday morning. Goodbye."

"Goodbye sir."

FBI Director Grey called Juan Pillar. Pillar's personal secretary put him through. "Hello Senator. How have you been?"

"Fine thanks and you?" He had no idea why Director Grey was calling him. "I am fine. Senator, there is something I wanted to discuss with you. As I am sure you have heard, we are investigating the Bernard case. We found DNA at the crime scene, and to make a long story short, some of the DNA found belongs to someone named Peter Marvin." Pillar's mind began to race.

"What are you suggesting? That my friend Peter Marvin, who lives in the DC area, is mixed up in the murder of Justice Bernard and his wife? I have known Peter Marvin for years, he has worked on several of my campaigns. This is an outrage!"

"Calm down sir. We are simply talking to everyone named Peter Marvin and eliminating those that we can. I am sure he will be removed from the list of suspects right away. I am calling you as a courtesy. In fact, I will make sure that we talk to him next so that this can be cleared up." Pillar was silent for a moment.

"Alright, Director. I appreciate you contacting me. Good day."

Director Grey called Ed Billet on Billet's cell phone. "Hi Ed. I just got off the phone with Juan Pillar and explained the situation with his friend Peter Marvin. He was indignant at first but calmed down. I told Pillar that we would contact his friend now to help him clear his name."

"There is a problem, Director. Juan Pillar's friend is a police officer with several incidents of police brutality. This guy has a temper, and that combined with his background in law enforcement make him a likely suspect."

"Whoa, Ed, backup. We are going to treat him like all the others. We will talk to him and verify his alibi. From a political standpoint, I am sure that he is in favor of foreigners being able to run for President, based on his association with Pillar. Which position would Bernard have taken?"

"He seemed to be against it. I maintain my suspicions though. Bernard's daughter is a bleeding heart liberal, and his wife had liberal leanings as well. I am sure they took every opportunity to wear him down. The bottom line is that we cannot rule out anyone of committing this crime based on their beliefs about this case."

"Point well taken. Please send an agent to talk to Pillar's friend. It's a priority."

President Harrington's press secretary, Rebecca, released the press release to the media. "September 23, 2039. President Harrington's administration has selected a candidate for the empty seat on the Supreme Court. They nominated Superior court judge Isaac Adler of Vermont. While Judge Adler has not formally accepted yet, President Harrington has every hope that he will make the right decision for himself, his family, and the country. President Harrington will be giving a press conference today at 1pm after which he will answer questions."

Isaac Adler's phone began to ring. He had just seen the special news report and was surprised. President Harrington told him he could use the weekend to decide. Maybe this was his way of encouraging Adler, or he thought that Adler would definitely say yes, which he probably will. He had a quick thought. He would call the President and try to arrange for his own press conference simulcast right after the President's. That way he could answer questions all at once and not be harassed for the next few days.

September 23rd, 1pm

President Harrington walked into the media room and stood at the lectern. Once he smiled and nodded, all the reporters took their seats. He began to speak. "My fellow Americans, today my administration has reached a decision on whom the next nominee for the US Supreme Court will be. As announced in the press release issued earlier, it is Isaac Adler. Isaac is a giant in the legal world, a brilliant legal scholar and a forward thinker. If you recall, he was in the original pool of people when Darren Conklin received the nomination. I have every confidence that his confirmation will be smooth, should he decide to accept the nomination, and that he will be able to familiarize himself quickly on the court's caseload. I will now answer questions. Miss Glock?"

"How long did it take for you to decide that the nominee should be Isaac Adler?"

"About a week. The fact that we had gone through this exercise a few months ago made it much easier. Yes?" The President pointed to a greasy haired reporter in the back from the Washington Post.

"Mr. President, were you trying to force Isaac Adler's hand by releasing his name before he has officially accepted?"

"Isaac knows that there is no pressure on him to accept this nomination. I simply attempted to facilitate the process by giving the public and Congress, who will be reviewing the nomination, as much information as possible as soon as it became available. One more question; Helen?"

"If Adler turns down the nomination, who is next on the list?"

"We are not conducting our search that way. We are focusing on one candidate at a time. Now, ladies and gentlemen, I have a surprise for everyone. Isaac Adler will be joining us live from Vermont with a statement and he too will answer some questions. Isaac?" Isaac Adler appeared on the screen next to the President.

"Hello Isaac."

"Hello Mr. President. Thank you for including me in today's conference. I would just like to express my gratitude for being nominated; I will give it every consideration and will give my answer on Monday. Questions?"

"Have you been railroaded into accepting because the President has already made your nomination public?"

"No, not at all. The President and his staff understand that I didn't reach a decision yet."

"Do you feel slighted at all that you were selected only after Darren Conklin was rejected?"

"No. Judge Conklin is a good man; each candidate is considered on his or her own merit."

"What is your opinion on the foreigners running for President?"

"I cannot form an opinion yet. If I accept the nomination and am approved by Congress, I will familiarize myself with all the material the Supreme Court has been reviewing. Good day everyone. You will be hearing from me on Monday."

Billet decided that he would handle this one personally, since the man was politically connected. He arrived at Peter Marvin's house around three pm, and thought about Isaac Adler. He had listened to the President's speech and it was clear from the President's comment about Adler being a forward thinker that he anticipated Adler would rule in favor of a foreign born person running for President. That would almost definitely tip the balance of the court. He knocked on Marvin's door. A woman came around the side of the house; it looked as if she had been gardening. Billet introduced himself and asked if Peter was home. The woman answered that he hadn't finished his shift yet and should be home around seven pm. Billet said he would come back then. Without saying what this involved, Billet got into his car and drove off. He looked at his watch. It was three pm and not really enough time to go back to FBI headquarters or home. He was hungry anyway, and knew he would probably spend some time on the case tomorrow, so he stopped for something to eat. He was used to eating alone. After a while, he became used to people looking at him and probably thinking, "What a loser, sitting all by himself." He had been engaged once, years ago. Everything seemed to be going along fine, the wedding date set, and then that fateful night happened. He came home early from his training class at Quantico because he hadn't been feeling well. As soon as he walked into their apartment, he heard the noises coming from the bedroom and realized what was happening. He walked in and turned on the light, surprising both his fiance and the woman she was with. His fiance turned bright red; he turned around walked out and never saw her again. It turned out to be a blessing in disguise; he decided to focus on his work from then on, and as a result has had a successful career with the FBI.

Refocusing back on his work, he thought about the case. His leading suspect right now was Kelly Visque. He drove back to Peter Marvin's house and took a nap in his car. When he heard a car pull into the driveway he woke up. He saw the man whom he assumed was Peter Marvin get out of his squad car; before he could make it to his front steps, Billet got out of his car and called Marvin's name. Marvin turned around with a surprised and angry look on his face. "Who the hell are you?"

"Ed Billet, FBI. I'd like to ask you a few questions about the death of Winston Bernard and his wife."

"What does any of that have to do with me?"

"We found DNA at the crime scene that matched a person named Peter Marvin, and you being in law enforcement grasp that we cannot keep each person's individual DNA sequence in our computers, just the matching name." (This was a decision by the US Supreme Court about twenty years ago.)

"Refresh my memory, when were they killed?"

"We believe they were killed on June 18th and their bodies were found on June 19th."

"I was out of town that weekend with a couple buddies on a fishing trip. We go a few time during the summer." How nice for your wife, Billet thought.

"Ok, thank you Mr. Marvin. When you get a chance, could you get me the names of the people you went fishing with, as well as where you stayed. I understand that you know Juan Pillar. Give him my best when you talk to him."

Monday, September 26th 11am
Isaac Adler dialed the President, who had given him his private number. The President's secretary answered. When she realized it

was him, she patched him through to President Harrington. "Hello Isaac. I trust you had a soul searching weekend?"

"Yes sir, and I came to a decision. I accept the nomination."

"Wonderful Isaac. I will alert the media, and I took the liberty of having Congress begin their background check on you so that we would not have to wait for the official announcement. This should go much faster than Conklin's confirmation, because more of our congressmen worked with you in the past, plus they understand the urgency here. Welcome aboard Isaac."

"Thank you sir."

The news about Adler spread like wildfire through the country. The members of the Supreme Court were in deliberations when one of their aides knocked. Justice Manucci went to answer the door; he was about to bite the aide's head off when the aide blurted out that Isaac Adler accepted the nomination. Manucci went back to his colleagues and told them. None of them were surprised, and they all seemed happy. First of all, Adler's name had been thrown out before Conklin got the nomination, and even though all the justices did not share the same ideologies with Adler, they all respected his intellect and grasp of the law and where the country should be going. Chief Justice Braxton spoke first. "I am sure we all agree that this is a positive move. Also, there is no doubt he will sail through the confirmation process."

Judith Lackey said, "Did you catch when the President said that Adler is a forward thinker? It is almost a guarantee that he will be in favor of foreigners running for President."

Alex Levitsky added, "Well, I believe we are all in agreement, once the clauses about being a resident for at least five years and taking a class about how our government works were mentioned." Everyone nodded. Samuel Kleinman spoke next and had the most insightful observation so far. "I wonder how long the President will give Congress to confirm Adler."

"The President has no control over that Sam," replied Irene Salkin. "

"Actually he does, Irene. Under the Emergency Act of 2019, the President has the authority to set a time limit of confirmation hearings of a Supreme Court justice, if he or she is not the first one nominated to fill an empty seat. This was passed to avoid the exact situation we are in right now," Andrew Turnbull and Danielle Sorensen said in unison,

"Two weeks." Sorensen continued, "The President wants to see this through quickly so the candidates get ample time to campaign."

President Harrington called Matt Eldridge, who was in charge of selecting the new justice and told him to let Congress know that they were being given two weeks to complete the confirmation process. "We are in a holding pattern Matt, and the election is just over a year away. I am invoking my executive power to get this done."

"Yes sir. I will make it clear that they must be finished by Friday October 7th."

"Thank you Matt. Job well done."

Wolf and Viper were on the phone together after hearing about Isaac Adler. "Everything is going perfectly," said Viper. "We will talk again after a decision has been made. Goodbye Wolf."

Ed Billet was meeting with his team; they had been given ample time to investigate Juan Pillar's friend Peter Marvin. Billet asked, "Did he really go fishing with his buddies like he said?"

"Well, his friends corroborate his story, but no one in the area where they were remembers seeing them, and they stayed in a cabin owned by one of them, so there is no financial trail."

"Are they all cops?"

"Yes."

"Well, what about gas? They had to fill up their tank, right?"

"They claim they paid cash."

"Ok, let's follow up on them. Fax their pictures to the gun store and haul them in to Quantico for questioning. I will talk to them myself. Anything turn up about Kelly Visque?"

"Not yet."

"Alright, back to work."

Congress held an emergency session today to discuss the time limit they had been given of two weeks to complete the process of confirming Isaac Adler. Many of them were up in arms, angry about the ultimatum. Mark Summers was defending President Harrington. "He has to keep the process on track. If nothing else, it is a disservice to operate with only eight justices." Cole Simmons became all red in the face at this.

"What are we, a bunch of children that need to be told what to do? I have been a senator for 25 years! How dare he! We realize what is at stake!"

Jo Sylvester stood up. "Calm down Cole. If President Harrington really wanted to usurp your authority, he would have skipped the confirmation hearings altogether, which he also has the power to do, so let's keep our eye on the ball." Cole Simmons turned even redder, but shut his mouth. He was a bully who would back down pretty easily. Sylvester, the President's chief of staff, continued. "The background check of Isaac Adler has come back clean. We will spend the remainder of this week talking to people from his past, and next week putting him through a series of interviews, and will arrive at a decision by that Friday. I arranged for the following people to appear here this week; three of his friends who knew him growing up, an old girlfriend from high school, his old college roommate, two of his professors from law school, two coworkers from his old law firm, and a member of his country club, with whom he has not always seen eye to eye with. If there is anyone who believes that this is not enough of a sample to determine what his character is like, speak up now and offer suggestions as to who we should add. Anyone?" The room was silent. "In that case, we will begin tomorrow with his old co-workers, who were able to get here on short notice."

Monday, September 26th 9pm

Isaac Adler and his wife were relaxing at home after a very hectic day of answering an endless stream of phone calls about Isaac's nomination when the phone rang yet again. At first they weren't going to answer it, but when Isaac saw who was calling he decided to talk. "Hello?"

"Hello Mr. Adler, this is Sondra Tristan."
"Sondra, how are you? How is Blake?"
"We are doing fine. I am sorry to be calling so late, but I just wanted to say that I am glad you accepted the nomination. I can't think of anyone more fitting to fill the seat left by my father."
"Thank you Sondra. That means a lot. Your father was a good man; if I am confirmed, I will do my best to live up to his reputation."
"Well, I will let you go, you must be exhausted. Goodbye Mr. Adler."
"Goodbye Sondra."

Tuesday, September 27th
Isaac Adler's old co-workers arrived at Congress by 10am. They were shown into the main floor where Congress had assembled. This was done on purpose and designed to intimidate. The President had insisted that the media be banned from these proceedings. He had seen too many times that the media became a participant when they were involved. In the interest of time, both co-workers were being interviewed at the same time; they would alternate answering questions. Congress compiled a list of questions that would be asked by Jo Sylvester. He read the first question. "When you worked with Justice Adler, did you ever witness him do anything that in any way was illegal?"
"No, he always practiced law with the highest ethics."
"Question 2, how did you find Justice Adler's morals while at the same law firm?"
"His morals were exemplary. He was always held up as an example of the proper way to conduct oneself." The questioning went on for a few more hours, and no one said anything that could be used against Adler in any way.
A small group of senators had gathered privately. "Today was no surprise; he sailed through with flying colors. Wait until we get a chance to talk to his college roommate and the person who goes to his country club. Then we may hear some real dirt. Let's prepare our statement to the media."

That night on the six o'clock news, it was reported that the first day of interviews during the confirmation hearings for Isaac Adler went very smoothly, and he was one step closer to gaining the nomination. In the oval office, President Harrington smiled to himself. He couldn't have been happier.

Friday, September 30th, 5pm
The first week of the hearings had passed, and the biggest controversy that came to light regarding Isaac Adler came from the fellow member of the country club where he played golf. The other man said that Adler used his position on the board of the club to give himself preferential treatment when it came to tee times, and that one time he bumped someone else off the list to allow one of his friends to play. When his college roommate spoke, he said that the only questionable thing he had ever seen Adler do was play a prank on some students down the hall in good fun. Unless he said something next week that would hurt himself, Adler was as good as confirmed.

Ed Billet was at his weekly meeting with his team who were investigating the Bernard murders. He started with the team responsible for investigating all the people named Peter Marvin. "What have you found? Any leads?"

"We narrowed down the list. We uncovered 8 people with that name in the DC area. Out of those eight, only one has an uncorroborated alibi. There are two people across the country that we are following most closely; a 46 year old from Oklahoma here on business for a week at the time the Bernards were killed, and a 35 year old from Florida here on vacation. We didn't look into their alibis yet."

"What about the Peter Marvin from DC? What alibi does he have that has not been corroborated?"

"He said he was working late, and the last one in his office."

"Where does he work?"

"He is an engineer for the state of Maryland."

"Keep looking into these people. Where do we stand with the friends of the cop that Juan Pillar knows?"

"The gun store in Atlanta did not recognize any of them, and we will be bringing them in for questioning on Monday, if you will be there."

"I will. Lastly, anything new turn up with Kelly Visque?"

"We recorded her railing against Adler's nomination. It seems she is vehemently against a foreign born President, and she has quite a temper."

"Hmm. Go back and talk to her friends. See if she has any experience with guns. We will meet again here next Friday."

Monday, October 3rd

Isaac Adler was being ushered into the same room where all of his character witnesses had appeared the week before to attest to his fitness for the Supreme Court. This week it was his turn. He prepared all weekend to answer any charges that arose, such as the ones that related to his country club position and the alleged abuses. Once that part was done, it should be smooth sailing. He was glad that his wife had come along too. The government put them up in a very nice hotel, and they did some sightseeing. She loved her first trip to Washington so far. Tomorrow night President Harrington had invited them to dine at the White House! He stopped his thoughts from drifting away, as the questioning was about to start. The format would be the same, with Jo Sylvester asking all the questions. "Mr. Adler, when you are reviewing a case, what is your approach to arriving at an opinion?"

"First, I try to gather all the factual information about that topic that I can. Next, I research what other experts in that field as well as what other judges have written. I try to place myself in that situation and keep in mind what would be best for society as a whole within the parameters of the law. Once I complete all this, I then am ready to formulate my own opinion."

"Would you say that you are easily influenced by what others believe?"

"I wouldn't say easily. I use other people's beliefs as a guide."

"How much time do you spend, on average, reviewing a case before you are ready to render an opinion?"

"Although each case in different, I would say from six weeks to two months." Jo Sylvester looked down at the list; there were fifty questions total. He groaned silently. It was going to be a long day.

Monday, October 3rd, 7pm
Ed Billet arrived at Quantico, and the three friends of Peter Marvin the cop were already in the interrogation rooms. He took a quick glance in all three rooms and chose to start with the biggest and meanest looking one. If the others heard him yelling they might be scared enough to provide more information. The first guy's name was Arnold; he acted real tough like he wasn't scared; Billet had seen guys like him before. "Well, Arnold, looks like you got yourself into some trouble. Were you told why you are here?"

"Yeah, some bogus trumped up charge about Pete killing the Bernards because DNA was found at the crime scene that matched up with someone name Peter Marvin. WELL HE IS NOT THE GUY!"

When Arnold stood up to shout, Billet swept his legs, pushed him down on the floor and put his foot on his throat. "YOU LISTEN TO ME! I DON'T GIVE A SHIT WHO YOU ARE OR WHO YOUR FRIEND KNOWS! WHILE YOU ARE IN THIS BUILDING YOUR ASS BELONGS TO ME! WHO DO YOU EXPECT EVERYONE WILL BELIEVE? A COP WITH AN ATTITUDE OR AN FBI AGENT WITH A STELLAR RECORD? IF I WERE YOU I WOULD SHUT THE FUCK UP AND ANSWER MY QUESTIONS!" Billet could see that Arnold would now cooperate. Billet took his foot away and Arnold gasped for air. He let him lay there for a minute and then grabbed him off the floor and dragged Arnold back into the chair. "Now, how is it possible that no one saw your group the entire weekend you were fishing?"

"We were in a very remote cabin owned by one of my buddies. All we did was fish while we were there. We go there every year and we never bump into anyone else."

"What about food? Are you going to tell me that you bring all your food from home?"

"No, but we cook and eat the fish we catch."

"There must be something that would tie you all to the cabin in the woods."

"We stop every year at the same bait and tackle store about half an hour away. Although we pay in cash, I am sure the owner will remember us."

"Great. Give the name of the store to my colleague on the way out." Billet did not feel the need to question the other two; he had gotten all the information he needed from Arnold. He told his people to check with the store that they claimed to frequent.

Tuesday, October 4th

Isaac Adler was back for day two. Yesterday the questions had been about his ethics and morality; he had no idea what the questions would be about for the next three days, but on Friday, the last day, he was scheduled to take an exam about the Constitution and Constitutional law. Once the exam had been graded, assuming he passed, Congress would then vote on his confirmation. He looked up. Congress had filed in and taken their seats. Jo Sylvester once again walked to the podium with the list of questions. Today's topic was to be about Adler's past, and he would be questioned about the things that the witnesses said last week. "Mr. Adler, what is your response to the allegations that you gave preferential treatment to your friends that were members of your country club?"

"Let me clarify what happened. One time when I inquired about tee times on a certain day and was told that the time slot I wanted was already full, I waited at the clubhouse for ten minutes, and the people never showed. We set out onto the course in their place, and when they appeared five minutes later, I apologized and offered them their spot back. They told us to continue and they would wait for the next opening in about two hours. So you see, it was a simple misunderstanding."

"Did you act according to the club's rules?"

"Absolutely. The members of the club would not have kept me on the board if I abused my position."

"Mr. Adler, did you ever do anything in your past that you are ashamed of?" He thought for a minute.

"Nothing major. I am sure I treated people with too little respect at times, but I always try to make amends if I know I wronged someone."

"What has been your greatest regret?"

"Not getting into politics."

Friday, October 7th

Isaac Adler awoke at 8am to prepare himself for the last day of the hearings, when he would take the written test. He collapsed last night after four days of questioning. On Tuesday, he was asked about his past, on Wednesday about his ability to work with others in various capacities, and yesterday he was interrogated about his legal knowledge and how he feels about various legal issues. He handled all the questions adeptly, and he would be very surprised if he did not get confirmed. He had gone over the material again last night which helped him relax. As he was leaving, his wife wished him good luck and told him they would celebrate tonight.

Adler went into the room where he was going to take the written test, and everything had been prepared for him. He would have four hours to complete the test and then it would be graded. He looked over the test and it was exactly what he expected. "Ok, here goes." Four hours later he finished. He handed the paper in and found out it would be graded in two hours. He went to find his wife and eat some lunch.

Ed Billet walked into his staff meeting and everyone was already there. He got right down to business. "Let's begin with the person named Peter Marvin who claimed to be fishing with his friends? Did you contact the store they claimed to frequent?"

"Yes, and they confirmed that they knew him, and also remembered them being there that weekend."

"OK, cross them off the list. Next, what about the Peter Marvin that lives in DC and claims he was working late?"

"We checked the logs at his building; no evidence of him signing out that night, and no videos of him leaving the building at all that day. He is seen going into the building in the morning, but that isn't until the next morning."

"What is his explanation for this?"

"He says he went out the private back entrance which is not monitored, because that exit is closer to the elevators."

"Sounds thin. Do a background check on him. What else?"

"Well, the 46 year old Peter Marvin came up with an iron-clad alibi. He says he attended a convention all day Saturday and we spoke to people that verified this."

"What about Sunday? He could have participated in dumping the bodies."

"No, he ordered room service Sunday morning at around 7am and it was delivered at 7:30. The clerk at the front desk says he then checked out around 9am to go back to the convention, after which he flew back home on a 3pm flight."

"Alright, no point in pursuing that. What about the 35 year old from Florida?"

"He was staying at his friend's house in Maryland while he was away in Europe and took advantage of DC during that time."

"What of his alibi?"

"He doesn't really have one, other than a waitress who remembers serving him at a restaurant in DC."

"What time was that?"

"Around 7pm on Saturday night."

"That would have given him all day Saturday to kill them and been back in time to his friend's house Saturday night to go back to DC the next morning where he placed the bodies. Did anyone check the toll records for the Beltway to see if his license plate came up?"

"He said that he took all local roads in and out of the city."

"What town does his friend live in?"

"Laurel Maryland."

"Did anyone see him while he stayed there?"

"We haven't gotten that far yet."

Billet's blood pressure rose, but he kept a lid on it. "This case is important, people. We need to step it up, even from our usual high intensity." He took a breath. "Lastly, anything new about Kelly Visque?"

"We spoke to her friends. They said she can be very volatile and has always been ultra conservative politically."

"If this is what her friends say, imagine what impartial people would disclose. Does she own a gun?"

"No, but she grew up with them apparently, and is comfortable with them."

"Well, she is still our leading suspect. Make it your business to track down her parents and see what kind of people they are. Ok, we will regroup here again next Friday."

Congress reviewed Adler's tests, and he passed all of them. They now gathered to decide on his appointment. Mark Summers, the Senator from Maine, opened the floor by saying how much he favored Adler. "He would make an excellent addition to the Supreme Court. He has extensive knowledge of the law and has a firm handle of where we want to go as a country. I motion that he be approved." Just about all of the members of Congress agreed; then Senator Simmons got out of his chair. Just about everyone in the room rolled their eyes.

"Adler does not speak for the masses! He has no idea what problems the average American has!"

"He is not going to be a legislator, Cole," said Jo Sylvester. "His job will be to interpret the law, which he has been doing effectively for many years!" Before Simmons could respond, Sylvester called for a vote; he was under pressure from the President. "All in favor of Isaac Adler raise your hand." An overwhelming majority did so.

"This is wrong. You are trying to rush this through the process to appease the President. I am not going to let that happen." The room became quiet; Sylvester sensed an opportunity.

"Senator Simmons, you are out of order. You are the only one opposed to this; I will not allow you to derail these proceedings based on some misguided power trip!" The senior senator from Alaska also voiced his opinion.

"We listened to your rantings for years, Cole. Well no more! I am certain that I speak for just about everyone here when I say that you burned any goodwill with your loud and ignorant tirades! We no longer care what you have to say. What's more, we do not need a unanimous decision to approve the nomination. Continue on with the motion Mr. Sylvester." Simmons sat back down; for one of the few times in his life he was speechless. His authority had been totally neutralized. Sylvester repeated his request for a vote. Only two people did not approve Adler. His work here was done.

Sylvester called President Harrington the minute he left the deliberations and the vote. "It is done, sir, and Adler passed easily. Senator Simmons tried to object, and he was put down immediately. He is finished in Congress; I wouldn't be shocked if he resigns."

"Excellent work Jo. Go ahead and notify the press."

Adler got back to his hotel that night and the reporters were camped outside the front entrance. "Justice Adler, congratulations! Congress reached a decision in record time! What are your thoughts?"

"It's an honor to serve on the U.S. Supreme Court. I will devote all my efforts to upholding the Constitution, while at the same time considering the direction that the fine citizens of this country want to take."

"When will you meet with the other justices?"

"On Monday morning. I will be attending my first session and we will be discussing Michael Harrington vs. the United States. Once I read all the material, I will return home to finish up any business that remains and then return to Washington to begin my duties full time. Now if you will excuse me I promised my wife a nice relaxing dinner. Good night."

Wolf called Viper right after the media broke the story about Adler's confirmation. "Our plan is working. I maintain every confidence that our boy Adler will come through for us."

"I agree. Remember, though, that we control the rules of this game." The line went dead.

Sunday, October 9th

Hayao was talking to Natsu, who felt very optimistic about Adler. "Everything is falling into place, Hayao. Provided Adler rules the way I am anticipating, I will expect you to get started right away, and with momentum."

"Yes, sir. I already began making preparations for my campaign, without letting on the specifics of my plans."

Monday, October 10th

Isaac Adler arrived at the Supreme Court building half an hour before the session was supposed to start. He wanted time to unpack a few things into Winston Bernard's old office; the janitor let him in. The floor creaked as he walked across it, making him jump. He hoped to change to a different office soon; he didn't care if it was smaller. Just then someone knocked on his door; Chief justice Braxton. "Hello, Isaac. Welcome. We are very excited for you to join us. I will see about making arrangements for another office as soon as possible. Is there anything you need?"

"I could use a cup of coffee."

"Sure, the coffee maker is right down the hall in the kitchen area. We will be meeting in the deliberation room at 9am." As Braxton turned to leave, Isaac Adler thanked him.

At 9am sharp all the justices convened and after welcoming their new peer, got right down to business. "Now, Isaac," justice Braxton said, "We are going to start with the case that is on everyone's mind. We, the eight of us, spent many hours deliberating, have concluded that part, and all written our opinions. We did not published them yet, as we were waiting for Winston Bernard's replacement. The protocol here is for us to provide you with a summary of our sessions where we discussed this, as well as the briefs we received, and the opinions we produced. We are sure that you possess a firm grasp of the law on this, and the access to our information will enable you to render an opinion on this. I arranged for the material to be delivered to your office. We thought that you could read it at your leisure while we get started on the next case. We know that you are going back home, and could arrange to have it shipped.

"That's ok, Jim, but then I will always be behind."

"Well, we would just be at the beginning of the next case, and it would not be such a huge undertaking for you to get caught up. We were wondering Isaac, and we won't hold you to it, but how long do you think it will take you to render an opinion?" Adler thought for a moment.

"Probably about three weeks." That would put them at the beginning of November, Braxton thought. Even if it took him an extra week, there would still be enough time to stage a successful campaign.

"Alright Isaac, that sounds great. What are your plans, now that we met?"

"I might as well head back home now, and have the documents related to the case shipped. That way, I can read them at home while I am making arrangements to live here permanently. I will devote as much time as possible to this and hopefully be back in a month. Now, does anyone know a good real estate broker?"

Wednesday, October 12th 10am

Isaac Adler was in his study, reviewing the three briefs that were submitted to the Supreme Court. This was all rhetoric, he thought. The country needed to move forward. The United States could not rely on natural born Americans anymore; they were not the best and the brightest, and no longer representative of the majority. This was not the same place as when the Constitution had been written! George Washington could never have foreseen the technology that allowed the world to become so much smaller. Adler did not need to read all this material. He read all the other justice's opinions; Braxton, Manucci, Sorensen, and Turnbull were against it, and Kleinman, Lackey, Salkin, and Levitsky were in favor. That made him the tiebreaker. Everyone suspected that he would rule in favor of the measure. President Harrington used his hatchet man, Jo Sylvester, to push the measure through, invalidating Senator Cole Simmons in the process. President Harrington amended the legislation to include the stipulation that any candidate must live here for at least five consecutive years and take a class about government. Adler suspected one of the eight justices told

Harrington that those clauses were obligatory. That was fine with him. He looked at the boxes of papers and was ready to write his opinion.

Friday October 14th

Billet was meeting with his team at their usual time. "Did you reach out to Kelly Visque's parents?"

"Yes. Her dad is a retired policeman, and her mother had been in the army, so it's clear where Kelly gets her militant attitude, and her comfort level with guns. Unfortunately, all the evidence regarding her so far is circumstantial."

"What about the Peter Marvin from Florida? Did anyone in the town of Laurel recognize him?"

"Not a soul." Billet took a breath and looked around.

"Does anyone have any ideas about where to go from here?"

"It seems like Kelly Visque is still our leading suspect. I suggest we continue our surveillance of her around the clock," one agent said. "We can do it subtly. If she lets her guard down, maybe she will do or say something to incriminate herself."

"Alright, let's do it," said Billet. "It's not like we are bursting with options."

Monday, October 31st

Three weeks went by since Isaac Adler had met with the Supreme Court and started to review the information they collected. Chief justice Braxton called him yesterday to see how things were going. Adler told him that he should be finished with his opinion in a few days, although he had written it two weeks ago. He then let Braxton know that he would be returning to DC on November 7th for good and would attend the Supreme Court session on Wednesday November 9th, at which time he would share his written opinion with the rest of the justices. That seemed to pacify Braxton, and would give him the rest of the week without being bothered to say goodbye to his family and friends. Right now he needed to continue packing, as the moving men were coming on Wednesday.

Todd Russell started to rely more and more heavily on Joe Berry. The appointment of Isaac Adler unsettled him, as Russell believed that he would rule in favor of a foreigner running for President; he needed to make sure his image received a drastic overhaul. Berry seemed to really know what he was doing; Russell's numbers had gone up quite a bit. There was much more to be done, however. Russell wanted Berry to start booking him on all the national talk shows to increase his exposure as the man who has gotten Illinois back on track. He needed to get started on this right away. He knew that of all the potential candidates for President, he had the most to overcome. Eric Layton possessed much more national recognition as a senator, and had a very good record with his constituents as well. It certainly was going to be an uphill battle, but Russell thrived on being the underdog.

Wednesday, November 9th
Isaac Adler had returned to Washington two days ago, and now was about to sit in on his first real session with the Supreme Court. He had his opinion with him, because he knew that would be the first thing they would want to hear. Alex Levitsky entered the room first and he greeted Adler heartily. By nine fifteen all the justices had convened. They all welcomed Adler back and then got started. Justice Braxton said, "Isaac, we hope that three weeks proved to be long enough to come to a decision. Have you been able to do that?"

"Yes. I reviewed the documents and finalized my opinion on the matter. I rule in favor of the measure of permitting persons not born in the United States to run for the office of President, provided that they meet the standards set forth in the opinions of those of you who support this measure." No one looked surprised, and justice Turnbull requested that Adler read his opinion aloud. Adler took out his opinion and began. "The Constitution was written more than 250 years ago, by men who extricated themselves from oppressive leadership. They had every reason to be fearful of foreigners, and drew strength from solidarity. If they somehow were able to travel through time to our day and age, they wouldn't even recognize it. We cannot continue to follow their values when we live in a world where not only do we not shun people and governments from other countries, we rely on them for our very survival for things such as natural resources and other commodities. Just as our economy is dependent on countries around the world, our demographics changed just as drastically. We can no longer deny the fact that someone not born here is just as representative of the population as someone who is. We are a nation of forward thinkers; that is one of the things we do have in common with those citizens from colonial times forward. It is only fitting that we continue that tradition here and now by expanding the definition of suitable Presidential candidates. I propose that the Constitution be amended to allow those citizens who were not born in this country to run for President, provided they have resided here for at least five years and taken a college course in United States Government." All the justices were silent; they knew that the measure had passed and that they just made history.

   When the media reported the results of the deliberations that night on the evening news, all the people in the know in Japan and Mexico celebrated with as much gusto as they could muster, for they recognized the enormity of this decision, with their candidates already in place.

CHAPTER 4

Monday November 14th

Hayao had hardly gotten any sleep since the announcement that the measure passed in the Supreme Court. Both Eric Layton and Todd Russell had already received nominations to be candidates from the nominating committees from the governing body of the Universal Party, the name of the merged Democratic and Republican parties. The day after the story broke, Hayao flew to DC to meet with President Harrington. It was just a formality, really. The President had promised him the nomination; any elected official could nominate for the office today, but it would mean so much more coming from the President. He knew that Juan Pillar had met with the President as well; in fact they had bumped into each other at the White House; they had been civil towards each other, but from now on they were adversaries. President Harrington planned to hold a press conference today to make the announcement himself. The President was going to nominate both Hayao and Pillar at the same time; that way, he would not be aligning himself with either of them in an obvious way. Hayao's plan was to wait a month before he made it known that Alex Ramirez would be his running mate. He hired an entire public relations team; money was not an object; he had the Moritu Corporation behind him. His aim was to focus on getting his name out there as much as possible; he intended to travel the country and shake as many hands as possible; he and Natsu had already agreed that he would turn over the reins of running Moritu in the United States to someone else; his job would be waiting for him once he was finished with politics, which he expected not to be for a while. He was about to start writing his acceptance speech for the nomination when the phone rang; his assistant said he had a call from someone who would not identify themselves but said it was important. He told her to patch the call through. When he picked up and said hello, he found it was none other than Louis Grenadine, the famous Hollywood actor. "Hello Hayao. How are you today?" Hayao crossed paths with Grenadine a number of years ago when he travelled to California and taken a tour of the movie studios there; Grenadine was there working on a movie and came across as a real asshole. "I am fine Louis, what can I do for you?"

"Let's talk about the Presidential race. I understand you have been interested in the Presidency for a while. I also know President Harrington is going to announce today that he is nominating both you and Juan Pillar for President, giving you both the opportunity to run." Grenadine paused, waiting for Hayao to ask how in the world he found out; Hayao never did, instead saying impatiently, "And?"

"And, I believe I can be an asset to your campaign. Things are going to heat up really quickly, and you will need to position yourself visibly right from the beginning. I am only interested in operating strictly behind the scenes, however." Hayao decided to play along and find out what Grenadine wanted; he wasn't doing this out of the goodness of his heart.

"What can you offer me Louis?"

"I command much respect in the movie industry, and in turn greatly influence the American people when I endorse a certain candidate; I can bring a lot of votes to your side."

"What would you desire in return?"

"Ah, you cut right to the chase, don't you? My son is looking to break into politics, and I would like you find a spot for him in your administration; perhaps a White House aide?" What a shyster! However, Hayao figured that Grenadine really could help him procure votes, and what would it hurt to give the snot-nosed kid a job?

"Alright Louis. Welcome aboard."

Sondra Tristan was driving to work with her mind drifting. There had been no news from Ed Billet in a few weeks and she desperately longed for an update. She would call him when she got to work. She sighed. Blake had been pushing her lately to try to have a baby; she just wasn't ready yet, she needed closure on her parents' murders first. Besides, it was their first year of marriage and she wanted to be free for them to travel for a year or two before starting a family. She would lay it out for him tonight once

and for all, as they seemed to bicker about this every day. She pulled into her office parking lot at the ACLU and called Billet as she walked to the building. He answered on the second ring.
"Hello?"
"Hi Ed, it's Sondra Tristan. How are you?"
"Hi Sondra, I am fine. How are you doing, and how is Blake?"
"We are fine; I am sure you know why I am calling."
"For my sparkling conversation, of course!" They both chuckled.
"I am sorry, I have not reached out to you about the case in a few weeks. Would you be free this evening to meet?"
"Sure that would be great. Would you like to come to our apartment? Say around 8pm?"
"That would be perfect. See you tonight."

President Harrington was preparing for his press conference. He expected to be criticized for his remarks, but he honestly felt it was best for the country. All of the United States' interests were much more intertwined with other countries, and the countries bordering the United States were even more critical. It was ironic, really, that the U.S.'s immigration and foreign affairs policies had created a type of 'super immigrant', those immigrants who surpassed natural born Americans in patriotism and national pride. These were the people politicians were pandering to lately; not only were they the fastest growing demographic, but they held the added bonus of currying favor back home at the respective countries. He devised a move he believed to be brilliant; nominating both Juan Pillar and Hayao Yamamoto; the ultimate hedge. Then he would surreptitiously support both of them, claiming to the press it would be unethical for him to endorse a candidate to replace him, until one of them had taken a clear lead, then he would get behind that person and when they won he would look like a genius. Eric Layton and Todd Russell didn't stand a chance in hell. People viewed them both as being a part of the same old political machine and even if they ran neck in neck, they would get blown away at the debates. Russell was naive when it came to national issues and Layton so full of himself that people would see right through him. Harrington had no doubt the next President would be a foreigner which would pave the way for Harrington to do the lecture circuit abroad as well as at home.

Monday November 14th, 3pm
President Harrington decided to hold this press conference on the south lawn since it wasn't brutally cold outside. After a brief opening statement by his press secretary he was ready.
"Good afternoon. We are living in historic times. The Supreme Court has recently produced a landmark ruling, and that is what I am going to address. More and more, we are interdependent on other countries. The United States must change with the times and the demographics of our country, which has changed as well. We are no longer a nation of homogeneity and this must be recognized in our political arena when it comes to leadership also. There should not be restrictions when it comes to finding the best and the brightest to run our country. We must realize that we are representing interests worldwide and not just between our shores. This is merely an extension of what is written on the Statue of Liberty, 'Give us your tired, poor, huddled masses,' is it not? The poem by Emma Lazarus does not continue to say we should accept immigrants and then keep them strictly as subordinates. Our country has always been one where anything is possible. Well, this is simply an extension of that. The next Presidential election is just under a year away. It my great honor to preside over such a groundbreaking political season, and contribute to it as well. I would like to nominate two fine people for President of the United States, Hayao Yamamoto and Juan Pillar, neither of whom were born here, but both of whom are fine citizens, and proved themselves to be worthy of holding such an office. I will now take questions."
"Mr. President, when did you decide to make these nominations?"
"I gave this matter a great deal of thought during the time of the Supreme Court's deliberations. Once the measure passed, I took steps to contact both Mr. Yamamoto and Senator Pillar to confirm they were both interested. When they said they were, I knew I had

to move quickly to give them both a chance to begin campaigning."

"What were their reactions when you asked them?"

"They were both flattered and received the news with appreciation and humility."

"How can you justify nominating two people for the same office?"

"It would not be ethical for me to do otherwise. Since the abolishment of our political parties, if I were to support only one person that would scream of impropriety."

"Who would you like to win?"

"The best person for the job."

"And who is that?"

"The one who gets the most votes by the American people."

Juan Pillar was at his condo outside of DC when he heard the press conference. He thought that the President had spoken very well and represented himself professionally, and would be able to hit the ground running. His first goal was to assemble a campaign staff. He possessed some contacts from the Senate, and he would try to find the right mix of Mexicans and Americans to appeal to both demographics. He felt certain he would receive plenty of backing from Mexico as well; the country is greatly interested in his success. He wanted to start creating television ads also; he would have his assistant contact that director she knew. His major concern remained Hayao, who would greatly cut into his pool of American voters that were progressive enough to vote for a foreigner. Pillar also would make sure his campaign staff would spend a good part of their time helping Mexican immigrants register to vote and then make sure they got to the polls; that might make the difference between winning and losing. He knew the other candidates and was not worried about them; besides, it would be a waste of time to compete with Russell and Layton; the conservatives who would vote for them would not be swayed and the liberals would be split between him and Hayao, not the old guard. He heard the first car pull up; the media had arrived. Showtime.

Hayao was at the offices of Moritu Corporation in Dearborn when his number two man knocked on his door with the news of the nomination. Feigning surprise, Hayao accepted the congratulations as they turned on the tv to watch the end of the press conference. "What are you going to do now, Hayao", asked Zachary.

"I am going to run for President, and turn the reins here over to you. Now if you will excuse me I need to get back to work, and so do you." When Zachary left, Hayao started preparing for the questions he would be asked when the reporters arrived. Sure enough, half an hour later they arrived. He agreed to answer questions outside. "Mr. Yamamoto, when did you find out that President Harrington intended to nominate you?"

"Yesterday, when he called me."

"Are you going to accept the nomination?"

"I already have. I will be taking time off from Moritu to conduct my campaign, and will leave Moritu in my associate's Zachary's capable hands."

"Did you clear this with your superiors in Japan?"

"Yes, and they are behind me 100 percent." Along with their money.

"What do you think about President Harrington nominating both yourself and Juan Pillar?"

"Well, the President must stay neutral when it comes to the candidates; by nominating more than one person he has upheld the integrity of the office."

"Who would have nominated you if the President hadn't?"

"I can't say for certain. Since our political process requires an elected official to nominate a person to run for President, there aren't too many politicians who support President Harrington's measure strongly enough to nominate a foreigner."

"Do you feel that you are qualified for this?"

"Yes. I have been a leader here at Moritu for quite a few years, and the way I see it, being President is being the chief executive of the federal government, so I would be trading one organization for another."

"Will Moritu hold your position for you?"

"Only if I should happen not to win, which is highly unlikely." The reporters chuckled.

"What is your first move?"

"Lining up a campaign team. By the way, if any of you wants to join a winner, I will find you a spot among the ranks. Thank you all, no more questions." Everyone listening was impressed; Hayao had been eloquent and confident without being cocky or glib.

Eric Layton was livid. The dual nomination by Harrington would really impede his progress as a candidate. First off, it would place both Hayao and Pillar in the limelight and take the spotlight off him. Second, they would be supported by the same people who would have backed him and would also acquire some momentum that would help them create an early lead in the race. He wanted to talk to his wife. He paged his assistant to get her on the phone. His son Jack answered. "Hey, Jack, it's dad! How are you kiddo?"

"I am fine dad. How are you?"

"I am doing great. How is school going?"

"It's school dad, how good can it be?" Layton smiled to himself.

"Do your best in school Jack. You'll be happy later in life. I'll be home in a few weeks for Thanksgiving Jack. Think about what you want to do while I am home."

"Won't you need to start campaigning?"

"Yes, but we can sneak in a little fun too. Can you ask mom to come to the phone now Jack?"

"Sure dad. See you in a few weeks."

Cindy Layton picked up the phone. "Hi Eric. I heard the press conference. Are you freaking out?"

"Yes." Forcing himself to calm down, he continued.

"Oh, Cindy. This adds a huge hurdle to our campaign. President Harrington is very popular; Yamamoto and Pillar will enjoy a big push from this."

"Well, then we must get a big push too. We need to find someone popular to endorse you. Any ideas?"

"There is one person I believe can help us. Justice Patrick Manucci. He was - is - opposed to the measure and the way the Supreme Court ruled. He also has connections that extend beyond the judicial arena, and if he is looking to flex his muscles, and get some retribution, I would be the perfect candidate for him to back."

"Have you approached him about any of this?"

"Not yet. I am sure he will jump right on board."

"You realize that you must offer him something in return. What are you willing to do for him?"

"I can promise a cabinet spot to someone close to him."

"Just be careful whoever it is has a wholesome reputation; you do not want that to be your undoing."

"I will be. I hope to meet with Manucci sometime before I come home."

"Good luck Eric. I love you."

"I love you too Cindy. Goodbye."

Todd Russell had Rose reach out to Joe Berry; fortunately he called Russell back a few minutes later. "Hi Todd, what's up?"

"Did you watch the President's press conference?"

"I did, and I came up with some ideas. We have to capitalize on your recent momentum in Illinois. The work you have done there will be a precursor to the job you can do in Washington. I would say that most people, all things being equal, would rather vote for someone who had been the person in charge of an organization rather than someone involved in the federal government at a lower level, like Layton or Pillar, because being President requires a great deal of leadership. The advantage you hold over Hayao, of course, is that he has no political experience at all. So, when you look at it strategically, you are the most qualified candidate as a whole. That's the angle we are going to take."

"Who are you considering as benefactors?"

"Perhaps some of the U. S. senators from the Midwest, some of them enjoy big bank accounts and more importantly, lots of contacts. They would be likely to support you as they would expect the Midwest camaraderie that would exist to make their lives easier while you were in office."

"What do you want me to do?"

"Continue to do a bang up job in Illinois, and hire a campaign team to set up public appearances for you and let me work in the background, lining up as many votes as possible. Now if you will excuse me, I will get started."

Billet arrived at the Tristans' apartment at five minutes to eight and sat in his car for a few minutes. At eight o'clock sharp he rang the buzzer at the outside door; he was buzzed in a minute later; he knew the way to their place. The door was open and he greeted Sondra and Blake. They offered some light refreshments, which he was happy to see since he hadn't eaten dinner. He could sense that they wanted to get right down to business. "Let me tell you what we discovered so far. There were two sets of DNA at the crime scene, one belonging to a man named Peter Marvin, and the other belonging a woman named Kelly Visque."

"What are their alibis?"

"Peter Marvin, who is from Florida said he was housesitting for his friend in Laurel Maryland and spent that day in DC."

"Has anyone corroborated his alibi?"

"A waitress where he had dinner that night, around 7pm."

"What about the other suspect, Visque, did you say?"

"She lives in Bethesda, Maryland and claims she was having lunch that day with a friend, after which she went to the spy museum alone."

"Did you confirm this with her friend?"

"Yes. We also spoke to some other of her friends, as well as people she works with, and her parents. The consensus is that she is very conservative politically, and she has quite a temper. She has long been against an open immigration policy, and is outspoken about it."

"Well, how did their DNA get to the crime scene? Did they admit being there while they were in DC?"

"No, neither of them did. You see, we found a dead bee at the crime scene, which contained human DNA inside. The DNA that was extracted led us to these two, and we are still trying to come up with something to link them to the crime."

"Who do you think is the more likely suspect?"

"Kelly Visque. She is strong enough to pull this off, as she is a personal trainer, she had motive, that being she was strongly opposed to foreigners running for President, she has experience with firearms, and she had opportunity, as she has no alibi for Friday night, when the kidnapping occurred."

"Why would she have kidnapped my father, when he has almost always ruled on the conservative side of the cases before the Supreme Court?"

"She probably thought you would influence him actually. You see, we know how important family was to your father and that you are a liberal, and a big supporter of the ACLU, as well as an employee. We believe Kelly Visque realized this too, and acted on a hunch that you persuaded your father to rule in favor of the case."

"Well, the FBI may possess some intelligence to that effect, but how could Kelly Visque have any idea about it?"

"Your family was in the news all the time, with information about how close you were and your position at the ACLU; it isn't a stretch to imagine that despite your father's conservative beliefs, he would have been swayed."

"Alright, but why him? Why wouldn't whoever did this kidnap a justice who has been consistently liberal over the years?"

"We suspect it's because your father kept a predictable schedule; he became the easiest target."

"If it's true that the people behind this wanted to prevent the passage of the measure, wouldn't they have tried to eliminate another justice once my father was replaced by Isaac Adler, who would certainly come down in favor of the case?"

"Since your father's kidnapping, the justices received protection around the clock, with security that never leaves their sides. It would have been impossible to get to them, and their families as well. We also had them change and vary their schedules." Billet paused, unsure if he should tell the Tristans this. He decided it would be ok. "As a matter of fact, there was another incident. Someone shot at me one evening when I arrived home. I am sure it was meant to scare me, because the gunfire wasn't really close to me."

"Oh my god! When did this happen?"
"Shortly after I took over the investigation."
"I am so sorry. But what makes you sure of the connection?"
"A smoke bomb was released that contained the words 'back off the Bernard case'."
"And yet you are going forward."
"That's my job, Sondra. What kind of agent would I be if I could be intimidated so easily?" Sondra nodded in agreement.
"That leads me to my next question Ed. What do you predict they will do now? Will they try to go after the foreign candidates? Or make another attempt on your life?"
"Both scenarios are possible. We accounted for all options."
"Well, where do you go from here?"
"Kelly Visque is our primary suspect. We are going to keep digging to see if we can find more information about her." Sondra offered him another cup of tea, which he declined, wanting to get home. Sondra and Blake thanked him and he left.

9am, Tuesday, November 15th
Billet was in Director Grey's office, waiting for the director to arrive so Billet could bring him up to date. He showed up two minutes later and dispensed with the pleasantries, asking Billet to get started. "Well, our best lead so far is Kelly Visque, a woman who lives in Bethesda and whose DNA was found at the crime scene."
"How does she explain that?"
"She says she may have walked by there during her day in DC."
"Well, what about her alibi for the day and time the Bernard's were kidnapped?"
"She worked until 5pm and then said she went home, where she lives alone."
"And?"
"And that would have given her ample time to kidnap Cecily Bernard, immobilize her somewhere, and grab Winston."
"Did anyone at the gun store recognize her?"
"No."
"What about anyone around the gun store?"

"Came up empty there too."

"Anything about the other person whose DNA was found at the crime scene?"

"No. We inspected the house where he stayed, and not a trace of evidence."

"What's his background?"

"A salesman in Florida who served in the military years ago. That's how he knew his friend in Laurel Maryland."

"What about the woman? If she had abducted the Bernards, where would she have taken them?"

"We are not sure yet. We checked her credit card receipts and there is nothing for gas."

"That doesn't mean anything. Ed, I am sure I don't have to tell you we need an arrest in this case. If you need more agents, let me know; make this case a priority."

"Yes, sir." He had been dismissed.

Sunday, November 20th

Juan Pillar was feeling confident, even cocky, about his chances for election. He recognized what a big Latino population existed in this country, and relations between the United States and Mexico had never been better. He maintained a great record in Congress and knew he could assemble a great team. His cousin Vicente would be his right hand man and would handle the day to day operations of his campaign. They would stick to the same political views he held all along, the ones responsible for getting him elected. He had to focus on the Midwest as they were the most conservative section of the country. He would also continue to serve the great state of Georgia; that would show he could handle multiple tasks and also show he finished what he started. Pillar was most concerned with Hayao, of course, as they would both be going after the same piece of the pie, but he came across much better than Hayao, who could be quite abrasive. Pillar also felt strongly about the southern states such as Texas with strong Mexican populations. He also had to pick a running mate; he would most likely choose someone from the Northeast to help draw in those voters who were opposed to a foreigner being

President. His campaign headquarters would be at his house in Atlanta which was big enough to control operations. Many people believed drug money paid for his house, but in truth his family owned legitimate businesses in Mexico, and he came to the United States as a young man to take advantage of the multitude of opportunities for advancement this country offered. He didn't want to spend his life working as an executive in his family's software company; politics had always interested him, and during his career he supported legislation which would make it easier for his family to do business in the States, which had always been consistent with his platform. He served his constituents with enthusiasm and vigor, and remained one of the few politicians Americans believed held their true interests at heart, and for the most part he did. Even though the political landscape changed drastically in America in the last twenty years, politicians hadn't, with a majority of them only caring about getting reelected and taking care of their cronies. The public hoped that doing away with bi-partisan politics and the Electoral College would make politicians more responsive to everyone's needs by eliminating some of the competition between Democrats and Republicans, as well as levelling the playing field in terms of the impact each state has in the election. Things didn't work out that way, however. The one aspect still not changed was the number of terms politicians could serve; the American people bought into the concept that more than one term was necessary for any real progress to be made. The concept of GRIP, Get Rid of Incumbent Politicians, picked up steam for a while under the two party system, but fell by the wayside when the Universal party was created, as people thought this would fix everything. There had also been an attempt to tie politicians' salaries to their performance while in office, but those in power proved to be sufficiently eloquent to convince enough of the public that this would not work as there would always be a faction who would not be satisfied. The incident which brought this to a head happened when a certain faction of Congress held the country hostage over an issue where they did not see eye to eye with the President, which caused a government shutdown and almost caused the economy to come undone. They lost the battle, and they ended up looking like idiots.

This occurrence was the last straw and caused such an uproar that great sweeping reforms became necessary. It had been right around this time that Juan emigrated from Mexico and started to work his way up the political ranks. An affable guy, people took a liking to him immediately, and after a start in local politics, he had been elected to Congress. The public started to lose faith in politicians, and their credibility began to weaken. That trend turned out to be very fortunate for Pillar, as his political career and ascendancy coincided with the fledgling movement to include foreigners in various government posts. He first served on the city council in Atlanta before being elected to the state legislature in Georgia, and then made a successful run for the U.S. Senate. During this time a concept known as 'distributed government' became increasingly popular, which was the practice of relying on officials in other countries to help make policy decisions and take some of the wind out of those who held elected office who put the people's interests last for so long. The few areas that were not affected were Congress's authority to confirm appointments, and defense issues, which the public thought was too precarious to seek the advice from those outside the U.S. Other areas however, such as the economy and health care, were now influenced by what countries around the world were doing. This delivered a big blow to the political status quo, who never expected such political outrage from the average American citizen and always counted on apathy for minimal opposition to its self-serving ways. There had been a massive awakening, however, and it was fitting that petulant politicians brought about their wings getting clipped themselves through their arrogance and stubbornness, finally motivating everyone to become more involved. Now Juan could reap the benefits from the sweeping reforms. He would show during his campaign that he could establish good relations with governments around the world; the game changed, and now campaigning had to be done globally, not because people in other countries voted, but because American voters were now influenced by how the candidates were perceived by the citizens in those countries. The world was more interdependent than ever, and Pillar intended to capitalize on that. He couldn't see Eric Layton or Todd Russell even coming close to him in that regard, as they were both so provincial having spent their careers focusing on being popular at home. That worked fine for them all along, as the positions of senator and governor did not command such global recognition. Now, however, they were on a much bigger stage. Pillar would use his Mexican background to his advantage, not only in South America but in Europe as well, where Spain cultivated excellent relations with the United States in addition to the rest of the continent. The Orient would be a problem of course, but he believed he could overcome it by being more popular elsewhere as well, such as the Middle Eastern countries, who more closely associated themselves with Europe. Americans would see he was the favored candidate abroad, and that would translate into higher approval ratings during the polls, and ultimately more votes on Election Day.

Monday, November 21st

Hayao stayed up all night working on his campaign lining up support across the country, as well as reviewing his position on the various issues. He planned to takes liberal stances right down the line which people would expect from him. He worried about the Midwest; that demographic usually produced more traditional views. His one advantage was that he worked and lived there, was well known and liked as a businessman, and would spend a lot of time shaking hands in those states. He also wanted to finalize his staff including having campaign managers in each state, all of whom would report to him directly; he did not want too many layers of administration, things get missed that way. In addition, he wanted a group of speech writers on his team, as well as political consultants to help his stance on the major issues. He had California covered with Louis Grenadine on board, and Alaska and Hawaii shouldn't be a problem, as they were usually looking for a change when it came to politics. He would focus his personal attention on the Midwest and South, the two regions least likely to vote for a foreigner. That left the rest of the West coast and the East coast for his campaigners. Hayao predicted those regions wouldn't need as much attention due to the large number of oriental people; the West coast would need more work because of the high concentration of Latinos, who would be leaning towards Juan Pillar. This disadvantage would be partially neutralized however, when they debated. Hayao believed he was much more eloquent than Pillar, and would have no problem showing him up in a debate. Todd Russell and Eric Layton didn't worry him either since he demonstrated way more charisma than they did. He also needed to reach out to Alex Ramirez to make sure she was still on board. He would wait a few more weeks before he announced she would be his running mate. Picking her showed brilliance, he had to give Natsu credit for that, she was the perfect complement for him politically. With her background, she would help him with several demographics at once; the female vote, the conservative vote, as Florida was a conservative state, and the southern vote, as Ramirez enjoyed much popularity in the South. He doubted if the other candidates could come up with such a winning combination. Her experience would also help him navigate the political terrain, plus she had an administrative staff in place to use as a launching pad. He asked his assistant to get Ramirez on the phone. When his intercom buzzed a minute later, he picked up the phone on his desk. "Hello Alex, how are you today?"

"I am fine Hayao, how about you? Congratulations on the nomination. Your mind must be moving in a thousand different directions. I understand you relinquished control of Moritu Corporation for the time being. Have you been organizing your campaign team? The election will be here before you know it. What can I do for you?"

"I intend to follow through on my offer, Alex. Are you still interested?"

"Yes I am. Is this your official request?"

"Yes it is, although I am not going to go public yet. I intend to in about three more weeks. The appearance must be made that several people were considered, as there is already speculation as to whom the Vice Presidential candidate will be."

"First of all, thank you for selecting me. I believe we have an excellent chance of winning. Between the two of us, we cover most of the voting segments, and we both also know how to get things done. When do you plan on making the announcement?"

"On December 14th in Florida. I want to do it there because it will show I am flexible and that we are a true team. I also want to campaign in the South at that time. We must be aggressive to attract the Mexican vote. I want to use your staff as base for our campaign team Alex. I will arrive a few days before to give the impression you have not decided yet, but we will really be discussing our strategy. How does Tuesday December 13th sound? Can you clear your schedule for those days?"

"Absolutely. Thank you Hayao, I will see you then." She could see herself on the national stage already.

Tuesday November 22nd

In a nondescript office building in Boston, MA on the fifth floor, resided a small accounting business which housed a CPA who was a sole practitioner. He did no auditing work and did tax work exclusively. He had the luxury of only taking the clients he wanted to, since he worked alone. It was the perfect front for a National Security Agency (NSA) operation, and the accountant doubled as a NSA agent. The NSA operated much like the terrorist organizations they were committed to thwarting, with cells all over the country and world. The agent in Boston went by the code name Kangaroo, and he controlled a cabal of 4 agents. All the cells communicated with each other through legitimate businesses and were experts at fading into the background. The phone in the accounting office rang; Kangaroo answered all the calls himself. "CPA office. How can I help you?"

"Hello, this is your Uncle George. I have a tax question. I am planning on doing some investing in Japan and Mexico in the near future, and I need to get continuous updates about the conditions there. How would I go about doing that?"

Kangaroo answered, "Let me look into it and get back to you." He hung up. Kangaroo was the agent in charge of Presidential candidates, and he just received the assignment by the NSA's director of setting up and maintaining surveillance for those individuals in Japan and Mexico with any dealings and contact with Hayao Yamamoto and Juan Pillar. He had to gather his agents and send them there right away.

President Harrington felt vindicated. He pushed very hard for the Constitution to be altered, and now that would be his legacy. Unlike Manny Sharpe, the President before him, he actually accomplished something. He loved the United States and hated what was happening to the political system. It had to be opened up to people from around the world before the country became too vulnerable. The dumbing down of America became so drastic that one bad leader could turn it into a third world country. He held selfish reasons for wanting the reform as well. Hayao Yamamoto was incredibly popular and very well backed by the Moritu Corporation in Japan. The top executives there would recognize the potential in having one of their own be one of the most powerful people on the planet and all the perks they would get from a business standpoint. The fact that Harrington nominated Hayao would be remembered and Harrington expected Hayao would win. He hoped his goodwill would be reciprocated. Harrington needed to think about his life when his tenure in the White House was over. What would he do with himself? He wanted to serve on the board of a major corporation. Ronald Reagan received $20 million to give one speech in Japan after his second term, and he had been on his way to senility. If and when Hayao won, that would be Harrington's request. Of course, he would also hedge his bets; his backup plan would be to seek a position from Juan Pillar. If they both lost, which was highly unlikely, his record as President would surely open many doors for himself. Just then his personal secretary buzzed him, and reminded him that a teleconference with the Prime Minister of Israel was on his schedule. He opened the cabinet and touched the tv screen. "Hello Naftali, my old friend!"

Sunday, November 27th - The Perry O'Malley show
Perry O'Malley hosted the hottest show on Sunday mornings out of New York, where viewers called in to give their opinions on various topics in the news. Today of course, the item everyone

would be discussing would be the Presidential race. He always found a way to interject his conservative opinions, no matter how well-spoken the caller sounded. After a short introduction to the audience, he took the first call. It was from a woman in Alaska strongly opposed to the measure of foreigners running the country. "What is the benefit of all this liberal progressive crap? So what if the demographics are different. The white person will be enslaved here if this trend continues. Yes, we are a melting pot. But make no mistake, just as the settlers from England took this country from the American Indians, so too will go the white man. Whichever country the President is from, that country's government will make their presence felt, and will slowly inject its influence here. All this will lead to a civil war, and the United States will be reduced to a puppet government run by the country whose contingent wins the civil war. That's the society we will be leaving for our grandchildren."

O'Malley cheered. "I couldn't have said it better myself! Next caller. It's Steve from New Jersey who would like to set our previous caller straight. Go ahead Steve."

"With regard to the woman from Alaska, what would she like us to do instead? The politicians in power now are only focused on themselves and taking care of the people who helped them get elected. They don't have a clue how to conduct themselves politically, and their knowledge of foreign affairs is dismal. Why would anyone want to continue with such an environment?" Perry O'Malley interrupted here.

"Because maybe, Steve, despite their lack of sophistication about diplomacy, they won't give the country away piece by piece as their loyalties won't be divided!" Steve countered,

"There are controls which could be put in place! Haven't you ever heard of checks and balances?"

"That is not the solution Steve. To all of you social reformers out there, once the floodgates are open, foreign born politicians will be in all branches of government, and then the system of checks and balances will fly right out the window. What needs to be done is to make politics prestigious again, so our top students will want to choose it as a career."

"I see. How exactly do we accomplish that Perry?"
"We change the system from within. We eliminate the lobbyists and special interest groups in Washington; they carry way too much influence and corrupt the political process. Second, we create guidelines about how much money each candidate can spend on his or her campaign, and each candidate can spend up to the same amount, based upon the candidate with the smallest fund, and three, we implement a one term policy across the board. People who continually get reelected become lazy and arrogant. If politicians know they only are allotted four years to accomplish something, they will be much more ambitious. Now folks, we conducted a poll asking people whether they would be in favor of these three measures. Out of ten thousand people surveyed in all fifty states, an overwhelming 72% said they would! What does that tell you? Stop this unpopular trend next election day! Vote for one of the candidates born on American soil! Your descendants will thank you! When we come back, we will turn our attention to the debate about those pests everyone loves to hate, Canadian geese!"

Monday, November 28th, 9am
Ed Billet gathered his team. "Anything new come to the surface about Kelly Visque?"
No one had anything new, surveillance did not turned up anything. "Ok, we are going to go back and talk to the Supreme Court justices again. Maybe one of them noticed her hanging around the building at some point. We can also show them the pictures of Peter Marvin too. We cannot afford to overlook anything. I want the surveillance to continue, and the rest of you split up interviewing the judges amongst yourselves. We will meet back here next Monday, same time. Dismissed."

Tuesday November 29th
The phone in the accounting office rang. "Hello?"
"Hi it's Uncle George. Have you had a chance to find out about investments in Japan and Mexico for me?"

"Yes. The information is quite lengthy however, and it would be easier to review face to face. Why don't we meet at that diner you like, say tomorrow at noon?"

"Perfect, nephew. See you then." The diner was code for the park, where they would be free to talk without the fear of being wiretapped.

Wednesday November 30th, noon, Boston Commons

No one would have suspected that the two men walking were spies; they had their disguises down pat. Kangaroo was dressed in business casual, and Uncle George dressed the same, except he added an overcoat, sunglasses, a hat, and a walker, so he appeared to be Kangaroo's father. The park was just crowded enough so that no one paid particular attention to them. Kangaroo said, "All the wiretaps are in place. We bugged Juan Pillar's and Hayao Yamamoto's offices, as well as those of Moritu Corporation's top executives and Pillar's family members in Mexico, such as his cousin Vicente, and his parent's house. The bugs have not produced any chatter yet worth reporting."

"We will meet here every week at this time. There will not be a need for Uncle George to call his accountant anymore." They walked in silence for the rest of the time, when Kangaroo put his 'father' into a cab and sent him on his way.

Tuesday December 13th, 8pm

Hayao Yamamoto was boarding Moritu Corporation's private jet to Florida at Detroit International Airport. The press followed him to the airport but he gave all his staff members, including the pilot, strict orders not to discuss their destination. It worked, for when he landed at Tallahassee there were no reporters there as they probably assumed he was going to Washington to meet with President Harrington. Governor Ramirez sent a limo for him and he spent the night at the Governor's mansion.

Wednesday, December 14th, 9am

Hayao and Governor Ramirez were having a quick meeting over breakfast before they would make their announcement to the world. Hayao wanted to make sure they were on the same page about the important issues. "So Alex, let's discuss a few things. What is your position about limiting politicians to one term? That is a policy I would like to implement."

"Oh, I don't know Hayao. You are going to be hard-pressed to get the politicians to pass that."

"I intend to include it on the ballot and let the voters decide. Are you on board?"

"Don't you agree it is better for politicians to maintain more continuity so more can be accomplished?"

"Continuity is important, Alex, but I have been nominated for a reason, to find the will of the people again. When politicians are re-elected, they spend their second term furthering their own agendas."

She thought for a moment, and then expressed her consent to the point. Hayao continued, "What about distributed government?"

"I can see the benefits, as we cannot get a real sense of what is going on in other countries without being there. In addition, more communication between governments will help to foster the current climate of peace among the world powers. Final decisions need to be made here however, after all the information has been processed and analyzed."

"Agreed." Hayao paused briefly. "I am planning to challenge Juan Pillar to a forum in the near future where we both express our views and courses of action. Granted, it is a little early for a debate, but I am fairly confident I will come out looking better than him, and that could be momentum to build on."

"What about Layton and Russell? Will they be invited to the forum?"

"No. By excluding them, I will be sending a message demonstrating I do not consider them to be real competition, although the reason I will give will be that they are not the outsiders to the Presidential race, having been born in this country, and Pillar and myself face more obstacles to overcome during our campaigns. Once Pillar selects a Vice Presidential running mate, I will expect you to do the same."

"Alright Hayao. Anything else?"

"No. I'll have my assistant call for a press conference today at noon, right here at the Governor's mansion."

Wednesday, December 14th, noon at the Governor's mansion in Tallahassee FL

Hayao decided to conduct the press conference outside since the weather was perfect today. All the local and national tv stations were represented as well as being broadcast worldwide. A rather large crowd of citizens gathered as well, for they could sense something big was happening. He stepped up to the microphone that had been set up and began to speak. "Hello everyone. Thank you for giving me your attention. As you know, I need a running mate, someone who shares my political views yet will complement my skill set. It gives me great pleasure to announce I have selected Governor Alex Ramirez as my Vice Presidential candidate. I can think of no one more qualified. Governor Ramirez has an impeccable record and is an inspiration to people all over the world." He paused. "Now, it is my honor to give you Governor Ramirez!"

Alex Ramirez walked up to the microphones and hugged Hayao before she began to speak. "Thank you, Hayao, and thank you all for being here today. I humbly accept this fine honor, and I can say I am grateful to the people of the fine state of Florida for believing in me. I believe in you too, and also that together we can do great things! Our country is at a crossroads, and together we can take the right path! Working with Hayao, I can continue to make a difference on a larger scale. I am asking for your support as we embark on this historic campaign! I will now answer questions."

"Governor, when did Hayao first approach you about being his running mate?"

"Shortly after he received the nomination from President Harrington."

"Were you surprised?"

"Yes, but in a good way. I respect Hayao as a businessman and know his success will translate easily into politics."
"How long did it take you to make a decision?"
"About 10 seconds."
"What about your responsibilities as Governor?"
"I will continue to serve as Governor until the end of the year, at which time I will hand over the reins to my lieutenant governor and turn my focus to campaigning and spreading the word about what Hayao and I, and our administration, will stand for."
"What do you stand for?"
"We stand for making this country great again. President Harrington has brought us in the right direction, but there is still much to be done. We cannot operate as if we, the government, exist in a vacuum; we must start listening to the people again and implementing the measures they want." Ramirez looked around. She saw the people believed in her, and decided this was a perfect place to end. "Thank you all very much. God bless America."

Wednesday, December 14th 6pm, The Washington Alive show
"Good evening everyone. I am Evan Shaw, the host of Washington Alive, where we discuss current events. Tonight we will be discussing what everyone is buzzing about, the selection of Alex Ramirez as Hayao Yamamoto's running mate. While Governor Ramirez has a formidable political presence, I for one did not anticipate Hayao selecting her. It was interesting that he decided to make the announcement on Governor Ramirez's turf, trying to show solidarity, and also to show he cares about his staff." He turned to his panel, who he never bothered to introduce by name, as Shaw always wanted the spotlight all for himself. "What do you all think?"
Wanda Price, a journalist and a regular on the show, spoke next. "Selecting Governor Ramirez was a brilliant move. Hayao is expanding his demographics by teaming up with someone of Hispanic descent and a woman as well. He will be cutting into Juan Pillar's votes in a big way."
Tom Dresden, a public relations person, chimed in next. "He was also wise in making his selection so early in the race. This will

give Hayao and Governor Ramirez time to gel and learn each other's styles. By the time the election comes, they will have a distinct advantage. Hayao understands how important public perception is." The show cut to a commercial. When broadcasting resumed, Evan Shaw made sure he got the last word before they moved on to the next topic. "It certainly appears Hayao has hit the ground running. We shall see if his momentum will continue."

Juan Pillar was fuming inside. Goddamn Hayao! He had gotten the drop on him. Pillar should have been more proactive. Well, he would begin putting more effort into his campaign. He would not pick a running mate just yet though. Besides not having anyone in mind, such an action right now would look desperate. Instead, he would focus on getting the word out about his policies and what he intended to focus on when he became President. He would stress his experience in government compared to Hayao's non-existent experience. How could people envision him as an effective leader with no background at all in politics? Pillar would hammer away at this. He calmed down. His phone rang, and it was Vicente. "Hi Juan. I am sure Hayao's announcement has been on your mind all day. Well, don't worry. We can easily neutralize any lead this may create. I assembled part of your campaign staff, and they are very strong. Also, we will highlight your service in government. I know you do not want to use negative campaigning and it won't be necessary. Your integrity will come shining through. Have you given any thought to a Vice Presidential candidate?"

"No. In fact, I propose we wait and concentrate on where I stand on various issues. I do not want to react to what Hayao does. I am confident I can go toe to toe with him on any issue. For now, let's stick to our plan."

Kelly Visque was furious. The stupid FBI would not leave her alone! She had nothing to do with the murders of the Bernards! Now they were bothering her friends and family. Yes she opposed foreigners running for President; the feds learned that she had a violent temper, and she did, but she was not a killer. She became so angry when Ed Billet questioned her she almost punched him, but managed to control herself at the last second. She wished she had just stayed home that day in June. Her phone rang, she saw it was her mother. "Hello mom. I am fine how are you? I'm sorry the FBI keeps bothering you and dad. Yes I told them you had served. What do you want me to do? I was in the wrong place at the wrong time. No I did not forget, I will be there tomorrow at 10am to take you to the doctor. Goodbye."

  Eric Layton and Todd Russell displayed similar reactions to Hayao's announcement; they thought it would elevate Hayao in the polls and would damage Pillar. They both also knew they had to do something fast to try to upstage Hayao. Russell was getting ready to call Joe Berry; he wanted Berry to help him create his first political ad. He would stress his experience as a seasoned politician, and while he wouldn't attack the other candidates, he would mention in general terms that running a business would not lead to success in the political arena. It would not be necessary to neutralize Juan Pillar. Hayao was the real threat. Just then Russell's intercom buzzed. His assistant announce it was Eric Layton calling. Russell hesitated for a second, then picked up the receiver. "Hello Eric."
  "How are you Todd?" Layton replied.
  "I am fine. What can I do for you?"
  "Well, I wanted to discuss the new developments in the campaign and the repercussions they will likely bring. In my opinion, Hayao has definitely strengthened his position at our expense. We need to fire back."
  "We? Since when are we in this together?"
  "Come on, Todd, it's obvious we are fighting an uphill battle. Here is what I am proposing, a non-aggression pact. Pillar is not an issue, at least right now. The fact that Governor Ramirez is Hayao's VP will cut into Pillar's votes. You and I must focus on Hayao."
  "What are you suggesting Eric?"
  "I am not going to perpetrate any attacks specifically on Hayao; instead I am going to stress that someone born elsewhere, no matter how long they lived here, cannot truly embody the national

pride which comes with being a natural born citizen. Such a person has no ancestral roots; theirs is a superficial belief that they understand what America stands for. This is the message I am going to spread. For my part, I will not engage you, Todd, in any confrontations if you will do the same. I don't know, and don't want to know, what your strategy will be, but we can help each other by subtly chipping away at the shortcomings Hayao embodies. What do you say?"

"Alright Eric, count me in. This doesn't mean, though, that we are a team. We are only agreeing to refrain from targeting each other. After today we will not speak about this again. One more thing, once we successfully derail Hayao, if that happens, all bets are off, and I will come at you with everything I have."

Layton answered sarcastically, "I expected no less from you Todd," and then abruptly hung up.

Wednesday December 21st, Boston Commons

Uncle George shuffled along again with his nephew, who was giving him an update on the surveillance. "Nothing terribly exciting yet, probably the biggest thing to transpire were several conversations between President Harrington and Natsu Hakituri, ostensibly about business but really for Natsu to keep tabs on Hayao and his progress in the race so far. Natsu anticipates that President Harrington has a vested interest in Hayao, due to the fact it was him who nominated Hayao. What Natsu is forgetting is the President also nominated Juan Pillar, thereby playing both sides against each other. One other small tidbit. We learned that Louis Grenadine is contributing money and campaigning for Hayao, although strictly behind the scenes. He agreed to endorse Hayao with all of his cronies in Hollywood in exchange for Hayao giving his son a job in the White House if he wins. I guess that is one demographic where Hayao needs all the help he can get."

"Anything about Pillar?"

"No. When he talks to his family, it's almost always about personal topics, except for his cousin Vicente, who is in Pillar's inner circle politically."

"Well, keep listening. Something of consequence could pop up at any time."

Wednesday, December 21st, 2pm
Juan Pillar was in his Congressional office when the phone on his secretary's desk rang. "Hello? Yes, this is his office. Oh, yes, I am fine. What can I do for you? A debate? I will have to check. I will call you back tomorrow morning."

Juan called, "What was that all about?"

"Hayao is inviting you to a debate, just the two of you. He has picked a date of Saturday January 7th at 8pm right here in DC at American University."

"A debate? Isn't it kind of early?"

"Well, yes, but it might give you a chance to demonstrate your superior knowledge of government and explain why you are the better candidate. I doubt Hayao has the extensive understanding of politics your experience has brought."

"Good point. Alright, make sure my schedule is clear for that day. When you call tomorrow to accept, find out who the moderator will be and where the questions will come from. I am going to take Hayao down a peg."

Friday, December 23rd, 9am
Billet was meeting with his team, and they all wore solemn expressions on their faces. "Can I assume, from the expressions on your faces, we struck out when we went back to speak to the Supreme Court justices? No one remembers ever seeing Kelly Visque hanging around the Court or even recognized her?" Everyone nodded their assent. "Well that's just great. We are dealing with a criminal mastermind here!"

"C'mon, Ed. We have been working really hard on this. Maybe we are looking in the wrong places. We focused on the DNA found at the crime scene. That could be circumstantial. We need to go back and expand our suspect pool. Let's question people in the DC area who spoke out against immigrants running for President, and while we are at it, perhaps consider the possibility the Bernards were killed for some other reason. I mean, the Supreme Court dealt with many controversial cases over the years, and touched millions of lives. It stands to reason that they made enemies."

"Are you suggesting we review all their old cases and try to track down everyone who may be unhappy about the way the Court ruled, and specifically, Justice Bernard?"

"I am suggesting we look at some of the Supreme Court's landmark cases that were decided while Bernard was on the bench, and determine if much public dissent existed about the issues involved."

Billet didn't respond for a minute. "Alright, I guess it can't hurt to investigate." He spoke to the agent who suggested all this. "You take the point on this. If you encounter any resistance let me know. In the meantime, I will meet with Director Grey and explain what we are going to try. We will meet back here next Friday, same time. Dismissed."

Friday December 23rd, 10am FBI Director Grey's office
Billet was waiting for the Director to finish his phone call and fidgeting a bit. Grey would not like to hear that they had made no progress. Ten minutes later the phone call ended. He turned his attention to Billet. "Well, Ed, what new developments are there to report?"

"Well, sir, we seem to be at an impasse. No one claims to have ever seen Kelly Visque near the courthouse, and without any eyewitness accounts, and no prints on the gun, we possess no hard evidence."

"What are you proposing to do?"

"We are going to go back and review some of the other controversial cases the Supreme Court had and see if they lead to anything."

"While your team is doing that, bring Kelly Visque in here, I will question her myself. Perhaps if I lean on her some she will crack. If she is as tough as she holds herself out to be, we won't lose anything, and then we will know we should look elsewhere. Let's also go back and talk to the support staff in the building again. I will meet Kelly Visque on Monday. Oh, and Ed, don't tell her ahead of time."

Monday, December 26th, 11am FBI Director Grey's office
Ed Billet and another agent escorted Kelly Visque into the Director's office. The three of them sat around the table, waiting for Grey to enter. Kelly was furious that they picked today to do this. It was the day after Christmas! She still wanted to celebrate with her parents at their house! Didn't anyone have any respect? She understood she was not required to come with them today, not being under arrest, and she almost didn't, but thought it would be wise to cooperate and hopefully clear this up once and for all. She felt as if she had been harassed. A man walked in who definitely possessed an air of superiority about him. He walked over to the table and the two agents got up and silently left the room. The man walked over to her and held out his hand. "I am Director Grey Miss Visque." She looked up at him.
"You don't have a first name?"
He ignored her and said, "You seem to have been able to evade being charged with the murder of the Bernard's. Very clever. What did you do, wear a disguise when you went to buy the gun in Atlanta? Very smart, paying cash. Consider yourself lucky that the gun store didn't record any information about the sale." He bent down and got right in her face. "You will not outwit the FBI! How did your DNA end up at the crime scene?"
"I already covered this with your other agents. Don't you people even talk to each other?!", she screamed back at him, refusing to be intimidated.
"I will ask you as many questions as I like, even if you repeated this over 100 times!"
Kelly composed herself, and answered. "I was stung by a bee, which I then killed."
"Why were you there by yourself?"
"I spent some time with a friend, and then went to a museum. Afterward, I wasn't ready to go home yet so I took a walk."
"I understand that you are quite the rabble rouser when it comes to foreigners and immigration issues."
"I attended several American Pride meetings. No, I don't approve of a foreigner running the country."
"What did you know about Winston Bernard?"

"Mostly what I have seen in the news. He tended to be conservative in his rulings, but his daughter works for the ACLU, so that probably influenced him to be more liberal as of late."

"Perhaps you killed him because you thought he would rule with the liberals."

"If that is what you believe, then why didn't I just kill the President? After all, he is the one who is pushing for this."

"I don't know, why didn't you?"

Kelly smiled a sinister smile. "He's harder to get to than a Supreme Court justice."

"You are not helping yourself with your sarcasm young lady", his words dripping with condescension.

"I hope the FBI is also considering those with liberal political ideologies as potential suspects as well."

"Our investigation does not concern you. You should be worried about clearing your name. Now, what were you doing on Friday, June 17th?"

"I worked at the fitness club, and then I went home."

"What time did you stop working?"

"Around 7pm."

"What about Saturday? After you took a walk around DC?"

"I went home."

"How did you get home?"

"I drove."

"Who do you live with?"

"I live alone."

"How convenient. What about Sunday?"

"I worked."

"It sounds like your time is pretty well accounted for."

"Yes, it is."

"Who were you working with?"

"Excuse me?"

"C'mon, you expect me to accept as coincidence that your DNA was found at the scene?"

"That's exactly what I expect you to believe, because it's true."

"You had motive, wanting to prevent foreigners from running for President, and opportunity, you work and live in the DC area. Even though you crafted an alibi for part of the weekend in question, you could have easily been working with one or more people to pull off this crime. Who was it? Other members of American Pride? Coworkers of yours? We are going to keep talking to these people until something linking you to the crime comes out, and it will come out."

Kelly Visque glared at him, and Grey thought she might ask for a lawyer, which would have demonstrated that she was worried and had something to hide. Instead, she asked, "Am I under arrest?" He was forced to say no, and she then demanded to be taken home. As she was leaving, Director Grey called after her, "Good day, Miss Visque. We will be talking again."

Monday December 26th 11am

Word had been leaked to the media earlier that Hayao Yamamoto and Juan Pillar would engage in their first debate in a week and a half, and all the tv networks broke the story during the commercials of their regularly scheduled programming. They reported the debate would take place on the campus of American University on January 7th at 8pm, and would be moderated by Theodore Punch, a professor of political science at American University. The questions would be selected randomly from an email pool, and the participants would not see the questions ahead of time. Each candidate would have five minutes to respond to each question, and the other candidate would get two minutes for a rebuttal. Questions would alternate, with Hayao answering first. For the most part, this was viewed across the country as a positive event, as it would give the nation an opportunity to see each candidate's views and judge how loyal they really would be to traditional ideals. Very few people seemed to think it was wrong that Eric Layton and Todd Russell were excluded, as they were not the ones who joined the game based on the new rules. The debate was already generating quite a stir, and people seemed interested enough to make an effort to watch it.

Tuesday December 27th, 9am

Juan Pillar was meeting with his advisors, and would spend the majority of his time over the next ten days going over various issues which might come up during the debate. He was expecting all the usual topics - the economy, environmental issues, etc., but this time there would of course be an added element, the foreign factor, which meant Hayao and him. They would undoubtedly get questions that went straight to the heart of the matter. Pillar intended to be ready to illustrate his connection with the American spirit. He maintained advantages over Hayao in two areas, his political acumen and his ability to make people accept him as one of their own. As popular as Hayao was, he still worked for a Japanese company; ultimately that is where his loyalty would lie. "Let's get started. What is a question which I might be asked about the economy?"

Vicente spoke first. "You might be asked something like 'How do you plan to sustain the current economic boon we are experiencing, after the terrible recession we just emerged from?"

"Ok, and I would answer something like this: 'We are ahead of every nation in the world when it comes to managing our infrastructure for distributing water across the country, and making it available to places that were in danger of losing their entire population twenty years ago due to drought. This has proven to be a solution to several problems; first, the rising sea levels are kept in check by drawing water from the ocean and being processed through our desalinization plants, and then being piped out everywhere, so we are helping the environment. Second, this process has created jobs, which has helped both the economy and made many parts of the country desirable again, due to both water availability and the presence of employment opportunities. Third, it has made doing business in the U.S. desirable again. I intend to expand this program by making sure all the equipment is up to date, as well as allowing companies from other countries to inspect our plants and processes. Such expansion will further stimulate the economy as the firms involved will get tax breaks. The U.S. government will benefit from this as well, as we will collect tariffs from those organizations looking to collect this information. So, you see, I plan on deepening the interdependency of the economy and environment!"

"Excellent, Juan. That is just the kind of answer we are looking for. You sounded authoritative without being patronizing, and integrated two issues masterfully. Lastly, you managed to work in a slight dig at Hayao, even if you didn't realize it, when you mentioned the point about making doing business here desirable. Well done!"

"Thank you. Now let's move on to how I should show I am tapped into the American consciousness and how to work that into the answers I give about other subjects."

Friday, December 30th

Ed Billet was hoping for some good news from his team of agents this morning. Their focus would be on discussing any of the cases the Supreme Court reviewed that could have led to the murder of the Bernards. They took one case at a time. The first one they considered was the one that led to the abolishment of the multiple party system; it caused quite a stir everywhere, and there were some extraordinarily powerful people who fought this vehemently. Even though it happened a long time ago, it was not out of the question for someone to want revenge. The second case that caught their attention involved the end of the Electoral College. This too generated much opposition, mostly from elected officials. People were so disgusted with politicians at that point, and there was such a public outcry for change the representatives could no longer dismiss the will of the people. Lastly, the appointment and confirmation of Alex Levitsky to the Supreme Court created a big red flag for the FBI because it was the first time the Constitution came under review in terms of a public official's birthplace of origin. When it was decided by the Supreme Court, rioting erupted in several major cities. Winston Bernard had been a member of the Court for all three of these cases. Billet listened to the report given by his agents, and when they were finished, gave them the green light to look back at old files during those time periods to determine which individuals or groups had been volatile. He felt magnanimous; he gave them two weeks this time to gather this information.

Monday, January 2, 2040

Hayao was spending his time this week campaigning with Alex Ramirez. He did not devote the same amount of time prepping for the debate as Pillar, convincing himself he would be able to come out ahead by using his eloquence and would be able to make due even though his knowledge of some of the issues about which he would be asked was somewhat superficial. They were on the West Coast working their way from North to South. Their travels would end in Southern California on Friday, after which Hayao would fly to DC on Saturday and Ramirez would go back to Florida at that time. They would formulate their next agenda on Sunday after the debate. Today they were in Seattle where they took a tour of the Boeing plant and of course, stopped at a popular Starbucks to fraternize with the locals. They were planning on adhering to the following schedule: Monday in Seattle, Tuesday in Portland Oregon, Wednesday in San Francisco, and Thursday and Friday in Los Angeles, where they would meet with Louis Grenadine and see what he had in mind for procuring votes. If he came up with a winning strategy, Hayao would try to implement it in the other parts of the country. Hayao also hoped to ingratiate himself with the people that lived out west, as he was most well known in the Midwest. Alex Ramirez was not a household name here either, and so far she succeeded in making a good impression. She could sense what made people tick and transform herself to say and do the right things. Hayao watched her and thought it was a real gift.

Alex continued to enjoy the trip immensely. She never ventured further west than Chicago, and liked the people so far. The majority of Seattle's citizens were young people, a stark contrast to Florida. They were also more humble than Floridians, who were a brash group. She certainly was glad the Electoral College had been abolished; now they could spend an equal amount of time in every state without worrying about delegates. The art of campaigning had changed. She felt Hayao was making a mistake by underestimating Juan Pillar. While she couldn't come right out and say that, she could subtly ask him his opinion about certain topics to determine how he expressed himself. Hayao did not need to hit a home run, as long as he made no major blunders during the debate.

She and Hayao got back into the limousine to return to their hotel. As she settled into her seat in the limo, her cell phone rang. It was the lieutenant governor who assumed Ramirez's duties, calling to tell Ramirez the occurrence of yet another alligator attack.

Friday, January 6th, 10pm
It had been a very productive week for Hayao and Alex, and the best part was that Louis Grenadine certainly seemed to have a handle on California. He knew everybody, even the non-showbiz people, as he grew up in the northern part of the state and retained ties there. Tomorrow they were leaving and were confident that they would win there come election time. Hayao could relax and turn his attention to the debate, which would take place in less than twenty four hours.

Saturday January 7th, 8pm
"Welcome everyone, to the first debate of the 2040 Presidential race." Hayao and Juan Pillar were already at their respective podiums. "My name is Theodore Punch, and I will be the moderator tonight. We have two participants this evening, Hayao Yamamoto and Juan Pillar. Our format tonight will be a traditional one, where I will be asking all the questions drawn from a pool sent via email from people all over the country. The candidate answering will get five minutes, which will be followed by a two minute rebuttal by the other candidate. The first question will be posed to Mr. Pillar. What is the greatest challenge facing the United States today?"

"The environment. The earth's natural resources are limited, and we must to continually find ways to stretch them. Countries around the world must put politics aside to work together. The U.S. has set an example when it comes to harnessing the power of technology to meet the needs of its citizens in terms of making various regions of the country habitable again where they weren't for a period of time, unlike other places around the world. When I am elected, my administration will seek to expand these efforts. We must continue to be vigilant before it is too late."

"Mr. Yamamoto?"

"Our relationship with other governments. We have made a giant leap forward politically by removing certain restrictions for the office of President; that is why I am here today. If we are the pioneers of this trend, we can show people from other cultures can be just as effective as those who are natives, and even inferior countries can emerge to be strong again." There was a murmur from the audience; they realized immediately that Hayao just put his foot in his mouth, and so did the rest of the people watching from home. Hayao looked around, perplexed. "What was everybody whispering about?" He started to feel self-conscious; meanwhile, Juan Pillar smiled inside. "Didn't Hayao know better than to refer to the U.S. as inferior? This would change the entire tone of the debate. The public would infer that Hayao still saw himself as Japanese first and foremost." Pillar now had a hook; he would hammer home the point that he would always put this country ahead of any nostalgia he held towards Mexico.

The crowd quieted down and Theodore Punch looked at the next question, this one for Hayao, who now had a sheen of sweat on his forehead. "If you could change one trait about yourself, what would it be?"

"My tendency towards tunnel vision when it comes to the project at hand. I become so focused I lose sight of everything going on around me. In that regard, I am a perfectionist and I will work on something until I get it right." He went on to cite several examples of this quality. Punch signaled when five minutes passed. "Senator Pillar?"

"My desire to attempt to make everyone happy. It is just impossible. In politics it is a fact of life that you will alienate some of your constituents no matter what you do. A good leader will make those difficult choices; a great leader will be able to make people see those decisions are for the common good. I will aspire to become such a leader."

"Mr. Pillar, what is the biggest obstacle facing our young people today?"

"I would say keeping up with all the changes in our society. Everything changes so rapidly, an individual must be vigilant to be successful. There is no clear path to success like there used to be, and people must be prepared to takes risks to get ahead, much more so than ever before. That is one of the things I intend to work on if I am elected, getting our education system back on track. There needs to be more cooperation between industry and the way students are taught, so studies are more practical, and it is not such a culture shock for people to enter the workforce."

"Mr. Yamamoto, rebuttal?"

Hayao was clearly unsettled and now off his game. "All of the temptations they have to deal with. Peer pressure can be blinding and if someone makes a bad enough mistake, it could affect them for the rest of their life." He stopped talking and Punch waited, clearly expecting more. When Hayao did not answer, Punch got ready to ask the next question.

The debate continued in this fashion, with Pillar taking every opportunity to demonstrate his love of the United States and how he considered it to be his home. He realized he had the upper hand, and Hayao was cautious about what he would say. He tried to be straightforward when asked about the economy and other issues, and Hayao's answers were vague if not downright evasive. When the first poll was taken minutes after the debate, it showed that people felt Pillar was the clear victor by a margin of 92% to 8%.

Sunday, January 8th

The next day, all the pundits on tv were praising Pillar's performance, and he was savvy enough to capitalize on that by getting out and campaigning, trying to be as visible as possible. Hayao did not leave his house, listening to the news and how he put his foot in his mouth by insulting the United States. He knew he was digging a bigger hole for himself, but he needed one day to lick his wounds and then he would begin damage control. At 10:45 in the morning his phone rang. Hayao answered; it was Alex Ramirez. She basically gave him what amounted to a pep talk. She told him the race had just started, and that people would remember those events which happened closer to the election. Hayao told her he would be able to bounce back from this and that he would work with his advisers to be more prepared in the future. They would confer tomorrow about what their next step would be, which would probably be more handshaking and kissing babies, old fashioned techniques. He needed to undo the negative publicity the debate generated, and right away. He would call for a meeting of his staff tomorrow. Just then his computer buzzed. It was an email from Natsu Hakituri, and said simply, "Fix this right away."

"Fuck!" thought Hayao. He became so frustrated that he hurled his coffee cup against the wall, smashing it into tiny pieces and not caring at all.

Friday, January 13th, 2040

Ed Billet was anxious to hear what his team had to say. When everyone arrived he nodded, signaling that they could start reporting. "Well, Ed, we came up with a few leads. For starters the folks at American Pride have been vehement about their opposition to many decisions handed down, and perhaps they saw an opportunity to prevent another one."

"Ok, what else?"

"Remember two years ago when the government finally stepped in and introduced sweeping legislation to reform secondary education, basically making an education at a private college or university accessible again for more Americans? Well, many people were furious and lawsuits were filed, a few of which were on their way to the Supreme Court. It's entirely possible that the Bernards were killed to make sure the lawsuits were decided in a certain way, to prevent the government from extending its reach into this arena."

"Well, how would Bernard have ruled on this case?"

"Probably in favor of the changes."

"And can you think of any people that may have done this?"

"Not yet, we must do more research."

"Is that all?"

"No, there is one more case. About five years ago there a bombing took place in Chicago, right in downtown. The man convicted of the crime, Carl Wiggins, was only prosecuted because he confessed while tortured. There had not been enough physical evidence to convict, and Congress rushed a case to the highest court in the land giving law enforcement agencies more options when performing interrogations. The public got behind this, realizing that having a safe society comes with a price. Winston Bernard proved to be the most definite of all the justices in his written opinion. After Wiggins was convicted, his brother, another lunatic, made public death threats against the justices, accusing them of being barbaric. He is definitely someone we should investigate."

"Where is he now?"

"We don't know."

Billet tried not to let his frustration show; after all, his agents had made significant progress. "Alright, good work everyone. I will see you in two weeks. At that time, let's try to have some specific leads regarding the lawsuits dealing with education reform, and also try to find the whereabouts of Carl Wiggins' brother. Dismissed."

  Despite all of his efforts during the past week, Hayao made no progress in undoing the fallout from the first debate. He visited factories, schools, churches, anywhere which would show he was in touch with the people across the country. He had been shunned. Didn't everyone realize he possessed genuine concern for the citizens of the United States? All he meant by his comment was in some ways the country continued to struggle. In the meantime, Juan Pillar's numbers had been rising in the polls, as he showed his patriotism whenever he could, while never actually attacking Hayao directly. Just then his private cell phone rang, which he kept off the grid and known about by only a few people. He saw the number calling was restricted. "Hello, this is Hayao."

"Hayao, it's President Harrington. How are you today?"

"I'm fine sir, how are you?"

"I am good. Listen, I am sure this past week has been difficult for you. Politics is a funny business; you can be riding high one minute and the next thing you know your campaign is gasping for air. Just remember people in this country are forgiving, and one good deed can erase a lot of negatives. My advice to you is to stay positive, act like you have not done anything wrong, and when you are asked about your remark at the debate, look the person asking straight in the eye, and explain the comment was a poor choice of words, it does not reflect how you feel, and that you are proud of all the United States has accomplished. Going forward, perhaps you should spend more time reviewing your responses with your advisers."

Hayao was slightly offended by the last thing the President said, but quickly reminded himself to keep his ego in check. "Thank you sir. Rest assured I will be more prepared next time. I want to thank you again for your support."

"You're welcome. Remember you can call me anytime with any questions Hayao. Goodbye."

"Goodbye Mr. President."

Sondra Tristan sat at her desk at the ACLU, and her mind drifted. It had been two months since she heard from agent Billet about her parents' case, and she was starting to get annoyed. He promised to keep her up to date with the progress; she didn't call that living up to his word. She tried to be patient, and Blake encouraged her to let the FBI do their job, but it was so hard! They missed her wedding, and they would never get to hold a grandchild. Thank god for the support of her coworkers, who had been wonderful. Her productivity declined since last June, but her superiors reassigned some of her cases. She still loved her job; someone had to be an advocate for the uneducated and downtrodden, and that was how she liked to see herself, as a champion for those who couldn't defend themselves. Blake wanted her to go to law school; according to him it would be the next logical step in her career, and would allow her to wield a much bigger sword than she does right now, as she currently investigates cases where there has been wrongdoing, gathers all the background information, and then passes it on to the attorneys who decide if it warrants further attention. Blake loved being a lawyer, but she wasn't sure if that would be for her. Three years seemed so long, and she hoped to start a family soon. Besides, once she graduated from law school, Blake would want her to go into private practice with him, he being on the fast track to wealth, power and prestige. That was why they were such a good couple; they complemented each other well. She would ask Blake to reach out to Billet on Monday. He might say no at first, but would come around when he saw how important it was to her. It also might go down easier at Blake's favorite restaurant. She called his cell phone; he answered on the second ring. "Hi Blake. How is your day going? Listen, we haven't been to Mezza Luna lately. Why don't we make a reservation for tonight? Say around 8pm? Ok, great. I will call them right now. Oh, and Blake, we will save our dessert for when we get home."

  Wolf was keeping company with a hooker named Gumdrop when the phone rang. Still in a fog from the triple play they just achieved, it took a minute to focus, which Viper noticed right away. "What are you doing you idiot! I am trying to tell you something important! Just call me back in an hour after you clear your head, and don't forget to use the secure line."
  One hour later, they were talking again. Viper got right to the point. "Things are not progressing the way we hoped with the campaign. I was hoping it would not come to this. You know what needs to be done. Please be discreet."
  "You do not have to keep reminding me, alright?"
  "Yes I do, for both of our sakes." Click.

Sunday, January 15, 2040, 7pm
  When it came to trying to reach people at home, as well as airing new tv shows and commercials, Sunday night was always the best because more people were home with their families than any other night of the week. During the first commercial break of the Disney movie being shown that night on ABC, Eric Layton chose to air his first political ad. He thought it brilliant. He refrained from attacking Hayao or Juan Pillar, instead working the angle of being a family man and being more in tune with the struggles that families face. The ad started with the camera fading in on Layton working at his desk with the narrator going over his stellar record in Congress, and how he has always been very responsive to the needs of his constituents, as well as for the common good. After about 20 seconds, the screen cut to a scene of Layton shaking hands outside a food bank, with people of all ages waiting in line

to meet him. At the end, the narrator simply announces, "Eric Layton, the people's representative." The ad went over very well across the country, and on the news that night at eleven, it was reported the Layton camp managed to score some points early on in a race dominated thus far by the foreign born candidates with the first of many commercials of the campaign. The reporter noted the importance for the candidates to pace themselves, as things could and often did change overnight in such campaigns. Todd Russell saw the spot, and cursed himself for getting left so far behind. Viper also watched a rerun of the advertisement on the news, and was glad the next part of the plan had been set in motion.

Monday, January 16, 2040

Ed Billet arrived at the office around 9:30 am, and when he looked at his messages, saw that Blake Tristan called him. After getting organized, he called Blake back. They exchanged pleasantries and then Blake asked for an update on the case. Billet explained how they had gotten nowhere with Kelly Visque and how they were exploring leads related to other controversial cases on which the Supreme Court ruled. Blake asked which cases, and Billet evaded the question by saying the FBI had nothing concrete yet. Billet heard the frustration in his voice and could empathize, as this case continued to elude him as well. He then asked when he and Sondra could expect an update, and Billet replied that he hoped to obtain more information in the next few weeks, promising to keep the Tristans in the loop. Billet did have other files, but he spent nearly all of his time on this one. He would try to spend the next two weeks catching up as much as possible, even though he played a minor role in the other cases. One thing still perplexed him regarding the Bernard murders. He really thought Kelly Visque had done it, even though it could not be proven yet. What he didn't know is how she gained access to the judge; he found it very difficult to believe she had worked alone. His team had been moving in the wrong direction, but he received the directive from Grey and there was nothing he could do. Once they exhausted these other leads, he hoped they could turn their attention back to focusing on this lawsuit. He had to admit he was glad to be back in the game, leading an investigation and proving to himself he still had the juice.

Wednesday, January 18, 2040
Kangaroo was meeting with Uncle George again, but today they were discussing the developments in the Bernard saga. The NSA kept an inside person at the Bureau and received information that the feds were now looking in a different direction. This affected the NSA as they already knew Carl Wiggins' brother lived in Canada, they kept tabs on him this whole time. They could save the FBI some time by sharing this information, but each agency still operated independently, and only shared information if forced. "Those morons at Quantico have apparently gotten nowhere when it came to finding Winston's murderer or murderers. Now it appears they decided there are two other paths to follow by looking through other decisions which the court has handed down that caused a stir. The first one has to do with the education reforms from a few years ago which upset many people, and the second deals with the Chicago bombing. "

"Ah, Carl Wiggins. Let me guess," said Uncle George, "the feds are going to try to find the brother but have no idea where to start looking?"

"Exactly."

"What about Hayao and Pillar? Anything new? "

"No. I don't believe either one is involved with the Bernards. They knew as well as anyone Winston was becoming more and more liberal. "

"That's why it stands to reason whoever killed them was doing so to stop a foreigner from running for President. Kelly Visque is their leading suspect. They would do well to focus on her." Switching gears, Uncle George inquired about how Hayao has acted after his major faux pas at the debate. "He brooded for a day, then got up and resumed his activities again. He did receive an ultimatum from Natsu, and a pep talk from President Harrington. His campaign has been sucking wind since then. There has been no sign of any impropriety though. As far as Juan Pillar goes, he is as clean as a whistle."

"It seems like President Harrington has a vested interest in Hayao's victory. As you reported earlier, he has business dealings with the Moritu Corporation, not to mention the fact that he was the one who filed the lawsuit."

Kangaroo could see where Uncle George was going with this. "We already tapped his phone, although I can't believe he would be dumb enough to say anything to incriminate himself on that line, he would use a one-time use cell phone which we cannot trace. I am sure Harrington is angling for something. This will be his legacy, and he will want to have a job when his term is up. That's why he is backing Hayao. Pillar does not possess nearly as much to offer."

"Presidents come and go, Kangaroo, but information is power, and is here to stay. That is our business, and the United States needs us to keep taking care of business."

"Agreed. Now I better hop on back to work. It's tax season, you know."

Thursday January 19th, 2040

Wolf approached the mailbox with the letter in hand, making sure not to be seen. It was two am and the street deserted. Hopefully this would be the last action necessary, but Wolf was ready if it wasn't, committed along with Viper to seeing this through. They made a good team, and covered their tracks well. Shoving the letter in, Wolf looked around one more time before getting back in the car and going back, undetected.

Todd Russell was feeling desperate. He had been bringing up the rear so far, even trailing Hayao in the polls. It was his lack of visibility. His PR team had been focusing on his responsibilities as Governor, which was fine, but he now needed them to switch gears. Perhaps he should divide them into two factions and hire a few more people. And what about Joe Berry? Russell was paying him a lot of money, what had he done? Offer a few suggestions about what to do. He was going to get him on the phone today and demand some personal attention. He buzzed Rose and asked her to get in touch with him. Two hours later he called, using Russell's private line. "Hi Todd. How have you been?"

"Well, Joe, I've been better. I am way behind in the Presidential race so far, and while it is still early on, I am losing momentum every day. We need to step it up, and fast. I need some concrete plans. What do you propose?"

"I am going to book you on some of the talk shows which deal with hard news. Then I will also schedule you for an interview on primetime with one of the top journalists. That will give you an opportunity to highlight your views, and make a good impression on the national stage. It will also be a different tack from the other candidates. You will be separating yourself from them."

"When are you going to make these arrangements?"

"I will do it this afternoon."

"Please call me back afterwards, and please get me these appearances as soon as possible."

"Yes, sir. Goodbye."

Joe Berry stopped the project that he had been working on and turned his attention to the Russell situation. Time to earn your money Joe. He was fortunate to hold a job with much flexibility and would be able to finish his work tonight after hours. He wanted to tackle the arrangements for Todd Russell during business hours because all the personal assistants would be gone after 5pm. He considered the Evan Shaw show, as it was the most popular of its kind. As far as the interview, there could only be one person that would do; America's sweetheart, Darby Killington. Darby was the southern belle who won every beauty pageant she entered since age three, all the way up to Miss America, where she had been runner up. She was no dummy. After she toured the world, she made sure she finished college before she entertained any job offers. All the usual ones came in, posing for adult magazines, working as a scantily clad waitress, but she was well spoken and savvy, and she accepted the proposal from media giant Google, who wanted to create her own web based show where she would interview celebrities and people in the news. Her program was extremely popular, and Berry grasped having her as the interviewer would guarantee a decent number of viewers. He looked up her number and called. Her secretary answered. "Hello, this is Joe Berry, to whom am I speaking?"

"Miss Killington's assistant. What can I do for you?"

"I am calling on behalf of Governor Todd Russell. I would like to schedule an interview between Darby and Russell. We can film it ahead of time and air it during the evening hours. What is her availability?"

"Well, she is busy every morning with her webcast. She usually does prep work each afternoon for the next day. An evening or weekend would be best. Now, let me check her calendar. She is all booked up through January 27th. I will consult with her to see if she is interested; if she is, I can schedule it for Saturday the 28th. Let me get back to you."

"When can I expect to hear back from you?"

"Sometime today."

It was 8pm when Berry's phone rang again. "Hello Mr. Berry. I spoke to Ms. Killington and she is interested. She just has a few stipulations. Number one, the taping will have to be done in New York, and number two, Miss Killington will decide on the questions which Mr. Russell will not see ahead of time."

Berry thought for a second. "This will benefit Darby Killington's career as well."

"Those are her demands. Take it or leave it."

Berry was fairly confident that Russell would go for it; he would probably be willing to do just about anything to gain some ground in the race. "Ok, it's a deal. What time on the 28th?"

"2pm."

As soon as he got off the phone, Berry went about making arrangements to air the interview. He called his contact at ABC studios; Berry managed to persuade him to air the program on Thursday February 2nd at 10pm, a popular time slot for adults. It would be billed as a special event which would drum up interest. He looked at the time - 9pm, which meant 8pm in Chicago. Russell would want to know. When he answered, Berry got right to the point. "I have the interview all lined up. You will be meeting with Darby Killington on Saturday January 28th at her studio in

Manhattan for the filming, and the interview will be shown on ABC February 2nd at 10pm. The questions will not be given to us ahead of time. As for the appearance on the Evan Shaw show, I will handle that tomorrow. I wanted to have this in place first, since your ratings will improve, provided you are prepared and perform well. We will be able to determine what to focus on after the interview is shown and we get some feedback by conducting some surveys about what people thought about what you said."

"Well done Joe. I hope you made it clear we don't want it leaked that you are working with me and you are the one who organized this and the Evan Shaw appearance. Also, when are we going to make my first commercial?"

"Let's get through these two events first, and yes, I did stress the fact that I am working for you behind the scenes."

"Thank you Joe. Goodbye."

Monday, January 23rd, 11pm
Juan Pillar pulled into his driveway after an exhausting but productive day of performing his duties as a Senator as well as campaigning. He grabbed his mail, walked inside, and was about to look through it when his cousin Vicente called him with his schedule for the next day. He quickly flipped through it while he was on the phone, and seeing nothing important, shoved it in the desk drawer. He finished his conversation and went to sleep, forgetting to look again at the mail.

CHAPTER 5

Thursday, January 26th, 2040
Todd Russell prepared all week for the interview on Saturday. His goal would be to project the image that he could be trusted, and that he was not afraid to make decisions. His advisers were optimistic that Darby would not be too harsh. Evan Shaw was another matter. He would be put through the ringer. He would focus on that after Saturday. Today he would get a massage, and then conduct some business with the mayor of Chicago, who would be attending a fundraiser for PETA, and Russell agreed to attend. It was being held at the new hotel on Lake Shore Drive for a good cause. He tried to split his time evenly between running Illinois and campaigning, without giving the impression that he was neglecting his duties. He made the wise decision of having two separate staffs and would keep his position as governor until he was elected President; he could multi task, unlike Hayao. Tomorrow he would get a haircut, facial, and manicure; he wanted to look and feel his best. He would also eat at one of his favorite restaurants in New York tomorrow night.

Saturday, January 28th, 2040 at 2pm, the taping of Darby Killington's interview with Todd Russell
The technician performed the last check on all the equipment; he then attached the microphone to Governor Russell's shirt. He met with Darby an hour ago; she had been very friendly and seemed genuinely concerned that he had been well taken care of by her staff. She was beautiful; it was no surprise that she had almost been Miss America. ABC's studio seemed very well appointed, as was his dressing room, with a refrigerator and microwave, and a butler to accommodate any special requests. Darby would be facing him in an armchair while he sat on a loveseat. He opted to wear an open collar shirt to avoid being viewed as too stiff, and Joe Berry agreed. He met Russell in New York but stayed at the hotel to preserve his anonymous role in Russell's campaign. Darby glided in two minutes later and took her place across from Russell. They smiled at each other; once she had her mike on, the

technician explained that there would be two cameras in use, one of which would be capturing both of them at all times, and one which would be focused on the person speaking. They were instructed to look at camera number one when they were speaking, and to look at camera number two when the other person spoke. Both cameras were labeled. He indicated that they would start in three minutes. Russell got himself settled and silently went over his strategy one last time. The woman on camera one motioned to them that they would start in...three, two, one. Darby began immediately. "Hello, and welcome to a very special event tonight. I am Darby Killington, and it is my distinct pleasure to welcome Governor Todd Russell of Illinois, one of the candidates for President. Governor, thank you for taking time out of your busy schedule to be here with us tonight."

"Thank you Darby, it is my pleasure."

"Well, you must be burning the candle at both ends, running a state and trying to campaign at the same time."

"It is difficult, but I am blessed with two wonderful staffs and a great campaign manager. I thrive on having several balls in the air at once."

"What made you decide to enter the race?"

"Well, my stint as Governor has been very rewarding, and I firmly believe that the buck stops here, with the person at the top. I hope to continue my career on a national level. My opinion is that all things being equal, the best preparation for being President is having been in charge of a smaller office, because being the final decision maker is a difficult skill to master."

"How did you get your start in politics?"

"I majored in political science in college and planned to go to law school. When I graduated, I began working as an aide for a Senator at the time and became enamored with it, being young and idealistic. Law school fell by the wayside, one thing led to another, and here I am. "

"What has been your greatest accomplishment in politics?"

"Getting reelected as Governor. That indicated that I was doing a good job, and that people trusted me to lead for four more years." Darby remembered the bonehead that ran against him the second time. "The other thing that I am proud of is getting Chicago to become the most livable city in the country. The mayor and I worked long and hard to accomplish this."

"What are some of your regrets?"

"After my reelection my approval ratings were down for a period of time. I guess I lost sight of the fact that I was in office to serve my constituents."

"How do we know that you won't do that if you are elected President?"

"I learned a valuable lesson. Stay true to your roots and remember that one person is not more important than the whole."

"What issue would you tackle first?"

"Continuing to make sure the economy is strong. Many, in fact all, of the issues that are foremost on people's minds are related to a healthy economy. If people are doing well financially, many smaller issues do not seem so important."

"How are you going to keep creating jobs?"

"Well, our higher education reforms have gone a long way to making college much more accessible for many more people. These additional skills will open up opportunities, and provide motivation as well. Much has been made of the 'redistribution of wealth'; there are more lower income jobs now than ever before, and I will always support these programs as our country is healthier for it. We live in a global economy and this has led to more chances for better lives everywhere." Darby and Russell discussed several other topics, including the environment and crime, and while Russell didn't say anything earth shattering, he didn't put his foot in his mouth either. When he met with Joe Berry afterwards, they both agreed it had helped his image. Now he needed to prepare for his appearance on the Evan Shaw show.

Monday, January 30th, FBI headquarters, Quantico VA

Billet's team reconvened last Friday, and they had some substantial leads this time. Carl Wiggins' brother had been found, living in a neighborhood called York in Toronto. Billet planned to pay him a visit personally, but first he had to obtain clearance from the Canadian authorities. The FBI had worked with the Royal

Canadian Mounted Police before, and it would only take one phone call from Director Grey to obtain any cooperation they might need. With regard to the case about higher education that possibly spurred someone to kill the Bernards, the name Ned Donato came out. He was the chief financial officer at Princeton University whose lawsuit on behalf of Princeton was on its way to the Supreme Court. He was known to have a real temper and to be very critical of the way the government became involved. Since Donato lived on the east coast and it would only take Billet half a day to get to New Jersey, he decided to tackle that today. He looked at his watch; 9:45 am. If he left right now he could be in Princeton by around 2pm. He would direct his team to get in touch with the Director to pave the way for his trip to Canada. He grabbed his coat and off he went to his car hoping to find no construction on I-95.

   Director Grey was going over some technical analyses from other cases when his phone rang. It was a member of Ed Billet's team working on the Bernard case. The agent seemed nervous speaking to him; he had probably only seen him on tv or around the building. The Director tried to make him feel at ease by engaging in some small talk. The agent then began to explain what he and the rest of the group had planned. "Director, sir, we are investigating other leads in the Bernard case as we have not turned anything up yet regarding Kelly Visque. We want to pursue two avenues; a person convicted of the bombings in Chicago, who was tortured to get a conviction and is serving a life sentence in Joliet. His brother was all up in arms about the treatment and vowed revenge. He is currently living in Toronto. The other lead we are following is for a Princeton University official who raised hell about the education reform a few years back."

   "Thanks for the update. What's the next step?" Grey realized what the next step was, but let the agent explain.

   "We can handle the fellow at Princeton, Ed is on his way there right now as a matter of fact. We need your assistance with the brother of the bomber in Toronto. If you would, please get in touch with the head of the Mounties and pave the way for us to talk to him. His name is Earl Wiggins."

"I shall take care of it today."

"Thank you sir."

The trip to Princeton did not involve too many traffic jams, and Billet arrived on schedule. He called the President's office immediately and was sitting in his office fifteen minutes later. He had not contacted the administration ahead of time believing they would be shook up by his visit and perhaps spill some information if he leaned on them a little.

The President of Princeton, Hoyt Millicent, worked in academia all his life and came up through the administrative ranks. It sometimes seemed like he was drowning in this job, where his first priority was always to make sure the university operated in the black, which became increasingly difficult due to the new laws governing tuition and other fees. There were other top officials at schools around the country with business backgrounds who were much more savvy about raising money, and Millicent often consulted the board of trustees for guidance. This was one of those times when he felt in over his head. This FBI agent, Billet, stayed in his office trying to intimidate him, demanding to speak to Ned Donato, the Chief Financial Officer; he complied and summoned Donato to his office. While they were waiting, the agent inquired about Ned, asking how it had been for him since the reforms in higher education. When Millicent wanted to know what this involved, all he got was a dirty glare.

When Donato arrived, he saw another man in with President Millicent. Donato started to get nervous. He could usually bully Millicent, a great professor for many years, but had been pushed into taking this job which he was ill suited for. This other man introduced himself as agent Billet from the FBI and his heart began to race. Forcing himself to remain calm, he sat down across from both of them at the conference table. Billet became combative.

"Mr. Donato, I am agent Ed Billet with the FBI. I summoned you here to discuss the education reform that took place a few years ago. Before the new legislation, Princeton University, like many other schools, was able to raise their tuition annually and more or less answered to no one. Now all of a sudden, the applicant pool comes from many different socioeconomic groups. It was only a matter of time that what happened in society at large and in government trickled down into the scholastic arena."

"We have never been a school for rich kids, Mr. Billet. We give out much in financial aid as well as scholarships."

"That may be true, but now, since tuition is monitored, your school must work hard to control expenses." Billet understood this was a farce; all these schools utilized many other ways to make up the difference, such as raise ticket prices for the athletic events, and Princeton enjoyed a substantial endowment; they were not hurting for money but he decided to play along. "How has your student body changed since the new regulations were implemented?"

"Well, we maintain a greater cross section of students from foreign countries than ever before."

"Yes, I have researched that. Do you resent the fact that Princeton now is more likely to be giving away free or partially free educations, as the penalties for financial aid default are not nearly as strict? Is that why admission requirements suddenly became more stringent?"

Donato felt his face get red, and Millicent tried to intercede. "Our top priority is to educate, Mr. Billet. Our impeccable reputation means everything here."

Billet turned back to Donato. "How much money do you make, sir?"

"That is none of your business."

"Is it straight salary, or do you get a bonus that is tied into how much the university takes in each year?"

"You obviously know nothing about the job requirements of a chief financial officer. I do not set tuition rates or raise money in any way. That is the President's job, and if you do even a modicum of research you would quickly learn that the President's position is salary only!"

"It's obvious you possess significant clout here. The President relies on the information that you and your staff supply to make decisions. Secondly, look at him. Your President is merely a pawn, put into this position strictly so everyone gets their agendas pushed through," Billet responded then paused a beat. "Look at him, I am standing here insulting him to his face and he doesn't even have the balls to stand up to me!"

"You get out!" screamed Donato.

Billet shouted back at him, "I found out you filed a lawsuit on Princeton's behalf to oppose the legislation. How far would you have gone to ensure that your lawsuit won, Ned? Up to killing a Supreme Court justice?"

Stunned, Donato was speechless. "What are you talking about?"

"Winston Bernard and his wife. He consistently supported education reform. Perhaps you killed them to help your cause!"

"That is just sick. There is nothing on which to base such an ugly accusation." Donato's response spoke volumes. Most people would have said something more like 'How could you think I am capable of such a thing'? That would demonstrate moral indignation. Donato's answer showed that his first reaction was to attempt to clear his name; a sign of possible guilt.

"Yes there is. The murders took place during June, a time when school is not in session. You could have easily slipped down to DC and carried out the killings! Come on Ned. You displayed quite a temper. How angry were you about the new laws? They changed the face of Princeton, one of the oldest and most exclusive colleges in the world."

"Your welcome is worn out here agent Billet. President Millicent's assistant will show you out."

Billet turned to Millicent. "Good day sir." Right before he walked out, he turned back to Donato and said "you haven't gotten rid of me yet. We will be digging into your past and figuring out how you pulled off the double murder."

Tuesday, January 31st, Washington DC

Eric Layton was running late which was a problem. Justice Manucci did not like to be kept waiting. Fortunately, traffic turned out to be really light and Layton's driver managed to make it to the Supreme Court building in record time. Layton had waited a long time for this meeting; he had made the appointment back before Thanksgiving but this was the first time they had both been available. He dealt with Manucci before; he liked to have his ego stroked. Layton didn't mind; Manucci could be a big asset to his campaign. He was the legitimate member of a not so savory family. Manucci knew enough at least not to attempt to try for an elected position. When he received his appointment to the Supreme Court the confirmation sailed through very quickly. The Manucci family maintained big ties in government and getting him confirmed proved to be much easier than getting him into an elected position would have been, as the average citizen was not indebted to the Manuccis as other elected officials across the country were. Once Patrick joined the Supreme Court, the Manucci's power increased tenfold, and they were able to expand their operations beyond New York. They had gotten smart and conceded to work with other ethnic groups in their criminal endeavors. Manucci's secretary escorted Layton into his office. "Patrick, how are you? It has been way too long. You are looking well."

"Thank you Eric. You as well. How are Cindy and Jack?"

"They are fine, and your family?"

"Thank God everyone is well. How is that golf game these days? We will play once the weather gets warmer. I know you play all year round, but I am not as hard core as you are." Manucci chuckled.

"Much has happened since we last saw each other. The Presidential race has expanded, and the killer of your colleague is still at large. Has the FBI made any progress?"

"No. I am not privy to any more information than you are Eric. Let's hope they get their act together soon. By the way, your commercial proved very effective. You definitely scored points across the country."

"Thank you Patrick." Time to get down to business. "Patrick, the election is about nine months away, and I have much work to do if I am to win. The other candidates are all going full steam ahead and so must I. My campaign would get a big boost from the support of a prominent public figure. We share a long history of working together. I would always put the United States first as President, Patrick." He knew that Manucci had opposed the measure to allow foreigners to run for president. "Let me not insult you by mincing words. I would like you to ask for your public endorsement."

Manucci sat back. He needed to ponder this for a minute. He liked Layton and agreed with his policies. Manucci's top agenda however was always 'what's in it for me'. "Eric, I cannot really back anyone publicly. That would only serve to undermine my impartiality on the bench. Let me make another offer, however. I will use my clout behind the scenes to spread the word that I am behind you. My message will be spread back home in Connecticut and my reach will extend to New York. You can count on carrying the popular vote in the states between Connecticut and Pennsylvania."

"That would be great Patrick." Layton was relieved; winning a good portion of the northeast would mean a lot.

Manucci cleared his throat, signaling that he had more to say. "You know me Eric, I do not give something for nothing."

"You are giving me your support, Patrick. It goes without saying that I would reciprocate."

"Excellent." Although it would have come to pass anyway, it was much easier to proceed with cooperation. "Eric, are you familiar with Steven Morris?"

"The junior senator from New York? Of course."

"He is an up and coming political star, and a close friend of my family. I would like you to make him your Vice Presidential candidate."

"Well, Morris is a fine man, and I am sure he would be an asset for my ticket. Quite frankly, however, I planned on picking someone from the south, and perhaps a woman. As I see it, I must do something to compete with Hayao and Alex Ramirez. They are my biggest competition, despite his flub at the debate. I already enjoy an advantage in the Midwest, and with your support, I will grab the Northeast. The western states will likely be split between Hayao and Pillar, due to the fact that there are large blocks of Orientals and Mexicans in those states, which will make extensive campaigning there a waste of time. That leaves the south, which I must pursue vigorously."

"Those are all valid points. Remember, though, that Steven Morris has a very high profile, and the two of you are both young and vibrant. If you two are a team, you will bring a renewed sense of vitality to the race, one that really hasn't been seen since Clinton-Gore back in the 1990's. You shouldn't encounter any trouble with the south, and might even cut into the votes out west."

Layton felt torn. Morris was not his first choice, yet Manucci brought much to the table and Layton wanted him in his corner. He sensed that this was a deal breaker, and he didn't want the Manuccis to back someone else who did agree to include Morris. A compromise became necessary. "Alright, Patrick. Let's do it. Steven Morris will be my vice president."

"Excellent, Eric. We will make a great team. Steven will be expecting your call in the next few days. The two of you can talk before it is announced to the media. Good bye, Eric. I am sure we will be speaking again soon."

Director Grey asked his secretary to get the head of the Mounties on the phone. His name was Michel Antwar, one of the most tenacious bastards Grey had ever met. That was how he rose through the ranks. He hailed from French descent and came from a long line of soldiers and law enforcement professionals. Once he became involved in a case he did not let go until he apprehended the perpetrator. The two worked together several times when the crime involved both countries, such as when a serial killer had murdered people both in Canada and the United States. Antwar was almost always receptive to Grey and today was no different. "Hello James! How are you today?"

"I am fine Michel, and you?"

"Never better. What's going on?"

"I am sure that you remember the murders of Supreme Court justice Winston Bernard and his wife last June. The investigation is still going on and now has taken a turn that involves a man in the Toronto area. His name is Earl Wiggins, the brother of the person who bombed Chicago a few years back. He has vowed to get revenge on the United States as his brother endured torture to get a confession with the Supreme Court the body who ruled that torture could be used in certain instances by law enforcement, and the Chicago bombing met those criteria. Bernard was one of the justices who ruled in favor of using torture, and we must speak to Wiggins. We need you to provide us access to him and to make sure the Toronto police don't get in our way."

"That may take me a few days, James. I will have to clear it with several people, such as the mayor of Toronto and the head of the Toronto unit of the Mounted police. I will present it to them as if you and I will be working together, so just help me spin it that way. I will also ask them to gather some background information about him so that we are aware of what we are walking into."

"Great. Thanks for your cooperation. Once we get him, we are planning to extradite him, as the crime was committed in the U.S. I will make sure, however, that Canada is recognized as being an integral part of the apprehension. Thanks Michel. I will be speaking to you later on this week."

Dearborn, MI

Hayao was meeting with his public relations team; he wanted them to start getting him more exposure. President Harrington set him straight, he needed to deal with this directly. The first thing that he wanted to do was go on one of the late night talk shows and perhaps poke fun at himself. That would break the ice and make it easier to grant interviews with more difficult questions. Another priority also needed to be finding people around the country to endorse him. That would be a task for his team of interns. He divided his time now between campaigning and reviewing old videos of politicians debating to pick up some pointers on how to turn questions around to his advantage and make certain points even when asked about other things. He had to retrain himself to stop answering questions like a businessman. Alex Ramirez would resume tutoring him upon her return from Vermont trying to ingratiate herself with the people there. He wanted to focus on the Northeast and be as charming as possible, for that was where he believed that he needed the most reinforcements. He would make his rounds there in a few months. His private phone rang; it was Natsu. "Hello, Natsu. How is everything?"

"I am fine. We have not spoken recently."

"Yes. Running for President is very time consuming. How is Moritu doing? Is Zachary handling things properly? I told him to contact me with any issues."

"Moritu is doing just fine; we are giving Zachary as much support as he needs from the home office." Natsu paused. "That is not why I called. What have you been doing to advance your campaign?" Hayao reviewed all the steps he had taken and tried to sound confident on the phone. While Natsu listened politely and told Hayao that he was on the right track, silently he felt pessimistic about Hayao's plan and became angry. There was much at stake.

Wednesday, February 1st

Ed Billet sent an email out to the agents on his team, explaining what had taken place at Princeton with Hoyt Millicent and Ned Donato. Donato definitely existed on their radar now. He charged his team with finding out as much as possible about Donato's past and his whereabouts when the Bernards were murdered. His agent talked to the director and the director agreed to use his authority to make Earl Wiggins available for questioning. He did not speak to the director yet since he got back from New Jersey, but assumed that he was waiting on the Canadian authorities. He went downstairs to the interagency room, where there were resources to find out what the CIA was involved with, although the information the FBI shared with the CIA and vice versa just scratched the surface. The CIA obviously held the upper hand in gathering additional information about the FBI and mostly constituted a show of good faith that they tried to cooperate. Billet wanted to see if they unearthed any new developments or reports about the Presidential race. He possessed a fair amount of clearance and could see some classified documents. He got to the computer screen where files were listed alphabetically and found the one for the 2040 election.

There were a few links in the file, each one pertaining to a candidate. First he looked at Hayao's information. He looked for something that resembled a motive, and something that might connect one of the candidates to either Kelly Visque, Ned Donato, or Carl Wiggins. The only thing of interest involved the amount of contact that Hayao had with Natsu Hakituri, who seemed to be running the campaign as well as the Moritu Corporation. Billet thought this through. If Hayao established connections with any of the three people of interest, it would most likely be Carl Wiggins as they were both from the Midwest. He looked at all the links and found nothing to tie any of the four to the three for whom the FBI was looking. The files were primarily composed of the people that they associated with and their roots going back to their childhoods. One thing all four had in common was the fact that they were all overachievers. They all worked hard to get where they are. The least flamboyant of them was Todd Russell, who seemed to rest on his laurels when possible. He spent two hours poring over the pages but found nothing in their early years that would arouse suspicion. He wanted to take a crack at Wiggins. Maybe he should be looking at their files.

   Steven Morris was working at his desk in his house in Ronkonkoma New York. He had come home for a week to see his family and stay connected to his constituents. He did that every few months; it was essential for doing his job effectively. His phone rang startling him as only a select few had this phone number. He answered and discovered it was Presidential candidate Eric Layton. What could Layton possibly want? "Hello Steven. How are you?" They worked together a few times on legislation in Washington, and Layton had always been very impressive.
   He quickly regained his composure and answered. "I am doing fine Eric, how are you?"
   "I am well. Steven. You must be wondering why I am calling you at home. There is something that I would like to discuss with you. Let me get right to the point. Steven, I would like you to be my Vice Presidential running mate." Layton waited a few seconds for a response; when Morris didn't say anything, Layton knew he had not seen this coming and that Patrick Manucci did not tell him that Layton might call him.

"I am honored, Eric. I must ask you though, why me? There are many more prominent people out there who would be an asset to your ticket."

"Well, Steven, we worked together on several occasions and I noticed your skill at dealing with people, and your knowledge of the issues at hand. I believe we would make a good team and would complement each other well."

"What about the demographics? You will cover the Midwest, and I can help us with the Northeast. We will need help with the other sections of the country. What is your plan for that?"

"We will be a formidable team, Steven. People will be drawn to our experience and vitality. We will not need the home court advantage. Let the other candidates go after regional votes. We will give people real substance."

Morris pondered that for a minute. Layton made a good point. The other three candidates either had no vice presidential candidate yet or they were having issues; if Layton and Morris appeared to be cohesive they could get out in front and sail past Juan Pillar, who led in the polls. Momentum was critical in politics. Morris still entertained doubts. He enjoyed a pretty soft job in Congress. He was wildly popular in New York and could come and go from Washington pretty much as he pleased. It would be hard to give that up. He never pondered taking his political career further; if and when he failed to be reelected, he could always go back to practicing law. Still, it would be very prestigious to be Vice President, and would elevate him to the upper echelon of those in public office. He thought he knew what his answer would be, but he wanted at least one day to consider it. "Let me get back to you Eric. I will give you an answer by the end of the week."

"Alright, Steven. Thanks for your time."

Juan Pillar was still flying high, coasting from the outcome of the debate. All of the campaigning he did since then had been very successful; he was way ahead in all the polls. He had to continue to project the image of being energetic and enthusiastic, people were drawn to that. Hayao has done nothing so far to make up any ground, and the two Americans were also getting nowhere, despite their recent public appearances. His campaign staff had increased too. People smelled blood in the water, and Hayao was hurting. For the time being, Pillar had to avoid any more face-offs with him, for he did not want to take the chance that things might go differently next time. There would come a time when it would be necessary to engage in another debate, but he would put it off as long as he could. If he continued to say all the right things, winning the White House would be in reach.

Friday, February 3rd, 9am
Steven Morris discussed the offer from Eric Layton with his wife and made his decision. He had his assistant call Eric Layton. When Layton got on the phone himself five minutes later, Morris got right to the point.

"Eric, I am sincerely flattered by your offer, and I thought about it seriously. I must decline, however. I am very comfortable where I am and very content to stay here. I believe I serve my voters well and am not looking for a new adventure right now. I wish you the best of luck; you can count on my vote and my support."

Layton was surprised; he thought that Morris would definitely come aboard. "That's ok, Steven. I understand. I don't blame you for wanting to stick with a good thing. I know that we will continue to work together successfully whether I win or not." They ended their conversation, and Morris couldn't help but notice the condescension in Layton's voice.

Eric Layton called Patrick Manucci the minute he got off the phone with Morris. "Your boy turned me down. Any suggestions as to whom I should choose now?"

"No. We have known Steven for years and watched each others' backs. The choice is yours now. Pick someone who will give you the best chance. Whoever you select is fine with me; you can count on my endorsement."

Layton breathed a sigh of relief. "Thank you Patrick. I will be in touch."

2pm

Director Grey just got word from Michel Antwar, the head of the Mounties, that the FBI received clearance to interrogate Earl Wiggins. He wanted to act as soon as possible. The Canadian police were good and for the most part reliable, but there were often leaks in any organization, and time was of the essence. He needed to find Billet and get him up there. He sent a text from the high priority FBI phone, reserved for special messages. That line used satellite technology to find the recipient immediately and bypassed the cell towers used for routine cell phone calls. However, since the technology only worked one way, Billet's return phone call took the standard 10 seconds. "Yes, sir?"

"Hi Ed. We just received clearance to see Earl Wiggins. I am sure I needn't tell you that the sooner we can get to him the better. When can you leave?"

"I can leave tonight. I will be able to use the plane this time, right?" For such short notice, one of the perks was using the Director's plane, as long as he wasn't.

"Yes, I already set it up. You will fly out of Dulles tonight at 6pm and land in Toronto between 7 and 8 pm. I want you to talk to Wiggins tonight. We need to catch him off guard. If you need to stay overnight the bureau will pay for it. The Mounties will meet you at his residence. Be careful Ed. This guy may be volatile."

Ed was aware of that. "Yes sir. I will report back to you afterwards."

Eric Layton was racking his brain. He expected it would be so easy to come up with a running mate, but it wasn't so. He wanted someone who would cover a different segment of the population and was experienced in government. Steven Morris sounded better and better. He wanted to reach out to Patrick Manucci and ask him to try to convince Morris to change his mind. Morris would make an excellent running mate and Layton considered himself lucky he stumbled upon it. He called Manucci. When he answered, Layton explained that he really wanted Morris. Manucci said he couldn't guarantee anything but he would use whatever influence he had.

He promised Layton he would provide more information in a week.

9 pm, Toronto

Billet's plane touched down, the flight had been slightly delayed. One hour later, he arrived at Earl Wiggins' house accompanied by two Mounties, and the Toronto police, who wanted in on the action, and it was just easier to include them than start a turf war. Billet knocked on the front door and waited. A man answered the door; Billet assumed it was Wiggins. He held up his badge. "Ed Billet, FBI. I would like to ask you some questions."

"You're a little bit out of your jurisdiction, wouldn't you say, agent Billet? I guess that is why you brought the entire posse."

"My jurisdiction doesn't concern you."

"What is this about?"

"The murder of Supreme Court justice Winston Bernard and his wife. We can do this here or down at the station."

Wiggins sighed. "Let's just get this over with." He motioned them in.

"I understand that you have been living in Canada for two years now."

"That's right, so why are you bothering me?"

"Because of the trips that you made to visit your brother. We checked the prison logs. You were there twice during the first half of 2039, once in February and once in the middle of June, about a week before the murders. You could have travelled to Washington, committed the killings, gone back to Chicago, and then returned here. The timeline fits."

"I hope you also checked for rental cars and train or airline tickets because you will find that I didn't purchase any of them."

"Don't give me that. You probably paid in cash. Train travel doesn't require any form of id."

"Fine. What do you want from me?"

"Where were you from Friday June 17th to Sunday June 19th?" Wiggins wanted to say he was fucking the agent's wife, but he bit his tongue.

"In Chicago going back and forth between the motel and the jail to see my brother."

"Well, what did you do when you weren't at either place? Joliet doesn't offer visiting hours all day long."

"I explored Chicago. I went to the Lincoln Park zoo and the Field Museum. You should visit Chicago. There is a lot to do, even for government types who don't get out much." Pretending not to hear that last comment, Billet said, "I want the name of the motel where you stayed."

"I stayed at the Holiday Inn outside of town."

"How did you pay?"

"I use cash exclusively. I don't even own a credit card. There is way too much information floating around out there."

"Then you would have had to show some form of identification."

"I own a passport and a provincial driver's license."

"Let me see them."

Wiggins brought them back two minutes later.

"I am going to take these down to the station when we are finished, scan them and bring them back. How did you get to Chicago?"

"I took the train."

"How did you get back and forth between the prison and your motel?"

"Taxis."

"Where did you take all of your meals?"

"Mostly at the motel, but I went out to restaurants a few times. You still haven't told me why I am a suspect."

"Do I really need to spell it out for you? Your brother's case was the impetus for the Supreme Court to rule that torture is acceptable to elicit confessions in certain instances, and you were very outspoken on his behalf, even promising revenge on a few occasions."

"Fine, yes, I did lose my cool a few times; who wouldn't if it were their sibling?"

"Your brother killed hundreds of people with his terrorist act! While no evidence exists to prove his guilt, the circumstances all led to him and him alone. Justice was served by his conviction no matter how it was obtained."

"That depends who you ask. To me, it made society at large just as bad as him."

"I am not here to debate politics with you, Wiggins. I have a job to do, and that means getting to the bottom of this. Justice Bernard was outspoken about the measure; you vowed retribution and I will either confirm your alibi or investigate you further. Now, I want a recent picture of you, as well as the papers you signed when you checked into the motel."

"Fine, but you are not getting them tonight. This has already been an inconvenience, and I am tired. Come back tomorrow. Good bye."

"We will be back in the morning. Have the requested items ready. Oh, and don't get any ideas about sneaking out. We will leave a patrol car parked right outside." With that, they left.

Saturday, February 4th, 10 am, Brooklyn, New York

Bruno Carmelli was at home looking at last night's winners at the track when his cousin Patrick Manucci called. "Well, hello Patrick. Long time no hear. What can I do for you?"

Ignoring the sarcasm, Patrick asked him how he had been, then got right to the point. "We have a friend who could help us with something, to all of our benefit. A little convincing is required."

Pause. "Ok, I'm listening."

"It's regarding Steven Morris. We want him to accept the offer of running for Vice President."

"Really? For which Presidential candidate?"

"That would be Eric Layton. Morris rejected his offer. That's where you come in. Explain to him that we would much appreciate if he would reconsider, but be nice. Ours is a mutually beneficial relationship. Try to stress all the advantages he will gain by such a new position, and hint at the fact that we might not be so quick to back him next time he runs if he doesn't work with us now."

"Alright. What do I get out of all this?"

"Think, Bruno. You will be personally connected to the Vice President. Imagine the doors that would open for the legitimate businesses you are involved with."

"Yeah, well, I am personally connected to him now, and it hasn't been that great."

"He will be playing in a much bigger league."

"Well, what if they don't win, Mr. Know-it-all?"

"He and I will owe you a favor, alright?" Patrick became getting impatient with his cousin's greed and stupidity.

"Don't get your balls in an uproar. I will call you back when I am done with him."

"Just remember, go easy. This is a job that needs finesse."

"I got it cuz. Bye."

Toronto, 11am

Billet and the officers from the mounted police returned to Earl Wiggins' house. They rang the bell and waited. After a few minutes Billet got nervous; maybe the officers out front fell asleep and Wiggins then fled. He then heard footsteps coming to the front door and took a breath. Earl Wiggins threw open the door and tossed the picture and the papers at Billet. "Here. Now leave me alone," he said, slamming the door. Billet looked at the documents and they were sufficient. He wanted to harass Wiggins further, but just took the papers and left.

Sunday, February 5th, New York, NY

Todd Russell just finished taping the Evan Shaw show to be aired next Sunday, February 12th, and it had gone very well. There were a few curve balls, but Russell believed that he handled them expertly. He had been well prepared and his staff agreed. He expected that to narrow the gap in the polls between him and Juan Pillar. His image was being repaired and people were seeing the old Todd Russell. He made strides in Illinois and the citizens there were believing in him again. He was really glad that he hired Joe Berry; he had gotten him back on track. Now there were two tasks on his plate; to keep his state on track and still begin to campaign. He would hire a campaign manager; he would talk to Rose about that. He needed someone with connections throughout the whole country. Except for Pillar, all the candidates hailed from the Midwest so they had to differentiate themselves somehow. Hayao tried to do it with his vice presidential pick, and Layton already created his first ad. They were clearly lining up support as well. He wanted to focus on the south; they were the most conservative section of the country and the region he could carry. He needed to come up with a way to make himself a more attractive candidate than Layton who had amassed a good record in Congress. Russell, on the other hand, would stress the work he accomplished as Governor, emphasizing his tenure as the chief executive of the state which would translate perfectly to his being President. When Layton mentioned his familiarity with the way that Washington worked as an insider, Russell would counter that he was part of the political machine and would highlight all the things that were wrong with the current leadership. He would also call on the support of other governors around the country with whom he built good relationships. They were a tight community and Russell knew he could count on them. He would also enlist the help of the senators and representatives from Illinois, who were well liked. That was one of the many advantages of doing away with partisan politics; no one voted or endorsed others solely on their party anymore. He called his lieutenant governor to see how things were going for the last few days. Once they reviewed everything that was pressing, Russell told him that he would be back tomorrow. He wanted to meet with Joe Berry before he left New York, and then would attend a fundraising dinner tonight on his behalf, where all the prominent politicians would be in attendance. He would be extra charming and ingratiate himself to as many people as possible. This could be his springboard to gaining a stronghold in the Northeast.

Monday, February 6th
Bruno Carmelli called Steven Morris. Morris wasn't surprised; Carmelli called him once in a while just to shoot the breeze.
"Hello, Bruno. How have you been? "
"Just fine Steve, and you?"

"Excellent."

"Steve, there is something I'd like to talk to you about. I was talking to Pat and he said that you declined the offered of the vice presidency. We were both surprised." Bruno paused, allowing Morris to respond.

"I am comfortable right where I am, Bruno. I am able to make a difference here. If I accepted this new offer I would be playing in a totally different league and would not be able to look after my constituents like I do now. Besides, if we don't win then I will be nowhere."

"Plenty of politicians hold their office while they run for another one; why can't you?"

"I will be travelling all over the country campaigning. I cannot effectively run things like that, especially since both Ramirez and Hayao already set precedents by leaving their positions."

"This could be big for us, Steve. The influence you wield now would pale by comparison compared to being VP. Plus, who can tell where that may lead? You will be able to take care of your people and bring a lot of positive attention to our area. Our businesses and towns will all profit from this. I just can't understand how you can say no." Morris suddenly recalled Bruno's tenacity. He was one of the brighter members of his 'family', but he could be dangerous as well as charming. He had been told to convince Morris to take the offer. There was no use trying to resist. These people still wielded substantial power in this country; not much had changed over the years, despite the efforts of the FBI.

"Thanks for the pep talk. I need at least one day to come to terms with all this, and then I will get in touch with Eric Layton tomorrow."

Smiling, Bruno thought how easy this was. "Great, Steve. By the way, how is your golf game these days? We will have to play sometime."

"Sure Bruno. I'll be in touch." They both knew he wouldn't.

Ed Billet just finished briefing his team about what he had accomplished in Toronto. He wanted them to turn their attention to verifying Wiggins' alibi. He also wanted to look into Ned

Donato's past. Billet divided his team in two and told them he wanted some answers by Friday. In the meantime, he would continue to look for other motives in justice Bernard's past, other cases that might have come back to blow up in his face.

Todd Russell was waiting at the airport to board the flight back to Chicago. He was going over things with Joe Berry, and they both believed that things were going extraordinarily well as of late. They definitely gained momentum. "Joe, we need to select a vice president. That is our next big task. Have you given it any thought?"

"A little. Clearly the Midwest is your stronghold, and that you need to focus elsewhere. Your running mate should come from an area where he or she will bring in more votes. Hayao is covering the southeast with Alex Ramirez, so I think we need someone from either the northeast or out west. I am leaning toward the west as I think you made strides here with your visit. Perhaps someone from academia; break the mold of the typical politician. I actually have two people in mind, Alphonse Darden, the commissioner of education in Washington State, or Vincent Weimetz, the President of Caltech. Weimetz also has the added advantage of being born elsewhere, which would help with some of the foreign vote. Both men are very bright, and would bring a different perspective to the administration."

"Interesting. I did not even considered selecting someone outside the political arena. Let's look at both of them. What would Darden bring to the table?"

"Well, he knows what it takes to run an organization. He most likely has many connections in the world of education, undoubtedly extending beyond Washington. He is very knowledgeable about political issues and would make many people believe that you would stress continued education reform were you elected. On the other hand, he is not as well known nationally as Weimitz, with a smaller political base. Weimitz is brilliant. He has increased enrollment at Caltech tremendously, which has enabled the school to keep tuition in check. He is practically a celebrity in scientific and technical circles, and as I said earlier, will help tremendously with drumming up foreign support. Weimitz's downside, however, is his ego. He will likely try to be active in running the country where some Vice President's take a back seat."

"Overall, who would you say would be a better choice?"

"I would say Vincent Weimitz."

"Do you think that he would be interested in leaving Caltech?"

"There is only one way to find out. I think you should ask him in person. Should I arrange for a trip to California?"

"Yes. Make it for next week; I will combine my visit to Caltech with some campaigning. We will fly there on Sunday, and stay Monday through Friday. That will give me this week to handle things in Illinois, and put procedures in place for next week when I am gone."

"You should also plan on going abroad before the election as well, Governor. People in other countries continually gain more and more influence over voters here. That factor cannot be overlooked, and if Weimitz decides to come aboard, having him accompany you, at least in Europe, would be a smart move."

"I will do that. First things first though. Let me know when the trip out west is in place, along with the stops we will make. Thanks Joe."

Hayao was getting nowhere. People were not letting his comment go. It haunted him everywhere he went; while he met people and shook hands, someone in the crowd always made a snide remark. He became more and more discouraged and angry. He apologized for it, explained it was not indicative of how he felt, but nothing seemed to make a difference. All of the people closest to him told him to just keep his head down, try to weather the storm, let any comment roll off his back, and eventually it would die down. That was easier said than done, however. People sensed it bothered him, and that simply incited them to belabor the point. He had to make up his mind to ignore it as best he could. He forced himself to concentrate on his campaign. There were plenty of politicians who overcame much bigger scandals than this one. He needed to be extra charming to try to win people over. No matter what, he would still enjoy the support of the Oriental people in this country. He had to make sure that he campaigned abroad as well as here in the states. He would also arrange for his public relations people to set up a commercial for him. Thank god Alex Ramirez resided in his corner. She still believed in him, in their potential. She was seasoned and knew how to play the game. He trusted her opinion; she had become his most valued adviser. They spoke at least once a day and she seemed to see ahead of the curve. He wished that he had consulted with her before the debate. He tried to listen to her; when she said that they could overcome this, he took it to heart. She would continue to go far in politics even if they lost. She projected an intensity rarely seen, but masked it with polish and sophistication. She has been telling him that the most important thing he can do is reverse his business mentality and remember that he is going to be serving the people. He cannot act like he is the ultimate authority anymore. This was difficult for him to understand, didn't the President possess the last word? Didn't everyone expect him or her to conduct themselves with confidence and self-assuredness? She explained the difference between confidence and arrogance, a fine line. In public life it separated the winners and the losers. She said that the best leaders come to the line without crossing it. That was the essence of what he needed to learn. She would be the best resource for this. He would ask her to come to Michigan today when he spoke to her. He needed an intensive session in diplomacy. While she was here, she could also guide him on how to use the media to his advantage. His PR people were good, but they would also benefit from her insight. She retained one of the best public images of any Governor. Hayao would be up to speed in a few weeks.

    Morris wanted to run that by his wife. He told her what happened and about the pressure being applied. He explained that it had to be this way for him to continue in politics. She was ok with it; their kids were older and out of the house, so moving to DC would not be an issue. Personally she hoped he would pursue this opportunity; to her, you don't pass up something like that. They were comfortable where they were, but it was time to leave their comfort zone. She supported him 100%. She harbored no illusions about what it would mean. Steve would be travelling extensively for the next 9 months campaigning, and if they won, he would be away a lot as well. She wanted this; it would be both a prestigious accomplishment to become Vice President and a stepping stone to the Presidency. Her role was to stay in the background, however, so she felt glad that Layton wanted him enough to use tactics bordering on coercion to get him to join the ticket.

Tuesday, February 7th
Eric Layton's phone rang, and it was the phone call he expected. "Hello?"
"Hi Eric, it's Steven Morris. Well, it seems you know some very persuasive people. You can count me in to be your running mate."
"Excellent, Steve. Welcome aboard. We will make a great team. We will appeal to a great many people out there. Our biggest assets will be our combined experience in national politics, and the fact that we both grew up in this country. That is a trait that cannot be duplicated, and people will recognize that."
"Thanks, Eric. I am excited too. The next step would be for us to meet, I suppose, to discuss what our strategy will be."
"That would be best, easier than doing it over the phone. I will come to you. When would be a good time for you? Perhaps this weekend?"
Morris looked at his calendar. "I am free on Saturday. Why don't we get together for lunch at a nice little Italian place that is near my house?"
"Perfect. Why don't I come by your house and we can go there together. What time should I come?"
"How about 11:30? I will introduce you to my wife and then we can go."
"Great. Now all I need is your address."
As soon as he finished talking to Morris, Eric Layton called his wife. "Cindy, I found my Vice President!"

Wednesday, February 8th

Kangaroo and Uncle George were having a quick meeting today as it was so bitter cold out in Boston. Kangaroo got right to the point. "I have not unearthed anything new about any of the candidates since we met last. Their campaigns are progressing normally. Juan Pillar has gained the most ground recently, still having momentum from the debate. Todd Russell is picking up speed as well with two successful television appearances under his belt. Hayao is still struggling, and I understand that Eric Layton has selected a running mate, Congressman Steven Morris from New York. That's all I can report right now."

"Ok, good. One thing I want to tell you. I noticed last week that INS has approved substantially more applications for immigration to the U.S. than they have in a long time."

"Did you learn the breakdown of those applications? Where are the people coming from?"

"That I am not sure about, but I will definitely keep an eye on this trend. We will meet again next Wednesday."

Friday, February 10th, 10am

Billet assembled his group of agents. He hoped they had some developments for him, particularly about Earl Wiggins. He didn't like something about him. They were all there now. With a wave of his hand he made it clear that he wanted to get started. "What have you found?"

"Wiggins was telling the truth. He really did visit his brother that weekend. The prison logs confirm it and the clerk at the motel does remember him, because he happened to leave no tips, whenever he ate in the restaurant there and also to the room steward. Cheap bastard."

"All that proves is that he wasn't in DC. Did you check his cell phone records as well as those from the motel where he stayed?"

"Yes, we checked both, and they came up clean. He could have just as easily been working with someone from Toronto."

"What about the first time he came? Did you check out his comings and goings then?"

"Again, nothing out of the ordinary."

"How about Ned Donato? Anything come out about his past?"

"He is a more likely suspect, Ed. He has a violent streak and he has connections in Washington in the education field. As the CFO of Princeton, he travelled to DC often to meet with senators and lobbyists."

"Was he there that weekend?"

"Possibly. I am still digging for information. The new legislation angered many people, and he was one. He has a reputation as a ball buster and is tenacious when he wants something. Maybe he became angry enough to try to do something."

"So neither Wiggins nor Donato is off the hook. It's also possible that the Wiggins brothers worked together."

"No, neither is off the hook. I don't see how Carl Wiggins could have been doing much of the planning from prison, however."

"I mean he may still retain connections from when he orchestrated the bombing in Chicago. We need to see if Kelly Visque had anything in common with any of the three of them. Go through her old phone records next. Also, see if any of the groups she was involved with such as American Pride show any record of the Wiggins or Ned Donato attending their meetings. You can divide up the tasks anyway you wish, and we will meet again next Friday. That's all."

Saturday, February 11th

Eric Layton arrived at Steven Morris's house, a modest split level design on Long Island. He hoped that the chit chat wouldn't take long and they could go get down to business. He rang the bell and the door was opened by June Morris, Steven's wife, an attractive blond woman with a nice smile. "Hi Eric. Come on in. Steven will be right down. Can I get you something to drink?"

"No, thank you June. We are going to eat lunch."

Eric saw Steve coming down the stairs. "Hi Steve." They shook hands.

"Thank you for coming here Eric. How was the drive from DC?"

"Not bad. Not too much traffic, mercifully."

"Good. Shall we go to lunch?"

"Yes, why don't we." He turned to June and kissed her hand, and Steve kissed his wife on the way out. They got into the car and ten minutes later were at the pizza place. They both expected to be recognized; Morris was very popular around here, and Layton's face has been in the news extensively since his candidacy was announced. Someone would call the local tv station and their meeting would be on the news in no time. That was good publicity, it would project the image that they were both in touch with the people that they represented. They would save their real discussion for when they got back to Steven's house. Steven shook the owner's hand when they walked in and introduced Eric Layton. They sat down and the owner tripped all over himself to serve them. They both ordered pizza and everyone in the place stared and whispered; just the reaction they were hoping for. During their meal, they made small talk and shook hands of all the patrons that stopped by the table. When they were leaving, the television cameras were there, and they tried to get them to answer questions, but both Layton and Morris simply smiled and walked straight to the car. They escaped quickly enough so they weren't followed, although the paparazzi would be camped out at Morris's house in no time. They hurried inside to get down to business. Eric spoke first. "I know we both tend to be liberal. That's good. We are living in a time when that is what the public is looking for. That's not to say that we will be off the charts; I still believe in traditional education, but am in full support of making education more affordable to everyone. Colleges needed to be reined in. What is your position? Education is a major political issue, if we don't agree about a particular issue we should iron it out now."

"I agree. Education is the force that will keep us competitive and maintain our status as a world leader. It will also keep people from other countries immigrating, which in turn will help the economy."

"Well put. What about the environment?"

"Well, I think we have done a remarkable job implementing a network of water delivery systems, allowing irrigation and the availability of drinking water all over the country. We were in dire straits before that. We also succeeded in reversing global warming, and I will always be interested in continuing this." Morris paused. "Now let me ask you Eric. How do you feel about the Vice President's role in the President's administration?" He thought

Layton would give the stock answer, but wanted to see how he delivered it.

"You will be an integral part of my team, and I will seek and value your opinion both on a day to day basis as well as on major issues. You will not be window dressing." Impressive, thought Morris. Let's test that. He knew that Layton felt strongly about keeping a close eye on other countries' nuclear capabilities, and really did not want most countries to develop nuclear weapons. This has been in the news a great deal lately due to the emerging of many former third world countries as powers on the rise.

Morris said, "I think it's great that there are so many countries now that are coming into their own, and able to be self-sufficient more and more. I have always believed that each nation has the right to defend themselves and needn't answer to others about the type of weapons that they are developing or possess."

Layton clenched his teeth but kept a calm exterior. "The only problem with that is that some of these countries either harbor zealots on the inside, or are greedy enough to sell their weapons on the black market to the highest bidder. How do you propose we deal with that?"

"I didn't say that we shouldn't keep an eye on arms buildups, but we should not be permitted to prevent them. We retain the governing bodies among nations as our watchdog."

"Point well taken, Steve." Morris recognized then that even if they disagreed, Eric would value his opinion and didn't need to feed his ego by being right all the time. Layton looked at his watch. It was 4pm and they had covered a lot of ground. Layton spoke again. "We will have to campaign in Europe and Asia. We need to try to cut into the vote that Hayao and Pillar spent time cultivating. When should we make our official announcement?"

"With the media following us today, people are going to be speculating everywhere. I think we should make the announcement tomorrow. We can break the news through a press conference; it would be best to break the news personally in a forum where we can answer questions as well. We both should be there; the best place to do it would be back in Washington. Hayao's press conference in Florida with Alex Ramirez sent the message that they were interested in convenience. We would be making a statement that we are willing to go above and beyond by hurrying back to DC together to gain support. We can make the announcement right outside the Capitol building."

"Perfect. We should probably leave now so we can arrange things for the morning. You can stay in a hotel, courtesy of the 'Layton for President' campaign. I will call my campaign manager to arrange that the equipment be set up outside, and we can alert the media tomorrow. What do you think about 10am?"

"Perfect. Now here is my suggestion for us leaving."

Sunday, February 12th

Juan Pillar was travelling through Europe, meeting as many people as possible. He decided to skip Spain, since he would undoubtedly have the support of the Spanish government and people, who would encourage all the Spanish emigres to vote for him. He decided to focus on France, Italy, England, Germany, and the countries that used to make up the USSR. Foreign regimes had a lot of influence over United States politics, due to the continued rise of technology over the years and the concept of distributed government. He was in London right now, meeting with the British Prime Minister, and tomorrow, the King. He hoped that although they might be partial to endorsing an American, the leaders in England would back him because of his popularity in Spain. He was counting on the fact that most of the countries in Europe were allies right now to bolster his support. On Tuesday he had a meeting with the Pope, and would consider it a major victory to get his backing, for Catholics back home would by and large support him then. The Pope likely would, as both Layton and Russell were Protestants, and Pillar had made it known publicly that he practiced Catholicism. In addition, having the Pope in his corner would mean that the Italian government would follow suit. Pillar would be in Europe for the rest of this week and then he would continue on to Asia, although he would stay out of Japan; there was no point to that. He would spend his time in China, and perhaps some of the smaller countries in the Orient such as Thailand. Even though they were all allies officially, resentment and strong competition existed for the top spot in that part of the world, and the citizens of the other countries might very well want to see Hayao fail. They would encourage their American peers to vote for him to claim their revenge for not having a candidate of their own. He would also make a trip to the Middle East sometime in the spring, to visit the countries who also wielded considerable influence. He was lucky that he had such a competent support staff back home, he counted on them to fulfill his duties in Congress in his absence.

The Capitol Building, DC
Layton and Morris were outside making sure everything was set up properly. They had been masterful in evading the press yesterday. This morning Layton instructed his press secretary to contact the media. They were all there already, watching the two of them get organized. Of course, everyone suspected what their announcement would be and the local newspaper on Long Island carried their meeting on their front page. Despite his reluctance initially, Morris was excited about this. It was a new journey; if it didn't work out he would have no trouble getting his old job back. He checked his phone for the time; 9:45 am. He felt like he could trust Layton; one thing that he neglected to ask Layton was who their financial backers would be for the campaign. The podium and microphone was ready, and mercifully the weather cooperated; it was 50 degrees and sunny, excellent for February. They decided to keep their plans for the campaign under wraps for now. They were going to report that they discussed their positions on various issues, and for the most part they saw eye to eye. When the reporters asked follow up questions, they would explain that it was the administration's stance that mattered, not any one individual. They decided they would answer questions for an hour, 30 minutes for each of them. He looked back to the entrance of the Capitol building, Layton motioned for him to come back inside; they would walk out together, exactly at 10am. That would show that they were a team and project the image of them standing united against any challenge that may come along. At precisely 10 o'clock they did so. The horde of reporters looked at them like

they were pieces of meat, salivating to get something more than their competitors. That was one thing that had not changed; the media remained just as aggressive and persistent as ever. Layton approached the microphone first. He smiled and everyone quieted down. "Good morning. I would like to thank you all for assembling here on this fine February morning. I could not think of a more fitting place to make this announcement." Layton paused; he sure had a flair for the dramatic when it was called for. "We live in a country with a magnificent and stellar past, filled with heroic people who did extraordinary things to protect our freedoms and advance our way of life. When I am elected President, I will strive to continue this tradition. To do so, I want someone by my side who shares my passion for the United States, someone who shares my deep commitment and loyalty to our home that comes from having lived nowhere else. I am honored to say that Senator Steven Morris will be joining me as my Vice Presidential candidate! Steven!" Morris walked up to the podium and shook Layton's hand. Two microphones were side by side so neither one of them would need to stay in the background at any time.

"Thank you Eric. I am very excited about working with you and the rest of your team. We will do great things in Washington, and will continue to lead our country through happy and prosperous times. Enough speeches, however. I am sure that you have a million questions for us."

One of the reporters in front raised their hand before first. "Mr. Layton, what made you decide to choose Mr. Morris?"

"Steven Morris has an exemplary record in Congress and his constituents hold him in the highest regard. He is just and moral and is a role model for our young people." Layton recognized a female reporter in the back and gave her the opportunity to ask the next question.

"Aren't you concerned that you are not targeting a wide enough demographic?"

"Not at all. You are making the assumption that everyone will vote based upon their nationality or that which is closest. People want quality, and between the two of us we accumulated extensive experience in federal government. That is one of the things that sets us apart."

"What do think of the progress and/or problems the other candidates met so far?"

"I am not going to comment on our opponents except to say that it is very early on in the race; whoever is ahead or behind right now absolutely cannot sit back and relax."

"Mr. Morris, you have been a fan favorite of the people of Long Island for years. Was it a difficult decision to leave your comfort zone?"

He bristled slightly at the question. Everyone knew the mafia unofficially ran Long Island. He resented the implication that things were easy for him as long as he cooperated with the local crime boss. "I weighed all my options. I have thoroughly enjoyed my tenure in New York. Now I am looking forward to representing the entire country with the same diligence and enthusiasm."

"Are you going to resume your duties as a senator should the election not go your way?"

"I am an optimist and am not going to make a contingency plan for a scenario which I don't believe will happen."

"Mr. Layton, back to you. How do you plan to counteract all the support that Hayao and Juan Pillar will get from their countries of origin encouraging their brethren here to vote for them?"

"Our message is clear. We, Mr. Morris and myself, were born in this country. In very short order it seems that has become a liability for U.S. politicians. Our country's interests depend upon the well-being of other nations everywhere; the 'PC' term is distributed government. While we were been working in Washington we saw firsthand the importance of this. Steve and I know the best ways to incorporate the needs of other governments and their people without compromising our interests. While all of the candidates undoubtedly have loyalty that is beyond reproach, it would not be difficult to lose sight of one's priorities if one felt beholden to another place or culture. It takes a lot of assistance to run a successful campaign, and many times promises are made along the way which can be hard to break."

"What promises are you willing to break, Mr. Layton?" Layton decided to turn his response into a joke. "None that I would make to you, ma'am." Everyone chuckled. "Two more questions please."

Monday, February 13th
Todd Russell waited for the plane to depart. This would be his first campaign trip out west, and it would be combined with another purpose. He wanted to meet with Vincent Weimitz. Joe Berry had contacted Weimitz, and he agreed to the meeting. He would come to Russell, not the other way around. That would make it easier to keep things under wraps. Weimitz would come to Russell's hotel when he arrived in San Francisco; he was very well known in California, but Russell would be under scrutiny constantly. He wanted to start his route up in Washington State, but Berry convinced him to meet with Weimitz right away, because it would be easiest and less likely for the press get wind of it if they met as soon as he arrived in on the west coast, as no one alerted the media about his visit. He traveled under an assumed name with the plan being to disclose his strategy after he arrived in Seattle just in case Weimitz wasn't interested. The plane was in line, waiting for the runway. He looked over his notes from his last interview, critiquing how to give better responses next time. The plane suddenly took off, and two minutes later they were airborne. Somewhere along the way he must have dozed off, because the next thing he knew they had arrived in San Francisco. He didn't want to be noticed, which meant that he needed to go through the exit screening process like everyone else. Three hours later, at 11 am Pacific standard time, they arrived at the hotel. He and Joe checked in and then Joe called Vincent Weimitz. He told Joe that he would be at the hotel at 3pm. The three of them would share a drink in the bar in the lobby, where it would be quiet at that time and they would be able to talk privately. He would make it clear to Weimitz that he needed his answer by tomorrow morning. If Weimitz turned the offer down, Berry would reach out to Alphonse Darden once they got to Seattle tomorrow. If Weimitz accepted, on the other hand, Russell would make the announcement from

Seattle, not feeling it necessary for Weimitz to be with him at the time. People would be impressed that he stayed at Caltech showing his conscientious nature in passing up such a momentous occasion to do his job. This was Joe Berry's idea; he really did have a gift for public relations. Russell checked his watch; 11:45. He decided to hit the exercise room and blow off some steam.

3pm

Russell and Berry were waiting in the hotel bar for Weimitz, who arrived five minutes later. The three of them shook hands and went back to the table in the cocktail lounge. Weimitz asked about their trip and whether they had ever been out west before. They both said yes and then got to the matter at hand. "Vincent, I am sure you were surprised that we contacted you, and are dying to find out why. Let me get right to the point. I would like you to be my Vice Presidential candidate." Russell gave him a minute to digest the request.

"Well, I am honored. I never considered myself a politician, Todd. There is a certain amount of glad handling that comes with being the President of a university, but my responsibilities are much more narrow, and I do not have to exceed the scope of what is best for Caltech."

"You developed an excellent reputation, Vincent. You are a celebrity in the field of engineering all over the world and would be a fantastic ambassador for the scientific community. Think about all the goodwill and awareness you would bring to people everywhere about those disciplines."

"I wouldn't have time for that. I would be making policy, dealing with Congress, and performing other administrative duties."

"That is not necessarily true. Different people who held that office were able to concentrate on different things. Your focus could be on projects that involve advancing our society and that of other countries using science and technology. That is something that we are desperately in need of. You would be filling a terrible void, and with the connections you built over the years would be able to accomplish much." Russell was appealing to his ego but the music sounded so sweet that he didn't care. It did sound very appealing. He would be able to pursue projects with a global impact with infinitely more resources at his disposal. Could he trust Russell to hold up his end of the bargain? He remembered how his popularity fell after he had been reelected as governor; would he go back on his word? Maybe he should ask to be the Secretary of Science and Technology instead. Russell wouldn't go for that. He needed a running mate. Maybe he should ask for some kind of agreement in writing.

"What assurance can you give me, Governor, that once I get into office I will not be bogged down with other tasks and will have time for all the fine work that you are describing?"

"Good question. Ordinarily I couldn't promise anything like that. However, I am going to take the unprecedented step of creating a new position on the Vice President's staff by executive order entitled the liaison to Congress, who will handle all the typical jobs that you would handle. I will take this action within the first 50 days of being inaugurated. I will sign a document right now to that effect, and if I don't follow through, you can simply resign and go back to the world of academia." Russell certainly had seen three moves ahead.

"I need to think about this Todd. Would I be able to hold on to my position until the election?"

"I don't see why not. We will be campaigning, and I will want you with me some of the time, and you will have to participate in at least one debate, but other than that there will not be too much asked of you." Russell saw doubt in Weimitz's face. "If you are worried about the debate, don't. I will make it clear to the media that you will be handling the technological end of my administration, and you will also enjoy the resources of my advisers at your disposal who can assist you with political issues and my position on each of them. You will be well prepared for the debate."

Weimitz was very tempted, but he refused to make a decision on the spot. "I will need to think about it, Todd."

"I understand, but unfortunately I am going to need a response by tomorrow morning; we have to keep the ball rolling."

Weimitz thought that did not give him much time, but he supposed that was fast paced politics. "Of course. I will call you first thing tomorrow."

Tuesday, February 14th

Joe Berry walked excitedly into Governor Russell's room. "We got him! Weimitz is on board. He wants the document you promised him before you go public with this. Did you draft it last night?"

"I wrote a rough draft. I don't want to make it so restrictive that I have no wiggle room if I want to ask him to do something that is slightly out of the scope of STEM (science, technology, engineering, and mathematics)."

"Be careful, Todd. He was adamant about his job description. If you try to pull the bait and switch on him, it could backfire. He has a reputation as being rigid. He might very well resign if he feels he was misled."

"Ok, point well taken. Even so, unless he has a lawyer read this over, I doubt he will realize that it is written in a vague manner. If he gives me a hard time once we are in office I can always back off. The important thing is that he took the offer. I will finalize the document, then you can email it to him."

Juan Pillar arrived at the Vatican on Tuesday at noon. It was quite spectacular; he always wanted to visit. Now that he had made a name for himself in politics, the Pope was anxious to meet with him as well. Pillar went through security and bypassed the crowds that came every day and stood on line for hours. Once inside, two ushers who seemed to be expecting him whisked him away. He was led down a hallway to a large room and told the Pope would be appearing in a few minutes. He sat down and waited. Soon after, a man walked in who turned out to be the Pope's handler. Behind him was the Pope. Pillar stood up and went over to shake his hand. "Holy Father, it is truly an honor. I anticipated our visit since it was arranged. There is much to talk about."

"How has your journey been, my son? I understand that you visited numerous countries. Have you had much time for seeing the sights?"

"Not as much as I hoped. The people that I met, though, have truly been extraordinary, and went out of their way to be helpful and are really interested in the United States' political process and customs that are used in our government."

"Many people believe in you and what you stand for, Juan. I am one of them. The world can no longer operate in provincial ways as we used to; our nations are all melting pots now. The United States is very brave as a country to accept that fact and incorporate it into their government."

"On behalf of the U.S., I thank you. I am certain you are aware, Holy Father, that there are many Catholics in our country, and they need some guidance as to whom they should vote for. There are many Americans that were born there that are opposed to this whole idea, and would vote against a foreign candidate just for that reason. There are many citizens of Latin descent, and I could probably count on their votes. However, I need an edge."

The Pope smiled and clasped Pillar's hands. "You are seeking my endorsement. All four candidates possess positive qualities, and each has the support of a certain segment of the population. No one has a greater feel of the interdependency that exists worldwide than you, Juan. You will lead them into the next phase of their evolution; the era where foreigners will be the majority, and one of the cornerstones of the U.S. Constitution will be changed forever. You are the most worthy of the candidates for this responsibility. You can count on my endorsement. I will support you publicly with a statement that I will issue tomorrow."

"Thank you. You are a wise, just, and compassionate leader."

"I have a question, for you, Juan. Why have you chosen to apply your efforts to the United States and not your homeland of Mexico?"

Pillar was taken aback. He had not expected such a question from the Pope. "Mexico is a fine country. I emigrated to the United States as a young man to take advantage of the more extensive opportunities available for professional advancement. My career advanced, and I became more and more entrenched in society. I now consider it my home, even though much of my family still is in Mexico. I have prospered there, and now I would like to repay that favor by helping the government and its citizens flourish as well."

"That's very commendable."

"This election will be different. People will be influenced by what the leaders and citizens of other countries believe. Voting will not be decided along political ideologies like it has in the past. Religion, culture, and international peer pressure will come into play. Having your support will not only help my standing with Catholics, but will likely align the governments in Europe with me as well." Both Pillar and the Pope recognized what this would mean.

"Do not discount the Asian countries either, Juan. The dynamic in that part of the world is very hard to read. I would recommend that you spend some time there as well."

"I plan to."

"Juan, once you win you will have great power at your disposal. The President has much discretion over many things. It will be the perfect time to implement change, gradually so that it will be easier to swallow."

He saw where the Pope was going, but he played dumb. "What are you getting at, Holy Father?"

"It will be the perfect opportunity to incorporate Catholicism into American society."

"It already is. People enjoy freedom of religion."

"That is not what I mean. We - sorry, I mean you, could start nudging the country in the direction of having an official religion."

"With all due respect, that is a battle that would not even get off the ground."

"It would if handled properly. It would need to be executed using baby steps, and with subtlety. You want the Catholic Church behind you; I need to know that you can be counted on to work with us." The Pope's face had turned dark; the kindly old man here a minute ago was gone. Pillar needed his backing; the politician in him came to the surface; promise now, find a way out of it later.

"Of course. We have an agreement. You understand that it will not happen overnight."

"I do. The fact that counts is that you will be working toward our goal. I wish you a successful campaign, Juan, and now I will pray silently for your victory. Please bow your head and join me."

Alex Ramirez arrived in Michigan last night. Hayao was really struggling and needed guidance. He made a special plea for her to come and help him learn to navigate the political minefield. They had been working all morning on the skill of using a question to stress one's strengths and further their agenda. It wasn't simply about giving the right answer but giving the answer that people wanted to hear. There was an art to this, and there were several cardinal rules. First, never come across as arrogant or holier than thou. People cannot identify with those traits, plus if you are ever caught in some kind of scandal, it will be that much harder for the public to forgive; they are infuriated by hypocrisy. If you think that you are giving that impression, make a self-deprecating joke or smile and try to explain your comments. Number two, never hold yourself out to be perfect or preach about morality. Remember that politicians are people; we are supposed to lead by example; it is not about do as I say, not as I do. Be humble; we all screw up, it's how you accept it that counts to the public; they will even find it endearing, as that is not how they are used to politicians behaving. Third, be modest whenever possible. Do not toot your own horn, and downplay your successes and achievements, while still appearing confident in your abilities. Everyone wants a leader to be sure of him or herself, but just to demonstrate that through their actions. Hayao wanted to hear an example. Alex told him to ask her a question about herself. He asked, "How were you able to so greatly improve Florida's image and still keep the state under budget for the entire time you were Governor?"

"I was fortunate. I worked with a wonderful staff who truly understood what the state needed. We also benefitted from a cyclical turn in the Florida's economy, thanks to increased tourism for which we could not take credit for but which we capitalized on. Our state is a wonderful place; like the United States, it is filled with wonderful people who want to be led in the right direction. By talking to my constituents, I managed to hone in on what was important to them and deliver and eliminate those programs that were outdated and unpopular. Once those changes were implemented, our state's financial health was back on track." Alex paused to allow Hayao a minute to reflect on her answer. "Do you see how I answered in general terms? Never be too specific, unless the question expressly calls for that. I gave credit to others on my team; never take all the credit for something. I also worked in the part about the people that I represent being wonderful, praising them and extending that to the rest of the country. Lastly, I demonstrated that I was in touch with what the masses want and not operating my administration without regard for my voters. Now, you try giving an answer." "Mr. Yamamoto, what has been your biggest accomplishment since working at Moritu?"

"I would say…", before he had a chance to continue, Ramirez made a hand gesture to slow him down. He took a deep breath and continued. "I was the top performer in Japan, and that is what led me to taking over the corporation's New York office, which turned into my springboard to taking over the U.S. operation. Advancing so quickly up the corporate ladder is what I would say."

"How has this prepared you to lead our country?"

"I have been the head of an organization. That will transition well into being the top official in government. Through my leadership I demonstrated I am capable of making decisions and of being able to follow through on my word. As President, I will be the final authority, and that is a power that is not to be entrusted lightly. Not everyone has the fortitude to make decisions that affect billions of people."

"Good answer, but not for a politician. All you did was pump yourself up. You did not include in your answer the fact that you worked with many different types of people and learn the art of compromise along with being the person at the top. You cannot give the impression that your style is to bark orders rather than to listen to your peers and subordinates. People are going to need affirmation that you value their opinions and that they are not being dismissed. I think that was one of the issues at your first debate. It's a fine line between being sure of yourself and being conceited. Try to project yourself as a team player, even if you don't feel like one. Let's try again. What do you think is the most important character trait to be President, and do you believe that you possess that trait?"

"Self-confidence. The leader of the free world must maintain enough confidence in his or her own abilities to make decisions, as well as to understand when to involve others in the decision making process and be big enough not to feel threatened when someone else has a better way of doing things than you. I do believe that I have this characteristic, as I constantly interact with many different levels of management, some above me and some below. I report to decision makers who depend on my information, and deal with employees that answer to me who provide me with information. Both roles require me to take a back seat at times, and put my opinions last. I know that I am making the right choice each time and that my job takes a group effort that calls for input from many different people, yet I am able to make a split second decision and stand by it if need be."

"That was much better. You incorporated teamwork and the ability to be sure of yourself into the answer. Let's try a few more."

Vincent Weimitz received an email from Joe Berry with the written agreement about his job requirements as Vice President attached. He opened it and took a look. It seemed to be straightforward, with not a lot of legalese. He did not think he needed an attorney to review it. He felt he could always resign if need be. There was a place for Russell's signature and a place for his. He signed it, scanned it, and sent it back. Soon everyone would know that he would be the top science guru in the world.

9pm, Central time
Alex Ramirez was in her hotel room, relaxing. It has been a somewhat productive but exhausting day. She had a lot of work to do with Hayao. Maybe it was partially cultural, but he seemed unable to grasp the concept of speaking with humility. Whenever

he was asked about himself, he always answered directly rather than bringing his response around to his supporting players as well. She reminded herself to stay positive; the election was still a long way off, she just needed to be persistent. Her phone rang; she recognized Natsu's number. They had been conversing about Hayao's progress; Natsu could get a more objective view from her. She told him tonight that they still had a long way to go; she knew by Natsu's tone that he was displeased. He expected results; if they did not happen soon, he would likely try to do something out of desperation. She must avoid that; he could really mess things up for them, having no idea about what was acceptable during the campaign season and what actions might be offensive. She and Hayao just had to keep on plugging.

11 pm, Pacific time

Todd Russell and Joe Berry were going over what their next step should be, now that they were in possession of the signed agreement from Vincent Weimitz. Tomorrow they would travel to Washington state for meet and greet sessions, and that would be where they would break the news that Weimitz would be the Vice Presidential candidate. There would be much hullabaloo about the fact that he had no political experience, but they would point out that Hayao didn't either. Weimitz was a brilliant man with administrative experience, and he would fill a specific role. His opponents would harp on this. How could Russell in good conscience pick a man who, granted, interacted with academics, but was not schooled in diplomacy, to be a heartbeat away from running the country? Russell would justify his decision by discussing the superb team of advisers Weimitz will have. Everyone knows Washington DC is a self-sustaining operation; like any organization, it's primary goal is to keep itself going. Weimitz would do a fine job as President with all this support around him. A video chat would also be set up for Weimitz to join the press conference from his office at Caltech. Russell would resume his task of visibly spending time with voters, working his way down the west coast. Having Weimitz on board would help him tremendously with the technical faction of voters. In addition, the citizens and governments of other countries who enjoyed a love for science would influence their comrades who lived in the States. This was a great move all around for Russell. He checked his email; everything seemed fine in Illinois; he would be back there on Sunday. He and Joe looked at each other; it had been a long day. Before Joe went back to his room, they shared a drink from the mini bar.

Wednesday, February 15th

Kangaroo saw Uncle George waiting for him at their usual spot. He hoped this meeting would be brief - he had much to do. "I have some more information about the rising trend in immigrants. Natsu Hakituri initiated the process. He called the Prime Minister of Japan, with whom he has a personal relationship. The prime minister of course, wants to see Hayao win. He in turn, called President Harrington to see if we could ease our immigration regulations. The President, of course, endorsed Hayao and Pillar, so he is looking to give them every possible advantage. If more people immigrate and can get approved as citizens before the election, they could seriously influence the outcome."

Kangaroo didn't say anything right away. "Why is President Harrington so invested in this?"

Uncle George replied, "He was the architect of the whole amendment. It stands to reason that he would want to see it succeed. President Harrington fancies himself a statesman; he wants this to be his legacy."

"Well, what do you think he will get in return?"

"He will get increased popularity all over the world. Don't forget that his term will be up soon, and a move like this will boost his popularity globally. He will be able to go out on the speaking circuit as a high priced lecturer with engagements all over the world. It's a win win situation for all the powers that be."

"Ok. Are any laws being broken, or is what they are doing simply unethical?"

"The President has the legal authority to change the requirements for entering the U.S. He has wiggle room here. He could say something like he wants more citizens to work on maintaining the new national water distribution and irrigation system, or some other project that is understaffed. There are any number of reasons he could conjure up, knowing that once they are here they will become citizens and be able to vote."

"Is this something we should expose?"

"I am not convinced it would do any good to do that. We would not be able to prove the connection between the wave of immigrants and the election outcome until afterwards, and how would we establish a connection between the new immigration requirements and a foreign born person being elected at all? I can bet what the President will do; he will reduce the amount of time that a person has to be living here before they can vote, under the guise that they are helping to keep our country strong, and they should be afforded the same rights as people who have been living here much longer. He will justify it by saying that if foreign born people can be President, then people who immigrate here legally should be given the right to participate in their own government. There may be some opposition initially, but remember that there are so many people here already from these countries, that there will be much support also."

"Well, what about the phone conversation between President Harrington and Japan's Prime Minister? I am sure the non-Japanese people here wouldn't be too happy about Japan's government having such an active role in setting U.S. policy."

"Not much there. The President would simply say that he initiated the conversation because we need more workers in this country."

"We can counter by asking him why he sought out Japan."

"Because many of them are strong in science and engineering, which is what our workforce requires right now. My point is that there is no smoking gun to point to a scandal."

"What about undue influence related to Hayao's campaign? That would certainly reflect poorly on him."

"Again, largely circumstantial. Hayao could always claim he knew nothing about it, and that would be hard to prove otherwise. We just have to wait. If something more definitive surfaces then we can pounce." Kangaroo smiled at the pun.

Todd Russell and Joe Berry boarded the plane to Seattle at noon. Joe had arranged a press conference at 5pm at the hotel where they were staying. The word spread that they were going to be there this afternoon, so when they landed and deplaned in the airport, they were mobbed by reporters in the terminal. "What are you doing here, Governor?" "Where did you arrive from?" What were you doing in San Francisco?"

Russell simply said "You will all find out today at 5pm," and kept on walking to his waiting car to take Joe and he to their hotel, leaving the media with no information to report back.

President Harrington was pleased with how things were progressing with the 2040 election process so far. Juan Pillar was shoring up support in Europe, Layton and Russell had both made selections that would advance their campaigns tremendously. Hayao. That remained the sore spot. He had done much damage at the debate, but he understood that Alex Ramirez was working with him closely to teach him the nuances of political rhetoric. There would also be more Asian people entering the country, and by the time the election came around, they would be able to vote. All in all it was shaping up to be a very competitive race. Of course, he knew who he would like to succeed him as President. More importantly, however, he would be remembered for orchestrating this gigantic change to the one of the most basic tenets of the United States Constitution. He would be viewed as a pioneer and a visionary, one of our finest Presidents. He had been a progressive President, implementing some projects long overdue, like the nationwide water distribution network, and maintained and improved relations with other countries' governments worldwide. This achievement would catapult him into the upper echelon, and he would be grouped together with Washington and Lincoln. He felt pretty good as he turned his attention back to the daily affairs, which included talking to FBI Director Grey for an update on the Justice Bernard case.

Ciarro Dispoti, the Italian Prime minister, just finished speaking to the Pope who told him that he would be backing Juan Pillar in his Presidential bid. Dispoti had a good relationship with the Pope, who understood that secular decisions needed to be made independently of religion; he could not say that about all previous Popes; some of them were downright rigid and obstinate regarding state affairs. Dispoti would endorse Pillar as well, and that would set the stage for the other countries in Europe. Pillar would represent Europe better than any of the other candidates, giving them a glimpse into the happenings of the U.S. government. He was scheduled to meet with Pillar later today, and now the meeting would be brief. Dispoti wouldn't make him wait in suspense. He would explain that after speaking with the Pope, he decided to follow suit, and that he would use whatever influence he maintained with the leaders of the other European countries. He heard what happened with Hayao, and there was widespread belief that Pillar would be the likely victor. He looked at his watch. He had an hour to get some work done before Pillar arrived.

    At four forty five Todd Russell went downstairs to the lobby of his hotel to meet the reporters. Joe Berry set everything up, including the live feed from Caltech, so that Vincent Weimitz could participate in the press conference. He would make his announcement and then accept questions, as would Weimitz. Joe Berry would stay in the background, although Russell expected he would be questioned about him too. He straightened his tie and ducked into the men's room to make sure his hair looked neat, then walked out to the microphones. "Hello, everyone. You are all too sharp for me, catching us at the airport. I am sure you are dying to know what's going on. Well, I have just come from San Francisco where I decided upon my Vice Presidential running mate. It will be Vincent Weimitz, the president of Caltech."
    There was a murmur in the crowd; no one expected this. Weimitz had no background in politics. "What made you select him?"
    "I wanted someone who has an impeccable reputation in the scientific community to help make my administration attractive to those who can envision all the progress that can be made in technology. He will focus on those projects that can advance our interests in fields such as engineering and mathematics."

"When did you approach President Weimitz with the offer?"

"Just the other day. We met in San Francisco and discussed the details, and he gave me his answer the next day."

"Can we speak to him?"

"Absolutely. He is available through a live feed right now. Vincent, are you there?"

"I am, Todd. How is everyone today? I am available to answer questions, presumably about my new status as Vice Presidential hopeful."

Everyone chuckled. One reporter asked, "You have devoted your life to science and its advancement. What made you decide to enter the world of politics?"

"An opportunity presented itself to continue that advancement on a worldwide scale with far greater resources than I currently have. Once we are elected, my main responsibility will be to oversee all the technological projects that are currently in the works, as well as to develop new ones. I want to share our knowledge and expertise with people everywhere."

"Governor Russell, having Mr. Weimitz as the number two person in federal government is very nice, but how will he help you run the country?"

"Vincent will be an invaluable adviser and expert when it comes to science, and his office will include staff members who will be able to analyze the geo-political ramifications of any decisions and policy we might make."

"Governor, what are you going to be doing next?"

"This is my West Coast campaign trip. I am working my way down for the next few days, and will be back in Illinois on Monday."

"You were seen with Joe Berry at the airport the other day. Is he working your campaign?"

"Yes. Joe joined my campaign a few months ago and we have been enjoying working together."

"What is his role?"

"He is handling public relations, his specialty."

"Perhaps also handling your schedule?"

"For right now, yes."

"Will he be joining your staff if you are elected?"

"You mean when. No. Any work Joe does for me after November will be just as it is now, as an independent client."

"Mr. Weimitz, what will become of your post at Caltech?"

"I will keep it for now, and will still be involved after November. After all, it is the best school of its kind in the world, and an incredible place to hang my hat."

Another reporter raised her hand. Todd Russell acknowledged her and announced that this would be the final question. "Governor, did you select Mr. Weimitz because he hails from Europe and you believe he can help with the European vote in this country?"

"I picked him because he is an intelligent man who will be a great asset to my team. Thank you all for meeting here today." He turned and went back inside.

Friday, February 17th

Billet was meeting with his team again, hoping for some good news. He spoke to the Director who leaned on him for some information because the President had asked him for an update. One agent spoke.

"We looked into the Wiggins brothers' past. They had been members of American Pride, but attended meetings in the Midwest. There is no indication that they ever came in contact with Kelly Visque."

"We know how those groups work. Their members can connect anonymously all over the world if they need something. The Wiggins brothers could have easily arranged for her to kill Bernard and his wife. Anything about Ned Donato?"

"If he became involved, it wasn't with Kelly Visque. He had never been part of any hate group."

Billet thought for a minute. "Where do you all suggest we go from here?"

"Let's look into the Wiggins' bank accounts around the time of the murder, with three months-time on both ends, and compare that to Kelly Visque's financial records. Even if they exchanged money as cash, her spending habits may have changed."

"Good. That's moving in the right direction. Tell me if you run into any opposition at the IRS or any other agencies. Look for any big ticket purchases made by Miss Visque, such as a car or new furniture. The Department of Commerce keeps records of large purchases like that. Check for any vacations she might have taken as well. Go back and look at her work schedule, check with the airlines, and her credit card companies. Even if she paid in cash, a credit card would be necessary to reserve the room. We will meet back here in two weeks."

Sunday, February 19th

Juan Pillar was exhausted, but also experiencing a kind of euphoric energy. His European trip turned out better than he hoped. He had not made it to the Soviet Union, which may have turned out for the best since Vincent Weimitz was in the picture now, and Pillar's strategy had to change. All of the other countries fell in line with him. France, Germany, England, and of course, Spain were all behind him. They all agreed to work with their ambassadors and citizens in the U.S. to cultivate votes. He had basically half of Europe in his pocket. All of the leaders gave their endorsements publicly as well, and Pillar heard from his cousin Vicente that all of this was being reported back in the States as well. He had tremendous momentum now which would be easy to build on. He was on the plane back to Washington right now, and all reports were that he would arrive to a hero's welcome. After that he would start planning his next campaign trip. He wanted to make his first stop in Atlanta; his constituents deserved that right. He was behind about picking his VP, but he honestly believed he had time for that. Right now he felt like nothing could stop him.

Wolf's phone rang; not surprisingly it was Viper. "Remember what we discussed? Things are really not going the way we envisioned. We cannot wait any longer. You know what needs to be done. How you handle it is up to you. We will not talk again until after." Viper abruptly hung up. The game was on; Wolf's juices were flowing again.

Friday, February 24nd, Washington, DC

Wolf arrived at Dulles airport ahead of schedule. Everything was in place with the target located and the route planned. Wolf now waited at an inconspicuous vantage point where nothing would be missed. This must not be mishandled; it was a valuable service to the United States, the work of a patriot.

Juan Pillar's plane from Atlanta landed at Dulles. His campaigning there worked flawlessly, meeting with local officials, business leaders, and conducting several high profile interviews. He shook more hands than he could count, and felt he set the tone for travels across the rest of the country. Next would be New England and the rest of the Northeast and he would save the Southwest for last, as that area would need the least amount of effort. He deplaned, was whisked through security, and saw his driver with his name on the placard. He bid goodbye to his press secretary, who lived in the opposite direction. He shook his driver's hand, and then they walked to car that waited to take Pillar home.

Wolf witnessed all this; it was time to act.

Saturday, February 25th 6am, Reston, VA

Jim, a lawyer, was out for his usual early morning jog. He didn't mind the cold and dark, it was quiet and gave him a chance to think. He ran by a private residence when he noticed something out of the corner of his eye. Turning around, he jogged in place for a minute to get a closer look. Oh my god! Two bodies were strung up over a tree, and they had both been hanged. He got a little closer, and when he did, he realized that one of them was Juan Pillar.

CHAPTER 6

Saturday, February 25th

This amounted to a national crisis the likes of which had not been seen in 39 years. Within hours, it seemed like society came to a grinding halt. A hole had been punctured in our country's consciousness. Pillar represented the traditional values from which the United States originated. His dream, along with that of his supporters had been snuffed out so callously and casually most likely to protect an archaic, narrow minded ideology that made whoever did this more at odds with the American way of life than the new laws they perceived as a threat and against which they were rebelling. Everyone seemed frozen in time; stores were deserted, businesses closed early, and of course all government entities in session adjourned themselves immediately. President Harrington was utterly drained but forced himself to remain composed and set an example for the nation and world. He would give an address today at 5pm. Even the media had the good sense not to crowd around the law enforcement personnel at the crime scene.

Director Grey was there and not fucking around this time; he would not waste valuable time allowing some other local bureau fumble the ball on this one, when the most critical time in finding leads for a crime were the first 48 hours. He wanted to get as much information as possible about Pillar and the driver, who almost certainly was collateral damage, but still had to be ruled out the main target. He wanted Billet to run this investigation. There was no doubt in the Director's mind that this scene and the murder of the Bernards was related. Juan's cousin Vicente, his closest relative in the States, came straight up to DC. He exhibited a mixture of anger and grief. He lurked around the crime scene until Grey asked one of the agents to arrange for a grief counselor. The bodies had not been cut down yet; it appeared they had both been drugged before being hanged. The car service's car had been found two blocks away and a charge set off inside that eliminated all fingerprints. Both men had their hands and feet tied. Whoever killed them clearly knew the area and would be able to easily slip away undetected. Very little physical evidence existed around the area of the murders. Alright. He assembled his team. "Here is how we will proceed. I want one agent to attend to Pillar's cousin Vicente and try to extract some information about Pillar when he has calmed down. I want someone else to check on the driver's parents and make sure they are aware of what's going on before they hear it on the news. Ed? Where is Ed?" Grey looked around and saw him, lost in his own thoughts, no doubt beating himself up over not catching the killer or killers. The Director walked over to him and tapped him on the shoulder. He would coddle him later. "Ed, would you join us for a minute? I would like you to go back to the airport and retrace Pillar's steps. Perhaps we will come across something of importance. I will be in my office orchestrating everything. Good luck."

Billet drove to Dulles airport to see if anyone saw anything. He sought out the security team working in the area where Pillar's flight de-planed. They had seen him but things were so chaotic that they were focusing on simply preventing him from being trampled. Next, Billet went to talk to the workers at the airline. The agent at the reservations desk called the airport in Atlanta to see if anyone made any unusual inquiries about Pillar or the flight in general. No one had. Billet then went to speak to the flight attendants on the flight. They didn't notice anything unusual nor had there been any unruly or peculiar passengers. No progress had been made and he wanted to talk to the dispatcher at the livery company. He wasn't sure how often the driver was supposed to check in. That would be his next stop.

Pillar's cousin Vicente was still partly in shock and couldn't really give too much information. He managed to communicate that Pillar had no real enemies, no one who would want to cause him such harm. Did the FBI have any leads at all? The agent didn't want to reveal that he believed this was related to the Bernard murders.

The U.S. Supreme Court justices gathered at their building for an unplanned session. "This cannot be a coincidence," said Andrew Turnbull. "It must be related to Winston and Cecily somehow."

"What good will it do to speculate," replied Sam Kleinman. "This groundbreaking Presidential race has forced us to reexamine what it means to be an American. Half the people born here are apathetic to the point of not even sticking their own necks out for themselves. This is the pool from which candidates are selected from? We finally work up the courage to change things and our leading candidate for reform is killed."

"There will always be individuals who are resistant to change, Sam," chimed in Danielle Sorensen.

"Well, the Bernards and Pillar have not died in vain. Regardless of the outcome of the election, they will be remembered as martyrs and they will always be symbols of the great and radical changes our country made to remain a superpower," replied Chief Justice Braxton. "Now, since we are all here, we might as well devote a few hours to deliberating about a few of our most pressing cases."

5pm

President Harrington stepped out in front of the podium in the room in the White House used for State dinners. Today it was filled with reporters. Harrington didn't want his speech to sound like a eulogy; that would be for the funeral. Instead, he wanted to speak about heartbreak and perseverance. "My fellow Americans, two lives were cut short today, a tragedy. No life is expendable. We cannot, however, let this horrible loss get the better of us. We are on the verge of something great, and must not be derailed. A precedent is being set for the whole world, and we must continue down this path without fear of intimidation. Following that course of action would make Juan Pillar proud; he would want to see his work finished. We are resilient and will bounce back from this. Such scoundrels as those who committed this reprehensible act will not be allowed to gain the upper hand. We are united; we all need time to mourn and nurse our vulnerability, for I know that is what I am feeling right now. Once that time has passed however, we must do our best to resume our normal routines, for if we do, we will have conquered not only our fears but also the part of our past we would like to forget. God bless us all." He turned and walked out of the room before any questions could be fired at him.

Billet came up empty again at the livery company. The dispatcher had spoken to the driver as he got ready to leave the airport and not after that. Many times the drivers brought the cars back after hours and dispatch didn't see them until the next day. That meant the perpetrator obtained their schedule and probably had been watching at the airport. He was wasting his time. It was late, around 9pm. He wanted to go through Pillar's house and look for any leads, but he understood how this worked. They would have the autopsy tomorrow and the funeral on Monday. Pillar's cousin would not be available until Tuesday. Well, it wasn't ideal but what he had to work with.

Sunday, February 26th
The bodies were at the morgue now, going through an autopsy. They had both been drugged so they could be hanged without putting up a fight. Other than that, the coroner didn't find anything out of the ordinary. Director Grey called an hour later for a report and didn't seem surprised.

Hayao spoke to Natsu last night, and for the first time since Hayao had known him, Natsu seemed unsure of himself. He actually wanted Hayao to decide what to do next now that Pillar's support was up for grabs. Hayao was not a monster, but how could he not feel lucky? He would have to make a statement, and he asked Alex Ramirez to write it for him. He also made arrangements to attend the funeral. That would help his cause with the populations in Central America, South America, and Spain. He now had a valid reason to visit there. He checked his email and saw the one from Alex. "I am deeply saddened by the loss of Juan Pillar. He was a loyal American, and a shining example to people from all over the world of how a person can overcome obstacles and achieve great things. My heart goes out to his loved ones who can be proud of the way he conducted himself, the universal respect and high esteem he commanded. He will be missed." That was perfect. He would release that statement through his press secretary. He wanted to formulate his plan to campaign abroad. Europe was wide open, but he could not count on the Pope's support the same way Pillar did, since he practiced Buddhism. He trusted however, that many of the countries would still support him even without the Pope. Hayao would likely consider what was best for European and Asian countries in his decision making much more than the other two candidates would. Most of the political pundits believed foreign countries would have a big impact on this election, and Hayao intended to make the most of it.

Eric Layton wanted to get in touch with Steven Morris to see what he thought about all of this. He sent Morris a text hoping to hear back from him soon. Layton's actions over the next few days would be very important as he would be judged by his demeanor and the way he carried himself during this difficult time for the country. He would seek out the endorsement from the Pope, but wanted to wait a little while so he wouldn't seem too anxious. Layton wasn't too worried, for if the Pope would back anyone now, it would be him, as he had ties to Italy through Morris's connection with the Manuccis. He felt confident about the rest of Europe too, as France and England would likely support him also. He wasn't going to spend much time or effort on Russia, as Russell would gain the support there due to the fact that Vincent Weimitz was on his ticket. As far the Orient, he would only make an attempt to gain a foothold in China, as Hayao would have a stronghold on all the other countries. It was fascinating now that one political party existed in the United States, the new expanded political field has created an entirely new method of competing for votes. The inclusion of candidates born abroad ironically created the reverse effect of diminishing the importance of the issues facing the U.S. This was because the country where the foreign born candidate emigrated from played an integral part in garnering support, as foreign countries and governments wielded a great amount of influence with their groups of immigrants living in the United States, as well as those U.S. citizens born in America and still swayed by the will of the countries from where their ancestors came. Layton realized he had to tap into this and also wanted to travel to the Middle East to cultivate relationships there. The phone finally rang; it was Morris. He of course knew what Layton wanted to discuss. Morris said they should both attend the funeral tomorrow. They did not want to seem uncaring, and he agreed they should spend time abroad, and perhaps leave the United States for last as the foundation will have been set by then in the other countries. Central and South America were also worth visiting, and they enjoyed an advantage there; Morris was Catholic and those in power would encourage their brethren to vote for them. Right after the debate, they decided they would go to Spain to get a jump on Hayao and Alex Ramirez. She would be the logical person to endorse; she had proven herself as a politician and leader, and would use whatever authority she could to Spain's advantage. All this travel would be expensive; Layton said he would call Patrick Manucci for a contribution to their campaign. They had not raised much money yet for their campaign; since President Harrington nominated both he and Russell together diminished the available pool of money the traditional political benefactors donated in half. They were relying more and more on larger contributions from private citizens, rather than large organizations. Through Manucci, they were fortunate to have a broad network of people to lend a hand financially. They agreed to meet up at the funeral tomorrow and bid each other goodbye.

Monday, February 27th, 11am
Half of the politicians in Washington gathered at Arlington National Cemetery for Pillar's funeral. Yes, it was a military cemetery, but Pillar had been such a hero to so many people it seemed fitting that he should be interred here. Only two people would speak, Pillar's father and his cousin Vicente. There would then be the firing of weapons which would end the schedule. Pillar's father got up and strode to the podium. He started to speak. "Juan was very proud of"; he struggled to stay composed but could not go on. Juan's cousin Vicente helped Juan's dad back to his seat and then went to the podium. He too worked to keep himself together. "Juan Pillar was a true and loyal friend, who rose above his environment. He was blessed with a loving family and determined to achieve the success he defined for himself at an early age. Along the way, he never forgot to help those less

fortunate than himself, and that in part made him a superior public servant. He set his sights really high, and though his dream was never realized, he remains an inspiration to us all and left a legacy of virtue and integrity beyond reproach. Juan, we love you and miss you." The soldiers fired their weapons and the shots placed a punctuation mark at the end of the life of a political pioneer.

Tuesday, February 28th
Vicente Pillar's phone rang. He didn't feel like talking, but he didn't recognize the number and thought it might be important; as it turned out he couldn't have been more right. "Hello?"
"Hi, this is Ed Billet, Mr. Pillar, and I am with the FBI. Would you have a few minutes now to talk?"
"Well, I have already been interviewed by some of your coworkers. What do you want to know?"
"Well, I have been to the airport and the livery company and have not gotten any leads. Perhaps you might offer some advice on where to go from here."
"Juan was squeaky clean, agent Billet. I am certain this was politically motivated, and not personal." His tone was biting, offended by the implication that Juan had dealings shady enough to make someone want to kill him for personal reasons.
"Well, perhaps we could get inside his apartment and look around. Would you possibly let us in?" Silence.
"I suppose," Vicente said reluctantly. "Meet me there on Thursday at 11am. Here is the address."

Wednesday, February 29th
Todd Russell, Vincent Weimitz, and Joe Berry were on a plane headed to Russia. They would visit all the countries that made up the Soviet Union while there. Having Weimitz with them was invaluable; he would be their ambassador, and Russell managed to entice him with the opportunity to collaborate with the top minds at each university in each of the countries they visited. They would also make stops in other European countries, and would be able to drum up support which would trickle down back to the U.S. They had planned to go anyway, but Juan Pillar's death forced them to

accelerate their trip. Russell made Joe Berry make the arrangements last Saturday, right after the story broke. He wanted to capitalize on the uncertainty people around the world must be feeling and wanted to make a good impression everywhere so he would gain the benefit of any available influence with the citizens back home. He hoped to be received as a caring person trying to allay fears that the U.S. remained in good hands. The one country they would not go to now would be Spain, as the wound was still fresh there and his presence would be resented. Joe Berry was sleeping, but that was ok, Russell wanted to talk to Vincent Weimitz. He said, "Vincent, there are a few things I would like to go over. We will be doing a good deal of campaigning, and I would like you to participate. We can accomplish a lot. There will still be ample time for you to devote to science. When we visit the other countries in Europe, your presence won't be as critical, but in the Slavic countries, you will be our ambassador. How do you think we should approach all this?"

"You're right, I will create much goodwill in those countries; they will appreciate the fact that I have been given the opportunity to hold such a high office. One thing we should try to do is convince everyone we are listening, and if we are elected will pay attention to how our decisions will affect them. We need to convey the message that we will remember our supporters and those who got us to the White House."

"Ok. I also want to meet with some government officials in each country to show they are behind us as well."

"We will have to settle for mid-level politicians, as the top leaders always want to give the impression they are too busy to meet."

"Alright. I will have Joe set up some meetings. It's shaping up to be a very productive trip. "

Thursday, March 1st

Billet arrived at Juan Pillar's home just before 11am and saw that cousin Vicente hadn't arrived yet. Five minutes later, Vicente arrived. They shook hands and went inside. Billet was not going to perform a full sweep as this was not a crime scene. Instead, he looked for clues. Vicente hovered over him; it was most irritating.

Billet suggested he go get something to eat and come back in two hours. Vicente wasn't happy about it, but realized a federal agent wouldn't be likely to steal anything. He left without a word. Now Billet could get down to it. He started with Juan Pillar's closet, going through his pockets, but not finding anything. He pulled down the boxes at the top of the closet, which contained a variety of items such as old pictures and Mexican artifacts that he collected over the years. Billet would take these things with him, and he would want Vicente to go through them and identify the people in the pictures. Billet focused on gathering everything that might come in handy so he wouldn't have to go through Pillar's home again. Next, he checked the kitchen drawers; he found the standard things, along with some letters. He went through Pillar's desk and grabbed everything and threw it into the box. He noticed a crawl space and pulled down the ladder and looked inside. There were more boxes, and Billet took them all. He finished his sweep of the rest of the rooms, and by then Vicente returned. Billet told him what he wanted, and Vicente seemed to be on board. He would do anything within his power to help catch the bastard who killed his friend and cousin.

Billet carted all of the boxes back to FBI headquarters in Quantico, and he and Vicente arranged to meet there on Saturday. He would have time to sort through all of the stuff in the meantime and be able to ask about anything that might give him a lead. Suddenly his phone rang. He answered and it was Sondra Tristan.

"Hi Sondra. How have you and Blake been?"

"Oh, fine, Ed. I am sure you can guess why I am calling. What do you make of the murder of Juan Pillar and the driver?"

"The driver was collateral damage and Pillar the target."

"Do you know that for a fact?"

"Not yet."

"Do you think this murder and my parents' murders are related?"

"Yes. I am talking without any real basis in fact here, but my hunch is they are."

"What do you think the link is?"

"I am not sure. We are at the beginning of the investigation. Speaking of which, let me give you an update. We are looking into the Wiggins brothers to see if there is any connection with Kelly Visque."

"What made you consider them in the first place?"

"We went back and looked at some of the past controversial cases the Supreme Court ruled on. Carl Wiggins was the bomber in Chicago a few years back who was tortured to get a confession, something which the Supreme Court ruled to be permissible. His brother is very volatile and threatened revenge after his brother's conviction."

"Isn't it possible he worked alone?"

"Yes, but there is no physical evidence linking him to the crime. If it comes out he knew Visque, we would have something."

"Are there any other leads right now?"

"Ned Donato from Princeton, who spoke out against the education reform that was passed. This is all premature. The thread from these two recent killings may lead us somewhere. I assure you I will keep you abreast of all developments."

"Thank you Ed. Good luck."

Friday, March 2nd

Eric Layton was in his office in Washington, DC. He had some pressing issues to confront. The crime rate in Denver was on the rise, and the people of Colorado were clamoring for more federal funds to help with the unemployment rate by reopening Buckley Air Force base which closed five years ago with other Air Force bases in surrounding states, the rationale being that we were at peace. It did not encounter too much opposition at the time, as the economy in Colorado was good and the employees at the base were reassigned and able to find jobs elsewhere. Times had changed however. More people were out of work, and with the several high profile assassinations in the last year, the defense of the U.S. was being questioned. Our western borders were vulnerable, and due to the increased unemployment in Colorado, people were desperate and taking whatever action necessary to put food on the table. The Governor made a few feeble attempts to get money from Washington but had been rebuffed, and being a political neophyte wasn't very effective. Layton recognized he must step in, and now that he was running for President, could use his national clout to get results, both for his constituents and for his image. He called President Harrington, and his personal secretary answered. "Hello Senator. The President is in a meeting now but will call you when he gets out."

"Thank you." He went back to drafting the paperwork to expedite things so when the President acquiesced and allocated money to Colorado, everything would be in place. He remained so focused on his work that he hardly noticed two hours passed when the phone rang. It was President Harrington. "Hello?"

"Eric, hi it's President Harrington."

"Hello, Mr. President. How have you been? I'm sure it has been a stressful week for you."

"That it has. What can I do for you?" Layton went over the whole scenario regarding Denver, and after his sales pitch, he explained they badly needed funds. He was requesting money from FEMA (Federal Emergency Management Act). It was something of a stretch, but many of the citizens there were in dire straits, and it was a major American city. He felt optimistic the President would go along with the plan. If he agreed, Layton would have the governor declare a state of emergency, a prerequisite to qualifying for FEMA funds.

"Now, Eric, FEMA usually is set aside for natural disasters such as earthquakes and the like. Increased unemployment hardly seems to qualify." Layton was silent for a minute, deciding what to say next.

"You're right. However, you haven't been to Denver recently. It's gotten really bad; there are parts of town even the police won't go to anymore. We are heading towards martial law."

"Are you sure you are not exaggerating, Eric? It seems a little coincidental that you are bringing this to me now, right in the middle of your campaign." Layton just shrugged off the snide comment.

"This is not political grandstanding, sir. We are desperate." Silence on the other end.

"Let me see what I can do. I will reach out to the people at FEMA and try to get them moving on this. In the meantime, you talk to the governor and tell him to get on top of this, and explain how we are trying to proceed." The President hung up, and Layton knew from past experience if he offered to make something happen, he would use all of his power to see that it did.

Saturday, March 3rd
Billet met Juan Pillar's cousin Vicente at FBI headquarters in Quantico at 9am. He had set up all the boxes in Director Grey's private conference room. Vicente brought two coffees for them. They anticipated staying there all day if necessary. They started with the first box of private letters. Most of them were from friends and family in Mexico, but there were also some from Juan's old love interests, none of which were ever very serious. He had always been married to politics. Billet inquired about all the people in the pictures confiscated from Pillar's home, but Vicente identified all of them and none of them jumped out as potential suspects. Still, they pressed on. They took a short break for lunch and then got right back to it. By 6pm, they were exhausted and had managed to go through just about all of his stuff, save for a few boxes, but there hopes of finding a lead were sinking. Billet pulled out a bunch of papers from a box he thought he filled with items from Pillar's desk. He sifted through them quickly and came across an envelope with Pillar's name and address on it with no return address. He tore it open, noticing the postmark was from California and froze when he saw the paper inside. It was a note that contained a threatening message pieced together from different magazines and newspapers:

YOU **ARE BEING** WARNED!

RECUSE *YOURSELF* FROM THE PRESIDENTIAL RACE!

IF YOU DON'T REMOVE YOURSELF, YOU WILL BE IN DANGER!

THIS IS NOT A THREAT,

THIS IS A FACT!

Vicente and Billet were flabbergasted. They stumbled upon a major lead and looked at the envelope. It was postmarked in Los Angeles and had been sent back in January. Juan must have grabbed it, got distracted by something else, and never opened it. If only he did, he might still be alive. Billet tried to focus. Thankfully the envelope was still intact. If Pillar had thrown it away they would be nowhere. Whoever sent this probably counted on that. He looked over at Vicente, who looked like he might pass out. Billet got him a glass of water. After a minute he managed to compose himself and asked Billet what the next step would be. Billet said he would send the letter and envelope to be tested for DNA, and also for any particles that might provide more information. Vicente said he was wiped out and he asked Billet to keep him posted. After he left, Billet went straight to the crime lab and put the evidence in an envelope and wrote priority all over it. He would come back first thing Monday morning when the technicians were here.

Todd Russell was ecstatic. The tour they were on around the former Soviet republic was going superbly. Everyone treated Vincent Weimitz like a rock star and they even managed to meet some politicians as well, who basically promised they would encourage all the U.S. citizens with Russian ancestry to support his candidacy. They also said as the election got closer the heads of state of each country would make time for him and publicly come out with endorsements. They were heading to England tomorrow and then France. He wasn't sure who those countries would end up supporting, him or Eric Layton. He had Weimitz, but Layton had Morris with ties to Italy through his association with the Manucci family. Those countries could go either way and possessed good relations with both. It would come down to which candidate had more to offer and was willing to reciprocate more in exchange for support. On his end, he was willing to ease the laws governing imports and exports, a point of contention among many European countries. That would be a big incentive for many of the European countries to endorse him. He also knew he needed to make inroads into China. The Pope would likely back Layton, and Hayao would of course dominate the Oriental vote, except that China hated Japan, so beating Layton there was crucial. Weimitz remained his secret weapon in his quest for China's support. Russell would want him to spend time in China developing a program to improve science education there, and to promote the sciences for adults as well. China was an unbelievable resource for labor which remained largely untapped; Russell wanted to seize this opportunity to work with them. As a country, they had not embraced technology like the rest of the world over the last twenty years, and Russell would look like a genius if he could help bring them up to date. He would discuss this with Weimitz later on, once he got a taste of having the world open up for him. He would also work the Middle East, and Africa, but knew to tread carefully. While relations were not so volatile now between Israel and the Arab countries, some of the more extreme Arabian leaders may support one of the other candidates out of spite if Israel backs him, which they are likely to do, as they are advocates of science and technology and are on good terms with Russia. His plan was to publicly court those countries first and then approach Israel behind the scenes. He believed he would get India's support, so he did not feel the need to visit. South America was not worth the trip either, as having Alex Ramirez on his ticket would practically ensure their support would largely go to Hayao. This was world diplomacy, and his tenure as governor of an ethnically diverse state had prepared him perfectly for this, just as planning and executing a successful campaign would prepare him for running the country, and interacting globally with a level of success never before seen.

Sunday, March 4th

Hayao wanted to make a commercial, and fast. He wanted to draw people's attention to the fact that Todd Russell was out of the country and that he neglected his responsibilities as governor, but wanted to do it subtly, without negative campaigning. He didn't want to resort to it unless absolutely necessary; people became disgusted with that tactic very quickly, himself included. He never wanted to hear what the other person didn't or couldn't do, he wanted to hear what you brought to the table. God, that always made him so angry! Slinging mud was not also permitted under his direction at the Moritu Corporation. It was counter-productive and only served to draw attention away from the issue at hand. There was no faster way to be let go at Moritu than to engage in finger pointing. This extended into American society as well and was one of the things which instigated all the political reform in the last two decades. People were simply fed up. Anyway, back to the commercial. He wanted both himself and Alex to be in the commercial, to send the image they were taking care of business. He wanted to shoot it in Alex's office, with her seated at her desk and him standing beside her. The dialogue would have a reassuring tone intended to put people at ease. The message would be clear, people would inevitably draw comparisons between the candidates, and Hayao's image would be partially mended. He talked to Alex about this, and she thought it was a great idea. She knew a director who would help them, someone she had used before in making tourism ads for Florida. They were going to film it next weekend, and hopefully have it broadcast within a few days. Once that was done, he wanted to spend some time in South America, to show his sympathy for Juan Pillar, and to ingratiate himself and Alex with the people and governments there. He was confident he would have their support because of Alex, but wanted to be the first candidate to visit those countries to show his compassion. They planned to be there in two weeks and stay for three. When they returned to the States, he hoped people would have more or less forgotten about the incident at the debate allowing him to start building on a successful trip with some campaigning in the Midwest, a region split between him and Todd Russell.

Monday, March 5th
Ed Billet arrived at Quantico around ten am, hoping to find the forensic techs already analyzing the letter and envelope, and he

wasn't disappointed. Those guys were committed. Ideally, they would find prints which did not belong to Pillar, but Billet knew that was highly unlikely. He knocked on the glass to let them know he was here. They came out about fifteen minutes later. "Hi Ed. There really isn't much to go on. The only prints we lifted belonged to Pillar, and there was no DNA or anything else that would help us identify the culprit."

"What about the envelope? Were there any particles found to help narrow down where it was mailed from?"

"Unfortunately not. It originated in Los Angeles. From a forensic standpoint, that's about all we can offer." Billet was disappointed, but he knew they had done their best.

"Thanks for all your efforts. Have a good day."

Billet got in touch with the head of the U.S. Postal Service, a woman named Eunice Washer. He hoped she was having a good day; he understood she could be quite cantankerous. "Hello?"

"Hello, this is agent Ed Billet, FBI. How are you today?"

"Fine. What can I do for you?" Bitterness and weariness filled her voice; she had been in charge for a good number of years and the Postal Service had taken a beating under her reign.

"I am investigating the murder of Juan Pillar and the man who was with him." By letting her into his confidence, he hoped she might be a little more cooperative. "There is a piece of evidence I would like to find out more about. You see, Mr. Pillar received a threatening note a while back mailed to him in January and I am hoping somehow we can trace it back to a location to determine where it originated." She was silent for a minute.

"When was it postmarked?"

"Thursday, January 19th."

"Where was it mailed from?"

"Los Angeles."

"I can't promise anything, but let me do some investigating. I will call you in a few days."

"Thank you. I know I can trust you to keep this as confidential as possible. Right now only five people know about this and I want to keep it that way to preserve the integrity of our investigation."

"I will do my best." Eunice wasted no time. This was a highly critical matter. She called the director of operations in Los Angeles. She couldn't remember the man's name, but that didn't matter, when she said jump her employees just said how high. "I would like you to ask the people who work in your operation if they remember seeing a letter addressed to Juan Pillar mailed from LA on January 19th. Please check with all the mail carriers who collect mail from the public mailboxes. We need to determine which mailbox it was deposited in. Let me know as soon as you come up with something, and make it a priority."

With such a directive, Milton, who was in charge of all the post offices in L.A. had to get some answers fast. He sent out a bulk text message to all the heads of the individual post offices to ask the mail carriers if they recall ever seeing a letter addressed to Juan Pillar. He hoped to hear back from them in a day or two.

Wednesday, March 7th

Kangaroo arrived a few minutes early, hoping Uncle George possessed some information to provide today. He wanted to find out if the trend regarding immigration had increased for people with Latino heritage lately as well. He arrived a few minutes later. They dispensed with the pleasantries and got right down to business. "What a wild week. We now have quite a few agents down in Mexico and South America looking for a lead from the various governments there."

"Why are we looking there? I would think the people and administrations down there would have been behind Pillar 100%."

"Alex Ramirez is of Spanish descent as well. With Pillar's increased momentum in the last few months, there could have been a group that decided to derail him permanently. Also, if it was someone from the Orient or United States, South America would be the perfect place for them to hide."

"How do you plan to flush them out?"

"We are the NSA, Kangaroo. We deal with information on a macro level; the details involved in solving crimes are left to the FBI. There are people out there who are trying to manipulate the process in our country, and it our job to expose them. Without sounding like a conspiracy nut, I do believe the murder of the Bernards and Juan Pillar have been done by the same person. Put yourself in their shoes. What would you be after?"

Kangaroo thought for a moment. "I would want the candidate that would most benefit me to win the Presidential election."

"Ok, good. Now, at this point, who is in the best position?"

"Todd Russell."

"Correct. And who would profit the most from his victory?"

"Well, everyone, from a technical standpoint. Considering his running mate is a god of science, all those science and technology aficionados and people who believe we need more capital improvement projects."

"Yes, but also citizens in Russia and other former countries in the Soviet Union who know they will be favored."

"Then what was your point about Alex Ramirez?"

"I am getting there, just give me a chance."

"Russia has a good relationship with many of the governments in South America, and there is no doubt they would harbor a Russian fugitive. Both regions would benefit if the South American countries' governments held a vested interest in Hayao and Alex Ramirez. That way, the assassin would get what they want and so would the government in question. Both sides would profit. Now, I am not saying there was any kind of planned arrangement, but it seems like the logical place to look, and we can follow both theories, the one that a group who wants Hayao and Ramirez to win was responsible, and the one that surmises a person or persons took Pillar out so Russell and Weimitz have a chance, and are now hiding in South America."

"What about the connection with the Bernard murders?"

"That is something we will have to discover." Kangaroo thought for a minute.

"Have you gotten any more information about the immigration numbers? Have they still been increasing?"

"Yes, but now they are up not only for people from the Far East, but for everyone. That way, it can be not be said any favoritism existed."

"Alright, I will activate five agents and send them to various countries. Their assignments will be to infiltrate the governments of those countries, and report back to me in three weeks." They parted company without a word.

Thursday, March 8th

Eunice Washer was in her expansive office at 10am when the phone rang. It was the supervisor from Los Angeles. Knowing her, he got right to the point. "One of my mail carriers does remember a letter going to Juan Pillar. He noticed it was routed to Washington DC and then looked at the name."

"Can you cut to the chase, please? Where did he pick it up from?"

"From a box in Beverly Hills."

"Thank you, goodbye."

Washer called Ed Billet immediately and told him what she found out. she just wanted to cross it off her list of things to do. He asked her if she knew anything about where that mailbox was located, in a busy area, etc., and she curtly said she had no idea. "Before you hang up, Eunice, I will probably want to visit the site and may call upon your employees to show me, so please give them a heads up." She agreed with a grunt and got off the phone as fast as she could.

Saturday, March 10th

Billet arrived in Los Angeles and the escort from the post office was waiting for him; they went directly to the mailbox from which the letter was supposedly mailed. He looked all around at the surroundings. The mailbox stood in the middle of a busy street in Beverly Hills. Why did they pick this mailbox? There must be a reason. He thought about Ned Donato and the Wiggins brothers. Would they go to such lengths to throw the FBI off their tail? Maybe. He would check with all the airlines to see if any of the three of them travelled to L.A. anytime in the last few months since Juan Pillar had pulled ahead in the Presidential race. If it turned out there were no matches, he would go a different route, one he wasn't crazy about, but would be necessary.

Hayao arrived in Tallahassee yesterday and spent the night in the governor's mansion. He and Alex Ramirez both woke up early today to plan out their commercial. The director knew Alex would arrive at 1pm. They changed their minds about it and now envisioned themselves outside in a crowd, shaking hands with those that surrounded them, which would include people of all different ethnicities. That part could be filmed in Florida, but the second half of the ad had to be filmed in DC, and more specifically at the White House. He would need special permission to film there, but any hoops he would have to jump through would be worth it when the commercial aired, as the image of the two of them standing on the south lawn with the White House behind them would remain with viewers for a long time. Hayao didn't care about the expense; he would fly himself and the other two straight up to DC to finish the commercial. The director arrived, and after going through introductions, they got to work. Hayao and Alex described what they envisioned, and the director liked it and only suggested some minor modifications. He helped them with the details, and when they were done talking, they agreed to start shooting tomorrow. The crew was already assembled and would be available. Tonight Hayao and Alex were attending a fundraising dinner at the statehouse sponsored by the teachers union in Florida; they were very powerful here, and the changeover to the one political party system had not diminished their clout. Politicians, especially local ones, could still be bought. Secondary education became more affordable through legislative reform, and primary education had taken a turn back toward basics, when teachers didn't have so many regulations to abide by, and there were not so many mandates or required standardized tests. Teachers were starting to have more leeway in the curriculum, as the adults who voted now had grown up during the years when school systems tied their budgets to the students' scores on those tests. The teachers and schools became obsessed with the children's performance, covering material only pertinent to the exam. The United States continually fell further and further behind other nations when it came to producing top students, a trend in no small part responsible for the fact that they had to look elsewhere for strong political leaders. It was fitting that the teachers' unions were doing so well, and both Hayao and Alex were happy to support them.

Sunday, March 11th
Todd Russell was on his way back to the States and coming back a winner. He had made a lot of progress in England and France, and would continue his tour around the U.S. after a few weeks in Illinois, where he would resume his gubernatorial duties. Weimitz would go back to Caltech, and Joe Berry would continue to plan out Russell's next moves. While they were in Europe they filmed a political ad, which would air in two weeks in the United States. He thought it was masterful and believed it would help his stock rise all over the world. He was shown promoting a message of tolerance and peace to which everyone across the globe could relate. They were not planning to campaign in South America, as Alex Ramirez would be the favorite, with Steven Morris behind being a Catholic. The only hope he retained for garnering any support down there was from those people who would want to see Weimitz in power to promote science. They would back him anyway, so it was pointless to seek out their endorsements. He would focus on this country next, as well as Canada, who enjoyed a big influence on the people that relocated here. At some point he would have to be interviewed again, probably in a month or two. He wanted to gain some ground in the polls first so he would have something to discuss. He didn't know what Hayao and Layton kept up their sleeves, but he was very confident about his hand.

The three NSA agents arrived in South America, all within an hour of each other, one in Brazil, one in Venezuela, and one in Colombia. They were all going to proceed the same way, by trying to infiltrate the main government buildings as janitors in the capital cities of Brasilia, Caracas, and Bogota, and place bugs in all the offices. Technology existed which the NSA owned that made bug detection next to impossible. They were all going in with fake identities, and they already had the jobs lined up through the foreign operatives already there. They would be listening in their apartments with cutting edge listening devices. If they learned nothing after a month they would move on to other countries, hoping they were focusing their efforts in the right places. These three countries were picked to stakeout first due to their easy immigration laws and the greed of their governments; they would be most likely to grant asylum to a person looking for a place to hide in exchange for money. Kangaroo was optimistic that if a connection existed between the assassin and South America, it would turn up in one of these three places.

Monday, March 12th
Eric Layton was just finishing up a meeting with his congressional staff when his secretary buzzed him that President Harrington was on the phone for him. Layton ended the meeting and made it clear he wanted privacy. When his office was clear, he answered the phone. "Hello, Mr. President. How are you?"
"I am fine, Eric. I am sure you know why I am calling. I made some inquiries about FEMA funds, and in my opinion, you do qualify. I gave that recommendation to FEMA's director and I am sure he will see to it you get the money." Layton knew the director of FEMA would fall in line with the President's wishes.
"That's excellent, sir. I cannot thank you enough. When can I expect to hear from him?"
"He should call you within the next few days. If you do not hear from him by Friday, please contact me and I will get on his case."
"That's very kind of you."
"Well, goodbye, Eric."
"Goodbye, sir." Excellent! This would reflect well on him with the people in Colorado, and would come at the perfect time politically, for he was planning a trip to Europe for Morris and himself on Saturday, March 17th, so he could point to his success with FEMA while on his trip. He would meet with the Pope; enough time had passed for him to seek the endorsement. This was good. He felt himself gaining momentum.

Ed Billet came up completely empty in Los Angeles. There were many different fingerprints on the mailbox of course and no surveillance footage anywhere. Time was of the essence here, so he would take the extraordinary step of enlisting Director Grey's help with a special request. He would go up to see him as soon as he got back to Washington tomorrow. For now, he wanted to formulate a plan regarding what to do once the Director followed through with Billet's request. Of course it would depend on what was disclosed, but he planned to act on it right away. He didn't foresee a problem with the director getting cooperation, and believed action would be taken quickly. The director wanted to resolve this as quickly as he did, and would put the pressure on the powers that be. If it turned out to be a bust, he would go back over past evidence again to see if anything new came up with a connection to Los Angeles. His mind going in ten different directions, he tried to focus on the task at hand, writing the report he would submit to Director Grey tomorrow.

Tuesday, March 13th

Billet arrived at Dulles and took a taxi directly to Quantico. He wanted to get the ball rolling immediately. When he went up to the top floor to the Director's suite, he was on the phone. Billet waited patiently for five minutes and the director finally ended the call. He waved Billet in and welcomed him back from California. Billet got right down to business. "I struck out in Los Angeles. There was no physical evidence of any kind."

"It's weeks later, Ed. Did you really expect there to be any?"

"I hoped. That's why I am here. I have a request. We are desperately in need of information, and the inter-agency room just will not do the job this time. I need you to contact the CIA and find out from them if there are any people who fit the bill for the murder of Juan Pillar, anyone they have been keeping their eyes on. Could you do that? Oh, here is my official report."

"Thanks Ed. I will call my contact there today."

Hayao and Alex Ramirez were in Washington after finishing the first part of the commercial, which they both believed came out very well. They shot a lot of raw footage showing both of them meeting people and conversing with them, and the crew the director travelled with did a good job of editing it. Their task over the next few days was to obtain permission to film at the White House. Alex Ramirez knew someone who worked at the White House, a young woman named Abigail who had helped her before. She was going to call her today. Abigail would be able to point her in the right direction being very close to the President. While Ramirez focused on that, Hayao and the director reviewed the script for the commercial. For this part, they had it written out, unlike the portion in Florida which was ad-libbed. Both Hayao and Alex will be standing with their backs to the White House, and they would be conveying the message they were ushering in a new era, with a new unique global perspective that would lift the U.S. to heights higher than ever before, with its impact resonating with allies all over the world. The location they picked was brilliant, in Hayao's opinion. Alex kept trying to get through to Abigail, and after 4 tries, she was finally successful. "Hi Abby. It's Alex Ramirez. How have you been?"

"I've been doing great, Governor. I have my dream job, am living in a great place in Georgetown, and love hobnobbing with all the politicos!"

"That's great. I understand President Harrington thinks you are a rising star in the governmental arena. Stick with it. Us women are a precious minority. The reason I am calling is that we, Hayao and myself, would like to film a commercial at the White House, and I know we need permission. Who would we need to speak to about that?"

"It would be Rebecca, the White House press secretary. I can handle it for you, if you would like. It shouldn't be a problem. Filming for political ads at locales around town, and certainly one for a Presidential candidate should be approved."

"Great. Here is my cell phone number. Give me a call when you get an answer."

"I will."

Rebecca noticed her cell phone vibrate and pulled it out of her pocket. She didn't recognize the number. "Hello?"

"Hi Rebecca, this is Abigail, an employee on President Harrington's staff."

"Hello, Abigail. What can I do for you?"

"I was contacted by Alex Ramirez, Hayao's running mate. She is requesting for them to film a commercial at the White House, and since we had dealings in the past, she contacted me to see what needed to be done and I said I would handle it for her. So, that's why I am calling, to arrange for them to film at the White House."

"Ok, that shouldn't be a problem. I just have to run it by the security team here and find out which day would be best. They have to be on duty whenever a dignitary comes in or if the President is receiving other guests. They usually have a copy of his schedule a few days in advance so they can get ready as well. I will call you back either tonight or tomorrow."

"Great, thanks."

Director Grey took out his private cell phone, one which contained top secret phone numbers. One of them was the off the grid number for the director of the CIA, who went by the code name Mata Hari when he talked to Grey, and Grey used the code name Hoover. He called. Mata Hari didn't answer, as was his practice. He would see the number and call back. That practice always gave him a chance to get to a secure location free from any listening devices. Grey went back to work. He only answered the phone he called from in his office, so if Mata Hari didn't call back in an hour, he would try him again tomorrow.

Wednesday, March 14th

Todd Russell was in his office at the Governor's mansion in Springfield, Illinois. Things had been handled well during his absence and he was being praised for having such a competent staff. He would be leaving in ten days for Canada, along with Weimitz and Berry again. Berry took a leave of absence from his job in Washington which did not change their arrangement. Berry was now a gun for hire. Russell knew it was incredibly early in the race, but he had a big lead in all the national polls and definitely was on a roll. His stops in Canada included Montreal, Toronto, and Vancouver. He would be highlighting his emphasis on science and technology, which would be very well received there, especially in the cities he would visit, where there were many cutting edge companies employing the latest and greatest practices available. He would also have Joe Berry book him on some talk shows. Once they were done in Canada, they would all return to their respective homes for a short while, before embarking on their next trip, this time to the Middle East, where he would also be taking advantage of being the favorite. This campaigning style would have been unheard of even just twenty years ago. The foreign born candidates added an entirely new dimension to the process of running for President. It was even more important for those candidates who were born in the United States to visit these other countries; paradoxically, they were now the underdogs. The factor keeping Russell in the lead now was Weimitz. Russell told Joe Berry to make that a priority.

   The three agents in South America communicated to each other using a device which transmitted brain waves to a receiver worn next to a person's heart, which powered the device using the heart's electromagnetic pulses. It was experimental, only for government use right now, and the brain waves were untraceable, unlike cell phones which still could be hacked by very experienced hackers. The agents were communicating now and all of the information exchanged indicated nothing important had been observed by any of them. They wanted to check in with each other before they sent this data back to the States. That way, if there were any consistencies they could narrow down their covert activities to zero in on more likely targets. They agreed to do this again in ten days.

Director Grey was in the middle of his lunch at the Capital Grille when his private phone rang; he knew it was Mata Hari. He needed to get to a secure, quiet location right away. He signaled to his driver that he needed to go, told his waiter to add the amount from his lunch to his tab, and was out the door. Twenty minutes later, he returned to Quantico. He called Mata Hari immediately, and fortunately he was still there. "I need some information, if any is available. Do you have any intelligence on anyone with a motive to kill Juan Pillar? We are thinking it was done for political reasons, not revenge. We also think it is somehow connected to the Bernard murders." Mata Hari took a moment to think.

"What do you have so far?"

"We know there was a threatening note mailed to Pillar sent from L.A. We think the perpetrator does live in that area, as the note was done in an amateurish way and does not look like the work of a pro who covered their tracks. Is there anyone who lives in southern California who could be working with Louis Grenadine?"

"The actor? Why would he possibly have wanted to kill Pillar?"

"He is a major benefactor for Hayao Yamamoto's campaign. We have a phone conversation on tape between the two of them that Grenadine initiated where he offers to be a contributor in exchange for Hayao giving Grenadine's son a position in his administration if he wins." Grey's mind was spinning. He almost started asking Mata Hari a million questions but realized they were questions for other FBI agents, not the country's top spy.

"As always, I appreciate your assistance."

"Goodbye, Hoover."

CHAPTER 7

Wednesday, March 14th, 2pm

Director Grey wasted no time getting in touch with Billet and summoning him to Quantico. This demanded immediate attention. Billet arrived about 2pm; he had been working on another case about an hour away. Grey said, "I have some information for you. We have a person of interest, a name you know. Louis Grenadine."

"The actor?"

"Yes. Apparently he is going to be contributing a substantial amount of money to Hayao's campaign."

"What is he getting in return?"

"His son will get a job in Washington if Hayao wins."

"I am sure Grenadine is also stumping for Hayao. He knows tons of people in California; I wouldn't be shocked if Hayao uses him in a commercial."

"You're probably right. People are swayed when a celebrity endorses a certain candidate or cause; they can't see past the bright lights. We are going to pursue this on two fronts; finding out more about Grenadine, and delving back into the lives of those people connected with the Bernards, to see if we can find a link between the killings."

Billet groaned silently. Why does he keep coming back to that? "Yes, sir. I will do my best to conduct my investigation behind the scenes, to avoid both the press and Grenadine from getting wind of it."

"Excellent. I have to meet with President Harrington tomorrow and I will brief him on this new development. You might want to approach Sondra Tristan also and inquire whether her dad had any dealings with Grenadine."

"I will, but what I think is more likely is Grenadine thought his best chance of securing his son a position within the government was with Hayao, He probably believed he had the most to offer Hayao, rather than the other three candidates. Hayao needs the most help on the West Coast. Grenadine didn't want to take any chances that Hayao wouldn't be able to run, so he chose the justice he thought would rule against the Constitutional change and killed him. He has starred in movies with plenty of killings; this is awful to say, but he probably picked up some pointers over the years."

"Certainly worth looking into. Make sure you also poke around Layton and Russell, just to throw off the press. With regard to the other people connected to the Bernards, this adds a new thread to be followed. If you come up with any physical evidence, or even something circumstantial, from Pillar that points to any of the people suspected of having some involvement with the Bernard murders it would seem to be an open and shut case. Do you have enough agents at your disposal for all this?"

"I should, if not I will let you know. Alright. Let me plan out how I am going to divide my troops."

Thursday, March 15th

Director Grey was waiting to enter the Oval Office. The President liked to play that little game of making people wait. One time he kept Grey waiting for 90 minutes. He looked at his phone to check the time. It was 10:20 am. Grey went over to the assistant's desk. "Excuse me, but if this is not a good time for the President, I could come back."

"No, he wants to meet with you. Let me see if he will be much longer." She came right back and told Grey it will only be a few more minutes. Ten minutes later the President was ready. They shook hands and with a nod but no apology, he silently told Grey to begin. "Well, I have some interesting new developments to report regarding the Pillar case. We have some evidence that led us to someone in California. We have also learned Louis Grenadine is working with Hayao."

"You're implying Grenadine was involved, his motive being to help Hayao win the presidency? Why would he do it now, so early on in the race?"

"He saw Pillar picking up steam. If Pillar gained enough momentum, and Layton and Russell started to move up in the polls also, maybe Grenadine thought Hayao could be squeezed out of the race." President Harrington shook his head. He started to speak, then stopped. He took a minute to collect his thoughts.

"I don't know Mr. Grenadine but have seen some of his films. Look, you guys are the experts. I am not going to tell you how to do your job. Thank you for bringing me up to speed, James. Good day."

Eric Layton received a phone call from the director of FEMA.
"Hello, this is Ozzie Urbanski, from FEMA. I understand Colorado is having some hard times."
"That's correct."
"Well, we are here to help you. I will be sending you a financial package amounting to about 10 million dollars, which will allow you to reopen Buckley air force base. More people will be able to get their jobs back and hopefully that will have a trickle-down effect. How does that sound?"
"That's a great start, Ozzie, but we need more. We have to invest in job training programs and educate people about ways to better themselves. We also want more money pumped into our schools. Students are dropping out due to the fact that there are less and less options for those who don't want to or can't go to college. We need around 30 million dollars."
"That's a bit more than I was expecting. Oh boy. I might be able to come up with it but will need a little time. In the meantime, how about I forward the ten million to Colorado's coffers?"
"Great, thanks. How much time are we talking about?"
"It will take me a few weeks at least."
"Well, I am leaving for Europe on Saturday, and will return on March 26th. Do you think you could have an answer for me by the time I get back?"
"I am going to need a little longer than that."
"Perhaps the President could help speed things along."
Goddamnit, this guy was a pain in the ass! He was trying to do as much as possible now to look good to the voters. See what I did! What could Ozzie do? He didn't want to get on the wrong side of the President, but he would need his support to acquire that kind of money so quickly.

"Ok, Eric. Let me get in touch with President Harrington and explain the dire circumstances Colorado is facing. I am sure he will throw his weight behind it and you will see results."

"Thanks Ozzie. I appreciate everything you have done." Ozzie raised his middle finger at the phone as he hung up.

Billet was in his office, collecting his thoughts. He needed to split his team into two groups, the first for investigating Grenadine, and one to go back and revisit all the material accumulated regarding the people interviewed in the aftermath of the Bernard murders. Thirty agents now reported to him. He would try to come up with a good mix of those respected in the field and those better on analysis. He spent the next half hour making the assignments and when he was done he thought the teams looked fairly well balanced. Next, he wanted to come up with game plans for each group. His plan to find out more about Grenadine involved delving into his past, talking to his peers to find out more about his character, and also to track his whereabouts when Pillar was murdered. If evidence was recovered to link him to the murders of Pillar and his driver in any way, the FBI would pursue those crimes first and then look for the connection to the Bernards. As far as those individuals associated with the murders of the Bernards, they would have to be approached again for additional information. All of these tasks would be very difficult to do without it becoming public pretty much right away. There was a tactic available, one the government employed before; creating a diversion. If a bigger story came along, the media would shift its focus and Billet and his team could start working behind the scenes, or at least to a much lower profile. He would talk to the Director about that, who would in turn have to approach the President for some suggestions. It seemed underhanded, but it was necessary for the government to operate effectively with reporters and paparazzi running around everywhere. He would instruct his teams to begin carrying out the portion of their assignments which could be done without alerting the people involved and not perform any overt investigation until they heard back from Billet. He contacted all the agents and scheduled a mandatory meeting for

Monday, March 19th at 9am. That would give him time to meet again with the Director and explain his plan.

Abigail, the White House assistant whom Alex Ramirez contacted about filming the commercial, just received permission from Rebecca, the press secretary, for Hayao and Ramirez to go ahead and film. The best day to do it would be this Monday, March 19th, according to White House security. If possible, they should try to finish it in one day, as Tuesday there were going to be some logistical issues with the President's schedule that would make filming difficult. If they didn't finish on Monday, Rebecca would work with the security staff again to see when they could come back. Abigail was pleased she managed to pull this off; it would make her look good in the eyes of Hayao and Ramirez. She would call them right now. She hoped they would remember this when and if they won the election. Alex Ramirez answered on the second ring. Abby told her they received approval and Ramirez was very appreciative. Abby explained they needed to really try to complete all the footage they needed in one day, and Ramirez said they would do their best. She thanked Abby again and got off the phone to start making the arrangements to film on Monday.

Ozzie Urbanski, the head of FEMA, called President Harrington.
"Hello, sir. How are you today?"
"I am fine Ozzie. What can I do for you?"
"I spoke to Eric Layton, and I offered him ten million dollars to help reopen Fort Buckley. He graciously accepted but said that will not be enough. He is requesting FEMA supply him with 30 million dollars. I told him that would take some doing. In order to get such a large sum for Colorado, I need your help. I need you to submit an executive order for increased funds. If we go that route, we have a much better chance of succeeding."
"Alright. I will put my efforts into getting this done. Thank you, Ozzie, for making this happen so quickly. I am sure we will be speaking again soon."

Friday, March 16th

Billet had spoken with Director Grey late last night and they agreed to meet today at 11am. He went into Grey's office at 10:55 and found Grey ready to start. "So, Ed, what brings you back here so soon?"

"I wanted to discuss how we will keep a lid on our investigation. We need to maintain secrecy if at all possible so as not to tip anyone off. Perhaps we could create a diversion. It's been done before. What do you think?"

"I agree. I think we will have to. I will talk to the President about a way to achieve that. I am sure he will understand how important this is and come up with something. I will get in touch with you as soon as I have more information."

"Excellent. Thank you sir."

Director Grey called President Harrington. He hoped to do this over the phone and avoid another trip to the White House. The President was in a meeting and would call Grey back. When he did, Grey would let him know this had to be a confidential call to be kept only between the two of them. He knew the President would find a way to draw the public's attention away from this; he was a master at the sleight of hand.

President Harrington wrapped up his meeting and saw there was a message from Director Grey. "What does he want now?" The President went to take a leak and then stopped to chat with several of his staff before he went back to endure Grey. He sat down at his desk, sighed, and made the call. Grey answered immediately; no doubt he had been sitting by the phone.

"Hello, Mr. President. Thanks for getting back to me. We need to talk about our budget." That was the code they used to indicate the conversation needed to remain classified. President Harrington answered he would send a car for Grey in two hours to bring him to the White House. In reality, they would meet at Camp David where they would be afforded privacy. The car from the Presidential fleet came at 1pm and took him to the White House, where a helicopter whisked Grey off to Camp David. When he got off, he was escorted into the President's private office. "Hello sir."

"Hello again James. Let's get down to business. What is so urgent?"

"It's related to our investigation of Louis Grenadine for the murder of Juan Pillar. We need to conduct it as quietly as possible which will be very hard to do unless the public is preoccupied with something else."

"I see. The FBI needs a diversion. I think I can help with that. Being in politics gives you such experience. I have some ideas. Leave it to me, in two weeks you will have your diversion. I appreciate you coming all the way out here. Why don't we have some lunch?"

Saturday, March 17th

Eric Layton and Steven Morris met up at JFK airport in New York for their flight to Europe. Their original plan had been to set up a debate between Layton and Russell and then go to Europe, but Pillar's death changed their plans, and both of them felt it would serve them well to go now and beat Hayao to the punch. They would be there for ten days, meeting with the Pope in Madrid where he would be for a conference right before they returned to the States. Before that they would tour Italy, France, and England and meet with the Presidents in each country, which would also help with foreign relations after they won in November. They knew better than to venture into Russia, as Russell and Weimitz monopolized the connections there. If they received the Pope's blessing, then many of the countries would get behind them, which would generate votes from many of the Catholics back home. Layton also wanted to see what the Pope would want in return for his endorsement as he was known to be an opportunist. They tried to keep their departure information quiet but were spotted at the airport and now were being hounded. They just kept their heads down and went into the VIP lounge available for those passengers flying business class. They both took deep breaths, found a quiet corner to talk quietly about their itinerary, and what they hoped to accomplish. Morris said, "Our message should be one of inclusion, where we will continue to make the environment for businesses much more attractive. We will also try to incorporate the interests of other governments around the world into our decision and policy making processes, as long as they don't interfere with our national security. It's a fine line but I think we can walk it. I think we have a chance to win Spain's support, despite the fact that Alex Ramirez is a Vice Presidential candidate. There are many Catholics in Spain, and many of the U.S. citizens who come from Spain are Catholic too." Layton agreed with just about everything Morris was saying and was impressed. He seemed to have a really good handle on geo-political issues. Layton needed the exposure. He and Morris did not have the name recognition globally that the other candidates did, so he needed these trips to display his superior interpersonal skills. He expected to come back home to great fanfare, especially after meeting with the Pope next weekend.

   President Harrington included two things on his agenda for today that he definitely had to accomplish. The first was a call to the head of the Senate Budgetary committee and the second the development of a plan for a news story designed to draw attention away from the Pillar case. First things first, he was hungry and wanted breakfast. He dialed his personal chef and requested one of his favorite meals, lobster bisque and salmon eggs benedict. While he waited he read the news online and once he finished eating he was ready to get started. He called Wally Cooper, head of the budgetary committee. "Hello Wally. It's been awhile. How are things?"
"Just fine sir, and you?"
"Excellent. Wally, I want to talk to you about appropriating some money from the Federal budget to the FEMA fund. You see, there is a lot of unrest in Colorado and they need money right away. We have given them some money from FEMA but it has not been enough. I am requesting you to enter an item in the budget for the State of Colorado to receive more federal aid."
"How much are you talking about, sir?"
"Twenty million dollars." Wally saw what was happening. Eric Layton had called the President and asked for money due to all the problems in his state that started when Fort Buckley closed. Since he was running for President, he wanted to look like a knight on a

horse riding in to save the day, and President Harrington wanted to ingratiate himself with all the candidates so he would be covered regardless of who won. Wally always liked the President, but he sure was an opportunist.

"Alright, sir. I will assemble the committee for an emergency session and see what I can do. I will set something up for Monday and call you back afterwards."

"Thank you Wally." Alright, on to task # 2. He had eased the regulations for immigration with the rationale being that more workers were needed for all the ongoing infrastructure projects. He would have conversations with industry leaders and top ranking government officials at countries affiliated in some way with the candidates for President and Vice President. His message would be to start encouraging people to emigrate to the U.S. Numbers were already up and people were already starting to question the trend. If the trend continued, it would certainly become a news story. He would be prepared to answer any questions. There would be a good cross section of people coming from different countries so there would not be any appearance of bias. This diversion was also part of a bigger master plan. Once all these additional immigrants arrived, the President planned to make them eligible to vote. They were here legally, doing work to help the country, why shouldn't they be afforded this right? There may be some opposition, but ultimately it would be approved. No matter who won, he would come out smelling like a rose. He had done something out in the open for each one of the candidates and would be paid back in kind. Once people started coming in droves, the media would largely forget about Juan Pillar.

Sunday, March 18th

Todd Russell was working at his desk when Joe Berry called him. "I have been finalizing the plans for Canada, Governor. We are going to have a very full schedule, with stops in each of the cities we will visit, and I have also incorporated a good mix of talk shows at each location. Weimitz will be giving a few lectures about technology, and of course we will be doing a lot of hand shaking." "Good work, Joe. We are on the same page about being as visible as possible. What separates us from the other running mates is the contrast in our backgrounds; we are not two people with the same past. That will give us a much broader voting base. We have to remember that whenever we are meeting with the public and highlight it. You have been doing a great job, Joe. Here is what I would like you to accomplish this week before we go away. Conduct polls in all the major regions of the country, namely the Northeast, Southeast, Midwest, Southwest, and Northwest. See how our numbers are, and in those regions where we are behind, delve into it more deeply and find out what we could be doing differently. I would like to have this information prior to our trip so we will be able to plan a strategy while we are together."

"Ok, sir. I will report back to you with the results."

Monday, March 19th

Ed Billet was going to see Sondra Tristan about whether she knew of any connection between her father and Juan Pillar. He would mention the fact that they were looking into Louis Grenadine, but only if she asked first. She agreed to meet at the ACLU offices where she reserved a conference room for an hour. He went to her cubicle and she gave him a nice greeting. They entered the conference room and after asking each other how they had been, got down to the matter at hand. "Sondra, I am sure you can surmise why I am here. I am looking for any information available about Juan Pillar's murder. Are you aware of any connection between him and your father?"

"No, I am really not. They may have crossed paths as prominent Washington figures, but my dad never mentioned him, except to say he believed he would be a Presidential candidate if the measure for foreigners to run passed. Obviously you believe the crimes are related."

"I do."

"What makes you think that?"

"I think both were politically motivated, due to the timing. Whoever did this had, and has, a certain agenda."

"You can trust me to keep this confidence, agent Billet. Is there anyone you are looking at as a person of interest?"

"As a matter of fact, yes. Louis Grenadine." A look of bewilderment came over Tristan's face.

"The actor? What could he possibly have to gain from all this?"

"I am only telling you this because I know you won't tell anyone, not even Blake. Grenadine is working with Hayao as a behind the scenes benefactor and will probably publicly endorse him at some point."

"Alright, but why would he have wanted my father dead?"

"We are not sure yet. We are just starting to look into him as a suspect. As more information becomes available, I will keep you posted. Also, please leave this to us. Please don't begin making inquiries of your father's colleagues to see if they know anything. That would just create problems, and I can assure you we will cover all the bases."

"Agreed. Thank you for coming here and keeping me abreast of what is happening."

"Of course, Sondra. Take care of yourself and I will be in touch."

Hayao and Alex were sitting in their cars waiting for the film crew to arrive. The director was on site as well and they had reviewed the script. Hayao would speak first, Ramirez would speak next, and then there would be a portion when they would speak together. The film crew arrived, and an hour later they were all set to go. The director suggested they stand with their backs to the front entrance of the White House and then try different camera shots. They wanted to create a classic feel, one intended to send the message of tradition and history. That image would be contrasted beautifully with both of them being born in other countries, and would demonstrate they were ready and able to lead the country into the next era, one which would usher in a new era of global political cooperation. That was what they intended to project; the U.S. was on the verge of new frontiers. They did take after take, and when they finished at 8pm, it was dark, and they amassed 10 hours of footage. The next step would be to edit all the footage and then meet with the director again to look at a rough copy of the commercial. Once that was completed, the final edit would be done and then it would be ready to be distributed to the networks. They hoped it would be on the air in three weeks. After that, Hayao and Ramirez would be heading to Mexico, where they expected to be greeted with open arms. They would also go to Europe, for they hoped to win some support in Spain, if not the other countries. Hayao hoped this advertisement would help to restore his image in this country. He could count on those people of Oriental descent not born here, for they would support him blindly because he was Oriental as well. The younger Orientals as the natural born U.S. citizens would be most critical. They would think he should have known better than to make such a major slip up, and would even go so far as to publicly endorse one of the other candidates. That was a trait drilled into them by the education system; people need to assimilate and become well versed in the customs and social mores of the society in which one lives. Hayao has been here for twenty years, they would say. He should have been aware that calling this country inferior was just not acceptable and they would not let it go. He had to work really hard to gain their favor again and that is what he was willing to do.

   Tuesday, March 20th

   Layton and Morris were having a great time. They had started in England, meeting with top government officials and attending a function at Buckingham Palace. They met with the British Prime Minister, Harry Edmunds while at the function, and he was very receptive to them. He did not come right out and say he would back them, but he said he agreed with their positions on the major issues. They were staying in a lovely hotel in London, and tomorrow were heading on to Paris. Morris had never been out of the country before and was loving it. He managed to do a little sightseeing yesterday for three hours, visiting the tower of London and Westminster Abbey. Today they would be out meeting people and shaking hands around downtown London. England was super; one thing they would change, however, would be the food. It wasn't bad, but many of their traditional dishes tasted bland and included limited offerings. As far as being a cosmopolitan city however, London even rivaled New York with way more history, which is something Morris enjoyed. He put it on his list of places to visit when he had more time. Layton obviously was also impressed with London although he had been here before. They were at their hotel right now, planning their schedule for when they arrived in France. They would be staying in Paris the entire time, and arranged to be interviewed on the most popular talk show in France, the Hard Edge. They would be there until Saturday, go to Italy for a day and a half where they would meet with Ciarro Dispoti, the Italian Prime Minister. On Sunday night they would cruise to Barcelona to spend some time with the Pope before heading home. They didn't feel it necessary to stay in either Italy or Spain longer than that, as once they secured the Pope's backing, Italy would be theirs too and Spain was a lost cause as they would fall in line with Ramirez. Layton was really glad he pushed Morris to be his running mate as he was the reason the Pope would give them his endorsement.

In Japan, there was a meeting going on that included the President and top officials from the foreign ministry. They were discussing the directive from President Michael Harrington about how he said it would be beneficial for more people to emigrate to the United States starting right away to increase the number of voters for the next Presidential election. Harrington had made it clear he would be able to justify the influx of people and the American public would accept it after an initial period of skepticism. There would be similar discussions in other countries in Europe, based on the information from the U.S. The governments all wanted to start getting the word out to their people that there were jobs available in the United States. The key to this plan, however, was that citizens of these countries had to come in a little bit at a time, with President Harrington being the quarterback. He would regulate who came in and when. Timing would be key, for if too many came all at once, there would be a logjam and supply would exceed the demand for jobs. This had to be coordinated with the new capital projects on the horizon. Obviously the biggest one was the maintenance and expansion of the national irrigation system, which was just starting to make its way into New York and New Jersey, where there had not been water issues. The system was an amazing engineering feat with pipes crisscrossing the continental United States drawing water from way out in the Pacific Ocean and then running through an enormous desalination plant in northern California, which disseminated water to all the states across the country. The plant was state of the art, with offshoot pipes that could be opened and closed with the push of a button that carried water to each state's original water source before such a shortage developed. Each major water source now contained sensors to indicate its capacity and what percent of its capacity it contained. If it fell below 70 percent water was automatically added. The system originated on the west coast and been built out, first going to the southwest into Arizona and Nevada, extending north into Oregon and Washington state, and then creeping eastward toward the Midwest, slowly being integrated into all the water sources one by one. Texas was next, as they were really suffering, and after that the southeast, including Florida and Georgia. Now the project was making its way north from Georgia, and east from the Midwestern states. The northeast would be the last section of the country to be done and the pipes would be connected on the other end to the Atlantic Ocean, with plans for another desalination plant in Delaware about two miles inland from the ocean. The entire project had cost about 20 billion dollars, with a good portion coming from private funding, and with many people donating their time as volunteers. More labor was needed now, however, as some of the equipment installed initially needed to be replaced and more people would be needed to help build and then man the power plant coming to Delaware. This was not the only project in the works, however. In the last ten years, much progress occurred in the field of turning waste into usable energy and methods discovered of turning even the most toxic chemicals into forms that could be recycled over and over again. These new technologies created an emerging new industry and would need a lot more labor in the years to come. In addition, primary education had undergone much change recently as well, with teaching once again becoming more prestigious as it was about 100 years ago.

Americans realized that as a nation, they could no longer afford for their young people to fall further behind, so a revolution of sorts took place. Many of the regulations imposed by state governments for standardized testing were done away with and instead teachers managed to get back to basics. Colleges placed more emphasis on knowledge again rather than on performance, and re-implemented a bunch of entrance exams designed to find out where the potential students' interests lie in addition to simply testing intellect. These three areas were what President Harrington needed to keep pace with in terms of allowing immigrants in and not grossly exceeding the demand. This would be harder than it sounded, since he also had to take into consideration the many different countries included in this rotation so it would appear there was no impropriety going on, as well as the changing vacancies from one month to the next. That had been explained to all the top officials the President contacted and they in turn had to make it clear that the process could not get out of hand to all of their staff at the foreign ministries to maintain an even flow into the U.S. They had to adhere to the changing quotas handed down continuously from the heads of state, who in turn would receive them from President Harrington. He kept in close contact with the people in charge of the capital projects, as well as the Secretary of Education. He knew the labor requirements at all times and could pass that information on accordingly. That was what they were talking about in Japan and elsewhere; how the process worked and what everyone's role was. The people involved also were shrewd enough not to ask too many questions.

Wednesday, March 21st

Billet received a report back from the half of the team investigating Grenadine. They found that he visited Washington D.C. at the time Pillar died. He attended a Screen Actors Guild convention; being the President he couldn't really miss it. The FBI agents found this out by checking with the airlines. They already knew Grenadine lived in Beverly Hills with access to the mailbox from which the letter to Pillar was mailed. He stayed at a posh hotel in D.C., and even though he didn't rent a car while in town, he could have easily collaborated with another person to commit the murders. The agents were poring over his bank accounts right now. Even if they didn't find a smoking gun, however, Grenadine commanded enough star power to have coerced someone to do this dastardly act for him for no money; who knows what he might have promised. Groupies were fanatical; some of them would do anything. The FBI managed to establish motive and opportunity, but they possessed no physical evidence. Yet. The second half of the team had not gotten back to Billet with any information. He hadn't really expected them to; they were retracing their steps but this time with the added caveat of trying to find a link to Grenadine. The next thing he wanted his agents to do was to look into Grenadine's background by talking to his family, friends, neighbors, coworkers in the industry, and acquaintances to see what kind of man he was and if he would really be capable of something like this. That included gathering information about whether anyone he associated with felt so enamored of him that they would become involved in such a serious crime. This had to wait, however, until they confirmed the President concocted a scheme that would preoccupy the press, and there were no indications in the news this had taken place yet.

    Hayao and Alex Ramirez were on their way to the studio in D.C. being used by the director of their commercial to edit the footage they assembled. He said over the phone that he managed to pare it down to 4 hours, and they needed to look at all the takes to see which one they liked best. They could mix and match and splice the best takes together. It helped that both Hayao and Ramirez knew what they were looking for; still, it was an exhausting task and Hayao had a new respect for people who did this on a regular basis by the time they were done. They agreed on what to use, however, and they would come back on Saturday to see the finished product. After that it would be distributed to all the major networks. That reminded Hayao he needed to get in touch with Natsu and tell him how much all this was costing so he could replenish the campaign funds set aside for this. They also started planning their trip to Mexico, probably in April. Moritu

Corporation was doing well, so fortunately he didn't have to turn his attention there. He was still working on his political rhetoric which Alex believed had improved quite a bit. He tried to learn to answer the question he wanted to answer rather than the one asked and to do it in such a way that the people listening wouldn't even notice the transition. They both agreed however, not to initiate another debate until the fall, and to avoid agreeing to one if one of the other candidates suggested it, unless they were backed into a corner and had no choice.

Thursday, March 22nd

Joe Berry had been working around the clock trying to conduct and organize the polls Todd Russell requested. He was grateful Russell placed a good portion of his staff at Berry's disposal. He dispatched people all over the country to gather the information while he stayed in Washington to act as the command center. Everyone was doing a fine job so far, both in getting the data and making it available to Berry. Russell's best showing was out west, largely due to Weimitz. The west coast contained a large population of people interested in science and to them, Weimitz was a God. Hayao ran a close second and surprisingly showed much popularity with people in the entertainment industry. Berry had a sixth sense Hayao and his team were up to something. Why would he have such an advantage in that demographic? Well, no sense trying to analyze that now. Russell wanted to have a conference over the phone later today and Berry still had work to do to prepare for that. Russell led in the northeast as well, thanks to Weimitz, as they liked to stay on the cutting edge of what was happening in the world. The Midwest was split between Layton and Russell as expected, as they were more conservative and the south overwhelmingly supported Hayao because he shared the ticket with Ramirez. Berry also wanted to break down the numbers by gender, race, religion, age, and ethnicity. Russell would also want recommendations about what to do to change things, so Berry tried to come up with some strategies on how to get more into the game. He had some ideas. Russell needed to ingratiate himself more with certain demographics, such as married people who viewed him as an outsider because he was single. He also must make more of an effort with the elderly, a group who did not support him due to the fact that many of his political views tended to coincide more with the younger generation. He would have to start visiting places that older adults frequented and addressing concerns important to them, such as health insurance and pension/retirement reform. Berry looked at his watch. It was 4 pm and he would be speaking with Russell at 7 pm. He felt good that he thought of some concrete ideas and suggestions about what Russell should do.

Friday, March 23rd

Eric Layton was handling himself wonderfully with the French, who could be a difficult bunch to win over. He employed a self-deprecating sense of humor which they found endearing. The United States has been good to France over the years and it stands to reason they would favor a ticket with two Americans on it. Paris was everything it was supposed to be; Layton had to bring Cindy here one day, it would knock her socks off. It was love in bloom here. He and Morris met with the French President and that had been a huge success; he all but guaranteed they would get his endorsement. That was nice, but it wasn't such a big thing. Having France in their corner wouldn't do so much for them at election time, as there were not nearly as many people with French backgrounds in the U.S. as other nationalities. The real benefit would come when they won the election and they could count on a friendly government to help further their agenda. What were they offering in return? That was what every government wanted to know of course. For one thing, they would continue the infrastructure work President Harrington began and would be looking for foreign workers to lend a hand. They also planned to expand the education initiatives to include strategies currently being employed by other countries proven to be most effective, such as having a more specialized education at a younger age and tailoring each student's experience according to their individual strengths. They would also include a push about science and technology, although they wouldn't stress that too much since they couldn't compete with Weimitz in that arena and they didn't want to look like amateurs. They would be meeting with other officials today, but they felt all the heavy lifting in France was done. They would have time for a little more sightseeing today, but had to keep in mind their every move would be publicized, which meant they couldn't do anything off color or wild. They would visit the Louvre and have dinner in the hotel restaurant. Tomorrow they were headed to Italy where they were sure to find support as well, considering it was widely believed they would receive the Pope's support. Their time in Italy would not be too intense either with time set aside for leisure activities there as well including of course the Vatican. They would be given a private tour at the Pope's request, as well as a guided tour of the city of Rome by Ciarro Dispoti. When Layton got back to the States, he owed a big thank you to Patrick Manucci for using his connections to help raise the money to pay for all this.

President Harrington had gotten some statistics back from the various departments and was ready to start the immigration process. He would set the events in motion to have Japan and other countries from the Far East start first, each sending 500 people early next week. The next people to emigrate would be from countries in the Middle East so as not to create a pattern. The media would undoubtedly catch on, report it in the news, and it would become the top story. The FBI would then be free to start investigating Grenadine freely without having to worry about being scrutinized. He also heard the Senate budgetary committee planned an emergency session tomorrow to discuss a request by Wally Cooper. He knew Wally would come through because he was well respected among his peers and tenacious when he wanted something and coming through on this would be to his benefit to ingratiate himself with both the President and Eric Layton. President Harrington would make sure one of his aides stayed around to report on their progress. He hoped to be able to let Eric Layton know the money had been appropriated when he came back to the U.S. on Monday.

Saturday, March 24th

Todd Russell, Vincent Weimitz, and Joe Berry all arrived in Montreal within an hour of each other to start their Canadian tour. Their goal was to win over the Canadian public, and unlike other campaign stops around the world, winning the government's endorsement, while important, was secondary to getting the people's approval as they were so closely intertwined with the U.S. That was why Berry arranged for Russell to be interviewed on tv, to make him seem accessible. They would be attending public functions and visiting workplaces and schools while there. They would be meeting with elderly citizens as well and demonstrating their commitment to change. Russell recognized all the work Berry put into the polls conducted last week and really seemed to be ready to work on the things that needed his attention. The first thing on their schedule in Montreal would be a walking tour of Old Montreal tomorrow. Tomorrow night Russell would be appearing on a webcast where people all over Canada called in and ask him questions, and on Monday he would hold a town hall meeting hosted by the mayor of Montreal. They were renting a tour bus for part of their stay and decided to make a stop in Ottawa as well, although that had not been part of their original plan, but they would be so close it wouldn't be prudent to do otherwise. They would be meeting with the Canadian Prime Minister, who agreed to arrange for two factory visits for them. Today they were visiting a senior center in Bossard, a suburb. They would spend three days in each of the east coast cities and then fly to Vancouver for three more days before returning home. Russell called Berry's room and asked him to come to Russell's suite for a strategy session. One thing they wanted to cover was the issue of how Canada handled the war on prescription drugs and kept them under control. That topic remained a problem in the United States. Doctors were much too quick to prescribe painkillers for ailments unnecessarily and it led to those people becoming addicted and then graduating to more powerful illegal drugs such as heroin, which basically took over your life once you tried them even once. Canada had tightened their laws regarding medical regulations, which was easier to do because their health care system was designed to make medications more accessible to people of all economic means, a change the U.S. adapted about twenty five years ago. Unlike Canada however, the hybrid plan in the U.S. still allowed doctors to operate without as many checks and balances, and therefore permitted more abuses which made those prescription drugs more readily available. The trick was to get people to understand the symptoms they suffered with did not require such powerful medications, but American society became one of such instant gratification that the only way to get people to change was through legislation which gave them no choice. Russell had been one of the few proponents of following this course; other politicians believed this stance would make it more difficult for them to be elected and reelected. He hoped Berry would be able to come up with a way to appeal to both sides of the aisle, those who wanted change and those who wanted to continue to give physicians more discretion. Honestly, there were merits to both. Socialized medicine was not without its problems with frequent long waits to see a doctor. On the other hand, the ills of a society with instant gratification were apparent also. There needed to be a balance. Personally, he thought state run medical care was not the answer, but rather elements of government assistance interspersed within a system mostly fueled by the private sector, so as not to place too much stress on the economy. The countries with the most efficient healthcare systems used this model, and it seemed to work better than any other combination. There was a safety net and yet people had to rely upon themselves to finance the majority of their medical care. Costs were lower because doctors were required to accept patients regardless of their ability to pay, and those who couldn't receive subsidies from the state's public funds. It wasn't perfect, but overall it seemed to work better than anything else. If anyone could put a spin on the issue that would encompass all of these factors, it would be Berry.

   The Senate Budgetary committee was in full swing and Wally Cooper once again seemed to be proving himself to be a capable ringmaster. He had begun the meeting with an overview of how there were certain sections of the country really hurting and tried to make it personal by mentioning all of our brothers and sisters in the armed forces who came back to this country only to be treated like second class citizens after risking their lives to protect our freedoms. He then segued into discussing Fort Collins and how so many people lost their jobs, and from there brought up Colorado's plight. He was so skilled at describing the sorrow that the committee would have been ready to allocate three times what he would be requesting. Sure, a few members were skeptical about the motives here, but even they knew better than to make waves. It was clear the President was behind this and he would be very powerful even from beyond the White House, so they decided to be a silent minority and emerge with their futures intact. The measure passed easily, and as soon as the meeting ended President Harrington's aide got in touch with him to tell him the good news. The President called Ozzie Urbanski personally and told him the money would be on its way. His next task was at hand now also and that involved letting the authorities in Japan know they could start sending people to emigrate, and he would suggest they start on Monday. He would cap it at 500 for now and then continue with the Middle East, and more specifically some of the Muslim countries. He would single out Israel in the next round to keep the balance. Director Grey would recognize all the media attention and understand the President's plan had begun.

4pm, FBI headquarters, Quantico, VA

Half of Ed Billet's team was having a meeting amongst themselves to compare notes and make sure they didn't go over the same ground unnecessarily. Mike, the senior agent in the room, spoke first. "First, let's run down the list of the Supreme Court justices to confirm we have interviewed them all again and inquired about any connection between Justice Bernard and Pillar." The agents didn't know anything about Grenadine. When they finished, Mike asked if any of the judges remembered a connection, but none of them had other than the fact they both moved in powerful circles. He knew Billet spoke to Sondra Tristan and received the same answer. They had not exhausted all the resources yet, however. They would go back and meet with all the other people who dealt with either Bernard or Pillar to see if any connections came to the surface. If nothing did, then they would interrogate the suspects again and delve back into their pasts to see if this new wrinkle with Pillar would shake anything loose. At this point that remained their best approach.

Sunday, March 25th

Layton and Morris travelled all over Rome, stopping at Tivoli Gardens, and enjoying some of the best food they ever tasted. Their tour guide had been Prime Minister Dispoti and naturally the entire day proceeded seamlessly. Today they were going to the Vatican for a private tour led by people on the Pope's staff. It would be a perfect lead in to meeting with the Pope himself tonight. They would have much to talk about and they would have the opportunity to express their gratitude for the arrangements made. They both believed they had captured Italy politically between their good relationship with Dispoti and the expected endorsement from the Pope and expected the support of the Italians back in the States who voted based on nationality. All in all, they would both rate the trip as being a huge success. They were taking a boat to Barcelona, opting for a change of scenery instead of a plane. It was a yacht generously offered by its owner, a rich Italian communications magnate. Layton and Morris were travelling in style. They had just finished eating a gourmet meal and found comfort in their cabins. The captain was a skilled sailor who got them to Spain ahead of schedule. They used the same route the cruise ships used between Barcelona and Civitavecchia, the port closest to Rome. They also had a much easier time getting cleared to enter the country as they were with someone who did it before. Once they entered Spain, a man who represented the Pope greeted them. "Welcome to Spain", he said with a thick European accent. "The Pope will be available to meet with you shortly. Our driver will take you to the mayor's office where the Pope is waiting for you." With that, they were shepherded into the car and whisked away.

The head of the immigration department in Japan was busy at work. He received the order to contact the first 500 people who applied for and been denied permission to emigrate to the United States; the list was much longer than that, and for those who no longer wished to leave, their names would be eliminated and he would keep working down the list until 500 had been reached. He also received instructions to give preference to adults only, not families. He assumed people were needed to work, so children were not desirable right now. He wound up staying in his office all day; because it was Sunday, many people were not home, so by the time he managed to come up with 500 adults willing and ready to leave, it was already nighttime.

Layton and Morris arrived at the mayor of Barcelona's office at 7pm, which had been graciously turned over to the Pope while he stayed in town. His Excellency was ready to receive them when they arrived and they were both very excited. They walked up to him and shook hands. He motioned for them to sit, and they expressed how much they appreciated the time he afforded them. He was glad they enjoyed Rome so much and the three of them discussed all the sights there were to see. The conversation turned serious when the Pope brought up Juan Pillar. "What a tragedy. He was such a role model to so many, a man who rose above his background to become a success, and was a credit to his heritage." Layton and Morris nodded their heads in silent assent. The Pope continued. "His death has changed the Presidential race in your country. It is not a secret I was going to endorse him, as a Catholic and as a fine leader." The Pope looked wistfully out the window, as if he recalled a lost opportunity. "So, what brings you here so we could meet?" Wow, he was a fantastic politician. The way he brought the conversation around to the reason why they were here was masterful, so smooth it was practically transparent.

"Actually, father, we do have some business to discuss", said Layton. The Pope had also opened the door for his endorsement request by mentioning Pillar. "We would like to ask for your support in the election that you mentioned a few minutes ago." The Pope stroked his chin. They all knew this was one giant game.

"The Pope doesn't typically get involved with specific candidates, gentlemen. There has to be a real special case."

"With all due respect, your Eminence, you did it for Pillar."

"Those were special circumstances. History is being made here. What is your proposal?"

Morris decided to explain. "I am a Catholic, your Excellence. Your support would go a long way for us."

"I do believe religion has a part in politics. The United States will be more of a melting pot than ever before, and will need some type of structure to help people make sense of things. Here is my arrangement. If I publicly back you both in your bid for the White House, in return I want Catholicism as the official religion." Layton pretended to think for a minute. He expected this would come up; the Pope was tenacious when it came to furthering his cause. Some of the Popes that preceded him were not so dogged in their quest, but he wanted to make the entire world practicing Catholics. He realized, however, he had no choice but to agree to it. Layton was much more slippery than Pillar and would try to find a way out when and if he became President. That's why the Pope took the extra steps of having the mayor's office wired for audio and video, so if it came to it, the Pope would find a way to leak it to the media. Layton had a plan, he could always say Congress opposed the idea and blame them for its demise. There were many ways to keep it from ever coming to fruition. That's why it was safe to agree to it now.

"Ok, holy father. I agree to your terms. I will introduce legislation to have a state sponsored religion."

"Excellent, Eric. You have my support." It was clear Layton would try to find a way out of it, as when Pillar had this conversation, he tried to explain the roadblocks he would encounter. Layton just went along with it, as if he expected this and had a strategy already in place. Looks like the Pope might need to use the recording at some point after all. The Pope then explained he would make his endorsement public tomorrow, and people aware of Layton and Morris's itinerary would not be surprised. All parties involved were happy, as they were all getting what they came to get. Layton was pleased he would go home on such a high note, not knowing he also had won the fight for the extra money from FEMA.

Monday, March 26th

People who worked at the customs offices at major airports around the country noticed something out of the ordinary. On a typical day, only about 4 to 5 people were processed to legally enter the U.S. Today there were about 15 and all were Asian. Well, one day could be an aberration. If this happened again tomorrow, it would constitute a pattern and would require further attention. Each airport had their own processing center, as well as the ones at the ports around the country, Boston, New York, Baltimore, and Miami on the East coast, Portland Oregon and San Diego on the West coast, Honolulu in Hawaii and Anchorage in Alaska. These were the only options except for those coming from Canada or Mexico, with people from those countries coming through Buffalo or Seattle, and Tucson, Arizona. The head of INS noticed this information at the end of the day and realized something was up, but was forced to wait one more day to see if this repeated itself. There were protocols in place to be followed and the people who emigrated today had all been pre-approved by the State Department. That meant someone high up had a specific reason for this, and depending upon what happened tomorrow, it was INS's obligation to find out why.

Layton and Morris had just arrived home after deciding to take the red eye on a specially chartered flight. They wanted to get back to work and managed to get some rest on the flight home. They landed in New York and then parted ways, with Morris taking the train back to Long Island and Layton taking a second flight to Washington. He longed to go to Colorado for a few days to see his family but that was not in the cards right now. He stopped at his apartment to freshen up and then went right into work. When he arrived, his aide was beaming. Layton knew something good had happened. "We were awarded the extra money from FEMA, sir. Ozzie Urbanski called as soon as he heard. We should be getting the funds in the next few weeks and then we can continue the rebuilding process."

"Fantastic. How were things while I was away? Any other major developments?"

"Well, everyone knows about the Pope's endorsement. That's the big news around here. How was the rest of your trip?" Layton could tell he was jealous.

"It was good, thanks. Have you ever been to Europe?" The aide shook his head no. "You definitely should go. Consider it as broadening your horizons, especially now with our changing political landscape. How do you think we should handle the news about the FEMA money?"

"I think you should reach out to the Governor and arrange a joint news conference. It will work to our advantage as the public will see the two of you working together when your views on the issues haven't always been in sync." That was actually a good idea.

"Alright, let's do it. Can you set it up please? Arrange it with the Governor's office and make it for Friday. We can leave for Colorado on Thursday later in the day and come back to DC on Monday morning. Also, please conduct some polls now to see what our public image is and then again next week after our announcement on Friday." This was perfect. Layton would come out looking like a hero as the person who will help get his state back on track, and he would get to spend the weekend with his family.

Hayao and Ramirez saw the commercial after the director completed all the editing, and they both thought it came out great. It was set to air this coming Sunday during the 8pm tv shows, first on ABC, then NBC, and finally CBS, during the first, second, and third commercial breaks. It would also be shown on all the leading internet streaming movie and tv websites, which reached people all over the world, and while it would be broadcast in English, it would appear with subtitles in whatever language that corresponded to the country in which it was being shown. Now, Hayao, who was back in Detroit had to get in touch with Natsu. He called him right now on Natsu's private number. "Hello Hayao," Natsu answered after the third ring. "How are things going?" Hayao was surprised; Natsu never acted this relaxed.

"I am fine. We just finished reviewing the commercial which Alex and I filmed, and it came out very well. It will be shown all over the world starting this Sunday. It sends a universal message of inclusion and tolerance that will resonate everywhere."

"Excellent. What else?" Natsu had his sixth sense going. "We are running low on funds, Natsu. The commercial we filmed was expensive, and we have travel plans coming up. We need a cash infusion."

"How much?"

"Ten million dollars for now. I can't promise we will not need more in the future."

"Of course." Hayao had to say Natsu was very liberal with Moritu's funds. "We need to run a competitive campaign which can't be done on a shoestring budget."

Tuesday, March 27th

Todd Russell and his entourage were now in Ottawa and while not everything ran so smoothly in Montreal, they still felt good and optimistic about the rest of their trip. They encountered some protesters in Montreal who had gotten in Russell's face, screamed obscenities at him and accused him of turning his back on the elderly and the infirm and that he wanted to take away programs which have been benefitting those groups for years under the guise they were too expensive. On the other hand, he came across very well in his interview and other public appearances, so he wasn't too worried about that incident and might even end up playing to his advantage with the sympathy factor. In Ottawa, he would be visiting a homeless shelter and a boys and girls club. He would be meeting with the Prime Minister and lastly, having a conference with some top political analysts. Berry knew the experts in the perceptions of politicians in other countries. They possessed an extensive web of correspondents in countries all over the world who would provide feedback about the happenings in those countries. This was a fairly new concept and one critical to winning the election. In the meantime, Weimitz focused on what he knew best, attending gatherings and functions involving science and technology, promoting the idea that Russell's administration would be progressive in their approach to global technological advancement. It was better to keep him occupied at those tasks, because while he was a brilliant man, he wasn't always the best at interpersonal relations and fared much better in situations where there weren't any unexpected interactions.

New York, 7pm

The head of INS, Mark Desmond, reviewed the numbers from today and wasn't surprised. They were similar to yesterday, with an influx of Japanese. Two days constituted a trend, and Desmond was suspicious about coincidences. He called the Secretary of State, Susan McBride and was told she was in a meeting and would get back to him. He cultivated contacts in other countries as well, people with comparable positions to him, but many times they enjoyed no real authority. Japan was one of those countries. Desmond understood they were a democratic nation, but decisions like this were handed down from above, just like in this country. If Desmond wanted any real answers, he would have to go to the top of the food chain here, and even then he would have to make some inferences. He was tired; who knew when Susan would be free. He decided to go home and resume this tomorrow.

Wednesday, March 28th

Uncle George and Kangaroo met at their usual spot and knew about Louis Grenadine. This time, they each anticipated what the other would say. Kangaroo would want to pull the agents in South America back right away, and Uncle George would agree, but he would also want to keep them close, just in case the information about Grenadine turned out to be a false lead. He would then want them to go back and resume collecting the intelligence on which they had been working. Uncle George wanted Kangaroo to take the lead on following what was happening with Grenadine, as well as continuing to monitor the activity surrounding immigration patterns. It would be easier for the NSA to infiltrate other governments as they were experts at protocols and customs around the world. They would not have to meet every week anymore; once a month would suffice. Kangaroo was glad about this as tax season was almost over and he would have more time to conduct his operation and not have to worry about producing status reports for Uncle George constantly.

Secretary of State Susan McBride was doodling, which she did when she was deep in thought about something. She needed to call Mark Desmond, as he was tenacious and would take it to the next level to get information. She had to tell him something, enough so that he would accept the explanation, and yet not too much for him to dig further. Of course, President Harrington managed to supply reasons as to why there had been such a sharp rise. It was a transparent ploy, but the one thing senior Administration officials wanted to avoid was people nosing around in the affairs of the countries with which these arrangements were being made. Alright, she was ready She dialed the number of his private line and Desmond answered on the second ring. They exchanged pleasantries and then Desmond asked her if she researched the trend in immigration over the past two days. She answered that she had and went on to say there were some labor intensive capital projects going on and the people from Japan had been waiting to enter the U.S. for a long time and they were next on the list. They acquired the skills necessary for the projects going on and the U.S. followed protocol by adhering to the rotation set up a few years back by President Harrington. Desmond asked why these jobs weren't being offered to Americans. McBride explained there were quotas; foreign workers had certain slots that needed to be filled. McBride went on to explain, as Desmond knew, there was much more reciprocity among foreign countries now and sometimes that superseded providing opportunities to citizens born here. He wanted to know who authorized this and she thought better than saying she wasn't sure, for if she was aware about this then people above her were as well. "President Harrington, Mark. He has to look at the big picture. This new arrangement is a factor in the global economy."

"What about our citizens going abroad to find work? Has any of that been going on?" He knew the answer; not nearly as much as people coming to the U.S. for employment.

"There has been some, but not to the same extent. You see, we are at the forefront of these new technologies, so the demand has not really taken off yet around the world. We are trying to educate other governments about some of the projects that have worked here, so right now most of the people going to foreign countries are going as liaisons for these capital projects, to help get them off the ground, and also to help raise money for them at the same time. The increased labor requirements will come later." Along with an increased approval rating for the President, thought Desmond. He felt some skepticism regarding the benefit of this measure for American workers, but if he voiced it, McBride would explain that he only saw one small picture of running the country and many factors existed that he, and she for that matter, were not authorized to know. He wasn't going to get anywhere further, so he thanked her for her time and ended the call.

Mark Desmond wasn't the only person who noticed the two day surge in Japanese people entering the country. The news bureaus also picked up on this as many of their correspondents travelled. Due to the large numbers, it became newsworthy and was the featured story on all the news websites and the lead story on the evening news. Director Grey was of course made aware of this as he kept up with current events and recognized the diversion the President created. He got in touch with Billet and told him they received the green light to begin investigating Louis Grenadine.

Thursday, March 29th, 10am
Ed Billet spread the word via email that the half of the team charged with finding out about Grenadine should get started. He suggested they begin with Hayao's entourage to see their impression of Grenadine. They could disclose the reason they were asking, as Hayao would not want it to get out that his staff included a potential murderer. Word would not get back to Grenadine from anyone in Hayao's camp. The FBI would also reveal Grenadine had been in DC when Pillar was killed. They hoped Hayao would have some information about their prior relationship. From there, they would pursue as many contacts as possible in the film industry as well as his friends and family. The team members

scheduled a meeting for themselves later that day at Quantico, as this was now an urgent matter. The media would be occupied with the immigration story and they should be able to proceed with minimal interference. The other half of Billet's group was working their way through the principals involved with the Bernards. They interviewed the security force in the Supreme Court building but no one unearthed any leads about a relationship between Justice Bernard and Pillar.

7pm

The phone rang in Hayao's campaign headquarters in Detroit and one his staffers answered. When he heard it was the FBI on the other end, he panicked slightly. The agent asked to speak to Hayao, who happened to be unavailable. The staffer offered to patch the caller through to Alex Ramirez, and the agent agreed. Ramirez picked up a minute later, having no idea why the FBI would be calling. "Hello?"

"Hello, Governor. Thanks for taking my call. I am calling about Louis Grenadine. I understand he is operating as a behind the scenes benefactor for Hayao." She hesitated, just for a split second.

"Yes he is. What is the situation?" She had dealt with the FBI before; they liked everything cut and dry. "He is a suspect in Juan Pillar's murder." Ramirez's mouth hung open.

"Are you kidding me? Why does the bureau believe that, because he is working with Hayao? He would go to such lengths to be on the winning team? I don't really know the man. You would be better off speaking with Hayao and he will not be available until tomorrow." Right, so you can call him and give him a warning.

"Ok, no problem. I will call him in the morning. Thanks for your time."

As soon as she got off the phone, Ramirez left an urgent message for Hayao explaining exactly what happened and to expect a phone call tomorrow. Little did she know the FBI would visit Hayao in person to catch him by surprise and watch his reactions.

The three NSA agents all received word around the same time that their mission was on hold as of right now and they were to return home immediately. Something big must be happening, they all thought. They would not pull the plug on this without a good reason. It would take them a few days to get home, but as soon as they did they all wanted to get to the bottom of this.

Friday, March 30th, 8am

The doorbell was ringing at Hayao's house. His staff had not arrived yet and he was in the middle of his morning coffee. Who in the world could be bothering him now? He quickly threw on some clothes and went to see. It was the FBI, and now it made sense. Alex tipped him off last night. He opened the door and pretended to be ignorant about why they were here. When they explained, he replied that he dealt with Grenadine only marginally throughout the years in his capacity as SAG President, and found him to be efficient and arrogant at the same time. They asked him if he thought Grenadine could be capable of murder, and Hayao said he couldn't really judge. He had not known Grenadine happened to be in DC when Pillar was killed, as they did not converse on a daily basis. The agents wanted to know what Grenadine was getting in return for his financial support and when he replied his son would have a position in Hayao's administration if he was elected, they were not surprised. The agents accumulated enough information to question Grenadine himself.

Eric Layton arrived in Colorado last night and it sure was good to be home! He had a great life and arrangement with his family, but he couldn't help feeling he was missing out at times, being away from his wife and son. Cindy invited all the extended family over on Saturday night, which would be a nice reunion and celebration for Layton's successful European trip. Right now he was on his way to meet with the Governor to plan out their press conference, scheduled for today at 5pm. They would share the credit; Layton thought that would work to his advantage. They would be lauded and praised, and the news of this feat would quickly spread all across the nation as a model of how to think outside the box in order to find solutions to the problems facing the constituents whom politicians serve. Layton felt he definitely had the momentum now and the determination to hang on to it. He was glad the Governor made time for this today, as he promised his son Jack they would spend Saturday and Sunday together, just the two of them, doing whatever Jack wanted.

Todd Russell and his inner circle were spending their last day in Toronto before heading to Vancouver tomorrow. Their meetings with the analysts in Ottawa had gone well and not surprisingly, they enjoyed the best following in Russia. Russell needed to work on his image in countries where technology wasn't stressed as much, as well as the Far East. He also had a strong showing in Muslim countries whose citizens maintained an interest in science. While he was in Toronto, he would actually have time for recreation, as they were going to a Blue Jays preseason baseball game and seeing a classical music concert. He wanted to get as much campaigning in as possible in the next few months before the summer, as that was traditionally a slow period in politics. Once September hit and school went back in session, the sprint to the finish line would begin. He intended to be at the front of the pack when that time came. He and Joe Berry would plan out their schedule for the next three months on their way back to the States from Vancouver. His aim was to visit as many countries which contained big concentrations of their citizens living in the US, such as India. He still believed the people from India would support him and initially had not planned at touring there, but a little reinforcement couldn't hurt. These countries could be divided into two categories; those invested in technology and those who weren't. Russell developed an approach for both. For those nations up on technology, he would initiate new programs related to science and help improve existing ones. The nations behind the technological curve were in need of education, which his administration would be committed to providing without seeking anything in return. Weimitz possessed many connections that could be tapped for these purposes, not only in the U.S. but all over the world, people who would be thrilled to work with him, and would offer their services just for the experience. He felt pretty good about his strategy. Back home, he had strong placement in the Midwest, and the technical strength of his administration would give him a strong showing in other parts of the country. He also felt skeptical about Hayao carrying California, even with Grenadine's help. Right now it was pretty even.

Saturday, March 31st
Ed Billet was at his desk, planning out what to say to the Director. He wanted enough agents at his disposal to swarm over Grenadine and many of his friends all at the same time so they won't have time to compare their stories. He believed the Director would authorize this without a fight, as he would want to maintain the integrity of the investigation as well. If he got the green light today, he could have the agents out to California by Tuesday. He would go as well; he wanted to handle Grenadine himself. The other reason he wanted to do this as quickly as possible was that Grenadine would undoubtedly find out about this sooner or later, and Billet wanted to preserve the element of surprise. He called the Director, gave his whole sales pitch, and the Director agreed this was the right way to go. He commissioned enough agents so they could all interrogate, or interview, all the people at once. The next step was to determine which people would be seen to find out more about Louis Grenadine. Billet had three days to come up with a list. He would stay away from family, only talking to them to gather Grenadine's whereabouts, for if they lied about that they could get in trouble too. He was trying to track down a list of SAG members and heard one time about a biographical book with information about all of the members. He would get a subpoena if necessary and couldn't imagine any judge who wouldn't grant him one under the circumstances. He had also googled a list of Grenadine's movies, went down the list and written down the names of the actors, actresses, and directors that had worked with him to contact them as well. He would have all the agents do these things while he met with Grenadine. The man was in for the shock of his life.

President Harrington had been besieged by reporters over the last few days about the new influx of people emigrating. He explained there was a demand for people from other countries, and these countries in turn were looking for Americans to go to their countries and join their workforce. "Mr. President, is there a certain rotation that will be employed? Which country will come next?"

"There will not be a fixed rotation. This will be based upon the needs of the projects, as well as the needs of the countries with whom we have this arrangement." One reporter picked up on that immediately.

"Oh, so there is an arrangement? With which countries do you have this arrangement?"

"There are too many to list, but we will post them on the INS website. The point is we are helping each other by creating jobs for the global workforce."

"What about the fact that we have many more jobs here than they do elsewhere? We will be taking in considerably more people than we will be able to place elsewhere."

"That is not true. We have people out of work in this country, yes, but the jobs we have available are ones they would not all be interested in. This new model is a panacea; it will create opportunities for all types of workers, skilled and unskilled alike. We have seen situations like this here before, when there were jobs available that Americans did not want to do. The difference now is we are allowing people to enter this country legally."

"And why is that, sir? Why have you gone about changing the requirements for immigration now and made them so much more lenient?" President Harrington had been waiting for this question and was ready.

"Excellent question. This change goes perfectly with our new more liberal political policies. We have entered a new age and this is the next logical step." Brilliant answer! He managed to illustrate the connection between his prior achievement of changing the U.S. Constitution, and reiterated his role as a statesman and pioneer. He knew people saw him and his actions as selfish and opportunistic and thought he simply wanted to secure his place in history and create a future for himself after he left office by performing acts as President that would put other people, governments and countries in his debt, but in his own mind he saw himself as a leader who had changed the world and made it a better place with altruistic intentions. He looked out at the group of reporters and saw looks on their faces which showed he had gotten through to them. He decided to take a few more questions before he ended this press conference. "Yes, Diana?"

"How are you planning to train workers from countries who have no skills at all?"

"That is part of the process. We will be sending teachers and other counselors to work with them at their homes to provide them with the background for them to come here and assimilate into our society. We will not be forcing anyone to participate. If anyone is thinking this is just another example of the United States imposing its will elsewhere in the world, it is not. We are working with other countries and their citizens, not against them. Thank you all. Good day."

Sunday, April 1st

Billet was on his way to California and all of the agents Director Grey had mobilized to work on this case were on their way also and were all going to meet at the FBI field office in Los Angeles. He had a stop to make first. He was going to the SAG headquarters and would be met there by the Vice President who would give Billet the list for which he was looking. Once he had the list, he planned to meet with all the agents, give out the assignments, and then expect everyone to find their people on Monday morning, which was when he would track down Louis Grenadine. He would start out questioning him at home. Grenadine would undoubtedly get in touch with his lawyer right away, and Billet would have to place him under house arrest, which would not be a problem, even with his attorney fighting against it, as once Billet explained the circumstances, there would be no judge who wouldn't impose the terms of house arrest. That would give him limited opportunity to eliminate anything to connect him to the murders. There were three categories of interviews he wanted to conduct; those with members of SAG that may have known Grenadine, those with actors and actresses in movies with him, and those with family and friends. He would have the most experienced agents do the ones with friends and family, as they would be most likely to elicit information helpful in providing clues as to Grenadine's activities leading up to the day Pillar was killed. All of this would happen tomorrow after Billet outlined precisely how he wanted things to proceed.

Hayao had one of his staffers check with all the networks to confirm his commercial would air tonight. He really thought it would be well received by the public. Next week they, he and Alex, would be heading to Mexico to spend some time campaigning there. The timing would hopefully be right, as they would be able to capitalize on the momentum of the commercial tonight, which would be seen all over the world via the internet. Hayao hired the firm Universal Linguistics to translate the ad based upon the country where it was being shown. Natsu would undoubtedly watch it as it would be morning in Japan. They would discuss it as soon as it was over and Hayao expected Natsu would have some new insights into how the campaign should proceed. Hayao learned to agree with him and then proceed in the way he thought best. If Natsu ever questioned him or became angry, Hayao would simply fake stupidity. Natsu was so desperate for Hayao to win the White House he would tolerate almost anything. Alex knew this too and also cooperated about humoring Natsu. Hayao often deferred to her, she was very skilled in navigating these shark infested political waters. He thought of her almost as a campaign manager. The downside to having her as a running mate meant she tried to take over sometimes and be heavy handed with her advice. He viewed this as a necessary evil, and hopefully would pay off.

Monday, April 2nd, 7:30 am
Roger Squelch, an FBI agent working on the Bernard part of the multiple murder case, was at Lorraine Corvino's apartment to interview her again, per Billet's request. She expected him and wanted him to come early so she could still get to her custodial job on time. She let him in and offered him some coffee, which he declined. They sat down and just as they were about to start going

over her background again, her phone rang. While she went to go answer it, Squelch got up and looked around. He wandered over to the bookcase and began inspecting her selection of books. He happened to glance behind the books and notice a picture. He took out his pen, and not worrying about a warrant as the picture stood in plain sight, bent down to take a closer look. It was a picture of Corvino and her bowling team holding up a trophy. "Oh my God!", he almost exclaimed out loud before he caught himself. One of the women in the picture, standing at the end, was none other than Kelly Visque.

CHAPTER 8

Monday, April 2nd, Lorraine Corvino's apartment

Roger Squelch was frozen. Everything suddenly came into focus. He had to get in touch with Billet, but needed to act natural so as not to let on that he knew. Boy, she must be pretty dumb not to hide the evidence that the two women interacted with each other and conspired to perform these deadly murders. That was something he never understood, how people didn't cover their tracks when they committed a crime. Oh shit, he heard her finishing her conversation! He hurried back to the chair and looked like he had been waiting for her. She came back and sat down and he forced his mind back to asking the questions which needed to be asked. "Miss Corvino", she interrupted him. "Please call me Lorraine."

"Lorraine, are you aware of any connection between the Bernards and Juan Pillar?"

"Not really. I am a custodian there, my contact with the justices is peripheral." Squelch knew that wasn't true, but now was not the time.

"Did you ever notice anyone suspicious hanging around the courthouse in the time leading up to the Bernards' murders?"

"No. I mean, there are protesters there sometimes, but they are just the usual wackos. No one really comes to mind."

"What about the justices? Have any of them been acting strangely lately?"

"Again, I just see them in passing. I don't know what would constitute strange behavior for them." Squelch resigned himself that he wasn't going to get any worthwhile information from this woman, so he decided to pretend to be frustrated with her lack of observation to end this conversation and go call Billet. He sighed and lifted his hands in the air.

"Thank you for your time Lorraine. If I need anything further I will be in touch." She extended her hand as he left, not knowing the FBI would probably be back later today, most likely to arrest her.

As soon as Squelch got into his car, he dialed Billet's private cell phone number, not even considering he would be asleep. A groggy voice answered. "Hello?"

"Hi, Ed, it's Roger Squelch." He gave him a minute to clear the fog away.

"Hi Roger. What time is it?"

"It's 5:45 am in California. I am sorry to bother you but this is big. I was meeting with Lorraine Corvino, the custodian who works at the Supreme Court building?"

"Yes, I remember, go on."

"Well, she went to answer the phone and I took that opportunity to look around and noticed a picture out in the open behind the bookcase of her with her bowling team holding up their trophy. Guess who else appeared in the picture? Kelly Visque." Billet understood right away what this meant.

"Oh my god, that's how Visque anticipated Justice Bernard's comings and goings!" Billet needed to process this. There could be numerous different scenarios here, but it was clear Visque was responsible for the murder of the Bernards. There was motive, to prevent a foreign born person from running for President, which Bernard would have likely supported in his ruling to amend the Constitution, there was opportunity, with Corvino feeding her information, and there was evidence, with Visque's DNA showing up at the crime scene. The extent of Corvino's involvement seemed sketchier. If she had grown weary of waiting for Justice Bernard, who was her lover, to leave his wife, she might have been looking for revenge. It was also possible she was an innocent pawn in this, with the conversations between her and Visque being innocent enough on her end, while Visque built a plan the entire time. This would require more digging. What about the connection to Pillar? If, as Billet believed, it was a matter of the heart for Corvino, then Visque acted alone when she killed Pillar, if in fact she did. Billet was getting ahead of himself, however. He had a job to do in California; to interrogate Louis Grenadine. Kelly Visque needed to remain on a back burner right now, except to get in touch with Director Grey and ask him to have her arrested. They clearly established enough suspicion to hold her in jail on bail.

Once that was done, they could take their time hearing what Visque would say, talking to Lorraine Corvino again, this time showing their cards, which might prompt her to throw Visque under the bus by revealing it was her idea, or that Corvino had no inkling Visque would commit such a horrible crime. The FBI would also go back and talk to their teammates on the bowling team to determine what kind of relationship the two women maintained. Billet was planning the next steps in his investigation. He could now look for evidence to link either Grenadine or Visque to the Pillar's murder. The net just got much wider. Alright, Squelch was still on the phone. He thanked him for the excellent job and told Squelch he would get back to him; for now, it was critical for him to get in touch with Director Grey. He dialed the Director's number reserved for emergencies. When he answered, Billet got right to the point. "We now have a real suspect for the Bernard murders." He went through the whole story and then said he would like to have Visque arrested. Grey agreed enough evidence existed to do so and said he would contact the Attorney General, who would undoubtedly issue an arrest warrant and very possibly prosecute the case himself. He told Billet he would get back to him later today and he should carry on with his plans to meet with Grenadine and all the others who were connected to him. Billet got off the phone and saw it was time for him to get ready to go see Grenadine.

Michigan, Monday April 2nd, 9am

Hayao was in his private study, very pleased with the reaction to his commercial. The 11 o'clock news turned it into a human interest story, revealing the results of their poll taken over the internet and showed an overwhelming majority thought the ad to be very effective. The feedback given expressed that both Hayao and Ramirez conducted themselves with grace and professionalism and would be two people that would be strong and competent leaders. Natsu had been thrilled with the ad as well, and the response seemed to be universal. Hayao felt his expectations were surpassed and made a promise to himself to use this director again. Now he could focus on his trip, and plan out his strategy for the rest of the spring political season. He had a substantial amount of work to do on his knowledge of political gamesmanship and that was something he was working on with Alex. He knew if he won in November, he would make an excellent President, as he was efficient and persuasive, and could compromise when necessary. Getting elected was an entirely different ballgame, however, and even though the general public revolted and demanded more accountability from their politicians, during the election season it was all about which candidate made people believe they could solve all the country's problems, and in a way vague enough to leave wiggle room after they were elected so they could always say they were misunderstood and their words taken out of context. That was just the opposite of the way he conducted himself as a businessman. Hayao was excited about this; it was a challenge. He had overcome many obstacles in his life and he was certain he would be successful at this too. He was not worried about the issue with Grenadine either. If it turned out to be true, Hayao would have no trouble showing that it was Grenadine who approached him, as he kept a recording of their conversation. It also wouldn't be hard to find someone else with influence in California to stump for him.

  Director Grey called Quinn Waller, the United States Attorney General, to request a warrant for Kelly Visque's arrest. Waller recognized the urgency of this, now that the FBI finally had a solid suspect for the Bernards' murders. Waller debated whether to pursue this as an act of terrorism, or just a federal crime. It really was not a stretch to consider this a terrorist act, as one of the clauses of the Patriot Act, enacted by Congress in 2001, states that an act intended to affect the conduct of government is terrorism. Waller could certainly make that case to a judge and he knew just the one. He envisioned this case playing out in his mind already, one that many people considered to be one of the finest legal minds in the country. Waller came from a blue collar background, but his grasp of the legal system, as well as how people work, was admirable. He truly deserved to be Attorney General. He took out a legal pad and wrote down where he thought this case would go, and detailed every move Kelly Visque and whoever she hired as a lawyer might make, accounting for every contingency. Just like a good chess player, Waller possessed the vision to picture legal strategies his opponents would employ throughout the trial, usually all the way to the endgame. The first decision he needed to make in this case was the charge to proceed with, either murder or terrorism. He tried not to think politically, but rather legally. Whichever charge he filed, he would receive criticism. The key issue was intent. More information was necessary for him to make a decision. He wanted to talk to Ed Billet and find out more about both Kelly Visque and Lorraine Corvino. If the Bernards were killed to influence the Supreme Court's decision, then Waller would consider it terrorism. He made some notes and then an unsettling thought popped into his mind. He could envision a conflict brewing, one that would be ancillary to the case, but might end up hurting a friend of his.

Los Angeles, 8am

Everything was in place. All of the agents were going to descend upon their targets, with Billet taking the grand prize. He knew Grenadine would be livid and would do everything possible to thwart the FBI's progress, but that would only add to his appearance of being guilty. Billet would make it clear he was just gathering information and it would be in Grenadine's best interest to be cooperative. With that in mind, he had instructed all the agents to wear casual clothes this morning without any FBI issued apparel, to avoid arousing any curiosity from any nosy onlookers. Billet knocked on the door of Grenadine's mansion high in the Hollywood hills and a maid answered the door. "It must be nice", he thought. He asked to see Grenadine, and when the maid inquired about what, he simply answered it involved a private matter. She went to retrieve him, came back five minutes later, and showed Billet into Grenadine's study, where he was told Grenadine would be right with him.

Grenadine was annoyed. Why would someone bother him at his home this early in the morning? He should rehire a security guard. He opened the door to the study and noticed a man dressed casually looking out the window. He asked him what he wanted as he closed the door, and the man showed his badge and introduced himself as agent Ed Billet. What could the FBI possibly want?

"What brings you here, agent Billet?"

"I wanted to discuss the murder of Juan Pillar and his driver." Grenadine turned white.

"What could that possibly have to do with me?"

"We understand you are working with Hayao on his campaign. What is your role?"

"I am helping him with his campaign on the west coast."

"Did he approach you or did you approach him?"

"I approached him."

"What did you request in return?"

"My son is interested in politics. I asked that if Hayao wins, he give my son a position in his administration."

"I see. Have you done any travelling lately?" Typical, asking questions for which they already knew the answers.

"Yes, I have. I travelled to Washington DC a few weeks ago."

"When, exactly?"

"In late February. Yes, I was in DC when Pillar was killed."

"What were you doing there?"

"I was there for a SAG convention."

"Are there people available to verify your whereabouts?"

"Yes, a whole slew. Many people from Hollywood were there. I can get you the SAG register, and I will mark off the names of people to contact."

"What about on February 24th and 25th?" Grenadine thought for a minute.

"The convention had ended by then. My wife and I were doing some sightseeing on our own."

"Which sights did you go to?"

"We took the water-downed tour of the White House and went to the Air and Space museum."

"Good times. I will just need to verify this with your wife. Is she home?"

"Yes, but she is getting ready to go out. You'll have to come back another time."

"It will only take a few minutes. Could you have the maid let her know I would like to talk to her?" Grenadine scowled, but complied. He buzzed the maid in and asked her to escort Mrs. Grenadine to the study. When she entered the room, Billet asked Mr. Grenadine to leave. He then turned to Mrs. Grenadine, a tall, thin woman, with very expressive eyes which looked to contain sadness and disappointment. Louis Grenadine was known to be quite the philanderer. Billet also knew Mrs. Grenadine was not in show business, so she probably didn't realize what she was getting into when she married him. He inquired about their schedule when they were in Washington, and everything jived with what Louis reported. They were not off the hook, yet, however. Louis Grenadine could have easily conspired with someone to handle this. Billet was anxious to hear what the other agents found out in their interviews when they all convened at the FBI's office in downtown LA. In the meantime, he wanted to obtain a subpoena for all the Grenadine's phone records, as well as financial records going back three years. Billet was looking for a pattern, or something unusual that would raise suspicion. Between his authority, fame, and fortune, it would have been simple for Grenadine to arrange for someone else to carry out a hit.

The FBI building, downtown Los Angeles, April 2nd, 6pm

Billet looked at all the tired faces. That was good; it meant they exhausted themselves getting the necessary information. There were 100 agents in the room and Billet was going to hear what each had to say, one at a time, so if there was anything relevant to what any other agent learned, it would be realized immediately. Billet pointed to the agent in the first row, in the seat on the far left, a man with the nickname Koko. Billet spoke first, giving some instruction. "We have much to get through tonight, and rest assured, we will get through it all. Here is how I would like to proceed. When it is your turn, I want you to state your name, say the name and relation to Louis Grenadine of the person you met with and anything worthwhile that you learned. We are looking for any information which reveals something about Grenadine's character that might suggest he is capable of murder, or arranging one, as well as anything told to you that either confirms or refutes his, and his wife's, assertion that they were in DC when Pillar was killed, but were out sightseeing both days. That is what I learned. As far as motive, Grenadine had offered to work with Hayao on his campaign in exchange for his son getting a job in Hayao's camp should he win. Koko, you may begin."

When the last agent finished, it was 2 am, and many of the agents were nodding off, but Billet had all he needed. It seemed Grenadine was ultra-competitive and tenacious. He would do whatever it took when he really wanted something, and he wanted something for his son. He would meet with Grey about this when he returned to DC tomorrow. Despite the alibi the Grenadines provided and corroborated by members of SAG that various agents spoke to, Grenadine remained a suspect. Billet had more investigating to do back at home.

Tuesday, April 3rd, 9am, LAX

Billet was exhausted, but this investigation now had taken on a life of its own, and absolutely no time could be wasted. He called headquarters in DC and arranged for round the clock surveillance on Visque and Corvino. They had no inkling the law was closing in, but Billet didn't want to take any chances that they would leave for any reason without the FBI knowing where they were at all times. He had two things to accomplish today. First, he wanted to meet with Director Grey and tell him what his plans were. After that, he would go see Quinn Waller and go over the profile he developed about Kelly Visque. That information would be used to determine which crime to charge her with. It was his turn at the counter to book his flight. At least he had five hours to sleep on the plane.

This was going to be an intense day. The plane landed at Dulles and a car waited to whisk Billet to Quantico. He went right into Grey's office and explained what he wanted. He thought the next steps in the investigation should be to interview Hayao about any involvement he had with Grenadine about his trip to DC for the SAG awards, with the objective being to observe how Hayao reacted to the thinly veiled inquiry about the Pillar murders, and to review the security tapes at Dulles airport for the day Pillar was kidnapped. Billet desperately wanted to make some tangible progress in the Bernard case. He sensed the glances coming his way from the other agents and heard the whispers. He was starting to look like a failure. It had been almost a year and to the people not familiar with the case, it appeared his team was spinning their wheels. Now that they had a real breakthrough, he was going to move as fast as he could. If he saw this through successfully, he could receive a promotion and have some input about his next assignment. Ten minutes later, he was seated in Grey's office, waiting for the Director to get off the phone. Once he hung up, Billet got started. He explained what they found in LA and even though Grenadine offered an alibi that was verified, he could not be ruled out yet. He had the opportunity, and intent would not be difficult to prove. It was also possible that he hired someone else to do it. Billet told Grey about the two things he wanted to do, view the tapes at Dulles Airport, and meet with Hayao to see if there was any involvement there. Grey pondered that for a minute, and then told Billet he would arrange for both to happen, but he would meet with Hayao himself, as Hayao would probably get offended at the suggestion that he was involved and it would be better coming from the Director. Grey also agreed the surveillance videos should be examined, but Billet's first priority should be to meet with Quinn Waller. He wanted to get together with Billet as soon as he was done with Director Grey. They would meet at the White House because President Harrington wanted to sit in on the conference as well. A secret service agent was waiting outside the FBI building. Half an hour later they were at the White House, and Billet noticed Waller was already there because he saw his car which was issued from the Department of Justice. They would be meeting in the Oval Office, which held a small conference table where the three of them could sit. Billet walked through the full body scan machine, which buzzed because of his firearm, and then proceeded to meet the other two. They all shook hands and then Waller began. "Ed, the first thing I would like to know is more about Kelly Visque and Lorraine Corvino. If, as you suspect, they are both implicated in the murders of Justice Bernard and Mrs. Bernard, what was their motive?"

"Well, Kelly Visque has been vehemently anti-foreigner for a long time. We have proof that she attended numerous American Pride meetings."

"Ok, so she was in bed with the white supremacists. Where is the connection to her wanting Bernard dead?"

"It's a straight line, Quinn. She probably realized that Bernard, while traditionally a conservative, would be heavily influenced by his daughter. When Visque held the Bernards hostage, she probably tortured them, either physically or psychologically, until Winston confessed as to how he would rule on the case."

"If he was tortured long enough, he would have said anything to make it stop. The kidnapper probably didn't truly know which way he would rule. Let's say he said he would rule against it. Even if the kidnapper believed him and wanted to prevent the Constitution from being changed, he or she would have had to kill them anyway just on the off chance that Bernard was lying."

"Maybe so, Ed. If that's the case, however, then why didn't he or she kidnap one of the judges who they knew were liberal?"

"Because Winston was the easiest to get to. He drove his own car to the Supreme Court building and did not have security around him like the others."

"Well, how would Kelly Visque have known this?"

"Enter Lorraine Corvino. She was Bernard's lover, and probably a scorned one at that. She undoubtedly had surmised he would never leave his wife, and was enraged, looking for revenge. She and Kelly Visque played on the same bowling team so they probably hatched this plan together. Corvino knew Bernard's schedule and tipped Visque off."

"So, Corvino was an accomplice. Do you think it's possible that Visque was the mastermind, that she obtained this information from Corvino who gave it up without knowing what Visque would do with it? Perhaps they engaged in conversations which Corvino thought were innocent and had no inkling this would happen."

"Maybe. We have to find out more information about her. We can talk to the people that work at Magnus Industries as well as the people at the Supreme Court building to see what her demeanor is like when she is there. Kelly Visque, however, is a cold blooded killer. She eliminated Bernard to prevent the measure from being passed by the Supreme Court, but much to her chagrin, President Harrington appointed another liberal. That's my view of Kelly Visque's profile, and personality makeup. Where do we go from here, Quinn?"

"We have to decide which crime to charge Kelly Visque with. To me, it seems the terrorism clause applies. We should really make an example of her. She is trying to derail the operation of government. I say try her as a terrorist. What do you think, Mr. President?"

"I agree. Justice Bernard, and all the U.S. Supreme Court justices, are instruments of our political process. This was not just murder. Visque has to be treated accordingly."

"Great. I am glad you feel that way. I will go ahead and draft the arrest warrant with the charges listed, and then some of your agents, Ed, can go bring her in." Waller paused. "Ed, I know you have started working on the Pillar murders as well and have made some headway with Louis Grenadine. I don't know what your next step is, but I need you to put that investigation on hold. I am going to need your undivided attention on this case for the next two months. You will have to be available for the initial court appearance, when we get an indictment, and when we start the trial, I will need you as a witness. Once you have been called to the stand, you will be able to turn your attention back to Grenadine." Billet observed the intense look in Waller's eyes. He realized there was no point in arguing; besides, Waller had a point. This case had been sitting out there for almost a year and it should be top priority.

"Of course, Quinn. Whatever you need."

"Thank you Ed." The three men looked at each other, each knowing where things would go from here and what each of them must do. They all stood up and left without a word.

Tuesday, April 3rd, 2pm

Waller went to see Albert Garner, a federal circuit court judge, known to be a pushover when it came to granting warrants and providing prosecuting attorneys the tools they need to do their jobs. In this case, it also helped that President Harrington had phoned ahead to explain what was happening. As a result, Waller was able to give him the abbreviated version. Half an hour later, Waller received his arrest warrant.

3pm

Waller arranged for the warrant to be hand delivered by messenger to Ed Billet who returned to FBI headquarters. Billet gathered three agents together and set out to execute the warrant. They drove over to Star Fitness where Kelly Visque worked and observed her giving a personal training session. Billet had decided to handle this quietly, so he approached the manager and pretended he was looking to set up an appointment for personal training. He found out Visque's last training session ended at 7pm, so they would come back then and take her into custody in the parking lot. In the meantime, Billet wanted to establish a game plan for checking into Lorraine Corvino's background. He scheduled a meeting with his team for tomorrow at 11am where he would assign them various tasks between talking to Corvino's coworkers and friends and researching if she had any dealings with any radical groups like Kelly Visque did which would add another layer to the motive that she had for wanting Bernard dead. He would also tell them that investigating Grenadine was on hold until his obligation to the Bernard case was done. He wrote all these notes down because he would be conducting this meeting remotely since most of the agents were still in California. He checked his watch and seeing it was 5 o'clock went to have some dinner before going back to Star Fitness.

5pm

Kelly Visque was having a great day, unaware her life would change forever in about two hours. All of her clients praised her efforts that day, telling her she was the one of the most knowledgeable trainers they had ever encountered. That was what she prided herself on, being the best in her business. Her father instilled that in her, along with his infamous bad temper which he always denied. She developed her love of exercise and weight lifting at an early age. She was never a beauty, and the boys did not notice her in school. She turned to bodybuilding as a way to separate herself from the other girls, but it did not make her any more popular with the opposite sex, not that it mattered to her now anyway. She came away with something much more valuable, however, a passion for an activity that she managed to turn into a career. She has been saving money whenever possible, someday hoping to open her own gym. She jokingly thought that if she did, no foreigners would be allowed. Looking at her schedule for the day she saw she had two more hour appointments. The first one was with a man with whom she had been working for six months who had shown incredible progress, and the second for an initial consult. She breezed through both of them, took a quick shower, and left for the night. When she got to her car some men came up on her quickly and she recognized Ed Billet from the FBI. Oh, shit, not him again! He must have more questions about why her DNA was at the crime scene. Her friend who was a lawyer said it was very difficult to win a harassment case against the feds as they enjoyed much leeway when it came to investigations. She would do her best to keep her cool. He walked over to her and simply said, "Kelly Visque, you are under arrest for the murders of Winston and Cecily Bernard." While he was speaking he was attempting to place handcuffs on her, and she snapped, which she would regret later. While she was very strong, there were four agents experienced at subduing unruly perpetrators. When she lost her cool, they threw her to the ground, one of them put his foot on her neck while another cuffed her. They then dragged her to her feet, and Billet finished reading her rights. They shoved her in the back of their car and off they went. When they started to drive away, she forced herself to stay calm. "What is going to happen to my car?"

"You can call someone to come pick it up. We will deliver the keys to whomever you want."

"Where are you taking me?"

"To the federal lockup in downtown DC."

"When can I call someone to bail me out?" She was obviously not familiar with the criminal process.

"You cannot be bailed out until your initial appearance before a federal magistrate, where you will enter your plea and your bail arrangement, if any, will be decided."

"When will I get a lawyer?"

"Do you have one?"

"No."

"One will be appointed for you at your first appearance before the judge."

"When will that take place?"

"Within 48 hours. You will remain in our custody until then." She was quiet and suddenly acting like a child caught by her parents. That was common actually. People gave law enforcement all kinds of grief until they were actually under arrest. Billet witnessed even the most belligerent, aggressive people become contrite and submissive in that situation. Of course, they didn't always stay that way. Once the shock had worn off, many people reverted back to type. They arrived at the federal lockup and got her processed. They put her in a private holding cell and left her under watch of the guard at the desk.

9pm

Waller had been keeping in touch with Ed Billet all day and knew Kelly Visque was behind bars. He was now going to make sure she stayed there through the arraignment. He called Judge Tim Fresco at home. He was one who always fell in line with what the A.G. wanted and could be counted on to deny bail. At first, Fresco was annoyed at being bothered at home, but Waller quickly squashed that with a no nonsense tone. "Tim, this is how it is going to go. You will make time in your courtroom tomorrow for this case. I am planning to charge her with a violation of the Patriot Act."

"Terrorism?"

"Yes. She killed the Bernards with the intent to interfere with the operation of the United States Government. That makes her a terrorist."

"You are breaking new ground here. I am glad I will not be the judge presiding over this case." That makes two of us, thought Waller. You are too much of a coward to set precedent.

"I will see you tomorrow judge." Waller hung up and was ready to go home.

Wednesday, April 4th, 10am, Federal Courthouse, downtown DC
Kelly Visque was being escorted to the U.S. Magistrate's courtroom. Billet learned the judge would be Tim Fresco, not that it mattered to Billet. That was Waller's area of expertise. He had every confidence Waller would get his conviction. They arrived and went into the courtroom where Waller was waiting. Once they had all been seated, the judge entered the room. "The honorable judge Fresco, please rise!" Kelly Visque was called first, and she and Waller stood in front of the bench where Fresco was presiding. "What is the charge here, counselor?"

"Miss Visque is charged with violating the Patriot Act, your honor. We are treating her as a terrorist." Kelly Visque turned white.

"What the hell is going on here? You are treating me like a terrorist?", she screamed.

"Quiet, ma'am. You had better calm down and listen to what Mr. Waller has to say. Continue, counselor."

"We are requesting that Miss Visque be held without bail."

"Approved. Do you have an attorney, Miss Visque?"

Still shaken, she answered in a small voice, "No, not yet."

Judge Fresco replied, "Does that mean you will find your own attorney?"

"No. I don't know any criminal lawyers."

"Fine. One will be appointed for you. Your arraignment will be in two weeks from today, on April 18th at 10am." He banged his gavel and Visque was led to the van that would take her back to the temporary jail where she would stay until the arraignment. Billet looked at his watch; ten thirty. Waller had promised him he would be done in time to make it to his 11 o'clock meeting and he was true to his word.

11am

Billet arrived back at Quantico just in time to begin his debriefing for the continued Corvino investigation. It would be quick. He just wanted to tell them to switch gears and start looking into Corvino's past and present relationships as they would be trying to find some kind of link between her and Kelly Visque in addition to the bowling team. Grenadine was on hold. The only path they would pursue with him right now was Director Grey going to see Hayao. He would focus his attention on getting Kelly Visque convicted. The first thing he wanted to do was hold a press conference to alert the public that the FBI had apprehended someone for the murder of the Bernards. He wanted to preempt any attempt by Visque's counsel to generate any sympathy in the media by implying she was wrongfully imprisoned or that her rights had been violated. He sent the Director a text explaining what he wanted to do, and the director responded with his approval a few minutes later.

  Kelly Visque was back in her cell, beginning to grasp the gravity of her situation. She did not have the connections or means to hire a lawyer and was grateful one would be appointed to represent her. She hoped whoever it was possessed some experience, as she was already at a major disadvantage. She had no idea what changed to make the FBI believe she was responsible for the two murders. How could she have been able to get to the judge? She wanted to call her parents; her dad might have some advice to give her. She knew enough to keep her mouth shut and control her temper, which could be volatile. She called for the prison guard, and when he responded she asked to make a phone call. He told her she would get to do that later. She prayed; it was all she could think to do right now.

1pm, FBI headquarters, Quantico, VA
  Ed Billet had arranged for the press conference to be conducted at 1pm. He would issue a short statement and then field questions.
  When the cameras for all the news stations started rolling, he began. "Good afternoon. My name is Ed Billet, and I am the special agent in charge of the Bernard case. We have made an arrest, a woman named Kelly Visque who is in our custody right now. We are at the beginning of the legal process and are still

trying to put together all the puzzle pieces. I will answer questions now."

"How long have you been watching Kelly Visque as a person of interest?"

"For about 8 months."

"Why did it take you this long to make the arrest?"

"There were still a few loose ends that recently came together and allowed us to close in."

"Do you suppose she did this on her own?"

"We are not sure yet."

"Was this politically motivated?"

"The FBI does not speculate, we simply enforce the laws."

"Well, what was her motive? Was she having an affair with the judge?"

"Those are questions best left for Ms. Visque herself."

"Do you think she was involved in the murders of Juan Pillar and the driver?"

"No comment."

"Does she have an attorney?"

"I don't know."

"Who is going to be prosecuting this case?"

"Attorney General Waller." A murmur arose in the crowd. Waller only prosecuted the cases he wanted to make sure went his way; he was one of the most thorough attorneys anywhere. All the reporters there were already on their phones telling their agencies to call Quinn Waller for an interview. Billet was waiting for more questions, but once they had Waller's name, the media expected he would provide way more information than Billet would.

An hour later, Waller began to be besieged by phone calls; he was not surprised. He expected Billet to alert the media that they had made a collar. He decided he would not reveal the fact that he planned to charge her with being a terrorist. He did not want to turn this into a three ring circus like some other high profile cases. The reporters would learn of it soon anyway, as the Grand Jury was being convened next week to hear the case and decide if the charges were justified legally, and to confirm the arraignment date. For now all he revealed was that the FBI had done a thorough job in pursuing and capturing Kelly Visque and now that they had handed the ball over to him, he was not going to drop it and would use all of the resources available to him to guarantee she ended up where she belonged. He told his assistant to hold all calls for the rest of the day.

Uncle George called Kangaroo on his office line and talked in code. There was no need for them to meet, at least for the time being. "I made use of the three deductions we talked about," said Uncle George. "I know they will come in handy again, especially when dealing with foreign interests. Oh, that reminds me, the next country we are going to do business with is Israel, so I need more information about their economic trends."
"Of course. I will get you that data as soon as I can." Kangaroo had just been informed the three agents were back, Uncle George might want to use them again, and Israel was involved in the next round of immigration. "Oh wow, I just caught another rat in the trap. I have been waiting to catch this one for a while. I think it's the culprit behind the trouble we have been having." He communicated the fact that the FBI had arrested someone for the murder of the Bernards.
"Don't be surprised if there are other rats like this one." Uncle George was saying Kelly Visque may have been working with others. Kangaroo had to get back to work.
"I'll be in touch."

Kelly Visque was in a daze; the minutes seemed interminably long. A man walked into the corridor and stopped in front of the bars of her cell. "Hello Miss Visque, my name is Lionel Ross and I am your court appointed attorney." Wow, he looked awfully young. "I have requested that the guard let us talk privately. There is an interrogation room down the hall. I will meet you there in five minutes." The guard brought her there and cuffed her to the table. Attorney Ross took out some papers and a pad from his briefcase. "Let me get some background. I spoke with the Attorney General and he told me what they have so far. Basically, they have your DNA which places you at the location where their bodies were dumped; they have intent, the reason why you would have killed the Bernards, and now they also have information about how you would have known his schedule."

"Wait a minute. What do you mean by intent? What motive do they think I had?"

"The FBI knew you were involved with American Pride and that you have a temper. Their theory is that you killed them because you believed Justice Bernard would rule in favor of a foreigner running for President and you were vehemently opposed to this and would stop at nothing to prevent it."

"Oh my god. Well, what about my alibi?"

"Let me see here. You ate lunch with a friend and then went to the spy museum by yourself. Was the FBI able to corroborate your alibi?"

"No. I asked them not to talk to Richard as he is married, and I paid cash when I went to the museum."

"I see. You know, we will probably have to call Richard as a witness during the trial."

"No, I am not interested in that. First of all, I promised Richard we would keep our friendship a secret, and second, even if we did call him, he would not be a very good witness as he can be quite high strung. He would crack under pressure."

"Alright, we can revisit that later. Waller is going to seek the formal indictment next week. That means he is going to explain all these things we just talked about to a group of people known as a Grand Jury, who will decide if the evidence is enough to justify a criminal trial. You will be expected to be there for that. Assuming they do find the evidence sufficient, the next step will be an arraignment, at which point you will have to enter a plea of guilty or not guilty. Do you know how you want to plead?"

"Not guilty, of course!" She looked at him like he was crazy.

"Don't be insulted. Just be aware that if you plead guilty the other attorney and the judge may have leniency on you."

"I did not commit this crime." Ross was quiet for a minute. He had to find the right way of explaining this.

"You and I are convinced about your innocence. The world at large, however, sees things differently. People will need closure from this ordeal, and you could end up being the sacrificial lamb. Remember the jury is drawn from everyday citizens and the Attorney General will do his best to sway public opinion before the trial starts to help his chances for a conviction. If you are convicted, there is a greater chance you will receive a harsher penalty than if you plead guilty, because you will be saving the prosecution time, money and energy."

"I don't care. I am not going to admit to something I didn't do. It's your job to make the jury see that!"

"Ok, take it easy. Remember, I am on your side. Let's go over a few things. How did your DNA show up at the location where the bodies were found?"

"I got stung by a bee and swatted it down on the ground where it died. I already explained that to the FBI. Let me ask you something. Why are they arresting me now? They knew about my DNA and association with American Pride a while ago."

"They were interviewing other people connected with the Bernards, and they found a picture of you and Lorraine Corvino at her place. She was having an affair with Justice Bernard. The authorities believe you found out about Bernard's comings and goings through her."

"They think she is involved?"

"They don't know yet. Either she told you willingly because she was jealous that he would not leave his wife for her or she unwittingly revealed things about him to you on which you capitalized. That is their theory and they are not sure which one it is yet."

"I can't believe this. Alright, what are the steps we need to take to prove my innocence?"

"Let's start with compiling a list of people who will agree to be character witnesses to paint a picture that you are incapable of committing such a horrific crime. Give it some thought. While your parents may come to mind, it should be people not so emotionally involved, such as coworkers and friends. Also, when it comes to American Pride, if there is anyone who would downplay your association with them we should use them too. Did you admit to the FBI that you killed the bee?"

"Yes."

"Ok. Try to work on those things. Maybe ask your mom and dad to reach out to them and let them know I will be getting in touch. In the meantime try to relax and if anything comes to you that might help us write it down and let me know about it when we meet next, which will probably be Monday as the Grand Jury meets next Wednesday. Take care Kelly."

Greg Driscoll was the national director of the ACLU and he had seen many things over the years. One of those things was American citizens' rights getting trampled upon when they were suspected of committing or being involved with a crime. They were not convicted yet, and still law enforcement did many questionable things during an investigation. He had a sneaking suspicion as he watched the press conference this morning about Kelly Visque that this was one of those times. She was being accused of a horrible double murder and Driscoll understood the amount of pressure the FBI had been under to catch someone. They likely cut some corners when it came to technicalities which could have violated certain civil rights. Driscoll was inclined to look into this, and perhaps even offer for one of the ACLU's lawyers to take over as counsel for Kelly Visque if she agreed. He knew his organization would catch a lot of heat for this. Number one, the American public would scream the Bernards' civil rights were stripped when they were murdered, so why should there be any concern for the civil rights of the people who ended their lives? Number two, Bernard was a national figure of strength. Why would they want to tarnish their image to the point where people would ostracize them, even people who were traditionally liberal? Number three, he needed to remember Winston had been a friend and his daughter was now an employee. Pursuing this would be a personal insult to her, and would likely cause her to quit.

CHAPTER 9

Thursday, April 5th

Hayao had just gotten off the phone with Natsu, who was insisting Hayao have increased security at all times and offering to pay for it. He was planning to hire a former member of the U.S. Special Forces team who now did security. Hayao didn't really want to travel with more of an entourage, but it was easier to go along with it than to argue. He and Alex were leaving for Mexico on Saturday. Hayao was already counting on the Hispanic vote, with Pillar out of the way and Ramirez on his ticket. At this point, he wanted to have a real strategy session as to how they would approach their campaign for the next seven months, which would take them right to Election Day. He could divide the remaining time into three parts; the time before Memorial Day, when many people started their summer vacations, the summer, from Memorial Day until Labor Day, and after Labor Day, which would be about two months and would be a sprint to Election Day. They were three vastly different seasons, and each one would require a distinct action plan. Tomorrow Ramirez was flying to Michigan, and the next day the two of them, along with the beefed up security force, were going to Mexico for two weeks. He anticipated using their time together tomorrow to discuss these things and come up with some concrete action plans. Politics, getting elected at least, may require a lot of rhetoric, but determining which rhetoric to use and when required solid planning which his successful background in business certainly made easier.

Mr. and Mrs. Visque had been at their home yesterday after dinner, watching a movie shown in the theatres two months ago which they missed because Mr. Visque had been sick. Their phone rang at just after eight and it was their neighbor, Mrs. Parsons from across the street. "I am sorry to bother you, but your daughter is in some trouble!" Oh god!
"What do you mean?"
"There was a press conference earlier today, and I just saw a recap on the news. Kelly has been arrested in connection with the

Bernard murders. Do you know anything about that?" Mrs. Visque turned red. Of course she had known. They endured several harassing visits by the FBI. She did not feel at all like talking to anyone right now.

"Uh, I will talk to you later Mrs. Parsons." Without saying goodbye, she hung up and turned to her husband. "Kelly's in trouble. She has been arrested."

"For the double murder?" Mrs. Visque nodded. "Well, where are they holding her?" Mr. Visque always stayed calm during a crisis, stemming from his training during his tenure on the force.

"I don't know."

"Well, let's see if we can track her down." He got up and put on his coat.

"Where are you going?"

"You mean where are we going? We are going to the police station in town. They will be able to point us in the right direction. It will be faster than trying to call the FBI and getting sent on a wild goose chase. I am sure they will show me some consideration as a former cop." Half an hour later they were at the local precinct. The sergeant on duty managed to track Kelly Visque down, and her parents managed to get word to her that they would come to see her tomorrow.

They arrived at the building where the FBI was holding their daughter around 9:30 am, and once they explained, they were allowed to go see Kelly. They were led to the same room where she had met with Lionel Ross and Kelly appeared five minutes later. They hugged each other before she was shackled to the table, and though they told her they were glad she was ok, she observed the contempt in their eyes. "I didn't do it!" she exclaimed plaintively. Her dad said they believed her and would help her in any way possible. She went over what her lawyer discussed with her and said she needed them to contact the people on her list and alert them that her lawyer will be getting in touch with them. They were relieved that an attorney had been appointed to her as they possessed neither the contacts nor the funds to get one for her. They took the list from her and asked what they should bring her. She said some of her clothes, and a nice suit for her to wear to court. She also wanted some of her books, and weights, but knew they would never be allowed as they could be used as weapons. All items needed to be approved by the lieutenant in charge of this jail and very strict criteria existed. Most of the things on her list were innocuous however, and her parents shouldn't have such a hard time providing them. They stayed around for a little while, but once Kelly seemed settled, they left and said they would come back tomorrow.

 Eric Layton was back in Washington, focusing on his duties as a representative. He continually received a lot of recognition for his efforts in Colorado and knew he remained the leading candidate among Catholics. He had been planning out the course he wanted to follow from now until November and came to understand the majority of his campaigning should take place in the U.S., unlike his rivals. They thought this election would be won by winning the favor of foreign governments who would greatly influence the masses of their citizens in this country whereas he wasn't convinced about that and theorized those who had emigrated here did so for the reason of wanting a different life and were not necessarily looking for the elements of the country they hailed from. He did recognize, however, the importance of highlighting his commitment to foreign affairs and acknowledging the interdependence of all nations. He needed to balance that with the United States holding on to its own identity. He thought, and Morris agreed, the best way to achieve that was to stress his policies which would enhance the quality of life for the people here now as well as for future generations. The one country he would visit was China, as previously planned, for the simple reason bitter jealousy existed between China and Japan and people of Chinese origin in this country would vote against Hayao simply out of spite. He would keep the open door for immigration and would also make technology a priority so as to create jobs. He did not fear losing workers to other countries, he understood it was a global economy. While he was interested in getting elected, he needed to make sure he could follow through on most of his campaign promises. He convinced himself people would see him as a man of integrity and served the people of Colorado with distinction, and that he would do the same from the White House.

Mr. Visque looked at the list of people Kelly wanted them to contact. There were a few from Star Fitness, some childhood friends, and Richard. He knew about Richard, the married man whom she was dating, but did not approve. Everyone talked about the fact that morals and values seemed to fall by the wayside after the Vietnam War and the counter-culture movement of the 1960's. Well, he had been a millennial and he considered himself a man of virtue. There were others like him. The problem wasn't with the population but with their leadership. The people tried to exercise their will, and some strides had been made, but in the end we were not getting our top young people to run for office anymore. In his opinion, a person did not break up a family, and yes, he realized Richard did not have any children. He still thought Kelly's actions were wrong. She didn't listen to him, just reached out when she needed something, and she sure needed their help now. He hoped her episodes with the white power group did not come back to haunt her, but he couldn't imagine it wouldn't. He started making phone calls. The people on the list knew about what transpired and some of them seemed receptive to talking to Kelly's attorney, who would be getting in touch with them either on Saturday or Sunday. He expected this case would generate a media storm, and as it would turn out, he would not be wrong.

Quinn Waller had delegated all his other active cases to his subordinates; this one commanded his undivided attention. He was preparing for the next step in the process, the Grand Jury, scheduled for next Wednesday. He would be surprised if they didn't grant the indictment. His team possessed strong physical evidence, the DNA, as well as a clear path from Kelly Visque to the Bernards through Lorraine Corvino. It should be a slam dunk. Once that was done the arraignment would be the following Wednesday, and he had an idea as to how it would go. She would plead not guilty and her lawyer would use the media to Visque's advantage as much as possible before the trial began. He tended to avoid the press as they usually portrayed the prosecution as the villain; he preferred to focus on the task at hand. Once the arraignment was finished, he would have approximately six weeks for discovery before the trial started, which should be ample time to collect all the information necessary to convict.

Friday, April 6th, 11am
Mr. and Mrs. Visque returned to see their daughter and found her in a fragile state. They asked her what was wrong and she said she just felt nervous about everything coming her way. They tried to reassure her she was getting good representation and that her friends would testify on her behalf and vouch for the fact she was not a murderer. They did not sound very convincing, however. Mr. Visque said he managed to contact everyone on the list Kelly gave him and they all expected a call from her lawyer. Kelly asked if her dad would call Lionel Ross and find out when he planned to see her friends and coworkers, and also when he was coming back to meet with her. He said he would. Her parents stayed for another half hour and then left, saying they would come again tomorrow, and in fact every day. Kelly appreciated that and bid them goodbye, having a little more of her strength renewed.

President Harrington was in the midst of planning his third round of increased immigration, and this time would be Spain. He and Spain's President had agreed to push through capital projects that would get awarded to companies from the other country. This was the perfect time for Harrington to do that since the country was caught up with Kelly Visque and the trial to come. He wanted Spain next since most of the people there would support the ticket of Hayao and Ramirez even if they were Catholic. Harrington predicted that for most of them their nationality would come before their religion. The process had been set in motion for their citizens to start coming on Sunday, and would work the same way as those from Israel and Japan before them. They would send people in over a few days and have them go to various parts of the country to set up living quarters. Once they became absorbed into society which usually took about a month, he would start the process again, this time with South Africa. He wanted to have all the people here from the countries which would help the candidates he endorsed by the beginning of August, so he would have time to pass legislation that would allow them to vote in the Presidential election. If he continued to do it quietly, no suspicion should be aroused, as long as he kept an explanation at the ready, which he always made sure he did. He understood Hayao was going to Mexico tomorrow, and Russell and Weimitz along with their lackey Joe Berry would be visiting India sometime next week. That was good. He wanted them to ingratiate themselves with governments abroad, even those whose citizens did not make up a big percentage of this country's population. It would show the world dialogue existed which would reflect well when it came to Election Day. It would show they were progressive candidates who would consider the global impact of their decisions, which captured the ideology of the future.

3pm
Alex Ramirez's plane landed in Detroit and Hayao's limo was waiting to drive her to Moritu's Dearborn office where Hayao would meet her. They would have a strategy session that afternoon where they would review their itinerary and the message they would try to convey.
Once they exchanged greetings, Hayao spoke first. "What are the places we are going to visit in Mexico?"
"We will start our tour in Mexico City, where we will meet with the President and spend two days meeting with various politicians and business leaders. From there we will go to Ecatepec to visit a factory or two. Ecatepec is a city but is very closely tied to Mexico City as many people who live in Ecatepec work there. We will do well in that area of the country. When we venture out further from Mexico City, you will be viewed as more of an outsider."
"What other places are we going to visit?"
"I want to hit all the major cities. That will give you a flavor of the country and will allow the people a chance to get to know you. We will spend two days in Mexico City and then one day each in the next nine cities before we end our trip in Acapulco for a day and a

half to let our hair down a little and show the country we are at home there. Hayao, I am sure I don't have to tell you the people there will be watching you very closely, so it's important to try to embrace their customs and ingratiate yourself into society as much as possible."

"I know that. I am looking forward to the trip and getting to know the fine people there!"

"Excellent. We will be travelling by bus with four security officers from the firm Natsu hired on our bus, and there will be two buses accompanying us that are being supplied by the federal authorities in Mexico, one in front and one behind us staffed with two armed guards each as well as assistants who will help us with our accommodations and any other details that may arise."

"Thank you Alex, for arranging all this. It's hard to believe the election will be here in seven months. While we are on the plane I would like us to come up with our course of action for the remainder of our campaign from a macro point of view. We don't have to iron out all the details yet but we should have a big picture. The way I see it we can divide the remaining time into three parts; from now until the summer, the summertime, and the two months after the summer until the election. Try to give some thought tonight about what we want to accomplish during each stretch and how we will go about it."

"Alright, I will. I have some ideas that we can discuss tomorrow. I understand we have dinner plans this evening."

"Yes, we will be dining with the Governor of Michigan at his mansion to secure his endorsement." Just then Hayao's assistant came in to tell him that FBI Director Grey was on the phone. Hayao answered. "Hello, this is Hayao."

"Hello, Hayao, this is James Grey. I am sorry to bother you, I know you are meeting with Alex Ramirez but I wanted to catch you before you went to Mexico. Would you have time to meet with me?" Is this for real, Hayao thought, but recognized he must comply. At least he could make Grey come to him.

"Sure, I am at Moritu Corporation's offices in Dearborn."

"Great. I will be there in 30 minutes."

Half an hour later, Grey was shown into Hayao's inner office. The displeasure at being inconvenienced showed on Hayao's face, so Grey got down to business. "I have to talk to you about Louis Grenadine. Let me be blunt in the interest of time. He is a suspect in the murders of Juan Pillar and his driver. We, the FBI, are aware he is working for your campaign. We have to follow every lead, so I need to know where you were on February 25th and with whom, as well as all your phone records, your office phone, your home phone, and your cell phone. I don't need them right now, but I would like you to arrange for all the information to be sent to me as soon as it is available."

"I will take care of it. Now if you will excuse us, we have things to do." Grey got up and left without a word.

Saturday, April 7th, 9am

Lionel Ross was on his way to see the first person on his list of potential witnesses for the defense given to him by Kelly Visque, and he was going into a poor neighborhood in DC to meet with Stefan Kurtz, a coworker and friend of Kelly Visque's from Star Fitness. He spoke with a strong German accent as if he had just arrived in this country and asked Lionel to tell Kelly he was thinking of her when the two men had spoken on the phone. Ten minutes later he arrived in front of Kurtz's building, a row house in the middle of a city block. He rang the bell and a tall blond man who looked like he started lifting weights the moment he came out of the womb answered the door. He shook Ross's hand with a grip that almost tore his arm off and invited him inside. They sat in the kitchen and Ross began his questioning. He wanted to know how Kelly was to work with, and Stefan said she took personal training very seriously and always gave her clients the best possible service. She had been doing this a long time and was very knowledgeable. She was easy to get along with but insisted on perfection when it came to using the equipment properly and preparing to exercise and came across as militant at times, including telling other trainers how to do their jobs. Did she ever preach about her political views or impose them on others? Kurtz replied she could be vocal at times and was clearly against immigration in addition to being a member of American Pride for a time. Ross said he was surprised he knew about that. Kurtz said she wasn't embarrassed about it and often came up in conversation. Ross next asked Kurtz if he thought Visque could have committed murder and he hesitated, then answered no. Ross wasn't keen on putting him on the stand as a witness, not because he would say anything incriminatory, but because the prosecution would likely be able to crack him open and get him to slip up and contradict himself. Ross would put him at the bottom of the list. They chatted for a few more minutes and then Ross left to go to the next person on the list, a man named Calvin, the manager at Star Fitness. He was at work so that's where Ross went to speak with him. Calvin embodied the exact opposite of Stefan, a thin build and medium height. They went into the office to conduct their meeting. Calvin described Kelly as a serious worker, sometimes too serious, as she had the tendency to push her clients too hard. He never heard her espouse politics at work though he understood she could be very opinionated and forceful. Did Calvin think her capable of murder? No. Ross asked if he would be willing to testify to that and he said he would. Ross expected him to make a good witness as he exuded self-confidence and did not vacillate. He would be the defense's first witness and would start them off on the right foot. Ross left and looked at the list to see who was next, and it turned out to be one of Visque's childhood friends. Her name was Margo and she lived out in Maryland. Ross checked to see if there was anyone else on the list on the way out to that part of the state, but unfortunately there wasn't. He would go there tomorrow, maybe the traffic would be lighter. He wanted to go meet her parents today since they lived near here and then he would call it a day. Tomorrow he would find Margo and the two white supremacists on the list.

The FBI agents investigating Lorraine Corvino had not uncovered much yet, except that she had indeed been fooling around with Winston Bernard. They were on their way to talk to her boss at Magnus Industries. His name was Cecil and he was in a hurry. They told him it wouldn't take long, just a few questions. When they started asking about Lorraine, he became nervous and wanted to know what it was about. They told him they were investigating someone that lived in her building and inquired if she maintained any contact with that person, but they could not disclose the person's name to Cecil. Did he trust she was credible? Would they be able to trust what she said? He said she had always been reliable and there had never been any complaints about her from their customers. When did she start working there? Cecil said about ten years ago. What did he know about what she did outside of work? He said nothing. The employees never discussed their personal lives outside of work. He suggested they speak with Rick Heller, who often worked with Lorraine. They asked Cecil about Heller's schedule and he told them he was off today and tomorrow and would be back at the Supreme Court building at 7pm on Monday. They thanked him and were on their way, planning to be there Monday at 7. Their next stop was Corvino's apartment, where they would tell her she was a person of interest and they needed to speak with her friends and family members to get more information. She was not under arrest, but she would be under surveillance to make sure she didn't flee. They asked her about the people they could meet with, and she said her mother and father were dead but she had a brother who lived nearby and two friends upstairs. They wrote down the names and went to find them.

4pm
Hayao and Ramirez were en route to Mexico City. They each had a drink to relax a little and now were ready to talk. Alex spoke first. "Each of the segments you mentioned has a different objective. The time from now until summer should be spent campaigning abroad and gaining as much support as possible from those countries for the citizens here. Much of the U.S. will be preoccupied with the trial going on, so trying to cultivate votes here will be futile. We can also spend this time analyzing the political climate and finding out which issues are important to the majority and decide which segments of the population we will pursue. This will be done through the use of polls, which will be conducted by the market research firm I have used in the past,

headquartered in Florida. Once we have the results, we can coordinate a consistent set of policies which will attract the largest block of voters across various demographics. That will lead us into the summer, when we will review debating techniques and interview skills, and spend some time on leisure activities so people can see a human side as well. Once the fall arrives, we will be poised to begin touring this country, using your charm and my preparation to inspire people and convince them you are the only candidate who can get the job done."

"Alright. That sounds like a good course of action. When we get back from Mexico, let's begin conducting the polls. We can run a few of them to make sure we obtain all the information we need. Once we are back from Mexico where else do you suggest we go?"

"We should visit a few of the countries in Europe, specifically Spain, France, and England. Even though many people there will follow the Pope, we can try to make some inroads in those nations. Spain will be ours but we should still visit to show we are not taking them for granted. We should also schedule a trip for the Middle East. Many of those countries have not decided who they will endorse. I know Russell is planning to visit India, and I am sure he will go to other countries in the region as well." She paused. "How confident are you we will carry the Orient?"

"Except for China, very confident."

"Do you suppose we should go to the countries there to show our commitment to them?"

"Let's tour the other places first, and then if we still have time, we can make a trip to the Asian nations. You know, Natsu is going to insist on coming to the United States for a period of time before the election, probably a month. He will say his presence will be beneficial as he will persuade people to vote for me."

"Are you worried he will get in the way and make things worse instead of better?"

"Exactly."

"Well, we can give him tasks to keep him busy and out of the way, and we can do it in such a way that he won't even realize it." Hayao looked skeptical. "Trust me, I have handled people like him before. Let's turn our attention to our itinerary for Mexico and what we will encounter at each location."

The FBI agents concluded their conversations with Lorraine Corvino's neighbors and her brother and learned she was a good neighbor, quiet and mindful of other people's needs. Her brother suspected she had been having an affair, because she remained uninvolved for a long time and she always said she was lonely when on her own, yet she has seemed much more upbeat for the last few years. Whenever he would comment on that, she would say she was happier with her job, enjoyed her freedom and realized she didn't need a man to feel fulfilled. They didn't get together too often, so he didn't know much about her daily schedule. He knew she worked at the Supreme Court building, but had no reason to suspect it was a Supreme Court justice with whom she was having an affair. Basically, the agents came away not knowing anything more than they had before today. They were hoping Rick Heller would have some inside information for them. They decided not to spin their wheels and would revisit this case on Monday when they met with him.

Kelly Visque was exhausted from all the anxiety. She wondered if she should just end it all and hang herself right here in her cell. The shame and guilt she felt was unbearable. She had always been someone who prided herself on not worrying what others thought and being tough, but this involved all the people around her as well. She had been opinionated about her opposition to immigration and had a volatile temper, she would admit, but she was not a murderer, and now her parents were being dragged into this. She hoped her lawyer would be able to project the image that she wasn't so fanatical about her views as the other members of American Pride. God, she had been so stupid to go to their meetings! She knew she would survive this; just take it one day at a time, she told herself. The worst was over; being arrested. The best way she could help herself was to remain calm and do her best to be cooperative through this process. She had to be her own advocate.

Sunday, April 8th

Lionel Ross was on his way to meet with one of the members of American Pride, a man who went by the name of Samson, not because of his physical strength, but because he always wanted to remember not to give in to temptation. He lived in a trailer park and was badly in need of a shower. Ross suggested they talk outside. He wanted to know if Samson recalled what kind of participant Kelly Visque was at the meetings she attended. Samson recalled a vague recollection of her as being an active participant but never a leader, and she didn't last very long. Ross asked him how long he has been associated with American Pride and he said ten years. Despite his appearance and lack of hygiene, he seemed well spoken, so Ross would consider using him as a witness if he agreed to clean up before taking the stand. Kelly's parents said last night there were members who were not so extreme, and while they did not condone the organization, they suspected some people joined out of a sense of jingoism but were not violent and wanted what they thought was best for the country. Ross just hoped Samson wouldn't lose his cool if the Attorney General tried to goad him on the stand. He had gotten all he could from Samson and went to see Margo, Kelly's childhood friend. After that, he would go see the other person from American Pride.

Ross got to Margo's apartment building around noon and he was glad he brought his umbrella as it was raining pretty hard. He found her apartment number and pressed the buzzer. A moment later she let him in and he trudged up the stairs to the third floor. She was a thin woman with a nice smile. She offered him a cup of tea which he declined. By looking around her apartment he surmised she was athletic and into sports. That must have been what she and Kelly had in common. Ross thought he should let Margo reminisce about Kelly, and lots of information would come pouring out. He started by asking her about her childhood and what kinds of things they enjoyed doing together. "Well, we were both tomboys, always playing outside. Kelly was so good at sports the boys usually didn't want her to play with them as she was better than many of them. She was also into working out a lot and

advocated fitness. She often said she would like to motivate people to be healthy; it's really not a surprise she ended up as a trainer."
"It sounds like she always knew what she wanted out of life."
"Absolutely."
"What opinions did she hold about foreigners and our government's policy on immigration?"
"She felt people who came to this country should have to pay their dues before they receive the same rights and privileges as others who have been here longer."
"How strongly did she feel about this?"
"She was never violent if that is what you are getting at."
"Why do you think she associated with American Pride?"
"She wanted to collaborate with those whom she thought had like mindsets. Once they started insinuating violent means be used she ended her relationship with them for good."
"I understand she can be volatile at times."
"Yes, she has a temper. I have often thought she needs to learn how to control it. Her temper comes from her passion. I am not saying that is an excuse, but sometimes she just cannot imagine how others could not see her point of view." They talked for another half hour, and when they finished Ross knew he would definitely be calling Margo to the stand.

4pm, Mexico City
 Hayao and Alex Ramirez were at a vigil at the Angel of Independence to make a statement that there would be greater collaboration between the United States and Mexico. Mexico's President was there of course as well as the Mayor of Mexico City and other key industry leaders and top government officials. They were both staying at Los Pinos while in Mexico City and tonight they were going to be President Carraval's guests for dinner. Mexico City was beautiful; a city loaded with history and culture. Hayao was thoroughly enjoying himself and looked forward to the rest of the two weeks. The people were super friendly and Alex was both acting and being received as the perfect ambassador, the woman who would help usher in a new era in worldwide politics. Yesterday when they arrived they had been given a tour of the

whole city and Hayao felt positive relations would be good were he to win the election. Tomorrow they would be visiting the Jumex headquarters in Ecatepec, the biggest producer of juice and nectar in Mexico, after which they would be taking their motorcade to Puebla where they would be participating in a parade at the Zocalo, where the government buildings were, and visiting the Volkswagen plant located there. The purpose of this trip was to interact with the public as much as possible and the itinerary Ramirez created included the right mix of that and governmental business as well.

Monday, April 9th, 10am
Lionel Ross arrived to meet Kelly Visque and was quickly processed through security. They wanted to review some strategies. He had met with all the people on the list and wanted to review the conversations. As far as a witness list went, he believed they should call the following people; Margo, her boss from work, Calvin, and Stefan Kurtz, the trainer who Ross interviewed. They would all provide favorable testimony. Kelly shook her head. "Margo will not make a good witness; she is very easily swayed. I do not want her testifying. Instead, we should call Samson and Richard, my friend."
"Are you sure about Samson? He may not fare so well when Waller cross examines him."
"He will be fine. He rises to the occasion."
"I saw the second American Pride member but he was really unstable and I will not put someone like that on the witness stand; he would damage our case so badly that we couldn't rebound from it." All this background was related to Visque's character which would be one of the building blocks of the prosecution's case. They were going to hammer away at the connection and relationship between her and Lorraine Corvino saying Visque used Corvino to obtain information about Justice Bernard and had motive to kill him, that being to eliminate the possibility of the legislation getting passed which would allow a foreigner to run for President. They, the prosecution, would of course point to her association with American Pride, omitting the part about her being

an ancillary member. Ross told her they needed to paint a picture of her simply looking to satisfy her curiosity and wanting no part of the more extreme aspects. She agreed with some of their philosophies but never advocated violence, and once she realized some of the members engaged in such acts then she was no longer interested in their organization. The other half of their case would involve the hard evidence, namely the DNA. They have a DNA sample from a dead bee that stung her. Ross asked her if she remembers being stung by the bee, and she said yes. Did she kill the bee? She swatted at it but is not sure if it died. He then asked if she recalled if the bee stung her while she was in front of the Supreme Court building and she thought so. Would she swear to that under oath? She took a minute to ponder and to try to jog her memory. It was when she was there! Her mind had been wandering, wondering if she really could build a future with Richard when she experienced the sharp pain and reacted by swatting the bee. She watched it land on the ground and then kept walking. She looked at Ross to make sure he believed her and he did. The prosecution would likely say the other person whose DNA turned up, Peter Marvin, had been stung elsewhere earlier. Ross needed to arrive at a sensible theory that refuted this. It was all about reasonable doubt. He made a note to find out if the time of the sting could be verified; if so, Kelly Visque might be exonerated. He would start looking for an expert on DNA extraction tonight. He felt optimistic right now. The information she passed on to him might lead to an advantage. He was really done with Kelly for now. Her parents were coming and he wanted to get going to allow the three of them some privacy. He told her he would continue on with his representation of her, and she should remain calm and write down anything else she remembered that could be relevant.

7pm
The two FBI agents who were investigating Lorraine Corvino showed up at the Supreme Court building to talk to Rick Heller. He was a skinny man with lots of tattoos and a ponytail. They showed him their badges and he realized why they had come to

speak to him. "You have more questions about Lorraine, huh? Well, fire away."

"How long did you work with her?"

"On and off for five years."

"Did you ever see her interact with any of the justices?"

"You mean was it obvious she was screwing Bernard? Yes it was. She would wait around till I left and I would sometimes see him lurking around the stairs on my way out."

"Did she ever talk about him?"

"Never. She would daydream though. Probably thought he would leave his wife for her. Fat chance. The guy had it too good. He strung her along the whole time. If she was involved, the bastard had it coming. Hey, any openings for a G-man? I could be an agent." The two agents kept a straight face, thanked him, and suggested he check the Bureau's website.

Wednesday, April 11th, 9am

Quinn Waller was all ready to present the evidence to the Grand Jury to obtain the indictment for Kelly Visque. The jurors filed in and sat down in the jury box. Waller introduced himself and started to speak. "We are here today to review the evidence against Kelly Visque, arrested for the murders of Cecily Bernard and Winston Bernard on June 18, 2039. I, as the prosecutor in this case, have one irrefutable piece of evidence. I have Miss Visque's DNA which the FBI extracted from a dead bee at the crime scene. There were two sets of DNA found in the bee, but Miss Visque had motive. She is a friend of the woman who was having an affair with Justice Bernard and who likely wanted revenge. Furthermore, Miss Visque attended several meetings for American Pride, which shows her political leanings and views on immigrants and those Americans with ancestry an American Pride member might find objectionable. There is certainly enough material here to indict." One juror raised his hand.

"Mr. Waller, what about the other person whose DNA was found?"

"He offered an alibi which was corroborated and none of the circumstances pointed to him."

"Circumstances? Are you saying some of the foundation of your case is circumstantial?"

"No, but let's also remember this is not a trial but a proceeding for an indictment. Your job is to decide if there is sufficient evidence to charge Miss Visque with a crime." Waller had finished his presentation, and the jurors got up to leave the room. They would go into the jury deliberation room to discuss the case. Waller went to make a few phone calls in the meantime.

An hour later, Waller got the call that the jury was back. He went into the courtroom and they filed back in. The foreman stood up in the jury box and addressed Waller. "We have reached a majority rule of ¾. We are granting the indictment for the charge of murder for the defendant Kelly Visque." Waller breathed a silent breath of relief.

"Ladies and Gentlemen, I thank you for your service today. You are excused." This was the easiest indictment he had ever obtained; the jurors did not even ask to see any witnesses or hear any testimony. This case presented such a high profile they could not have ruled any other way.

Lionel Ross went by to see Kelly Visque at lunchtime. He told her Waller had gotten the indictment, but that she shouldn't worry, he lined up good character witnesses and was on the way to finding a DNA expert. He had done some reading and believed no current way existed to determine when DNA was captured by bees that had stung a person. That would work to their advantage as the prosecution could not claim she was stung at a certain time and Ross would make the argument she had been stung earlier at another location and someone else killed the bee. That was reasonable doubt. He asked her how she was coping. She was doing ok under the circumstances, but remained anxious to get the trial underway. He tried to explain to her as gently as possible that there would be a period of discovery after the arraignment. She asked how long, and he told her up to two months. She let out a sigh at the thought of being stuck in this cell for that long, plus the time during the trial. Ross knew she was in denial about the possibility of spending the rest of her life in a cell. He made a mental note to talk to the sergeant about getting her some privileges here and would request she be transferred to a medium security facility after the arraignment. Visque asked him what time it was and he told her it was almost one pm, which cheered her up as her parents would be here in about an hour.

Director Grey's phone rang and his assistant told him there was a woman on the phone with some information for him about Hayao. He told her to patch the call through. The woman on the other end explained she had Hayao's phone records and a sworn statement from Zachary, the number two man at Moritu Corporation's headquarters in Michigan that Hayao had been with him that day all day from 11am until 10pm when they stopped working for the night. He asked her to email it to his private account at the FBI and thanked her for the prompt response. The email arrived a few minutes later and he checked the signature against the signature on file in the FBI database for Zachary, and noticed in the phone records there were no calls to Louis Grenadine, the DC area, or any number that could have been considered remotely suspicious. He would let Billet know further investigation of Hayao was not necessary.

Kangaroo had not been home in two days due to the tax return filing deadline of April 15th looming over his head. Once he was done being a spy, he would be done doing this tax crap too. It was boring and monotonous, and his clients became more demanding each year. His phone rang and he recognized the voice right away. "Hello, I am calling to check on my tax return. I have some more documents I need to give you. Would you please meet me and pick them up, say today at 4pm?"

"Of course. I will meet you at the halfway point and review them before we part ways." Their meeting had been set for their usual spot.

4pm, Boston Commons

Uncle George labored down the street with his walker and went to usual bench. Kangaroo came two minutes later. "The FBI is interested in another woman for the Bernard case. Her name is Lorraine Corvino and she knew Kelly Visque from a bowling team on which they both participated. They are not sure if she was complicit in the murders or the unwitting provider of information. They are looking into that. The feds also understand she was having an affair with Justice Bernard which will certainly become public information very soon." He paused. "There is something concerning Kelly Visque we must make President Harrington aware of. She had been associated with American Pride. There very well may be demonstrations during the trial and some of them may turn violent. I will have to let him know we have intelligence on this. He will likely want us to keep an eye on American Pride to see if they are planning any disturbances. We should set something up so when he asks we will be ready. Why don't you contact the agents who are back from South America and give them a heads up. That will give them a chance to find out where they need to go and what they need to do. We will talk again next week."

6pm, Washington, DC

Sondra Tristan had been itching to get an update from the FBI about the case since the press conference given by Attorney General Waller, and now she couldn't wait any longer. After work, she drove to Quantico and went up to see the Director. She hadn't called ahead but knew he would meet with her if possible. Fortunately it was and she went in just a few minutes later. She got right to the point. "I am sorry to barge in like this, but I really need to be brought up to speed on the latest developments in the case. I am aware Kelly Visque has been arrested; has she pleaded yet?" The Director kept a solemn expression on his face.

"From what I understand, no, but that would be a better question for the Attorney General. I can tell you we are investigating another person who may have been involved in this crime along with Kelly Visque." Sondra looked surprised for a moment.

"Who would that be?"

"Her name is Lorraine Corvino, and she is a custodian at the Supreme Court building." Director Grey could see the wheels turning in Sondra's mind.

Warily, she said, "What does that have to do with my father?"

"It seems they were involved." Director Grey noticed the transformation right before his eyes. Sondra's face turned red and she got a dark expression on her face. She spit out the words, "My father was not a philanderer or unfaithful to my mother!" She was so angry she was grinding her teeth while talking.

"I am sorry Sondra. I cannot imagine how hard this must be to hear. This information became necessary to uncover so that we will be able to put Kelly Visque behind bars. Without it the Attorney General has no case as there is no opportunity for Visque to have had access to your father."

"This custodian, Corvino, she could have known my father's schedule just from working in the building."

"We spoke to the other custodian that works with her. He said even though they were never caught in the act, it was obvious what was going on."

"I am telling you nothing like that ever happened. Please don't tell me you are going to accept the word of a janitor over me!"

"The evidence points to it being true. Even if our side didn't use it to our advantage it would have come out as the defense would find a way to make it work for them."

"You are supposed to have been my father's friend! How could you drag his name through the mud? Go to hell!" With that said, she turned on her heel and stormed out.

Thursday, April 12th, 10am

Kangaroo got in touch with one of agents who was back in the States after being pulled from his assignment. He explained the situation with Kelly Visque and how American Pride needed to be watched. Kangaroo said he would leave it up to the agent as to how to proceed, whether he wanted to try to infiltrate the organization or simply use surveillance. He told the agent they should meet in three weeks from today, on May 3rd, and the agent should have a game plan at the minimum.

Todd Russell's office, Chicago, noon

Governor Russell was flying high. People were recognizing his administration would be the one to lead them into the future with technology. Illinois was in good shape, and the national polls conducted recently all showed him being in the lead. Vincent Weimitz already expressed ways to improve upon the initiatives President Harrington had undertaken since entering office almost eight years ago. As an example, Weimitz suggested incorporating sensors into the cross country irrigation and water source system to more efficiently distribute the water and ultimately to anticipate hydration needs. He also developed an idea for taking traffic software to the next level by incorporating more factors into the software such as vacation trends, holidays, and construction projects to name a few. He wanted to build the most comprehensive traffic program yet and configure it to be used in just about any metropolitan area. Russell was thinking more and more he would simply let Weimitz run with technology and not count on him for any government functions, instead relying on other members of his cabinet to perform the duties of the Vice President. That was an unorthodox strategy but it would make use of Weimitz's strength. He also expected to gain even more ground in India and the other countries he planned to visit because they were fascinated by all the technology the countries in the Western hemisphere retained. He would also continue to focus on making sure Illinois stayed strong, for if he neglected his duties as governor people wouldn't care what else he did. Lastly, he would devote the last three months of the race to campaigning right here in the U.S., and as long as he made no major mistakes, he truly expected the White House to be his.

Blake Tristan called his wife on her cell phone and when she answered, he knew she was still in bed. She said she didn't feel well; he checked his calendar for the rest of the day and saw he didn't have any more appointments so he decided to go home and check on her. When he walked into their apartment 45 minutes later, the door to the bedroom was closed and it was really stuffy when he opened the door. Sondra pretended to be asleep and he walked over to her and shook her a little. "Hi honey." She squinted at the clock.
"Blake, it's 2:45 in the afternoon. What are you doing home?"

"I was worried about you."

"This thing with my dad upset me terribly. I didn't even want to go out today."

"I am really sorry. Your father was a good man." Sondra sat up and the blanket fell away, she was naked.

"I thought Director Grey was on our side. Why would he perpetrate such sordid allegations?" Blake just listened, not knowing what to say. After a few minutes of silence, she asked him what he thought.

"Let's do something to take your mind off this. Let's go away for the weekend. We can find a nice bed and breakfast in Virginia. How does that sound?"

"It sounds great."

"Excellent! I will go make the arrangements." He got up to go to the computer when she grabbed his hand.

"Not so fast counselor!"

Hayao and Alex were in Juarez, in the state of Chihuahua visiting a children's museum there after spending a few days in Puebla. Ramirez had been correct, the people outside of Mexico City were not as trusting of him being a foreigner. He was patient, however, and sensed them starting to warm up a bit. Each stop turned out slightly better than the previous one, as the news reported his interactions in a positive way. Their itinerary for the remainder of their trip was as follows; they were staying in Juarez until tomorrow, driving to Chihuahua for two days, leaving for Monterrey on Monday, staying there until Wednesday morning, driving to Victoria for a day and a half, and then heading to Acapulco until Saturday afternoon for a little relaxation. Later on Saturday they would be chauffeured back to the airport in Mexico City for the flight home. They both felt the trip had been a success and were anxious to see what the reaction would be when they arrived back home in Detroit.

Saturday, April 14th

Kelly Visque was reading quietly in her cell, reflecting that the last few days had been an improvement. Her attorney arranged for her to be allowed to lift weights for an hour a day which was a big comfort. Her parents visited each day, and Richard even stopped by once. He seemed uptight, more than usual, and she wouldn't be surprised if she never saw him again. She was deep in concentration when an officer told her she had a visitor. She wondered who it could be as her parents said they would be back tomorrow. She was led into the room down the hall and handcuffed to the table. Five minutes later a well-dressed man arrived. He waited for the officer to leave before he introduced himself.

"Hello, my name is Glen Aaron, and I am a lawyer for the ACLU. I was sent by Greg Driscoll, who is the director." Kelly looked surprised. What could the ACLU possibly want with her?

"What can I do for you, Mr. Aaron?"

"I am here to take over your case, if you would like me to. We believe we could provide you with better representation than you will receive with the public defender that you currently have."

"Ok, but doesn't the ACLU take cases where someone's civil rights have been violated?"

"Yes."

"Well, how do you figure mine have been then?"

"The search the FBI made of Lorraine Corvino's apartment when they found the picture of the two of you on the same bowling team. They did not have a warrant."

"How did they think they could get away with it then? I mean, they are seasoned detectives."

"They are claiming it was in plain sight so a warrant was not required. That is something I will address at your arraignment on Wednesday if you decide to have me represent you." She thought for a minute.

"Do I have to decide right now?"

"No, I can give you until Tuesday."

"How much are you going to charge me?"

"Nothing. We are going to take your case pro bono." Of course, she realized, they wanted the publicity for their organization.

"Well, my lawyer has done some background work. Would you meet with him before the arraignment so you can pick up where he left off?"

"Absolutely. I looked around when I came in. Perhaps we can have you transferred to a facility with less restrictions while you await trial. In the meantime is there anything you need?" Wow, this guy was smooth.

"No thanks. I am good. Why don't you come back on Monday and I will have an answer then. Good day."

"Fine. One thing, we do not want this news getting out just yet, so if you decide to discuss this with anyone before Wednesday, please make sure it stays between you and them." She yelled to the guard right outside that they were finished.

Sunday, April 15th

The NSA agent Kangaroo made operational again decided not to try to go undercover within American Pride. It would take too long and the members were wary of strangers coming around looking to join without being sponsored, so it would be hard to come by any valuable information that way. Instead, he decided to mobilize ten of the top surveillance agents to tail American Pride's top leaders to see if anything incriminating surfaced. The agents were scattered around the country, mostly in rural areas where the group typically met and lived. That made it more difficult to spy, but these operatives would find a way, even if they had to bury themselves in the woods.

Kelly Visque's parents got to the jail at around 1pm and Kelly had been waiting all day. She wanted to see what they thought about the lawyer from the ACLU. They took a few minutes to ponder, and then her dad said he thought she should switch. Her public defender might be competent and have her best interest in mind, but he did not have the resources they did, and they also possessed experience about using the media to their advantage before the trial started, which would have an impact on the jury selection process and those ultimately selected for the jury. Overall, he said, they were simply a more formidable opponent and her mother agreed. Kelly decided she would follow their advice so when Aaron returned tomorrow, she would tell him he was hired. Her mother said she had spoken to the lieutenant on duty and obtained permission to bring some food from a restaurant for dinner if she wanted, and of course she did. An hour later, Kelly and her parents were dining on three perfectly cooked steaks and baked potatoes from a local steakhouse, and Kelly thought a meal had never tasted so good.

Tuesday, April 17th, 10am
Lionel Ross had called Kelly Visque to tell her he would be stopping by tomorrow to review some last minute things for the arraignment. Aaron suggested she not tell Ross over the phone that she was switching lawyers as he might try to destroy some of the information he had gathered out of spite. When Kelly informed Aaron yesterday that she wanted him to be her lawyer he said he would wait for Ross to arrive first and then he would come in a few minutes later. That way, Ross would have displayed all his notes on the table and could not deny he had them there. Aaron would be able to demand either Ross turn over the original documents to Aaron or they would both go together and make copies. He told Kelly not to worry if she had told him anything in confidence as that was protected by privilege. Ross arrived and went into the meeting room and Aaron came in fifteen minutes later. Kelly felt a little guilty not saying anything until Aaron got there, but she knew Ross was a professional and would bounce back. Aaron walked in and Ross told him this was a private meeting and he would have to leave. Aaron said he was not leaving as he was Kelly Visque's new attorney and introduced himself to Ross as Glen Aaron, attorney for the ACLU. Ross looked at Visque and demanded to know what was happening. She explained he had done a great job so far but she needed someone with more clout behind them and she was sorry he found out this way. He turned red in the face and started to gather his papers when Aaron requested that he leave them. Ross scooped them all up and flung them in the air so they scattered all over the room, picked up his briefcase, told them both to go fuck themselves, and stormed out.

CHAPTER 10

Wednesday, April 18th, 9am

Kelly Visque's arraignment had arrived, and strangely, she felt more in control since this whole ordeal started with her arrest. She had strong representation and Glen Aaron believed they possessed a strong witness base who would be convincing to a jury. The arraignment judge entered. Aaron had explained the judge today was really not important. Their only function, besides accepting the plea and setting a trial date involved asking for any pretrial motions, which Aaron planned to submit. He was going to try to have the results from the search of Lorraine Corvino's apartment thrown out with a motion to suppress the picture of the bowling team based upon the doctrine of illegal search due to the lack of a search warrant. The prosecution's team seemed focused on the man sitting next to Kelly Visque as that was not the same lawyer assigned to her from the public defender's office. Waller wondered what was going on and didn't have to wait long to find out. The man sitting between Visque and Lionel Ross stood up and introduced himself as Glen Aaron, an attorney for the ACLU who was taking over as Kelly Visque's counsel, replacing Lionel Ross. The judge addressed Kelly Visque and asked her if she had made this decision of her own free will and she said she had. The judge asked the court stenographer to enter this into the record, and once they had, excused Mr. Ross and requested Waller to state the formal charges. He stood up and read the charges as terrorism and murder, of which terrorism brought an automatic sentence of death. That, however, amounted to the only fundamental difference between a trial for a terrorist and that of a murderer. The judge next addressed Kelly Visque and asked her for her plea. Her plea of not guilty was entered and the judge set a trial date of Monday June 4th, giving both sides ample time for discovery. He asked if there were any pretrial motions, and Aaron stood up and said he wanted to introduce one. He handed it to the judge who remarked that he would pass it on to the trial judge and added that the deadline for any more pretrial motions would be Friday, May 25th. No one voiced any objections so the judge banged his gavel and called the next case. Quietly, in the back of the courtroom, Tom

Sirois, a reporter for WNTL here in DC, slipped out to go report on what he had just heard.

10am

All the major news networks, as well as all the internet news websites and email news alerts were breaking the story about the Bernard case and the ACLU swooping down to come to Kelly Visque's defense. The commentators attempted to explain that obviously those in charge there convinced themselves Miss Visque's rights had been violated. At the ACLU office in Washington DC, one of Sondra Tristan's co-workers walked by her cubicle and quietly suggested she go listen to the news. She ran out to her car and opened up an internet session on her phone. She didn't have to look long to see the story. After reading it, she went right home.

Friday, April 20th

Greg Driscoll, the director of the ACLU, had not spoken to reporters yet about his decision to defend Kelly Visque. He intended to wait a few days until he and his staff were no longer the top story. He was working at his desk when an email popped into his inbox. He saw it was from Sondra Tristan. He sighed, knowing it would only be a matter of time until she reached out to him. He opened it and saw her request for two weeks' vacation starting Monday. He approved it right away, understanding this was difficult for her. He went back to work for an hour when he received another email from her. This one tendered her resignation effective the last day of her vacation, sending a statement that she would not be able to train any replacement the ACLU might be able to find on such short notice. Driscoll thought it quite vindictive of her, but didn't really care. No one was indispensable. Approved.

Sondra Tristan was not taking this betrayal without planning some kind of retaliation. She and Blake arranged for her to be interviewed on the news magazine show "In Depth" which aired Sunday at 7pm. The interview would be taped tomorrow with Heather Evigan, the lead correspondent for the show. She would get her point across that the ACLU joined the fight to further their own agenda and not to help Kelly Visque for altruistic reasons. She might end up coming across as bitter but she didn't care. Who would blame her after being stabbed in the back by her employer? No, public opinion would be on her side.

Sunday, April 22nd, 7pm

Sunday remained the one day that most people could be expected to be home and spend time with their families, so the networks often saved their family fare for Sunday evening and Sunday night, as well as shows that would interest a large cross section of the population such as In Depth. Tonight, Sondra Tristan's interview would be covered first. They had been advertising it like crazy and people were curious as to what she was going to say. The first question Evigan asked was did Tristan believe that Kelly Visque was guilty. "Yes. The FBI conducted a thorough investigation and pursued every lead. They are professionals and would never advance their own agenda at the expense of the job at hand." That was a jab at the ACLU and Greg Driscoll.

"I understand that you tendered your resignation right after you heard the news. What were you thinking when you did that?"

"The ACLU is selling out. There is no reason to think that the defendant's civil rights were violated. The decision to defend her came from the top and let me just say they are looking on this as a chance to advance their own individual careers."

"What is the most unfair part about this?"

"That my organization is more concerned about the rights of an accused terrorist and murderer than they are about my parents, who are the real victims. Who was protecting their rights?"

"Do you regret resigning?"

"Not at all. I would not want to work for such a hypocritical organization."

8pm

Greg Driscoll watched Sondra Tristan's interview and felt the need to defend himself and his decision. He issued a statement through a spokesperson that the nation seemed to care about the rights of immigrants and foreigners more than they did about native citizens, and he regretted people assumed they had no business getting involved, but a large segment of the population still existed that didn't want a foreigner as President. Besides, if Kelly Visque was guilty then the legal system would work to arrive at the just outcome. Any personal gain he was being accused of remained a complete fallacy and a feeble attempt to discredit him by shifting attention away from the reason why the ACLU exists in the first place.

Monday, April 23rd

Sondra Tristan made her way up to Quinn Waller's office in the Justice Department's building; she did not have an appointment. He was doing some paperwork and she got right to the point. "I want to join the prosecuting team to work to help put Kelly Visque away."

"Sondra, you are not a lawyer."

"Perhaps I could assist with the investigating or even do clerical work. I don't care, I just want to be involved."

"Alright." He realized he had to help her, her dad was an old friend and she had really been through the ringer lately. "Alright, come back tomorrow. You will be my special assistant and will handle special projects related to the case."

"Thank you, Quinn."

"Don't mention it. See you tomorrow, and be prepared to jump right in."

CHAPTER 11

Tuesday, April 24th

Glen Aaron arrived at the prison facility to see Kelly Visque. There was one thing he needed to explain to her. She had been charged with two separate crimes, those of terrorism and murder. She could be convicted of one, both, or none. If she was charged with terrorism that carried an automatic sentence of death. The murder charge would require a separate sentencing hearing, on the other hand. For the prosecution to prove she was a terrorist they had to prove she had violated the Patriot Act which dictated the criteria for terrorism. The clause Waller would most likely pursue was the one that stated a terroristic act intended to influence the government's conduct. He would argue that Visque was looking to prevent people not born here from running for President and she expected Bernard to vote in favor of the measure. He was the one she kidnapped instead of one of the other justices because of her relationship with Lorraine Corvino. Aaron's task, besides of course proving Visque's innocence, was to discredit the prosecution's theory that Visque was so hardcore in her beliefs that she would resort to murder. Yes, she opposed immigration and the measure the Supreme Court had passed but she was not so fanatical as to commit such a heinous act. She asked him if he thought they had a chance of having the picture of the bowling team thrown out as evidence. He told her honestly he wasn't sure; a lot of it depended upon the judge they got, but he promised to try. He was definitely going to file a pretrial motion to suppress. He was also going to reduce the impact the DNA inside the dead bee had by finding a DNA expert who believed that older DNA inside a bumblebee's stinger was just as likely to show up prominently as fresh DNA. Aaron predicted if their side managed to refute both of those things they had a good chance of taking the bite out of the prosecution's case. The next step was for Kelly and Glen to discuss possible witnesses for the defense. Lionel Ross had spoken with numerous people and Aaron wanted Kelly to consider which ones would make good witnesses. First of all, Kelly wanted Aaron to make contact with Richard again and ask him to visit her one more time.

Kelly felt she could convince him to testify on her behalf, not about her whereabouts, but about her character and the fact that she was not a murderer. Richard knew her well and was a person people believed and trusted; he had an air of being beyond reproach. Aaron said he understood; he also understood what a good prosecutor Waller was and that he would be able to lead Richard to contradict himself and unravel his entire testimony. Aaron was also interested in Samson, the former member of American Pride. Samson had remarked that he thought Visque was not unstable emotionally and had quit the organization just like he had. Aaron planned to have Visque examined by a psychologist and thought the testimony would seem more credible to the jury if it was corroborated by a lay person, even one with a background in a vile organization such as American Pride, because after all, everyone makes mistakes, and the jury would definitely be able to identify with a reformed delinquent. Kelly looked like she had another question and Aaron told her she could always say what was on her mind to him. They would have a much better chance of winning if there was an open dialogue between them. She wanted to know how long he had been practicing law and he told her ten years. She then remarked about the two charges against her, terrorism and murder. According to her, Aaron had explained how he would come up with a defense for the terrorism charge, by refuting the image of her presented by Waller as a xenophobic hate monger with disdain for anything new. She inquired about the murder charge. What was Aaron's plan for that? "Much of the physical evidence that they, the prosecution, have is circumstantial." Trying not to sound condescending, he asked, "Are you familiar with the two types of evidence?" Because she wanted an elementary explanation, Kelly shook her head no. "There is direct evidence and circumstantial evidence. Direct evidence are such things as fingerprints, DNA, eyewitness accounts, etc., that irrefutably link the defendant to the crime. Circumstantial evidence is basically second hand or coincidental situations or occurrences. Both are regarded by the jury, but direct evidence is much more difficult to refute. In this case, the prosecution has no direct evidence." Aaron paused to allow Visque a minute to ponder.

Kelly said, "I thought you just said that DNA is direct evidence."

"I did. I am glad you picked up on that. In this case however, I am treating it as circumstantial, because your DNA found in the bee at the crime scene does not mean the bee stung you at that location. It will be easy for me to argue, which I will, that you very likely were stung somewhere else and the bee just happened to die there. The statement you gave to the FBI was sufficiently vague enough for me to make that argument. You said you remember being stung and swatting at the bee but don't recall if the bee died. That gives me plenty of wiggle room to say the bee may have lived until another person killed it later on. I am planning to find a DNA expert to find out more about how DNA is processed and tested, and how long DNA lasts in a bumblebee before it breaks down. As I understand it the bee was tested for DNA quite a while after the bodies were found, so it may not have been possible to discern anything about the DNA other than whose it was. If that's the case then we come out ahead as I will be able to propose the scenario which I just described." Aaron paused. "There is one more thing Kelly. The FBI took Justice Bernard's body to their crime lab right after the murder to examine his brain and found he did not know his assailant." She looked incredulous.

"How could they tell?"

"They have technology that can read brain waves and detect emotions such as joy and anger. This has to be done within the first 48 hours from the time of death, and the subject had to have submitted to a baseline brain scan so there would be something to compare the new one to. Obviously, Bernard had done a previous brain scan. The judge's brain after he died most closely resembled the model scan that he submitted to when he had been subjected to frightening situations. Waller will infer from this that Bernard was afraid and did not know the kidnapper or kidnappers. That's circumstantial evidence. It has room for interpretation, but can still be helpful for the side who introduces it, usually the prosecution. We are getting ahead of ourselves. For now your job is to decide who our witnesses will be. How are they treating you in here? Do you get to exercise each day? Let me know if the guards start to give you a hard time. Is there anything you need? I understand you have contact with the outside world through your parents, but if there is something you don't want to ask them for tell me and I will see what I can do. I'll do some research over the next few days and be back to give you an update on Monday. Take care, Kelly."

Sondra Tristan arrived at Quinn Waller's office at 10am excited to get started. He was on the phone so she waited right outside his office. He hung up about ten minutes later and came out to greet her. "Hi Sondra, how are you today? I hope you ate your Wheaties, I have a lot planned for you. Why don't we go into the conference room. I will introduce you to my team and go over everything." They walked into the adjacent conference room and the other members were already there. Waller went around the table and did the introductions. "Roberta, Victor, and Joy, this is Sondra Tristan. She is going to be joining our group and helping out in any way she can." They all greeted her warmly and shook her hand. Waller spoke again. "Let's get started. Kelly Visque has been charged with two crimes here, terrorism and murder. Proving each one is completely different, and it is possible for us to get a conviction on both, one or the other, or neither. The criteria for being considered a terrorist is dictated by the Patriot Act, and the clause we will pursue is the one that says someone who performs an act intended to influence the operation of the U.S. government can be considered a terrorist. Kelly Visque fits that description in my mind. The four elements of a crime are intent, conduct, concurrence, and causation. Out of the four of them, which one do you predict will require the most effort to sell to the jury?" No one answered. Waller addressed Sondra for a minute. "This is how I work, Sondra. I try not to give orders. Instead, I get my staff involved by making them think. It is the method used in law schools and I believe it quite effective." He turned his attention back to everybody. "So, which one will demand our focus? Joy, what do you think?"

"I believe it is intent, Quinn. The criteria of conduct and causation are based upon the direct physical evidence of the bee and picture of Visque and Corvino, and concurrence will be present once we establish intent."

"Very well put, Joy. I must correct you on a few things, however. The defense will likely argue that neither of those are direct evidence and instead should be considered circumstantial. As a result, conduct will not be based solely upon the evidence, but rather a combination of that along with the intent. Causation will follow from that as well, as it was Visque shooting the gun which resulted in both Justice and Mrs. Bernard dying. So you see, it is critical that we convince the jury of the factor of Visque's intent to disrupt the operation of the government in order to demonstrate that she is in fact a terrorist." Victor raised his hand.

"I have a few points to make, Quinn. First, why are you intent on trying her as a terrorist?"

"She attempted to derail an entire political process. As a nation, we need to make progress, and we cannot do that with our current band of underachieving, self-absorbed boobs we call politicians! We are on the verge of a new era. I am sure you have all heard the term 'distributed government'. We need to integrate worldwide, geo-politics is no longer a theory, it must be put into practice. Kelly Visque is an example of those Americans who are protecting an archaic concept that was fine when we broke away from England, but no longer applies. She must be made an example of." Victor continued.

"Two additional points I want to raise. First, how do we illustrate that she held the beliefs you are describing, where she wants to maintain America for native born Americans? Second, how do we prove she fired the gun that was used when we have no fingerprints, DNA, or even any witnesses who remember her buying the gun or even seeing her anywhere around the gun store in Atlanta?"

"We will talk to people associated with American Pride, the paramilitary right wing organization in which Miss Visque was a member for a short while. With regard to the firearm, while it is true there is no connection, we know her parents both worked in professions that involved weapons, so she was exposed to them since she was a child. We all acknowledge there are ways to purchase them anonymously." The associates stared at him in awe. Sondra found her voice first. She knew her way around a trial.

"What are we going to discuss next, Quinn?"

"The evidence we will be able to use. There are four items we can use; 1. The bee containing the DNA, 2. The picture of Visque and Corvino, 3. The brain scan the FBI ran against Justice Bernard's brain, and 4.The gun. Let's address them one at a time. Glen Aaron will likely find a DNA expert who will testify that the time the DNA was extracted can be determined to the minute, so that Visque's DNA in the bee would have been there since a few hours before the bodies were dumped," Waller looked at Sondra, then said, "uh, sorry I meant placed, at the crime scene. We need to find an expert who will refute that concept and testify that no test exists yet that is so precise." He started to continue but was interrupted by Sondra.

"If nobody minds I could use a short break. Can we regroup in ten minutes?" Everyone nodded, and on their way out, Sondra whispered she would like to have a word with Quinn. They went into his office and she closed the door. "Quinn, I just want to get this out of the way now. I know some awkward topics will come up about my parents, and I want to say I can handle it. There is no need to tap dance around the issues or discuss it when I am not around. I realize what I signed up for, and I assure you I am prepared to hear whatever it is. We are all working toward the common goal of making sure justice is served." She saw from the look in his eyes that he understood and there would be no more sugar coating, which was what she wanted. They went back to the conference room, and once the other three came in, Waller began where he had stopped. "So, we need an expert to back our theory that Visque was stung by the bee at the time she left the bodies in front of the Supreme Court building; in other words to refute any notion that DNA testing can be done with such precision. This will also mean the bee will be circumstantial evidence to back up our case as well as that of the defense. If Aaron cannot find an expert to support that stance, they will still most likely treat the bee as circumstantial rather than direct because then their argument will be that Visque was stung somewhere else and the bee was killed in front of the Supreme Court building. If we as a team attempt to use the bee as direct evidence and argue Visque was stung at the time the bee was killed, the defense could easily counteract that she may have thought she killed the bee but just stunned it at a different place, and the bee stung another person before it was killed where the bodies were found." Sondra noticed Roberta was writing all this down. "Ok, moving on to the picture. The two of them in the picture together demonstrates Visque had access to inside information about Justice Bernard. Lorraine Corvino worked in the Supreme Court building; she knew his schedule and when would be the best time to grab him. She passed that on to Visque. That connection shows opportunity. We need to speak with the other people in the picture on the bowling team to verify the kind of relationship the two women had, and also to get a sense of their characters. The FBI is going to be conducting the same inquiries, so perhaps we can obtain some preliminary data from them. Next, the brain scan performed on Justice Bernard a few days after he died. A few years back, the FBI developed cutting edge technology to read brain waves and decipher a person's emotions. Several top Americans participated in the initial rounds of testing to create baseline results as a comparison if they ever needed to have their brain scanned again for situations such as this one. Two days after his body was found, the top secret crime lab at Quantico ran these tests on Justice Bernard, as he was one of the people to undergo the testing several years back. The results from the updated scan after he died showed he was experiencing fear and uncertainty and did not know his attacker. This works to our advantage as it does not eliminate Visque as a suspect, as she and Bernard did not know each other. Lastly, the gun found in the Potomac with the serial number filed off in one place. The FBI was able to view the serial number using chemicals called reagents and trace it to the gun store in Atlanta, as Victor mentioned. That will not help us at all. We need to forget about this specific gun and instead stress her comfort level with firearms in general and make it clear this was her method of choice to carry out the murders. We can also point to the fact that the serial number was filed away as an indicator

that someone who understood police procedures was involved."
Waller paused for a moment. Roberta raised her hand.

"How are we going to divide things up?"

"We are not quite finished yet, Roberta. We have laid out our case for the terrorism charge, now let's address the murder indictment. Three of the elements are the same, the different one being intent. We must show Visque planned to kill Justice Bernard because he would have ruled in favor of the measure to allow naturalized citizens to run for President. We must first prove this and then build on it for the intent portion of the terrorism charge. The two intent criteria are related. Once we demonstrate Visque had the intent to murder the justice, we can then delve into the reason why which will give us the material we need to show her motive for killing him violated the Patriot Act. We will then have made the intent clear for both of the crimes." Joy spoke next.

"Who do you plan on having provide the testimony that will convince the jury of her intent?"

"Lorraine Corvino. I suspect she will be indicted on a lesser charge once the FBI has a chance to question some of the people on her bowling team. We can squeeze her to testify against Visque in return for a deal from us. We will then have intent for murder." Joy jumped in again.

"Ok, but how do we make the leap from that to terrorism? I mean, justice Bernard was known for being conservative. Wouldn't Visque have wanted to assassinate someone more liberal?" Before continuing, Waller glanced at Sondra.

"We can use Corvino again for that, and someone else. Winston was conservative, that's true. Remember, however, his daughter worked for one of the most liberal organizations in the country and they had a very close relationship. She influenced him greatly and I am sure she tried to make him see our political system needed an overhaul. I knew Winston. He always had an open mind. Sondra, I am planning to call you as a witness. Do you have a problem with that?"

"Absolutely not, but Quinn, wouldn't that be a conflict of interest since I am working on your team?"

"Ordinarily, yes, but since you are not a lawyer, and since you will not be getting paid, you are volunteering your time, so no, there is no conflict. You will be answering questions about how your father was coming around to see your point of view about expanding our options as a nation."

Sondra pondered that, but then asked, "That's all fine, but how would Kelly Visque have known this?"

"Two ways. First, she is no dummy. It was public knowledge that you worked for the ACLU and yours was a close knit family. Combining that with the fact she had Corvino as a resource made your father the obvious choice." Waller paused.

Roberta asked, "What was the second way?"

"Through Lorraine Corvino. It is rumored that Lorraine Corvino was having an affair with Justice Bernard. Part of our deal with her would be to confess to it. I am sure during the times they were together, Bernard opened up about some of the cases before the Supreme Court and how he planned on ruling as well. It probably finally dawned on Corvino he never would leave his wife, so she passed that information on to Visque out of spite, which was her whole motive for conspiring with Visque in the first place." Everyone stole a glance at Sondra, whose expression remained impassive. She spoke.

"That sounds like a good plan. We, my dad and I, did talk politics and he seemed to be coming around to my point of view. What Quinn has laid out makes sense."

"Excellent. Now, Roberta, we are ready to divide up the tasks. I will get in touch with the leadership at American Pride to see what they can tell me about Kelly Visque during her time with them. Sondra, why don't you handle the bee and the brain scan. Find a DNA expert who is of the opinion that testing has not progressed to the point yet where DNA can be pinpointed down to the minute. We want to keep the information about when the bee likely stung Kelly Visque as vague as possible. Also, set up a meeting with Director Grey at the FBI to review the brain scan, and have him explain the results. We will hold off on speaking to the bowling team until after the FBI does and we have more information. Victor, you handle the portion of our case related to the gun.

Consult with the FBI and find out who they have spoken to, such as people who knew Visque when she was younger to see if she was always interested in guns and her comprehension about police procedure. I doubt we could rely on her parents to provide honest information. Joy, why don't you find a psychologist who has an expertise in extreme patriotism and how it can cloud a person's judgement. Talk to some acquaintances from her past and find out if she has a temper and has expressed her views about immigration. Investigate her employer, Star Fitness. Perhaps she has had some customers as a trainer she rubbed the wrong way. Roberta, you will be responsible for the portion of the case related to Lorraine Corvino and the bowling team. You can reach out to Ed Billet. He is our point of contact and he will keep you posted as to their timeframe and what they find. You will be in charge of working up the case for trying Visque as a terrorist, as that hinges on the information we get about and from Corvino. If it turns out Corvino really had no part in the plot and was an unwitting pawn, we can still use her as a witness who will say that Visque was always inquiring about Bernard and his beliefs and schedule. Ok, is everyone ready and excited to get started?" They all smiled and nodded. "Great. We will meet back here next Tuesday at the same time for an update. Good luck everyone and be careful."

2pm, FBI headquarters, Quantico, VA

Ed Billet had assembled his team to see what they had done. They rehashed their progress, and Billet was not impressed. He had expected them to have met with the people in the picture by now, and told them so. The agents said they were waiting for a warrant to go back to Corvino's apartment and confiscate the picture to permit them to question her about who was who. Billet told them impatiently he would arrange for the warrant tomorrow so they could return and get the ball rolling. He called the next meeting for this Friday at 10am and let the agents know he wanted some answers.

Billet went back to his office. Ten minutes later his phone rang. It was a woman named Roberta from the Attorney General's office. She was asking about the bowling team; what a coincidence. He told her he would have more information on Friday, and she said she would be back in touch then.

8pm, Blake and Sondra Tristan's apartment
The couple were finally sitting down to dinner. Blake was working really long hours these days; it was a big effort to get ahead at the big law firms; we are talking 80 hours per week.
"How did it go today with Waller," asked Blake.
"Very well. He made me feel like an integral part of the team right away and gave me an assignment already."
"What does he want you to do?"
"Two things, find out more about the brain scan the FBI performed on my father, and track down an expert on DNA who will support our case with regard to the DNA extraction." She filled him in on both topics and for the first time in a long time, she felt proactive in helping to bring her parents' murderer to justice.

Wednesday, April 25th
Todd Russell had just seen the results of the national Gallup poll which reported he and Weimitz were way ahead of the other candidates overall across the country. Russell recognized it was because of the technological expertise Weimitz brought to the table. People everywhere believed many of the issues facing the world could be handled using advances in science and Weimitz was the person to accomplish that. He had a great legacy, having been heavily involved in the planning and construction of the federal irrigation system and was a pioneer in helping to make the electric car more readily available to the masses. Technology was associated with increased and better employment opportunities and the jobs lost due to obsolescence were more than compensated for by progress. Russell had always been a champion of subsidized job training for those workers whose jobs had been fazed out and this was the perfect platform on which to expand his philosophy nationwide. By instituting this training, workers in the U.S. would be able to perform the tasks the increased technology called for, and as a result, the economy would thrive as less people would be out of work and have the ability to support themselves and in turn

fuel the economic engine. It would be a process that would feed on itself. Once Russell had implemented that here, his administration would bring the same model to other countries around the world. It was simple yet brilliant at the same time. With regard to the other issues to be addressed in a political campaign such as abortion, immigration, etc, he would follow the liberal approach right down the line. He thought that was in keeping with the expertise he and Weimitz were bringing with technology, and consistency was a huge factor in politics. He would be staying in Illinois until the end of May, concentrating on his gubernatorial duties, before going on a trip to India with a side trip afterward to Israel.

Sondra Tristan called Director Grey at the Hoover building. She was put on hold for about three minutes before he answered. "Hello?" "Hello, Director Grey, it's Sondra Tristan." "Hi Sondra." He was somber. Alright, let me get this over with, she thought.

"I am sorry for our last exchange. I was out of line and you are just doing your job." She hoped he would accept it and move on; she was in no mood these days to wallow.

"Already forgotten. How are things?"

"Good. I don't know if you heard, but I am working with Attorney General Waller on the Visque case." Without missing a beat, he responded.

"Good for you. I hope doing so will bring you closure and a feeling of vindication."

"Thank you sir. I was wondering if you could help me with something."

"Of course, what?"

"I need some information about the brain scan you performed on my father. I know nothing about it so please start at the beginning."

"Your father was a subject in a series of experimental tests involving people's brains several years ago. He was asked to participate because he was a public figure and a friend of mine. Basically, what we did here at our crime lab was subject the people who were part of the test to various scenarios designed to evoke different emotions and then monitor the blood flow in the brain to see how it differed with the various stimuli. The goal was to create a baseline to compare with should we ever need to for forensic purposes, like if they were ever the victim of a crime. When your father died, we knew we had to perform the same test to glean any information available. We only had 48 hours; that is the time frame before the test will no longer work. We borrowed the body from the Supreme Court police and ran the test. The results showed he was experiencing fear and bewilderment; we surmise he did not know the kidnapper."

"So you are saying the scan performed after he was dead was closest to the baseline in which he was exposed to frightening and stressful situations?"

"Exactly."

"Would this test be admissible in court?"

"I believe so, but you would have to ask Waller. Would you like me to send you the report?"

"Yes, that would be great. Thank you, sir. Perhaps one day we can get together for lunch?"

"I'd like that a lot."

Maitland, Florida, just outside of Orlando, 2pm

One of the NSA agents working the American Pride case believed he just hit on something, something big. He was painting the office of a small employment agency which was a front for NSA surveillance. The place they were listening in on was a travel agency down the hall. This travel agency also happened to be the front for the southeastern headquarters for American Pride. They used a fake company because even though American Pride was ostensibly an organization on the up and up, they planned their nefarious activities for this region of the country in this location. It just so happened one of the top assassins in the country was working out of Florida and was associated with American Pride. The agent had picked up chatter in code of course which was a plan for the execution of Quinn Waller. No specifics were discussed but it was clear as to what they were referring. The man on the phone was talking to another American Pride member, someone equally high up on the food chain. Agent X would be able to capture the phone number and find out where the call went to, then send one of his colleagues there. Once they had more concrete information, they would take it to Kangaroo for review and for him to decide what to do next.

Offices of the ACLU, Washington, DC, 3pm

Glen Aaron had two important tasks to do. He had to find a DNA expert who would explain the position of the blood that contained the DNA inside a bee's stinger determined when it was drawn. He realized this was a departure from the strategy which he had discussed yesterday with Kelly Visque, but now believed it to be a better course of action. The bodies of the Bernards were likely left at the Supreme Court building at night, so the fact the other person's, Peter Marvin's, DNA was closer to the end of the stinger might cast reasonable doubt in the minds of the jury. Aaron felt it was his best shot. Most of the evidence pointed to Visque and Waller would make this as airtight as possible. He performed a search online and came up with 16 names. He had to find someone reputable as Waller would crucify them. Aaron had to remember he had the full weight of the ACLU behind him; he was not in private practice where he had to watch every penny. He wanted to beat the prosecution to the punch and find the best person out there. He went down the list and read each of their biographies and the types of research they had done. After an hour, he was completely frustrated. None of them had concluded DNA testing was precise enough to testify the position of the fluid containing the DNA determined when it was obtained. Think, he commanded himself. He recalled one of the people on the list had worked with an assistant with whom he had a falling out and the assistant left to open his own lab. Scrolling through the list of articles, he found the assistant's name, Otto Lampf. It only took Aaron a few clicks on the internet to find where he was working; at a lab he had set up for himself in Albuquerque New Mexico. Aaron had a feeling this could be his guy, but he wouldn't reach out for him yet. He would sit on it for a few days. The other thing he had to do was find a psychologist to examine Kelly and say that her patriotic feelings were not so extreme they would have caused her to commit these crimes. He suspected that would be easier to do, as there were psychologists with very varied schools of thought. Once he had those two components of the case lined up, Aaron would then start interviewing potential witnesses.

Washington, DC, 8pm

Victor from the Attorney General's office had spoken to Margo, Kelly Visque's childhood friend, last night on the phone and they agreed to meet tonight at 8pm at a pizza place near Margo's apartment. He arrived first and kept his eye on the door. At about five minutes past nine a small, mousy looking woman walked in, and Victor was betting that was Margo. She looked at him, walked over, and introduced herself. They shook hands and he asked her if she wanted anything. She said she would like a diet coke, and he got one for her and one for himself. When he came back, Victor was all business. He started by saying he wanted Margo to know she wasn't doing anything wrong or disloyal by talking to him and that Kelly would get whatever help she needed to come through this. She said she understood. He asked her to describe what Kelly as a child. Margo thought for a moment and said she was always a type A personality who was used to getting what she wanted. Victor wanted to know if she had a temper. Margo answered that she did. Was she comfortable with guns? Absolutely, Margo replied. How close were they when they were younger and what about now? When they were kids they spent a lot of time together as they were next door neighbors. These days, they saw each other sporadically but when they did it was very pleasant. "Did Kelly try to impose her opinion on others?"

"Sometimes."

"Would she get mad if someone disagreed with her or failed to take her advice?"

"Yes, at times. In recent years, however, she seemed to calm down and become more tolerant."

"Did she ever belong to American Pride?"

"Yes, for a short period of time, but found it to be too extreme and violent."

"What kind of parents were Mr. and Mrs. Visque?"

"They were strict but fair. Kelly learned a lot about how to take care of herself, and her parents always wanted her to be strong."

"Did they talk about their jobs much?"

"I am not sure, what are you getting at?"

"I am wondering if she was familiar with police procedure and the steps law enforcement goes through when they are trying to solve crimes."

I would imagine she is. Growing up as the child of a police officer would lend itself to obtaining that kind of knowledge, unless the parent was so closed off there was no discussion. Mr. Visque was not like that, he enjoyed communicating about his work."

"How does she feel about foreigners and the rights they should have?"

"She is not opposed to people emigrating here in search of a better life, but she does expect them to earn their rightful places in society."

"How strongly opposed was she to the measure of an immigrant running for President?"

"Very opposed. I am sure you already knew that."

"Do you suspect she could have been angry enough to carry out this crime?"

"Let me say this, I have seen her get so angry at times that she has done things I didn't think her capable of doing."

Friday, April 27th, 10am, Quantico, VA, FBI headquarters

Billet's team had executed the search warrant he had arranged for to legally confiscate the photo. Lorraine Corvino wasn't happy about it but begrudgingly cooperated; she provided the names of the people in the photo. It was a female only league so there were five women on the team. Besides Corvino and Visque, there was Sophie Tingle, Gwen Botch, and Helen Sawyer. They had retrieved their addresses but had not had a chance to meet with them yet. That was the goal for this weekend. Billet accepted that and set the next meeting for this coming Tuesday, same time and same place.

1pm, Starbucks coffee store, Downtown DC

One of Billet's agents had tracked down Gwen Botch, an employee at Starbucks right in town. It was in the middle of the lunch craze but he managed to get Botch's attention when he flashed his badge and asked to speak with her. She asked him to come back at 2pm and since she wasn't a suspect but a witness who could be of service to him, he agreed. He returned an hour later. He showed Gwen the picture of the bowling team and asked her the names of all the people at first to break the ice and make her more comfortable. She understood why he was asking, Kelly Visque's face was everywhere. He wanted to know what kind of relationship Visque and Corvino seemed to have. Botch said they appeared to be close, they talked to each other often and believed they went out after the matches to a bar or something like that.

"Did you ever hear Kelly Visque express her political views? More specifically, did she say anything about how she felt about a foreigner running for President?"

"Are you kidding? She railed about it all the time. We, except for Corvino, all got tired of hearing about it."

"Corvino didn't seem to mind?"

"Just the opposite. She seemed to revel in whatever Visque said."

"What about Corvino? Was she very talkative during your bowling matches?"

"Not as much as Visque, but yes, she did her fair share of yakking, mostly about her job as a janitor at the U.S. Supreme Court. She claimed to be sleeping with one of the justices, but tried to be so cool and discreet by not mentioning his name. You are obviously here because the FBI has reason to believe it was Winston Bernard. Wow. I guess she wasn't making the whole thing up like we originally thought."

"Did she sound bitter at all?"

"Yes, as a matter of fact. We could tell he was giving her the run around."

"Do you think she would have wanted to harm him?"

"Maybe, if she thought she could have gotten away with it, she probably would have gone for it."

"Did the other two women on the team feel the same way?"

"I would think so, it was pretty nauseating, but you would have to ask them yourself." Indeed I will, he thought.

"Would you happen to know how I might find them?"

"Yes. Helen is a librarian at the Library of Congress, and Sophie is a beautician. I will text you her phone number and the name of the salon where she works." He received the text a minute later, along with Gwen's phone number and the message 'Call me!'.

The FBI agent didn't want to waste any more time in tracking these women down, especially since the Attorney General's office was looking for the same information. He spent the remainder of the day finding them and confirming Gwen Botch's story, which both of the other women on the bowling team did. He called Billet right away and filled him in about what the women had reported. Billet asked him about what he thought of the relationship between Visque and Corvino, and if they had been planning it together or if Visque had simply used information she had gleaned from Corvino. The agent said he had a hunch they had worked together and asked Billet if he wanted him to arrest Corvino. Billet said not yet, the FBI did not have enough information. He told the agent to pass the message to the other two he was working with and for the three of them to canvass the neighborhood around the bowling alley and see who saw the two women together. "Go to the local bars, restaurants, etc. You know the drill, find out how they acted when they were with each other, etc. You can give me the update on Tuesday."

Ed Billet called Roberta, the woman from Waller's team. He passed on the information he now had, and told her more would be forthcoming next week. She was appreciative and wished him a good weekend.

Agent X from the NSA had tracked down the phone number of the person on the other end of the line of the conversation in Florida. It was to a private residence in Tucson Arizona. He didn't recognize the address or phone number as being someone to watch. He would use one of the other agents, probably agent Z. Agent Z would stake out the residence and find a way to see what the person who lived there was doing.

Joy, the lawyer who worked at the Attorney General's office was searching for a psychologist to examine Kelly Visque. She needed someone who would conclude that a person who was excessively patriotic, a fanatic, could be driven to commit murder. Extreme patriotism could be thought of like a drug and cause a person to act irrationally. Joy was searching through past trial transcripts to find ones that had used a psychologist to provide a similar opinion, as in trials for other terrorists. She trolled through 10 case notes before she found one she thought might have a possibility. Alan Wentworth, a professor of psychology at the University of Michigan and the author of several books, had given opinions about how the enhanced love for one's country influenced a person to act in unexpected ways. Joy looked at her cell phone to see that the time was 4pm; with any luck he would still be at his office. A woman answered on the third ring. Joy explained who she was and the woman put her right through to the professor. "Hello, Joy, how are you?" He spoke to her like they were old friends.

"I am fine, doctor, how are you?"

"I am great, please call me Alan."

"Alan, I am involved in a case that you may have heard about. I am one of the prosecutors for the Kelly Visque case." If he was surprised, Joy couldn't tell.

"A person would have to be living under a rock not to know about that case." He paused to allow her to continue.

"You see, Alan, my team is looking for a psychologist to meet with the defendant and provide a professional opinion about her. We were wondering if you would be interested."

"Do you know anything about my work, Joy?" They both knew she did.

"Yes I do. Miss Visque is going to be tried as a terrorist and we know that you have experience with those crimes, having testified before." Wentworth was interested but was late for another appointment.

"Why don't we talk on Monday when I have more time. Is Monday good for you?"

"Monday is fine. I will call you at ten am. Enjoy your weekend."

"Perfect. Goodbye."

Saturday, April 28th, 8 am, Hayao's house in St. Clair Shores, Michigan

Hayao was very happy with the reception he and Ramirez had received since they had gotten back to the U.S. from Mexico a week ago. The Hispanic community had felt they had shown a sincere interest while they were there and now Hayao had won their loyalty and support. He had really enjoyed Mexico and had felt rewarded when the people began to warm up to him. The places they visited were somewhat of a blur, but the people really were memorable for their kindness and genuine nature. Once they warmed up to him, they went out of their way to be friendly. In Acapulco, for example, Hayao's suitcase had somehow been left behind at their previous stop and the hotel staff had seen to it right away that he had clothes to wear until his suitcase arrived. He had loved Acapulco; what scenery! It had been really nice to end his trip with a stay at a resort. He was able to relax by the pool and enjoy a few really good meals. He was proud to call the people of Mexico his friends and looked forward to representing the Mexican Americans in the White House and having a good working relationship with the Mexican government. Hayao turned his attention back to the future and planning the next trip he and Alex were going to take. They would be going to Europe on May 10 for 2 weeks to visit three countries, England, France, and Spain. Spain was a must to show their solidarity for Ramirez's heritage, and they hoped to pick up some support in the other two countries by stressing their superior grasp of worldwide inter-dependency among nations, economically and otherwise. None of the other candidates had Hayao's experience in business and in dealing with cultures globally and would bring such an understanding of how to relate to other governments. Despite Russell's popularity and lead as of late, Hayao knew he was the complete package and was confident people would come to realize that by election time.

Eric Layton was in Washington, DC, going about his duties as Colorado's representative. He too believed he was just where he wanted to be in this Presidential race. To him, the best way to get ahead was to do the job in front of him. His strength was job creation and the economy, so that was what he would do. He had a big feather in his cap with the Pope's endorsement and expected on carrying the Northwest as that was his territory and the Northeast as Morris hailed from there and had lots of support through the Manucci family. His record in Congress and his integrity were his strengths and the factors which would carry him to the White House.

10am, Sondra Tristan's apartment

Sondra had enlisted Blake's help in finding a DNA expert. They were combing through science journals online, looking for articles about genetic testing and forensics, when Sondra came across one about insects and how they could be used in criminal prosecutions. She didn't read the whole thing, skipping down to see who wrote it. It was a woman by the name of Edna Jillow, PhD and her thesis seemed to coincide with what Waller was proposing about DNA testing not being able to be so precise to pinpoint exactly when the DNA was produced and extracted. Blake and Sondra looked her up through a google search and found her contact information. They called her, noting she lived in Pennsylvania. No one answered. When her voice mail picked up, Blake left a message briefly explaining what they were looking for and requesting she call them back. Blake was willing to take Monday off from work to accompany Sondra to this woman's house if those were to be the arrangements. They continued reading about other DNA researchers but none of them had the same credentials as Jillow. Fortunately they didn't have to wait long to hear back from her. She said she had been in the shower when they called. Sondra explained what they were looking for and she seemed very receptive. Some of the answers she gave were somewhat offbeat, but Sondra and Blake chalked that off to her simply being eccentric. They inquired if she was available to meet on Monday and said they would come to her. She gave them her address, it was in the Poconos in Pennsylvania. Blake quickly looked it up on an interactive map on the Internet and determined it would take them about three and a half hours to get there. Sondra asked if they could meet at 11:30 am and Edna said that would be fine and she would have lunch ready for them. Sondra bid her goodbye and hung up. "Great, we are all set, and now you will be ready for your meeting with Waller on Tuesday. Hey, I have an idea. Let's spend a few nights in Hershey on the way to the Poconos. We can leave this afternoon, stay in a cute motel, hit Hershey Park, and eat copious amounts of chocolate!" Sondra wasn't as gung ho as he was.

"Blake, we just went away for the weekend and I thought we were trying to save money to buy a house."

"Aw, c'mon, let's have some fun! Besides, you just sold your parents' house!" How could she say no to chocolate?

"Alright, let's go for it! I'll make the arrangements this time, and I'll be sure to include a heart shaped bed!"

Glen Aaron had decided he would get in touch with Otto Lampf and see if he seemed like he would be able to give solid testimony about DNA. He had gotten the number to his lab through Greg Driscoll's connections and had also asked Driscoll if he knew a psychologist. Driscoll gave him the name of the one the ACLU uses for their legal work. Aaron dialed the number for Otto Lampf's lab and no one answered. He decided to call back in about an hour. In the meantime he would track down the psychologist. His name was Malcolm Kelsey, based in the DC area. Aaron called his office and he happened to be in; he said he was catching up on paperwork. Aaron began by saying that Kelsey had worked with his office before. He explained the case he was involved with and of course Kelsey was familiar with it. "Would you be interested in meeting with Kelly Visque? One of the charges against her is that of terrorism. I anticipate the prosecution to attempt to meet the burden of proof of one of the clauses of the Patriot Act to convict Miss Visque of being a terrorist. To paraphrase the clause, it says a person must have committed an act that he or she would believe would disrupt the operation of government. The Attorney General, Quinn Waller, who is prosecuting this case, is going to argue that Miss Visque killed Justice Bernard thinking and hoping his replacement would not be in favor of a foreigner running for President and would rule against it, therefore preventing the measure from passing. I am looking for someone to give the opinion that Miss Visque was not so patriotic to have done something like that in order to commit an act she saw as protecting her country. Are you interested?" Kelsey thought for a moment. Kelly Visque was not very popular right now; he would likely be perceived as a villain if he worked with her defense. On the other hand, he had never shied away from controversy which had allowed him to become well known and respected within his field. He made his decision.

"I will be happy to meet with her, Mr. Aaron. When is the trial date?"

"June 4th. Your testimony probably won't be needed until July, however, what with jury selection and the prosecution presenting their case first. When would you be available to meet with my client?"

"How about two weeks from this coming Monday, which would be May 13th."

"Could we make it sooner? I need time to assemble all the elements of my case."

"Ok, let me take another look at my calendar. If she could be available early in the morning this Friday, say 5am, I will meet her then."

"I am sure that could be arranged. She is in the federal correction center in downtown DC. Here is the address. Thank you very much doctor. I will see you Friday at 5am. Goodbye."

"Goodbye, Mr. Aaron." Excellent, thought Aaron. One more piece in place. Alright, let me try Otto Lampf again. He called back and this time Lampf was available. "Hello?" He sounded wary; the experience he had just been through with his old boss must have made him suspicious of strangers.

"Mr Lampf? My name is Glen Aaron." Lampf interrupted him.

"It's doctor Lampf. What can I do for you?" Aaron explained what was going on and that he was looking for a DNA expert to support the theory of the possibility of determining the chronology of multiple sets of DNA inside a bee's stinger. "I have worked with DNA before, but never specifically with bees. I would have to perform some experiments", said Lampf.

"Are you interested in doing that?"

"I am, but experiments require equipment." Aaron was expecting the subject of money to come up and he was prepared. The ACLU was well funded.

"I am able to offer you $20,000 upfront to cover all your expenses related to this case including your airfare and hotel accommodations for when you come to DC from New Mexico to testify." Twenty thousand!! Wow! Lampf would have done this for way less. Still, he saw an opportunity here.

"Make it twenty five and we have a deal." Aaron grasped this guy was a bandit, but he didn't have a lot of choices; besides, it wasn't his money.

"You have a deal. Do you have a bank account I could wire the money to?" Lampf gave him the account number.

"As soon as the money is in my account I will get started. When I have some results I will be in touch."

"The money will be there on Monday."

"In the future, Mr. Aaron, please call me on my cell phone, here is the number."

Agent X with the NSA had made contact with Agent Z, who was on his way to Tucson to begin shadowing the assassin for American Pride. He told Agent X he would report back in a few days.

The three FBI agents were canvassing the neighborhood near the bowling alley and had picked a good time of day to go, in the afternoon when the regulars were in the seedy little bars rather than the nighttime when couples came out to spend the evening respectfully, by enjoying a nice meal. They had decided to stay together on this one. They went into the first dive bar and had to adjust their eyes to the dim atmosphere after being outside. There were five people in the bar drinking and they all gave the agents dirty looks. The bartender was in the corner drying glasses when they approached him. One of the agents flashed his badge which made the bartender take notice. The agent produced the picture of

Corvino and Visque. "Have you seen either of these women in here?" He took a closer look.

"No, I haven't, sorry." The agents looked at each other. They exchanged unspoken communication to approach the people drinking. The first customer was an older fellow, about 60, who looked like an over the hill construction worker. They showed him the picture. "Have you seen these women?" He shook his head no. Even if these people were lying, the FBI would have no way of coercing them. They went over to the second patron, a younger woman of around 30 who looked like a school teacher drowning her sorrows from a career that didn't turn out as planned. She too denied having seen them. The agents decided to leave; they went three blocks over to an Irish pub which was more crowded as it was now lunchtime. Many of the people were having sandwiches along with their beers. This time the agents took seats at the bar and ordered soft drinks. The barkeep must have thought them to be local businessmen as he made a sarcastic comment about them being lightweights who should be tossed out of the place for ordering soda. He changed his tune when they identified themselves. He did not know the women, but added that he just started there as an employee and went to get his manager. They came right back and the manager took a quick look at the picture and identified them right away. "Oh yeah, they would come in together often. They always seemed like a happy couple."

"You mean they behaved intimately toward each other?"

"Oh yes. Very affectionate."

"When they were with each other, did they seem to engage in deep discussions?"

"Absolutely. Many times they seemed oblivious to their surroundings, totally engaged with each other." The agents recognized they had what they needed. They took the manager's name and thanked him. They had to get this information to Billet.

Victor from the Attorney General's office took a ride over to Star Fitness where Kelly Visque works. He wanted to meet with some of her coworkers to hear what type of impression they had of her and to see if they knew her comfort level with guns. He went in to see the director of the facility, and explained why he was there. He asked the director to call the employees in one at a time and for him to leave during the interviews. The manager said that would take time as they all taught different classes today, and Victor said that was fine. The first person Victor met with was an aerobics instructor named Carla. She gave the impression that Kelly was constantly talking about her activities with firearms. He asked her if Kelly ever talked about her upbringing and the fact that she had been exposed to guns since she was a child. Carla said no, they weren't that close, he should talk to the other personal trainers who spent more time with Kelly, they tended to stick together. Victor looked at the list of employees with their job titles next to their names. There were 10 personal trainers. It was going to be a long day.

Victor finished meeting with all the employees he wanted to right before the gym was set to close at eight 'o'clock. The overall impression he got was in line with what Margo had told him the other day; that Kelly had been exposed to guns, how to use them, and the methods police use from early on, and she still enjoyed pursuits with guns such as hunting and riflery. When he presented his findings to Waller on Tuesday he would make it clear he thought Visque would have been capable of trying to make the gun used in the murder of the Bernards untraceable, and known how to dispose of it. Two of the employees had agreed to testify, which was a huge step in the right direction of putting the pieces in place to secure a conviction.

Ed Billet's home, 4pm

Billet's private phone jumped, and he saw it was a text from one of the agents on his team. The message said please can you meet us at Quantico right away. Billet knew his men. They wouldn't ask to meet if it wasn't urgent. He texted back they could meet at 6pm. Two hours later the four of them were in Billet's office. He told them to get right to the point. "Ed, we spoke to the manager at a bar near the bowling alley. He said Corvino and Visque would come in there together all the time and be real chummy. We felt certain you would want this information immediately." Billet's head was spinning. He wanted to go arrest Corvino right now for conspiracy, but had learned enough law over the years to understand several things had to happen first. They needed a warrant of course. Second, this manager had to agree to testify. That was a job for the Attorney General's team. He wanted to call Waller.

"Excellent work! I knew you could do it. Now, if you will excuse me I have a few phone calls to make." As soon as they walked out he dialed Waller. "Hello, Quinn, it's Ed Billet. I have some news for you. The manager at a bar near the bowling alley identified Corvino and Visque and said they were there often. We need to move on this right away. You probably want to send the woman who called me, Roberta, over there right now to confirm his account and make sure he would be willing to testify." Waller was silent for a moment, not liking anyone telling him how to run his office, but then realized Billet was just excited and anxious to make progress.

"Absolutely. Let me get in touch with her. Would your agents be willing to meet her there since they know who the manager is?"

"I will see to it they are there. Can she be there by 8pm?"

"If you don't hear from me then she will be there at 8. What is the name of the place?"

"The Leprechaun."

"Good work, Ed." Quinn tracked down Roberta and apologized for bothering her on the weekend but explained what was happening and of course she agreed. She got to the Leprechaun at ten to eight and the FBI agents were already there. They briefed her on what they had learned and the four of them entered the bar. The place was jumping. They asked the hostess to find the manager, his name was Ryan. He walked over five minutes later looking harried. He recognized the agents of course and Roberta introduced herself and asked if they could talk. "I am swamped right now. Why don't you come back at ten pm? That's when things start to slow down." Roberta said of course; she would see him then.

Waller was waiting to hear back from Roberta, and his phone finally rang at 11pm. "Hi Quinn. I spoke to Ryan, the manager, and

he repeated everything he had told the FBI. He agreed to testify. We now have Lorraine Corvino on conspiracy to commit murder."
Yes! Waller cheered silently. "Quinn? Are you there?"
"I'm sorry Roberta, I was just thinking. Great news. First thing on Monday I will obtain a warrant for her arrest. You must be exhausted. Go home and get some rest, you earned it. I will see you at our meeting on Tuesday." Waller's mind was going at a mile a minute. He wanted to try Corvino concurrently with Visque, using the same judge and jury, as the two crimes were related. That would take some doing, and he and his staff had to move fast. He would push Corvino's indictment and arraignment through as quickly as possible, calling in some favors if need be. His legal team would pick up the slack of the additional case, which would be manageable as some of the witnesses would be the same. Waller recognized what he had to do, and went to his liquor cabinet to have a belt of scotch to help him sleep.

Monday, April 30th, 8am
U.S. Magistrate Tim Fresco had just arrived to his office at the Federal Courthouse when there was a knock on his door. "Who is it?" He looked up and saw it was Quinn Waller. "Hi Quinn. Come in."
"Morning Tim. How have you been?"
"Just fine. What's up?"
"I need an arrest warrant. It's related to the Kelly Visque case. She had an accomplice, a woman named Lorraine Corvino. We have evidence to charge this woman with conspiracy to commit murder. I need the warrant right away."
"Is she a flight risk?"
"Probably not, but I don't want to take any chances. My goal is to try her along with Kelly Visque."
"That's going to be tough, but if anyone could do it, you can, Quinn. Ok, I will fill it out. Come back in fifteen minutes. By the way, I will be on the bench today if you want me for the initial appearance, and I am also available two weeks from today if you want to schedule the arraignment."
"Thanks Tim. I will do just that."

Lorraine Corvino's apartment, 10:30 am

Lorraine Corvino was eating her breakfast, getting ready to go to work. Today she was working the noon to 8pm shift for Magnus Industries, probably splitting her time between a few locations. She saw a car pull up in front of her building; two men dressed in suits got out. She pegged them as feds, and thought they were here to ask her more questions so she hit the buzzer to open the door. When she let them inside her apartment, she got the surprise of her life when they placed her under arrest.

CHAPTER 12

Monday April 30th, 11am

Quinn just got word that Corvino was in custody, in the same facility as Kelly Visque, one floor below. The press did not know about the arrest yet. Waller was going to schedule a press conference for tonight at 8pm. He knew that his team had tasks to accomplish today and he didn't want them getting distracted by the news.

Edna Jillow's house in the Poconos, 11:30 am

The Tristans arrived right on time after a very enjoyable weekend and they both had a pleasant flush about them. The house was a quaint little cottage that looked like something from a fairytale. Jillow answered the door and gave them a warm welcome. She was a petite woman who seemed genuinely happy to see them. They walked in and were surprised at the beautiful lunch she had prepared. She had finger sandwiches, fresh scones, and soup. They decided to save their business until after they ate. Once they were done and the table cleared, they got started. Sondra spoke first. "I am involved in a murder case and some of the key evidence has to do with DNA. You have written numerous articles about DNA extraction and are very knowledgeable. I was hoping you would review the evidence we collected."

"I would be happy to." Sondra handed her the envelope with the bee inside that she had gotten from Waller as well as the reports from the FBI's crime lab. Jillow looked them over briefly and said that she will be in touch.

"We would like to know if you think there is a way to determine which of the two sets of DNA inside the stinger was drawn first." Jillow nodded without looking up from the notes. "When can you let us know about that?"

"Well, today is Monday, so how about Thursday? That should give me plenty of time."

"Perfect. I will call you on Thursday morning. Thank you for this delicious lunch. Enjoy the rest of your day." Jillow remained so engrossed in the reports that the Tristans took it upon themselves to leave.

Attorney General's offices, Washington DC, 1pm

Joy, the lawyer from the Attorney General's office, had been trying to get in touch with Alan Wentworth since 10am with no luck. All she could do now was hope that he would hear her message and call her back. She dove back into the other cases on her schedule and fifteen minutes later her phone rang. "Hello?"

"Hi, this is Alan Wentworth. We spoke the other day? I am sorry I was unavailable earlier but I had an emergency situation to deal with. When we spoke on Friday you gave me the big picture about the case you thought I might be interested in. Could you give me some more details now?"

"Of course. Kelly Visque, the defendant who my team will be prosecuting, will be charged as a terrorist for the murders of Justice Bernard and Cecily Bernard. We are looking for an expert to evaluate Miss Visque and give an opinion as to whether she understood that her actions would affect the workings of the government, as that is the basis for the clause in the Patriot Act that we are maintaining she violated. We are impressed by your extensive experience in this area and would like you to take this case, which would include testifying as a witness for the prosecution at the trial." Joy gave Wentworth a minute to respond.

"I am interested, Joy. When is the trial set to begin?"

"June 4th, but the first few weeks will be devoted to selecting the jury. Your presence probably wouldn't be required until early July, and we could conduct a taped deposition ahead of time if you would be unavailable in July." Wentworth looked at his calendar.

"As of now, July is wide open. I will block out the whole month for now until you have a better idea of when you will need me. The first step however, as you mentioned, is for me to meet with Miss Visque. I could be in Washington next Monday, one week from today?"

"Let me check with her lawyer and I will get right back to you. What is your email address?" He gave it to her and they bid each goodbye. Joy wasted no time calling Glen Aaron and arranging the appointment for her psychologist to examine Kelly Visque on Monday May 7th at 11am. She fired off a quick confirmation email to Doctor Wentworth, pleased that she would have something concrete in place for their meeting with the rest of the team tomorrow.

2pm
Agent X of the NSA received word from Agent Z that he had been observing the assassin and knew how to get to him. He enjoyed the services of a prostitute each night. "I need you to find someone, a female agent, to pose as a hooker to get into his house. She can place the bug inside while she is there. He will never suspect a thing as he uses an escort service."

"That's a good plan, but it may take me a little longer than one day to set this up. What is the name of the escort service?"

"Luck be a Lady. It's a business that sells and repairs slot machines. They deal with casinos and are a front for this escort service."

"It will take me a few days to find someone to do this and infiltrate the operation. Probably more like a week. In the meantime, stay focused on the assassin." Agent X would do what he could, but he may need Kangaroo's help to make this happen. He would be speaking to him on Thursday and would ask him then if he didn't have anything in place yet.

3pm
Waller wasted no time in processing Lorraine Corvino's paperwork and arranging for her initial appearance before Judge Fresco that same day. The judge asked Corvino if she had an attorney. She said she did not and Fresco asked the bailiff to get in touch with the public defender's office. Forty five minutes later, a lawyer arrived. It was none other than Lionel Ross, the one whom Kelly Visque had replaced with Glen Aaron. Waller laughed to himself and wished he would be able to see the looks on the faces of Visque and Aaron when they heard. No matter to him. Ross spoke to Corvino for a moment and then asked for ten minutes privately with Waller. The court granted the request. The two

lawyers went into a private room out off the hallway. Waller spoke first. "Back for another bite at the apple, huh, Lionel?"

"Yes, I got screwed out of my first opportunity. This processing of Corvino seems to be happening quickly, Quinn. Are you planning on trying her alongside Kelly Visque?"

"Absolutely. Everything is already in place, and the crimes are intertwined together. To make matters even easier, you are coming aboard as counsel, and are already familiar with part of the case."

"When is the trial set for?"

"June 4th."

"Has a judge been assigned yet?"

"No. That will happen on May 24th."

"Fine. Thanks for the update. Ready to go back?" Back in the courtroom, Fresco was ready to resume. "The people are requesting that Miss Corvino be held without bail, your honor. She has been charged with a crime in a high profile case and the people maintain concerns that she may try to flee", said Waller.

"I have not had the chance to meet with my client yet, your honor, but once people learn about this in the news, Miss Corvino will not achieve anonymity anywhere, so there is nowhere for her to flee", replied Ross. Fresco pondered this for a minute.

"The defendant will be held without bail. I am not going to take the chance that she has arrangements in place. The arraignment date is set for two weeks from today, on Monday May 14th at 11am. Next case!" Ross knew that he had to get moving. He asked where they were going to hold Corvino, and he learned that it was the same building where Visque remained incarcerated. He told Corvino that she would be put through some administrative processes and that he would come down to meet with her later on to go over what their game plan would be.

4pm, Albuquerque, New Mexico

Otto Lampf checked his bank account and the money that Glen Aaron had promised had been transferred. Fantastic! He could now get started. The first thing he had to do was to capture a bee and find a way to get two DNA samples into its stinger. He had a plan. He would allow himself to be stung and would ask one of his neighbors to be stung in exchange for $50. He would then take the bee back to his lab where he would begin the extraction and analysis. Perfect.

5pm
Agent X was racking his brain trying to think of an agent that he knew to double as a prostitute. He worked with women, of course, but he needed someone that the assassin would be interested in. The hard part was finding the right woman. Once that was done, getting her into the mix at Luck be a Lady wouldn't be a problem, it would simply take a little strong-arming, a practice the NSA did all the time. He had encountered prostitutes over the years, but he couldn't use civilians for operations. He decided not to wait until Thursday and sent a message to Kangaroo on his secure line. "It's X. We need to meet tonight. Usual place and time."

6pm, Washington DC federal building
Lionel Ross passed through security on his way to see his new client. He found her one floor down from where Kelly Visque had been and hoped he would encounter more success this time. He went to Corvino's cell, asked her how she was doing, and then went to get the guard to arrange for them to use the visiting room. When they were both situated with Corvino handcuffed to the ring on the table, Ross got started. "Let me get a little background. The Attorney General is charging you with conspiracy to commit murder. That means that they possess evidence that you were working with Kelly Visque to carry out the murders of Mr. and Mrs. Bernard. They are not saying that you actually performed the killings, just helped plan them. Apparently they believe that you had ties to the Bernards and to Kelly Visque. What information do they have Lorraine? Please call me Lionel."

"They found a picture of myself and Kelly along with the rest of our bowling team at my apartment. They are also saying that I was sleeping with hizzoner."

"Were you?"

"Yes."

"So, they are going with the scenario of a scorned lover working with a zealot to prevent a sweeping change to the U.S. Constitution. It sounds pretty convincing to me. Fortunately for you, I represented Miss Visque briefly, so I am well acquainted with the government's case against her. She is being tried as a terrorist as well as a murderer. Waller will employ a DNA expert, a psychologist, people from Visque's past, and folks who saw the two of you together to paint an unfavorable picture of her. He will try to do the same to you using some of the same individuals and evidence as well as some different ones, perhaps such as a co-worker of yours who can testify about the affair, or an old nemesis of yours who will say that you are the jealous type. The trial is scheduled to begin on June 4th, which gives us ample time to prepare, but we need to jump right in. You can give it some thought, but I need to know what the prosecution will find when they go looking for these things. Who will they want to testify for them to show the jury you wanted to harm the Bernards? Conversely, our side needs witnesses also. Therefore, I need you to come up with people you know who will say that you are not the kind of person who would ever be involved in something like this. Could you have this information ready for me by Thursday?" Corvino nodded. "Great. I am also going to swallow my pride and reach out to Glen Aaron, who is Kelly Visque's lawyer. We should try to use the same DNA expert and psychologist. That would expedite things. Let's plan to regroup on Thursday. Hopefully by then we will have both made progress. Is there anything you need?"

"No, I am ok. Actually I will need a pencil and paper to take notes about what you asked me."

"Sure. I will mention it on my way out and see you on Thursday." Ross talked to the guard who said Corvino could have crayons instead of a pencil and that he would bring the items to her shortly.

7pm, Kelly Visque's cell

Glen Aaron showed up right when she was finishing her dinner. Her parents had brought her some candy which she looked forward to having once she asked the guard to bring it. Now it would wait.

Tonight Aaron said they could talk right there instead of going to the room. He told her that he had found a DNA expert who would hopefully provide testimony to back their case, and a psychologist who would be meeting with her this Friday at 5am. Was he serious?! Aaron definitely was; Dr. Kelsey had a great reputation and had time then. Aaron told her she could always go back to sleep. Dr. Kelsey would ask her about how she felt about the United States and try to see how she reacted to various stressful situations to discern if she had a temper. Aaron went on to say that the prosecution wanted Visque to meet with their psychologist Monday at 11am and were looking to demonstrate that she was extremely patriotic and knew the direct connection between killing justice Bernard and affecting the operation of the federal government so she could be tried as a terrorist. Visque understood; she had to seem like she loved the U.S. but would not break the law for her country and did not believe the death of one person, even a very influential one, would change the outcome of governmental policy. "What else do you know about the case that they are building?" Kelly asked.

"Not much right now. I should understand more in a week or two when we exchange notes, which will include witness lists and the evidence they will present, which are referred to as exhibits. In the meantime, I am going to start speaking to our witnesses. Here is a copy of the people on our list." Kelly read the names on the paper that Aaron handed her:

"The DNA expert, the psychologist, a member of American Pride who would testify that Kelly never took their organization seriously and never was interested in violence of any kind, her friend Richard who would provide his testimony through a deposition, a member of the bowling team that Corvino and Visque played on, one of her coworkers at Star Fitness, her boss, and Kelly Visque." She looked at him incredulously. "You want me to take the stand?"

"Sure, why not? You are convincing as innocent. We will go over the questions that Waller might ask and how to remain calm even when he is baiting you."

"Alright. Forget about the bowling team as witnesses. They never liked Corvino or myself and were always jealous. What evidence are we going to use?"

"The report from the FBI detailing the DNA in the bee. The data in the report will be explained in our DNA expert's testimony and will show that your DNA wasn't the one drawn closest to the time when the bodies were dumped. That should be sufficient for reasonable doubt." Kelly was impressed. Aaron seemed to have a well formulated strategy.

"When are we going to meet next?"

"I want to hear back from Otto Lampf, the DNA person, and get the results from the two psychologists. While we are waiting for those things, I will be interviewing the witnesses and learning their personalities so I can question them effectively. We will talk again sometime next week."

8pm, Quinn Waller's office

Waller had arranged for the press conference a few hours ago, and the media suspected it had to do with another arrest in the Bernard case. By holding the conference at his office, he was precluding the smaller tv networks from attending and forcing them to obtain the news secondhand. He started to read his prepared statement precisely at 8pm. "Good evening everyone. We have made another arrest related to the murders of Justice Winston Bernard and his wife Cecily. We have in custody a woman named Lorraine Corvino who has been charged with conspiracy to commit murder. She is being held along with Kelly Visque and they will be tried at the same time using the same resources which will reduce the cost to the taxpayers." The reporter present from ABC News raised her hand first.

"Yes?"

"What led the FBI to the other woman?"

"Evidence was found that linked her to Kelly Visque."

"Is it true that this new defendant was having an affair with Justice Bernard?" asked the CBS correspondent.

"No comment."

"What is the relationship between these two women?"

"No comment." Waller fielded questions for five more minutes, most of which he answered with 'no comment'. The reporters left wondering why he had bothered holding this press conference at all.

9pm, a secret location somewhere in Boston
Agent X was waiting for Kangaroo, and they both would come disguised. They would identify themselves using a prearranged phrase. This was a crowded place so no one would become suspicious. A person, impossible to determine the sex, walked up to Agent X and muttered the second half of the phrase, to which Agent X responded with the first half. Once done, they were able to talk. "I need a lady of the evening from inside our house to give us ears on the man in Tucson, and fast."

"I will have someone suitable tomorrow. Have her assignment ready." That was it, and they parted company.

11pm
"Good evening, my fellow Americans, and thank you for tuning in to the nightly news here on ABC. I am Evan Shaw, here with a special report. A few hours ago we had breaking news delivered during a press conference given by Attorney General Quinn Waller. He announced that another arrest had been made in the case of the murders of Winston and Cecily Bernard. Please stay tuned after the news at 11:30 as we cover this story in more depth. The Late Show will be delayed for half an hour and will start from the beginning at 12 am. Thank you and we hope to see you at 11:30."

Tuesday, May 1st
Lionel Ross was awake at 8 am; he hadn't slept well during the night, feeling anxious about calling Glen Aaron. He had watched Evan Shaw's special report and had not been surprised that the commentary reinforced what he already knew; he would be hard-pressed to find 12 jurors who would be sympathetic to Corvino. She was accused of conspiring to kill a person admired as someone of integrity and conviction. Shaw's message had been that he

thought that Visque had worked with an accomplice, someone who possessed inside information. The show did a hatchet job on Visque, rehashing her time with American Pride and portraying her as a right wing fanatic. Ahh, he was driving himself crazy. He went out for a walk to clear his head and would call Aaron when he returned.

  Kangaroo had his work cut out for himself trying to find an NSA agent to pose as a whore on such short notice. Fortunately, since he was running this operation he had some clout. He went to the proprietary NSA intranet and brought up the field office page. He started with the one in L.A. where the Agency assigned the better looking women as they would blend in more naturally. Scrolling down, he encountered several women whom he thought would work. He printed out the pictures with their names so he could recognize who was who when he spoke with them. He also checked to see how long each one had been an agent as this was a sensitive and potentially dangerous mission. After an hour he had narrowed it down to five; Amy, Betsy, Candace, Fiona, and Gladys. He would question each of them and then decide. It was still too early to call California so he busied himself with some tax work for a few hours.

  Lionel Ross bit the bullet and called Glen Aaron. "Hello?"
  "Hi, Glen, this is Lionel Ross." Aaron just about fell off the chair.
  "What can I do for you, Lionel?" Aaron knew he was representing Corvino but never expected to hear from him, at least not so soon. "Perhaps we can both benefit from working together. We could probably both use the same experts and combine our strategies to come up with ways to beat Waller and his team. I happen to possess a decent amount of experience with criminal trials." Aaron was used to working alone, but they did share a common goal and he did feel somewhat guilty about what had happened to Ross with Visque.
  "Alright Lionel. I still have some groundwork to do, so why don't we meet one week from Thursday?"

"Actually I was hoping to make use of the experts you have in place if you have gotten that far. Do you have a DNA expert and psychologist yet?"

"I do."

"Well, perhaps I could use the DNA expert as a witness also and arrange for your psychologist to talk to Lorraine after Kelly."

Aaron was going to say yes but let Lionel sweat for a minute.

"Ok. My DNA person is Otto Lampf in Albuquerque and my psychologist is Malcolm Kelsey who is meeting Visque this Friday at 5am and should be done around 7am. I would call both of them and explain the situation. Here are their numbers and I guess I will see you on Friday. The prosecution's psychologist is examining Visque on Monday at 11am, and I would expect that they will arrange for him to see your client right after, so don't be surprised if they call you. I will keep you informed as I get information back from anyone and let you know if it is favorable for my client and hope you will do the same."

"Absolutely. See you on Friday."

11am

Waller had assembled his team for a strategy session that would last most of the day. He wanted to get an update from each member, go over the witnesses, review the evidence that they would present, and hand out assignments for their next meeting including the additional tasks now that Lorraine Corvino had been arrested. They all had to fight through the gauntlet of reporters that had camped out in front of the building. They all made the right decision and kept their mouths shut. Waller virtually never spoke with reporters; justice and what happened inside the courtroom was compromised by the media. They all made a mental note to start using the side entrance. He started with Victor. "How did you make out with delving into Kelly Visque's past and finding out about her comfort level with guns?"

"Good. I spoke to an old childhood friend and several of her coworkers. Her friend said that it only stands to reason that after growing up in a home exposed to guns and with gun safety stressed a person would feel comfortable handling them. She also said that

Visque's parents did discuss their jobs so Kelly heard about the ways in which police solve crimes so she would have had the knowledge to evade the law. Lastly, her coworkers said that she was against foreigners enjoying the same rights as native born Americans without working for them."

"Did they believe her capable of these horrific acts?"

"The consensus was yes if she became angry enough. She has quite a temper apparently. She had a customer once who she berated in the middle of his workout."

"So, we have established that she knew how to use a gun, she is familiar with how law enforcement works in the course of their investigations, meaning that she understood enough to wipe her fingerprints off the murder weapon and file off the serial number, she fancied herself a patriot and could be unpredictable when she was angry enough.", said Waller. "How did you do Joy?"

"I was able to find a psychologist based out of Michigan, Alan Wentworth. He specializes in the area of jingoism and how it can make people act erratically. He is going to be meeting with Visque this coming Monday at 11am, and I will reach out to him today to request that he evaluate Corvino right after."

"Excellent. Make sure you let Lionel Ross know. I will want to speak to Dr. Wentworth before he meets with the defendants so please text me his contact information."

"Of course, Quinn."

"Moving on. Roberta, anything new?"

"The FBI made my job very easy. They arrested Corvino!" Everyone chuckled. "I will backtrack this week and interview members of the bowling team to get their statements about the relationship between the two women."

"You and Victor can work together on that. Sondra, what did you find?"

"I found a DNA expert in Pennsylvania, Quinn. Her name is Edna Jillow and she seems competent. She has experience in DNA extraction, and I delivered the evidence to her personally on Monday for her to examine." Waller interrupted her.

"She has the bee in her possession?"

"Yes, is that a problem?"

"Well, we need the bee to stay intact for the trial. Please call her today and make that clear. Did you manage to obtain a copy of the brain scan report from the FBI?"

"I did, and it shows that my father exhibited fear and that he likely did not know the assailant."

"Good. When you get a chance, please forward a copy of the report to me. I am sure you are all wondering what I accomplished this past week. Well, I managed to bring Corvino into custody and set up the Grand Jury appearance for this Monday and her arraignment for May 14th. This Friday I am going to talk to Albert Cross, the national director of American Pride to get some high level information about Kelly Visque. Why don't we take a ten minute break before we dive into dissecting the witness list and the evidence we will present."

Sondra Tristan took this opportunity to call Edna Jillow immediately; fortunately she answered. Sondra told her that she wanted to make sure Edna knew that they still would need the bee back after Edna was finished with it, and Edna said that she understood and Sondra could come get the bee or Edna would mail it, whichever was easier. Sondra thanked her and told Edna she would let her know and hung up the phone with a sigh of relief.

Lionel Ross had a couple phone calls to make, but as he began to dial, his phone rang. He saw it was Joy, the lawyer from the Attorney General's office. He realized the reason for the call.

"Hello?"

"This is Joy, a prosecutor working on the case against your client."

"What can I do for you Joy?"

"We would like to have our psychologist examine Miss Corvino. He will be coming by this Monday, May 7th at around 1pm. Please see to it that your client is available and expecting him."

"Ok. I would like to request that I am given notice when and if he is on your witness list."

"I will see to it. Goodbye."

The team reconvened to discuss the evidence they would present, but before they started Sondra alerted Quinn that the bee was intact and that Jillow would make sure it stayed that way. Quinn threw out the question to all of them. "What should our evidence be, first against Visque and then against Corvino?" Joy spoke first. Besides Waller, she had the best formal legal training.

"The bee will have the biggest impact on the jury and that is what we should lead off with for the case against Visque. I am confident that our DNA expert will report that the position of the DNA in the stinger of the bee is not indicative of when the DNA was captured there. If the defense produces an expert who says otherwise, I am sure Quinn will have no problem discrediting him or her."

"I am not sure if the DNA should be what we stress", said Victor. "I mean, I could see the defense creating doubt in the jurors' minds pretty easily by offering scenarios like the bee stung Visque elsewhere and was simply killed at the location where the bodies were found."

"That's true, Victor, except we have a statement from Miss Visque saying that she was stung at the Supreme Court building", answered Waller.

"What if we receive an unfavorable report from Edna Jillow?" asked Sondra.

"That's possible", remarked Waller. "We would then look for another expert. We should also ask Jillow about the behavior of bees and how far they typically fly after stinging a person."

"She might not know that", said Tristan. "We would have to research that separately."

"Would you look into that Sondra?"

"Of course Quinn." She added it to her list.

"Ok, what else? Roberta?"

"Let's address the gun. We are aware that Visque has extensive experience with guns and how to dispose and conceal evidence. While we have nothing tying her to the gun store in Atlanta, we can point to the fact that the serial number was filed away as a practice that someone with her background would be aware of. It isn't direct evidence, but definitely can be presented as strong circumstantial evidence."

"What do the rest of you think?"

"She is right. Her handling the gun the way it was is consistent with her background and temperament", said Joy. Excellent, Quinn thought. He had planned to do just that but felt proud that one of his proteges had come up with it.

"Exactly. Joy, check Wentworth's background and see if he has ever testified about forensics and the psyche of criminals. If not, please go out and find a forensic psychologist. What is the next piece of evidence?" Sondra decided to answer.

"The brain scan. We can explain that the emotions my father exhibited, fear and bewilderment, demonstrate that he had never met his assailant and that he grasped he was in danger. He did not know Kelly Visque and I am sure she behaved in a threatening manner so as to intimidate them. Once we admit the report and establish what it means we can easily make the transition to the next piece of evidence, the picture of the bowling team showing Visque and Corvino." Victor was nodding his head.

"Since we are trying both of them at the same time with the same jury that is perfect. We can then call Lorraine Corvino's coworker, Rick Heller, as a witness to the affair that she and Justice Bernard were having to make the connection that Kelly Visque had access to information about the judge." Victor looked over at Waller to see what he thought; he had a tight smile on his face.

"I like it. Victor, write all this down so we can replicate the order at the trial. What other evidence do we have to support the charges against Visque?" Each person took a few minutes to review their notes. No one spoke, meaning that there were no more exhibits. "What about against Corvino?" Roberta cleared her throat as she was the most familiar with Corvino.

"Right now all we have is the picture. I think in the case against her we need to focus on the testimony of our witnesses." Everyone nodded in agreement.

"That leads us to the discussion of who our witnesses will be." Waller looked at his watch. "It's now twelve thirty. Let's break for lunch and resume in an hour."

Lionel Ross had called both Otto Lampf and Malcolm Kelsey to introduce himself and to request for Kelsey to meet with Corvino after he finished with Visque. They were both cordial on the phone and Kelsey agreed, even with the knowledge that he wasn't going to be paid to examine Corvino, as Ross was a public defender. He understood that the fee he would receive from the ACLU for Kelly Visque plus the exposure from working such a high profile case was well worth it. Ross felt relieved when Kelsey told him he would see him this Friday morning at the prison. He could now resume his research into the potential witnesses he would use and hoped that Corvino was doing the same to prepare for their meeting on Thursday.

9:35 am, Los Angeles

Kangaroo was on the phone with the agent in charge of the L.A. office of the NSA. He explained the top secret assignment and asked who would be the best option. The agent said Gladys would be best as she was a looker and a seasoned field operative. Would she be willing to have intercourse? Yes, apparently she had posed as a hooker on other assignments. Perfect, thought Kangaroo. "I would like to speak to her to make sure she knows what she is in for. Is she there now?" asked Kangaroo. The agent went to get her.

"Hello?"

"Good morning. I want to brief you on the assignment. You will be pretending to be a prostitute, and you will have to sleep with the target. You will infiltrate a brothel in Tucson Arizona, where the mark will select you tomorrow night and want you to accompany him back to his house, which is his M.O. You will stay there the entire night and he will want you to leave first thing in the morning. While he is sleeping, you will plant the bug in the house. I have the blueprints which I will forward to you for review. This man is dangerous and this is a matter of national security; the bug you plant must go undetected. Any questions?"

"How do you know he will pick me?"

"His pattern is to pick the newest hooker available. You will be meeting up with another agent in Tucson. When you go to the brothel together, which is a secret operation behind a legitimate business, be persuasive about them letting you in, and use any means necessary, including the threat of exposure. You can use any name you would like for your alter ego, and the disguise is up to you as well. Good luck."

1pm, Washington DC, the Oval Office

President Harrington's personal assistant brought in a message for him. It was encoded and he knew who it originated from. Natsu Hakituri was the only person who sent cryptic messages through his assistant. Harrington understood. Natsu believed it to be secure enough to do that, and he was right. The message read 'Big shipment leaving U.S. from Moritu and going to Tokyo. Please check on it if you can.' Natsu had requested that the President call him in Tokyo on his private cell phone number today. It was the middle of the night in Japan right now, but Natsu was obviously awake. The President went to his private office and took out his off the grid phone. He dialed the number and Natsu answered on the third ring. "Hello?" Amazing; he always sounded wide awake and full of energy.

"It's POTUS. I received your message."

"Thank you sir. I have a request that will be in both of our interests. We both realize that the one country in the Far East that will not support Hayao in his Presidential bid is China. He needs their support. The U.S. has a good relationship with China right now. Would you consider going there to meet with the President and attempt to get him to back Hayao?" Harrington thought for a moment. It would definitely be a big advantage to win China's support. He hadn't travelled to that part of the world in a while and could have his staff come up with a reason for his trip pretty easily. He was sure something could be offered in return for their support and really didn't have anything to lose. He could leave in a few weeks, which was a slow time of year politically.

"Alright, Natsu, I will go and see what I can do. Try to get some sleep and I will brief you on how things went when I return."

"Thank you sir. You are a most reasonable and accommodating man."

Waller's team had all returned by one fifteen except for Waller. He was on the phone with Alan Wentworth. "Mr. Wentworth, your credentials are top notch. One important aspect of our case against Kelly Visque is that she understood the connection between getting rid of Justice Bernard and affecting the operation of government, specifically the U.S. Supreme Court. She wanted to change the outcome of the case before the court involving the right of foreign born citizens to run for President. By killing Bernard, who she expected to rule in favor of the case, she hoped that his replacement would end up being someone who would be against it. When you speak to her on Monday, please determine if that type of cognitive reasoning is something of which she is capable."

"Of course. That is part of my job. I hope to have my report back to your office on both women by the end of next week."

"That would be great. Thank you doctor."

Waller joined the meeting ten minutes later, ready to discuss the potential witnesses. "Let's first list them and then we can dissect them one at a time." Roberta spoke first.

"Agent Billet can be our first witness and he can provide testimony against both Visque and Corvino."

"Not to interrupt, Roberta, but we will come back to the order later on", said Waller. She nodded then continued. "We can ask the agents that are part of his team to provide the details of which he may not be aware. That approach will be better than having fragmented testimony from several different agents."

"Visque's friend from when she was younger, Margo", chimed in Victor.

"Edna Jillow", said Sondra.

"Alan Wentworth", chimed in Joy.

"The old customer of Visque at Star Fitness who claimed she verbally abused him", added Victor.

"The bowling alley team member who we will speak to", called out Roberta. No one said anything for a minute, so Waller knew they were done.

"I have two more. A member of American Pride, whom I will interview after I meet with Albert Cross this Friday, and as we discussed earlier, Sondra Tristan. That should complete our list for Visque. In the interest of time, let me add the witnesses I foresee us using against Corvino. I thought of three; her coworker at the Supreme Court building, Rick Heller, her friend from when she was younger who said she tended to be obsessive when in a relationship, and the manager in the bar that Visque and Corvino frequented together. He can be a witness for both women. Now, let's delve into each person and start developing our strategy."

They finished at around 7pm, and Sondra Tristan's head was spinning. They sure were thorough, and even though she was exhausted she felt she had a good handle on where they were headed as a team. Waller had also given out the assignments for each person for their next meeting, which would be in two weeks on Tuesday May 15th, also at 11am. The tasks went as follows: Victor - meet with the following people; Margo, Visque's childhood friend, and Visque's old customer. Get their testimony in writing, along with the questions and answers exchanged during their sessions. Work with Roberta regarding the bowling team member and the manager at the bar. Roberta - in addition to being the lead for interviewing and documenting the testimony of Rick Heller, the bowler from the team and the bar manager, meet with Billet and explain that we want him to represent the FBI as their witness. Once he has all the information, set up a time for the two of you to meet. While meeting with him, obtain the gun and the picture of the bowling team as evidence. Joy - Oversee the psychologist that is meeting with both women and get his evaluation in writing. Find another psychologist if necessary to speak about how Visque's background prepared her to cover her tracks. Sondra - Follow up with Edna Jillow and get her written report and the bee. Find a bee behaviorist to offer the opinion that bumblebees usually stay in a small perimeter. Start preparing her own testimony and send a copy of the brain scan report to everyone. Waller - meet with Albert Cross, the head of American Pride, and find a member who remembers Kelly Visque as gung ho. They all bid each other good night and went their separate ways.

8pm, the Oval Office
President Harrington was having a briefing with two people, his Chief of Staff and his Secretary of State. "Thank you both for meeting on such short notice. I have to go to China sometime soon. I need you both to work together to arrive at a two week period this month for me to go and also come up with a reason for my trip."

They both jotted down what the President needed and knew better than to ask any questions. They waited for him to continue speaking but he was finished. He thanked them, sent them on their way out and requested that they get back to him soon.

Wednesday, May 2nd
Gladys was on her way to Tucson Arizona on a ticket she bought using cash and a fake name. She would meet Agent Z there, work up her disguise, and then they would go to Luck be a Lady. The technician in Los Angeles had given her a bug that fit inside a computer mouse. She would quickly take the mouse apart while he was sleeping and insert the bug. Satellite technology was used to transmit the data to the NSA office in Boston so Kangaroo could hear. Gladys had chosen to be a woman from New York who came out here to escape the cold winters. She had accepted this assignment knowing she would have to stay for a while as a prostitute so the assassin would not become suspicious. Hopefully he would not request her every night. She would be living at a hotel that offered extended stay arrangements. She reviewed her story again in her mind, and after a few more times felt pretty comfortable with it.

The Secretary of State, Susan McBride, was working with the President's chief of staff, Jo Sylvester. "First let's pick a time frame for the President to go, then we can work on the purpose of his trip", said the Secretary of State. "That's your department, Jo. Do you have his schedule handy?"
"Yes. The best time for him to go would be from May 20th to June 3rd. That will be over the Memorial Day weekend and should be quiet. I will block out that time. Now, as to the reason for his trip, over to you, Susan."
"We can tell the press that it is a combination business trip/vacation. I have given it some thought, and China is well versed in dealing with the issue of rising sea levels and how to preserve their shorelines, and that is also something we are going to be facing sometime soon. We could say he is going to meet with their leaders to view their strategies and perhaps hire a company

from China to handle the operation and bring their workers with them." McBride had a feeling that this trip had something to do with immigration and she wanted to give the President an avenue to accomplish his task. Sylvester was nodding, unaware of her agenda, but willing to cooperate.
"That's a good plan Susan. I will go ahead and make all the arrangements for his trip and meet with Rebecca, the press secretary so that she can alert the media about the upcoming plans."
"Thank you Jo. I will draft an explanation of the reason for his visit and send it to you in a day or two. We can meet with the President again after that and brief him on the plans."

Joy was researching psychologists who had expertise in the behavior and actions of criminals once the crime had been committed. There were many; it was not as specialized as extreme patriotism. She narrowed her search by looking for someone locally and got a list with 16 names. She decided that she would sort them alphabetically and use the first one that was free. Don Barcan. Ok, Don, here goes. The phone rang six times and voicemail finally picked up. "Hello, this is Dr. Barcan. I will be unavailable from May 1st through May 15th. Thank you and have a good day." Joy did not bother leaving a message and instead called the next name on the list, Sean Cardillo. A man answered on the first ring. "Hello, Dr. Cardillo speaking?"
"Hello Dr., my name is Joy and I am from U.S. Attorney General Quinn Waller's office." She went on to explain what she was looking for and when she had finished he certainly seemed interested. He said he could meet her client anytime this week, and since Joy knew time was of the essence she arranged for the meeting to take place on Sunday at noon. Lionel Ross wouldn't be happy about having to work on a Sunday but his schedule was of little concern to her. It was a done deal.
Sondra Tristan could not find any information on the internet about whether bumblebees travelled after they had stung someone or something. She was unable to locate anyone who classified themselves as a bee behaviorist, so she found the next best thing; a

beekeeper. She found that there were only three bumblebee keepers in the country; all the others worked with honeybees. The closest one resided in Nevada with the other two in California and Hawaii. For some reason, she had a hunch about the one in Hawaii and called him first. His name was Willy Detrop and his setup was in Honolulu. Sondra sent him an email asking if he had skype or facetime so they could talk. She checked her watch; 10:30 am. Blake was at work and she didn't really have much to do until he came home tonight. She decided to go into town and treat herself to lunch and a museum. Hopefully she would have a response from Willy Detrop when she returned.

Tucson, Arizona, 3pm

Gladys had breezed through the airport and met up with agent Z. They went to the motel where he was staying to allow her to get into costume. At four pm they went over to Luck be a Lady. A woman in a kimono whom they assumed was the owner and the madam for the brothel in the back answered the door. "Can I help you?"

"Yes, we are looking for a poker table for our home. Could you show us your wares?"

"Of course." Agent Z thought this woman looked like Elvira, the actress from some old campy horror movies. "Follow me over here to our selection." They looked around for a few minutes then told the owner that they would like to talk in her office. She gave them a peculiar look but led them to her sparsely decorated room. They all sat and then agent Z got right in her face.

"We know what's going on here!" The woman was startled but managed to press the button for her security guard. He arrived one minute later but by then both agent Z and Gladys had flashed their ids, so when the guard banged on the door, she told him never mind. "Here's the deal. This woman here, you can call her Eros, she is going to be your new girl. When a certain customer comes in tonight you will make sure that he chooses Eros." She started to speak. "Shut up! If you tell anyone about this or us, we will make sure the authorities find enough violations to put you out of business forever and behind bars for a long time. Do you get it?"

She nodded. "Good. Eros will go over her cover story and then will be back at 7pm."

Washington, DC 6pm
Sondra got back home intending to start dinner, but then checked her email and saw one from Willy Detrop. He had answered that he would be free tonight at 11pm her time and they could video chat then. She had to organize her notes; Blake would have to fend for himself tonight.

Tucson, 7pm
Eros returned to Luck be a Lady at 7pm and went into the concealed entrance to the back where the brothel was. The madam was expecting her and took her around to meet the other girls. She had the bug tucked into her purse, sewn into a pocket and surrounded by paraphernalia. She would rip it out when the time came. If it turned out that the assassin did not have a computer with a mouse that Gladys could slip the bug into, she would look around and find another place for it. The johns had starting trickling in and the phone began to ring also. Elvira the madam said that things really began picking up around 9pm, so Gladys calculated she had some time to prepare mentally.

The Tristan's apartment, 11pm
Sondra was online at 11pm when her computer buzzed. She opened up the video chat window and there was Willy Detrop. He had a full beard and beady eyes with glasses. She introduced herself and asked him how long he has been working with bees. "About twenty five years", Detrop replied.
"And you have worked exclusively with bumblebees?"
"Yes. They pollinate flowers and are critical to the health of my gardens."
"Would you consider yourself an expert on bumblebees' behavior?"
"If anyone could, it's me."
"Super. Here is what I am looking for. A written report explaining the life span of bumblebees with an emphasis on how

far they travel during the course of their life and whether or not they stay close to home each day. If your report is favorable to our case, then we will need a recorded deposition from you in which you explain what you write in your report. Are you interested?"

"My fee is $500."

"Ok. You will be paid after the deposition is recorded, which will also include questions from the other attorney. When can you get me the written report? "

"Probably by this Saturday. I will email it to you."

"Once we review it we will be in touch. Thank you Willy."

Luck be a Lady, 9pm

It was getting busy now. Eros was waiting in a side room so as not to allow the johns to see her. She would get a signal from Elvira when her mark arrived. He came every night, so she wasn't worried. At ten o'clock, she received the sign to come out and join the other girls. The man she was to go home with was walking around the room, evaluating whom he would take home tonight. His eyes stopped when he saw her. "I haven't seen you here before. What's your name honey?" Gladys didn't like him already; she hated being called honey. She used a quiet whisper to answer him.

"Eros." He had to lean in to hear and he reeked of cologne. It would be a long night.

"Well Eros, you are in for a treat. We will be spending the night together." He motioned to Elvira as they were leaving.

They arrived at his place after a 20 minute walk during which time he asked her about her past, and she answered with her made up story. She came from New York looking to escape the cold weather. She got here and couldn't find a job so she resorted to turning tricks. She looked around when they arrived and saw the computer in a room. She was all set. All of a sudden he grabbed her and started shoving her toward the back of the house. They entered a bedroom and he pushed her down on the bed. He didn't even give her a chance to take off her boots, and she tried to put her purse down on the floor beside her as gently as possible. He held her head down as he unzipped his pants and before she knew it he was inside her; she wondered if he had ever raped anyone. Ok, it was time to show him a thing or two about rough sex.

Three hours later he finally drifted off to sleep due to the combination of nonstop bumping and grinding and the pill she had slipped into the scotch she made for him. She waited ten minutes, poked him to make sure he wouldn't wake up, then went to plant the bug. It was almost too easy and she was back in bed ten minutes later, anxious for sleep herself.

Thursday, May 3rd, Boston, 7am
Kangaroo's cell phone buzzed, and he knew from the hour that it must be something important. He checked the text message and it was from agent X, stating that the bug was planted at the assassin's house with whom the head of American Pride had spoken about killing Waller. Kangaroo texted back "Good work. Let me know when you hear something."

11am
Sondra Tristan was at the supermarket when she got a call from Edna Jillow, the DNA expert. "Hello, Edna. Why don't I give you a call back in an hour?"

As soon as she had put the groceries away an hour later, Sondra called Edna back. "I am sorry about before, I was at the store and couldn't hear you very well. What did you find with the bee I gave you?"

"I examined the bee thoroughly and extracted the DNA from different parts of the stinger. There is no way to determine which DNA was acquired by the bee first based on its location." That was good news, Sondra recognized. It meant that Kelly Visque was not necessarily stung before the other person. That gave validity to the notion that Visque was stung when the bodies were left outside even though her DNA was not at the tip of the stinger.

"Thank you, Edna. When can I expect your findings in writing?"
"I should have it ready sometime tomorrow. I will also mail the bee back to you and you should receive it by early next week."
"Ok. I will be in touch in a few weeks about the trial schedule and when we will want you to testify. Enjoy the rest of your day."

The White House, 1pm

Jo Sylvester, the Chief of Staff had just finished up a delicious lunch in the executive dining room and went back to his office to check his email. He saw one from Secretary of State McBride. He opened it and saw the attachment that had the explanation for the President's trip to China. It was just what she had said the other day; that he was going to get information about how to combat rising sea levels. He would discuss this with the Press Secretary and explain that the President had an ulterior motive here. He called Rebecca and left a message telling her he wanted to meet sometime today.

Federal Penitentiary, Washington DC, 3pm

Lionel Ross was meeting with Lorraine Corvino to review what they had arrived at for witnesses and experts. He asked her how she was doing and she said fine, but she looked nervous and like she hadn't slept. He would see about getting her additional privileges like Kelly Visque had. "Lorraine, I want to make sure that you understand the charges against you. You are being accused of conspiracy to commit murder. If you are found guilty you could spend the rest of your life in prison. It's important that we work together to use all the information available to help prove your innocence. Your part will be to tell me which people to talk to that will paint you in a positive light and my job is to ask the right questions to convince the jury that a reasonable person would not think you to be guilty." Corvino nodded. "Good. Before we go over our homework assignments, there will be a few people that you will be meeting with over the next few days. Tomorrow a man named Malcolm Kelsey, a psychologist that is working with Glen Aaron and myself will speak with you to get a sense of your personality and how it relates to dating and the way you act when you are in a romantic relationship."

"What does that have to do with the crime I am being charged with?"

"We want an expert opinion to show that you do not become obsessive with the men you date or have relationships with and try to do them harm in any way."

"I see. This is about my relationship with Justice Bernard and the possibility that I would have tried to hurt him because he would not leave his wife." Ross saw her getting mad and he diffused that. "This practice is common. It will reflect well on you when our expert says that you are not that way." Corvino took a deep breath.

"Won't the prosecution want to do the same thing?"

"Yes, and they are sending their psychologist to meet with you this Monday for the same purpose, to show that you were obsessive."

"Won't the two experts cancel each other out in the eyes of the jury?"

"Not really. You see, I will ask their psychologist, Dr. Alan Wentworth, questions after their lawyer is finished asking questions, and I will discredit him in front of the court. After I have done that, our witness will seem much more believable." Corvino seemed relieved. "Now, remember our goal is to demonstrate that you would not have been capable of conspiring to commit this awful crime. To do that, we need an expert, which I have arranged for, and we need character witnesses, which you must provide. That is what I requested that you have ready for today. Have you had a chance to put that list together?" She handed him a list and also had one for herself. Ross read the list out loud. "My brother, my neighbor, and myself." Ross thought for a minute. This small list would probably be alright. "Lorraine, we have an advantage here. Kelly Visque also has strong representation and if she is found not guilty it would be almost impossible for you to be found guilty. I will talk to both your brother and neighbor. Once I have done that, we should meet again and start assembling the bottom layer of our case, and build on top of that. Your appointment tomorrow will be at 7am and the meeting on Monday will take place at noon. Your arraignment will take place on Monday as well, at 3pm. I will be with you for all three appointments, so don't worry. I should be able to meet with both people by Monday, so maybe we can talk again after your arraignment, which is nothing more than a reading of the formal charge against you, the conspiracy charge. We can discuss the conversations I had with the people on the list you gave me and the questions I and the prosecution will ask you when you testify. If you recall anything else relevant to this case, bad or good, please let me know, and you can call me anytime. Get a good night sleep and I will see you tomorrow at 7am."

The White House, 6pm
Jo Sylvester went up to Rebecca's office as this was a good time for him and she said she would make herself available. He strode in and dispensed with the pleasantries. "Rebecca, the President is planning to go to China for two weeks from May 20th to June 3rd. We understand that you will have to alert the media as it gets closer, and the reason you should give is that he is going there to learn about how to combat rising sea levels and bring back some technological know-how with him. I have his itinerary and will email it to you right when I get back to my office. Do you have any questions?" She did not. "If you think of anything you are not sure of or are just curious, please call Secretary of State McBride or myself. Thank you Rebecca, and you may want to put out a press release soon. Good night."

Friday May 4th, Washington DC Federal Penitentiary, 5am
Dr. Malcolm Kelsey met both the attorneys for Kelly Visque and Lorraine Corvino at the prison and the defendants were both ready. Visque would go first. Kelsey set up his video recorder and was ready to begin five minutes later. His first question was, "How do you feel about this country, Kelly?"

"I love our country. It was built by people who had vision and integrity and who crafted a framework that endures the test of time."

"Do you think that the same criteria should apply today as did 260 years ago?"

"No. While the foundation of guidelines should stay the same, people and times change and so should the specific regulations we live by." They talked for almost two hours and Kelsey believed he had plenty of information to render an opinion. Next up was Corvino, and her interview proved to be equally as productive with

Kelsey drawing her out about her past relationships and what outlets she had to cope with the times when men had broken up with her. She answered sincerely and when they were done both Aaron and Ross were pleased with the outcomes. They met with Kelsey after the women had returned to their cells and he told the lawyers his written reports would be ready on Monday.

Washington DC, National headquarters of American Pride, 9am

Albert Cross was a consummate executive, able to pander to people from all walks of life that he dealt with as head of this organization. When his secretary buzzed him that the Attorney General was here to see him unannounced, it only took him a minute to prepare. He opened his door a minute later and went out and warmly greeted Waller. "Quinn, what a pleasant surprise. Good to see you." He managed to sound pleased to see him without seeming fake.

"Likewise, Albert. How have you been?"

"Fine thanks. Why don't we continue this conversation in my office." Once the door was closed, Cross asked, "What brings you here today?"

"Well, I wanted to talk to you about Kelly Visque. Unless someone was living under a rock, they would know of what she was being accused. She also has a connection to your organization, being a member of American Pride several years ago."

"Yes she was, briefly."

"Here is what I am looking for. I need you to find me a current member who recalls Miss Visque from her days when she participated in the meetings as the gung ho patriot who would stop at nothing to protect the values upon which this nation was founded."

"That might be difficult, Quinn. You are asking me to help you find a witness that will provide testimony to assist proving your case. While I never condone violence, American Pride does not want a foreign born person as President, so you can see my dilemma here."

"Oh, I am sure that your morals have been compromised before, Albert. I'd hate to see your operation come under such scrutiny that it couldn't function or worse, be disbanded. Who knows what would be unearthed." Cross knew he had no choice the minute Waller arrived.

He smiled and said, "No problem Quinn. There are many people who have been around for years and will be glad to be on the right side of law and order."

"Excellent, Albert. When can I expect to hear back from you?"

"How about at the end of next week?"

"That's perfect. Have a good day." As Waller left, Cross's eyes bored into the back of his head in a stare of hatred.

The White House, noon

Secretary of State McBride and Chief of Staff Sylvester were on President Harrington's schedule for today to discuss his trip to China and they were proud and relieved that they managed to pull it together so quickly. They met in the President's private office again and had all the schedules and itineraries ready. They knew enough to just give him the big picture now and fill in the details later. He finished his phone conversation and turned his attention to the two of them. "Hello Mr. President", they said in unison.

"How are you both doing today?" They both said they were fine and then got down to business.

"We have worked together to determine a reason for you to visit China and create an itinerary as well. I think you will be pleased with both. You will ostensibly be going to discuss strategies for combatting our rising sea levels as they have dealt with this problem for some time now. While you are there you will be meeting with businesses that would be interested with sending employees to emigrate here to work on those projects." President Harrington smiled and McBride caught on that his trip was in part to encourage immigration from the government. Sylvester continued. "You will be going to Beijing at first and will be met by President Wang Jie. You will spend a few days there, go to Shanghai for a few days to meet with other dignitaries, and finish your trip in Hong Kong. The trip will be from May 20th to June 3rd and will include time in each location to discuss business as well as do some sightseeing."

"Job well done. You both have included the things that I wanted to accomplish as well as some down time too. Jo, let's get this information to the media as soon as possible so that it doesn't seem like I am trying to pull a fast one on anybody."
"Yes Mr. President."
"If you both will excuse me now I have another appointment in a few minutes." They took their leave silently, knowing this had been a victory.

Sondra Tristan had been volunteering at the library shelving books all afternoon and once she got settled at home checked her email. There was one from Edna Jillow and it contained the written report she had promised. Sondra opened it up and browsed the report; it was exactly like Jillow had promised on the phone. This was good news; another piece had fallen into place for the prosecution. Once she heard back from Mr. Detrop, hopefully tomorrow with a favorable write-up about bumblebees and the way they behaved, she would feel validated that she had done her part to help put her parents' killers away. She felt good for the first time in a long time.

The White House, 8pm
Rebecca, the press secretary who worked at the White House, had just gotten the green light from Jo Sylvester to alert the media about the President's upcoming trip to China with instructions to send it out as soon as possible, which she would right now to allow it to be broadcast on the 11 o'clock news tonight. She would just give an overview; President Harrington could fill in the blanks at his weekly press conference. She dashed off her press release and emailed it to all the news bureaus. As expected, it was one of the top stories across the country that night.

Saturday, May 5th, 8pm, the Tristan's apartment
Sondra and Blake had spent the first part of the day waiting around the apartment for the email from Willy Detrop. Once it had come and Sondra saw that it was just what she had hoped for, they spent the rest of the day at the movies seeing the newest

blockbuster that had just come out, and then going to their three favorite restaurants ordering takeout which they would eat at home in front of the tv while catching up on some of their favorite shows. They watched until ten pm, then decided that their time would be better spent on other activities. Newlyweds.

Sunday, May 6th, 9am, the Perry O'Malley show
"Good morning America. Today we are going to discuss President Harrington's upcoming trip to China and what this will mean for U.S foreign relations. It is clear that this is his, President Harrington's, way of extending the olive branch over past 'misunderstandings', let's say. It's a brilliant move from a diplomatic point of view. China gets to feel as if they got the better of us because we are the ones making the first move towards reconciliation, and we win because we get the benefit of their expertise when it comes to saving our ports, and we possibly also get the labor to actually do the job. Ok, let's take some calls. Betty from Maine, you are on the air."

"Thank you for taking my call. The President is also helping his case for easing our immigration laws by demonstrating the advantage of that. Workers from other countries have different skills. He is promoting his agenda on two fronts."

"Very well put. He is trying to solidify his legacy in the time remaining in his term. Ok, let's break for commercial and when we return it will be Duane from Oregon on the line."

Federal Penitentiary, Washington DC, noon
Sean Cardillo, the psychologist who specializes in criminal behavior, was there to evaluate Kelly Visque and determine if she had the background, training, and knowledge to take the steps to cover her tracks for the crimes she was being accused of that were performed; namely disposing of the weapon, wiping off the fingerprints, and filing off the serial number in the chance that it was recovered somehow. Both Glen Aaron and Joy were there to make sure that both sides were not mistreated. Dr. Cardillo began by asking Visque about her childhood. "What line of work were your parents involved in?"

"My mother was in the military and my father a policeman. I have answered these questions already. Couldn't you review the notes the FBI took and come back another day so you don't waste my time?" A smirk crossed Cardillo's face; Visque knew what he was thinking.

"Oh, since I am in custody my time isn't valuable? Go fuck yourself." Joy stepped in.

"Miss Visque, part of Dr. Cardillo's job is to observe your reactions." Visque had a vulgar retort pop into her head, but determined that now was not the time to antagonize.

"Fine. Continue, doctor."

"Do you have any brothers or sisters?"

"No."

"Do you feel that as an only child, your parents treated you more as a peer than as an offspring?"

"They only raised me once, I have nothing to compare it to."

"Surely you must have seen the way some of your friends were treated by their mom and dad. Was it similar or different to the way you were treated?"

"I suppose my parents exposed me to things that I wasn't ready for at times."

"Did they give you details about what happened to them at work?"

"Yes. I found it interesting."

"Did they also explain the reasons why they thought the people they dealt with did what they did?" Visque nodded.

"As I got older, they offered more and more about motives and their impression of how the criminal mind worked."

"Did you ever consider joining either the force or the military?"

"I did, but then I became interested in weight training and bodybuilding and wanted to pursue that instead."

"What do you know about forensics?"

"It's the science that law enforcement uses to identify evidence."

"Did, and do, your parents share the techniques used?"

"First of all, my mother was never a law enforcement officer. She performs duties in the military that are completely unrelated to what you are asking me about. My father is retired now but worked

as a patrolman and later a lieutenant, which meant he managed other officers, so he was not an expert in forensics."
"Tell me about your time in American Pride."
"What do you want to know?"
"What went on at the meetings? Surely there were members that were knowledgeable about circumventing the police."
"American Pride is an organization interested in preserving the integrity of the U.S., not one which plots out crimes."
"If you were unwittingly involved in a crime, what would you do?"
"I would like to think I would turn myself in."
"What if you knew that if you took certain steps you would get away with it?" She thought for a moment.
"I guess it would depend on the type of crime involved. If it were a victimless crime I would probably try to avoid being caught. If people were injured by it, I would try to ensure that justice was served even at my own expense."
Cardillo looked at her for a minute, then said "Thank you miss. Good luck to you." He left the room followed by the two lawyers and told them he would have his results to them by Monday May 14th.

Monday, May 7th, 8am, American Pride offices, Washington D.C.
Albert Cross was talking to his number two man, Jonathan Rope. "We have to find someone who can testify against Kelly Visque. The Attorney General came to see me and made it clear we have no choice."
"That won't be easy. Virtually every member thinks she is a hero as Bernard likely would have ruled in favor of the legislation that we hate to support his daughter."
"That's why we have to find someone who has nothing to lose by doing this, as his or her life won't be worth shit." Rope closed his eyes; he was deep in thought. He knew just about every member as he continually traveled around the country. A minute later he got it.

"There is a man named Terry Strauss who is in his sixties out at the Wyoming branch. He has terminal lung cancer and truly believes in our cause."

"Great. Forward me his contact information and I will get in touch with him."

9am
Glen Aaron and Lionel Ross both received an email from Dr. Malcolm Kelsey, their psychologist. He had included his evaluations of both Visque and Corvino. Each attorney looked at the attachment that related to his client first. Kelsey's report about Visque was exactly what Aaron hoped for; it stated that she was patriotic but not so extreme that she would commit a crime to get what she wanted. Furthermore Kelsey wrote that Visque understood that there was no guarantee as to which way Bernard would rule so killing him would not necessarily have prevented the measure from passing. The examination of Corvino was equally favorable as Kelsey documented that she did not exhibit signs of being obsessive about her romantic partners. Ross was relieved; he hadn't been positive as to how things would go. He knew he still had a long and bumpy road, but at least now he had his expert in place.

Things were firing on all cylinders for Todd Russell. He was leading in all the national polls, Illinois was thriving, and he was going to India and Israel in a few weeks. He would be visiting India first, from May 25th to June 1st, and then Israel from June 2nd until June 9th. This would likely be his last trip abroad before the election, as he planned to spend his summer in Illinois making sure the state was doing well for the remainder of the time before November, for if people saw him neglecting his job it wouldn't matter how much campaigning he did. Starting in September, right after Labor Day he would hit the campaign trail hard and also prepare for the debates. Now, however, he had to plan his itinerary for the two countries he was going to visit. In India he would be splitting his time between Bombay and New Delhi, and his goal was to demonstrate the ways to improve technology in order to enhance the quality of people's lives everywhere. He would leave it to his staff to arrange for the hotels and other logistical information. He was asking Vincent Weimitz to handle the technology part and also to research the areas where India was lacking and in what the citizens were most interested. Russell expected that would be in the areas of education and infrastructure. India's government tended to invest in many high profile projects that looked good to the world but ignored many of the problems its citizens faced. Once Weimitz had done that Russell would have Joe Berry make the appointments with the appropriate groups and individuals. Their approach would be the same for Israel with stops in Jerusalem and Tel Aviv. He contacted both Weimitz and Berry and scheduled a meeting for this Friday at 10am.

Federal Penitentiary, Washington DC, 11am
Alan Wentworth had arrived to meet with both Kelly Visque and Lorraine Corvino. Joy from Waller's office, Glen Aaron, and Lionel Ross were also in attendance. The two defendants knew that this inquiry would be much more intense than the one they each had on Friday with Malcolm Kelsey. Visque was scheduled first. Just as Kelsey had, Wentworth was recording everything. "Good morning Miss Visque. I am sorry we are meeting in such unpleasant circumstances. Shall we begin? Why don't you start by telling me about your childhood and what it was like growing up." Visque took a liking to Wentworth immediately even though he was aligned with the opposition.

"I was an army brat, we moved a few times until my mother settled in DC. My dad managed to find a good job as a policeman and this is where we set up shop. I am sure you won't be surprised when I say that they were both very conservative in their politics. We lived comfortably but were never rich, and I am sure they were relieved when I decided to live at home while I got my associate's degree and then got a job."

"What kind of values did they instill in you?"

"They always wanted me to have a strong work ethic, be honest, and do my part to help those less fortunate than myself."

"Do you think you live up to their expectations?"

"No. They would have liked me to follow in their footsteps but I have a passion for exercise and couldn't see myself in another career."

"Do you sense you disappointed them?"

"Yes."

"Do they make you feel inadequate?"

"I am comfortable with my choices." Wentworth made a mental note to study that section when he watched the video later today. He continued with the dialogue between them both, asking her about her feelings towards our government and the policies in place. He took her through her past chronologically to the present, trying to run parallel lines of questions about her life while interweaving national events. After another 90 minutes he had all the information he needed. Waller had stressed the point that he needed to verify that Visque grasped the connection between her actions and the effect on the government.

Lorraine Corvino proved to be much more transparent. Wentworth was a master at making people at ease when he spoke with them, but he hardly had to try at all with her. She demonstrated from her answers that she was super jealous when in a relationship and became possessive almost right from the start. Wentworth shlepped out the interview longer than he needed to because he didn't want to tip his hand, but he knew Corvino's lawyer had his work cut out for him.

FBI headquarters, Quantico, VA 2pm

Waller's staff member Roberta met with Ed Billet at Quantico, to make it easy for him. She wanted to review what the legal team expected of him and that they wanted him to represent the FBI as a witness. She requested that he put his account of the cases against Visque and Corvino in writing, including all the evidence, what made them arrest Visque in the first place, and what led them to Corvino. She also wanted the gun and the picture of Corvino, which Billet said he would give her before she left. He said he was up to the task of testifying on behalf of the Bureau, and would have his report to her by Saturday. She sensed he wanted to end the meeting and she had addressed all the items she had gone there for, so she waited while he went to retrieve the gun and the picture, then showed herself out when she had them in her possession.

Washington, DC Federal Court building, 3pm

Lorraine Corvino was in court appearing in front of the grand jury for her indictment. While he sometimes sent an associate to handle indictments, Quinn Waller was handling this one himself. He stood up and walked over to them. "Ladies and gentlemen, I am sure you are all familiar with the case against Kelly Visque, who will be tried for the murders of Cecily and Winston Bernard. Well, the woman before you today, Lorraine Corvino, was also involved in these crimes. She did not do any of the physical work, but provided information about how to get to both of the victims as she was having an affair with the judge. On the other side, she was a friend of Kelly Visque who participated on the same bowling team as Miss Corvino. We have witnesses who saw them together several times and we also have accounts that Miss Corvino was very jealous and angry when she came to the realization that justice Bernard never planned to have a future with her. It is my contention that she knowingly helped orchestrate these killings, so I am planning to charge her with conspiracy to commit murder. Thank you." It took the jury only a few minutes to issue the indictment.

Lionel Ross had been at the grand jury assembly with his client, Lorraine Corvino, even though his presence wasn't required. He had wanted to hear what Waller would say as to the connection between the two women and how Corvino had paved the way for Kelly Visque. That information would help him prepare his opening statement. He took out his notes and spread them out over the table in the room down the hall from her cell. He was pleased with what he had learned from the two people with whom he had spoken. "How are you holding up?"

"I'm ok. As far as prisons go, this one doesn't seem so bad. I have my own cell and have my meals brought to me; the guards are not abusive. Let's hope it isn't much different wherever I end up."

"I will do my best to make sure that doesn't happen. Now, I met with your brother and neighbor over the weekend. They both will make good witnesses on your behalf and I intend to put them on the stand. Your brother said that the two of you don't really see each other that often and told me what you were like as a child. He explained that you were very caring and watched over him a lot as your parents worked long hours and you and he fended for yourselves. He talked about the fact that you have had many boyfriends over the years and when you called him less often he realized that you were dating. He did not know that you were involved with Justice Bernard but is absolutely certain you were not the one who was part of this crime in any way. Your neighbor reaffirmed this and said that you were always very polite, kept to yourself, and helped her whenever she needed anything. She never saw you with either Bernard or Kelly Visque and said she never noticed any inappropriate behavior."

"Excellent. I knew I could count on them. I am still planning to testify as well."

"Ok. We can review your testimony ahead of time. We don't really have any evidence to introduce, but I will work with Glen Aaron to decide if any of the evidence that they are using would help us as well."

"What about the picture of our bowling team?"

"That could backfire on you as you look very friendly in that picture." Ross paused. "Let me think about it. I will be in touch after I get together with Aaron again. Is there anything you need in the meantime?"

"No, I am alright."

"Call me if anything comes up."

Sondra Tristan came home late that night from the library where she had been doing research about criminals tried as terrorists and the associated conviction rate. Blake had beat her home and told her a package had arrived for her and he left it on the front hall table. She saw it was from Edna Jillow and breathed a sigh of relief that she had gotten the bee back.

Thursday, May 10th, 6am, flight to England

Hayao and Alex Ramirez were very excited about their trip. They were staying in the biggest city in each of the three countries they were visiting; London, Paris, and Madrid. They would be meeting with top government officials in each place, and for Hayao the highlight would be the night they stay at Buckingham Palace. They would be doing some sightseeing as well as mingling with the citizens in each place. He was hoping to spread his message of efficiency of government and Hayao would point to his success at Moritu Corp. as a model for what he could do with the U.S. and it's relationships around the world. Being an expert in technology was fine, but without the knowledge of how to apply that technology it was useless. He and Ramirez were the most complete team and he would do what it took to make people understand. Tomorrow they were meeting with Harry Edmunds, the British Prime Minister, and Hayao would offer advice about how to tackle some of the problems England has been having as of late with their economy and unemployment rate.

Federal Penitentiary, D.C. 9am

Glen Aaron's head was spinning. He knew that the prosecution was building a very strong case. Public opinion was also working against him. While part of their evidence was circumstantial, the accounts of the witnesses that Aaron expected would be very powerful and he would spend much of his preparation time planning how to discredit them. That's not to say he had no witnesses; he did, but he felt that the character witnesses on his side, including the testimony of the DNA expert and the psychologist, would be outweighed by his opponent. He was brought back out of his fog by Kelly Visque who asked him if he wanted to get started. "Right, here we go." He was there to review the analysis from his experts and the others he would put on the stand. "I heard back from both Dr. Kelsey and Otto Lampf. Let's start with Dr. Kelsey. He was supposed to determine if you were patriotic to the point of being a danger to others in society, as well as evaluating whether you understand that the crime committed by killing the Bernards was intended to impede the operations of the

U.S. government and prevent the legislation for a foreigner to run for President from passing. He concluded that you do understand the cause and effect relationship but the point is moot because you did not exhibit the signs of jingoism."

"So you are pleased with the report?"

"I am."

"This Dr.Kelsey, he is highly thought of in his field?"

"Yes. I would predict the prosecution will have a difficult time impugning his expertise."

"That's great. What about Otto Lampf?"

"He is our DNA guru, as you are aware. He had been working with a top scientist until they had a falling out. His new lab is in Albuquerque New Mexico and according to him he is at the top of his game."

"What did he find", Visque asked impatiently.

"He examined a bumblebee that is the same as the one that stung you; that is one of the pieces of evidence the prosecution is using. I wanted to know if the location of the DNA in the bee's stinger bears a relationship to when it was extracted by the bee when there are multiple sets of DNA present."

"What did he say?"

"He ran a slew of tests and found that the order the DNA was pulled into the stinger does determine where the DNA is positioned in the stinger. That is good news for us because your DNA was towards the bottom of the stinger, which according to Lampf is where the older DNA resides. That explanation will allow us to argue that since your DNA was older than the other person's, you were stung elsewhere by that bee, thought you killed it but did not, and then the bee stung this other man and then was killed. This theory is based upon the word of an authority in the field, and provides sufficient reasonable doubt for an acquittal." 'Until Waller crucifies him on cross examination', thought Aaron, but kept his mouth shut. He was here today to boost Miss Visque's ego. "Their accounts will put us in a good position. After we call Lampf to the stand, we can introduce the report about the DNA and the bee prepared by the FBI, as it will lend credence to what he had just said. The character witnesses that we have who are laypeople will go over well with the jury, as they all are sincere and reputable people. We have a strong foundation." Kelly Visque was reassured that she had a real chance at being acquitted.

Washington DC office of the ACLU, 1pm

Glen Aaron had finished with his client around 11:30 am, which gave him time to have a quick lunch on the way back to his office where he had about an hour to prepare for his meeting/strategy session with Lionel Ross. They would go down the witness list one by one, discuss which points they would try to convey to the jury, and anticipate what Waller would do. Next the two of them would review all the evidence they would present and how to nullify what the prosecution illustrated as well. Trying a case like this required the synergy of a strong offense and a subtle defense in which the lawyer came across as forceful without being vindictive. In that sense it was much like politics. His secretary buzzed him that Ross had arrived and Aaron told her to send him in. They exchanged greetings and Aaron offered a cup of coffee, which Ross declined. "Shall we start with my witness list?" asked Aaron. Ross nodded. "First, we have Otto Lampf, the scientist who examined the DNA inside the bumblebee's stinger. He sent me a report which unequivocally states that the DNA closest to the top of the stinger is the one that is the most recent."

"That's good. Do you envision him coming across as credible?"

"He will be fine during direct. Who knows how he will do on cross. Waller will go after him hard and hammer away at his past. He will imply that Lampf is a quack and bait him into losing his cool. We will have to work with him on that, he strikes me as the type of guy who will lose it if someone calls his work into question."

"I am assuming he was paid well for his services?"

"Yes he was."

"We can remind him that he was well compensated and that he will be expected to finish the job like the professional that he is."

"Of course. He will probably be paid extra to testify anyway. My director, Greg Driscoll, really wants to win this one and will spare no expense."

"Great. Who is next on your list?"

"Malcolm Kelsey. Should be no problem there. He is very polished and has been to court many times."

"What was his conclusion about your client?"

"He thinks that she is not so patriotic to have acted in such a way and believes she understands the connection between Justice Bernard's death and the outcome of the Supreme Court's decision. Ordinarily, his assessment would play into the prosecution's hands as it would reaffirm that she should be tried for terrorism except for Kelsey's opinion that her views about the issue of a foreign born President were not so extreme. That is the paradox that Kelsey's testimony will create that will work in our favor; he believes that Visque possesses the intelligence to understand the chain of effects that this crime would set in motion which is what the prosecution wants, but then our witness, who seems to be playing right into Waller's hands, turns around and says that she was not so fanatical as to kill for her country, taking away all the momentum from Waller."

"That's brilliant, Glen. We just have to make sure the jury can connect the dots."

"Don't worry, my line of questioning will make it clear."

"That will also help my client; if the jury sees Visque as innocent then they will by default have to believe Corvino is too. We get two for the price of one. That takes care of the experts. Who else do you have?"

"A man who goes by the nickname Samson, who is a member of American Pride and knew Visque when she was involved with them."

"Are you sure that's a good idea?"

"He will corroborate Dr. Kelsey's account that Visque was not super gung ho."

"I am sure, but will he do more harm than good? Will the jurors be turned off by him automatically?"

"He is well spoken and intelligent. I think if he wears a suit he would be an asset. He will talk about how she was opposed to violence and spoke out against it at the meetings."

"Will he be able to withstand the onslaught from the Attorney General?"

"I think so." Aaron looked at his list. "We come to Stefan Kurtz, who says that Visque is passionate about fitness, is a great coworker and very supportive, and genuinely wants her customers to succeed. She doesn't bring her politics to work, and he had never seen her push a client past the point of safety."

"Ok, probably not much to trip him up on."

"We follow him with Calvin, Visque's boss at Star Fitness. She was a model employee, did everything asked of her, was always willing to go the extra mile, never talked about her personal life. Fitness was her life. He didn't know that she had been in American Pride, and he would hire her all over again." Aaron paused, and Ross thought he had no more witnesses. "I am going to call Richard, the man she was seeing and was with on the day the bodies were found. We will depose him ahead of time to help protect his anonymity as he is married. He will talk about how open minded Kelly is, and although she may have strong opinions, she is always willing to listen and is not violent by any stretch. Before you ask, he will be able to handle the cross examination."

"How do you plan to prevent him from looking completely underhanded and dishonest as a philanderer?"

"I will have him explain that he is in a relationship that disintegrated long ago and they are staying together for the sake of the kids. He understands that doesn't make what he is doing right, but he has no validation at home so he is filling his needs elsewhere. I imagine he will come across as sympathetic. Who hasn't felt unappreciated at times? My last witness will be Kelly Visque, and she will walk us through what happened that day and explain her schedule. It may be risky for her to take the stand, but I also don't want anyone concluding she has something to hide. As far as evidence goes, I will have one exhibit; the FBI's report that states the bumblebee's stinger had two sets of DNA, with Visque's closer to the bottom. I will not be asking anyone except for Lampf about that as it is not germane to anyone else's testimony. That's it on my end. You're up."

"I have Dr. Kelsey as well, and then I have Corvino's brother, her neighbor and herself. I was hoping to use her co-worker, Rick Heller, but after talking to him he is obviously not on our side. He spilled the beans about her sleeping with Justice Bernard immediately; she probably rebuffed his advances and he is pissed at her and looking for revenge. I have a feeling he will be a witness for the prosecution. Her brother will be a good character witness because he will say that she is very nurturing and kind; she is not the kind of person who would be involved in something like this. The only downside that the prosecution will hammer away at is the fact that they didn't see each other very often and he wasn't up to date about what was happening in her life. Corvino's neighbor will be equally flattering but probably ineffectual as well. I don't have a lot to choose from. My best chance is to shed doubt on their case rather than hope to convince anyone through the use of our witnesses. I have no evidence to introduce. My last witness will be Corvino herself, and I hope she will be able to project the air of caring and sweetness our witnesses will attest to." Ross paused. "We also have to coordinate how the two women will characterize their relationship. I suspect it will be that they were friends who enjoyed each other's company after the game."

"Waller will no doubt insinuate that they were lovers, which we should probably address on our direct questioning to steal their thunder. I agree with you, our best bet is to shift the focus away from our clients and put it on the credibility of their evidence and witnesses." Aaron looked at his watch, it was two thirty and they had accomplished much.

"I think that's good for today. Why don't we plan to meet again on the weekend before the trial to practice with our witnesses and discuss jury selection. I will call you to arrange the time. In the meantime, if you think of anything that could be helpful to us, please call me and I will do the same."

Green River, Wyoming, 3pm

Terry Strauss was working in his garden as he did most afternoons. That was something he missed when he worked full time. He had just finished putting in the last tomato plant when his phone rang. That was unusual. He didn't get many phone calls these days, which suited him just fine. "Hello?"

"Mr. Strauss, this is Albert Cross, from American Pride." Strauss knew who he was, the national director. He wondered how Cross had gotten his name and what he wanted. "I got your name from Jonathan Rope. I hope I am not bothering you."

"Not at all."

"Good. How are you enjoying retirement?"

"Very much. How are things back east?" He remembered Cross's office was there in Washington DC.

"Just fine. I am sure you are wondering why I am calling. I, we, I mean American Pride, needs a favor." He paused to see if Strauss had any comments. "I am sure you are familiar with the murder trial that will be starting over the summer involving Kelly Visque who is accused of killing Supreme Court justice Winston Bernard and his wife. Miss Visque had been a member of American Pride, and we know that you and she crossed paths on several occasions at meetings and rallies. Well, the U.S. Attorney General is trying to build a case against her and is looking for witnesses. They want someone to say that she was gung ho at the meetings and committed to the cause above everything else in her life. She would risk it all to help preserve the American tradition and way of life." Oh, he understood. Rope knew he was terminal and they need someone to testify against the murderer of the person who could have prevented this abortion of the Constitution. Why should he help put Kelly Visque away? She was a hero! He caught his breath for a minute. Why would American Pride be looking to work with the prosecution? Only one reason could exist; they were getting squeezed by the Attorney General's office. They probably told Cross that all their dealings would be scrutinized if they didn't play ball. Cross and Rope recognized that whoever did this, went against the doctrine of their organization, their life wouldn't be worth 25 cents. He fit the bill to the tee. His gut reaction had been to tell them to piss off, but he knew that he would be performing a valuable service by agreeing to do this. He had to act as a traitor to the organization he loved in order to protect that same organization. He was dead anyway, he might as well do something good with the time he had left.

"Alright, I am in. I assume that I will have to meet with Attorney General Waller to explain what I knew about her. Why don't you give him my phone number and tell him to call me."

"Thank you, Terry. I am sure you recognize what a valuable service you are performing here. Thank you and good luck."

Boston, MA, 10pm

Kangaroo was watching his favorite tv show that he missed the other night; he had recorded it.

He got a text message from agent Z saying that he had audio about the assassin in Arizona and they had him dead to rights. He sent the audio file in an email and told Kangaroo to get in touch with him if he had any questions.

Friday, May 11th, 10am

Todd Russell was meeting with Vincent Weimitz and Joe Berry at the Governor's mansion. "We need to plan out who we are going to meet with in India and Israel. Technology has to be the tool that we use to make improvements to the people's lifestyles. India's two main issues seem to be education and infrastructure. The government is very slow to spend money that has been appropriated for those two purposes for which it was intended. They spend the money on projects that are self-serving, just like all governments do. While we are there, we must show the people ways to address these issues in a cost effective way. If we can do that, it will translate into votes for us back home come November. Vincent, do you think you can handle that?" He nodded. "I want you to do the same for Israel, only you will have to research the areas in which they are lacking. Joe, once Vincent comes up with the proposals then you will pounce into action and set up appointments with the appropriate people. Why don't we meet again on Tuesday and have some concrete plans. Same time, same place. See you both then."

Sunday, May 13th, 10am, London England
Hayao had enjoyed himself immensely over the last few days. He had attended a gala dinner on Thursday, the day he arrived, had met with Prime Minister Edmunds and had accomplished much; they had established a rapport and had a mutual understanding that Hayao would have his support at election time. England and France were not super important for support, as people from their countries did not make up a huge portion of the population in the U.S., but Hayao wanted to show that they mattered by visiting, more for goodwill if he won the election. He liked Edmunds, a down to earth man who understood how politics and business should merge. Tomorrow he would be attending a Parliament meeting and from there he would visit John Lennon's house in Liverpool. The highlight of his trip so far, however, was his visit with King William and his overnight stay at Buckingham Palace. Hayao was well off financially, but these people sure knew how to live! Everything was at their beck and call 24-7! They had really made him feel welcome. He predicted they would also use whatever influence they had to tell people to vote for him in November. He made a mental note that if he were elected, one of the first things he would do would be to extend an invitation for William to be his personal guest in Washington and would see to it his staff went above and beyond.

1pm, Attorney General Waller's office
Albert Cross had called Waller on Friday and given him the name of a former American Pride member who had known Kelly Visque, Terry Strauss. He was terminally ill with cancer and and had agreed to do this knowing that he would be a marked man and be hunted down if the disease didn't take him first. Waller wanted to talk to him about how he would portray Kelly Visque in his testimony. He called Strauss and introduced himself. "Yes, I have been expecting your call." Waller started to fill him in but Strauss cut him off, knowing he did not have to be polite.

"I see what you are trying to accomplish. Kelly Visque was an extremist, even among the zealots of American Pride. She would incite others to violence and try to get everyone riled up. She spewed forth much hatred for non-Americans and was one of the worst xenophobes I have met."

"If all this is true, then why did she leave?"

"I suspect it's because people were growing weary of her tirades and she grew impatient when no one was taking any action."

"Why did you stop attending their meetings?"

"I came down with an incurable disease." Strauss said it with as much disdain as he could. He didn't give a shit. If Waller didn't like it let him find some other stoolie.

"Will I be giving my deposition ahead of time, or will you want me at the trial?"

"At the trial. I will arrange for your travel to DC and your accommodations as well. You could go into the witness protection program afterward if you want."

"What about my medical care?"

"You will have access to health care. The difference is that you will have a new name, but I will see to it that you have access to the top doctors."

"Great. What is the next step?"

"Right before the trial starts in a few weeks, we will review your testimony more extensively over the internet. Then you will come here when I have a better idea of when you will take the stand."

"Great. I will wait to hear from you, and try not to die in the meantime."

Monday, May 14th, 1pm, Liverpool, England

Hayao and Alex were taking the guided tour of Mendips, John Lennon's house. Hayao got chills while walking through the rooms. He had always enjoyed the Beatles' music and appreciated the legacy they left. He and Alex believed they had accomplished what they set out to do in England, and that was to ingratiate themselves with the populace there. Tomorrow they would visit Stonehenge in the morning and then leave for France, where their goal was the same. They would have a bigger impact in Spain, where they hoped to make serious inroads into the Pope's influence. They hoped that people realized if Layton won he would feel beholden to the Pope and would favor him, which might lead to problems, even if that favoritism were subconscious. They were counting on people to vote along nationalistic lines rather than religious ones.

11am, Washington, DC, Federal courthouse

Lorraine Corvino was being arraigned and knew what to expect from talking to Lionel Ross. The formal charges were read aloud, and the judge, Tim Fresco, the same one who presided over her initial appearance, granted the formal indictment. Corvino wasn't really paying attention as she understood this was a formality. The whole process took 20 minutes. Ross escorted her back to her cell along with the guards and told her they had some things to discuss. He went to see about using the meeting room and came back to get her. "I met with Glen Aaron last week and we mapped out some of the strategies we are going to use during the trial. Our goal is to try to discredit their witnesses and make their theories about the crime seem implausible to the jury. I am going to use the three witnesses that we discussed, and I think that will create a favorable character profile of you, Lorraine. Aaron also has a strong case and if the jury does not convict Visque, then by default you will also be found not guilty."

"What is our biggest hurdle?"

"Demonstrating that our explanation of the DNA is more plausible than the prosecution's and that our psychologist is more on point than theirs. Both sides will have character witnesses that will support their side, so it really comes down to the experts and who comes across as more genuine."

"What about the evidence?"

"Again, it depends on who explains it more coherently."

"Have you and Aaron discussed these issues?"

"Yes, and we have some ideas about how to proceed." Ross stopped talking; after a minute Corvino said, "Care to enlighten me?"

"I can't yet, I have not seen their witness list. Once we determine who they are using we will be able to research their credentials and come up with a line of questioning."

"Well, have you at least checked out Dr. Wentworth?"

"Not yet. I have been trying to get our case in order before I look at theirs. My style is to tackle everything at once." Ross saw she had a disbelieving look on her face.

"I have plenty of time. Are you familiar with the chronology of a trial?" She shook her head. "Our trial is set to begin on June 4th. The first step is to select a jury. Have you ever been called for jury duty?"

"Yes, five years ago. I was there for one day and the judge told me I was dismissed at the end of that day."

"Probably because you work at the Supreme Court building. Anyway, all of the key players are there for jury selection, the two lawyers and the trial judge. By the way, the judge that was at the arraignment today will not be the same judge at the trial. That judge has not been assigned yet. Then, everyone who was called for jury duty is at the courthouse that day. They will call people from the jury pool and the lawyers will ask them questions about themselves to determine if they can be impartial about the case. If the lawyers for both sides find that person acceptable, then he or she is on the jury, which is made up of 12 individuals plus one alternate juror who hears the case but does not participate in the verdict unless one of the regular jurors becomes incapacitated. The jury selection process can take a few weeks. No statements are made by the lawyers and the witnesses are not called until the jury is in place. So you see, I have ample time to get information about all their witnesses."

"Ok, that makes sense. What's the next step for us?"

"I will be going to look at our witnesses from all angles and trying to anticipate some of the traps the prosecution may try to set for them during the cross examination, which is when they get to ask our witnesses questions. If I can make those points when I am asking the questions, it will not seem so horrible if I give them a chance to explain."

"Could you give an example?"

"Let's say that the prosecutor asks Kelly Visque if she was ever a member of American Pride, which has a reputation for being a militant group who uses violence at times to further their agenda. The jurors will already form an opinion about a person for simply being a member. It is a yes or no question. If I ask that same question however, I would allow Miss Visque the opportunity to explain that she was only a member for a short time because she did not agree with their methods. By explaining this, the prosecution cannot make her look like a radical in front of the jury because she already elaborated on the circumstances so the impact was lessened from the prosecution."

"That makes sense. When do you suppose you will get their witness list?"

"I expect in a few weeks, probably right before the trial."

"When are we going to meet again?"

"How about next Monday? I will update you with what I have accomplished during this week."

"Thank you counselor. I will see you then."

3pm, offices of the U.S. Attorney General

Joy was looking through her email and she saw emails from Alan Wentworth and Sean Cardillo. Skimming through the report from Wentworth, she noticed it was what she expected. He concluded that Visque was so in love with the United States she would do anything to protect its integrity. Furthermore, her thought process was such that committing an act such as the one she is accused of would alter the government's operation. His report was succinct, but addressed all the issues that were necessary. Next she scanned Wentworth's report about Lorraine Corvino. She was characterized as obsessive and demanding of all a person's attention when involved romantically. She believed that person belonged to her. Wentworth explained that it represented an all-consuming psychosis. Corvino practically demanded her partner give her all their time and attention and if her expectations were not met, she became irrational. Lastly, she read Cardillo's report about Visque addressing state of mind regarding criminal behavior, and found that his opinion concluded that she was very well versed in how law enforcement works and how to circumvent their procedures with the intent of breaking the law. This definitely was consistent with their case against her, as it had not been anything that Visque did to seal her fate, but carelessness by Lorraine Corvino when she left the picture out that Agent Squelch had seen. All three reports were supportive of the approach that the prosecution was taking. Waller was going to be very pleased.

An hour later, Joy was finishing up some paperwork when her phone rang. She didn't recognize the number. "Hello?"

"Hi Joy, it's Glen Aaron."

"Hello Glen. What can I do for you?"

"Have you heard back from Alan Wentworth?" Is he going to be on your witness list?"

"You are asking the wrong person. Attorney General Waller is the one to speak to about that."

"Can you transfer me to him?" Knowing that Waller would not give Aaron an answer as he would force Aaron to wait for the witness list, she kept her mouth shut and transferred the call.

Tuesday, May 15th, Governor's mansion, Springfield Illinois

Weimitz was ready, he had done a fair amount of research in the last few days. "The best way to assist the people there would be to set up a corporation in India that would contribute money to the government in exchange for the freedom to operate the way we would like. It would be a nonprofit organization that would take contributions from people back here. I would be the director and would oversee operations. That is the most efficient way as the government will be more cooperative if it benefits them financially. We would fix the roads ourselves and look into building charter schools and hiring from the existing pool of people who are already in the education field. That's what we should be offering."

"That's all fine and good, Vincent, but as Vice President your duties cannot be so focused on one country. We will have to use someone else to act as director. Do you envision this nonprofit entity working in other countries?"

"I hadn't thought about it but I suppose it's possible."

"If that were the case then it could become one of your responsibilities. It could be a humanitarian effort and when you travelled to the countries to make the arrangements you could assess the technological requirements as well. I propose we have Joe Berry here be the head. Let's not get ahead of ourselves, however. We are here to discuss our plans for our trip which is in ten days. We know what we will focus on in India. Joe, have you made an itinerary?"

"Yes. We will be splitting our time between New Delhi and Bombay. Now that we know what we want to accomplish I will go ahead and set up meetings with the appropriate officials."

"Excellent. What about Israel?"

"We all acknowledge that they are very advanced. One area they need some assistance with is solar power and how to maximize its potential."

"Ok, then that will be our focus. Joe, what part of the country will we be in?"

"We will be in Jerusalem and Tel Aviv. I will find the right people for us to meet with."

"Great. We are on the right track. Let's meet again on the day before we leave to finalize our plans. Thank you both."

11am, Attorney General Waller's office

"I hope everyone is doing well today", Waller said to the team. They all nodded their assents. "Who wants to go first today?" Joy raised her hand.

"I received feedback from both of the psychologists. Their reports back up our case 100%. Wentworth also thinks that Visque suffers from jingoism and would do anything to uphold our traditions. She fits the definition of a terrorist that you are planning to use, Quinn, so no problem there. He is likewise on point with Corvino, reporting that she would not have wanted to share him and that she had acted the same way in her past relationships. He has an excellent reputation and can't see the defense being able to trip him up. The other psychologist, Sean Cardillo, who is the expert about the psyche of criminal minds, will testify that Visque possesses the nature to take the steps to elude the police after committing a crime of this magnitude, and would have gotten away with it had it not been for a stupid mistake on Corvino's part."

"Good work, Joy. Please send those reports to me when you get a chance. Sondra, how did you do?"

"Pretty good. I received the bee back from Edna Jillow and had a discussion with a beekeeper who has worked with bees for many years. He sent me an analysis of how bees behave and the bottom line is that bumblebees do not stray far from their home base each day, so the likelihood that Visque was stung far away from the Supreme Court building is unlikely. His name is Willy Detrop, and we would want to have a live feed to allow him to testify as he lives in Hawaii."

"Ok. Would you be in charge of making sure that he has the necessary equipment? We will pay for him to obtain it if we need to. Oh, and we received the brain scan report from the FBI. Thank you. Who's next?" Victor cleared his throat.

"I met with Margo, Visque's friend from childhood, and took notes this time while we spoke. She portrays Visque as a type A personality who always had strong ideas and was very traditional in her views, which she learned from her parents. She enjoyed guns and activities that involved them. I think if we don't push her too hard she will help us make our case. I also have an old customer of Visque's at Star Fitness who says that she became belligerent toward him during their session and attacked him verbally when he couldn't perform up to her satisfaction."

"Is he willing to be a witness?"

"Yes. His name is Angelo Forte. He lives locally so getting here won't be a problem."

"Moving on, that leaves you, Roberta."

"I got the gun and the picture of Visque and Corvino back from Billet and got his report detailing the FBI's chain of events in charging both Visque and Corvino. I also got the accounts of the bar manager, Corvino's coworker, and another member on the bowling team in writing. They all agreed to be available for the trial. The only one who we cannot count on now is Corvino's friend who developed a conscience and now will not be a witness."

"No problem. We have a strong case without her. Well, I am sure you are curious as to how I fared. I spoke with a former member of American Pride, Terry Strauss. He was convinced to testify, in large part due to the fact that he is dying and has nothing to lose." Everyone wondered why someone associated with an organization which would seemingly applaud the slaying of a potentially liberal Supreme Court justice would be helping to convict his killer, but they knew better than ask Waller what had happened to bring it about. "I am very pleased with our progress. Here is my task for everyone. The trial begins with jury selection on Monday, June 4th. Don't make any plans for Saturday and Sunday June 2nd and 3rd. We are going to be meeting with our witnesses during those two days and reviewing their testimony. For those people that live far away, get their IP addresses so that we can set up video chats, which is how we will also do it during the trial. I will send out the schedule of when I would like each person to be available by this weekend so you will all have ample time to make sure they are here at the assigned appointment. We will also talk about selecting our jurors that weekend. Good day everyone."

Friday, May 18th, 12pm, Paris, France
Hayao and Alex were making their way through the Louvre. They were not enjoying France as much as they had enjoyed England. The people were not mean, but they found an air of superiority around them. Yesterday they had gone to the Eiffel Tower; that had been quite an experience. The day before that they had met with some high ranking government officials who had seemed to agree with the positions that Hayao's administration would take on quite a few of the issues facing the U.S. One thing he had to say, the food was outstanding. He would gain five pounds in the time he was here. He wasn't overly concerned about winning over the French, however, as they did not have a huge voting block back home. He had a bigger stake in Spain, which carried more influence with more U.S. citizens. With Alex Ramirez in his corner, he could count on Spain's support.

2pm

Aaron, Ross, and Waller had all agreed to exchange their lists of witnesses this afternoon. Aaron sent his first, Ross sent his at 3pm, and at 4 o'clock Waller finally sent his. Waller was not surprised by the two he received, but Aaron had not expected the prosecution to use Dr. Sean Cardillo. Aaron had not thought that Cardillo had come away thinking that Visque possessed the background or devious nature to commit these horrific acts. His cell phone rang; he saw it was Ross. "Hello Lionel."

"Hi. What do you think of the prosecution's witnesses?"
"Pretty much what I expected except for Sean Cardillo."
"He is using him?"
"Yup. Cardillo knows where his bread is buttered."
"How are you going to handle it?"
"What do you mean?"
"There are two ways to go, try to undermine the witness they have or hire your own."
"I am going to find my own expert to refute what Cardillo says. We need to stay proactive to remain credible to the jury. If we attack all the time we will lose that."
"I can do the legwork of finding someone who specializes in this. I hope to have someone by Monday."
"Ok. Keep me posted."

6pm

Attorney General Waller chuckled to himself as he dined in a posh restaurant in downtown D.C. He had hoped that Aaron would use Otto Lampf. Waller couldn't wait to rip him apart on the stand; the guy was a total quack. The fact that they chose him demonstrated how desperate they were.

Sunday, May 20th, Dulles Airport, 5am

President Harrington was leaving for China amidst much fanfare. This was a voyage to obtain knowledge and resources that the United States needed. The public just couldn't look behind the curtain. Immigration would be a part of this trip, but for self-serving reasons that would happen when no one was looking. Jo, his Chief of Staff, had planned a great itinerary. Tomorrow he would arrive in Beijing and be greeted by President Wang Jie. The President was staying at the Shangri-La World Summit, a five star hotel. He would be in Beijing for a few days before going to Shanghai. On Tuesday he would meet with Wang Jie to discuss the election when everyone thought they would be talking about how to combat the rising sea levels which China had mastered. Indirectly they would, as Harrington suspected President Jie would want the contract to do the work. That would mean that Chinese citizens would have to emigrate to the U.S. These people would be enticed to vote for Hayao. It was quid pro quo; Harrington would award the contracts for the jobs of combatting the rising sea levels to the Chinese company in exchange for the workers' votes. Everyone was getting what they wanted; Americans were getting protection from the elements, China was helping their economy, and Harrington was protecting his legacy.

9am, France

Hayao and Ramirez were getting in some sightseeing before leaving for Spain later today. Yesterday they had toured the Notre Dame Cathedral which was impressive and today they were headed to Chateau de Fountainbleau, which everyone said was stunning. It was a palace that had been maintained by monarchs over the years and today housed an academy for the arts. Alex, for one, would be happy to get to Madrid. France was nice, but she would feel more at home in Spain. She felt that she and Hayao had ingratiated themselves here as much as they could. She believed most of the French citizens in the U.S. would be more interested in what each candidate could offer them than in what another foreign government thought was best. There was also another large faction of people that were Catholic in the States who would align themselves with the Pope, and she thought the best thing for Hayao to do for the remainder of the campaign would be to visit the countries that had large voting blocks back home, become more polished as a politician, and campaign around the U.S. He agreed with her, and he also accepted that he had to keep his hand in the operations of Moritu Corporation to show that he could multi-task.

They knew that Russell was in the lead right now, but that didn't worry them too much. November was light years away when it came to politics, and they believed with the course of action they had laid out they would peak at the right time and demonstrate that they were the best choice for the White House.

10am, Eric Layton's office, Washington DC
Eric Layton and Steven Morris had been keeping their heads down and doing their jobs as members of Congress believing that by serving their constituents they would gain favor with voters. They also knew that they had to spread the word about their platform and that is why they decided to visit China. They wanted to gain a foothold with the Asian population here. They were planning to go for two weeks in June, from June 10th to June 24th. Layton had been consulting with some friends that had visited China numerous times and gotten some advice. He wanted to spend time in each of the three major cities, Beijing, Shanghai, and Hong Kong. The influence that these three metropolises wielded over the whole country was great and they would get the most bang for their buck by doing that. They would spend a little time in the outer regions to show a good faith interest in these areas as well. He would plan on meeting with both politicians and business leaders in each area as well as visiting public places like schools and museums to take part in their culture. He was planning on bringing one of his aides as well to handle all the administrative details. He buzzed him in right now. "Robert would you come in here please?" "Robert, please sit down. Mr. Morris and I are planning to go to China in June for a few weeks. We would like you to make all the arrangements, and second, would like you to come with us." Robert tried to contain his excitement but couldn't.

"Oh wow! That sounds great!" Robert was in his early twenties and single. "When would we be leaving?"

"In early to mid June. Let us finish up here, then the three of us will sit and we will tell you what we want to accomplish and how and then leave it to you to take care of the plans to make it happen."

4pm, Boston, MA, Boston Commons

Uncle George and Kangaroo didn't usually meet on Sundays but Kangaroo did not want to wait. He had listened to all the tapes from the assassin's house and he had definitely incriminated himself. He needed to let Uncle George know. They didn't have to talk today; Kangaroo simply left the package on the bench and Uncle George took it when he left. He knew what was on it and Kangaroo had briefed him already. Kangaroo would hear back when it was time to proceed.

8pm, Dulles Airport, Washington DC

Ed Billet finally had some time off from the Bernard case, having submitted his report to Roberta. Since it was Sunday night the airport was a little slower so he went to view the surveillance tapes from when Juan Pillar was murdered. He made his way down to the security office where they were expecting him. All of the files resided on a dedicated server only for surveillance and labeled by the location they viewed, date and time. He started with the footage from inside the terminal but found nothing. He then looked at the files of the outside of the airport hoping to be surprised. An hour later he was about to give up when he saw it. A car from the service that Pillar had reserved. In the driver's seat, though wearing sunglasses and a baseball cap, was a person that looked just like Kelly Visque, done in once again by being captured on camera.

CHAPTER 13

Monday, May 21st, 9am, Attorney General Waller's office
Waller's phone was blinking, he saw that there were 15 missed calls. He checked the numbers and 14 were the same, Ed Billet. He didn't even bother checking the message, just called Billet back.
"Hi Quinn. I have big news. I saw a video of Kelly Visque on the security cameras outside Dulles on Friday, February 24th, the day of Juan Pillar's kidnapping." They both understood it was not a coincidence, but Quinn had to be sure.
"Did you get the license plate?"
"Yes. It's the car from the livery company."
"How do you know it was Visque?"
"There was a blond in the driver's seat with sunglasses and a baseball cap, and the driver on the schedule was a dark haired man." Waller closed his eyes to focus. It was definitely consistent with her motive. Killing Bernard hadn't worked so she had to resort to eliminating the front runner who represented everything which she opposed. It was not a stretch by any means.
"What about the letter found in Pillar's drawer that came from California?"
"During our investigation we learned that Visque has a friend in the San Diego area. She could have mailed the friend the letter and asked her to send it to Juan Pillar." Quinn decided that Kelly Visque would be tried for the murder of Juan Pillar and the driver as well. Waller knew what had to be done.
"Thanks Ed. Could you forward me the name of the friend in California?" He called Judge Tim Fresco to see if he was sitting today. Waller found out he was and made some calls to get this new charge on the docket for today. It wasn't an abuse of power as Visque already faced indictment for other murders and terrorism charges; Waller was simply requesting the formal charges be amended. He would contact Glen Aaron and meet him at Kelly Visque's cell to read the charges against her now, as the arraignment to modify the indictment was scheduled for 3pm.

10pm, Beijing

Air Force One had just landed at a special section of the airport reserved for dignitaries and was quickly deemed secure, China's President, Wang Jie, waited with his entourage and gave Harrington a royal greeting. The two leaders made small talk for a few minutes and then bid goodbye as they were both exhausted and wanted to be at the top of their games tomorrow when they negotiated with each other.

6pm, Royal Palace of Madrid

Hayao and Ramirez were attending a fantastic banquet with top leaders from around Spain. Hayao observed Ramirez totally in her element and the Spanish people adored her. They viewed her as a success story and she was their savior, even more so now that Pillar was gone. She in turn loved Spain and its people. They were kind and generous and knew how to enjoy themselves. The one thing that she objected to was their passion for bullfighting, which she saw as cruel. Madrid was a great city and had grown in international influence in the past ten years. President Lobato stood up and approached the podium. "Ladies and gentlemen, may I have your attention please!" It took a few minutes for everyone to become quiet. "I would like to welcome our special guests to our country and our fiesta." Everyone cheered. "We are behind you 100% in your bid for your Presidency and hold every confidence that you will be successful! Now let's get back to the festivities!" He signaled to the band to resume the music, many people got up to dance and the party lasted until the wee hours of the morning.

10am, Los Angeles, the home of Louis Grenadine

Louis Grenadine and his wife were having a leisurely breakfast when the phone rang, destroying the silence. "Hello?" said Louis.

"Mr. Grenadine, this is agent Billet with the FBI. How are you today?" Billet's attempt at being cordial fell on deaf ears.

"What do you want?"

"I wanted to tell you that you have been cleared as a suspect in the murder of Juan Pillar and the driver of the car."

"Cleared? What does that mean? Have you arrested someone else?"

"I can't say, except to tell you it will become public knowledge later today." Grenadine was silent for a few seconds, then simply hung up the phone without saying another word.

3pm, Washington DC, Federal Courthouse

"Please rise, the honorable Judge Tim Fresco presiding!" Judge Fresco went in and sat down, allowing everyone to do so as well. Waller had told Fresco that he wanted to go first, and Fresco agreed. "The United States vs. Kelly Visque." Waller had contacted Aaron and had explained what was happening; they had met at Visque's cell today at 1pm. Waller had detailed the new charges to her; she of course started to protest her innocence and Aaron told her that they would discuss that later. He had done that so that he could skip the initial appearance and jump right to the arraignment and indictment proceedings. "Your honor, there is already an indictment existing against Miss Visque for terrorism and first degree murder. I am simply adding two people to the charge in light of new evidence that came to my attention. There is no need for a separate trial, this new development can easily be incorporated into the one that is already scheduled, eliminating extra expense to our taxpayers, and there is still ample time for the defense to prepare for this unforeseen event."

"What is this new evidence, counselor?"

"The people discovered a video of Miss Visque at Dulles airport on the day that Juan Pillar was abducted. This act demonstrated consistency with the reason that the prosecution believes she killed Justice Bernard."

Aaron spoke up to object. "This is baseless Your Honor. I saw the video. The person could have been anyone with long blond hair."

"That's true, your honor. What Mr. Aaron is forgetting to mention however, is that the person with blond hair was sitting behind the wheel of the car that had been arranged to pick Mr. Pillar up, and the driver on duty that day had short dark hair." Fresco nodded; Waller smirked, and Aaron had known he never stood a chance.

"This modification is granted to the indictment with the new charges being combined at the existing trial. Bailiff, next case!" As soon as Waller left the courtroom, he called Joy, the lawyer on his team for the Bernard case, and the best investigator of the group. "Hi Joy. I have a job for you. As I am sure you ascertained from the news reports about FBI Director Grey's press release, we charged Kelly Visque with the murders of Juan Pillar and the driver. We decided that we will not answer any questions about this as it would contaminate the trial proceedings. Anyway, here is what I would like you to do. Kelly Visque has a friend in California that I believe assisted her in mailing something to Juan Pillar. I need you to go to California, find her, and get a taped deposition while you are there. She will probably find a local lawyer. You can depose her at his or her office. We will use the deposition at the trial rather than having her testify live." Waller wanted to get this done quickly before her friend really had time to compose her alibi.

"Sure Quinn. I will handle this."

"Great. Can you leave tonight?"

4pm, Federal Penitentiary, Washington, DC

Lionel Ross was meeting with Lorraine Corvino to go over the general approach he would use at trial. He also wanted to discuss what the new development with Kelly Visque meant for them. Ross believed that it would make it less likely that a jury would convict Corvino, as she would have had no reason to go after Pillar, lending credence to the notion that Kelly Visque had acted alone on all the murders. Of course, Ross still wanted to work as a team with Aaron. "We believe that we should try to poke holes in their case rather than to spend a lot of energy building up our character witnesses. We, myself and Glen Aaron, believe that we can make the jury grasp how disjointed their case is." Corvino felt good. "Lorraine, I am aware you are planning to testify and I think that's great. When you do, it would be best for you to project an air of kindness and love, as if you were not the type of person who could ever be involved in something like this." She understood.

"My demeanor in the courtroom will reflect my true nature, and the jury will have a hard time buying that I helped plan a double murder."

"Very good, Lorraine. I think that about covers it. Our plan is to meet with the witnesses on the two days before the trial starts to review their testimony. Aaron and I will also meet then to map out a strategy for jury selection. I will touch base with you then. If anything comes up before, use your phone call to reach me."

Waller had put together his schedule for the witness meetings on the weekend before the trial. He was not concerned with making it convenient for his attorneys; he wanted to meet with the witnesses in a certain order, starting with the professionals and finishing up with the character witnesses. He would go in the order that he would actually call them to the stand during the trial. In his experience, juries tended to focus more on the witnesses at the beginning of the trial. That gave the prosecution an inherent advantage, but it also made it important to present the witnesses who would have the biggest impact first. The jury took the witnesses who were there to discuss what kind of people the defendants were with a grain of salt; they would not be used by the prosecution if they said things the prosecution didn't want. The experts however, had more of a standard to meet and were under more of an obligation to tell the truth. That's why Waller wanted the psychologists and the DNA experts to give their testimonies first, and as a result to be the first to meet with him to keep the consistency. He could hear the groans all over town about the broken up times and the fact that the staff would have to leave and then come back throughout the day. He chuckled to himself.

11am, Tuesday, May 22nd, Beijing

Presidents Harrington and Jie were going into a private meeting, ostensibly to discuss the issue of rising sea levels that was happening in the United States. China had been dealing with this for some time now and Harrington wanted to hear what he had to say. His approach would be to negotiate to have several Chinese companies bid for the jobs and to accept the lowest bid. He would want as many workers as possible to come do the work which would be part of his ulterior motive. The Chinese government would appreciate the fact that the U.S. is giving them all this business, and would undoubtedly be eager to reciprocate in some way. Harrington laid out his plan to President Jie who listened attentively and acted as if he really liked what he heard. When Harrington finished, Jie got up and shook his hand and said that he would do whatever possible to help make this happen, which was basically everything. "I will make some calls and set up some appointments for you to meet with the executives at some of the businesses that do this type of work. You can compare notes and see."

"Excellent, sir. Thank you." Harrington paused. "There is something else I would like to discuss. As you know we have an election coming up with people who are naturalized citizens eligible to run for the first time. Our pool of qualified and reputable people who are entering politics has been dwindling, and in my opinion we must look elsewhere for qualified candidates. I have been the architect for this measure and want to see it succeed. One of the candidates is from Japan and I recognize your nation is not on good terms with them right now. Despite this, I am requesting that you encourage the workers that end up coming to work on the rising sea levels to vote for Hayao at the elections in November, as well as the citizens of Chinese descent that are already in the United States. It can be done behind the scenes, but if I have your word that you will deliver this endorsement, I will go ahead with the plan to employ one of the companies from your country." In his younger years, President Jie would have thrown Harrington out of his office for having the audacity to dictate the terms of an agreement. He had mellowed with age, however, and could see the benefit in this for him. One method which would help him would be to use his network of government employees to spread the word about the arrangement with the instructions to keep it quiet. It would be a big help to the Chinese economy.

"We have a deal sir. I will go ahead with my plan and alert you about when and where the meetings will be." He showed

Harrington out and instructed his secretary to arrange for transportation to take President Harrington back to his hotel.

10am, Wednesday, May 23rd, the Great Wall of China
President Harrington and his entourage were sightseeing at the Great Wall of China, and it really was a most impressive landmark. Later he would visit the Imperial Garden, but it didn't really matter, he would have been content to do nothing today. He was filled with such a sense of accomplishment that he had been able to persuade President Wang Jie to agree to his plan. His legacy was a step closer to coming to fruition. He, and the U.S., were winning twice by also getting expertise in combating the rising sea level issue. He considered himself a true statesman. He had every confidence that President Jie would arrange some contacts for him by the end of the day.

Noon, Tucson, AZ
Agent Z had just gotten the green light from Kangaroo to take the necessary steps to obtain information from the assassin, and once he had information to go ahead and place him under arrest. Agent Z had also been congratulated, along with Gladys, for pulling off a flawless operation. He did not want to waste any time. He got all his equipment together and drove over to the assassin's house. No one would ever suspect him of being what he really was; he had his cover down pat. He pulled up to the house in the plumber's truck and everyone would think he was a plumber there to do extensive plumbing repairs and would not be suspicious if he were there all day. He rang the bell and waited. It took the man quite a while to come to the door, he must have been asleep. When he finally opened the door, Agent Z started his sales pitch about checking for problems with plumbing and as expected, the assassin started to slam the door in his face. He had his tazer ready and he shot him with it right before the door shut. Agent Z pushed his way inside and watched the man squirm on the floor. When he stopped, Agent Z pulled out the barb and quickly handcuffed and shackled his legs and dragged him outside to the van.

Two hours later, Agent Z arrived at a federal holding facility outside of Tucson where he had arranged for some FBI agents he knew he could trust to meet him. The assassin had been formally arrested with all the proper paperwork so that there was no room for a judge to throw the case out, but no one knew he was here. Agent Z went in to talk to him. "Listen up, I am sure that you have been trained not to talk. No one knows that you are here, however, and you have been arrested in accordance with the procedures set forth by the state of Arizona."

"What I am being charged with?"

"Planning to kill the Attorney General. It is a conspiratorial crime. We possess audio of you discussing it and making the arrangements."

"Who are you people?" The seriousness of his predicament had begun to sink in.

"Agents of the United States. That's all you need to know."

"Well, you violated my civil rights when you used the tazer gun on me."

"Not true. You were resisting arrest. You are in deep here, buddy. What's your name, anyway?" The assassin didn't say anything. "You are going to spend the rest of your life in jail. Do you want to make that time easier on yourself?" Again, no response. "Fine. Let's find out if a few days in solitary confinement with change your attitude."

7pm, greater San Diego

Joy had managed to find where Maggie Evers, Kelly Visque's friend, lived and arrived at her house. She was tired from the trip, but wanted to get this over with so she could get back home. She rang the bell and heard a dog start to bark. The door opened a minute later and a brown haired plain looking woman appeared. "Can I help you?"

"Are you Maggie Evers?"

"Yes, who's asking?" Joy introduced herself and explained she was there to get her account of whether Kelly Visque had ever contacted her about a letter to be mailed to Juan Pillar. Evers of course knew about Visque being arrested for the murders of the

Bernards and the additional charges of Juan Pillar and the driver from the other day as that had been all over the news as well. Joy asked if she could come inside and Evers reluctantly allowed her to enter.

"We know that Visque never travelled to California during the period when the letter might have been mailed and that it was mailed from this state. It is our theory that she involved someone else to help her with her plan." Joy paused to allow Evers put two and two together.

"I don't know nothing about any letter."

"This would be a lot better for you if you cooperate."

"Don't threaten me."

"I am sure you didn't know what the letter said. If you try to lie to protect your friend you could be charged with perjury, which will mean that you could go to jail too."

"Get out! This is my house!"

Before she left, Joy said, "I will be back with a subpoena, and when I am you will have no choice but to talk to me", and with that she left, knowing that she would have Waller call the federal magistrate in San Diego first thing tomorrow.

10am, Thursday, May 24th, Shanghai, China

President Harrington was attending a meeting with a man named Zheng Yang, the head of the region of Shanghai. They would discuss how both countries would make it possible for the workers associated with the company that would do the work to emigrate to the U.S. They wanted to have this in place today as tomorrow Harrington would be meeting with the CEO of the company that would likely get the job. "President Jie and myself will see to it that the employees get special papers permitting them to leave China. The documents will be open ended so that they will be able to come back when the work is done, if they choose. That will be optional; if they do come back, they will retain their full rights as citizens." "I will likewise ensure that they will encounter easy entry into the U.S. as workers and will obtain all the rights and privileges associated with citizenship. Once the work is done, they will be able to remain in the country if they choose, and should have no trouble finding new work."

"Great. I am glad we are on the same page. It will help when you meet with Li Yan tomorrow. She can be a tough negotiator. How about some lunch Mr. President?"

11am, Federal Courthouse, Washington D.C.

The lawyers for both the defense and prosecution had convened to find out whom the judge for the trial would be. There was a rotation of numerous judges on the federal circuit. The announcement would be made by Tim Fresco, the judge that had handled the proceedings so far. He entered the courtroom and called everyone to order. He was not one for fanfare, so he simply said, "The judge presiding over the trial of the people vs. Kelly Visque and Lorraine Corvino will be Clinton Alfonso." Glen Aaron and Lionel Ross groaned, and Waller smiled. Alphonso was a major league conservative and had a heavy hand when it came to defense attorneys. This round definitely went to Waller; he was already winning and the fight hadn't even started yet.

1pm, Chicago, the Governor's office

Russell was meeting with Berry and Weimitz to hear with whom they would be meeting. "In India we will arrange for several open forums in which we explain how the country would benefit from better roads and highways and how education reform would be advantageous to all. Once we have whetted their interest, we can meet with the leaders and explain about how our nonprofit corporation will work, how it will generate money for the country and create jobs as well. We can also explain about our charter school proposal and how schools run with private funds tend to be more efficient." Weimitz finished and looked at Russell to see what he thought.

"I like the concept, Vincent, but it seems like you are leaving much to chance. We need to schedule definite meetings with their leaders so we can leave with commitments about their support. That is why we are going. We can dazzle them with our ideas but must make it clear that we want something in return." Russell sighed. "Well, you still have today and the time on the plane. We are ambassadors of the U.S. and they will want to accommodate us. Please set up some face to face meetings with their top officials in both cities." He turned to Berry, confident that he had fared better, and he turned out to be right, as he had arranged for several closed door sessions with Naftali Levy, Israel's prime minister.

3pm, San Diego city courthouse

Joy was going to meet with a judge named Janet Torch to obtain the subpoena for Maggie Evers so that they could get her testimony. It had only taken one phone call from Waller to make this happen. Joy went into her chambers and they got started. Judge Torch had already heard about the case of course. "What is the purpose of getting Miss Evers' testimony?"

"We believe that one of the defendants in our case, Kelly Visque, mailed a letter to Miss Evers to be re-mailed to Juan Pillar. The letter in question, which had never been opened by Pillar, contained a threatening message. We want to question Miss Evers about it."

"Off the record, I hope the jury finds her guilty of the terrorism charge and she gets the death penalty. How dare she consider herself a patriot! She weakened the country with her actions!" Joy took advantage of the judge's pause to get her back on track.

"When could the subpoena be carried out, your honor?"

"Oh, right. Let's see, today is Thursday. How about Tuesday morning at 9am? We can take her testimony right in my courtroom."

"That would be great. Thank you, your honor."

Joy called Waller immediately and told him when the deposition would take place. He told that he would arrange for a live feed to be set up inside the courtroom so that he could observe and participate if need be. "I will handle all that, you just make sure that the subpoena is served today and that you are back at the courthouse ready to proceed on Tuesday. Thank you Joy. I will see you, literally, Tuesday morning."

9pm, O'Hare airport, Chicago

Hayao and Ramirez just arrived from Europe, and it was a successful trip. They had made the most impact of course in Spain, but felt that they had ingratiated themselves in the other two countries as well, and would get the support of their citizens here for those that were not going to follow the Pope's endorsement and vote along secular lines. The next action they would take would be to conduct some polls to determine which demographics on which to focus. They would also visit Israel and India, and arrange for some training for Hayao on debating techniques. It would be a busy summer but they would be well prepared when September came and the home stretch to Election Day arrived.

1pm, Friday, May 25th, Shanghai, corporate headquarters of Sea Lift

President Harrington was in Li Yan's office, she was the CEO of Sea Lift, the company that had met the challenges posed by global warming's effect on the polar ice caps. Her company had come up with the revolutionary process of digging trenches around the shoreline and diverting water back to the middle of the ocean through the use of tremendous pipelines that ran along the ocean floor. That was the kind of technology the United States needed for its coastal areas. She had a beautiful office overlooking downtown Shanghai. "I am honored to be meeting with you, Mr. President. Please help yourself to some refreshments." He got a cup of coffee.

"Li, we are experiencing issues at home that would benefit from your expertise. We have to address the rising sea levels and fast. Everyone says Sea Lift is the best."

"What do you have in mind, Mr. President?"

"My administration wants your company to come to our country and analyze and implement the necessary equipment to keep those areas at risk from becoming underwater. I would want you to tackle all the areas at once which means that you will need quite a large crew. I have already cleared the immigration issues with President Jie and Mr. Yang. I could help with any additional workers while I am here." Harrington saw her turning over the proposal in her mind.

"What will happen to the workers when the jobs are finished?"
"They will be American citizens and will be offered permanent residence if they choose. With the experience they will have after completing the sea level project they should encounter no trouble finding jobs."
"What amount of compensation will we receive?"
"This is a government bid job, which means that the award will go to the lowest bidder. However, this is such specialized work that it will probably turn out that your company will be the only one bidding." Yan understood; she could name her price.
"Well, today is Friday, I should have an answer for you tomorrow. How about we meet back here at 3pm? We can finalize the terms and then go out for a nice dinner. How does that sound?"
"It sounds great. I will see you tomorrow."
2pm
Li Yan got a call from President Jie. "Hello Li, how have you been?"
"Just fine sir, and you?"
"Excellent. Li, I understand you have met with President Harrington. Has he gone?"
"Yes, sir."
"Ok, so he explained his plan. What do you think?"
"I think it will be good for both Sea Lift and China."
"Did he explain how the bid process works?"
"Yes. The contract will be awarded to the lowest bidder. He also said we are the only company with the knowledge and equipment, implying that we could pretty much name our price."
President Jie paused. "That is true, however, I would recommend against quoting a very high number so as not to scare him off. This will be a great thing for China; we will show the world that we are at the forefront of this technology, and just as importantly, will be providing opportunities for our citizens for years to come." This arrangement was brilliant; everyone knew that politicians, even in the current climate of public disgust with their leaders and the illusion of appeasement, as elected officials did not give something for nothing. The exchange here would appear to be the solution to the higher sea levels for the U.S., and increased recognition as a

cutting edge nation as well as financial security for its citizens and government. No one would need to know that President Harrington was also solidifying his own future once he left office by finding ways to ensure that the candidate he backed would end up winning, making him high in demand as an adviser and lecturer for years. Li Yan didn't like to be told how to run her business, but when the federal government stepped in, she realized she didn't have much choice as her life could be unpleasant if she did not cooperate.

"Of course, sir. I will keep my bid reasonable as it will benefit us all. If you will excuse me, I must meet the deadline that I set for the meeting."

4pm, Washington D.C. Federal Courthouse

Judge Alphonso wanted to meet with the attorneys from both sides to size them up. He told them to submit any pretrial motions that they had and he would rule on them shortly. Both Aaron and Ross were trying to get on his good side, looking to catch his eye and smiling while Waller was just going about his business. The defense lawyers each had a motion to suppress the picture found at Lorraine Corvino's place on the grounds that it was an illegal search as they were lacking a search warrant and the picture being in a different room from where the conversation between the agent and Corvino took place. Waller wasn't worried. Agent Squelch was a seasoned FBI man and would know what would pass for a legal search. Besides, Alphonso tended to be liberal in supporting the government and the tactics they used. They both handed the briefs to the judge who announced he would render a decision tomorrow via email, and instructed the attorneys to give the bailiff their email addresses before they left. The hearing was adjourned.

8pm, Federal holding facility outside of Tucson, AZ

Agent Z went to check on the assassin who had been in solitary confinement for over two days. He yanked open the door to the cell and the man shielded his eyes from the sudden light. "All right asshole, let's go." He and one of the prison guards hauled him to his feet and dragged him to the interrogation room where he was handcuffed to the table. Agent Z went at him hard. "Who was the other person on the line!?" he screamed in the man's face. The man didn't flinch. "Why don't you make this easy on yourself. Whoever you are covering for is just going to throw you under the bus when you are prosecuted. Don't tell me you are really expecting anyone to speak up and take the rap for you."

Agent Z spent another hour trying to break the assassin but was getting nowhere. "Fine. Since you are not in a talking mood, let's accommodate you and put you back in solitary." He was pulled and pushed back to the cell and shoved inside. Before the guard closed the door, Agent Z said to him, "Make it a week this time. One meal a day and just water." Slam!

3pm, Saturday, May 26th, Li Yan's office, Shanghai

President Harrington and his entourage arrived 10 minutes ago and Miss Yan was ready for them. She had come up with a fair offer and had prepared a prospectus for Harrington to review. They sat down at the conference table and Yan handed a copy to the President. He leafed through it quickly as she stood up and waited for him to signal that he was ready to talk. He looked at her after a few minutes and she began. "There will be a significant amount of preparatory work to be done at each location to determine the size of the trench, how deep it should go and how much reinforcement it will need. The amount of piping will be extensive to propel the water far enough away to be effective. I do not want to bore you with the details, but our bid for each location is $3 billion dollars." Harrington wasn't surprised. This was a major engineering project, and there had been much smaller projects that had cost proportionally much more. Plus, Yan knew as well as he that it wasn't his money, the United States was already trillions of dollars in debt and his citizens would be blinded to how much it had cost if their coastlines were saved. This was a fair number and she had probably been encouraged to keep it reasonable. Normally he would not accept the terms of a project this size on the spot, but he was only going to be in China for a short time and time was of the essence, not only for the rising water but to get the additional people into the country so that they would qualify for the legislation he would introduce that would enable them to vote.

"I would like to accept your offer, Miss Yan, and I thank you for your expediency in handling this matter. When do you think you can begin?"

"Thank you Mr. President. We will guarantee that our work will be done safely and that it will last. The first step is to do the evaluation that I mentioned to determine what is involved. Which location did you plan to tackle first?"

"Miami. The situation there is dire. I really would like to have the coastline saved there even before we do any preliminary work anywhere else. Please devote as many resources as possible there right away."

"We can have our equipment there in two weeks and have our divers complete their analysis in the meantime. We will work there exclusively until we are done. If you are satisfied at that point which I am sure you will be, we can discuss what the next site will be."

"Terrific. Now, what was it that you mentioned about a celebratory dinner?"

12pm

Aaron, Ross, and Waller were all hovering over their email accounts waiting for the judge's decision about the motion to suppress the picture. Without it the defense didn't think much of a case existed against their clients as they were both puzzle pieces that didn't add up to anything unless they were both present. Without Corvino, Visque would never have had the information necessary to be able to get to justice Bernard, and without Visque, let's be honest, Corvino never would have had the nerve to exact revenge on the lover who jilted her no matter how jealous or obsessive she was. Ten minutes later all three got it. Aaron opened it as quick as he could and any feelings of hope he held went right out the window. Both motions were denied on the basis that Agent Squelch was not looking for anything specific, just wandering around while Corvino had been on the phone and the picture had been conspicuously placed so that anyone would have noticed it. Aaron and Ross knew right then that this would be the tone of the whole trial and they would have to work extra hard to appeal to the jury as judge Alphonso would take every opportunity to undermine them. There was more information in the email. Alphonso intended to ban all media from the courtroom for the duration of the trial and would issue a strict gag order for the defendants, the attorneys, and the jury to not breathe a word about what happened to anyone, including spouses. All offenses would result in removal from the case in the instance of the jury and attorneys and the banning of the defendants except for the time when they were going to provide testimony. He was determined that this trial, and his courtroom, would not be turned into a circus like some other high profile trials had become.

6pm, Sunday, May 27th, Hong Kong

President Harrington had just landed at the airport in Hong Kong and was met with a representative from the hotel where he would be staying. The secret service agents were doing a good job of shielding him from the crowd as security was somewhat lax here. This leg of the trip would be more leisurely, as his only real duty here would be to promote the exciting new opportunities that Sea Lift was offering and to encourage people to take advantage of it. There would be enough promotion elsewhere in China so that he could focus his efforts here. He was looking forward to just sitting by the pool for a few of the days that he was here. The hard work had been completed and that had been getting Li Yan to come on board with her company. Tomorrow Harrington was going out on a fishing boat, a popular activity in Hong Kong. He knew when he arrived back home in a week his schedule would be crazy busy until January when the next President was inaugurated so he had made up his mind to relax and enjoy himself and not worry if it seemed like he was shirking his Presidential responsibilities.

3pm, New Delhi, India

India's Prime Minister, Mayank Sarin, was hosting the trio of Russell, Weimitz, and Berry at his official residence. Weimitz had hustled to set up meetings with the right people after getting dressed down by Russell the other day. He had even sat separately on the plane so he could finalize things without the Governor knowing that he was scrambling. It turned out alright as their schedule was full now with presentations. Tonight would probably be their most important one as they would be meeting with Sarin. Tomorrow they would be repeating it to the country's President, Parth Tambe, but the position of President was largely ceremonial. Russell had decided to focus only on education during this trip. He did not want to appear overwhelming or that he was trying to come in and dictate how things should be done. There would plenty of time to address the infrastructure and other issues once he was in office. Weimitz took a few minutes to set up his equipment; he had prepared a video containing footage about charter schools and how they were run by private companies using funds from individuals and organizations and were quite successful in preparing young people for careers. They would demonstrate how technology could be used to enhance learning, such as with interactive discussions with experts from around the world on whatever topic is being covered. The video lasted about an hour and Prime Minister Sarin clapped when it was done. "Most interesting. However, just because it works in the U.S. doesn't mean it will be a success here. We do not have the kinds of resources that you do. Many of our children do not go to school at all. All this technology is great, but it is like you are trying to build on a foundation that doesn't exist." Russell decided to do the speaking here.

"We have worked that into our plan. We will bring the education to the children, not the other way around. We will go into all the sections of the country including the poorest ones. We will bring our own computers with us as teaching aids and conduct our lessons wherever we can. Our model is a very flexible one."

"Who is going to pay for all this?"

"We are going to set up a nonprofit organization and receive contributions from the government and private citizens."

"What is the advantage to the government here?"

"Your citizens will become literate and educated and that will help India become more competitive with other countries. The people here will also be able to contribute more to society, and our company will be able to give money to the government from the endowment we receive. The world will view this as a humanitarian effort and we will be praised for it." Sarin liked what he heard. He would end up looking like a hero for working to bring his people the tools to better themselves. He did not give his approval right now, however. There were other people to be consulted and Russell was going to be spreading his message to other influential people while he was here so Sarin did not want to appear to be too anxious.

"Let me think about it. I expect you will be meeting with other people. Why don't you contact me on the day before you are scheduled to leave? That will give me time to ponder this, and we will still have time to iron out the details." All four men shook hands and knew they had an unwritten agreement.

12pm, Tuesday, May 29th, Bombay, India

Todd Russell and company had arrived here this morning for the next round of meetings. This afternoon they were hosting a luncheon for local community leaders to spread the information about their plan for revolutionizing the education system. They felt like missionaries. Yesterday they had met with President Tambe and had won him over quickly, though that had just been a formality to foster unity among the various government factions. In the middle of the presentation Russell looked up and saw the Prime Minister standing in the back, observing. They wrapped it up half an hour later and then fielded questions about the logistics of their proposal, such as where they would hold classes and how they would be able to power the electronic devices that they kept speaking of when electricity was not prevalent in many poorer areas of the country. Weimitz managed to answer that with an explanation about the new solar powered batteries that were available. Many devices already made use of them and were becoming more prevalent every day. That would enable classes to be held anywhere really, which would make it easy to gather groups of children together. Weimitz was very well prepared to field all the questions that came up and by the end had removed all doubt that this would work. All that remained to do was obtain the formal go ahead from Sarin when they met with him again before they left for Israel.

11am, Representative Eric Layton's office, Washington DC
Layton and Morris were expecting Layton's aide Robert any minute with the itinerary planned out for their trip to China. They had explained what they wanted to accomplish while there and he said he would make it happen. He came in ten minutes later and they all greeted each other. "So. Robert, my boy, what have you got for us?" Robert opened his folder and gave each man a packet. They glanced at it and were both surprised at first and then annoyed. Hadn't he listened at all to what they had said? "What is this Robert?" Layton asked, raising his voice slightly.

"I know this is not what you were expecting, sir. Let me explain. With the Constitutional change about Presidential eligibility also comes a game changing way of campaigning. The candidates must court those citizens that hail from other countries that still are influenced by their birth countries' opinions. However, when it comes to China, I believe that field has already been plowed, recently by President Harrington. Look at the deal he made. A Chinese company coming here to save our low lying coastal areas and bringing with them thousands of employees. Who do you think those employees will vote for?"

"Hold on, they won't able to vote."

"There is no doubt in my mind that Harrington will somehow get legislation passed or use an executive order to say that since they are living here, how can we deny them basic rights when people no longer have to be born here to hold the highest office in the land? Remember who Harrington nominated; both Hayao and Pillar. Only one remains; what do you think he asked for in return for accepting the bid of Sea Lift? The behind-the-scenes endorsement of his candidate. President Jie will spread the word to all the Chinese loyalists here to back Hayao. Going to China would be a colossal waste of time politically and would be completely transparent to those of Chinese descent here with disdain for their ways and want someone who will not resort to diluting the population to win votes but instead will focus on improving the situation of those already here using our established policies. My suggestion is to concentrate on campaigning in this country and focus on the issues that have made you successful all along such as job creation and education." Layton and Morris looked at him incredulously. They were amazed that this kid had the nerve to ignore their instructions! Thank God he did. His advice was brilliant; that had been Layton's original plan but somehow lost sight of his path when he thought Hayao would be getting the upper hand after Harrington had gone there on Hayao's behalf. Layton walked to the window in his office and looked outside for a minute.

"Ok Robert. Where should we campaign?"

"Well, we already secured the support of the Pope, which translates into devout Catholics. We should run some polls to determine which segments of the population to concentrate on. This is the perfect time to do that; many people are on vacation now so by conducting these polls and assembling the information over the summer we will be preparing ourselves for the critical two months before the election." Layton kept his back to Robert.

"Robert, please give us a minute. You can wait in the outer office." When the door closed, Layton said to Morris, "What do you think?"

"He's right on the money. His strategy will differentiate ourselves from the other candidates and prevent us from looking like typical politicians. We both have good reputations; we should build on that. Let Robert take the lead on the polls and see what the results show. We will then be able to build a plan as to where to campaign as well as what issues to prepare for when we have our debates." They called him back in and told him to run with his plan. They would want to hear back from him in a month with some hard statistics.

2pm, Hayao's house, a suburb of Detroit

Hayao and Ramirez were meeting to go over the polls they would conduct to determine the areas in which they were lacking. "Ok, we need to administer these polls strategically around the country. First, let's select the geographic areas."

"Hayao, I think we should include all the major regions of the country, including Alaska and Hawaii. For the continental U.S., we have the northwest, the west, which includes California, Arizona, and Nevada, the Midwest, the southwest, the south, the southeast, and the northeast. That makes nine distinct areas in total."

"Alright, we can use census data to gain access to people's email addresses, which would probably be the easiest way to make the polls as comprehensive as possible. I will designate a point of contact for each region, someone who will be in charge of sending out the mass emails and keeping track of who responds. Now, let's formulate the questions we will ask so that everything will be uniform."

"We will want to know such information as their age, sex, race, and religion, for starters. Then we will continue to their country of origin, how long they have lived in the U.S., and then move on to their stance on various issues. We should ask about the economy, the environment, whether they support the right of naturalized citizens to be President, and immigration. Once we get the results and organize the data, we will have an easy time of knowing what to zero in on." Hayao was really impressed with the handle Ramirez had on what their focus should be and how to go about it.

"Would you take the reins on this, Alex? Design the questions and collate it. Once you do, I will make sure it gets in the right hands."

"Of course. I should be able to complete it by Sunday."

"Great. Why don't we meet Sunday afternoon to put together the final draft and send it out. While you create the poll, I will put a team together to send it out, gather the results, and create a report analyzing the data. I will see you on Sunday."

4pm, San Diego courthouse

Maggie Evers was about to be deposed. The deposition had been scheduled for this morning, but the judge had another matter come up so they pushed it back to 4 o'clock. Attorney General Waller would ask the questions via a live satellite feed and Joy was there to make sure everything ran smoothly and to observe Miss Evers' demeanor. Her lawyer was some local hustler who must have owed her a favor. They were just about ready to start. Judge Janet Torch entered the courtroom although she was not here in an official

capacity. Waller began and addressed Evers. "Please state your name."
"Margaret Evers."
"Where do you live?". She gave her address. "Do you know a woman named Kelly Visque?"
"Yes, we grew up together."
"How would you characterize your relationship since you became adults?"
"We mostly talk on the phone."
"When was the last time you saw each other?"
"I think three years ago." Joy noticed that Evers was very nervous, wringing her hands and playing with her buttons.
"Did she come to visit you?"
"Yes, as a matter of fact."
"If she were in trouble would you help her?"
"I would try to."
"Did Miss Visque ever mention a woman named Lorraine Corvino?"
"No."
"Would you say that Kelly Visque could be driven to kill someone?"
"I don't know. Are we almost done?"
"Not too much longer. What were her views on politics?"
"She had old fashioned views."
"She believed in keeping traditions?"
"Exactly."
"Did she ever ask you to mail a letter for her, perhaps passing it off as a prank?"
"No."
"Remember that you are under oath, lying is perjury. Didn't she send you something to be forwarded to Juan Pillar?"
"Never."
"This is serious, Miss. You could get in trouble too."
"I told you I don't know anything." Waller realized this was going nowhere. Maybe Joy would have an idea. They could always depose her again.
"Alright Miss Evers, you are free to go."

Fifteen minutes later, when the courtroom had cleared out, Waller spoke to Joy. "What was your impression of Evers?"

"She acted in a very nervous manner, like she was hiding something. As soon as her deposition finished I saw her bolt outside to smoke."

"Do you think she was telling the truth?"

"It doesn't matter. The jury will think that she is lying in her testimony. She will end up helping us because she came across so tense. We should definitely use her in our case." Waller had to go with her opinion, as she had spent more time with the woman.

"Thank you Joy. I will book you on the first flight out tomorrow and send you the information."

4pm, Thursday, May 31st, New Delhi, office of Prime Minister Sarin

Todd Russell had chosen to attend this meeting by himself, giving Weimitz and Berry some time to sightsee before they went to Israel tomorrow. Sarin had some notes he was consulting when Russell walked in and motioned for him to sit down. "How was your time in Bombay? There is much to see there. Did you have a chance to explore at all?"

"We enjoyed the Gandhi museum. A fascinating man, and very effective in his methods. We enjoyed some fine meals as well, and had enough of a taste to entice us to come back again. Have you had a chance to ponder our proposal?"

"Yes." Sarin paused for a minute. He slid a document over to Russell. He looked at it and nodded. Sarin was asking for a flat amount of 10 million dollars a year from the enterprise Russell would create. That could be handled easily. Russell was expecting large donations as this was clearly an altruistic, humanitarian effort which would develop support worldwide. He didn't even have to seek out an endorsement from Sarin overtly; the East Indian population in the U.S. were still loyal to their homeland and would be grateful that Russell was taking steps to improve things there. They were the one cultural group that still embraced their old customs universally and had left purely in search of better economic conditions. He felt confident they would be in his corner once this arrangement became public. That was well worth the ten million annually. "Mr. Prime Minister, we have a deal!" They shook on it and then joined each other in a glass of Cholai, a potent Indian drink.

3pm, Friday, June 1st, Todd Russell's flight to Israel
The three men had spent last night celebrating their victory in India, but now it was time to get back to work. They had to review their schedule for the second leg of their trip. This time, Berry had the ball. "Our focus is going to be new and better energy sources, as Israel as a country is somewhat behind. The biggest push of course will be for solar energy which would be perfect for them being in the desert. We will also expose them to new ways to recycle as a power source. The biggest obstacle they will face is finding the room for these new facilities as space is even more of a premium here than back home." Russell reminded him that these new buildings could take the place of existing ones that are less efficient.

"Who are we going to be meeting with, Joe?"

"Tomorrow we will be in Jerusalem and be getting together with Prime Minister Levy. We will also attend several Knesset sessions in order to involve the various political parties over the next few days. We will then head to Tel Aviv for some downtime and a few presentations to national and local business people. We will be in the country for a week." Russell was pleased; Berry had done his homework. He decided to allow the men the rest of the flight to relax and sleep if they wanted.

1pm, Offices of the ACLU, Washington, D.C.
Glen Aaron heard his email account beep. He saw a new email from Waller. He knew what it was, the list of additional witnesses and evidence for the trial. He was surprised when he opened up the document and saw only one additional witness, a woman named Maggie Evers from California. He would have to ask Visque about her as the name had not come out during discovery. There were two more pieces of evidence; the note found at Juan Pillar's house, and the airport tape showing the blond woman in the car outside

the terminal where Pillar's plane had landed. This would prove to be the more damning piece as the woman was sitting in the car that had been sent to pick meet Pillar. On the bright side, he had ample time to prepare for these additions. Looking at the original list he had received, he was reassured that most of them were character witnesses. He had two ways to counter them; by shaking their credibility and by utilizing his own character witnesses. He would be spending the weekend, along with Ross and undoubtedly Waller as well, practicing with his witnesses and making sure they would appear confident on the stand. On his way home tonight he would stop by the jail and find out exactly who Miss Evers was, knowing that she represented a link to the charges against his client that were related to Juan Pillar.

2pm, Tucson AZ

Agent Z was heading in to see the assassin. He had been in solitary confinement with very severe restrictions and probably was ready to talk. The prison guard let him in; the assassin was slumped in a corner. Agent Z walked over to him and nudged him with his foot. Suddenly the assassin jumped up and grabbed him and pushed him back against the wall. Agent Z kneed him in the balls and he went down right away. Now he was mad. He had wasted enough time with this piece of shit. He instructed the guard on what he wanted and said it should be ready in fifteen minutes.

When Agent Z went upstairs and out behind the jail the assassin had his hands and feet shackled and was kneeling in front of a bucket of water. He walked over and knelt beside him. "Now, tell me who was on the phone with you?" The assassin merely spit at him. He grabbed him by the neck and shoved his face in the water and held it there. Ten seconds, then twenty. He pulled him up and asked him again. No response. Back into the water. Agent Z had been through this before; eventually they all talk. On the fourth time he held him for 45 seconds and kept increasing it a little more. He could sense the man was getting close to breaking. When Agent Z was about to dunk his head for the tenth time, he said "Wait. I'll tell you. It was Albert Cross."

12pm, Saturday, June 2nd, Beijing
President Harrington had just said his goodbyes to Prime Minister Jie and boarded Air Force One. This trip had been an unqualified success as he had gotten China behind Hayao and been able to hire Sea Lift, Those had been his two goals, The path was almost clear.

1pm, Jerusalem
Today was Shabbat, so no one in government was working. Russell and the others were going to use the day to go to the Western Wall and go through the underground passages that were there. Tonight they were going to a light show which was supposed to be quite spectacular and tomorrow they would get down to business.

9am, mock courtroom at the U.S. Department of Justice
Waller was ready. He would spend the whole day reviewing the testimony of his witnesses. He prided himself on his preparation and would not be surprised during a trial. The first one up was Dr. Alan Wentworth, who examined both Visque and Corvino and determined that they both possessed extreme cases of the characteristics that drove them to engage in these criminal acts. For Visque it was jingoism and for Corvino extreme jealousy. Waller had to make sure that Wentworth would not paint a rosier picture of the two defendants than what they were really like. "Good morning doctor. I am just going to take you through some of the questions that I plan to ask you when you take the stand. How many years have you been in practice?"
"22 years."
"What was your impression of Kelly Visque?"
"She is a very headstrong woman who often will put her thoughts and beliefs into actions." Excellent answer, thought Waller. This guy was a pro. He asked him a few more things that the defense attorneys could bring up and Wentworth handled each one perfectly. Waller excused him and checked the schedule for the rest of the morning. He had Sean Cardillo, the psychologist who who was an expert on the workings of the criminal mind and then Edna Jillow, the woman from Pennsylvania who would testify

about the bee's DNA. They would then take a short break for lunch and spend the afternoon reviewing with the character witnesses.

12pm, ACLU offices, Washington, DC
Aaron and Ross were spending the day the same way as Waller, going over the accounts of their witnesses. Today they would be meeting with the two experts, Otto Lampf and Martin Kelsey and tomorrow be talking to those that would provide accounts about the defendants' character. Ross had made good on his word and found a psychologist to refute Dr.Cardillo's testimony. Her name was Lucy Rauch and in addition to being a PhD she had also worked as a profiler for the FBI. Ross had found her through a friend of his. She did not feel the need to meet with Kelly Visque. Her specialty was studying the facts involved in a crime and arriving at an outline of the type of person likely to have committed that crime. She had a credible record, and her testimony would probably carry as much if not more weight than that of Cardillo. She should be here any minute. Once the two of them were done with the witnesses, they would spend some time talking about jury selection and what they were planning to look for in the potential jurors. A few minutes later they heard a knock. Aaron opened the door and saw a fifty something woman. She extended her hand and introduced herself. Both men would describe her as chic. "Very nice to meet you, Doctor Rauch. Please come in and sit down. Can we get you anything?"

"No, thank you. I am ready to get started. I went over the report that you sent me from the FBI. My conclusion, which I will present in court, is that this crime was carried out by someone who was sloppy, and had no experience with how police work and investigate criminal activity. The perpetrator did not cover their tracks, they left DNA at the scene, and they did not account for even the most blatant evidence coming to the attention of the authorities."

"What about the sex of the person?"

"That I could not say for certain, but the fact that Juan Pillar and the driver were hanged suggest someone with much upper body strength and the skills learned in traditionally male pursuits."

"Thank you. Would you give us a few minutes to discuss?"

"Of course. I am going to get a cup of coffee at the snack bar downstairs and will be back in twenty minutes. Just so you know, my fee is $1000 per day regardless of how long I am needed."

"Well, what do you think?", asked Ross.

"She is perfect. The person she described is the exact opposite of Kelly Visque. She would neutralize any testimony given by the defense's witnesses about Visque's predisposition to crime. It will be money well spent. I am ready to accept her terms."

The two attorneys finished up with Rauch and then moved on to discussing potential jurors. They agreed that they would look for people who were politically conservative like Visque and wanted those involved in technical fields as well, who could grasp the concept that much of the evidence the prosecution had was circumstantial and could be explained away. "I am hoping for a predominance of jurors that are intelligent and understand that there was tremendous pressure to solve these crimes", said Aaron. He stopped short of actually saying that Visque had been railroaded by the FBI. Ross nodded his assent.

"Let's hope that the jury pool will meet our needs. We may end up with a bunch of liberals and then it will a matter of selecting the least likely to convict. We can only wait and see." It was 3pm. Once they finished with Kelsey and Lampf they would stop off at the prison to meet with their clients and would then reconvene tomorrow for the remainder of the witnesses.

6pm, Federal Penitentiary, Washington, DC

Glen Aaron was meeting with Kelly Visque to brief her on the witnesses and also to find out about Maggie Evers. Lionel Ross was meeting with Corvino also, to calm her nerves and reassure her that everything was in place. "Hi Kelly. How are you?"

"Fine. How did it go today?"

"Very well. We met with the experts and had a discussion with a woman named Lucy Rauch who had worked for the FBI. We are going to use her as a witness to refute the testimony of Sean Cardillo."

"What is she going to say? I mean, she hasn't even met me."

"Her usefulness will come from her experience at coming up with a profile of the type of person likely to commit a crime. You do not fit the attributes she listed."

"What type of success rate does she have?"

"An excellent one. She worked some famous cases with the information she provided helping to lead to arrests. It will be difficult for the prosecution to discredit her as she was employed by the FBI."

"Ok. You said there was something else?"

"Yes. Who is Maggie Evers?"

"An old friend who lives in California. We talk to each other but haven't seen each other in a few years. What does she have to do with this case?"

"There is a piece of evidence, a letter mailed to Juan Pillar that came from California. Waller's theory is that you mailed this letter to Miss Evers and told her it was a prank and would she send it to Pillar." Visque's face got red.

"That's ridiculous!" She took a breath and calmed down. "Have they spoken to her?"

"Yes. I don't know what she said but apparently they will be using her as a witness."

"There's nothing to say. These charges are trumped up; the only thing I can think of is that she appeared nervous and like she has something to hide. You should call her, and when you do try to reassure her that she did nothing wrong and that she will not get in trouble. When will you question her?"

"Probably in the next week. I will call her tomorrow and break the ice. I will cross examine her on a live feed so she will not have to travel here. Don't worry, I will establish a good dialogue with her."

9pm, Quinn Waller's office

Finally, it was quiet. He thought the day had gone well, except for Rick Heller, Corvino's co-worker. He was so arrogant. Waller would have to find a way to make him seem less cocky on the stand. He decided he would be direct; he would insist that Heller act humble or Waller would excuse him right away. Tomorrow he would review the testimony of the remaining witnesses and then go over his plan for jury selection, which of course was to include as many liberals as possible. He was going to enlist the help of his team to size up each potential juror and see who they thought would be good. He just realized how tired he was. He didn't feel like going home; he decided to go out for a drink and then come back here and sleep on the couch.

7am, Sunday, June 3rd
President Harrington was on Air Force One and would land at McGuire Air Force Base in about two hours. The phone on the plane rang and he answered it right at his seat. "Hello?"
"Mr. President, it's Li Yan. How are you doing?"
"I am fine, how are you?"
"I am great. I wanted to give you an update on what's going on in Miami. The divers performed the reconnaissance and have a handle on what needs to be done. The equipment should arrive in about a week."
"That's perfect, Li. I can't believe you organized this so quickly. Once you get the project underway I will definitely take a trip down to see."
"Thank you, sir. I will call you next week once we have our machinery."

10am, Detroit, MI
Hayao and Ramirez were having brunch at a nice hotel in downtown Detroit and discussing the poll that she had created. He had gone over the poll and thought it was great. It was not overly long and yet comprehensive in that it covered all the important issues of the campaign and incorporated every demographic as well. The poll would be distributed all over the country and would be analyzed from every perspective, so that they knew as much information as possible about every segment of the population. Hayao had arranged for teams of analysts to process all the data. He thanked Ramirez for putting all this together and said he would be distributing the questionnaires later today. "I wanted to discuss the training that we have pondered for me to take about debating

techniques and communication strategies during interviews. Probably the best resource would be a spin doctor who has worked with a wide range of politicians over the years."

"I was also thinking of someone in public relations. I have some connections at the same firm where Joe Berry works, and they are one of the biggest in D.C. I think we should hire someone to come out here and work with you on your turf, which will disrupt your life as little as possible." She knew that the cost was not an issue. It would be more expensive to do it this way, but Natsu would gladly pay for it if he thought it would be beneficial. Hayao liked the idea. Ramirez said that she would set something up today. Hayao got up to get some food from the buffet. "One more thing, Hayao, before we eat. In light of Russell's successful trip to India and Israel, perhaps we should rethink our agenda for those countries when we visit ourselves. Russell has ingratiated himself into their societies and won the support of the U.S. citizens with Indian and Israeli nationalities by emphasizing his administration's strength on technology and its use to improve aspects about both countries. In India for example, I understand that Russell is going to set up a nonprofit organization to help rework the education system there and generate money for the government. People who hail from India in the United States will really appreciate that as they want to see India succeed. What I think we need to do is work with the governments of both countries at a high level to let them know that we will be open to doing business with them, both politically and commercially. Perhaps we can talk with Natsu about expanding Moritu's operations. Such a move will help raise those countries to be much stronger economically. That will translate into votes for us." Hayao was impressed. She had some great ideas. It had been a brilliant idea to bring her aboard. He may have the business acumen but she sure has the insight into what motivates people and the best diplomatic measures to use. She also has the resources and connections to go along with it.

"Alright, Alex. That's the course of action we will follow. I will line some things up with Natsu before we leave for Israel, so that when we get there we will have the approval to make the offers that you are suggesting."

"Great. You'll see Hayao, this will work. Now, let's eat."

12pm, San Diego, Maggie Ever's house
Evers was relaxing on the couch after what had been a stressful week when her cell phone rang. She saw it was a number from Washington DC and realized that it involved Kelly Visque. She thought about just letting it ring and then decided there was no use in prolonging the agony. "Hello?"
"Hello, Maggie, I am Glen Aaron, Kelly Visque's attorney. How are you today?"
Cautiously, she said "Fine. What can I help you with?"
"I wanted to talk to you about the deposition that you gave the other day. First of all, you did fine. It must have been very stressful and both Kelly and I are sorry you had to go through it. You see, the prosecution is on a witch hunt to prove Visque's guilt and will resort to any means necessary. You were very brave to tell the truth with such conviction." Evers was happy to hear this; the last thing she wanted to do was make it easier for the Attorney General to convict.
"Thank you. How is Kelly holding up?"
"She is ok. She knows that she has the support of family and friends and that is helping to keep her staying strong. Maggie, you realize that you will be called as a witness during the trial, right?"
"I do. I wish that wasn't necessary."
"Well, the good thing is that you will be able to testify from San Diego and will not have to make the trip here. We will talk again before that time, but remember that the best way to help Kelly will be to remain calm during the questioning and try to keep your answers short so that the other lawyer won't be able to take something you said and use it against us. Anything that you find is misconstrued we can fix when I cross examine you, so don't worry. Treat it like a conversation with a friend." Maggie felt more at ease already.
"Ok, Mr. Aaron. Thank you, and please tell Kelly that I am thinking of her."

8pm, the Oval Office

President Harrington had arrived back earlier today and had a slew of paperwork to conquer. He would probably be doing this until midnight. He saw his email light register. It was from Uncle George requesting that the President call him as soon as he could. Harrington picked up his private cell phone and dialed; Uncle George was not prone to contacting him unless absolutely necessary. When Uncle George answered, Harrington said, "It's POTUS. What's going on?"

"We have confirmed intelligence that there is going to be a hit on Waller. You need to step in and quash it."

"Please be more specific."

"We have apprehended an assassin in Tucson who was talking on the phone about carrying it out."

"Was this plan imminent?"

"No. It was still in the works and would have coincided with the trial."

"Well, you caught the guy. Why involve me?"

"Because of who was on the other end of the phone call; Albert Cross. You have sufficient clout to make sure he simply doesn't find another hitman."

CHAPTER 14

7am, Monday, June 4th

Judge Clinton Alphonso was at home getting ready to go to the courthouse. Only one topic dominated the news and people's minds today; the trial of the century. It certainly would make the lives of reporters across the country, indeed around the world much easier for however long the trial continued. News during the summer typically consisted of local crime and sports in the various metropolitan areas. This would certainly liven things up, although the press didn't yet know about the closed courtroom policy. They would certainly be up in arms about this and he would undoubtedly get flak from politicians who would try to persuade him to change his mind. He was a tough guy, however, and one who stuck to his decisions. He felt absolutely certain this was the right choice; he held old school beliefs about the judicial system and absolutely refused to have this trial be compromised by the media effect. The jurors would be under the tightest security possible; each time they travelled between the hotel, which was right across the street, and the courthouse they would be accompanied by security at all times. Alphonso had also decided he would travel with the jurors and stay in the same hotel for the duration of the trial except for the three weeks when he would be on vacation, and during that time the jurors would be transported to a fine resort in Virginia right on the Potomac where they would be the only guests. The judge had arranged to pay for all this through private donations from wealthy people that he knew wanted to see justice served without corruption. While they were at the hotel they would all be on the same floor. There were cameras at each end of the hallway and in front of each room and all communication including cell phone use and email would be captured and monitored on a real time basis. In addition, the hotel had agreed to leave the rooms directly above and below the floor they were staying on vacant as an added level of security. The people who would be accompanying the jurors and lawyers would be FBI agents, courtesy of Director Grey, which remained the best scenario Alphonso could have hoped for; their sense of commitment would be much greater than a private security firm's. All their meals would be eaten together; he believed he had thought of everything. The judge was not concerned about not being able to find twelve people who would not want to be excused from such seemingly restrictive conditions, either. There were retirees who had always been curious about being on a jury and would appreciate the opportunity to serve; young single people who would look upon this as a way to get a vacation; those folks who were unemployed and would like the fact that they would make a little money during the summer when it was a slow time for hiring anyway. This would be done by the book and he planned to keep the attorneys under his thumb, including Waller. He went in to say goodbye to his wife and told her he would see her tonight.

9am, Federal Courthouse, Washington DC

All the players had assembled. Once the judge had entered and taken the bench, he summoned the attorneys forward. "Good morning. Please give me your witness and evidence lists." Waller, Aaron, and Ross went to get them and handed them to Alphonso. Aaron had added one witness from his original list, Lucy Rauch. He put them in his folder. "First things first. I do not hold court on Fridays. I will be on vacation from July Saturday July 28th through Saturday August 18th so we will be on hiatus then. The jurors, the three of you, and myself will all be sequestered for the entire length of the trial, no exceptions." Waller started to interrupt but Alphonso quickly and sternly silenced him. He would set the tone right from the beginning. "We will be staying at the Marriott across the street and extraordinary security measures are in place. For the period when I am on vacation, everyone else will be transported to a beautiful getaway nearby where you will be the only people there." They all looked like they were about to have strokes. The judge decided to let voice them their concerns. Aaron went first.

"Your honor, that is going to be a huge expense to the taxpayers. There will be a major uproar! This regulation could adversely affect my client's opportunity to be afforded a fair trial. The jurors will consciously or subconsciously blame her for such strict conditions."

"No, they won't. I will make it clear this is my decision and is not typically how things are done. I will also let everyone know this is being funded privately and not through the government. I expect there will be plenty of citizens who would take an opportunity such as this to trade a public service in exchange for living in a nice hotel and a fancy vacation." Waller was next to address the judge.

"How am I supposed to conduct my business while I am sequestered?"

"There will be full office support and a messenger service available at no charge 24x7. If anything comes up that we are not ready to handle, I will consider the request and see that it happens unless it will lead to a security breach." Alphonso's tone indicated the discussion was finished. "You all have this time period to get everything in place and prepare your families for your absence." He motioned to the bailiff. "Please bring in the first group of potential jurors." Turning back to the lawyers, he said, "You will each be entitled to five peremptory challenges, use them wisely." There were two categories of challenges the lawyers had at their disposal when it came to selecting jurors; challenges for cause and peremptory challenges. The jurors would be questioned and some of the answers they gave would allow the attorneys to dismiss them for a valid reason, for example if they revealed they had dealt with one of the defendants in the past they would be excused with cause. These challenges were unlimited but had to be approved by the judge, and Alphonso had a reputation of really making the attorneys work for each one. The peremptory challenges were those without cause and used for those jurors whom the lawyers thought would rule against them but had no specific reason why they didn't foresee them being impartial. The defense had an advantage here as they were working together and would combine their peremptory challenges. The door opened and the bailiff led them to the jury box.

10am, office of Albert Cross at American Pride
There was a knock at the door leading from the hallway into American Pride's offices and he didn't hear the receptionist get up to answer it; she must be in the bathroom. Albert Cross went to open it himself and when he did he was greeted by two men in dark suits who pushed him back. He started to protest until he saw who stood behind them; President Harrington! Oh my God! He knew the President was not a fan of his or the organization so he couldn't imagine what he wanted. Cross offered his hand which the President ignored. He growled at Cross, "Let's take a ride." Without closing the door to the hallway, the men whom he assumed were Secret Service agents escorted him downstairs to the car. He hoped the receptionist was coming right back. Cross was pushed into the Presidential limousine which travelled by itself so as to attract less attention than his normal fleet would. The President was sitting next to him and the two agents were in a separate compartment on the other side of the glass. "What's new Albert?" Cross started to answer but the President grabbed him by the collar. "I know what you are planning you infinitesimal parasite! We have you on tape talking about killing Quinn Waller!" Harrington let that sink in for a minute. "If anything happens to him, or anyone, for that matter, and it comes out your group was involved I will make sure you never see the light of day again and the collection of misfits you call an organization will be dismantled piece by piece. Do you get me or is that too lofty a concept for you, you moron!" Cross just nodded. "Good. Now get out of my sight." They had circled the block and pulled up again in front of his building. The driver waited for him to get out which he did without a word.

5pm, Judge Alphonso's courtroom
The first day of the jury selection process had come to a close. After interviewing numerous people and asking them such questions as what their political leanings were and whether or not they owned a gun, the lawyers had agreed on 2 jurors. That was not great but at least they had made some progress. Everyone wanted to get home for some leisure time as they knew they would

have to be back here first thing in the morning to do it all over again.

10am, Tuesday, June 5th, Tel Aviv

Vincent Weimitz was in the middle of his demonstration about the ways which solar energy could be harnessed. Israel had not made the most of this, which was unusual for them as they were typically at the forefront of technology. Russell believed his visit with Naftali Levy in Jerusalem had gone very well and they had an unwritten agreement to work together on diplomatic issues in the Middle East. He was very impressed with Tel Aviv as well; it really could have been any major city in the United States. They were staying at a great hotel right on the beach and had gone to several museums which had exhibits about Israel's history. He sensed those in attendance today were impressed with what Weimitz was showing them and expected they would encourage Jewish people in the U.S. to vote for him. Russell regretted he didn't have more time to explore the country; Israel was a beautiful place.

11am, Saturday, June 9th

Todd Russell was very pleased with how his campaign seemed to be progressing and his image back home. Having such an expertise about technology was really paying off as his administration was seen as having the best combination of political experience and scientific expertise to lead the United States into the future and face all the challenges ahead. It was true that Russell had no experience in politics at the national level, but he had been the top man in Illinois and was accustomed to being the final authority. That proved to be an invaluable skill and many people regarded it to be more important to have the experience of leading than being able to navigate the shark infested waters of the federal government in Washington. It was true that as governor he had not dealt with heads of state from around the world which amounted to an entirely different set of rules. He learned quickly, however, and diplomacy had always been one of his strong suits. He believed he had the momentum now and could coast through the summer until

September when it would be a sprint to the finish. He wanted to focus on matters in his state so everyone would know he was not shirking his responsibilities, and he would combine two vacations with campaign trips, probably around the northeast and south, two areas where he accepted he trailed the other candidates. During the last two months he would conduct a few polls and concentrate on the areas where he was lacking. Next year at this time he fully expected to be firmly ensconced in the Oval Office.

3pm, Quinn Waller's home

The first week of the jury selection process had ended, and while it had been far from pleasant and at times downright combative, he was pleased with the five jurors that had been selected. The five jurors so far included an older woman who had worked for the biggest cell phone company in the country for twenty years, a college student, a bartender, an unemployed violinist, and a recently discharged soldier who had served a tour in Syria twenty five years ago. There were three men and two women, and Waller believed the balance worked in his favor so far. More importantly, judge Alphonso continued to give the two defense attorneys a tough time. They complained about a few things and as a result the judge formed an opinion of them as crybabies. Waller could see that. It would be very hard for them to undo that image now in the judge's eyes. Waller almost felt sorry for them and their clients. Alphonso's well known sense of stoicism extended to the type of demeanor he expected from those who appeared before him and it was clear he would be berating them for even small instances of behavior he thought were out of line. Waller knew that this might backfire, however. If the jury thought the judge was picking on the defense, they could become more sympathetic towards them. Waller had to form a strategy to deal with such a scenario. He might have to commit a transgression to get on Alphonso's bad side himself, just enough to draw some of the ire towards him and level the playing field in front of the jury. If it came to that, he had no doubt he would think of something.

11am, Sunday, June 10th, the Oval Office
President Harrington was taking a break for a few minutes and having a cup of coffee when his intercom buzzed. His assistant said Li Yan from Sea Lift was on the line. He picked up the phone.
"Hello, Li. How are things going in Miami?"
"Very well, sir. All of our equipment has arrived and we have all the blueprints and maps created so we are ready to begin. We will be laying pipe along the ocean floor to divert the water twenty five miles away from shore. That distance is far enough to prevent the coastline from being submerged."
"Excellent work, Li. When the project is complete I would love to come down and inspect it myself and help unveil it to the whole country as a success. Please keep me informed as to your progress."
"I certainly will. Goodbye Mr. President."

4pm, Friday, June 15th, Federal Courthouse, Washington DC
The process was complete. All the jurors had been selected in what had been a very arduous task. The court ended up having to interview five hundred people to be able to agree on just twelve and one alternate. Both sides were content with the makeup, however, despite some heavy pushing by the judge to keep the process moving. All three lawyers had faith that the people picked would be accepting of the fact that their lives would be drastically different for the near future which was very important as well, as they didn't want any resentment if their part of the case took a long time. Everyone came back inside after taking a short break; the judge was going to explain about the living arrangements now.
"Jurors, I would like to speak to you as a group. As you know, the crimes the two women on trial are being charged with have touched our nation like nothing has in a long time. I am not here to give a political speech, but I wanted to remind you of that. Because of this, there are many groups and individuals who would like to influence the outcome of this case. I will have none of that. I am banning any outsiders into the courtroom. Furthermore, your living conditions during the trial will be tightly controlled. We will make you all as comfortable as possible, but you will basically be

watched and supervised all the time until a verdict is rendered. I am taking the unusual step of including myself and the lawyers in the same boat as well so as not to take any chances that the proceedings will be compromised. You may end up hating me, but I will not turn this into a farce. The whole world is watching." The thirteen citizens all digested what Alphonso had just said. "Therefore, to allow you make any arrangements, I am postponing the start of the trial from this Monday to the following one, June 25th. Please take that time to spend time with your friends and families. Thank you in advance for your service and I will see everyone back here on the 25th at 9am sharp." The judge headed back to his chambers, feeling many pairs of eyes penetrating the back of his head. He sat at his desk and saw he had a message. It was from the President of the ABC network, and they wanted to schedule an interview with him on Sunday, June 24th during prime time with Darby Killington, America's sweetheart, to discuss the upcoming trial. Who was he to say no?

  10am, Saturday, June 23rd, Governor's mansion, Springfield, IL
  Todd Russell was meeting with his advisers and discussing his upcoming campaign trip set for July 2nd. He would be travelling to the Northeast for 2 weeks and be covering New England. He would be making stops in each state from Maine to New York. He expected that part of the country to support Layton and Morris, as Morris hailed from Long Island, but Russell believed he could drum up some support for himself there, particularly in the northernmost states. This was a good time of year to go there as most of the folks were on vacation and therefore more relaxed. It was the perfect environment for him to show his personable nature and let people see him as just another average person rather than an untouchable politician. Joe Berry had come up with this strategy and Russell thought it was a great idea. He would employ the same tactic in the South a few weeks later. If it worked there as well in ingratiating himself into their lives he would have a commanding lead in the regions where he was now trailing.

1pm, Dearborn, MI

Hayao and Alex Ramirez had gotten the results of the polls they had distributed and there were some surprising results. Across the whole country, among liberals, Russell was ahead with Hayao not even close to him. Among those who classified themselves as conservatives Russell held the lead as well. Hayao supposed that was because Illinois remained a state whose demographics hadn't changed much in recent years and people across the country probably held the perception that Russell held mostly traditional viewpoints. Layton had a sizable lead with Caucasians and those born in the U.S. with Russell second. Those who favored more lenient immigration were strongly behind Hayao, and Layton was way ahead among women with Russell being the leading candidate among men. Breaking things down geographically, one thing that bothered Hayao was his showing out west, where Louis Grenadine should have been drumming up support for him. If the election were held today, Russell would get 57% of the vote out west with Hayao only getting 33%. That was dismal. He must have a conversation with Grenadine. He had a slight advantage in the Midwest, which pleased him, being Russell's home turf as well. The rest of the country was pretty much what they had expected, with Hayao's best showing in the southeast thanks to Ramirez's influence there. The regions of the country where he would have to put forth the most effort were the South, Northeast, and Alaska.

"Where do we go from here Alex?"

"We need to come up with some strategies to boost our ratings among the segments where we are behind. For example, how do we increase our appeal to women as a whole?" Hayao remained silent for a minute while he was thinking.

"I truly value your opinion, Alex. Many times the Vice President is not the most important member of the President's staff. What if we stress and demonstrate how invaluable you are to me, and that you will have a very active role after we are elected?"

"That will work. Regarding the results with men, we could highlight your advantage when it comes to international matters as you are the only one of the three candidates that has lived and worked outside of the U.S. You will approach the economy with a business person's perspective; many people will be drawn to that. Americans are tired of the status quo which isn't producing the best society we can be. Our administration is the one most poised to shake up the system. That is the message we will send."

8pm, Washington, DC
What lawyer in their right mind would be working at this time on a Saturday night? One that has the trial of the lifetime coming up in a day and a half. The scenes at Waller's office and the ACLU were the same; a group of people reviewing their stories and loading up on coffee. It was round two for the witnesses to get their testimonies straight. This was not a full dress rehearsal like last time but rather a chance to smooth out any rough edges. Both sides would wrap up tomorrow by lunchtime and then the attorneys would spend the remainder of the day writing their opening statements. It was critical that the statements they give be flawless; they have a big impact on the jury; the lawyers knew from experience the jurors couldn't remember everything and tuned out some of the information. They were extra alert at the beginning, however, and determined to do a good job. What each lawyer said would be burned into their memories. This was one of the times that Waller accepted the help of his team to help make his presentation the best it could be.

1pm, Sunday, June 24th
Hayao was just boarding the plane with Alex Ramirez for their trip to Israel and India. They chose to leave now so that with the time difference they would arrive tomorrow morning, and figuring in being able to sleep on the plane, they would be able to start conducting business right away. They had discussed what they wanted to accomplish ahead of time and both planned to take some downtime on the plane. They were using Moritu's jet which was very comfortable and had every possible amenity. This would be their last campaign trip out of the country before the election and they were determined to make it count.

8pm, ABC studios, New York, and Judge Clinton Alphonso's home, outside of Washington, DC

Just as the normally scheduled program was about to begin at 8pm, the network broke in with a special report about the interview coming up next which they had been advertising for the last two days. Virtually every household across the country tuned in to find out something about the trial which had been such a closely guarded secret. Alphonso had agreed to do this interview because the network had agreed to use a satellite feed so he could do it right from his house. The camera was on Darby Killington and she began. "Good evening everyone, welcome to a special edition of ABC News. I am Darby Killington and tonight I will be speaking with Judge Clinton Alphonso who will be presiding over the trials of Kelly Visque and Lorraine Corvino, charged with the murders of Cecily Bernard, Winston Bernard, and Juan Pillar. Welcome, judge."

"Thank you Darby." Short and sweet.

"How long have you been sitting on the bench?"

"Sixteen years now."

"Do you still enjoy it?"

"Oh yes. I feel very lucky to be able to do my part to keep the justice system moving."

"What types of cases do you find the most rewarding to be involved with?"

"Ones which are resolved with the guilty party being convicted."

"Do any cases that you handled stand out?"

"Probably the one where those crooks from Wall Street were prosecuted. Now that was satisfying."

"What is your role in the process?"

"To guarantee that procedures are followed to the tee and no undue influence is brought to bear." That was the perfect segue to her next question.

"I understand you are instituting very strict regulations about who will be allowed into the courtroom."

"That's right. Only those directly involved will be permitted. I am excluding even family members. I will tolerate no leaks or information about what goes on to become news and compromise the trial."

"How could that happen?"

"If the media finds out what's going on, they will report it which might lead to the jury being influenced in their opinions. People may think I am going a bit overboard, but this way I can be certain that the process will not be corrupted."

"How do you plan to prevent them from outside contact?"

"I can't divulge that."

"Are you planning to sequester them for the entire trial?"

"Yes."

"How can you justify doing something so restrictive?"

"Societies have certain codes which make them functional. This society wouldn't work without a legal system, and such a legal system wouldn't be effective if people didn't do their part, including making sacrifices. Living without outside contact for a short period of time is not really too much to ask. It's not like they will be living in squalor. I have gone to considerable lengths to see to it that their needs will be met, and I will be living in the same environment as the jurors and attorneys."

"Do you feel this case is your legacy?"

"My career is my legacy. I hope I will be remembered as having adhered to the highest standards. The difference here is this case is being so widely scrutinized that I felt the need to protect it."

"Like it or not, this case has catapulted you into the spotlight. Do you see yourself writing a book after it is finished?"

"While I never say never, I have no plans to do that. Any celebrity status I enjoy is purely circumstantial."

"Thank you very much, judge. This is Darby Killington, bidding everyone a good night."

10 am, Monday, June 25th, Jerusalem

Hayao and Ramirez were going to be spending the day in this wonderful city with Israel's Prime Minister, Naftali Levy. Hayao greatly admired the Israelis. They were moral and virtuous and never started a conflict but made sure that they finished it. Hayao had requested a private meeting for just the three of them to

explain his plan. He and Ramirez regretted they would not be able to do any touring. They all sat at the conference table in Levy's private office. "Would either of you like something?" Ramirez said she would like some coffee. Hayao was ready to start immediately.
"Naftali, we appreciate you welcoming us so graciously. We are looking forward to having a fine working relationship for a long time to come. We all know that you are very influential with the Jewish population in the United States and would want to see their support go to the best candidate. We don't know what types of arrangements you have made with anyone else, but we are prepared to offer you a very attractive deal. We are interested in opening a branch of the Moritu Corporation here in Israel which we believe would benefit your country greatly. It would help your economy and put Israel on the path toward becoming a dominant economic force."
"Well, that is an extremely generous offer. I would love to say yes right off the bat, but I would want to iron out some of the details first. Have you received approval for this from your higher ups at Moritu?"
"Yes, we have."
"Where do you plan on building the facility?"
"We were thinking between Tel Aviv and Caesaria, right on the Mediterranean Sea. That would give us options to ship our product either by ship or by plane out of Ben Gurion Airport."
"Would you hire Israelis in the factory?"
"Absolutely, one hundred percent."
"That would be fantastic. It would certainly help with our unemployment issue. In return for this you would want my endorsement?"
"That's correct." Levy turned it over in his head. This would definitely be more beneficial than what Russell had been willing to give.
"Let me contact some of the people this would affect. What are your plans for the rest of the time you have here?"
"We would like to go to explore Jerusalem today and head to Tel Aviv tomorrow. Unfortunately we have to leave on Wednesday."

"Let me accompany you to Tel Aviv. I will introduce you to some people there who could help decide on a location for Moritu, and I will be able to give you an answer by Wednesday morning before you leave. How does that sound?"

"It sounds just fine."

"Now, let me lend you my driver for the day to be your tour guide."

9 am, Monday, June 25th, Washington, DC

"The honorable judge Alphonso entering, please rise!" Alphonso walked in, all business. He sat down, glanced around the courtroom to make sure everything was in order, and then addressed the Attorney General.

"Mr. Waller, are you ready to give your opening statement?"

"I am, your honor." Waller stood up and strode to stand about three feet away from the jury box. "Ladies and gentlemen, thank you for your service. We are here to address four crimes the defendant Kelly Visque is being charged with, and two crimes the defendant Lorraine Corvino is being charged with. Let's start with Miss Visque. She committed four murders, those of Cecily and Winston Bernard, and Juan Pillar and his driver. She is being charged with four counts of murder; in addition, the prosecution will show her motive makes her in violation of a clause of the Patriot Act. That means she committed an act of terrorism; she will be tried for both. As I will stress throughout the trial, her acts of murder and terrorism, while connected, should be viewed separately. I will be calling expert witnesses to explain how she would do anything for her country and has the mentality of a criminal. I will be introducing evidence that will place Miss Visque at the location where the bodies of the Bernards were discovered and a professional who can attest to its validity. The gun used to kill the Bernards has been retrieved as well and once again I can show how the shroud of mystery surrounding it relates to her past. We will show the second defendant, Miss Corvino, who is being charged with conspiracy to commit murder, which means she knowingly helped plan and execute the slayings of the Bernards, was having an affair with Justice Bernard. We will also demonstrate Miss Corvino's motive for wanting him dead and her link to Kelly Visque. We possess evidence that shows Visque planned out the murders. Finally, we have numerous character witnesses who will testify she is a loose cannon with a hair trigger temper. Now let's look at Juan Pillar and his driver, During the proceedings here it will become evident the target was Pillar and the driver happened to be exceedingly unlucky. He was abducted from the airport upon returning home from abroad; his schedule had been made public. We have hard evidence that Kelly Visque was the perpetrator. Now, the defense will try to argue the evidence we obtained is circumstantial, but don't you believe them. We will explain that Miss Visque's motive is politically motivated; as a result, according to the law, she is a terrorist. Once you have heard all of the witnesses' testimony and seen our evidence, there will be no doubt in your minds about Kelly Visque's or Lorraine Corvino's guilt." Waller quietly returned to his seat. His assistants noticed that the jurors followed him with their eyes. Glen Aaron was next to give his opening statement.

"Mr. Waller did a fine job of portraying my client, Kelly Visque, as a monster. In fact, she is not; instead she is a much maligned woman who is the victim of our federal police force under a great deal of pressure to apprehend someone for these high profile crimes. The prosecution has no credible direct evidence, as the DNA they have which matches Kelly Visque's cannot possibly be hers as the timing is off which the professional who works in the industry will explain. The Attorney General also said she is ultra-patriotic and has the mindset of a criminal. We will produce witnesses to refute this very idea. With regard to the gun that was mentioned, there is no direct link to my client, only speculation. Let me address the relationship between Miss Visque and Miss Corvino. They were friends who participated on the same bowling team. Oh my god, let's convict them right now and skip the trial! Yes, they were seen together having fun, and yes, Miss Corvino might have been intimate with Judge Bernard. However, it is a completely unsubstantiated leap to go from that to murder, and one for which there is no proof or even conjecture." Aaron paused for a minute for dramatic effect. "When it comes to the murder of Juan

Pillar and the driver, you will be told there are several pieces of damning evidence against my client which shows her threatening Mr. Pillar and then places her at the airport. These two events are strictly circumstantial. It will also be said that Miss Visque committed these acts out of some sort of misguided political agenda as a fanatic. We will show you the real Kelly Visque, a strong willed woman who loves her country, yes, but would never resort to harming others to achieve her means. Once you are presented with all the facts, the only conclusion you will be able to reach is that Kelly Visque is not guilty."

"Mr. Ross, you are next." Lionel Ross stood up and approached the jury.

"Thank you judge. Good morning ladies and gentlemen. My client, Lorraine Corvino", he pointed at her, "is a sacrificial lamb. The FBI and Attorney General's office had built a weak case against the other defendant here today, Kelly Visque, and had one piece missing. Their farfetched theory that has no validity of her kidnapping the Bernards and killing them for which they have no hard evidence, makes no sense because she would never have managed to obtain the justice's schedule to plan out her attack. What do they do? They find a link they can exploit to their advantage. They find out my client and justice Bernard shared intimacy and use the coincidence that she and Kelly Visque were friends to arrive at the trumped up charge against my client of conspiracy to commit murder. It is completely without merit. They needed to plug one hole in their circumstantial case against Kelly Visque which they were under enormous pressure to solve, and that plug was my client. We will refute everything the prosecution says and do so with hard facts and reputable witnesses who will explain why my client couldn't and wouldn't ever have been involved in these god awful events. Your only choice will be to return a verdict of not guilty. Thank you."

CHAPTER 15

6pm, Monday, June 25th, Tel Aviv

Naftali Levy had contacted the mayors of Ceasarea and Tel Aviv to disclose Hayao's plan. They both thought it a great thing for Israel as it would create a large number of jobs to the area, badly needed as students were graduating from university with no career prospects. The two mayors enjoyed a good relationship, so the only thing left to do involved approaching the landowners to make sure they would be interested, which Levy was certain they would be once they understood it would be in their best interests to cooperate for the sake of Israel.

7pm, Washington, DC, Federal Penitentiary

Glen Aaron and Lionel Ross decided to meet with their clients to reassure them everything had gone well in court that day and to explain why the judge decided to end the proceedings after the opening statements. Kelly Visque asked Aaron who he thought came out ahead after the opening statements, and he responded he thought they did, as they managed to poke several holes in the prosecution's arguments. For example, when Waller rambled on about her having a predisposition toward criminal behavior, Aaron refuted this by saying the government was desperate to convict someone for the crimes and she had been unlucky enough to meet the criteria through several coincidences. He believed she appeared most sympathetic to the jury. Judge Alphonso decided to postpone the first witness until tomorrow because he hadn't known how long the opening arguments would take so he didn't want the witnesses to show up for nothing and waste their time. The prosecution would start fresh tomorrow. "Can you predict who their first witness will be?" "I am expecting it to be one of the experts. I am sure Waller's strategy will be to start with the strongest weapon in his arsenal to cause the most damage to our case. How are you holding up?"

"I'm ok." She felt she was in good hands. "I wonder how Lorraine is?"

"Ross is meeting with her right now as well. I will talk to him and then come back if you like."

"That would be great, I am worried about her and I don't get a chance to speak to her during court."

"I will be back shortly." Aaron waited for Ross at the exit and inquired about Corvino. Ross said she seemed ok but nervous. They both agreed Visque handled the pressure much better and they would have to help calm Corvino down before she testified. Aaron went back to his client's cell, gave her the update, and then headed home to relax a bit before day 2.

9am, Tuesday, June 26th

The prosecution would present Alan Wentworth as their first witness and Waller thought he would hit it out of the park. He would describe what a fanatic Kelly Visque was and how she participated in an extremist group which has stayed with her even though she is not involved with them anymore. He was a nice looking man and seemed smooth without coming across as glib. Judge Alphonso entered the room and everyone went through the custom of standing and then sitting when he sat down. Waller was ready for the judge to tell him to call his first witness when instead Alphonso requested all three lawyers approach the bench. When they did, he told them that before they begin he had some information he wanted to share with the jury. They all looked surprised, and Waller asked what it was regarding. Alphonso told him not to worry, it was nothing which could be taken as prejudicial or would reflect poorly on their clients or the prosecution's case in any way. Waller felt skeptical but kept his mouth shut. The three of them went back to their seats and once they sat down the judge addressed the jurors. "Ladies and gentlemen, I have some information to pass on to you. This trial has two defendants as you know. They are being tried for different crimes, although they share two of the victims in common. That will be incorporated into this trial's procedures. We will be hearing the testimony of witnesses in both cases together rather than all the witnesses for one case and then the other. This is being done because some of the witnesses are here for both defendants so this will save time. The court will make it clear which witnesses will be doing double duty. If anyone of you have any questions you may submit them in writing to the bailiff who will make sure I get them. Now, let's proceed. Mr. Waller, are you ready to call your first witness?"

"Yes, your honor. The people call Dr. Alan Wentworth." The jury watched as a tall handsome man walked to the jury box and be sworn in. "If it pleases the court, Dr. Wentworth will be providing information about both defendants." Judge Alphonso glanced at the jury to make sure they picked up on this, and they seemed to from the looks on their faces. "Dr. Wentworth, how long have you been a practicing psychologist?"

"Over 20 years."

"What is your specialty?"

"I possess extensive experience analyzing those people charged with domestic terrorism."

"When you say extensive, what does that mean?"

"I have been an expert witness at over 50 trials."

"Do other psychologists seek out your opinion as well?"

"Absolutely."

"Where can people find your opinions?"

"I have written several books on the subject of jingoism and am a professor of psychology at the University of Michigan."

"How does a person who suffers from extreme patriotism become that way?"

"It usually can be traced back to their childhood. They came from an environment in which their caregivers were typically conservative in their political views and often were paranoid about foreign ideas and people."

"How does this cause them to act?"

"They will engage in activities designed to promote the traditional values of the nation in which they live."

"Are they usually law abiding citizens?"

"Extremely patriotic people all harbor the potential to commit criminal acts depending upon what the political and social climate is."

"In other words their behavior is dictated by the times they live in."

"Exactly."

"What types of activities would they engage in?"

"They would do whatever it takes to make sure the ideals of the country being compromised are kept in place."

"Does that include interfering with the operation of government if said person thinks the government is at odds with tradition?"

"Absolutely. They will go to great lengths to preserve what they perceive as important." Waller paused to let his comment sink in; he had just described the definition of a terrorist according to the Patriot Act. He wanted the jury to remember this as he would be coming back to it when Ed Billet took the stand.

"Doctor, did you meet with Kelly Visque?"

"Yes, I did."

"What was your impression of her?"

"She is a very headstrong young woman who has very traditional views when it comes to politics."

"What were her parents like?"

"Extremely conservative. Her father was a policeman and her mother is in the military."

"What were their views on the United States?"

"That we should stick to the ideals this country was founded on."

"And Kelly?"

"She feels the same way."

"Was she pleased that a person not born in this country is eligible to be President?"

"She couldn't be more against it."

"Do you think she would resort to derailing our government's process to try to stop it?"

"Without a doubt."

"Thank you. Let's switch gears now. It is obvious your area of expertise is extreme patriotism. You are also a psychologist who sees all types of patients, is that correct?"

"Yes. I treat a wide range of patients."

"Did you also meet with the other defendant here today, Lorraine Corvino?"

"I did."

"What was the purpose of your discussion?"

"To determine if she harbored so much jealousy and possessiveness in her romantic relationships that she would go so far as to help plan the demise of a lover who she felt had betrayed her."

"What was your conclusion?"

"She does indeed possess these personality traits."

"What do you think caused Miss Corvino to participate in the plan to kill the Bernards?" Before Wentworth managed to answer, Ross leapt to his feet.

"Objection, your, honor. That question calls for speculation on the part of the witness."

"Sustained."

"In a case such as Miss Corvino's, would the person be driven to murder by being lied to and told by their lover they would marry them someday but that day never comes?"

"Absolutely. That is exactly the type of betrayal which would cause the person to seek revenge."

"Thank you Doctor. I have nothing further." Aaron got up to conduct his cross examination.

"How did you arrive at your diagnosis that Kelly Visque suffers from extreme patriotism?"

"She has the typical upbringing, her parents both held positions in which they were responsible for protecting the United States, and she has a quick and volatile temper."

"In other words, she fit the profile of those people you have classified in this category in the past."

"Precisely." Aaron realized he had Wentworth in trouble now.

"The world is made up of patterns, wouldn't you agree, doctor?"

"I suppose so."

"There are patterns all around us, and we need patterns to help us make sense of things. Do you look for patterns in your work when you are evaluating people?"

"I do."

"What pattern did Kelly Visque fit?"

"As I said before, she fit the pattern of an extreme patriot."

"Because she grew up in a home where the parents served in the military and law enforcement and were conservatives?"
"Yes."
"Is part of the pattern of being a super patriot also associating with like-minded people?"
"Yes, and Miss Visque was a member of American Pride."
"Yes, but she hasn't attended any of their meetings in years and she rejected their fanaticism. Did you even ask her about her ideologies or only about her parents?"
"I asked her about those things."
"You seemed to have missed much. Did Mr. Waller provide you with the list of questions he wanted to be asked?"
"Objection!" Before judge Alphonso could say sustained, Aaron withdrew the question and said he had nothing further for this witness, but he thought he managed to show Wentworth's evaluation of Kelly Visque had been incomplete. Next it was Ross's turn.

"I realize you are a leader in your field, doctor. Your professional opinion about my client includes the observation she is obsessive when involved romantically with someone and she gets jealous and possessive when she cannot have them all to herself. Would you say that's accurate?"
"Yes."
"Have you ever dealt with other lovers who fell into this category?"
"Yes."
"What types of actions did they follow?"
"They demonstrated possessive behavior which becomes abnormal and they try to exert more and more control over that person. It is really a form of abuse."
"What happens when the other person in the relationship leaves them?"
"It puts them over the edge."
"What are some of the typical responses?"
"Many times the jilted party will become violent or begin planning their demise."
"Do they stay uninvolved in the process?"

"Just the opposite. They may not commit the crime itself but they want to be part of the process and be there to see the person get what they consider he or she deserves."

"So they want revenge and want to see the deed be done?"

"Usually."

"That's interesting. You see, Lorraine Corvino cannot be placed at the crime scene of the Bernards and she has alibis for both the time they were kidnapped and for when they were left outside the Supreme Court building. What do you make of that?"

"There are always exceptions to every rule."

"You didn't seem to feel Miss Corvino represented one of those exceptions until I told you about those two facts about her case. Do you believe your examination of her was complete?"

"I'd say so, yes. There is no doubt she becomes irrationally possessive when she is in a relationship."

"She does not fit the pattern you described as she was not with the victims when they died. Based upon your testimony here today regarding both my client and the defendant Kelly Visque, you did not conduct a thorough enough evaluation to offer an expert opinion which you claim to espouse. Nothing further." Wentworth's face turned red for the jury to see as the judge excused him.

10am, Wednesday, June 27th, Tel Aviv

Naftali Levy had heard back from the landowners outside of Tel Aviv and Caesarea about selling their land to Moritu Corporation. He was in his limousine on his way to Ben Gurion Airport to bid Hayao and Ramirez goodbye and to let them know the sale had been approved. They met with the buyers yesterday to discuss the terms of the sale and how beneficial it would be for Israel. In addition to the jobs that would be created, it would bring untold revenue as well. He got there just as they were boarding the plane and Hayao told him Moritu would be starting to build the factory in the next few weeks. He expected it to be done around the time of the election and thanked Levy in advance for his support. Levy was a man of his word and Hayao knew he would use whatever influence he had in the United States to help. Hayao boarded the plane and he and Ramirez were on their way to India.

9am, Washington D.C.

Waller had nursed his wounds last night; round one had gone to the defense as they really damaged Wentworth's credibility when they were able to show he had not been thorough enough in his questioning of their clients. That had been Waller's oversight; he met with Sean Cardillo, who would be today's witness, last night to review any pitfalls which may arise. Cardillo was the psychologist who met with Kelly Visque to determine if she possessed the mentality of a criminal and the ability to elude police. Cardillo was sworn in and Waller got started with his direct examination. "Doctor Cardillo, what is the single biggest factor that criminals who commit crimes other than out of self-preservation have in common?"

"Their background, and by that I mean the people they had contact with throughout their past. These people maintained some kind of contact with individuals who have worked to prevent crime in some capacity, either as law enforcement directly or in the legal system in some capacity."

"Do you mean to tell me everyone who came across a police officer or someone else in the legal system will turn out to be a criminal?"

"No, of course not. The criminals are a subset of those who had contact with these upstanding citizens. They are the ones who rebelled or deal with some kind of issue." Cardillo paused. "That's not to say every single criminal knows someone in law enforcement, but it is a common thread."

"What about the defendant Kelly Visque?"

"Well, her father worked as a policeman. I am sure she grew up hearing about his cases. The talk around the dinner table undoubtedly included the ways which the police succeeded in solving crimes and the ways criminals tripped up and got caught." That was the statement Waller needed to admit his first piece of evidence.

"The people offer exhibit A, your honor." He approached the bench to show the evidence. The judge looked at it and handed it back. "We are submitting a note recovered from Juan Pillar's house by the FBI when they were searching it after he had been killed." He held it up for the jury to see. It was a note pieced together from magazines to create a threatening message. The note was letting Pillar know he should remove himself from the Presidential race or else. The members of the jury could not fathom what this had to do with Kelly Visque. Waller continued, and as if reading their minds said, "I am sure you have no idea why this death threat is relevant to the defendant. This note, found still sealed in the envelope and unopened by Mr. Pillar, was mailed from California, and we will illustrate how that connects Kelly Visque to it later on in the trial. Doctor Cardillo, mailing a note from a place far away from where a person lives, wouldn't you say that is the thought process of someone who thinks like a criminal and has an idea of how to elude the police?"

"Absolutely. She devised some kind of plan to get it there, to Juan Pillar."

"She did, which will become clear as this trial unfolds. Would you be surprised to learn also that no DNA existed on the letter, except for Juan Pillar's?"

"No. Again, the work of someone familiar with police procedures."

"Thank you doctor. I have nothing further." Aaron stood up and went towards the witness box.

"I didn't realize we were in the presence of a mastermind, did you doctor?" Cardillo looked confused for a moment. He regained his cool demeanor and looked over at Visque.

"No I didn't."

"Oh wait, you thought I meant my client?" Aaron chuckled. "No, I am talking about the Attorney General. You see, he has us believing that two occurrences which anyone can learn from watching any halfway decent crime drama on tv or from a few clicks on the internet can pick up are advanced methods. The two practices he talked about, mailing a letter from a distant place and making sure no incriminating evidence existed on the letter are

quite elementary. Miss Visque is either on par with a first grader or she is innocent." Now it was the jury who was smiling. "One last question doctor. When you referred to the statistic that criminals who committed crimes for reasons other than self-preservation had a common bond of contact with law enforcement officials, how big was your sample?"
  "About 150 people."
  "Were they from all different parts of the country?"
  "They were from the DC area."
  "Were they a mix of women and men?"
  "Mostly men."
  "So, this homogenous test group is supposed to be representative of the entire law breaking country?" Aaron understood that Cardillo didn't have to answer, everyone knew he screwed up. "Nothing further." What Aaron didn't realize, however, was that he had played right into Waller's hands with his line of questioning about Juan Pillar and the note from California.

  10am, Thursday, June 28th, New Delhi
  Hayao and Alex were in their hotel rooms freshening up after the plane ride. While they were here in India, they hoped to accomplish the same deal they had in Israel, offering to build a Moritu plant and help boost the country's economy by creating jobs and increasing the gross national product in exchange for Prime Minister Sarin's support at election time. Hayao believed if he could obtain that, he would really be in great shape politically.

  9am, Washington DC
  Waller was finishing reviewing his notes one last time for today's witness, Edna Jillow, the DNA expert. Judge Alphonso called the court to order and Jillow was sworn in. "Hello Miss Jillow. The court appreciates you travelling here from Pennsylvania. How long have you worked with DNA?"
  "For over thirty years."
  "What type of DNA have you handled?"
  "Human DNA exclusively."

"You were asked to examine the human DNA extracted from a bee in this instance, is that correct?"

"Yes."

"Have you ever worked with bees before?"

"No."

"When you work with DNA, where is it most often extracted from?"

"From humans, either after they are dead or if they are the ones being charged with the crime, while they are still alive."

"This must have been a real learning experience for you then. What task were you presented with?"

"To determine whether the physical position of human DNA inside a bumblebee's stinger determined the chronological order in which it was drawn into the stinger by the bee stinging the parties' in question."

"The people introduce exhibit B which they would like to admit into evidence, your honor." The judge nodded. Waller went to the table and grabbed a plastic bag with a bee in it. "This is a bee that stung the defendant Kelly Visque on the day the bodies of the Bernards' were left in front of the Supreme Court building. The bee was found at the same location as the bodies and contained the DNA of Miss Visque. It was a bumblebee which means it could sting more than once and would not die after one sting. There were two sets of DNA found inside the stinger and Miss Visque's resided to the bottom." Waller turned back to Miss Jillow. "What types of techniques did you use to determine whether the chronological order was related to the physical location in the stinger?"

"I conducted some experiments involving inserting multiple sets of DNA into the stingers of bumblebees to determine where each one would be positioned."

"What was your conclusion?"

"That the location of the DNA remained independent of when it obtained by the bee."

"In other words Miss Jillow, one has nothing to do with the other and for all we know the more recent DNA might be at the bottom of the stinger."

"Exactly correct, DNA testing is not so precise."

"What about the length of time between when the DNA was inserted into the stinger and when it was tested?"

"That had absolutely no bearing on the outcome. The placement of the DNA did not change over time."

"So this scenario is entirely possible, person A was stung by a bee at 10am, and person B stung by the same bee at noon. Person A's DNA might very well be at the top of the stinger just as easily as person's B's."

"Yes, that is correct."

"I understand you are a leader in your field, Miss Jillow. There have been magazine articles about you as a pioneer. Have you ever had any falling outs with any of your employers?"

"At times I have thought certain things should be handled differently, but am always able to work these things out amicably." Waller was setting up this point he would make when he cross examined Otto Lampf.

"Nothing further." It was now Aaron's turn to conduct his questioning.

"Miss Jillow, you said it is inconclusive whether or not the location of the DNA in a bee's stinger corresponds to when it was obtained. Isn't it possible the DNA at the top was and is more recent?"

"Yes is it possible."

"Thank you, nothing further."

2pm, Eric Layton's office

Layton, Steven Morris, and Layton's aide were gathered in Layton's office to review the results of the polls that Robert, the aide, conducted. He tried to get information based on the issues rather than geographics. He believed they already had a good handle on which areas of the country they needed to concentrate. Layton and Morris both looked at him, silently telling him to get started. "The polls I conducted are grouped by the topics important to voters right now and have been tallied so that the numbers shown reflect the country as a whole." He gave each one of them a sheet showing the breakdown. They each took a few minutes to review it. The numbers were as follows:

The Economy - Layton, Hayao, Russell

Immigration - Hayao, Russell, Layton

Education - Russell, Layton, Hayao

Health Care - Layton, Hayao, Russell

Technology - Russell, Hayao, Layton

Environment - Layton, Russell, Hayao

Layton sat back in his chair to contemplate these results. He addressed both Morris and Robert; they had decided to include Robert in their future strategy sessions as they admitted he could provide a different perspective. "It seems like the area we should focus on first is immigration. We are at an inherent disadvantage here."

"The one demographic where we are leading with is those containing opposition to an open door policy; the problem is they are the minority. We need to find a way to keep a stronghold there and still pick up some points with those who favor immigration", Robert elaborated.

"We could work on projects designed to create jobs for people entering the country", said Morris. "Our platform could be that we are on board with increased immigration provided there are enough opportunities for those that come. Eric, you are seen as a champion of the unemployed, so that would fit perfectly into your image." Morris looked hopeful, and Layton smiled.

"That's perfect Steve. Robert, this will be your next task. Do some research about what and where there is large scale job creation and employment potential, and let's meet again in three weeks. Thank you both."

9pm, the hotel where the judge, lawyers, and jury was staying
Juror number three, the bartender, was in his room where he stayed basically whenever he wasn't in the courtroom. The first week of the trial was over and he thought the prosecution enjoyed a slight edge so far. The jurors developed a silent system of communicating with each other in the jury box, the only place they had any breathing room at all from being scrutinized and isolated. The judge was living up to his word of having their every move under wraps. They were allowed to go to the hotel gym, but only one at a time and the place was wired for video and sound with the feed going to the judge's hotel room. They used a series of hand gestures in the jury box as their method of communication. While being basic, it worked. They used the thumbs up sign when they thought a witness succeeded in getting his or her point across, the thumbs down when they didn't, and they scratched their noses when they thought the lawyer doing the questioning failed to convey the intended message or if they had done a poor job of questioning. They were including these opinions in their notes so it make it easier when it came time to deliberate. They heard the judge say they would be allowed out one at a time each day this weekend for an hour to get some fresh air and all hoped he would keep his promise.

10am, Sunday, July 1st, New Delhi
Hayao and Ramirez were headed home after what turned out to be a somewhat frustrating trip. They really tried to get India's government on board to endorse them when the election came around, and they were interested, but in the end they said they aligned themselves with Todd Russell and his plan to help them with technology. He had simply gotten to them first. Hayao wanted to kick himself for not visiting there sooner. His offer was just as attractive but came a little too late. He left on good terms, however, and agreed if something should change with Russell, the Indian government would adopt Hayao's proposal. That was all he could do for now. When they arrived back home, he would start working with the coach they hired to help handle himself better and start travelling around the country to make up ground in the

areas they were trailing the other candidates. Right now, however, he wanted to call Natsu and tell him Israel was in but India was not.

9am, Monday, July 2nd, Washington DC

The second week of the trial had arrived, and Waller was starting things off strong with two witnesses today and three pieces of evidence. He was ready for his first witness and wanted to get him on the stand while Waller's instructions were still fresh in his mind, like not to be cocky and not to try to engage the defense in a battle of wits or words. "The people call Rick Heller. Mr. Heller, how do you know the defendant Lorraine Corvino?"

"We work together."

"Where did you work together?"

"At the Supreme Court building."

"You are both custodians for Magnus Industries?"

"Yup."

"How long have you been partnered with Miss Corvino?"

"On and off for a few years."

"Has that time been consistently at the Supreme Court?"

"Yup." Wow, this guy was a real charmer! At least Waller had insisted he covered up his tattoos.

"Was she a good worker?"

"She was ok. She was always trying to talk to the people who worked there. Trying to get on their good side, like she was hoping they would do her a favor or something."

"Did the two of you ever see any of the Supreme Court justices?"

"All the time."

"What about Winston Bernard?"

"Yes."

"How did Miss Corvino act around him?"

"Sometimes she would be goofy, other times normal. Anyone could tell there was a thing between them."

"What do you mean by thing?"

"I mean they were ...", Heller started to say they were screwing each other, but then he remembered the pain in the ass attorney had kept telling him not to use such language in the courtroom. "They were having an affair."

"How can you be sure?"

"She would always linger around when we finished working, taking her time getting ready to leave. I always left before her."

"Did you ever notice any unusual behavior by Justice Bernard?"

"A couple times I caught him lurking around the stairwell, waiting for me to leave so he could run downstairs to meet Corvino." Waller wanted to continue the questioning to ask Heller about Corvino's personality and if she ever acted jealous or possessive, but then decided he would quit while he was ahead and not give the defense too much ammunition to discredit Heller now when they cross examined him.

"Nothing further." Heller started to get up, but the judge instructed him the other lawyer now had some questions for him. Ross got up and went over to the witness box.

"Mr. Heller, are you married?"

"Nope. Don't subscribe to marriage."

"Why is that?"

"Life is too short to be tied down with one person."

"I see. Would you consider yourself to be promiscuous?"

"What does that mean?"

"Do you sleep with many different women?" Heller developed a lopsided grin.

"I suppose you could say that."

"Did you ever sleep with Lorraine Corvino?" His smile disappeared just as fast as it had come.

"No."

"The change in your expression tells me you tried, however. What happened, she shot you down?" Heller didn't say anything; Ross pushed harder. "Come on, Rick. A stud like you isn't good enough for her? Who the hell is she right? She thinks she is too good for you, right, trying to land some rich and powerful prick." Waller needed to try to stop this before Heller imploded.

"Objection! Counsel is badgering the witness and trying to get him to admit to something by harassing him."

"I am simply attempting to break through the rehearsed answers Heller has been providing and get to the truth."

"The objection is overruled." Ross seized this opportunity to keep going.

"I request permission to treat this witness as hostile."

"Granted."

"How many times did she rebuff your advances Rick?"

"I never asked her out."

"You expect us to accept that? Three times? Four times? You probably bothered her so much she stopped talking to you altogether!" Heller couldn't take it anymore, looking like a loser in front of all these people.

"I am just as good as that judge she was pining for! I would have shown her a good time!"

"She never gave you the chance, right, so you became jealous and decided to get even by exaggerating about how she cavorted with Judge Bernard. We know they were having a tryst but I am sure they were infinitely more discreet than you would have us believe." Heller denied it up and down for five minutes, but it didn't matter. The damage to Heller's testimony and credibility had already been done. He might as well have been a witness for the defense.

1pm

The judge declared a recess until after lunch, and now that they were back it was Ed Billet's turn. Waller intended to introduce three new pieces of evidence during his testimony. "Mr. Billet, please tell the court what your profession is."

"I am a special agent with the FBI."

"How long have you been a special agent?"

"19 years."

"Approximately how many cases have you worked in that time period?"

"Around 200."

"How many have you taken the lead on?'

"About thirty."

"So it's fair to say you are very experienced."

"I suppose so."

"What was your role on this case involving the murders of the Bernards, Juan Pillar and his driver?"

"I was called in to take over when the case was transferred to the FBI."

"Who asked you to come on board?"

"FBI Director James Grey."

"He clearly places much faith in you."

"We have worked together in the past."

"What was your first lead in the case?"

"DNA extracted from a bumblebee found dead at the crime scene."

"How many sets of DNA were there inside the bee?"

"Two."

"Who did they belong to?"

"Kelly Visque and another man named Peter Marvin."

"Once you had their names, what did you do?"

"We started interrogating people with those names across the country. We eventually identified the people the two sets belonged to, a man named Peter Marvin who was in town on vacation, and the defendant Kelly Visque."

"Did they have alibis?"

"Yes. Mr. Marvin was seen by a waitress at a restaurant in town that evening and Miss Visque ate lunch with a friend and then says she walked around town until evening time when she went home."

"Did anyone see her arrive home?"

"We spoke to her neighbors and no one managed to place her at home that night."

"At this point who was the more likely suspect?"

"Miss Visque. We suspected it was her from the time we were able to verify the DNA was hers."

"Why?"

"Primarily at this point in the investigation because of her background. Both of her parents were very conservative and as we have heard were familiar with weapons and how law enforcement works. We learned she also was very physically fit with a volatile temper." Waller paused.

"Did the FBI recover the murder weapon?"

"We retrieved it around that time out of the Potomac River."

"The people admit exhibit C, the gun used to kill the Bernards. Were there fingerprints on the gun?"

"No."

"What information were you able to obtain from the gun?"

"The serial number had been filed off but we were able to view it using reagents, chemicals used on metal to reconstruct indentations."

"Where did the serial number lead you?"

"To a gun store in Atlanta."

"What did you find when you went there?"

"There was no record of the person who purchased the gun when the sale was made."

"Isn't that information supposed to be kept?"

"Yes."

"In lieu of that, what did the FBI do next?"

"We showed pictures of Marvin and Visque to the people who worked in the gun store and at the surrounding homes and businesses but we did not get any positive ids."

"What happened next?"

"Our investigation was at a standstill; we went back and widened our field of possible suspects to include political dissidents and such, and we met again with friends and acquaintances of the deceased."

"Did you make any progress?"

"Not for a while."

"When did your breakthrough come?"

"One of our agents was meeting with Lorraine Corvino at her apartment and noticed something."

"What did the agent see?"

"He saw a picture of the bowling team Corvino played on."

"What was it about the picture which piqued his interest?"

"One of the women in the picture was Kelly Visque."

"What did the FBI do with this new development?"

"We placed Miss Visque under arrest and charged her with the murders of Cecily and Winston Bernard."

"What did the picture illustrate that led to this arrest?"

"The fact that Miss Visque and Miss Corvino knew each other and Miss Corvino worked as a custodian for the company that cleaned the U.S. Supreme Court building where Justice Bernard worked."

"Did you believe Miss Corvino helped in the planning of the murders?"

"We didn't know. There were rumors floating around that the two of them were having an affair. It could have been Corvino had unwittingly provided information about Judge Bernard's comings and goings."

"Did the FBI have any other evidence at this time?"

"Yes. We conducted a brain scan of Winston Bernard's brain and compared it to a baseline scan created years before. We were able to see where the brain fluid pooled in his brain at the time of death and ascertain what his emotions were at that time. From the results he experienced fear and confusion, and we managed to conclude he almost certainly did not meet his attacker, which is in line with Kelly Visque."

"The people introduce evidence item D, the readout of Winston Bernard's brain scan. Agent Billet, let's get to back to Lorraine Corvino's involvement. When did you think she became involved?"

"We never thought she had actually been part of the physical kidnapping. We learned from talking to people who know and knew her that she tended to become quite jealous and possessive when romantically linked with someone. We spoke to their teammates on the bowling team and the employees in a bar they apparently used to frequent who said they were quite close and appeared to have fun together often. These factors were enough for us to charge her with conspiracy to commit murder."

"Alright, why don't we turn our attention to the last charge, that of the two murder counts against Kelly Visque for the killings of Juan Pillar and his driver. Lead me through the steps the FBI took here."

"Well, we first considered those individuals who would gain from having Pillar out of the picture." Billet went through the whole story of how Louis Grenadine was a suspect and ended his account with the discovery of the airport tape containing the footage of the blonde woman who looked like Kelly Visque, and at this point Waller admitted the tape into evidence as exhibit E which was shown to the jury right away. Once the video finished Waller was done with his questioning of Billet and it was time for the cross examinations. Once again, Aaron went first.

"Agent Billet, are you familiar with the term circumstantial evidence?"

"Yes."

"Would it surprise you to learn the three pieces of evidence Attorney General Waller introduced during your testimony are all circumstantial as they pertain to my client? There are no fingerprints, DNA, or eyewitness accounts. Those are direct evidence which is needed for a conviction."

"Three pieces of circumstantial evidence add up to a coincidence which cannot be ignored when they all point to the same person."

"That's why you are not a lawyer."

"Objection!"

"Sustained."

"Let's talk about the bodies of the Bernards. When do you suppose they were left in front of the Supreme Court building?"

"At night, so it would be less noticeable."

"Please tell me, agent, what you believe to have been the sequence of events involving the bee, Miss Visque, and Mr. Peter Marvin on the day of Saturday, June 18, 2039." Billet stole a quick glance at Waller; Waller noticed it and hoped no one else did.

"I believe, and the official position of the FBI is that Peter Marvin was stung first earlier in the day by the same bee which later stung the defendant Kelly Visque. She swatted the bee and believed she killed it but in fact did not, as she could have been stung anywhere and not necessarily at the building where the bodies were found. The bee either died on its own or was killed by a third person."

"What makes you so sure that's how it happened?"

"Mr. Marvin does not admit to having swatted the bee after being stung while Miss Visque does. It is more likely the bee was able to sting again without having been swatted at all." Aaron had his own version of the sequence but decided to disclose it later in the trial.

"We all saw the video at the airport. I saw a blonde woman with sunglasses in a car. How does that add up to Kelly Visque?"

"She was in the car that had been arranged to pick up Juan Pillar. His schedule for returning from his trip was public information. Miss Visque could have easily overpowered the driver and deposited him in the trunk."

"Were there fingerprints in the car?"

"No. That means nothing. She could have been wearing gloves."

"Is there any more to your explanation?"

"No."

"Then we are right back at the beginning of our conversation when we talked about circumstantial evidence, which is what the tape is. Nothing further." Ross got out of his seat.

"My client, Lorraine Corvino, is charged with conspiracy to commit murder. Does the FBI have any evidence of that?"

"We can offer eyewitness accounts of her and Kelly Visque together; everyone knows Corvino worked at the Supreme Court. She would have had access to the judge's schedule." Billet stopped short of mentioning the alleged affair; he recognized that would come in a follow-up question.

"What motive would she have for getting involved with the double murder?" Billet took a sip of water.

"She was rumored to be sleeping with him and be incredibly jealous. You do the math."

"That does not mean she was involved."

"How else would Visque have known when to kidnap the judge?"

"She could have learned the information from their conversations. Try that scenario on for size. No further questions."

5pm

Todd Russell had just arrived in New York. The next two weeks were supposedly a vacation, during which time he and Vincent Weimitz would be meeting as many people as possible. Their itinerary, organized by Joe Berry, had them visiting all the New England states, and their tour would end in Portland Maine. They were spending tonight in Manhattan and heading out to the Hamptons tomorrow, a fancy area at the end of Long Island. They would spend a few days there and then take a ferry across to Connecticut. They would go to Yale University in New Haven where they would meet with some of the top technology professors there. Next, they would travel on to Boston and Cambridge for Weimitz to lead a symposium at MIT, Caltech's rival. After that it was on to Cape Cod, a resort area south of Boston where they would stay in Provincetown, a community of artists. They would end their trip in the states of New Hampshire, Vermont, and Maine, hopefully having shaken enough hands to make an impact and usurp that region away from Layton and Morris.

8pm, FBI building, Quantico, VA

Ed Billet was finishing up some paperwork when he saw an email pop up from Director Grey. He opened it to reveal Grey was congratulating him on a good job testifying. He managed to get inside the courtroom; Grey was so good that Billet had not even seen him. He wondered if the judge even knew Grey had been there.

10am, Thursday, July 5th, Dearborn, Michigan

Hayao and Alex were reviewing which parts of the country they should tour as part of their campaign in the fall. They would first head out west to California. Hayao spoke to Louis Grenadine and told him in no uncertain terms he must put more of an effort into promoting Hayao. His other problem spots were the South, where the people were more traditional in their political views, and the Northeast, where the people favored Layton because of the connections Steven Morris held in New York and the surrounding states. They had come back with a poor showing in Alaska, but the population there was small enough that campaigning there was not so critical. They planned one sweep through the areas they mentioned in September. In October they were going to travel the entire continental U.S. to visit all the areas they missed thus far in the campaign and to go back to the regions where their showing needed assistance. With regard to the issues Americans were most concerned about, Hayao knew he was behind in education; his strategy there would be to point to all the recent grads Moritu hired each year and the scholarships they gave to support those children just entering college. They were also going to produce more commercials to highlight their strengths which would start to air in September. They told Natsu the Israelis were on board for a manufacturing plant but India was not due to their arrangement with Todd Russell. Natsu would get the ball rolling right away, and Hayao had left the door open with President Sarin if they reconsidered.

10am, Sunday, July 8th, the Perry O'Malley show
"Good morning my fellow Americans. It's a steamer out there today! Speaking of heat, we have the man at the center of the hottest happening right now, judge Clinton Alphonso who is presiding over the trial of Kelly Visque and Lorraine Corvino, accused of killing the Bernards and Juan Pillar and his driver." An image appeared with Alphonso's face on it. "Welcome judge."
"Thank you, Perry."
"How is the trial going so far?"
"As you well know, protecting the integrity of the courtroom is a priority for me and my staff and myself have gone to great lengths to preserve that."
"I understand practically everyone involved with the trial is residing in a hotel and arrangements are being made for them to stay at a resort when you go on vacation. Who is paying for all this?"
"The funds are all coming from the private sector; Joe taxpayer will not be on the hook for any of this."
"What can you say about what has gone on in the courtroom?"
"I can say the trial is moving along expeditiously and I have every confidence justice will be served."
"Are you planning to write a book about these proceedings once it is over?"
"I cannot predict the future, Perry. I am concentrating on the task in front of me, which is ensuring my court runs smoothly."
"How has it been living in quarantine?"

"Oh, it's not so bad. I went to great lengths to provide as many amenities as possible, and for those who enjoy dining out, it has been paradise!"

"Do you see the jurors becoming impatient at all, anxious to return to their families?"

"I am sure they are feeling that way, but I am confident they will conduct themselves professionally and not rush through their deliberations when the time comes by remembering how important our justice system is."

"Thank you judge."

"My pleasure Perry. God bless the United States."

9am, Monday, July 9th, Washington DC

The prosecution was going to present its last expert witness today before they started with their character witnesses. Willy Detrop would be taking the stand, he was the beekeeper from Hawaii who had agreed to come to DC. He was not tops when it came to hygiene but Sondra Tristan managed to get him looking presentable. He was staying at their apartment and enjoyed the hot tub at the gym Sondra belonged to, after which he took a shower, probably the first one in months. "Mr. Detrop, thank you for coming all this way. How have you enjoyed your stay?"

"Very much. Sondra and Blake have been really nice."

"Excellent. Tell me about your experience as a beekeeper."

"I have been working with bumblebees for about twenty five years." Waller waited for more, but Detrop was clearly a man of few words.

"Are bumblebees known to travel long distances each day?"

"Just the opposite. They stay close to their nest."

"What about the time of day they return to the nest? When is that?"

"Usually around dusk."

"So, it would be later during the summer?"

"Yes, it's not like it's the same time all year round. Bees don't wear watches." The jury chuckled.

"To sum up, Mr. Detrop, even if a bee stung someone, it would stay in the same general vicinity?"

"Exactly."
"Thank you. Mr. Aaron will now ask you some questions."
"Hello Mr. Detrop. You know, I have always wanted to visit Hawaii."
"You should, it is beautiful and we love visitors."
"I am sure. I am confused about something. As a beekeeper, wouldn't you work with honeybees exclusively?"
"Not exclusively. I work with bumblebees as well and use them for greenhouse tomato production in my greenhouse."
"Would that involve allowing the bees to leave the enclosure you built for them?"
"No."
"Then how could you ascertain whether they travel far from their nest?"
"Over the course of 25 years, I have seen many bees escape and then return a short time later."
"How can you be certain it is the same bee?"
"We tag them all."
"What makes you positive bees behave the same way when they are in the wild?"
"Captivity does not change a bee's behavior."
"Have you observed this personally?"
"No." Looking smug, Aaron said he had no further questions.

10am, Dearborn Michigan

Hayao was meeting with Glenda Pimental, the specialist who would help him improve his communication skills and sell himself as a candidate. The first lesson would deal with how to take a question and manipulate it so that information favorable to Hayao could be included. Hayao was a businessman and accustomed to giving straight answers. Pimental told him he could draw on his experience as a businessman and having an agenda. When running a company, one has a road map of where he or she wants the company to go. Answering a question is no different. The key is to create an outline for the information you want to convey for every topic which may arise and then to bend the question to incorporate that information. "Let's try an example. Ask me a question about any topic you wish." Hayao thought for a moment.

"If you could fix one thing about the environment, what would it be?"

"There are many aspects to the environment issue. One of the most pressing is corporate responsibility. Much of the pollution that is harmful to the ozone layer is produced by corporations and many still have not taken steps to minimize the damage they cause. Moritu has always been a leader in 'green' technology and has won several awards for environment friendly practices." She paused. "You see how I brought that around to Moritu and made you look like a saint? It's all about being well informed on all the topics. Now, you try one."

Three hours later, Hayao was exhausted, but getting the hang of it. He had fielded questions from Pimental about all subjects; he knew what he needed to do; more research about each one to include information to make him look favorable. Alex said she could and would help him with that. He was looking forward to his next session in a week.

9am, Tuesday, July 10th, Washington DC

Waller was going to start with his character witnesses today. The first one would be Helen Sawyer, the librarian at the Library of Congress who had been on the bowling team with Visque and Corvino. "Hello Miss Sawyer. I appreciate you taking off from work today. Please describe your relationship with the two defendants?"

"We were teammates on the same bowling team."

"Would you say you were friends?"

"No. Kelly and Lorraine spent most of the time together and didn't mingle with the rest of us."

"Were they unfriendly towards you?"

"At times, yes."

"Why did you stay on the same team with them then?"

"They both happen to be great bowlers."

"I see. So the two of them would talk amongst themselves?"

"Yes."

"What would they discuss?"

"From the parts I overheard, they would talk about politics and the men they were dating."

"Did you know what kind of jobs they had?"

"I knew Lorraine worked at the Supreme Court building as a janitor."

"What else did she say?"

"She would brag that she was fooling around with one of the justices. None of us believed her."

"Does that include Kelly Visque?"

"No, I mean myself and my other teammates, Gwen Botch and Sophie Tingle."

"Did it seem like Visque thought it was true?"

"Absolutely."

"Nothing further." This time, Lionel Ross performed the cross examination first.

"Miss Sawyer, were you ever jealous of my client?"

"Why would I be jealous?"

"Because she was so much better than you at bowling and you thought she was running around with a Supreme Court judge."

"No, I was not," she said a little too emphatically.

"Of course not. You would never fabricate such a story to get back at her for being arrogant." Ross withdrew the question before Waller could object and said he had no more questions. Aaron only asked one question of Sawyer, whether she ever heard Kelly Visque say she believed Corvino about dating a judge, and Sawyer had to answer no.

2pm, the White House

President Harrington was in a meeting with Susan McBride, the Secretary of State. They were meeting about the next and last wave of immigration they planned. "I want this one to be from Mexico, Susan. Russell is ahead in the national polls which is threatening my plan. I developed an explanation we can sell to the media. With the construction to fix the rising sea levels, the fishing industry will need to be overhauled. Fisherman in Mexico are experts at improvising and we could offer many opportunities that would extend out from this such as more canneries and the increased need for boats, etc. Would you be the liaison on this and get in touch with President Carraval and explain we would like him to authorize emigration to the U.S. of those individuals who are experienced fisherman and can provide advice and expertise. Let's push this through as soon as possible before the three month mark is here."

"Yes, Mr. President. I will get right on it."

9am, Wednesday, July 11th, Washington, DC
This morning, when judge Alphonso entered the courtroom, he saw all the equipment that had been set up. "What's going on?" Waller explained,

"It's for our witness, your honor. She lives in California and will be testifying using video chat."

"Alright then. Bailiff?"

"Please rise." Five minutes later, Maggie Evers came through on the screen. Even though she denied sending the threatening note to Juan Pillar at Kelly Visque's request and would undoubtedly do so again, she came across as being nervous which equates to having something to hide. He could already tell she was on edge. "Miss Evers, how long have you known the defendant Kelly Visque?"

"Since we were kids."

"When was the last time you saw each other?"

"I guess about three years ago."

"What kind of relationship do the two of you have?"

"What do you mean? I just said we are old friends."

"I mean, does she boss you around, and did she when you were younger?" At this question Evers became visibly distraught. Good. Waller knew now he had her right where he wanted her.

"We were equal." Her voice was shaky when she said it.

"Come on, Miss Evers. Weren't there many times you resented her?"

"No."

"You wanted to be her friend because you thought she was cool." Maggie Evers was barely able to keep from imploding. "You still feel that way, which is why you are protecting her, isn't that right?" She couldn't contain herself any longer and started to cry.

"She never sent me a letter to mail!" Her denial was so futile that the questions which Glen Aaron planned to ask her on cross examination would have seemed moot, so he did not even bother, and the video chat, which documented Miss Evers becoming a teary mess, was finished.

5pm, Monday, July 16th, Chicago, Illinois

Todd Russell arrived back home a few hours ago after a very successful trip through the northeast and New England. He had been a big hit everywhere he went, and his emphasis on technology made him a hero at many of the places he visited such as MIT where Vincent Weimitz met with the top people there. His vacation had been reported nationally and his image reinforced as a forward thinker with the ability to lead this country into the future. He would be staying in Illinois for a while to run the state, and then he would be travelling through the South to meet the people there and spread the same message.

9am, Wednesday, July18th, Washington, DC

This morning, Waller would be calling his final witness, Sondra Tristan. Over the past week he had called several witnesses who testified about various aspects of Kelly Visque's and Lorraine Corvino's lives and admitted one final piece of evidence; each one representing another nail in the coffins of both defendants, and today he was going to be sealing those coffins shut. The witnesses who testified in the last few days were: Margo, Visque's childhood friend who said Visque had always been against different people coming into this country and always possessed an aggressive streak, and Ryan, the manager of the bar Visque and Corvino would visit frequently after bowling and were seen being friendly and having a good time laughing together. Waller also admitted his last piece of evidence at this time, which was the bowling picture of the team showing Visque and Corvino standing next to each other looking happy. The next two character witnesses Waller called included Angelo Forte, the old customer of Visque at Star

Fitness who reported how unprofessionally he had been treated by her and how arrogant and militant she had been, and Terry Strauss, the former member of American Pride who reported how gung ho Visque acted at the meetings and how she was so patriotic she would resort to anything to protect the ideals in which she trusted. The defense attorneys tried unsuccessfully to discredit these witnesses, and only partially succeeded with Margo by having her describe what a loyal friend Visque had been. Waller believed his case was very strong and couldn't imagine Aaron and Ross being able to convince the jury otherwise. Sondra Tristan had taken the stand and was waiting. "Hello, Miss Tristan. How are you today?"

"I am fine."

"I can't imagine how difficult this must be for you." She nodded silently. "I will try to keep this brief. Defendant number 1, Kelly Visque, is on trial for murder and terrorism, and defendant number 2, Lorraine Corvino, is on trial for conspiracy to commit murder. The victims are your parents. Let's talk about Miss Corvino first. There has been testimony during the trial that she carried on an affair with your father. While that is hard for you to hear, do you believe it is true?" Tristan took a sip of water.

"I do. I loved my father dearly, but I regretfully admit he had an eye for the ladies. Miss Corvino was working in his building and I am sure their paths crossed many times. One thing led to another and they developed a relationship."

"Do you imagine your father led her to believe he would leave your mother and stay with her?"

"He probably insinuated that as things progressed."

"Is it possible Miss Corvino might have misinterpreted what he meant?"

"Yes. From what I understand, she could be jealous and possessive."

"Now, let's turn to Kelly Visque. Do you ever remember your father mentioning her?"

"No."

"Were you close with your father?"

"Absolutely."

"Did you talk about politics and current events?"

"All the time."

"What about the case involving the ability of foreign born people to run for President?"

"Yes, we discussed that extensively."

"What was his position?"

"My father was a conservative and felt the Constitution should be upheld."

"What do you feel about that?"

"I think times change and our society needs to adjust to what is happening. Our political system needed an overhaul and that change was necessary."

"Did he understand how you felt?"

"Absolutely."

"In your opinion, was he coming around to your point of view?"

"Yes."

"Mrs. Tristan, how do you suspect your father would have ruled on the case of President Michael Harrington vs. the United States?"

"I honestly believe he would have ruled in favor of the plaintiff."

There was a murmur in the courtroom and the judge banged his gavel. Waller continued once things had quieted down.

"Thank you Miss Tristan. I have nothing further."

"Hello Miss Tristan", said Aaron as he stood up. "I understand you are working with the prosecution on this case."

"That's correct."

"What exactly are you doing?"

"Gathering information for the Attorney General."

"Was your father a man who was easily intimidated?"

"No."

"Did he fold under pressure?"

"No."

"Was he honest?"

"Yes. He prided himself on that when it came to his duties as a Supreme Court justice."

"At the time of his death, how do you believe your father would have ruled on the issue?"

"At that point he would have ruled against it."

"I see. You just testified your father was honest about his responsibilities as a judge, is that correct?"

"Yes."

"After hearing all the testimony about Kelly Visque, would you agree she was vehemently opposed to the measure?"

"I would."

"Whomever kidnapped you father, why do you think they did?"

"To prevent this proposed change to the Constitution."

"Do you suppose that person asked your father how he would rule?"

"Yes."

"Remember, you are under oath. Being the honest person he was, what do you suppose he said?"

"He probably told the truth, that he would rule against it."

"If he had, knowing what you do about Miss Visque, would you expect her to have released your parents?"

"I suppose that's possible." Suppressing a grin, Aaron turned Tristan over to Ross.

"Mrs. Tristan, I am truly sorry for your loss. Do you need a moment?" She took a sip of water again and said she was ready to continue. "Ok. You speculated here that your father was having an affair with Miss Corvino, correct?"

"Yes."

"As we all just heard, your father was an honest man."

"Also true."

"If those two things are right, what makes you certain he was not telling her the truth about his intentions?"

"He probably conveyed his message in a way to make it seem he would eventually be with her exclusively."

"The same way he led you to believe he would change his mind about foreigners running for President?" Sondra turned beet red at this remark, and Ross concluded this was the perfect place to end his questioning, leaving that image of her in the jurors' minds. Waller gave her a minute to compose, and once she had returned to the aisle behind where he was sitting, he stood up. "The prosecution rests, your honor."

"Thank you, Mr. Waller. We will resume on Monday, July 23rd, at which time the defense of Kelly Visque will call their first witness. We are adjourned."

CHAPTER 16

9am, Monday, July 23rd, Washington DC
The defense was going to present their case now. The two attorneys had decided to present Kelly Visque's defense first. Tomorrow, when Malcolm Kelsey, the psychologist who has examined both women, would be on the stand, Aaron would go first followed by Ross. They had both met with their clients last night and had reassured them that even though the prosecution had made some valid points, several of the witnesses they presented had been discredited and ended up looking unsure of themselves, specifically Wentworth, Cardillo and Sondra Tristan. They would continue to chip away at the theory about the crimes proposed by Waller to create reasonable doubt. The lawyers told both women that all it takes is one juror to disagree for a hung jury. Their jury consultant felt optimistic so far; that was the one exception judge Alphonso had made, to allow jury consultants in the courtroom even though they were not technically essential to the process. Aaron's first witness was Otto Lampf, the DNA guru from Albuquerque New Mexico. Aaron hoped he had checked his ego at the door. "Good morning, Mr. Lampf. Thanks for coming all this way."

"You're welcome."

"What is your scientific background?"

"I have worked in labs all over the country for the past ten years for some top people. A while back I decided that I didn't want to toil in someone else's vineyard so I started my own in New Mexico."

"How is that working out for you?"

"So far so good."

"What area of science is your specialty?"

"Chemistry; lately I have become involved in forensics."

"Who are some of your customers?"

"I do work for several police departments in the area. Their projects keep me quite busy."

"Have you dealt with DNA before?"

"All the time."

"Where do you typically extract it from?"

"From such places as clothing, fingernails, and furniture. I deal with crime scenes, and those three things are common sources for DNA."

"Have you ever obtained DNA from animals?"

"Twice."

"When were those times?"

"I was involved in one case about a year ago where the perpetrator had broken into a house and was bitten by a dog, so I took DNA from the dog which matched that of the intruder."

"And the other time?"

"For this case, when I drew it from a bee."

"Do you consider yourself to be a thorough technician?"

"Absolutely. That is something I pride myself on."

"Why did you leave the job you held before you set up shop in Albuquerque?"

"The proprietor of the lab conducted things in a way with which I did not agree."

"What was your objective for this case?"

"To determine whether the position of multiple sets of DNA inside a bee's stinger was based on the chronology of when the people were stung."

"How did you go about gathering data?"

"I created an environment where both my assistant and I were stung by a bee at different times to see how the DNA was arranged."

"Your assistant is certainly committed and loyal to agree to be stung repeatedly for her job." Lampf barely cracked a smile; Aaron was glad he didn't work for him. "How many sets of data did you use?"

"Seven."

"Were the results the same each time?"

"Yes."

"What were the results?"

"The DNA from the person stung later in the day was always the one closer to the top of the stinger." It was time for the defense's first piece of evidence.

"The defense would like to admit exhibit A, the official report from the FBI about the DNA contained inside the bee." Aaron gave a copy to the judge and read from a second copy. "The official results show that there are two sets of DNA inside the bee's stinger. The one at the bottom belongs to a Miss Kelly Visque and the one at the top is from a man named Mr. Peter Marvin." Aaron turned back to Lampf. "Mr. Lampf, if Mr. Marvin's DNA was closer to the top of the stinger as the FBI is asserting, please tell the court what that means?"

"It means he was stung later in the day."

"Thank you, nothing further." Waller got up and adopted a swagger that made him look like he was about to announce that he had found a cure for cancer.

"Mr. Lampf, you have done a fine job of explaining why your research is unassailable."

"Thank you."

"Who was your previous employer?"

"I worked for a chemist known all over the world."

"Sounds like quite an opportunity. Why did you leave?"

"As I said earlier, we approached science differently."

"I understand you possess quite a reputation in the scientific community as being a rebel who has argued with several of your old co-workers."

"I believe that there is a right way to conduct a lab."

"Is your way the only way?"

"Well, everyone thinks they know best."

"So, you are more knowledgeable about science than the people you have worked with, some of whom are leaders in their fields, is that right?"

"Many of them were old fashioned." Waller noticed Lampf begin to crack.

"Isn't it more accurate to say that you are a troublemaker who can't get along with others and the only environment you could exist in is one where you are working solo?"

"No, that is not true!" Lampf proclaimed, his voice rising.

"You are not a scientist, you are a radical with no foundation in reality! The experiments you conducted with the bees were totally bogus. Your results cannot be relied upon!"

"Fuck you! I am better than you will ever be!" Judge Alphonso banged his gavel.

"Bailiff! Remove this fouled mouthed hooligan from my courtroom immediately!" Once Lampf was forcefully escorted through the doors, Alphonso gave everyone a moment to calm down. "Alright, everyone. Why don't we adjourn and resume tomorrow when everyone has had a chance to regroup."

11am, Eric Layton's office

Layton's staff member Robert was going to explain his plan for a project which would reinforce Layton's commitment to job creation nationwide, just as he had done in Colorado. "Gentlemen, I am sure you have heard that President Harrington is planning to work with the Mexican government to allow their citizens with backgrounds and experience in the fishing industry to emigrate to the U.S. to help our country make the transition to the new ways that fishing will have to be done with the rising sea levels and the new pattern the ocean will take in those areas where the water will be rerouted out to sea. What I propose is that we introduce legislation for the government to fund training and subsidize those businesses that already are involved in the fishing industry to allow them to make any necessary changes to their businesses. For example, the companies that make boats may now need to modify the types of boats that they build, and this endowment from the government will allow them to perform research and development as well as hire new employees. This project will show that we are looking out for our fellow Americans, that we are forward thinkers, and that we are willing to put our political differences aside with the President and work with him even though he endorsed Hayao."

"I like it. It will also show that we care about the environment as the fishing business is one that has been overhauled to make it more ecologically friendly. Good work, Robert." Layton turned to Morris. "What is your opinion, Steve?"

"I agree. It will make us look good on several fronts."

"Great. I am glad we are on the same page. The next step is to draft a bill. Robert, do you want to take a crack at it?"

"Sure. I could have it on your desk in a week."

"Perfect. After you email it to me and I review it, I will send it on to Congress. Thank you both."

9am, Tuesday, July 24th, Washington DC
Dr. Malcolm Kelsey was ready to testify. He had been thorough in his evaluations of both Visque and Corvino and expected to be above reproach. This time, Ross would conduct the direct examination first. "Good morning doctor."

"Good morning."

"While I reviewed your background, I noticed you developed a unique approach to analyzing your patients. Could you elaborate about that?"

"I believe that the patient has valuable input about their diagnosis and their opinion should be taken into account."

"How does this differ from other psychologists?"

"Most psychologists conduct an analysis of their patients in the form of an interview. They ask questions designed to provide them with an opinion about the person and allow them to reach a conclusion about their diagnosis and how they should be classified. That method does not include the patient's opinion about their own situation and what would be best for themselves."

"What do you think of this approach?"

"I think it excludes vital information. People know themselves best; unless a person is clinically insane, they are the best source to determine the issues they are facing and what steps should be taken to assist them to achieving progress."

"Wouldn't that eliminate the need for trained professionals?"

"Absolutely not. Experts are still necessary to guide the patient toward getting the appropriate help."

"What about if the person you are analyzing is not being honest, trying to fool you in what they believe is their own best interest or to get away with something?"

"Any halfway decent therapist would be able to see right through that."

"What was your impression of my client, Lorraine Corvino?"

"She strikes me as being a very passionate person who gives whatever she is involved in her all."

"Are you convinced she was being truthful when you met with her?"

"Yes, I am."

"Would you classify her as jealous?"

"No more than the average person."

"What about obsessive?"

"Again, not outside the normal range."

"Do you think she would ever be capable of plotting a murder?"

"No. She is a moral person, and her moral compass would prevent her from engaging in such an action."

"Thank you, doctor. Nothing further." Aaron stood up to begin his line of questioning. The groundwork had been set about Kelsey's philosophy about the patient's involvement so there was no need to rehash that.

"Dr. Kelsey, have you ever worked with people who had been accused of committing acts of extreme patriotism?"

"I have."

"What are the common bonds?"

"The biggest common denominator is the lack of a strong authority figure when they are young. Without this they are easy prey for undesirable influences who can make whatever ideology they are a proponent of seem attractive."

"What else?"

"A temper so strong that it prevents the people in question from thinking rationally."

"Did you see these traits in Kelly Visque when you examined her?"

"No. As we heard during prior testimony, Miss Visque had two very authoritative role models in her mom and dad. They led her through her childhood with strict rules and a disciplined upbringing."

"What about a strong temper?"

"Yes, it's true that Miss Visque has a temper, but it is not nearly as volatile as when she was younger and she has been able to keep it in check as she has matured."

"What about the fact that she had been a member of American Pride?"

"She managed to move past their beliefs and put that part of her life behind her." Aaron felt satisfied that he had shown his client was not a zealot who would protect the U.S. at any cost. He looked at Waller.

"Your witness."

"Would you say that your approach is in the mainstream Dr. Kelsey?" Kelsey took a minute to respond.

"I am in the minority. My methods are considered unorthodox."

"Isn't it true you have been called a radical by many publications?"

"All new ideas are met with suspicion and mistrust at first."

"Tell me, how can you justify allowing someone to evaluate their own psychological case when you, as a professional, are involved? Wouldn't that be akin to allowing a criminal to decide whether he or she should be eligible for parole?"

"We are not talking about patients who typically have been charged with crimes."

"In this instance we are, and you are placing her in the same group as the people you have seen on which you are basing your theory, that of letting them determine their own fate." Waller walked over to Visque and pointed at the jury box.

"Why don't you just go sit over there? Nothing further, your honor."

9am, Wednesday, July 25th

Today was Kelly Visque's big day; she would take the stand. She had hardly slept last night. Glen Aaron had reassured her that she would do fine but she couldn't wait to put this behind her. Initially Visque had resisted testifying, but her attorney had persuaded her to do so as it would show she had nothing to hide. Ross had done the same with Corvino. She was sworn in and Aaron smiled at her, trying to make her feel more at ease. "Miss Visque, why are you here today?"

"I have been accused of four counts of murder and one count of terrorism."

"Are you innocent of what you are on trial for?"

"Absolutely." Aaron pointed at Quinn Waller, returning the favor from when he pointed at Visque yesterday.

"Attorney General Waller has been leading the government's charge against you and has offered evidence and witnesses in support of their claim that you committed these heinous acts. Let's start with the gun." Aaron had wanted to refute this first because no direct link existed from the gun to her unlike the bee. "Have you ever shot a firearm before?"

"Yes."

"How many times?"

"I used to shoot often when I was growing up."

"Whom did you shoot with?"

"My parents. We would go to a rifle range a few times a month."

"Have you ever owned a gun of your own?"

"Never."

"Why not?"

"Guns have never been a hobby of mine."

"Were they important to you mom and dad?"

"They both were very comfortable with guns, if that's what you mean."

"Why did they have such a comfort level?"

"They both used them as part of their professions."

"What were their professions?"

"My mom was in the Army and my dad was a policeman."

"What was it like growing up?" Aaron would use these questions to transition into the next topic.

"I am an only child; my parents were quite conservative and very strict."

"How did they feel about the changes that American society has seen during their lifetimes?"

"They believed that the founding fathers had a good handle on how things should be even today."

509

"So they were against many of the new policies, including having a foreigner being able to run for President?"
"That's correct."
"Did your parents ever advocate the use of violence to achieve goals?"
"Only if was officially sanctioned by the government, or in self-defense."
"Did they want you to become a police officer or join the military?"
"Yes. They believe both to be both noble and critical careers."
"Why didn't you?"
"As a teenager I developed an interest in weightlifting and bodybuilding and decided to pursue that instead."
"Were they disappointed?"
"Yes."
"How did they feel when you belonged to American Pride?"
"They wouldn't speak to me during that time, and we had no contact until I told them I had cut all ties."
"I am confused, didn't they agree with the ideas that American Pride stands for?"
"Not at all. American Pride are extremists who preach that America is only for the white people. My parents are not against people from other countries emigrating here, they just believe that the Constitution should be preserved."
"What made you leave American Pride?"
"I realized that they were spreading a message of hate and intolerance."
"Miss Visque, you have been portrayed as a zealot who would do anything for her country. What is your response for that?"
"I do love my country. However, I will not operate outside the law, the very law that my parents and our ancestors worked hard to create and maintain since our country was founded."
"What about your infamous short temper?"
"That's true. As I have gotten older, however, I am able to keep it in check."

"The prosecution has also produced witnesses who have met with you and said under oath that you possess 'a criminal's mentality', whatever that means. Do you have a predisposition to crime?"

"Because I grew up in a household with people sworn to uphold our freedoms and trained in the prevention of crime? As a result I learned what not to do in order to break the law? That's ridiculous. My parents passed on their good values to me."

"Please describe your relationship with Lorraine Corvino."

"Lorraine and I are friends and are on the same bowling team."

"How did you meet?"

"We both joined the league around the same time, ended up on the same team, and found that we really hit it off."

"Did you realize that she worked at the Supreme Court?"

"Yes, of course."

"How do you feel about the change to the Constitution?"

"I was opposed to it."

"Are you familiar with the various justices serving on the Supreme Court when the Bernards were killed?"

"Probably not as much as I should have been."

"What about Justice Bernard?"

"I only knew who he was."

"Did Lorraine Corvino ever talk about him?"

"Not exclusively."

"Did you ever get the feeling that she was having an affair with him?"

"No. She never said anything remotely like that."

"How do you believe justice Bernard would have ruled?"

"I don't know. The media portrayed him as pretty traditional in his opinions over the years. On the other hand, his daughter seemed to wield considerable influence over him. I suspect he would have ruled in favor of it." She knew she was providing a possible motive against herself, but she and Aaron felt it was more important to be honest.

"Did you ever try to obtain information from Miss Corvino either in a sneaky way or out in the open regarding justice Bernard's schedule?"

"Never. She wouldn't have had that kind of information anyway."

"One of the pieces of evidence presented was a note sent to Juan Pillar mailed from California. Have you ever been to California Miss Visque?"
"Yes, a few years ago."
"Do you know anyone there?"
"Yes, a friend named Maggie Evers."
"Did you send her the note to be mailed to Juan Pillar?"
"Absolutely not."
"Juan Pillar was abducted from the airport and then killed. While anyone could have known his schedule as it was reported in the news, how do you explain the picture of the blond woman at the airport waiting in the car scheduled to pick Juan Pillar up?"
"I don't know. I wasn't involved in any way. I could not hazard a guess as to what that was about." Aaron was now ready to ask about the bee, the one piece of direct evidence available.
"Miss Visque, the bodies of the Bernards were found right in front of the Supreme Court building. There was a dead bee found at the crime scene as well which contained your DNA inside the bee. Do you remember being stung that day?"
"I do. It was sometime in the afternoon, if I remember correctly."
"Did you kill the bee?"
"I swatted it and thought I had killed it."
"What did you do when you were done in DC for the day?"
"I went home and spent the evening resting alone."
"Thank you Miss Visque. I have no further questions." Aaron believed he had covered everything and had not left anything for Waller to use to poke holes in her testimony. Visque's testimony had been quite long so the judge granted a ten minute break. Visque stood up, stretched, and had a drink of water. She mentally prepared herself for the cross examination. Waller was now ready to begin. He started his questioning from his table.
"Would you ever like to live in a world without rules, Miss Visque?" She looked puzzled, but answered.
"I don't think so. There would be chaos everywhere."
"I believe in rules as well. Rules are all around us. Take this courtroom for example. There is a certain etiquette that I must abide by, even if I was to treat you as hostile. The judge would

reign me in if I went too far. Countries at war follow rules as well. Human nature necessitates this, wouldn't you say?"
"I would."
"Who should decide on the rules we follow?"
"Whoever is in charge of the group to which the rules apply." Everyone in the courtroom began to look perplexed.
"What should happen to those who break the rules?"
"I suppose the punishment received should fit the transgression that was committed."
"What do you think of the Constitution?"
"It is a document that was written by people with great foresight."
"Should the tenets it contains still be upheld today?"
"I believe they should."
"So, in your eyes President Harrington was breaking the rules, and the Supreme Court planned to legally allow that to happen. Is that how you see it?"
"No. They were using legal channels to change the rules, not break them."
"That's just semantics. According to you, the Constitution is the final authority and anything that goes against it is a violation. Did President Harrington break the rules?"
"No."
"Was he trying to change something you viewed as unassailable?"
"Objection. That question has been asked and answered. Mr. Waller is badgering the witness."
"Sustained."
"Request permission to treat this witness as hostile."
"Granted."
"You snapped. You couldn't sit by and watch as a basic premise this country was founded on was tossed away. What did you ask of Lorraine Corvino?"
"Nothing."
"You asked her pointed questions about her lover, Justice Bernard, isn't that right?"
"No! They were not lovers!"

"Was she jealous and devious enough to join this deadly plot or simply an unwitting accomplice?"

"Neither of us were involved!" Her voice was rising. Aaron tried to catch her eye to motion at her to calm down but she did not look in his direction.

"Come on, Miss Visque, admit it! You couldn't stand to see this country, the one that your mother fought for and your father spent his career protecting, be diluted more than it already has been!"

"I had nothing to do with it! My family is above reproach!" She was shouting now.

"What would you know about it anyway! I know about you! You and your family have no honor!" Waller had won and he knew it. He had gotten her to lose her temper.

"Is this the same reaction you had when you first heard about President Harrington bringing this case before the Supreme Court? I guess your temper is not so in check as you would have us believe. No further questions." Aaron felt sick inside; his client had just done major damage to her own case. The judge ended the proceedings for the day and reminded everyone that he was going on vacation until August 20th and that everyone would be taken to a resort. On the bright side, Aaron had a few weeks to plan out his damage control and hope that the jurors wouldn't remember what a bad showing Visque had made.

7pm, Boston Commons

Uncle George was meeting with Kangaroo at the usual place. He wanted to discuss the President's new arrangement with Mexico. "I bet this will be his last wave of immigration. Harrington has made it look like many different countries have been represented and at the same time helped fortify Hayao's position. Sometime in the near future he will introduce the legislation I have been predicting, you wait and see." Kangaroo agreed; Uncle George seemed to be able to see into the future when it came to the moves of politicians.

"Switching gears, what is your opinion about the trial of the Bernards and Pillar?"

"I think the right people in custody. By the way, have you heard any more chatter coming from American Pride about having Waller killed?"

"Not a thing", replied Kangaroo. "The President must have really put the fear of God in Albert Cross. I don't think we will be hearing too much from them in the near future."

"What's next?"

"Let's continue to focus on any undue influence about the campaign. I can see Russell picking up steam which may turn into a problem for the powers that be."

9am, Dearborn, Michigan

Hayao was having his fifth and final session with Glenda Pimental, the debate specialist. Today's topic was how to sell yourself. Hayao was no stranger to this skill set and many of the traits that made him a successful businessman applied here too. She was really good. The other lessons she had gone over with him were: 1. How to speak without 'uh' and other utterances, 2. Making good eye contact, and 3. Body language. Each one was helpful and truly had made him a better speaker. He had also spent time getting more familiar with the issues. "When someone asks you a question, Hayao, try to determine what their angle is. That way you can tailor your answer to what they want to hear. Speak with confidence. Those are two things that will help you sell yourself. Let's try a practice question." Pimental adopted a forceful, almost belligerent pose as she asked the question. "What makes you think you are qualified to be President?" Hayao answered, saying that his tenure as the head of U.S. operations for Moritu and the decision maker prepared him for running the country. When he finished, Pimental critiqued his response. "I was looking for some evidence that you will be a strong leader. Did you notice my demeanor while I was asking? I was challenging you and being almost combative. When people ask a question, they usually like to see the responder answer in a manner that is similar to the one they are demonstrating. If I am calm, I want you to be calm. If the person asking the question is aggressive, then you should be too. That's not to say that you should be out of control.

Simply put a little of whatever they are giving you back into your answer."

"Ok, Glenda. Let's try a few more."

3pm, Washington, DC, Congress

Robert, Eric Layton's staffer, had drafted the bill about the federal funding for the fishing industry and related businesses. Layton had gone over it and he thought it was really comprehensive. They were asking for 3 billion dollars for training and subsidies so that existing businesses could expand. Many of the people on the floor were staunch supporters of President Harrington, and since this legislation was closely tied in with his agenda to fix the rising sea levels, Layton couldn't see his bill not passing a vote. He had decided to wait outside, choosing to vote by proxy. He didn't want to hear the negative things some people might be saying about him or his proposal. An hour and a half went by. He expected the discussion to take a long time; he was asking for a lot of money. Finally, about 5pm, Morris came out and gave him the thumbs up sign. "It passed with a 97% approval. It was a definite victory, and now we can point to our success regarding trying to bolster the economy during the campaign."

"Excellent. Robert came through. I am expecting him to take on more and more in our administration as time goes on. What's next on our agenda?"

"I think we have to tackle immigration. We had a poor showing there."

"We are at an inherent disadvantage because we do not have a foreign born person on our ticket. Our work with the fishing project will help us on the immigration issue since it goes hand in hand with workers from Mexico. We are covering two issues at once. The next step is for us to tour the country once the summer is over and to prepare for the debates." Layton paused. "Tonight I think we should take Robert out for dinner."

10am, Saturday, August 11th, Chicago

Todd Russell was getting ready for his second campaign trip. This time he would be travelling through the South to the states between and including Georgia to Texas. Weimitz was unavailable this time so he would be going with just Joe Berry. Joe had made quite a few campaign stops this time, and they would be focusing not so much on technology but other issues that were important to voters. They had a couple of stops at college campuses, which they hoped would lead to the students there talking about how much they liked what Russell stood for to their families and word would snowball from there. He was planning on stressing how his policies would create jobs and how strongly he believed in education. Russell's goal was to complete this trip having gained five percentage points in the area of the country.

9am, Monday, August 20th, Washington, DC
Judge Alphonso's vacation was over, and everyone except for him thought it wasn't a moment too soon. The resort was beautiful, no doubt about that, and they were treated well, but the jurors as well as the lawyers wanted to get back to the task at hand so they could all get back to their lives. When the judge bid everyone good morning, as a result of his energetic demeanor which seemed a little condescending, no one answered back. "Good morning!" he boomed. This time everyone responded half-heartedly. "Mr. Aaron, are you ready to call your next witness?" Lionel Ross stood up.

"The next witness is mine. The defense calls Lorraine Corvino." She walked up to the witness stand calmly and with confidence. "Miss Corvino, let's recap for the jury the charge against you. You are on trial for conspiracy to commit murder. What do you think that means?"

"That I helped plan the execution of the victims."

"Exactly right. By victims you mean the Bernards, right? You are not on trial for the killings of Juan Pillar and his driver."

"I understand."

"Why do you suppose you are being charged with these crimes?"

"Because I worked at the Supreme Court building."

"Were you questioned at the beginning of the investigation?"

"I was."

"Do you believe you were a suspect?"

"Maybe for a short while."

"Why do you suppose you were not considered to be a suspect for very long?"

"There was no direct physical evidence against me."

"Did you know the other defendant, Kelly Visque, before she was arrested?"

"I did. We bowled on the same team."

"Would you say you are close?"

"Yes. She is a good friend."

"Did you ever discuss your work at the Supreme Court or the people that you came into contact with?"

"Yes. She was curious about the goings on and whether I ever got to see a sneak peek at anything behind the scenes."

"Did her interest seem unusual or like she had an ulterior motive?"

"Not at all."

"You know her well. Would you say she is capable of murder?"

"No. She can become agitated at times but she is a moral, just person."

"How would you explain the evidence that was presented here during the trial?"

"Coincidences and circumstantial."

"What about the airport video?"

"That seems fishy to me. Kelly, I mean Miss Visque, has an alibi for that day and time anyway."

"I know, she was home which was verified by her neighbors."

"Miss Corvino, it's been alleged that you were having an affair with Justice Bernard. Is that true?"

"Yes." There were a few gasps from around the courtroom.

"How long had you been engaging in this activity?"

"About two years."

"What were your expectations?"

"Initially, I believed him when he would tell me he planned to leave his wife for me. I kept waiting and waiting. He never did. I came to realize that he had no intention of doing so."

"Did you become jealous?"

"Yes, at first."

"What changed?"

"I grew to like the arrangement. There were no strings attached and I could still see other people."

"Miss Corvino, did you participate in any plot to kidnap and kill Justice Bernard or Mrs. Bernard?"

"No, I did not."

"Thank you, nothing further." Waller was ready.

"How long have you been a custodian?"

"About 15 years."

"If you could switch to a different job, would you?"

"Objection! The Attorney General is trying to bait my client into losing her temper by insulting her."

"I am trying to make a point, your honor, not patronize anybody."

"Overruled. The witness may answer." Ross quietly gestured to her to keep her cool.

"The work can be tedious at times, but I work with decent people."

"But if someone came along and offered you a chance to train for a different position, would you take it?"

"Probably."

"I wonder if that is how you saw Justice Bernard. Your meal ticket. Your chance for upward mobility."

"After the initial period when I thought we had a real relationship ours devolved into a strictly physical one."

"You expect me and everyone else here to believe that you didn't want anything from Justice Bernard, one of the most powerful men in the country in return for some hot sex?" Corvino turned red but recovered quickly.

"Not everyone has your twisted psyche, sir."

"Right. You were physically attracted to a man twice your age. What has your relationship been with Kelly Visque since she was arrested?"

"The same as it always was."

"Really? How many times did you visit her before you were arrested yourself?"

"I don't know, a few."

"Try once. Sounds more like you coerced and used her to do your dirty work. I am finished with this witness."

12pm, the Oval office
President Harrington was online at one of the most popular news websites and the top story was Todd Russell's progress. He was making great strides in the South and was now the frontrunner across the country. There was a picture of him shaking hands and smiling. His itinerary down there had been brilliant. He had gone to those places that were the most liberal and ingratiated himself with the people there, knowing that they would spread the message of how terrific and genuine he was. He spoke about technology but only in general terms as Weimitz was not there. He also seemed to be getting the support of the citizens from India who appreciated what he had done while he was there about trying to help modernize the country. The President thought for a moment. If he didn't do something Russell would ride his momentum right to the White House. Harrington knew what he had to do. Tonight he would call the person who could help him make sure that his candidate had a clear path to victory.

2pm, Chicago, Illinois
Hayao believed it to have been a productive summer. He was on his way to becoming a masterful politician and had picked up support in several foreign countries as well as out West where he had challenged Louis Grenadine to do a better job. Today he would be studying interviewing techniques with Glenda Pimental again. The other candidates had done some campaigning over the last few months but Hayao had believed that not to be worth the time and instead would hit the campaign trail in September once everyone's routines went back to normal. His major concern right now was Todd Russell, who had hit his stride with some of the moves he had made recently. He had beat Hayao to the punch in India, and having such a strong foundation in technology was a godsend to him. The fact that Vincent Weimitz was from abroad helped as well. Russell was way ahead in the polls right now but Hayao had every confidence that he could overcome the deficit he faced.

4pm, The Oval office
President Harrington was ready to make the call now. He used his off the grid cell phone. Even though Treetop knew who was calling him he said hello instead of his customary 'yeah'. "Hi. I found a job for you. Have you been following the Presidential campaigns?" Treetop replied that he had. "Good." Treetop listened as Harrington explained to him what he was to do.

6pm, Washington DC
Aaron and Ross were meeting with their clients together to give them an update about how they thought the trial was proceeding so far. The fact that Waller had been able to get a rise out of Kelly Visque had not been good, but overall the jury consultant they had hired believed things to be pretty even as the defense had been able to discredit several of the prosecution's expert witnesses. The remainder of the witnesses they were going to present were character witnesses except for one, the former FBI profiler Lucy Roach. "How much weight will the jury give to their testimonies?" asked Visque, referring to her and Corvino's friends that would testify on both of their behalf.
  "Not as much as to the expert witnesses."
  "How do you think we have done in that regard?" asked Corvino.
  "Both sides seem pretty even. Otto Lampf came away with egg on his face, but so did their people. We were also able to poke some holes in their theories when Ed Billet was on the stand, and we portrayed Bernard as a philanderer and a liar, which can put doubt in the minds of the jurors that someone else out there had another motive for committing these crimes. That's all we need, one person with that element of reasonable doubt. I think we will get that." Ross nodded in agreement. "These are all points that we will cover in closing statements." Both the defendants felt more at ease now; it was too bad the attorneys didn't feel the same way about the prospects of the outcome, despite what they were telling Visque and Corvino.
  Waller was reviewing the progress of the case so far with his team as well. He was cautiously optimistic. He believed that even though some of the witnesses he had presented had not come

across in the best way, the evidence favored the prosecution. "The defense has not put on a very strong case regarding their experts", said Victor. "We seem to be way ahead."
"Yes, but the evidence we presented could be viewed as circumstantial. I mean, it seems pretty damning but I could also see it the other way", Waller replied. "They have a few more witnesses and then I will have the chance to put on a strong closing argument which might make all the difference." Roberta and Joy nodded in agreement.
"What are you going to talk about in your closing?" Sondra asked.
"I am going to review the facts of the case, review the evidence to the jury, and explain why our witnesses are more reliable than theirs. This is a big enough case that will compel the jury to come to a unanimous verdict. I believe that for two reasons: one, they will not want to be remembered collectively as the group who let two murderers go, and two, I am sure they know I would poll the jury and neither would anyone want to be remembered as the individual who let two murderers go." The others looked at Waller in awe.

9am, Thursday, August 23rd, Washington DC
The defense was going to call Richard, Kelly Visque's married lover only identifiable by his first name, to testify by video chat. That was the only way he would agree to do so. Aaron had called three witnesses during the previous two days; Samson, the former member of American Pride who had corroborated Malcolm Kelsey's testimony about Kelly Visque not being overly patriotic from when they were both involved, Stefan Kurtz, Visque's co-worker at Star Fitness who said that she was always courteous and very helpful to the clients she worked with, and Calvin, the manager at Star Fitness who sung Visque's praises as a model employee and the best personal trainer that he had. Customers would request her by name for her expertise, passion, and her ability to push them without seeming aggressive. Both Stefan and Calvin stressed that she was always friendly and never really lost her cool. They would not in a million years think she was capable

of these horrific acts. Their testimonies were convincing but overall would not mean much as they only saw a part of what made Kelly Visque tick. Richard was ready to begin and had taken great pains to assure his anonymity would be retained. He was conducting his end of the live chat from a totally nondescript location with a white background. The camera focused only on his shoulders and above so there was no way to tell where he was, and he wore a baseball cap and sunglasses. Aaron was ready to begin.

"Please tell us what you were doing on Saturday, June 18th, 2039?"

"I spent the early part of the day in Washington DC taking in some of the sights."

"What else did you do?"

"I ate lunch."

"Do you remember where?"

"I don't recall the name of the place."

"Were you by yourself?"

"No."

"Who were you with that day?'

"Kelly Visque."

"What time did the two of you part company?"

"Sometime in late afternoon."

"Did she say what she was going to do then?"

"No."

"Thank you. Your witness."

"You seem like an honorable fellow, Richard. Can I ask what your last name is?"

"You can ask, but I am not going to tell you." A few of the jurors laughed and Waller did too.

"That's very clever. Why did you choose to conduct your testimony through a feed rather than appearing in the courtroom?"

"I would rather keep my identity private."

"Ah. Why is that? Are you a spy or some top secret government operative?"

"I am married."

"Oh, you are married! If you would, could you please show us your ring finger?"

"Objection, relevance."

"It is relevant to the witness's character, sir."

"Overruled." He held up his ring finger and everyone observed it was bare.

"Where is your wedding ring?"

"I forgot it this morning."

"You take it off on a regular basis?"

"I took it off to clean it and was rushing so I failed to put it back on."

"Or perhaps you remove it when you leave your wife's presence."

"That's not true", he responded a little too defensively.

"Of course not. I am sure, however, that during the day that you and Miss Visque were together she saw more than the Washington Monument." Now the jury chuckled at Richard. "Your infidelity, or at the very least, impropriety, doesn't make you seem very trustworthy or a credible witness. Would you trust yourself?"

"Yes, I would", he answered, but his words rang hollow.

"Nothing further, your Honor."

"We are adjourned. I will see everyone back here on Monday."

11am, Saturday, August 25th

Todd Russell was on his way back from his campaign trip to the South which had turned out better than he had hoped. The media had reported that he was way ahead in the polls now consistently in most parts of the country. His governorship was going well and Joe Berry remained at the top of his game when it came to public relations and promoting his candidate. They had already talked about what they were going to do from now until Election Day. Until after Labor Day he was going to concentrate on running things in Illinois and during that time conduct some polls of his own with more specific questions that would determine which geographic and fundamental areas needed his attention. Once the results were received, he would act on them right up until November 6th and also engage in the traditional debates with the other candidates. He truly felt nothing could stop him now.

9am, Monday, August 27th, Washington DC

Today it was Lorraine Corvino's brother's turn to take the stand and she hoped that he would be able to handle it. He had a tendency to crack under pressure. She had told Ross to be gentle with him and he promised he would be. "What was your sister like when she was growing up?"

"Very nurturing. She was always taking care of those in need and was very kind as well."

"Was she ever overly jealous?"

"No, not really. She was usually happy for other people's successes."

"Did she have many boyfriends?"

"She had some. None were ever really serious. She always seemed to enjoy hanging out with her girlfriends more." He was starting to fade; mercifully Ross picked up on the signs that she had said to look for.

"Nothing further." Waller started his questioning from the chair he was sitting in.

"How often did you and your sister see each other?"

"Not too often."

"Once a month? A few times a year?"

"I would say once every two years."

"Really? And how many times a year did you talk on the phone?"

"Two or three."

"When you did talk, did she tell you what was happening with her? Did you even know where she worked?"

"Yes, I knew where she worked." He started to twitch. "She didn't talk about her personal life much with me."

"What did you talk about?"

"Just day to day stuff. We would call each other on our birthdays and reminisce about our childhoods."

"Congratulations. You knew your sister as well as you know the checkout person at the supermarket. I can see why the defense asked you to be a character witness. This witness may be excused." It was just in time, as her brother had started to grind his teeth.

11am, Dearborn Michigan
Alex and Hayao were plotting out their next step on their way to the finish line. Earlier today he had participated in a seminar on campaigning tips and how to come across as more attractive to people. "We have to go to Alaska, Hayao. We do not seem to enjoy much support there."

"Alright. There are a large number of people there who work for Moritu. I think if I show a genuine interest in the issues facing them, which I have, that will go a long way towards gaining their trust."

"As a whole, they are concerned about the environment. That's definitely something we need to stress."

"We have come out in support of President Harrington's initiative on the rising sea levels. That I am sure is critical to them. Fishing is an integral part of the economy there."

"What about after that?"

"Perhaps the South. After Alaska, however, we should probably conduct a new series of polls to obtain a more updated view of where our problem areas lie. We also need to set aside time to prep for the debates; there will be three for you and one for me. You'll see, Election Day will be here before you turn around and the next two and a half months will be a blur."

9am, Wednesday, August 29th, Washington DC
The defense team of Aaron and Ross were presenting their last witness today, Lucy Rauch, the FBI profiler who had interviewed Kelly Visque. Yesterday Lorraine Corvino's neighbor had attested to Corvino's quiet lifestyle and the fact that she was always polite. Aaron wanted Lucy Rauch to hit a home run as her testimony would be fresh in the minds of the jurors˙ when they went to deliberate. She seemed like a tough lady and he hoped she would be a match for Waller. "Dr. Rauch, what is your background?"

"I worked for the FBI for many years as a profiler and am currently a psychologist doing that same type of work in the private sector."

"What does a profiler do?" "We look at the information about a crime and determine which personality traits the perpetrator would most likely possess."

"What do you do now?"

"I am a practicing psychologist. I have private patients and I also serve as a consultant to law enforcement agencies and as an expert witness in criminal cases such as this one."

"So, you still perform profiling services?"

"Yes."

"How do you go about reviewing the information that is available about a case?"

"I study the evidence and look at similar crimes to provide insight about ways to narrow down the search for the person or persons responsible for the search."

"Doctor, when you are hired as a witness in a criminal case, do you typically meet with the defendant?"

"No. Hardly ever."

"Why is that?"

"I am able to get all the information I need from the specifics of the crime."

"Did you review the evidence in this case?"

"I did."

"What is your conclusion?"

"These crimes were very sloppy; clues existed everywhere around the crime scenes and very little care was taken to avoid detection. The defining characteristic that I came away with was that whoever did this had very little knowledge about police procedures."

"Thank you Dr. Rauch."

"Dr. Rauch, you said that you hardly ever meet with the defendant. Has there ever been a case when you did?"

"I have met with two defendants in my career. They were both early on before I was experienced and had developed procedures to be followed."

"What percentage of the cases that are you involved with did it turn out that you were correct about the person or persons caught?"

"I'd say about 25%."

"That's it?"
"It's not an exact science."
"Don't you believe you could make it more precise if you met with the people arrested in the ones where you are going to testify?" Rauch said not necessarily but looked weak as she said it and now Waller smelled blood in the water.
"Isn't it possible that the defendant Kelly Visque would have intentionally made the crimes look like they were performed by someone inept?"
"It's possible but unlikely."
"Why is that?"
"Because even though the crime scenes were not clean, they did not have the feel of being staged."
"I see. You were able to come to that conclusion without even meeting with Miss Visque once?"
"Yes I was."
Putting a skeptical look on his face, Waller looked at the jury and said "No further questions." Judge Alphonso addressed both the defense attorneys.
"Next witness."
They both said simultaneously, "The defense rests, your honor."
"Alright. We will hear closing arguments tomorrow. We are adjourned."

9am, Thursday, August 30th, Washington DC
The day had arrived; the end of the trial. This was the chance for the lawyers to pull it all together; Waller was up first. "Ladies and gentlemen of the jury, it has been a long and arduous process. We have arrived at the conclusion and it is very important for you all to remember what is important. Let's review what we have established; Kelly Visque, who is on trial for four counts of murder and a charge of terrorism, is guilty! Her DNA was found at the crime scene of the Bernards, and that is not circumstantial, that is direct evidence which Edna Jillow's testimony expanded on by explaining that the position of each set of multiple DNA inside the stinger is immaterial as affirmed by Edna Jillow. That alone is enough to convict for those two murders! We heard the testimony

of Sean Cardillo, who said that Visque has the mindset of a criminal and with her background would be able to fool the FBI. Miss Visque was able to file away the serial number on the gun and avoid detection at the gun store, things a person well versed in criminal procedures would have known. Those things show that Kelly Visque had the ability to carry this out. Now let's talk about the means. We saw the picture of Visque and Corvino, and heard about how friendly they were from numerous witnesses. We verified Corvino was having an affair with Justice Bernard and would have known his comings and goings, so that gave Miss Visque the opportunity. I presented the brain scan of Winston Bernard as well to show that he did not know his assailant. Why did she do it, people may ask. Allow me to explain. We learned that she was in American Pride, grew up with parents who support conservative ideals, and listened to Dr. Wentworth say that she exhibited jingoism. She knew that justice Bernard, while having been conservative in the past, likely would have ruled in favor of the measure for people born elsewhere to run for President as a result of his daughter's influence. She was vehemently opposed to this and willing to do anything to prevent this from happening. If she hadn't been caught, who knows who else she would have tried to kill. What about Juan Pillar and his driver? His driver was simply unlucky as her target was Pillar. We retrieved the note sent to him from California, which her friend denies but appeared agitated like she was hiding something. There is also the tape at the airport which shows her there in the car intended to pick Pillar up. The motive is the same; extreme patriotism. That takes us to the last charge against Miss Visque, terrorism. She violated a clause of the Patriot Act which states, in my own words, that an act intended to influence or alter the operation of government is terrorism. This certainly qualifies. Now let's turn our attention to Lorraine Corvino. She is on trial for conspiracy to commit murder. She admitted to having an affair with Justice Bernard. Several of our witnesses portrayed her as the jealous type and has characteristics of being obsessive when in relationships. We saw the picture of the two women that I mentioned earlier. How much more proof do we need? They planned the murders of the Bernards together, with

Visque carrying out the task, and then Visque took it upon herself to eliminate Juan Pillar when he was pulling ahead in the race. The only verdict that you can return that will allow you to sleep at night is guilty on all counts. Thank you." Aaron was next.

"None of the evidence regarding Kelly Visque is conclusive. The expert I presented, Otto Lampf, clearly explained the location of each set of DNA inside the stinger denotes which was obtained by the bee first. My client was a member of American Pride for a period of time when she was younger, something that the prosecution referred to repeatedly. So what? Hasn't everyone done something they are ashamed of? In Miss Visque's case, it was done out of a sense of idealism, twisted as it may be, and once she really understood what they were all about she ended her association. This was reiterated by Dr. Malcolm Kelsey, who concluded after a thorough examination that Miss Visque was grounded and not so extremely patriotic as to commit these crimes. We had numerous character witnesses who spoke very highly of her and we had a former FBI employee who attested to the fact that the way whoever carried out these horrible acts seemed to be tripping all over themselves and was not the conduct of a person as well versed in police procedure as my client. Let's explore the relationship between the two defendants. Aren't people permitted to be friends without having an ulterior motive anymore? Miss Visque did not use Lorraine Corvino to get access to Justice Bernard, the notion is preposterous. The prosecution is simply trying to grasp at a few coincidences and shoehorn them in to fit because this was the best they could come up with. Send the message that justice is not about settling for the closest explanation possible, but rather is about proving guilt beyond a reasonable doubt, which Mr. Waller has not even come close to establishing. I implore you as citizens to uphold your oath and not be swayed by the smokescreen the prosecution has placed before you. Not guilty is the only verdict that is based on the facts presented here. Thank you." Lionel Ross stood up.

"Earlier, I referred to Lorraine Corvino as the last piece of the puzzle. Like my colleague Mr. Aaron said, justice cannot be predicated on the best available scenario. It must be proven, and that was not done here. Miss Corvino admitted to having an affair with the deceased justice Bernard; it was implied that she was trying to sleep her way into getting some kind of favor. Did they have any evidence? Any eyewitness accounts? No and no. All they, the prosecution, managed to produce was the testimony of one of her coworkers bent on revenge for rebuffing his advances. She was evaluated by Dr. Kelsey, an expert on obsessive people who unequivocally stated that she is not clinically jealous or obsessively unbalanced. She has had numerous long relationships over the years and always managed to keep things in perspective. The worst mistake she has made with regard to the charges levied against her was having Kelly Visque as a friend. The prosecution attempted to conjure her guilt out of thin air. Don't buy into this trickery. Return a verdict of not guilty. Thank you." Judge Alphonso wasted no time.

"Jurors, the next phase of the trial is upon us, the deliberations. You will go and discuss this case until you reach a decision. You are entitled to read any part of the transcript of all the testimony and statements in order to render a verdict. You will be escorted to the jury room now." Alphonso went on to instruct them on the relevant law that they needed to know to come to a verdict, and then nodded to the bailiff, and all he, the defendants, and the lawyers could do now was wait.

11am, the Oval Office

President Harrington was just finishing the legislation he was going to submit to Congress today. The bill would allow everyone who had emigrated to this country in the last three months or earlier prior to November 6th, Election Day, to vote in the presidential election. It would be met with some opposition, but in the end he knew the legislation would pass. The members of Congress could not very well argue with the notion that one of the most basic rights of our society, the right to vote, be denied from such a large and now influential segment of society. Allowing a person born elsewhere to become President and then denying someone else with the same background a basic freedom could never be justified. He knew he had already won.

7pm
The news story that had broke about the new legislation had been reported across the country and everyone was buzzing about it. This was big; the bill removed the importance of citizenship and going through the proper channels. Uncle George sent Kangaroo a text message saying that he had predicted this all along.

9pm, the Governor's mansion, Springfield IL
Treetop was parked in his car receiving a video transmission from Todd Russell's bedroom. He had set up surveillance equipment on a silent drone that he had launched a few minutes ago when the man had been escorted into the mansion. The robotic drone was hovering outside the window, as unobtrusive as could be and would never be detected. A few minutes later things got started upstairs, and Treetop knew that Russell would be finished in politics for good.

2pm, Friday, August 31st, Washington DC
Treetop sat on a park bench across the street from CNN's building in downtown DC. He was sitting because he did not want to be remembered and his height made that hard. He saw two high school kids walking towards him. Perfect. He stopped them. How would you each like to make twenty bucks?" "They both nodded. "Take this package across the street to that building over there and ask that it be given to the news department."

"Ok", they said together. They walked a few steps, turned around to ask him a question and saw that he was already gone.

CHAPTER 17

10am, Saturday, September 1st

It was Labor Day weekend, the unofficial end of summer, and half the country was on vacation. Wherever they were however, they kept their smart phones with them so they could follow the story of Todd Russell, his male lover, and the pictures which surfaced. They had been sent anonymously to the news bureau in Washington DC. The story was being broadcast worldwide and the pictures had found their way on to some adult websites. Reporters were camped out at the Governor's mansion in Springfield Illinois but Russell had not surfaced yet.

The Governor was holed up inside, mortified and paralyzed with fear. He had taken no action as of yet and didn't have any plans to do so. He wanted contact with no one right now. Joe Berry had called and he hadn't even spoken to him. He needed to process this by himself before he could face the public. Russell decided he would stay in his private quarters until tomorrow and decide what to do.

All the news correspondents were giving an update now as the staff at the Governor's mansion were changing shifts. The reporters tried to ask questions of the workers who were leaving but no one said a word. That left the media with the mandatory update to their news bureaus reporting no one who might have had any contact with Governor Russell was talking and all they could do was wait.

11am, the White House

President Harrington was having coffee with his Chief of Staff, Jo Sylvester. "This is quite a drama, Mr. President. What do you suppose Governor Russell will do?"

"If he is smart he will address this right away. He may still have a chance if he comes clean; the American public accepts that sexual orientation is a person's choice and is not relevant in any way to a candidate's potential. Russell needs to come out of hiding and face this to show he did nothing wrong, which he didn't and that it is his business and his alone. The longer he waits the smaller his chances are." President Harrington was exuberant on the inside, but gave no indication it was him who set Russell up for this scandal.

12pm, Washington DC
Layton, Morris, and Layton's aide Robert were having lunch at a posh restaurant in DC. Naturally they were talking about Todd Russell. Robert asked, "What do you both expect to happen?" Layton answered first. "It seems like he is panicking. He hasn't come out with a statement or anything yet. I am shocked that it is being handled so poorly. If he had gone on about his normal routine right away, he could even have turned this into an advantage for himself by proclaiming his privacy and civil rights were violated. Most Americans see no difference between homosexuality and heterosexuality; this is not the 1950's. He is acting like he did something wrong. I can't believe he is not getting any advice about this from his staff, especially Joe Berry."
"I agree. That's what he hired him for, to help with the campaign but also to handle situations such as this one. I think we won't hear anything from Todd Russell today. He seems like he has to decide what to do next and is too shook up to make any kind of rational decision today."

3pm, Dearborn MI
Hayao and Ramirez had gathered their entire staff for a strategy session. Hayao addressed everyone. "This recent development will affect our campaign and how we proceed drastically. While we don't know yet, I want to set up a team to focus on a new course of action should he resign. What I would like you to do if you hear your name called is to meet in the conference room next door to craft a plan. Some suggestions I have; draft a statement that we will issue if he should bow out of the race to the effect that Governor Russell is a fine Governor and we wish him all the best. A few days later we should conduct a new poll to see where people stand now between myself and Layton. The poll should contain components based upon demographics, geographics, and the issues." Hayao paused to make sure everyone was paying

attention, and they were all taking notes. Good. "Ok, the following people will work on that task."

10am, Sunday, September 2nd, the Governor's mansion, Springfield IL
Todd Russell still felt shaken, but he was thinking more clearly today. He was finally in a state of mind where he could talk to someone and knew who he needed to call. He didn't know what he was going to do yet, but he had the rest of the day to decide and was sure he would have his mind made up by tomorrow. He dialed the number. Joe Berry answered on the first ring. "Governor, I have been trying to reach you! I called so many times I am surprised your phone isn't broken!" There was a touch of annoyance in his voice. Russell got right to the point.
"Joe, I want you to alert the media that I will be prepared to make an announcement tomorrow morning at this time, but will not be answering questions."
"Governor, what are you going to say? We need to formulate a plan about what to do from now until Election Day!"
"That is all Joe. Goodbye." Berry started to protest, saying he could not run the campaign effectively without more information, but Russell had already hung up.

10am, Monday, September 3rd
All the reporters were ready, having been camping out at the Governor's mansion since the story broke the other day. Russell came out dressed in a three piece suit and looking very Presidential. He walked up to the podium he had arranged to have ready. The whole world was listening. "Good morning my fellow Americans. The other day, I was sharing some intimacy with my male lover, who everyone knows by now was photographed with me and that he is Brad Milsen, a union representative. I demand that his privacy be protected. We have done nothing wrong and we care for each other just like any heterosexual couple. We kept our relationship private not because we are ashamed but because it is nobody's business. When this story became public information the other day, I was humiliated and experienced a wide range of

emotions from disappointment to anger. As a result, I handled the aftermath very poorly. Rather than confronting and dealing with this head on, I isolated myself from the outside world. That is not a quality a leader should exhibit. I wouldn't vote for myself. Therefore, I am withdrawing from the Presidential race." A murmur rippled through the crowd of reporters and chaos all over the world. Russell had represented a new era in technology to people everywhere because he had Weimitz on his team. This represented a major betrayal to them. The citizens of India in particular were up in arms because they had been very optimistic about the work Russell was planning for them. The government leaders were very disappointed as well. "I will, however, finish my term as Governor. Thank you all for indulging me today, and God bless the United States."

9am, Tuesday, September 4th, Washington DC

Today was the first day back from summer vacation for a good part of the country with school starting tomorrow. It was still way too soon to determine how Russell's departure from the race would affect the other candidates, but Layton did not want to waste any time trying to decipher the way the battle lines would now be drawn. He asked Robert, whom he now considered his right hand man, to come into his office. "Robert, the game has changed. All of the segments of the voting population that were behind Todd Russell are now up for grabs. I want to make sure we position ourselves to get as much of that support as we can. Here is what I want you to do. Review the results of the last poll you conducted and see where Russell held the lead. Once you have done that, draft a new one which targets these areas whether they are based on geography, a defining characteristic, or political issues. We will take the results and use it to form a plan. Good luck; let me know when the poll is ready to be sent out."

11am, Dearborn, MI

Hayao had suspected Russell would withdraw from the race. He was glad he had set the plan to conduct another poll in motion. This morning he also posted a statement on his official campaign website saying Todd Russell is a fine man and governor and Hayao wishes him all the best in his future endeavors. Hayao firmly believed he would pick up the majority of Russell's vote.

4pm, Washington DC, Federal Courthouse

The jury continued to toil conducting their deliberations and had reconvened about an hour ago. The foreman, a former soldier, was trying to keep the discussion organized. "Why don't we talk about the case the prosecution presented first. To me, they seemed to present a much stronger explanation of how these crimes were committed than the defense did of refuting it. I mean, look at all the evidence they collected and presented, from the bee containing the DNA to the picture of the two defendants to the tape of the blonde woman at the airport. I don't think the defense presented any evidence exhibits at all."

"The defining characteristic of the trial for me was the undermining of the witnesses on both sides. The cross examinations were very effective in chipping away at their credibility. Take Dr. Wentworth, for example. Both Aaron and Ross demonstrated his evaluations of both of them to be incomplete, and Agent Billet came away looking incompetent when asked about circumstantial evidence and the explanation for how Visque would have known the judge's schedule. It seems like each side was trying harder to distract us from the facts and more towards not listening to the other side's witnesses", remarked juror number 2, the college student.

"I agree", said juror number 11. "I have another point as well. The evidence presented was virtually, no, completely circumstantial. The burden of proof is the prosecution's responsibility and to me, they didn't really prove anything. They described a series of coincidences. The defense managed to explain away each one."

"That may be, but if you have enough coincidences added together, don't they equal presumption of guilt?"

"Kelly Visque was certainly portrayed as someone who would have wanted this measure to be rejected and would have taken extraordinary steps to make sure it was. Does everyone remember how she lost her temper during her testimony? Her connection with Corvino makes her guilty in my book."

"Yes, but has it been proven beyond a reasonable doubt? That is the standard it must pass", said one of the other jurors. "As far as I am concerned, yes, it has been. I also think Corvino was involved to an extent of more than just unknowingly providing information. I imagine she was jealous and obsessive and expecting something from justice Bernard."

"I don't think these two women would have been so naive as to imagine they could get away with something like this with all the circumstances pointing so blatantly at them", another one of the female jurors contributed.

"Perhaps that is what they would be expecting and hoping a jury to think", said someone else. The room fell silent for a moment as the foreman looked around at everyone. He saw different looks on each face, from skepticism to anxiety to an eagerness to continue discussing this. It was going to be awhile before they were finished, if ever.

9am, Friday, September 7th, Miami, FL

Operation Sea Lift had been completed and was working like a charm. The water from around the shoreline in Miami was being syphoned out to sea and the city no longer faced imminent danger of becoming submerged. President Harrington was present to view the success and offer his congratulations and gratitude to Li Yan who had run the whole project for her company. The President presented her with a plaque shaped like Miami. "We are all grateful to you, Li Yan, and the workers who have accomplished this great engineering feat. You have prevented a natural disaster with some brilliant man made ingenuity." He handed her the plaque and they shook hands. President Harrington then continued. "We have an announcement, Li and I. As a result of the seamless implementation here, Sea Lift will be performing the same task in San Diego next, another city desperately in need of this service. They will be starting the process there on Monday, with a target completion date of December 31st. Let's give them a big round of applause!"

4pm, Washington DC

Attorney General Waller, Glen Aaron, Kelly Visque, Lionel Ross, and Lorraine Corvino had all rushed to the courtroom. They received word that the jury was back. While they were glad the wait would be over, all three attorneys had actually thought it would take them longer than this to come to a decision. The judge went through the normal procedures and then asked the foreman if they had reached a verdict. "We have, your honor."

"On the count of murder against Kelly Visque for the murders of Cecily and Winston Bernard, how do you find?"

"We find the defendant guilty."

"For the count of murder against Kelly Visque for the killing of Juan Pillar and his driver how do you find?"

"We find the defendant guilty."

"On the charge for the violation of the Patriot Act, the crime of terrorism, how do you find?"

"We find the defendant Kelly Visque guilty."

"Lastly, on the charge of conspiracy to commit murder against the defendant Lorraine Corvino, how does the jury find?"

"We find the defendant guilty." Visque and Corvino were speechless, they had put their fates in the hands of their lawyers who had failed them who were now sitting there with somber looks on their faces. Judge Alphonso spoke next.

"The sentencing hearing will be in ten days on September 17th at 10am. Bailiff, please take the two defendants into custody. We are adjourned."

Sondra Tristan breathed a sigh of relief and felt like a weight had been lifted off her shoulders. She realized this would not bring her parents back, but she felt she had received closure. Waller strode out of the courtroom as quickly as he could to talk to the reporters who had been waiting for two and a half months to get some information about the trial. Aaron and Ross went into a room at the back of the courthouse to talk. "Lionel, we need to do something. We cannot see our clients end up like this."

"We can file an appeal."

"I think we have to. We should start right away. We can use the grounds that the search of Lorraine Corvino's apartment was unlawful as it was without a warrant. That is probably our best chance. I will get started on the paperwork and we can file on Monday."

"Ok. I am going to meet with my client and I will tell her that is the plan."

"Alright. I will do the same."

7pm, Lee U.S. Federal Penitentiary, Virginia

Both Visque and Corvino had been sent to Lee Federal Penitentiary, and this is where they would stay until they were sentenced on September 17th. Their lawyers arrived to make sure they were ok and to explain what they were planning to do. Since this was a maximum security facility, it took about half an hour for them to get through security. When Kelly Visque was finally led into the room where Aaron was waiting for her, she looked as if she finally comprehended the gravity of her situation. "Hi Kelly. I want you to know Mr. Ross and myself have a plan."

"What is it?" Her voice sounded far away, like she thought any effort on her behalf would be futile at this point.

"We are going to file an appeal of the verdict delivered by the jury on the grounds the search of Corvino's apartment was illegal. The FBI agent saw the picture of the two of you and judge Alphonso upheld it as valid because he agreed the photo had been in plain sight, and for that a warrant is not required."

"What makes you think the search would be overturned by another judge?"

"I am confident it can be argued that the photo was not really in plain sight, as the agent entered another room which was when he saw it."

"Ok, when are you going to file the appeal?"

"I am going to draft it this weekend and file it first thing Monday morning."

"Do you think we have a chance?"

"I do."

"I have a question. I was charged with violating the Patriot Act, correct?"

"Yes."

"Doesn't that mean the death penalty?"

"Yes."

"I thought Waller had said that at the beginning of the trial. If the appeal fails, what next? Is there a way to try to have my sentence changed to life in prison?"

"Unfortunately, the only way would be for you to receive a pardon. If we end up exhausting all of our appeals, we can certainly try working on President Harrington to grant you a pardon."

"I see. Well, let's hope for the best. Let me know when the appeal is filed." Visque had no more to say, and asked to taken back to her cell. Ross had gotten a similar reaction from Corvino, although she had less to worry about, as she would likely spend the rest of life in jail.

10 am, Saturday, September 8th

Both Hayao and Layton's teams had sent out their new polls, and although they were different in scope with Hayao's being all encompassing to analyze the entire country again and Layton's zeroing in on those areas where Russell held the advantage, both would be the polls each camp used to determine the direction they would take for the sprint to Election Day.

11 am, Sunday, September 9th, New York, NY the Perry O'Malley show

"Good morning, America. I hope everyone out there enjoyed a great summer and is ready to face the world again. Much has happened in the news recently, and we are going to discuss two topics today. The first is the Presidential race and how the events of the past ten days will affect things. Let's delve right in. Now that Todd Russell is out of the running, it has become a much more traditional race with the two candidates left each representing the values of the traditional political parties before the Democrats and the Republicans went by the wayside and the Universal party emerged. Hayao Yamamoto embodies the ideals of a liberal by virtue of the fact that he is running under new legislation which passed and Eric Layton is the established politician who, while not conservative across the board on every issue, would seem to be the choice for those who are more traditional when it comes to politics. That would seem to be the case at first glance. If you dig a little deeper, however, as my staff has done here on the show by conducting several surveys, it seems people who entered this country and have been here for a generation or more favor Hayao as he would be more likely to implement some of the customs from other countries around the world and be more open to other traditions. Younger immigrants, however, want their politicians to uphold the governmental practices they found attractive and enticing enough to want to come to the United States in the first place. That segment of the population, which an observer would expect to be more liberal, actually prefers the methods that have been in place. The political lines have been blurred. In conclusion, the demographics Todd Russell seemed to control appear to be up for grabs for either candidate at this point." O'Malley paused. He looked at the cameraman who signaled it was time for a commercial. "At the beginning of the show, I indicated we would be talking about two things today. When we return after this short break, we will be discussing the trial of the century, which just came to a close." "Welcome back. We have a special guest caller, right now. Attorney General Quinn Waller, welcome."

"Thank you, Perry."

"Congratulations on your recent victory. You must feel very relieved that the trial is over."

"I am glad justice was served, Perry."

"Did you at any time have any misgivings that you had the right perpetrators?"

"Never. The evidence pointed to both Kelly Visque and Lorraine Corvino right from the beginning, and we owe that to our fine men and women at the FBI."

"How do you feel about the way the trial was conducted? It seemed to the outside world that Judge Alphonso was being overly strict and controlling."

"It may have appeared that way, but in fact he insured the trial would be handled professionally and not become a farce like some other media spectacles. I admire him for the way he handled things; he stood up to a lot of public criticism about his refusal to allow the media in the courtroom. He didn't back down and that is commendable. Our society should look to people like him as role models."

"Thank you very much Quinn, for taking the time to speak with us today. Thank you to all you folks at home for joining us, and we will see you next week on the Perry O'Malley show."

1pm, Monday, September 10th, Tel Aviv, Israel

Moritu Corporation had completed their new factory and would open its doors today to much fanfare. Prime Minister Levy was there as well as Natsu Hakituri, Moritu's CEO. People in Israel were very excited about the influx of jobs. Natsu led a tour of the facility; they would start interviewing potential workers and begin operations in earnest tomorrow.

10am, Dearborn, Michigan

Hayao and Ramirez were getting ready to take their trip to Alaska tonight and were packing up when his phone rang. He didn't recognize the phone number. "Hello?"

"Hello, this is Mayank Sarin. How are you Hayao?"

"I am fine." He knew what the Prime Minister wanted. Now that Russell was out of the picture, India was willing to negotiate to get something in return for their endorsement.

"I wanted to talk to you about the offer you made to me while you were here a few months ago. We would be interested in working with you to have a Moritu plant, probably near Bombay." Hayao wanted to tell him to stick it where the sun don't shine, but knew that would not be prudent.

"I am glad to hear you have come around. I will tell you what, I am just getting ready to leave for a trip but I will pass your message on to Natsu Hakituri and I sure he will be in touch."

"Great. Thank you Hayao. You can count on my support as you continue your quest for the Presidency."

12pm, Washington DC, White House private dining room

President Harrington was having lunch with Jo Sylvester, his Chief of Staff. He wanted him to check the legislation's progress through Congress. He wanted to discuss this in a relaxed setting so Jo would be more receptive to the idea. "How is the family, Jo?"

"They are fine, sir. The kids had a nice summer vacation this year and were sorry to see the school year start." They shared a chuckle. The waiter brought out the plates of food they were having today, it was surf and turf, lobster and filet mignon. "This looks delicious. Thank you very much sir."

"My pleasure. Jo, I asked you here today for a reason."

"Yes, sir?"

"It's regarding the legislation I introduced to Congress about the voting rights of immigrants. It is crucial that it be passed by Election Day. I have publicly endorsed Hayao Yamamoto for President and sincerely believe he is the better candidate to lead our country in the rapidly changing global environment."

"I am with you so far."

"I need you, Jo, to make sure it gets pushed through. I have not heard anything about it lately, and I am concerned that it got put at the bottom of the pile."

"Of course Mr. President. I will get right on it. I will take a trip over there this afternoon and find out what is going on."

"Thank you, Jo. I knew I could count on you. What would you like for dessert?"

6pm, Detroit Metropolitan Airport

Hayao and Ramirez were on the plane waiting for the takeoff to Alaska. They would be there for a week, splitting their time between Anchorage, Fairbanks and Juneau. Hayao hoped to spend the majority of his time talking about his business experience and trying to capitalize on the presence of Moritu Corp. as a means to ingratiate himself with the citizens there. When they returned next Monday he hoped and expected to have the results from the polls. While he was waiting for the plane to leave, he called Natsu and told him India was now interested in having Moritu build a plant there, and Natsu answered gratefully that he would call Prime Minister Sarin and start the process right away, for he understood his attentiveness would translate into more support on Election Day.

10am, Wednesday, September 12th, the Oval office
"Mr. President, I have Chief of Staff Sylvester here to see you."
"Thank you. Please send him in." The two men shook hands and then Sylvester got right to the point.
"I met with the Speaker of the House about the voting legislation and he assured me it was on the agenda for the Senate Immigration Committee. They are scheduled to meet again this coming Monday, September 17th. I will check with them later Monday afternoon to see if they agreed to move the bill forward."
"Excellent. Please keep me posted Jo. Thank you."

9am, Monday, September 17th, U.S. Appellate Court, Federal District
Glen Aaron and Lionel Ross were at the Appellate Court ready to submit their appeal. The document they were handing in was succinct, and they both had wanted to be there as the appeal would affect both their clients. The reason they were giving was what they discussed, that the search of Lorraine Corvino's dwelling violated the Constitution without a warrant. They were hoping the Appellate Court would hear their appeal so they could explain the chain of events which would never have happened without the unlawful search.

10am, Washington DC, Judge Alphonso's courtroom
The time had arrived for the sentencing hearing. Mr. and Mrs. Visque were present along with Lorraine Corvino's brother. Everyone looked nervous. Judge Alphonso indicated he was ready to speak. The two defendants and the lawyers stood up. "Lorraine Corvino, I hereby sentence you to life in prison to be served at Hazelton Penitentiary in West Virginia. You will be eligible for parole in twenty years. Kelly Visque, I sentence you to death based upon your conviction of terrorism as a violation of the Patriot Act, which comes with an automatic death penalty. Until that time you will also reside at Hazelton, in their death row section. May God have mercy on your soul. We are adjourned." Kelly Visque couldn't believe her ears. She grasped intellectually what the

penalty was going to be, but hearing the words was a different story entirely. Glen Aaron pulled her aside. "We filed the appeal, which means nothing can happen until that is finished. There are numerous steps we can take to get the sentence changed. DO NOT LOSE HOPE! I will be there fighting with all I have every step of the way." That was all he had time to tell her; she wanted to say goodbye to her parents before being led away.

1pm, Washington DC
Jo Sylvester had been waiting all morning to get an update from the Senate Immigration Committee. He saw the email from them and opened it immediately. He was pleased and President Harrington would be too. They had approved the bill and were forwarding it to the full Senate. He called the President right away to tell him.

3pm
Hayao and Ramirez were on their way back to Detroit from Alaska, and both believed it had been a productive trip. They capitalized on Moritu's presence there to their advantage and the people had responded. The Alaskans understood that Hayao is a good businessman who realizes a big part of governing is keeping an eye on the bottom line. They also received good vibes about Ramirez, she projected the image of someone very astute politically and would be able to help steer the administration through shark infested waters. Hayao's staffers also received the results of the polls they had conducted. While he had done poorly again in Alaska, he wasn't worried because of his reception there. His biggest problem spots geographically were still the South and the Northeast, two areas where he would campaign in again. He had grabbed most of Russell's share in the other regions around the country and also led among both conservatives and liberals. Layton was leading across gender lines, however, and that was surprising. Hayao had expected to be winning among the men as his perspective was more practical than Layton and men tended to see things in black and white. The next step would be to plan out the

strategy for the next seven weeks, but they wanted to digest this for a few days first and decided to regroup on Thursday.

7pm, Washington, DC

Eric Layton was reviewing the poll results with Steven Morris and his staffer Robert. They had conducted the poll in the same way as last time back in June, based on topic rather than population segments. They had also taken the extra step of focusing on those issues where Todd Russell had been in the lead. The two main ones had been education and technology. Layton managed to gain ground when it came to education, getting a good part of the support that had gone to Russell. He was still lagging behind in technology, however, most likely due to Hayao's background at Moritu Corporation. Hayao was also leading on the immigration issue as a result of both he and Ramirez being born elsewhere. He remained in front when it came to the economy, health care, and the environment thanks to his record in Congress. Morris spoke first. "You did a great job here Robert. This information will really allow us to isolate where we need to do the most work and create a game plan." Layton nodded in agreement.

"Thank you. Are you both up for a strategy session?" They both were. "Let's talk about technology which seems to me where we have the most ground to make up. Hayao has Moritu behind him. That, however, could work to our advantage. We can point to the fact that Moritu hasn't always been the most environmentally friendly company with some questionable practices about not employing green and reusable energy sources. That is one part of my two pronged approach. The other will be for us to introduce a new high tech job bill that will appropriate a substantial amount of money to attract more high tech workers. We can also stress what a big supporter of education you are and how that could go hand in hand with training our younger generations for the future and the new initiatives coming down the pike."

"Excellent." What else did you come up with?"

"Well, we can talk about your support for the President's immigration voting bill."

"How did we fare based on gender?"

"I don't know for sure, but I imagine we would be leading among men as they would favor running mates who both had backgrounds in politics."

"Robert, we also should highlight the fact that I will be more likely to maintain more traditional policies both for ultra conservatives and those liberals who came here for a change to American values." Robert wrote that down. "Where should we spend the remaining time campaigning?"

"I think we should go to those areas of the country where our support is lacking and spend less time, although some, where our backing is stronger."

"Good idea. Steve, what is your opinion?"

"I agree. Why don't you come up with a schedule until Election Day, keeping in mind there will be three Presidential debates and one Vice Presidential debate. We also want to spend a decent amount of time continuing on in our current responsibilities to show we do not get distracted from our tasks at hand."

"Ok", answered Robert.

"Let's meet again on Thursday at the same time to review the calendar."

10am, Thursday, September 20th, Hayao's office at Moritu Headquarters

Hayao and Ramirez had both been giving the next seven weeks a lot of thought and had been working since 7am this morning. They believed they arrived at a winning schedule and plan. They successfully integrated the locations they needed to visit most with the issues they needed to address at each place. Here was their campaign schedule:

September 27th - October 5th, the South,
October 8th - October 14th, the Northeast,
October 17th - October 22nd, the Pacific Northwest and the northern part of the West Coast,
October 25th - October 31st, the Middle Atlantic States,
November 2nd - November 5th, the Midwest.

The first two stops they were going to visit were the ones where they were furthest behind. They were ahead in the other regions but wanted to reinforce their advantage. Their focus would be different at each of the regions. For example, when they visited the Southern states, they would stress the economy, as Layton was considered to be more experienced on that issue and the people in the South as a whole were having a harder time professionally and financially than folks elsewhere. Hayao planned to talk about how Moritu was expanding abroad, in Israel and India and how the U.S. economy was interdependent with nations such as these. There were other ways to help things than just job creation domestically. Ramirez suggested they also point out how much he has been an advocate of education over the years, seeing to it that Moritu offered scholarships in various countries, including this one, for many different courses of study. When they were in the Northeast, they planned to stress the health care issue and how their administration would appropriate funds for those who needed subsidized health insurance. This was a system which had been revised and tweaked over the years. Overall, there was a good system in place; if one thing could and should be modified it would be the amount of public assistance the lower income families and individuals received. They had both been able to come up with the topics they wanted to highlight during each leg, and by the time November 6th came around they would have covered all the major ones and made their positions and courses of action clear on each one.

7pm, Washington, DC

Robert had completed his analysis of Layton's situation in relation to Hayao's and was quite optimistic. Geographically, Hayao was the frontrunner, but those statistics were not nearly as important as they used to be when candidates were voted in based upon the Electoral College. With the popular vote, the mantra 'Politics is local' became much more important, and Robert believed Layton was much more skilled than Hayao in making people feel like he cared about their concerns. When Russell bowed out of the race, the technology vote became wide open and Hayao seemed to have inherited the crown. Robert needed to think of a way to close the gap. The other topic that Layton had to work on was immigration, and endorsing the President's legislation was a big step in the right direction. Robert wanted to match the issue to the region in the country where they were trailing as well. As a result, he wanted Layton to visit the Southwest, the Pacific Northwest, the Southeast, California, the Midwest, and the Mid-Atlantic states. Each one of these sectors held a different purpose that Layton had to take advantage of; each one signifying part of the bigger puzzle of getting elected of course, but each one also served as its own autonomous unit that needed to be conquered. Robert went over all this with Layton and Morris and they liked his approach. Robert tied each individual campaign trip to a separate subject and illustrated how they came together, just like building a house. You started with the foundation, and if that were strong, the house would be sturdy as a whole when completed.

10am, Tuesday, September 25th, Washington, DC, U.S. Senate session

The Senate subcommittee on immigration had approved the President's legislation on voting rights of immigrants, and today would be voted upon by the full Senate. Jo Sylvester had been working with Senate leadership to ensure it would be included in the agenda. The topic had been discussed already, although only the Senators knew everyone's stance. The issue had already been decided; this was just a formality. Sylvester was not permitted to be in the meeting but waited right outside to find out right away and report back to President Harrington. He wasn't sure how long the session would take as there were several initiatives that needed to be reviewed; the President's was not the only one. Sylvester went to make a few phone calls and get a cup of coffee. He came back about 45 minutes later and they still had not emerged. He went through his emails, and he was just about done when the doors opened. He found his contact from the subcommittee and asked him what had been decided. "It passed", the man answered. They shook hands. Sylvester was relieved but not terribly surprised; another hurdle had been completed. The next step was the House of Representatives; that could prove to be more challenging; President Harrington might have to get involved personally. He went to let the President know the good news.

2pm, Wednesday, September 26th, Washington DC, U.S. Federal Court of Appeals

The panel of judges was reviewing the briefs submitted by the attorneys for Kelly Visque and Lorraine Corvino regarding the grounds for appeal they were proposing based upon the search of Corvino's apartment which they were saying was unlawful. The prosecution in the case claimed the item in question was in plain sight so a warrant had not been necessary. "These briefs are pretty sketchy", said judge A, the one with the most seniority.

"Of course", said another judge. "They want to provide just enough information so that we will see the miscarriage of justice but not so much that we would dismiss the argument right here and now."

"What are the grounds for a search to be legal? Why don't we review that first", suggested the third and last judge. "If the FBI agent entered the residence with consent, that changes everything but is not mentioned anywhere in the brief", she continued. "It's obvious they want the opportunity to state their arguments in person. We should grant them the chance to do that. What do you both think?" The other two judges agreed, and judge A went to tell his clerk to notify both Glen Aaron and Lionel Ross and to set a date.

7pm, Dearborn Michigan

Hayao was filming another commercial, this one having a friend of Louis Grenadine's as the director. His name was Chad and he specialized in political ads. He was a surfer dude but was skilled at this. His notion was to film it at Moritu Corporation's headquarters and to showcase Hayao in his element of running operations there. Most of the commercial would contain footage of Hayao dealing with the tasks he normally did such as checking on the operations around the plant and working at his desk. At the end, he would provide commentary as to how he conducts himself and how that would translate into his role as President. The message of the ad would be to stress Hayao's ability to synergize many different tasks and integrate them seamlessly. There were many parallels between running a fortune 500 company and running the United States. Chad was hoping to get enough footage and have the filming completed in a week. Once that was done, he would have Hayao do his commentary about the scenes shown in the commercial. Hayao would be resuming his old responsibilities at Moritu for a week so that he could be filmed as he conducted himself and managed his affairs.

7am, Thursday, September 27th, Hazelton Penitentiary
Kelly Visque had just finished getting ready to go to breakfast when she received a message from one of the guards. She opened it up while she walked and saw it was from her attorney. Reading quickly so she didn't get in trouble with the guards, she got the point that their appeal had been granted and Aaron would discuss it further with her during their weekly phone call Sunday morning. He also let her know Lorraine Corvino had received a similar letter from Ross so if they saw each other they could discuss it.

11am, Detroit, Michigan
Hayao and Ramirez were leaving today for their nine day campaign trip through the South which would encompass the states from Texas up to Tennessee and down to Florida where they would arrive in Miami on October 5th for the first Presidential debate the next day. Tonight they would be in Austin where Hayao planned a speech at the statehouse. They would be visiting one state each day so every stop would become critical. This would be their only trip to this region and they were behind except for Florida so they had to make up ground. He would be fine tuning his speech on the plane today and reading it to Alex who would help him perfect it.

7pm, Austin, Texas
Hayao was about to address the state legislature of Texas and the entire world as his speech was being telecast everywhere. His goal was to demonstrate his steps to improve the lives of the people in the South and employ his background to promote growth there as

well. "Good evening ladies and gentlemen. I am glad to be in Texas and I want to thank you all for your hospitality. I have some definite ideas about how to promote commerce and increase job growth. I am planning to capitalize on my experience in business to bring foreign interests here. That will stimulate job growth and help fuel the economy in general, which is becoming more and more dependent on countries abroad. Moritu has expanded its operations into Israel and will do the same in India in the near future; I possess the connections and familiarity with cultures all over the world to take advantage of the opportunities they can offer. Many times there are hidden options available that only people who know where to look are aware of. I am one of those people. I aim to pass that insider's knowledge onto all of you! I will be your biggest advocate! Another matter I plan on handling is health care. The one factor lacking about our ever improving managed care system is that we do not provide many options for those living paycheck to paycheck. I will work tirelessly to change that. We are at a crossroads; our government must make decisions now to help seal a bright future for the United States; I am ready, willing, and more than able to do just that! Remember to vote for Hayao and Ramirez on November 6th! Good night!" He strode off the stage to a standing ovation.

9am, Monday, October 1st, U.S. Federal Appellate Court, Washington DC

Aaron and Ross were inside the courtroom about to make their presentation to the judges. They agreed ahead of time that Aaron would be the one to speak. They only needed one oral argument, as if the search was ruled to be illegal, a domino effect would be in place which would have precluded Corvino from being arrested and would have left the prosecution without a motive with which to convict Visque. Much rested on this which was why Attorney General Waller decided to show up to offer his side of the story to support the FBI's actions. Aaron stood up and walked to the lectern. "Good morning. We are here to review the evidence in People Vs. Kelly Visque and Lorraine Corvino. The specific piece of evidence we are here to discuss is the picture found in the defendant Lorraine Corvino's apartment. The photo was one of the bowling team which both defendants played on. It was found by the FBI agent, Roger Squelch, there to interview her to get more information about Justice Bernard since she worked as a custodian in the building. They were talking in the front of the residence when Miss Corvino got up to go into the other room. She did not invite agent Squelch to look around and expected him to stay in the room where they had been talking as she assumed this was just an informal interview. He wandered around the residence looking for something and saw this picture behind the bookcase, not exactly what I would call plain sight. At that point agent Squelch scurried back to the room where they had been chatting and continued on with their conversation. As soon as he left he contacted his superiors at the FBI about this bogus search and seizure. The picture was not in plain sight and he was clearly on a fishing expedition. Send the prosecution the message that they cannot circumvent the law. He knew exactly what he was doing. Thank you." One of the judges addressed both Aaron and Waller.

"While this is not typically the protocol for this type of proceeding, we would like to hear from the Attorney General. Mr. Waller?"

"This was not an illegal search. Agent Squelch simply looked around the dwelling and saw the picture. It was out in the open, not tucked away in a drawer. If Miss Corvino did not want anyone to notice it she would have hidden it away. Mr. Aaron mentioned a fishing expedition, I wonder to whom he was referring." Waller sat back in his chair.

"Thank you to both sides. We will be in touch when we have reached a decision. Good day."

11am, the White House
Jo Sylvester was in his office when his cell phone buzzed. "Hello?"

"Hi Jo." It was Daryl Wallace, the Speaker of the House. "We have voted on the President's measure. I am sorry to report it did not pass."

"What? How can that be?"

"Many of the representatives believe it is in the best interest of the United States that there be a longer probationary period for those who have emigrated for them to become familiar with our political process."

"I see. Voting for a candidate need not require hours and hours of research, The way the candidates conduct themselves is just as important as having an in depth perspective on how things work." Wallace didn't say anything further. Sylvester sighed. "Alright, I will inform the President. He won't be happy."

"Goodbye Jo."

"Bye."

1pm, Phoenix, AZ

Eric Layton was making his way through two states for the next few days, Arizona and New Mexico. He would be travelling to Miami on October 5th for the Presidential debate the next day, so additional campaign stops were not really possible. Robert had an agenda for him. He wanted Layton to stress how supportive he was of the rights of immigrants. There were two reasons for this. First of all, there was a large Mexican population in this region of the country, and Layton would be gaining support from those who were expected to vote for Hayao and Ramirez. The second reason involved creating the foundation mentioned earlier. There were people born elsewhere all over the United States. Hearing Layton say he backed President Harrington's new legislation would go a long way toward gaining their support. This would work for both the older generation and the newer generation as their viewpoints were different. The older folks wanted the values from the places they came from, which Layton's platform on immigrants' rights would pacify, and the younger people as a majority wanted the traditional policies of the U.S. government, which Layton represented much more so than Hayao. This strategy Robert thought of was brilliant. Once Layton had made his position clear, all the subsequent campaign stops he made would be all the more productive, as he would be able to address the most pressing issues at hand at each location due to the fact that the citizens would already be looking upon him favorably. He was feeling very confident; all he had to do was convince people about his viewpoint. Tonight he and Morris would be attending the Carnival of Illusion show in Phoenix, and tomorrow would be giving a press conference and meet and greet session at the Governor's residence, after which he was going to see the Diamondbacks play. The meet and greet appointment would be good practice for the debate on Saturday, Layton thought as he reviewed his notes for the press conference.

10am, Wednesday, October 3rd, the Oval Office
President Harrington was feeling better after hearing the news from Jo Sylvester on Monday about the House voting down the new legislation and calming down. He had been livid; they were just being obstructionists! He wanted to go confront Daryl Wallace immediately but fortunately Jo Sylvester persuaded him to wait. He had collected his thoughts and was now ready to contact him. Wallace wielded quite a bit of influence over the other members. Harrington dialed his phone. "Hello?"

"Hi Daryl, it's President Harrington. How are you?" Wallace had been expecting this call but still felt anxious about it.

"I am fine, sir. How are you?"

"Just fine. Daryl, I wanted to talk to you about the vote the House of Representatives took the other day."

"Yes, sir?"

"I was surprised by the outcome, quite frankly. This is an important matter for our nation, Daryl. We have someone running for President who would have not been permitted to do so in the last election; how can we deny others with similar backgrounds the basic right to vote?"

"We believe three months is not enough time for people who have emigrated here to have enough information to be able to make an informed decision on Election Day, sir."

"Just because someone doesn't live here does not mean they are not well versed in our political system and knowledgeable about our candidates. Information is at our fingertips 24/7."

"That's all fine and good sir, but sound bites do not give a person the complete picture."

"Since when is it our job to decide what people base their vote on? Every person has their own unique reason for voting a certain way; it is a subjective process. The person who does all the research in the world is no more correct than the person who votes based upon what each candidate is wearing on Election Day." Harrington paused. "This is the future, Daryl. Don't get in its way. Call for another vote and let me know when it will be. I want to take a personal stake in this measure." Wallace could hear the intensity in Harrington's voice.

"Ok, sir. I will let you know." Harrington got the call an hour later that the House of Representatives would reconvene and vote again on Monday October 8th. The President fully planned to be actively involved.

3pm, USS Alabama Battleship Memorial Park, Mobile, Alabama

Chad, the director who was filming Hayao's advertisement, had flown to Mobile to meet up with Hayao and Ramirez. Chad had decided to film it here to capture the contrast between Hayao's background and something so closely associated with the U.S. as a warship. Hayao would deliver his commentary with the ship in the background. It worked perfectly; his campaign trip had gone as well as could be expected in the South, where traditional values were the majority. Tomorrow he would be in Tennessee and then on to Miami for the first debate. Chad had almost finished setting up all the equipment and he told Hayao to go ahead and put on the mike. He motioned to Hayao a minute later to start. "Good afternoon. It's a pleasure to be standing here in front of the USS Alabama, used so valiantly during World War II. My background is in business, and I am used to having many balls in the air at the same time. Politics is the same, and my experience at Moritu Corporation has been excellent preparation for the Presidency. As you can see from the commercial, I am responsible for many different functions and must integrate them so the company as a whole flows smoothly. If one part is off course, the entire organization is affected. Running the country may seem to be a daunting task, but if all the facets can be brought together then there is harmony. Being a leader takes practice and training; great leaders are made, not born. There is no substitute for experience, and when it comes to being at the top I have plenty. Break away from the self-serving political machine, and give your vote to the candidate who can and will affect change. Thank you and God bless the United States." Chad made the 'cut' sign, and he was done. Everyone in the crew congratulated him and there was no need to even do another take. Chad would edit it, and told Hayao it should be ready in time for Sunday.

1pm, Friday, October 5th, Miami, FL

Both Hayao and Layton were now in Miami and would spend their time today and tomorrow preparing for the first Presidential debate, scheduled for tomorrow night at 8pm. The debates carried an enormous amount of weight for voters; it was a chance for them to see the candidates side by side responding to what the other said in an unrehearsed environment. Sure, as politicians they would bring the question around to get in the message they wanted, but they would not be able to be completely scripted as they often were. Their approaches would be like night and day. Hayao would try to stress his leadership qualities and undermine Layton for his lack of a global perspective. Layton would point to his stellar record in Congress and his recent increase in the population sectors that had been favoring Hayao, such as the Southwest. Both of them were feeling confident about the campaign trips they had just completed, but if either of them enjoyed an advantage, it was Hayao, due to the fact the debate was taking place in Miami, in Ramirez's domain. There was no doubt there would be a subconscious bias from the moderator. They were both going to be working with cosmetologists tomorrow to look their absolute best on tv. They both understood how critical their appearance came into play; that lesson went all the back to when JFK ran for President against Richard Nixon; for those who watched the debate, they believed Kennedy won, and those who listened on the radio thought Nixon was the clear victor. Right now Hayao was ahead in the nationwide polls by 5 percentage points; after tomorrow night, that could be completely different.

6pm, Friday, October 5th, ACLU offices, Washington, DC
Glen Aaron focused on his paperwork when he saw an email from the Appellate Court. He opened it with a sense of foreboding. It was not good news; the appeal request had been rejected. Dammit! He still firmly believed the search to be invalid. Corvino had been really dumb to leave the room. Roger Squelch had no right to snoop around the apartment, but this was such a high profile case the fact that both Visque's and Corvino's civil rights were trampled didn't matter. He was sure Ross knew also as they had both been waiting anxiously to hear. Well, no point in dwelling on this. They still had one more chance; the United States Supreme Court. He had to sell it to Visque, but why wouldn't she want to try? Aaron sensed they would agree to hear the case since their colleague was one of the victims. They would want to do his memory justice by seeing justice served. If there were any court that could be impartial, it was them. Aaron knew if he got the chance he would have to knock it out of the park.

CHAPTER 18

3pm, Saturday, October 6th, Detroit MI
Natsu Hakituri had arrived in the United States ostensibly to help Hayao get elected. He would do whatever he could to help the cause. Hayao and Alex tried to tell Natsu he could help just as well from Japan, but no one told Natsu what to do. He could be an asset here and wanted to make sure good decisions were made. He would be meeting with Hayao when he returned tomorrow after the debate.

8pm, University of Miami, Florida
"Good evening, and welcome to the first of three Presidential debates. My name is Marlon Crisp, I am the President of the University of Miami and I will be your moderator tonight. I will be asking questions of the candidates submitted to me by people across the country. The format will be as follows; I will have thirty seconds to ask each question, the responder will have two minutes to answer, and then the other candidate will have one minute for rebuttal. Please rise for the pledge of allegiance." Once that was completed, Crisp resumed control. "Representative Layton won the coin toss and has elected to go first. Mr. Layton, what makes you more qualified to lead our country?"

"I have served in our federal government for many years with the people's best interests at heart. I have the ability to change with the times, and understand that just being in charge of an organization does not necessarily mean a person is ready for politics. Running a company does not prepare you for dealing and interacting with heads of state from around the world, even if you have done so while in the operation of the business. Diplomacy is a tricky thing; say or do the wrong thing and relations could be compromised. That is much more difficult than building a new factory or seeking to sell your product in a foreign country, where you can offer something in return. Putting your foot in your mouth could be disastrous which is the last thing we want in a leader." That was a dig at Hayao for the time last February when he made an inappropriate comment when he debated Juan Pillar. "My

detractors will reiterate I have little experience in international affairs; that is a falsehood. I have interacted with many foreign dignitaries over the years in Washington and am well versed in cultures and customs around the globe." Layton had finished.
"Mr. Yamamoto, rebuttal?"
"Yes, it's true that being a businessman is different than being a politician; it is harder. I have tons of competition out there and have to make sure I am the best. I have to do whatever it takes to ingratiate myself with the people who make decisions. If that is not diplomacy then I do not know what is. Mr. Layton said he has interacted with important people from other countries here in Washington. That makes him a neophyte. He has not experienced other cultures first hand. Why would anyone want someone like that as the leader of the free world, especially in today's ever increasing globalization and distributed government."
Layton bristled at being called a neophyte, but kept himself in check. Hayao would answer first next, and then he would have a chance to retaliate. "Mr. Yamamoto, how do you plan to continue to preserve the earth's environment?"
"Well, let me start by saying Moritu Corporation is much more environmentally conscious now than when I joined the company. The U.S. has set an example to the rest of the world on how to go green, and with Moritu's influence in the countries where we already do business and those into which we are expanding such as Israel and India, I will use those relationships to educate and make those countries aware of the importance and methods of doing things in an environmentally friendly way."
"Representative Layton?"
"I have supported all of President Harrington's initiatives, such as Sea Lift right here in Miami. I have also made it a priority to crack down on those organizations that violated safety codes as well as those that refrained from staying current about the best practices available. When I take office, I will apply my tenacity to the country as a whole." Layton took a sip of water and looked at his watch. It was already 8:15 with an hour and 45 minutes to go.
At 9:55 Hayao was fading fast. The two hours drained his energy and he wasn't sure if he would still be five points ahead tomorrow.

His training over the summer had helped, but the real thing was much more taxing. He felt his performance tonight had only been fair and that Layton came out ahead as he had been more effective at exposing Hayao's weaknesses and the ways Hayao was lacking compared to himself. Layton was now just starting his closing remarks and then it would be Hayao's turn. "As a representative from Colorado, I have been involved with every major relevant political issue important to the people of this country and also how those issues affect our relationships with other countries around the world. There is no way to learn your way around Washington other than by being a part of it. Being the leader of an organization is not an easy job, and Mr. Yamamoto has been a success, but running a government is not just about maximizing the bottom line. There are layers upon layers of agendas to contend with. In a company such as Moritu, everyone is working towards a common goal. That is not the case in our federal government where there are many different motives and special interests involved and one must juggle multiple balls at the same time." Layton was very happy with the way the debate had gone. He managed to convey the message that technology remained a priority to him and believed he had done a good job at reaching those supporters of Todd Russell.

"Mr. Yamamoto?"

"Mr. Layton was right, as a CEO I am in charge of an organization that does work toward a common goal. The federal government is no different as their goal is to further the interests of the United States and their citizens. That takes strong leadership, the kind I am well prepared to provide. I am also well versed in how to marry technology with our society's needs as I have done at Moritu for our customers. There are political issues associated with every group of people; I have dealt with many varied personalities in the course of doing my job, and I am the chief decision maker for the U.S. for my company. I am ready to lead our country into the future in our ever increasingly complicated and interdependent world."

9am, Monday, October 8th, ACLU offices, Washington, DC
Glen Aaron was hard at work on the appeal for Kelly Visque to the U.S. Supreme Court. He knew he must be flawless this time. He had to present the search in a new way so the justices would understand exactly what a miscarriage of justice it had been. Ross offered to help him write it but he said he would complete it himself and show it to Ross for his opinion. He would make Corvino's expectation clear, that she never thought agent Squelch would wander around the apartment during the brief moment she left the room. He would paint a convincing argument during the oral presentation to the Court. His written brief would simply explain that the defense believed the search to be unlawful right from the time the evidence, the picture, was obtained during that search and used to indict Kelly Visque.

10am, House of Representatives session
Daryl Wallace felt quite nervous. He had basically been ordered by President Harrington to make sure the legislation for the voting rights of immigrants be pushed through. Wallace expected the President to call him the second the session ended. Wallace liked his job; he did not want to cross the President. Pushing this through would not be so easy, however. Many of his colleagues believed people needed to be here for years before earning the right to vote. To Wallace that seemed unreasonable; why should a country with so many freedoms not permit those who entered the country recently and most likely were knowledgeable about our government one of the most basic rights of a democratic system? Wallace went up to the podium and called for order. "Our first agenda item today is the measure which we voted on last week, the one of immigrant suffrage. Please think about this. These people are here as upstanding citizens looking to be productive members of society and we are denying them one of our basic rights. They arrived through legal channels and are entitled to participate in their own government. Remember we all had ancestors who came here and struggled as well." Numerous people started speaking at once and Wallace suddenly dreaded the hours ahead.

Three hours later Wallace emerged. The first thing he had to do was call President Harrington. He found a quiet alcove on the second floor and called the President's private line. Wallace kept it short and sweet just in case anyone was listening. "It's done, the measure passed."

4pm, Dearborn, MI
Hayao was getting ready to go on his next campaign trip, this one to the Northeast. His goal was to gain some ground there as Morris held a stronghold. He would stress his superiority when it came to technology and wanted to discuss his plan for keeping the economy healthy which was important to the people there. He and Ramirez also successfully dealt with Natsu by asking him to handle the volunteers working for Hayao to make sure they were being utilized effectively. He would be starting in New Jersey and working his way up the coast through New England. Hayao's plan was to emphasize his firm belief in education as the basis for his stance on technology. The scholarships Moritu has sponsored for technical courses of study such as computer engineering over the years are evidence they support trends for the future. That was the backbone of their position on technology combined with the new technical jobs they would be creating at their state-of-the-art plants in India and Israel. This would also be a perfect connection to their approach regarding the economy, as they would stress the international interrelationships that were so integral to the fiscal and financial health of nations everywhere. Hayao and Ramirez would be touring these states until October 14th at which time they would fly to Wake Forest University in North Carolina for the Vice Presidential debate the next day.

7pm, set of TV news show Washington Alive, Washington DC
"Good evening, America, welcome to another edition of Washington Alive! I am your host Evan Shaw. What an historic time we are in right now. Regardless of whomever our next President will be, history has been made. We are going to cover two related topics tonight; the first Presidential debate, and Hayao Yamamoto's political ad that aired the other night. Hayao may

have given his share of speeches as a Moritu executive over the years, but he still needs work in the political arena." Shaw took his first call. "Henry from Hartford Connecticut, the insurance capital of the world! Speak to me Henry! What did you think of the debate?" Henry began in a monotone,

"Eric Layton was much more effective in conveying his assets and experience while at the same time pointing out Hayao's shortcomings. He sold himself much better than Hayao did."

"Thank you, humdrum Henry. I happen to agree with you. One thing Hayao didn't come away with are any salesmanship skills during his years in business. Monica from Terre Haute, what say you?"

"I say Layton was the one who looked worse. He came across as vague and on the defensive; he spent just as much time attacking Hayao as telling us what he intends to do. Hayao may not know the nuances of political rhetoric yet, but he seemed more honest."

"Well put, Monica. Let's break for a quick commercial, and when we come back we will switch gears and analyze the commercial."

"We're back." Shaw turned to the panelists; two journalists and a lobbyist for the auto industry. "What about the ad the other night?"

"I thought it was brilliant. Hayao married his past as a business leader with his future by doing the narration in front of a war ship. It effectively illustrated the transition he will make", said the first panelist.

"I agree. It also showed the Hayao that was respected and liked by his employees which speaks volumes about the type of leader he is and will be", explained the lobbyist. "Did the commercial make up for his lackluster performance at the debate? I would say yes. His numbers went down about five points on Sunday but bounced back today according to the daily national poll. The key for him now is to give better performances at the next two debates. The American public will get behind him if he improves."

"What does Representative Layton have to do to stay competitive?"

"He needs to continue to address the issues on which he is weak, such as technology and immigration. The key for him is to grab as much of Todd Russell's votes as he can."

"Well, we are out of time. Thanks to our panelists and our callers from the audience. This is Evan Shaw and we will see you all back here tomorrow night when we will once again make politics come alive!"

1pm, Tuesday, October 9th, Denver CO
Eric Layton and Steven Morris were on their way to Seattle and several other stops in the Pacific Northwest. Robert remained back in Washington for this trip as he continued to analyze the data being collected about Layton's public image and the areas requiring the most attention. The two men would be stopping in three states on this trip; Washington, Oregon, and Idaho. Hayao was ahead in this region, but not by much. They would be focusing on environmental issues while here, an extremely important topic to the people he would be meeting. Layton enjoyed a good record with environmentalists. He had cracked down on those companies in Colorado in violation of health and safety laws, and had supported the Sea Lift operations in Miami and now in San Diego. He believed he could overtake Hayao in this area of the country. They were making two planned stops in each state, at each state's capital, and then at the University of Washington, at the Museum of Science and Industry in Portland Oregon, and the Botanical Gardens in Boise, where they would be hosting a fundraiser. Robert selected the locales they would be visiting to demonstrate nature was a priority to them. They would also be travelling around each state and making more informal stops where they would be accompanied by each state's governor who would guide them about where to meet and greet people. Today and tomorrow they would be in Washington, Thursday and Friday in Oregon, and Saturday and Sunday in Idaho. Late Sunday they would be flying to North Carolina for the Vice Presidential debate at Wake Forest University. Layton hoped to arrive at Wake Forest being tied with Hayao in the latest national polls. The election was less than a month away and he wanted to pull ahead and maintain that momentum. There were three more debates and four more campaign trips before November 6th and Layton knew he had to improve with each one and build on the debates and previous

campaign stops to improve his public perception with each round, take the feedback he received from his appearances and use it to perform at a higher level next time. That ability was what winning politicians were made of.

7pm, Sunday, October 14th, Winston Salem, North Carolina
Hayao and Alex Ramirez just arrived at their hotel outside Wake Forest University where tomorrow night's Vice Presidential debate would take place. Their trip through the states in the Northeast which included New England had been productive and they believed they created good impressions despite the fact that Morris had a stronghold in the area. Hayao had spoken with authority about the economy and seemed to foster trust in his message. He projected an air of authority at each of his stops; they both believed this had been the most effective and successful leg of their campaign. He now felt confident and like he was getting the hang of running for President. He came across as much more personable this time. They learned Layton and Morris had arrived earlier today, but they were not worried. Ramirez was a seasoned debater and could easily handle Steven Morris. They were going to have a leisurely dinner tonight and just relax, and spend most of the day tomorrow reviewing their platform on the various issues. This represented her chance to show that she and Hayao complemented each other and would be able to handle the wide range of problems which would arise during their term. Ramirez planned to work that fact into her responses; Layton and Morris were like twins politically and their range as a team was extremely limited.

9am, Tuesday, October 16th
The talk around the corridors and water coolers all over the country centered around last night's Vice Presidential debate. Debates between potential Vice Presidents had not generated nearly as much buzz as this one, obviously due to the fact that the game had changed. Many people believed the Vice Presidential candidates in general were superfluous; that was certainly true in this election as both Hayao and Layton were young, physically fit, and in good health. There was a growing movement, however, that

thought Ramirez would have significant pull in Hayao's administration. She was cultivating votes on her own appeal. The same could not be said for Morris who was basically a clone of Layton from the opposite side of the country. He had been tremendously overshadowed and outshone by Ramirez last night. That opinion was pretty much universal. He answered the questions asked of him but seemed like a dead fish, which was not like him at all. He had been intimidated. The positions he and Layton held on such things as immigration and technology made him appear ashamed of them and continually trying to justify their platform. Ramirez, on the other hand, seemed confident and proud of the work she and Hayao accomplished.

11am
Layton was really disappointed in the performance Morris turned in last night and he didn't even want to see him. Morris knew he had messed up and hoped in the days remaining before November 6th he, and they, could compensate for that. Tomorrow they were heading to the Southeast for five days and would visit three states; North Carolina, South Carolina, and Florida. It would be difficult to rev up support there as Ramirez was extremely popular and beloved as Florida's governor, but the two issues they would stress were immigration and the environment. Layton believed he could get a fair share of the popular vote down here thanks to Robert's plan for him to publicly support President Harrington's legislation while in Arizona and New Mexico and to back the construction project in Miami Beach as well. He took a deep breath and went to ask Morris if he wanted to go out for lunch. If they were going to work together for the next four years, amends had to be made.

10am, Wednesday, October 17th, Wake Forest University, Winston Salem, NC
Hayao and Ramirez had spent yesterday on campus meeting with students and in general savoring the victory from the previous night. Hayao found the students in general to suffer from a sense of entitlement that he also saw in his younger employees. It resulted from being raised in an environment where they were praised for

every little thing they did and coddled as well. He swore if he ever had kids he would not be the kind of parent who swooped in and fixed everything for them. He put on a kind face, however, and ingratiated himself at every turn. They would be leaving in an hour to go to Washington State, followed by Oregon and then work their way down the California coast. He wasn't really worried about carrying that part of the country, as there was a large Japanese population in the Pacific Northwest and Louis Grenadine being very visible and vocal lately about endorsing Hayao. He carried much weight in California. The one thing that made him wary was the successful trip Eric Layton recently had there. He seemed to have an excellent strategy which involved pandering to the immigrants all over the country by supporting their right to vote, and they in turn seemed blinded by which candidate was more competent when it came to the actual issues. He would discuss his leadership at Moritu and how he guided the company to employ more environmentally sound methods and play up his edge when it came to international affairs. That momentum would take him into the next Presidential debate in Sacramento on October 23rd.

5pm, Monday, October 22nd, Hazelton Penitentiary, West Virginia

Kelly Visque's dinner had just been brought to her and passed through the opening in the door of the jail cell. That's how it went when you were on death row; they brought things to you instead of the other way around. There was no light left in her eye. Oh, she knew Glen Aaron filed the writ of certiorari for the appeal to the U.S. Supreme Court but understood the odds were not good they would agree to hear the appeal, and even if they did, even less likely they would overturn the lower court's verdict. She looked at her tray with apathy. She had lost most of her muscle mass since being incarcerated; the little motivation she still retained to do a few pushups each day just didn't cut it. Lorraine had been allowed to come by a few times, but they had little to say to each other. Visque was allowed to have her e-reader, but spent most of her time daydreaming and thinking about various milestones in her life.

8pm, Sacramento, CA

Layton had just arrived at the airport. Morris returned to New York at the last minute to attend to some business which suited Layton just fine. Being alone would give him a chance to think and better prepare for the debate tomorrow night. He planned to bring each question around to work in his strength on the trends most Americans wanted to see. He knew Hayao was arriving tomorrow morning, giving the impression he was casual about this and confident enough to show up and only need one day to prepare.

10am, Tuesday, October 23rd, Quantico, VA, FBI Headquarters

Ed Billet sat at his desk reviewing his paperwork on several different cases with which he was involved. His schedule had certainly quieted down since he testified at the trial of Kelly Visque and Lorraine Corvino. The investigations he was conducting now dealt with robberies committed in multiple states, therefore becoming a federal matter. They were not high profile cases, however, and while he liked having the break, he missed the excitement as well. He had gotten into long distance running again since he had more time and was training to run the Boston Marathon in April. He had been quite good when he had been younger, leading his college team to the conference championships. He started to remember what it felt like to conquer a hill and run over the crest; it was such a feeling of accomplishment! He was daydreaming when his phone rang. "Hello Ed?" It was his assistant. "I am sorry to bother you, but there is a lieutenant from Florida on the phone who says he needs to speak with you."

8am, Wednesday, October 24th, Sacramento, CA, Hayao's hotel

Hayao hit it out of the park last night at the debate. He knew before-hand he needed to be confident and self-assured and that was exactly the demeanor he exhibited. He stressed his experience dealing with all kinds of people internationally and discussed diversity and how his team was the one with the know how to best meet the needs of all the various ethnic groups. He was very pleased with his performance. He flipped on the morning talk show on ABC. The host was talking about the debate, of course, and was saying this second debate was like night and day when compared with the first one. Layton held his own, the gentleman said, but Hayao had been like a different person. He answered the questions with conviction and managed to work in his points and demonstrate his advantage over Layton without seeming condescending or holier than thou. He was definitely getting the hang of it. Here was an excerpt from the debate: mediator - "Mr. Yamamoto, you seem to do better with those who emigrated to this country more than a generation ago, and Representative Layton seems to be better with the younger set. What is your explanation for that?" Hayao - "Many younger people have the misconception that I will immediately try to incorporate laws and customs from other countries which would come to supersede our current ones. That is not the case. Yes, I will try to deal with other countries with the concept of ever increasing interdependence among nations with the goal of always doing what is best for the United States." The host of the show went on to say that Layton gave adequate responses but didn't have any grand slams. "Layton neither made or lost ground based on last night's performance whereas Hayao seemed to take a quantum leap forward", the host of the show said in conclusion.

10am, Eric Layton's hotel room
Layton realized he remained stagnant after last night. He would remain in Sacramento for the next two days to try to break the chokehold Hayao held in California due to his association with Louis Grenadine. Layton was aware he needed to step things up and not seem so stiff. He needed to come across as more energetic and lively. He would have his staff make him an account on the newest social media site so he would be more accessible to his voters and also show he was current with technology.

9am, Thursday, October 25th, U.S. Supreme Court building
The justices on the Supreme Court were discussing the appeal of the convictions of Kelly Visque and Lorraine Corvino. The issue was the legality of the search. The appellate court had upheld the

verdict and now the lawyers wanted the Supreme Court to take a look. They had to have a session to decide. "Why should we entertain this case? Just because it involves one of our colleagues?", said Judith Lackey.

"We should entertain it because of its far reaching implications", replied Chief Justice Jim Braxton. "Kelly Visque was tried as a terrorist and her motive was ostensibly to prevent a foreign born person from running for President. The same cause whose legislation we ruled in favor of and which resulted in an amendment to the Constitution."

"The search does sound questionable", chimed in Patrick Manucci. "As Jim said, it is directly related to the amendment which we supported."

"Illegal searches take place every day. Does the fact that it relates to something we were involved in warrant our opinion? ", spoke Andrew Turnbull. This was an emotional issue; everyone remembered Justice Bernard and knew a decision would not be reached quickly.

11am, Dearborn, MI

Hayao stopped home for one day to look in on the operations at Moritu before jetting off to the next campaign stop, the Mid-Atlantic states such as New Jersey, Pennsylvania, Delaware, and so on down to DC. His focus there would be the economy and how Moritu's international presence would help the United States. The people in this region were very interested in doing well financially and represented a microcosm of the entire country as the diversity in those states was high. If Hayao finished his stint there with good numbers in the polls that would be a positive sign.

10am, Friday, October 26th

Eric Layton was on his way to Chicago where he would meet up with Steven Morris to campaign in the Midwest. They would stress their commitment to education, both quality and keeping costs affordable. People here tended to be more conservative and very family oriented, so that would strike a chord with them. Layton definitely felt the adrenaline rush now with the election so close.

That was good. He needed to appear energetic. He could refer to the fact that Colorado's state universities maintained one of the lowest average tuition rates in the country and yet were rated well academically, He also hoped to take ownership of Todd Russell's turf in Illinois as the more conservative candidate. Once they had spent the day in Chicago, he and Morris would travel throughout the Midwest to Indiana, Minnesota, Iowa, and Missouri stopping in each state for one day until October 31 when they would fly to Washington DC for the third and final Presidential debate the next day.

10am, Monday, October 29th, the Supreme Court building
The Supreme Court justices finally reached a consensus last Thursday night around 10pm. They agreed to hear the oral argument from the attorney who represented the defendant on death row due to the far reaching implications of this case. The other attorney was not going to speak; Kelly Visque's lawyer was familiar enough with the facts to represent both of them. The illegal search applied to both of them anyway, because if the search was found to be illegal then the picture of the two women together would be inadmissible, and it would be that much more difficult to show they knew each other, and without that relationship Kelly Visque would not have possessed the access to Justice Bernard. Glen Aaron had been preparing for this for the last few weeks and believed he hit upon all the points that would help persuade the court to reverse the ruling. He was ready to begin. "Honorable justices; I am honored to be here, presenting the evidence I have carefully prepared. The grounds I have for reversing the lower court's decision is the search performed by the FBI which was conducted without a warrant and therefore had severe limitations. The FBI is claiming the object which incriminated the defendant who lived there and subsequently my client was in plain sight and therefore no warrant was required." Aaron went through the explanation about how Lorraine Corvino had left the room, etc. He wanted to get to the important part of the argument, that being this case was intimately related to the ruling this same court had given which led to the U.S. Constitution being

amended. "I would like to say to all of you, that this case, if you review the prosecution's explanation of the motive, came to pass in response to the enormous change in our federal policy which had been in place since our country's inception. My client's life hangs in the balance because she was tried as a terrorist who is believed to have committed the murders of the Bernards and Juan Pillar and his driver out of a misplaced sense of patriotism. There are several reasons you should scrutinize the details of the search which I am claiming was unlawful. First, one of your colleagues was involved. He helped decide which way the legislation would go and placed his stamp on it just like all of you." Aaron quickly acknowledged Justice Adler was the exception. "This is not some petty theft. This is a crime with far reaching implications, was ostensibly politically motivated, and intended to alter the course of history by whomever performed these horrific acts. We have a responsibility to ensure proper procedures were followed by our law enforcement community. That's the second reason why this should be reviewed." Aaron paused for a second for dramatic effect. "The third and last reason I have to offer is that the FBI faced tremendous pressure to solve this case, and it is not out of the question that this agent, agent Squelch, could have become overzealous and tiptoed outside the law in the execution of his duties. I know that when you take into consideration all the factors at work here, you will come to the conclusion the search was indeed illegal. Thank you."

11am, Wednesday, October 31st
Hayao and Layton were both scheduled to arrive in Washington DC today and they both had productive trips respectively. Layton felt he created inroads in the Midwest and the latest polls reflected that. He would spend his time in DC up until the debate tomorrow night relaxing and preparing his strategy. He would stress that he was the seasoned candidate who could bridge the gap between the new paradigm of genuine concern for the people of this country and the ideals upon which the United States was founded and maintaining that integrity. Hayao, conversely, would be trying to demonstrate those traditional values had been corrupted by the

people within over so many years that it had become a caricature of itself. Politicians had been interested in serving one segment of the population for some time now; themselves. Having him as a candidate signified a radical change but a necessary one. His message would be that the U.S. needed to find the right balance of where she stood worldwide in the ever increasing synergistic relationship among nations.

9am, Thursday, November 1st, New Delhi, India

Moritu Corporation's new plant was opening today and while Natsu couldn't be there, he sent his number two man in the organization and participated via satellite link. Hayao obviously had not attended either, but made sure his name was mentioned as the person who helped broker the deal. He did appear briefly via satellite as well to offer his congratulations and good wishes. The opening had been planned perfectly to happen at the most beneficial time for him. He would show his commitment to his campaign by missing the opening of the project he had gotten off the ground. Furthermore it would show he was influential in making things happen all over the world; definitely a quality Americans coveted in their leaders. The ceremony went on for about an hour with both India's President and Prime Minister in attendance and was covered on the midday news. Hayao definitely held the momentum going into tonight's debate.

3pm, Washington, DC

Eric Layton spent the morning reviewing all the points he wanted to make tonight and trying to rehearse the demeanor he wanted to project. This was most likely his last chance to reach a national audience before Election Day and he was super determined to make the most of it. His wife Cindy arrived this morning and she would be with him until the election; their son Jack was staying with his grandparents. After the debate tonight they were headed to the Mid-Atlantic states for a few final days of campaigning and then were flying back to Denver where they would spend Election Day. She could see how tense he was. They had planned to go out for an early dinner; instead she suggested they order room service and she would help him relax. He readily agreed.

8am, Friday, November 2nd
"This is Chip Nesbit, coming to you live here in Washington DC. Today we are out in the street getting people's reactions to last night's final Presidential debate." He walked over to a gentleman who looked to be about sixty. "Sir, what was your impression of the two candidates last night?"
"I thought Hayao did much better than Layton. He seemed to convey the steps he will take if he is elected rather than bashing his opponent which is what Eric Layton did. Layton also seemed to give choppy, disjointed answers like he had certain points to make regardless of the question being asked."
"Thank you sir. Ma'am, what did you think about the debate last night?"
"I am planning to vote for Hayao."
"Were you before last night?"
"I was leaning toward him but wasn't sure."
"What specifically helped you make up your mind?"
"Layton's demeanor during the debate. He seemed to be trying too hard and didn't really answer the questions asked of him. It was not a stellar performance." Similar surveys were going on all over the country today and would produce opinions very much like the ones in DC.
  Both Hayao and Layton were observing the news throughout the day and naturally their reactions were like the two sides of a coin. Hayao was off to the Midwest where he would focus on education and reiterate his commitment to scholarships and trying to balance the quality of secondary education with keeping it affordable. He would continue to prohibit exorbitant salaries for administrators and limit tuition hikes. There were only four days left until the election and the third debate had been the last big hurdle. He remained very, but cautiously, optimistic.
  Eric Layton was pissed at himself. Just about everyone who watched the debate viewed him as the loser. He watched it himself and thought he could have done many things differently. The most

glaring mistake was his lack of responsiveness to the questions asked. He would have liked to believe he still was ahead overall but couldn't be sure about that. He hoped to salvage the last few days when he would be in the Mid-Atlantic states. His solid campaign up until last night combined with his exemplary record in Congress should be enough to win him the White House. He had just introduced a new high tech job bill which would appropriate 10 billion dollars annually for subsidized training in state of the art technology from around the globe. That would hopefully demonstrate his commitment to integrating the health of the economy with the area in which he trailed by the biggest margin, technology. If he had a really strong finish then perhaps the impact of last night's debacle would be diminished.

9am, Monday, November 5th, Washington DC, the U.S. Supreme Court

Glen Aaron and Lionel Ross had been summoned to hear the Supreme Court's ruling. They walked into the courtroom to find the justices already assembled. They stood in front of the bench where the judges sat and waited. Chief Justice Braxton spoke first. "Thank you gentlemen, for your continued efforts to ensure justice is served. We have reviewed the documents which you have submitted and have reached a verdict. We are upholding the search as constitutionally sound. The FBI agent looked around the apartment when Miss Corvino left the room. She did not ask him to stay in that section of her residence and did not close off the area where the picture was discovered. Miss Corvino could have moved the picture prior to allowing Agent Squelch inside. There is no impropriety here." Aaron and Ross both wore looks of defeat. "Do you have any questions?" asked Justice Braxton. They both answered no, understanding it was futile. "In that case, we are adjourned." Braxton banged his gavel, putting a definitive end to the cause, which was saving his client's life, that Aaron had been consumed with for the last six months. Both attorneys left the courthouse and without saying a word to each other, knew what they must do. They drove straight to the prison to see their clients.

12pm, Hazelton Penitentiary

Aaron thought it would be better to meet separately, so Ross pulled Corvino off of her work detail and Aaron asked that Kelly Visque be brought in from the exercise yard. He was waiting for her in the meeting room and of course she knew the outcome right away. She walked to the corner of the room and just faced the wall.

"What happens next?"

"A date will be set for your execution."

"How will it be done?"

"Lethal injection." Aaron waited for Visque to say something.

"Do we have any more options?"

"I could, and will, request leniency from President Harrington. He may be willing to change your sentence to life in prison through an executive order."

"Is there a reasonable chance he will do that?"

"He might. The fact that you are a woman may influence his decision."

"When will you meet with him?"

"I will have my director do it. He has significantly more clout."

She said she was ready to go back to her cell. An emptiness existed in her eyes which Aaron had not seen before. As he was leaving, he met with the warden to request Kelly Visque be put on suicide watch.

2pm, the White House

President Harrington was meeting with his staff when Abby, one of the interns, felt her phone vibrate. She took it out to look (she was one of the few people who could get away with that; the President took a special interest in her). "Mr. President, I just received an alert that the Supreme Court upheld the search in Kelly Visque and Lorraine Corvino's case!"

"Good. The FBI followed procedure and did not drop the ball."

"You know that you will be petitioned to have her sentence commuted from the death penalty. What will you do?", Abby asked.

"I don't know yet. I will want to hear the arguments given. Let's continue on with our agenda so we can finish before dinner."

5pm

Both Hayao and Layton were in transit to the destinations where they would spend Election Day. Hayao had decided to make New York his home base which caused a small uproar back in the Detroit area. He chose New York because it has been the port traditionally associated with the immigrant experience and that was the statement he wanted to make. His headquarters would be at Madison Square Garden.

Layton had chosen to stay closer to his roots and would be at the Brown Palace Hotel, one of the fanciest in Denver. He wanted to be surrounded by his constituents, win or lose.

CHAPTER 19

6am EST, Tuesday, November 6th, 2040

The day had finally arrived and brought with it a change in the fabric of the United States that many believed was inevitable. Regardless of the outcome, history was being made today. The polls on the East Coast were opening now and all the polling places across the country would be open from 6am to 8pm. There was an additional option for people to take advantage of this time around: voting from home. In the last Presidential election four years ago, it was used on a trial basis in several polling places and seemed to work well. People would submit a DNA sample ahead of time which was kept on file by the government in the cloud. When it was time to vote, the individual would be captured on camera in their home providing another DNA sample using a method of their choice, either the root of a strand of hair or saliva. They would place the DNA sample into a DNA reader purchased ahead of time which would decode the DNA and connect to their computer to transmit the unique code to the cloud where it would be matched against the sample provided. This option was available across the country but remained completely voluntary; there were still the traditional polling places where people could go to vote using the ballot machines. Once their identity was verified, their DNA code would allow them into the Board of Elections website where they would be able to cast their vote, after which they would be identified as completed. This option was expected to greatly increase voter turnout, particularly among the elderly. Political analysts expected this factor to favor Eric Layton more so than Hayao. It also allowed the polling places to close earlier than they had in the past, ending their day at 8pm instead of 9.

9am EST, Hotel Pennsylvania, Manhattan

Hayao was in his hotel room getting ready to cast his vote. He would vote remotely, of course, and was starting up his DNA reader and laptop. When he was ready, he invited the camera crew in from the national news as they would film him performing the process. When they were ready, the anchor started the broadcast.

"This is Jean Morton, coming to the entire country live from the Hotel Pennsylvania in New York City where Presidential hopeful Hayao Yamamoto is getting ready to vote. He will be using his DNA along with the required electronic equipment to do so. Hayao, thank you for allowing us to participate in this process with you."

"I am happy to do so, Jean. As a candidate, my actions are an open book." He pointed to the item on the table. "I have already taken a strand of my hair and placed it in the DNA reader." The cameraman zoomed in on that.

"Go ahead and turn it on whenever you are ready", said Jean. Hayao did, and a minute later a message appeared on the screen of his laptop that simply said confirmed. The Board of Elections website appeared next and went right to the screen to cast the vote. At this point Hayao blocked the view of the camera as he made his selection and submitted it. Once he was done he turned back to Morton. "Hayao, what are your foremost thoughts right now?"

"I hope that voter turnout will surpass that of all prior elections and that we set a record. Everyone should make their voice heard!"

"If someone had told you two years ago that you could be the next President of the United States, what would have been your reaction?"

"I would have dismissed that person as being foolhardy, probably with a little hostility", Hayao said, smiling. "I have learned that life can take some unexpected and wonderful turns."

"What are your plans for the rest of the day?"

"Well, I am going to be spending some time in the lobby downstairs today for those people who would like to come in and meet with me, I will be conducting another interview this afternoon from Ellis Island, and then I will be heading back uptown to my campaign headquarters at Madison Square Garden, directly across the street."

"That sounds like a full day, which is good practice for a potential President. Thank you, Hayao, and good luck!"

11am, Denver Colorado

Eric Layton decided to vote in the traditional way, travelling to the firehouse that had served as his polling place for the last 25 years. Although his process was not as dynamic as Hayao's, it generated the same amount of fanfare; a camera crew broadcasting his actions and the interview after he cast his vote. He too, described his schedule for the rest of the day, which included meeting and greeting his constituents, attending a reception at the statehouse, and then going to the Brown Palace hotel to await the election results. "If you could go back and change one thing about your campaign, what would that be?", the reporter asked.

"I would have employed the use of social media to a greater extent than I did. Perhaps that would have allowed me to reach a greater number of our younger voters."

"If you end up not winning, will you be looking for a position in President Hayao's cabinet?" Layton smiled.

"Let's think positive! Hayao will be seeking a spot in my cabinet!"

2pm PST

"We interrupt this program to bring you a special report"; all the networks were airing the updated election results, momentarily stopping all the daytime soap operas. "With eight hours left for people to vote in Hawaii where the votes will be tallied last, the percentages are 50% for Hayao Yamamoto and 50% for Eric Layton. We will continue to monitor the numbers and will keep the American public up to date throughout the day. We now return to our regularly scheduled program."

9pm EST

Live election coverage was going on now and all the evening television shows had been preempted. The polls had been closed on the East Coast for an hour and were now closing at those locations that were in the Central time zone. Hayao had pulled ahead and lead by a margin of 3 percentage points, 51.5% to 48.5%. Reporters were attempting to interview Layton, but when asked about what he thought, all he said was that he wouldn't be discounted until the final vote had been tallied.

12am EST
All the polls were closed except for those in Hawaii, and Hayao was the projected winner. He was ahead by 4.5 percentage points now nationwide and was winning in Hawaii as well. Eric Layton was disappointed and resigned himself now to the fact that he would lose. He was not upset however; all in all he honestly believed that he had conducted a strong campaign that highlighted his strengths and placed him in the best light possible with as many people as possible. Besides, he was a young man who still could anticipate a bright future in politics. He went to start drafting his concession speech.

1:15am EST
All the votes had been counted. It was official. Hayao had received 53% of the popular vote and Layton 47%. It was a new era. For those that were still awake, a sense of exhilaration along with a sense of trepidation existed. All change comes with a price. Both Hayao and Layton were exhausted yet fueled by adrenaline. Layton gave the standard speech by the candidate who lost, complimenting Hayao on his campaign and thanking all the people who had worked with him. Hayao was celebrating as expected and didn't provide a formal speech except to thank his campaign workers and the American public for exercising their right to vote and making themselves heard. His victory party was expected to last all night.

2am, Madison Square Garden
Wolf was wiped out and decided to leave Hayao's victory celebration and go back to his hotel. He would sleep briefly and then be on his way. He sure fooled them all! He was staying at the Wellington hotel about twenty blocks away. The candidate that he wanted to win did, and he was home free. He decided to walk, thinking the fresh air would do him good.

He arrived at the Wellington about 40 minutes later and felt a renewed sense of strength, so he decided to leave right now. He would stop in Laurel Maryland as his friend was away again and crash there for a day or two and then finish his trip back down south. When he went up to his room, he suddenly got paranoid and drew his gun as he opened the door. He swept the room but had been worrying for nothing, his mind playing tricks on him. He packed his one remaining bag, as he had packed up his car earlier today except for the few things left, went downstairs and settled his bill. He had found street parking on the west side earlier today; parking in those exorbitant parking garages drove him crazy. He got to his car and five minutes later was heading down to the Lincoln Tunnel when a voice from the back seat made him jump two feet in the air and almost hit a parked car on the side of the street. "Hello Peter Marvin, I am Agent Ed Billet with the FBI, and you are under arrest for the murders of Winston Bernard, Cecily Bernard, Juan Pillar, and his driver. Pull over to the side of the road immediately, shut off the car, and put your hands on the steering wheel." Wolf did what he was told; Billet came around to the driver's door, aiming his gun at Wolf the entire time. He pulled Wolf out of the car, frisked him, and removed Wolf's firearm from the holster around his waist. He cuffed Wolf with his hands behind his back and placed him in the back seat. Billet got behind the wheel and continued in the direction of the Lincoln Tunnel; he was taking Marvin to Washington DC tonight where he would be kept in a holding cell until tomorrow to be processed through the system. "You have been quite an adversary, Mr. Marvin, and you almost got away with it. Why did you do it?"

"I am not a squealer. If you know anything about my background you realize I have been trained to keep my mouth shut."

"Yes, I am aware you were in the military, congratulations. Do you want to know how you were caught?" Wolf suddenly thought of a plan which involved keeping Billet talking and distracted.

"Sure, go ahead. You're dying to gloat."

"About two weeks ago, I received a call from a Florida policeman. He said that they received a complaint about a foul odor coming from a townhouse and went to check it out. When they investigated, they found a few dead mice in the attic. They removed the mice and the smell went away. Can you guess who owns the townhouse?"

"Spare me the games. It was mine."

"Right. Do you know what else the police found in the attic in a box that they came across in their search for the source of the odor?" Marvin knew, but needed more time.

"What?"

"They found a photo id with the name Frank Evans on it. They discovered that the townhouse was owned by you, Peter Marvin, and recognized your name as being connected with the investigation into the four murders that I mentioned. They took it upon themselves to contact my office." Billet paused to let Marvin squirm. They were stopped at a red light; even at this hour there was plenty of traffic.

"Go on", said Wolf.

"I went down to Florida to check it out personally. I confiscated the id of Frank Evans and went to the gun store in Atlanta where we had struck out before. Guess what? They recognized you immediately. After that, we tracked you down. You got sloppy with the use of your credit card in Frank Evans' name; we had you under surveillance from that moment on. We also had your townhouse wired. When you were there last week we found out about your plan to attend Hayao's reception at Madison Square Garden. It was like shooting tuna in a barrel!" Wolf had heard enough. He glanced at the street sign; they were at 35th street. This was the perfect time to make his move. He had managed to slide his arms over his legs so they were now in front instead of behind his back. He took out the knife that Billet missed when he frisked him. He stealthily held it to Billet's throat.

"Don't move, you arrogant son of a bitch! Give me both my gun and yours right now or I swear to God I will cut your throat!" Billet did as he was told, handing both weapons to Marvin. Wolf took the clip out of Billet's gun, put it in his pocket, and kept his gun trained on Billet. Wolf got out of the car and came around to the driver's window. "Give me the key." Billet handed it right over and Wolf uncuffed himself and shackled Billet to the steering wheel, throwing the key down a nearby sewer grate. He shot one of the tires on the car, and took off running toward the tunnel. Now that he had escaped, he had more options but was making this up as he went along. Billet had a few tricks up his sleeve as well. When Marvin had held the knife to his neck, he had slipped a spare handcuff key into his palm which he now used to free himself, and then he grabbed the extra gun he had strapped to his ankle. He took off after Marvin. Billet was a fast runner and closed in on him quickly. He fired his gun but Marvin was too far away. He kept after him on foot. Wolf got to the entrance to the tunnel and went in, running toward New Jersey. He went up on the walkway that ran parallel to the road that the cars went on. The traffic leaving the city going towards New Jersey was bumper to bumper but there was no traffic going into Manhattan. Wolf looked behind him and Billet continued gaining ground. He fired at Billet but missed. Billet fired back, narrowly missing Marvin's head. "Give it up Marvin, there is nowhere for you to go!" He had gotten to the center of the tunnel.

"I'll never be taken alive!" He fired his remaining shots at Billet, hitting him once between his shoulder and chest. When he was out of ammunition, Wolf threw his gun at Billet, now crouched in pain against the wall, hitting him in the arm.

"Marvin, don't!" Billet managed to yell as Wolf climbed over the railing.

"One thing, agent. I am just the tip of the iceberg!" Wolf crossed the gridlocked traffic leaving the city and saw an oncoming car entering New York. Once it got close enough, he threw himself in front, getting thrown ten feet, landing on his back, and smashing his skull.

EPILOGUE

1pm, Saturday, November 10th, Jersey City Medical Center, Jersey City, NJ

Ed Billet had been rushed to the closest hospital after he had been shot which ended being the one in Jersey City. He had lost a lot of blood and had been in intensive care for a few days but was now in a regular room. He was just finishing his lunch when he heard a knock at the door. He was glad, longing for some company. Director Grey walked in slowly, wanting to see Billet's progress.

"Hi Ed, how are you?"

"Hello sir, I feel ok."

"Let me tell you, Ed, you are a certified hero! You captured the real person behind the murders intended to derail our nation's political process. President Harrington has already announced that he wants to give you a special commendation."

"That's very nice, but I am not looking for such recognition."

"I know. Right now just focus on getting better." Director Grey paused. "How did you come to realize Marvin was the murderer?"

Billet went through the whole story, how he had gotten a phone call from the police officer in Florida, how he went down there and got Marvin's fake id and confirmed he was the one at the gun store in Atlanta. "With regard to Juan Pillar and his driver, we traced Marvin's credit card receipts under the name Frank Evans to California right around the time the incriminating note was sent, more than a coincidence. We believe he simply donned a blond wig when he arrived at the airport as it was public knowledge by then that Kelly Visque was a suspect. Speaking of which, have she and Lorraine Corvino been released yet?"

"No, that will take place on Monday. They both owe you, Ed. They each owe their life, one literally and one figuratively. Look, I am sure you are going to want some time off after this, but I want you to know your job will be waiting for you."

"Thank you sir. There is some unfinished business. Right before Peter Marvin jumped in front of the car and killed himself, he said, "'I am just the tip of the iceberg'."

"First get well, Ed, then we can work together to get to the bottom of this." Billet was grateful, and he could see the Director was getting antsy.

"Sir, if you don't mind, I am feeling tired and would like to rest."

"Of course, Ed. I will talk to you next week." Ten minutes later, there was another knock; it was Sondra Tristan. "Sondra, come in. How are you?" She walked over and gave him a big hug.

"Oh, Ed, I have been calling the hospital every day, and when they told me you could receive visitors, I made the trip up from Washington right away. Thanks to you, I have real peace. How is your wound?"

"Getting better. I lost much blood; that was the most pressing issue. I hope to go home early next week. I am glad you can finally have closure, Sondra, and get on with your life. How is Blake, by the way?" She walked over to the window.

"It's funny you should ask about Blake and comment about getting on with life." She turned around with a big smile on her face and was blushing. "I am pregnant!"

Made in the USA
Middletown, DE
09 November 2015